GREAT Vampires
& OTHER HORRORS

GREAT VAMPIRES

& OTHER HORRORS

CHANCELLOR
PRESS

First published in Great Britain in 1992 by
Chancellor Press an imprint of
Reed International Books Limited
Michelin House
81 Fulham Road
London SW3 6RB

ISBN 1 85152 235 2

Printed in Great Britain by The Bath Press

Contents

Contents

6

But first on earth, as vampire sent,
Thy corpse shall from its tomb be rent,
Then ghastly haunt thy native place
And suck the blood of all thy race.
LORD BYRON

On horror's head horrors accumulate.
WILLIAM SHAKESPEARE

For the Blood Is the Life
F. Marion Crawford

We had dined at sunset on the broad roof of the old tower, because it was cooler there during the great heat of summer. Besides, the little kitchen was built at one corner of the great square platform, which made it more convenient than if the dishes had to be carried down the steep stone steps, broken in places and everywhere worn with age. The tower was one of those built all down the west coast of Calabria by the Emperor Charles V early in the sixteenth century, to keep off the Barbary pirates, when the unbelievers were allied with Francis I against the Emperor and the Church. They have gone to ruin, a few still stand intact, and mine is one of the largest. How it came into my possession ten years ago, and why I spend a part of each year in it, are matters which do not concern this tale. The tower stands in one of the loneliest spots in southern Italy, at the extremity of a curving rocky promontory, which forms a small but safe natural harbor at the southern extremity of the Gulf of Policastro, and just north of Cape Scalea, the birthplace of Judas Iscariot, according to the old local legend. The tower stands alone on this hooked spur of the rock, and there is not a house to be seen within three miles of it. When I go there I take a couple of sailors, one of whom is a fair cook, and when I am away it is in charge of a gnomelike little being who was once a miner and who attached himself to me long ago.

My friend, who sometimes visits me in my summer solitude, is an artist by profession, a Scandinavian by birth, and a cosmopolitan by force of circumstances. We had dined at sunset; the sunset glow had reddened and faded again, and the evening purple steeped the vast chain of the moun-tains that embrace the deep gulf to eastward and rear themselves higher and higher toward the south. It was hot, and we sat at the landward corner of the platform, waiting for the night breeze to come down from the lower hills. The color sank out of the air, there was a little interval of deep-gray twilight, and a lamp sent a yellow streak from the open door of the kitchen, where the men were getting their supper.

Then the moon rose suddenly above the crest of the promontory, flooding the platform and lighting up every little spur of rock and knoll of grass below us, down to the edge of the motionless water. My friend lighted his pipe and sat looking at a spot on the hillside. I knew that he was looking at it, and for a long time past I had wondered whether he would ever see anything there that would fix his attention. I knew that spot well. It was clear that he was interested at last, though it was a long time before he spoke. Like most painters, he trusts to his own eyesight, as a lion trusts his strength and a stag his speed, and he is always disturbed when he cannot reconcile what he sees with what he believes that he ought to see.

'It's strange,' he said. 'Do you see that little mound just on this side of the boulder?'

'Yes,' I said, and I guessed what was coming.

'It looks like a grave,' observed Holger.

'Very true. It does look like a grave.'

'Yes,' continued my friend, his eyes still fixed on the spot. 'But the strange thing is that I see the body lying on the top of it. Of course,' continued Holger, turning his head on one side as artists do, 'it must be an effect of light. In the first place, it is not a grave at all. Secondly, if it were, the body would be inside and not outside. Therefore, it's an effect of the moonlight. Don't you see it?'

'Perfectly; I always see it on moonlight nights.'

'It doesn't seem to interest you much,' said Holger.

'On the contrary, it does interest me, though I am used to it. You're not so far wrong, either. The mound is really a grave.'

'Nonsense!' cried Holger, incredulously. 'I suppose you'll tell me what I see lying on it is really a corpse!'

'No,' I answered, 'it's not. I know, because I have taken the trouble to go down and see.'

'Then what is it?' asked Holger.

'It's nothing.'

'You mean that it's an effect of light, I suppose?'

'Perhaps it is. But the inexplicable part of the matter is that it makes no difference whether the moon is rising or setting, or waxing or waning. If there's any moonlight at all, from east or west or overhead, so long as it shines on the grave you can see the outline of the body on top.'

Holger stirred up his pipe with the point of his knife, and then used his finger for a stopper. When the tobacco burned well he rose from his chair.

'If you don't mind,' he said, 'I'll go down and take a look at it.'

He left me, crossed the roof, and disappeared down the dark steps. I did not move, but sat looking down until he came out of the tower below. I heard him humming an old Danish song as he crossed the open space in the bright moonlight, going straight to the mysterious mound. When he was ten paces from it, Holger stopped short, made two steps forward, and then three or four backward, and then stopped again. I knew what that meant. He had reached the spot where the Thing ceased to be visible – where, as he would have said, the effect of light changed.

Then he went on till he reached the mound and stood upon it. I could see the Thing still, but it was no longer lying down; it was on its knees now, winding its white arms round Holger's body and looking up into his face. A cool breeze stirred my hair at that moment, as the night wind began to come down from the hills, but it felt like a breath from another world.

The Thing seemed to be trying to climb to its feet, helping itself up by Holger's body while he stood upright, quite unconscious of it and apparently looking toward the tower, which is very picturesque when the moonlight falls upon it on that side.

'Come along!' I shouted. 'Don't stay there all night!'

It seemed to me that he moved reluctantly as he stepped from the mound, or else with difficulty. That was it. The Thing's arms were still round his waist, but its feet could not leave the grave. As he came slowly forward it was drawn and lengthened like a wreath of mist, thin and white, till I saw distinctly that Holger shook himself, as a man does who feels a chill. At the same instant a little wail of pain came to me on the breeze – it might have been the cry of the small owl that lives among the rocks – and the misty presence floated swiftly back from Holger's advancing figure and lay once more at its length upon the mound.

Again I felt the cool breeze in my hair, and this time an icy thrill of dread ran down my spine. I remembered very well that I had once gone down there alone in the moonlight; that presently, being near, I had seen nothing; that, like Holger, I had gone and had stood upon the mound; and I remembered how, when I came back, sure that there was nothing there, I had felt the sudden conviction that there was something after all if I would only look behind me. I remembered the strong temptation to look back, a temptation I had resisted as unworthy of a man of sense, until, to get rid of it, I had shaken myself just as Holger did.

And now I knew that those white, misty arms had been round me too; I knew it in a flash, and I shuddered as I remembered that I had heard the night owl then too. But it had not been the night owl. It was the cry of the Thing.

I refilled my pipe and poured out a cup of strong southern wine; in less than a minute Holger was seated beside me again.

'Of course there's nothing there,' he said, 'but it's creepy, all the same. Do you know, when I was coming back I was so sure that there was something behind me that I wanted to turn round and look? It was an effort not to.'

He laughed a little, knocked the ashes out of his pipe, and poured himself out some wine. For a while neither of us spoke, and the moon rose higher, and we both looked at the Thing that lay on the mound.

'You might make a story about that,' said Holger after a long time. 'There is one,' I answered. 'If you're not sleepy, I'll tell it to you.' 'Go ahead,' said Holger, who likes stories.

Old Alario was dying up there in the village behind the hill. You remember him, I have no doubt. They say that he made his money by selling sham jewelry in South America, and escaped with his gains when he was found out. Like all those fellows, if they bring anything back with them, he at once set to work to enlarge his house; and, as there are no masons here, he sent all the way to Paola for two workmen. They were a rough-looking pair of scoundrels – a Neapolitan who had lost one eye and a Sicilian with an old scar half an inch deep across his left cheek. I often saw them, for on Sundays they used to come down here and fish off the rocks. When Alario caught the fever that killed him the masons were still at work. As he had agreed that part of their pay should be their board and lodging, he made them sleep in the house. His wife was dead, and he had an only son called Angelo, who was a much better sort than himself. Angelo was to marry the daughter of the richest man in the village, and, strange to say, though the marriage was arranged by their parents, the young people were said to be in love with each other.

For that matter, the whole village was in love with Angelo, and among the rest a wild, good-looking creature called Cristina, who was more like a gipsy than any girl I ever saw about here. She had very red lips and very black eyes, she was built like a greyhound, and had the tongue of the devil. But Angelo did not care a straw for her. He was rather a simple-minded fellow, quite different from his old scoundrel of a father, and under what I should call normal circumstances I really believe that he would never have looked at any girl except the nice plump little creature, with a fat dowry, whom his father meant him to marry. But things turned up which were neither normal nor natural.

On the other hand, a very handsome young shepherd from the hills above Maratea was in love with Cristina, who seems to have been quite indifferent to him. Cristina had no regular means of subsistence, but she was a good girl and willing to do any work or go on errands to any distance for the sake of a loaf of bread or a mess of beans, and permission to sleep under cover. She was especially glad when she could get something to do about the house of Angelo's father. There is no doctor in the village, and when the neighbors saw that old Alario was dying they sent Cristina to Scalea to fetch one. That was late in the afternoon, and if they had waited so long, it was because the dying miser refused to allow any such extravagance while he was able to speak. But while Cristina was gone, matters grew rapidly worse, the priest was brought to the bedside, and when he had done what he could he gave it as his opinion to the bystanders that the old man was dead, and left the house.

You know these people. They have a physical horror of death. Until the priest spoke, the room had been full of people. The words were hardly out of his mouth before it was empty. It was night now. They hurried down the dark steps and out into the street.

Angelo was away, Cristina had not come back – the simple woman servant who had nursed the sick man fled with the rest, and the body was left alone in the flickering light of the earthen oil lamp.

Five minutes later two men looked in cautiously and crept forward toward the bed. They were the one-eyed Neapolitan mason and his Sicilian companion. They knew what they wanted. In a moment they had dragged from under the bed a small but heavy iron-bound box, and long before any one thought of coming back to the dead man they had left the house and the village under cover of the darkness. It was easy enough, for Alario's house is the last toward the gorge which leads down here, and the thieves merely went out by the back door, got over the stone wall, and had nothing to risk after that except the possibility of meeting some belated countryman, which was very small indeed, since few of the people use that path. They had a mattock and shovel, and they made their way here without accident.

I am telling you this story as it must have happened, for, of course, there were no witnesses to this part of it. The men brought the box down by the gorge, intending to bury it until they should be able to come back and take it away in a boat. They must have been clever enough to guess that some of the money would be in paper notes, for they would other-wise have buried it on the beach in the wet sand, where it would have been much safer. But the paper would have rotted if they had been obliged to leave it there long, so they dug their hole down there, close to that boulder. Yes, just where the mound is now.

Cristina did not find the doctor in Scalea, for he had been sent for from a place up the valley, halfway to San Domenico. If she had found him, he would have come on his mule by the upper road, which is smoother but much longer. But Cristina took the short cut by the rocks, which passes about fifty feet above the mound, and goes round that corner. The men were digging when she passed, and she heard them at work. It would not have been like her to go by without finding out what the noise was, for she was never afraid of anything in her life, and, besides, the fishermen sometimes came ashore here at night to get a stone for an anchor or to gather sticks to make a little fire. The night was dark, and Cristina probably came close to the two men before she could see what they were doing. She knew them, of course, and they knew her, and understood instantly that they were in her power. There was only one thing to be done for their safety, and they did it. They knocked her on the head, they dug the hole deep, and they buried her quickly with the iron-bound chest. They must have understood that their only chance of escaping suspicion lay in getting back to the village before their absence was noticed, for they returned immediately, and were found half an hour later gossiping quietly with the man who was making Alario's coffin. He was a crony of theirs, and had been working at the repairs in the old man's house. So far as I have been able to make out, the only persons who were supposed to know where Alario kept his treasure were Angelo and the one woman servant I have mentioned. Angelo was away; it was the woman who discovered the theft.

It is easy enough to understand why no one else knew where the money was. The old man kept his door locked and the key in his pocket when he was out, and did not let the woman enter to clean the place unless he was there himself. The whole village knew that he had money somewhere, however, and the masons had probably discovered the whereabouts of the chest by climbing in at the window in his absence. If the old man had not been delirious until he lost consciousness, he would have been in frightful agony of mind for his riches. The faithful woman servant forgot their existence only for a few moments when she fled with the rest, overcome by the horror of death. Twenty minutes had not passed before she returned with the two hideous old hags who are always called in to prepare the dead for burial. Even then she had not at first the courage to go near the bed with them, but she made a pretense of dropping something, went down on her knees as if to find it, and looked under the bedstead. The walls of the room were newly whitewashed down to the floor, and she saw at a glance that the chest was gone. It had been there in the afternoon, it had therefore been stolen in the short interval since she had left the room.

There are no carabineers stationed in the village; there is not so much as a municipal watchman, for there is no municipality. There never was such a place, I believe. Scalea is supposed to look after it in some mysterious way, and it takes a couple of hours to get anybody from there. As the old woman had lived in the village all her life, it did not even occur to her to apply to any civil authority for help. She simply set up a howl and ran through the village in the dark, screaming out that her dead master's house had been robbed. Many of the people looked out, but at first no one seemed inclined to help her. Most of them, judging her by themselves, whispered to each other that she had probably stolen the money herself. The first man to move was the father of the girl whom Angelo was to marry; having collected his household, all of whom felt a personal interest in the wealth which was to have come into the family, he declared it to be his opinion that the chest had been stolen by the two journeyman masons who lodged in the house. He headed a search for them, which naturally began in Alario's house and ended in the carpenter's workshop, where the thieves were found discussing a measure of wine with the carpenter over the half-finished coffin, by the light of one earthen lamp filled with oil and tallow. The search party at once accused the delinquents of the crime, and threatened to lock them up in the cellar till the carabineers could be fetched from Scalea. The two men looked at each other for one moment, and then without the slightest hesitation they put out the single light, seized the unfinished coffin between them, and using it as a sort of battering ram, dashed upon their assailants in the dark. In a few moments they were beyond pursuit.

That is the end of the first part of the story. The treasure had disappeared, and as no trace of it could be found the people naturally supposed that the thieves had succeeded in carrying it off. The old man was buried, and when Angelo came back at last he had to borrow money to pay for the miserable funeral, and had some difficulty in doing so. He hardly needed to be told that in losing his inheritance he had lost his bride. In this part of the world marriages are made on strictly business principles, and if the promised cash is not forthcoming on the appointed day the bride or the bridegroom whose parents have failed to produce it may as well take themselves off, for there will be no wedding. Poor Angelo knew that well enough. His father had been possessed of hardly any land, and now that the hard cash which he had brought from South America was gone, there was nothing left but debts for the building materials that were to have been used for enlarging and improving the old house. Angelo was beggared, and the nice plump little creature who was to have been his turned up her nose at him in the most approved fashion. As for Cristina, it was several days before she was missed, for no one remembered that she had been sent to Scalea for the doctor, who had never come. She often disappeared in the same way for days together, when she could find a little work here and there at the distant farms among the hills. But when she did not come back at all, people began to wonder, and at last made up their minds that she had connived with the masons and had escaped with them.

I paused and emptied my glass.

'That sort of thing could not happen anywhere else,' observed Holger, filling his everlasting pipe again. 'It is wonderful what a natural charm there is about murder and sudden death in a romantic country like this. Deeds that would be simply brutal and disgusting anywhere else become dramatic and mysterious because this is Italy and we are living in a genuine tower of Charles V built against genuine Barbary pirates.'

'There's something in that,' I admitted. Holger is the most romantic man in the world inside of himself, but he always thinks it necessary to explain why he feels anything.

'I suppose they found the poor girl's body with the box,' he said presently.

'As it seems to interest you,' I answered, 'I'll tell you the rest of the story.'

The moon had risen high by this time; the outline of the Thing on the mound was clearer to our eyes than before.

The village very soon settled down to its small, dull life. No one missed old Alario, who had been away so much on his voyages to South America that he had never been a familiar figure in his native place. Angelo lived in the half-finished house, and because he had no money to pay the old woman servant she would not stay with him, but once in a long time she would come and wash a shirt for him for old acquaintance' sake. Besides the house, he had inherited a small patch of ground at some distance from the village; he tried to cultivate it, but he had no heart in the work, for he knew he could never pay the taxes on it and on the house, which would certainly be confiscated by the Government, or seized for the debt of the building material, which the man who had supplied it refused to take back.

Angelo was very unhappy. So long as his father had been alive and rich, every girl in the village had been in love with him; but that was all changed now. It had been pleasant to be admired and courted, and invited to drink wine by fathers who had girls to marry. It was hard to be stared at coldly, and sometimes laughed at because he had been robbed of his inheritance. He cooked his miserable meals for himself, and from being sad became melancholy and morose.

At twilight, when the day's work was done, instead of hanging about in the open space before the church with young fellows of his own age, he took to wandering in lonely places on the outskirts of the village till it was quite dark. Then he slunk home and went to bed to save the expense of a light. But in those lonely twilight hours he began to have strange waking dreams. He was not always alone, for often when he sat on the stump of a tree, where the narrow path turns down the gorge, he was sure that a woman came up noiselessly over the rough stones, as if her feet were bare; and she stood under a clump of chestnut trees only half a dozen yards down the path, and beckoned to him without speaking. Though she was in the shadow he knew that her lips were red, and that when they parted a little and smiled at him she showed two small sharp teeth. He knew this at first rather than saw it, and he knew that it was Cristina, and that she was dead. Yet he was not afraid; he only wondered whether it was a dream, for he thought that if he had been awake he should have been frightened.

Besides, the dead woman had red lips, and that could only happen in a dream. Whenever he went near the gorge after sunset she was already there waiting for him, or else she very soon appeared, and he began to be sure that she came a little nearer to him every day. At first he had only been sure of her blood-red mouth, but now each feature grew distinct, and the pale face looked at him with deep and hungry eyes.

It was the eyes that grew dim. Little by little he came to know that some day the dream would not end when he turned away to go home, but would lead him down the gorge out of which the vision rose. She was nearer now when she beckoned to him. Her cheeks were not livid like those of the dead, but pale with starvation, with the furious and unappeased physical hunger of her eyes that devoured him. They feasted on his soul and cast a spell over him, and at last they were close to his own and held them. He could not tell whether her breath was as hot as fire or as cold as ice; he could not tell whether her red lips burned his or froze them, or whether her five fingers on his wrists seared scorching scars or bit his flesh like frost; he could not tell whether he was awake or asleep, whether she was alive or dead, but he knew that she loved him, she alone of all creatures, earthly or unearthly, and her spell had power over him.

When the moon rose high that night the shadow of that Thing was not alone down there upon the mound.

Angelo awoke in the cool dawn, drenched with dew and chilled through flesh, and blood, and bone. He opened his eyes to the faint gray light, and saw the stars still shining overhead. He was very weak, and his heart was beating so slowly that he was almost like a man fainting. Slowly he turned his head on the mound, as on a pillow, but the other face was not there. Fear seized him suddenly, a fear unspeakable and unknown; he sprang to his teet and fled up the gorge, and he never looked behind him until he reached the door of the house on the outskirts of the village. Drearily he went to his work that day, and wearily the hours dragged themselves after the sun, till at last he touched the sea and sank, and the great sharp hills above Maratea turned purple against the dove-colored eastern sky.

Angelo shouldered his heavy hoe and left the field. He felt less tired now than in the morning when he had begun to work, but he promised himself that he would go home without lingering by the gorge, and eat the best supper he could get himself, and sleep all night in his bed like a Christian man. Not again would he he tempted down the narrow way by a shadow with red lips and icy breath; not again would he dream that dream of terror and delight. He was near the village now; it was half an hour since the sun had set, and the cracked church bell sent little discordant echoes across the rocks and ravines to tell all good people that the day was done. Angelo stood still a moment where the path forked, where it led toward the village on the left, and down to the gorge on the right, where a clump of chestnut trees overhung the narrow way. He stood still a minute, lifting his battered hat from his head and gazing at the fast-fading sea westward, and his lips moved as he silently repeated the familiar evening prayer. His lips moved, but the words that followed them in his brain lost their meaning and turned into others, and ended in a name that he spoke aloud – 'Cristina! With the name, the tension of his will relaxed suddenly, reality went out and the dream took him again and bore him on swiftly and surely like a man walking in his sleep, down, down, by the steep path in the gathering darkness. And as she glided beside him, Cristina whispered strange sweet things in his ear, which somehow, if he had been awake, he knew that he could not quite have understood; but now they were the most wonderful words he had ever heard in his life. And she kissed him also, but not upon his mouth. He felt her sharp kisses upon his white throat, and he knew that her lips were red. So the wild dream sped on through twilight and darkness and moonrise, and all the glory of the summer's night. But in the chilly dawn he lay as one half dead upon the mound down there, recalling and not recalling, drained of his blood, yet strangely longing to give those red lips more. Then came the fear, the awful nameless panic, the mortal horror that guards the confines of the world we see not, neither know of as we know of other things, but which we feel when its icy chill freezes our bones and stirs our hair with the touch of a ghostly hand. Once more Angelo sprang from the mound and fled up the gorge in the breaking day, but his step was less sure this time, and he panted for breath as he ran; and when he came to the bright spring of water that rises halfway up the hillside, he dropped upon his knees and hands and plunged his whole face in and drank as he had never drunk before – for it was the thirst of the wounded man who has lain bleeding all night long upon the battlefield.

She had him fast now, and he could not escape her, but would come to her every evening at dusk until she had drained him of his last drop of blood. It was in vain that when the day was done he tried to take another turning and to go home by a path that did not lead near the gorge. It was in vain that he made promises to himself each morning at dawn when he climbed the lonely way up from the shore to the village. It was all in vain, for when the sun sank burning into the sea, and the coolness of the evening stole out as from a hiding-place to delight the weary world, his feet turned toward the old way, and she was waiting for him in the shadow under the chestnut trees; and then all happened as before, and she fell to kissing his white throat even as she flitted lightly down the way, winding one arm about him. And as his blood failed, she grew more hungry and more thirsty every day, and every day when he awoke in the early dawn it was harder to rouse himself to the effort of climbing the steep path to the village; and when he went to his work his feet dragged painfully, and there was hardly strength in his arms to wield the heavy hoe. He scarcely spoke to any one now, but the people said he was 'consuming himself' for love of the girl he was to have married when he lost his inheritance; and they laughed heartily at the thought, for this is not a very romantic country. At this time, Antonio, the man who stays here to look after the tower, returned from a visit to his people, who live near Salerno. He had been away all the time since before Alario's death and knew nothing of what had happened. He has told me that he came back late in the afternoon and shut himself up in the tower to eat and sleep, for he was very tired. It was past midnight when he awoke, and when he looked out the waning moon was rising over the shoulder of the hill. He looked out toward the mound, and he saw something, and he did not sleep again that night. When he went out again in the morning it was broad daylight, and there was nothing to be seen on the mound but loose stones and driven sand. Yet he did not go very near it; he went straight up the path to the village and directly to the house of the old priest.

'I have seen an evil thing this night,' he said; 'I have seen how the dead drink the blood of the living. And the blood is the life.'

'Tell me what you have seen,' said the priest in reply.

Antonio told him everything he had seen.

'You must bring your book and your holy water tonight,' he added. 'I will be here before sunset to go down with you, and if it pleases your reverence to sup with me while we wait, I will make ready.'

'I will come,' the priest answered, 'for I have read in old books of these strange beings which are neither quick nor dead, and which lie ever fresh in their graves, stealing out in the dusk to taste life and blood.'

Antonio cannot read, but he was glad to see that the priest understood the business; for, of course, the books must have instructed him as to the best means of quieting the half-living Thing forever.

So Antonio went away to his work, which consists largely in sitting on the shady side of the tower, when he is not perched upon a rock with a fishing line catching nothing. But on that day he went twice to look at the mound in the bright sunlight, and he searched round and round it for some hole through which the being might get in and out; but he found none. When the sun began to sink and the air was cooler in the shadows, he went up to fetch the old priest, carrying a little wicker basket with him; and in this they placed a bottle of holy water, and the basin, and sprinkler, and the stole which the priest would need; and they came down and waited in the door of the tower till it should be dark. But while the light still lingered very gray and faint, they saw something moving, just there, two figures, a man's that walked, and a woman's that flitted beside him, and while her head lay on his shoulder she kissed his throat. The priest has told me that, too, and that his teeth chattered and he grasped Antonio's arm. The vision passed and disappeared into the shadow. Then Antonio got the leathern flask of strong liquor, which he kept for great occasions, and poured such a draught as made the old man feel almost young again; and he got the lantern, and his pick and shovel, and gave the priest his stole to put on and the holy water to carry, and they went out together toward the spot where the work was to be done. Antonio says that in spite of the rum his own knees shook together, and the priest stumbled over his Latin. For when they were yet a few yards from the mound the flickering light of the lantern fell upon Angelo's white face, unconscious as if in sleep, and on his upturned throat, over which a very thin red line of blood trickled down into his collar; and the flickering light of the lantern played upon another face that looked up from the feast – upon two deep, dead eyes that saw in spite of death – upon parted lips redder than life itself – upon two gleaming teeth on which glistened a rosy drop. Then the priest, good old man, shut his eyes tight and showered holy water before him, and his cracked voice rose almost to a scream; and then Antonio, who is no coward after all, raised his pick in one hand and the lantern in the other, as he sprang forward, not knowing what the end should be; and then he swears that he heard a woman's cry, and the Thing was gone, and Angelo lay alone on the mound unconscious, with the red line on his throat and the beads of deathly sweat on his cold forehead. They lifted him, half-dead as he was, and laid him on the ground close by! then Antonio went to work, and the priest helped him, though he was old and could not do much; and they dug deep, and at last Antonio, standing in the grave, stooped down with his lantern to see what he might see.

His hair used to be dark brown, with grizzled streaks about the temples; in less than a month from that day he was as gray as a badger. He was a miner when he was young, and most of these fellows have seen ugly sights now and then, when accidents have happened, but he had never seen what he saw that night – that Thing which is neither alive nor dead, that Thing that will abide neither above ground nor in the grave. Antonio had brought something with him which the priest had not noticed. He had made it that afternoon – a sharp stake shaped from a piece of tough old driftwood. He had it with him now, and he had his heavy pick, and he had taken the lantern down into the grave. I don't think any power on earth could make him speak of what happened then, and the old priest was too frightened to look in. He says he heard Antonio breathing like a wild beast, and moving as if he were fighting with something almost as strong as himself; and he heard an evil sound also, with blows, as of something violently driven through flesh and bone: and then the most awful sound of all – a woman's shriek, the unearthly scream of a woman neither dead nor alive, but buried deep for many days. And he, the poor old priest, could only rock himself as he knelt there in the sand, crying aloud his prayers and exorcisms to drown these dreadful sounds. Then suddenly a small ironbound chest was thrown up and rolled over against the old man's knee, and in a moment more Antonio was beside him, his face as white as tallow in the flickering light of the lantern, shoveling the sand and pebbles into the grave with furious haste, and looking over the edge till the pit was half full; and the priest had said that there was much fresh blood on Antonio's hands and on his clothes.

I had come to the end of my story. Holger finished his wine and leaned back in his chair.

'So Angelo got his own again,' he said. 'Did he marry the prim and plump young person to whom he had been betrothed?'

'No; he had been badly frightened. He went to South America, and has not been heard of since.'

'And that poor thing's body is there still, I suppose,' said Holger. 'Is it quite dead yet, I wonder?'

I wonder, too. But whether it is dead or alive, I should hardly care to see it, even in broad daylight.

Antonio is as gray as a badger, and he has never been quite the same man since that night.

The Vampyre
John Polidori

It happened that in the midst of the dissipations attendant upon a London winter, there appeared at the various parties of the leaders of the *ton* a nobleman, more remarkable for his singularities, than his rank. He gazed upon the mirth around him, as if he could not participate therein. Apparently, the light laughter of the fair only attracted his attention, that he might by a look quell it, and throw fear into those breasts where thoughtlessness reigned. Those who felt this sensation of awe, could not explain whence it arose: some attributed it to the dead grey eye, which, fixing upon the object's face, did not seem to penetrate, and at one glance to pierce through to the inward workings of the heart; but fell upon the cheek with a leaden ray that weighed upon the skin it could not pass. His peculiarities caused him to be invited to every house; all wished to see him, and those who had been accustomed to violent excitement, and now felt the weight of *ennui*, were pleased at having something in their presence capable of engaging their attention. In spite of the deadly hue of his face, which never gained a warmer tint, either from the blush of modesty, or from the strong emotion of passion, though its form and outline were beautiful, many of the female hunters after notoriety attempted to win his attentions, and gain, at least, some marks of what they might term affection: Lady Mercer, who had been the mockery of every monster shewn in drawing-rooms since her marriage, threw herself in his way, and did all but put on the dress of a mountebank, to attract his notice – though in vain; – when she stood before him, though his eyes were apparently fixed upon hers, still it seemed as if they were unperceived; even her unappalled impudence was baffled, and she left the field. But though the common adultress could not influence even the guidance of his eyes, it was not that the female sex was indifferent to him: yet such was the apparent caution with which he spoke to the virtuous wife and innocent daughter, that few knew he ever addressed himself to females. He had, however, the reputation of a winning tongue; and whether it was that it even overcame the dread of his singular character, or that they were moved by his apparent hatred of vice, he was as often among those females who form the boast of their sex from their domestic virtues, as among those who sully it by their vices. About the same time, there came to London a young gentleman of the name of Aubrey: he was an orphan left with an only sister in the possession of great wealth, by parents who died while he was yet in childhood. Left also to himself by guardians, who thought it their duty merely to take care of his fortune, while they relinquished the more important charge of his mind to the care of mercenary subalterns, he cultivated more his imagination than his judgment. He had, hence, that high romantic feeling of honour and candour, which daily ruins so many milliners' apprentices. He believed all to sympathise with virtue, and thought that vice was thrown in by Providence merely for the picturesque effect of the scene, as we see in romances: he thought that the misery of a cottage merely consisted in the vesting of clothes, which were as warm, but which were better adapted to the painter's eye by their irregular folds and various coloured patches. He thought, in fine, that the dreams of poets were the realities of life. He was handsome, frank, and rich: for these reasons, upon his entering into the gay circles, many mothers surrounded him, striving which should describe with least truth their languishing or romping favourites: the daughters at the same time, by their brightening countenances when he approached, and by their sparkling eyes, when he opened his lips, soon led him into false notions of his talents and his merit. Attached as he was to the romance of his solitary hours, he was startled at finding, that, except in the tallow and wax candles that flickered, not from the presence of a ghost, but from want of snuffing, there was no foundation in real life for any of that congeries of pleasing pictures and descriptions contained in those volumes, from which he had formed his study. Finding, however, some compensation in his gratified vanity, he was about to relinquish his dreams, when the extraordinary being we have above described, crossed him in his career.

He watched him; and the very impossibility of forming an idea of the character of a man entirely absorbed in himself, who gave few other signs of his observation of external objects, than the tacit assent to their existence, implied by the avoidance of their contact: allowing his imagination to picture every thing that flattered its propensity to extravagant ideas, he soon formed this object into the hero of a romance, and determined to observe the offspring of his fancy, rather than the person before him. He became acquainted with him, paid him attentions, and so far advanced upon his notice, that his presence was always recognised. He gradually learnt that Lord Ruthven's affairs were embarrassed, and soon found, from the notes of preparation in Street, that he was about to travel. Desirous of gaining some information respecting this singular character, who, till now, had only whetted his curiosity, he hinted to his guardians, that it was time for him to perform the tour, which for many generations has been thought necessary to enable the young to take some rapid steps in

the career of vice towards putting themselves upon an equality with the
aged, and not allowing them to appear as if fallen from the skies, whenever
scandalous intrigues are mentioned as the subjects of pleasantry or of
praise, according to the degree of skill shewn in carrying them on. They
consented: and Aubrey immediately mentioning his intentions to Lord
Ruthven, was surprised to receive from him a proposal to join him. Flattered by such a mark of esteem from him, who, apparently, had nothing in
common with other men, he gladly accepted it, and in a few days they had
passed the circling waters.

Hitherto, Aubrey had had no opportunity of studying Lord Ruthven's
character, and now he found, that, though many more of his actions were
exposed to his view, the results offered different conclusions from the
apparent motives to his conduct. His companion was profuse in his
liberality; – the idle, the vagabond, and the beggar, received from his
hand more than enough to relieve their immediate wants. But Aubrey
could not avoid remarking, that it was not upon the virtuous, reduced to
indigence by the misfortunes attendant even upon virtue, that he
bestowed his alms; – these were sent from the door with hardly suppressed
sneers; but when the profligate came to ask something, not to relieve his
wants, but to allow him to wallow in his lust, or to sink him still deeper in
his iniquity, he was sent away with rich charity. This was, however,
attributed by him to the greater importunity of the vicious, which generally prevails over the retiring bashfulness of the virtuous indigent. There
was one circumstance about the charity of his lordship, which was still
more impressed upon his mind: all those upon whom it was bestowed,
inevitably found that there was a curse upon it, for they were all either led
to the scaffold, or sunk to the lowest and the most abject misery. At
Brussels and other towns through which they passed. Aubrey was
surprized at the apparent eagerness with which his companion sought for
the centres of all fashionable vice; there he entered into all the spirit of the
faro table: he betted, and always gambled with success, except where the
known sharper was his antagonist, and then he lost even more than he
gained; but it was always with the same unchanging face, with which he
generally watched the society around: it was not, however, so when he
encountered the rash youthful novice, or the luckless father of a numerous
family; then his very wish seemed fortune's law – this apparent abstrac-
tedness of mind was laid aside, and his eyes sparkled with more fire than
that of the cat whilst dallying with the half-dead mouse. In every town, he
left the formerly affluent youth, torn from the circle he adorned, cursing,
in the solitude of a dungeon, the fate that had drawn him within the reach
of this fiend; whilst many a father sat frantic, amidst the speaking looks of
mute hungry children, without a single farthing of his late immense
wealth, wherewith to buy even sufficient to satisfy their present craving.
Yet he took no money from the gambling table; but immediately lost, to

the ruiner of many, the last gilder he had just snatched from the convulsive grasp of the innocent: this might but be the result of a certain degree of knowledge, which was not, however, capable of combating the cunning of the more experienced. Aubrey often wished to represent this to his friend, and beg him to resign that charity and pleasure which proved the ruin of all, and did not tend to his own profit; but he delayed it – for each day he hoped his friend would give him some opportunity of speaking frankly and openly to him; however, this never occurred. Lord Ruthven in his carriage, and amidst the various wild and rich scenes of nature, was always the same: his eye spoke less than his lip; and though Aubrey was near the object of his curiosity, he obtained no greater gratification from it than the constant excitement of vainly wishing to break that mystery, which to his exalted imagination began to assume the appearance of something supernatural.

They soon arrived at Rome, and Aubrey for a time lost sight of his companion; he left him in daily attendance upon the morning circle of an Italian countess, whilst he went in search of the memorials of another almost deserted city. Whilst he was thus engaged, letters arrived from England, which he opened with eager impatience; the first was from his sister, breathing nothing but affection; the others were from his guardians, the latter astonished him; if it had before entered into his imagination that there was an evil power resident in his companion, these seemed to give him almost sufficient reason for the belief. His guardians insisted upon his immediately leaving his friend, and urged, that his character was dreadfully vicious, for that the possession of irresistible powers of seduction, rendered his licentious habits more dangerous to society. It had been discovered, that his contempt for the adultress had not originated in hatred of her character; but that he had required, to enhance his gratification, that his victim, the partner of his guilt, should be hurled from the pinnacle of unsullied virtue, down to the lowest abyss of infamy and degradation: in fine, that all those females whom he had sought, apparently on account of their virtue, had, since his departure, thrown even the mask aside, and had not scrupled to expose the whole deformity of their vices to the public gaze.

Aubrey determined upon leaving one, whose character had not yet shown a single bright point on which to rest the eye. He resolved to invent some plausible pretext for abandoning him altogether, purposing, in the mean while, to watch him more closely, and to let no slight circumstances pass by unnoticed. He entered into the same circle, and soon perceived, that his Lordship was endeavouring to work upon the inexperience of the daughter of the lady whose house he chiefly frequented. In Italy, it is seldom that an unmarried female is met with in society; he was therefore obliged to carry on his plans in secret; but Aubrey's eye followed him in all his windings, and soon discovered that an assignation had been appointed, which would most likely end in the ruin of an innocent, though thoughtless girl. Losing no time, he entered the apartment of Lord Ruthven, and abruptly asked him his intentions with respect to the lady, informing him at the same time that he was aware of his being about to meet her that very night. Lord Ruthven answered, that his intentions were such as he supposed all would have upon such an occasion; and upon being pressed whether he intended to marry her, merely laughed. Aubrey retired; and, immediately writing a note, to say, that from that moment he must decline accompanying his Lordship in the remainder of their proposed tour, he ordered his servant to seek other apartments, and calling upon the mother of the lady, informed her of all he knew, not only with regard to her daughter, but also concerning the character of his Lordship. The assignation was prevented. Lord Ruthven next day merely sent his servant to notify his complete assent to a separation; but did not hint any suspicion of his plans having been foiled by Aubrey's interposition.

Having left Rome, Aubrey directed his steps towards Greece, and crossing the Peninsula, soon found himself at Athens. He then fixed his residence in the house of a Greek; and soon occupied himself in tracing the faded records of ancient glory upon monuments that apparently, ashamed of chronicling the deeds of freemen only before slaves, had hidden themselves beneath the sheltering soil or many coloured lichen. Under the same roof as himself, existed a being, so beautiful and delicate, that she might have formed the model for a painter, wishing to pourtray on canvass the promised hope of the faithful in Mahomet's paradise, save that her eyes spoke too much mind for any one to think she could belong to those who had no souls. As she danced upon the plain, or tripped along the mountain's side, one would have thought the gazelle a poor type of her beauties; for who would have exchanged her eye, apparently the eye of animated nature, for that sleepy luxurious look of the animal suited but to the taste of an epicure. The light step of Ianthe often accompanied Aubrey in his search after antiquities, and often would the unconscious girl, engaged in the pursuit of a Kashmere butterfly, show the whole beauty of her form, floating as it were upon the wind, to the eager gaze of him, who forgot the letters he had just decyphered upon an almost effaced tablet, in the contemplation of her sylph-like figure. Often would her tresses falling, as she flitted around, exhibit in the sun's ray such delicately brilliant and swiftly fading hues, as might well excuse the forgetfulness of the antiquary, who let escape from his mind the very object he had before thought of vital importance to the proper interpretation of a passage in Pausanias. But why attempt to describe charms which all feel, but none can appreciate? – It was innocence, youth, and beauty, unaffected by crowded drawing-rooms and stifling balls. Whilst he drew those remains of which he wished to preserve a memorial for his future hours, she would stand by, and watch the magic effects of his pencil, in tracing the scenes of her native place; she would then describe to him the circling dance upon the open plain, would paint to him in all the glowing colours of youthful memory, the marriage pomp she remembered viewing in her infancy; and then, turning to subjects that had evidently made a greater impression upon her mind, would tell him all the supernatural tales of her nurse. Her earnestness and apparent belief of what she narrated, excited the interest even of Aubrey; and often as she told him the tale of the living vampyre, who had passed years amidst his friends, and dearest ties, forced every year, by feeding upon the life of a lovely female to prolong his existence for the ensuing months, his blood would run cold, whilst he attempted to laugh her out of such idle and horrible fantasies; but Ianthe cited to him the names of old men, who had at last detected one living among themselves, after several of their near relatives and children had been found marked with the stamp of the fiend's appetite; and when she found him so incredulous, she begged of him to believe her, for it had been remarked, that those who had dared to question their existence, always had some proof given, which obliged them, with grief and heartbreaking, to confess it was true. She detailed to him the traditional appearance of these monsters, and his horror was increased, by hearing a pretty accurate description of Lord Ruthven; he, however, still persisted in persuading her, that there could be no truth in her fears, though at the same time he wondered at the many coincidences which had all tended to excite a belief in the supernatural power of Lord Ruthven.

Aubrey began to attach himself more and more to Ianthe; her innocence, so contrasted with all the affected virtues of the women among whom he had sought for his vision of romance, won his heart; and while he ridiculed the idea of a young man of English habits, marrying an uneducated Greek girl, still he found himself more and more attached to the almost fairy form before him. He would tear himself at times from her, and, forming a plan for some antiquarian research, he would depart, determined not to return until his object was attained; but he always found it impossible to fix his attention upon the ruins around him, whilst in his mind he retained an image that seemed alone the rightful possessor of his thoughts. Ianthe was unconscious of his love, and was ever the same frank infantile being he had first known. She always seemed to part from him with reluctance; but it was because she had no longer any one with whom she could visit her favourite haunts, whilst her guardian was occupied in sketching or uncovering some fragment which had yet escaped the destructive hand of time. She had appealed to her parents on the subject of Vampyres, and they both, with several present, affirmed their existence, pale with horror at the very name. Soon after, Aubrey determined to proceed upon one of his excursions, which was to detain him for a few hours; when they heard the name of the place, they all at once begged of him not to return at night, as he must necessarily pass through a wood, where no Greek would ever remain, after the day had closed, upon any consideration. They described it as the resort of the vampyres in their nocturnal orgies, and denounced the most heavy evils as impending upon him who dared to cross their path. Aubrey made light of their representations, and tried to laugh them out of the idea; but when he saw them shudder at his daring thus to mock a superior, infernal power, the very name of which apparently made their blood freeze, he was silent.

Next morning Aubrey set off upon his excursion unattended; he was surprised to observe the melancholy face of his host, and was concerned to find that his words, mocking the belief of those horrible fiends, had inspired them with such terror. When he was about to depart, Ianthe came to the side of his horse, and earnestly begged of him to return, ere night allowed the power of these beings to be put in action; – he promised. He was, however, so occupied in his research, that he did not perceive that day-light would soon end, and that in the horizon there was one of those specks which, in the warmer climates, so rapidly gather into a tremendous mass, and pour all their rage upon the devoted country. – He at last, however, mounted his horse, determined to make up by speed for his delay: but it was too late. Twilight, in these southern climates, is almost unknown; immediately the sun sets, night begins: and ere he had advanced far, the power of the storm was above – its echoing thunders had scarcely an interval of rest; – its thick heavy rain forced its way through the canopying foliage, whilst the blue forked lightning seemed to fall and radiate at his very feet. Suddenly his horse took fright, and he was carried with dreadful rapidity through the entangled forest. The animal at last, through fatigue, stopped, and he found, by the glare of lightning, that he was in the neighbourhood of a hovel that hardly lifted itself up from the masses of dead leaves and brushwood which surrounded it. Dismounting, he approached, hoping to find some one to guide him to the town, or at least trusting to obtain shelter from the pelting of the storm. As he approached, the thunders, for a moment silent, allowed him to hear the dreadful shrieks of a woman mingling with the stifled, exultant mockery of a laugh, continued in one almost unbroken sound; – he was startled: but, roused by the thunder which again rolled over his head, he, with a sudden effort, forced open the door of the hut. He found himself in utter darkness: the sound, however, guided him. He was apparently unperceived; for, though he called, still the sounds continued, and no notice was taken of him. He found himself in contact with some one, whom he immediately seized; when a voice cried, 'Again baffled!' to which a loud laugh succeeded; and he felt himself grappled by one whose strength seemed superhuman: determined to sell his life as dearly as he could, he struggled; but it was in vain: he was lifted from his feet and hurled with enormous force against the ground: – his enemy threw himself upon him, and kneeling upon his breast, had placed his hands upon his throat – when the glare of many torches penetrating through the hole that gave light in the day, disturbed him; – he instantly rose, and, leaving his prey, rushed through the door, and in a moment the crashing of the branches, as he broke through the wood, was no longer heard. The storm was now still; and Aubrey, incapable of moving, was soon heard by those without. They entered; the light of their torches fell upon the mud walls, and the thatch loaded on every individual straw with heavy flakes of soot. At the desire of Aubrey they searched for her who had attracted him by her cries; he was again left in darkness; but what was his horror, when the light of the torches once more burst upon him, to perceive the airy form of his fair conductress brought in a lifeless corpse. He shut his eyes, hoping that it was but a vision arising from his disturbed imagination; but he again saw the same form, when he unclosed them, stretched by his side. There was no colour upon her cheek, not even upon her lip; yet there was a stillness about her face that seemed almost as attaching as the life that once dwelt there: – upon her neck and breast was blood, and upon her throat were the marks of teeth having opened the vein: – to this the men pointed, crying, simultaneously struck with horror, 'A Vampyre! a Vampyre!' A litter was quickly formed, and Aubrey was laid by the side of her who had lately been to him the object of so many bright and fairy visions, now fallen with the flower of life that had died within her. He knew not what his thoughts were – his mind was benumbed and seemed to shun reflection, and take refuge in vacancy; – he held almost unconsciously in his hand a naked dagger of a particular construction, which had been found in the hut. They were soon met by different parties who had been engaged in the search of her whom a mother had missed. Their lamentable cries, as they approached the city, forewarned the parents of some dreadful catastrophe. – To describe their grief would be impossible; but when they ascertained the cause of their child's death, they looked at Aubrey, and pointed to the corpse. They were inconsolable; both died brokenhearted.

Aubrey being put to bed was seized with a most violent fever, and was often delirious; in these intervals he would call upon Lord Ruthven and upon Ianthe – by some unaccountable combination he seemed to beg of his former companion to spare the being he loved. At other times he would imprecate maledictions upon his head, and curse him as her destroyer. Lord Ruthven chanced at this time to arrive at Athens, and, from whatever motive, upon hearing of the state of Aubrey, immediately placed himself in the same house, and became his constant attendant. When the latter recovered from his delirium, he was horrified and startled at the sight of him whose image he had now combined with that of a Vampyre; but Lord Ruthven, by his kind words, implying almost repentance for the fault that had caused their separation, and still more by the attention, anxiety, and care which he showed, soon reconciled him to his presence.

His lordship seemed quite changed; he no longer appeared that apathetic being who had so astonished Aubrey; but as soon as his convalescence began to be rapid, he again gradually retired into the same state of mind, and Aubrey perceived no difference from the former man, except that at times he was surprised to meet his gaze fixed intently upon him, with a smile of malicious exultation playing upon his lips: he knew not why, but this smile haunted him. During the last stage of the invalid's recovery, Lord Ruthven was apparently engaged in watching the tideless waves raised by the cooling breeze, or in marking the progress of those orbs, circling, like our world, the moveless sun; – indeed, he appeared to wish to avoid the eyes of all.

Aubrey's mind, by this shock, was much weakened, and that elasticity of spirit which had once so distinguished him now seemed to have fled for ever. He was now as much a lover of solitude and silence as Lord Ruthven; but much as he wished for solitude, his mind could not find it in the neighbourhood of Athens; if he sought it amidst the ruins he had formerly frequented, Ianthe's form stood by his side; – if he sought it in the woods, her light step would appear wandering amidst the underwood, in quest of the modest violet; then suddenly turning round, would show, to his wild imagination, her pale face and wounded throat, with a meek smile upon her lips. He determined to fly scenes, every feature of which created such bitter associations in his mind. He proposed to Lord Ruthven, to whom he held himself bound by the tender care he had taken of him during his illness, that they should visit those parts of Greece neither had yet seen. They travelled in every direction, and sought every spot to which a recollection could be attached: but though they thus hastened from place to place, yet they seemed not to heed what they gazed upon. They heard much of robbers, but they gradually began to slight these reports, which they imagined were only the invention of individuals, whose interest it was to excite the generosity of those whom they defended from pretended dangers. In consequence of thus neglecting the advice of the inhabitants, on one occasion they travelled with only a few guards, more to serve as guides than as a defence. Upon entering, however, a narrow defile, at the bottom of which was the bed of a torrent, with large masses of rock brought down from the neighbouring precipices, they had reason to repent their negligence; for scarcely were the whole of the party engaged in the narrow pass, when they were startled by the whistling of bullets close to their heads, and by the echoed report of several guns. In an instant their guards had left them, and, placing themselves behind rocks, had begun to fire in the direction whence the report came. Lord Ruthven and Aubrey, imitating their example, retired for a moment behind the sheltering turn of the defile: but ashamed of being thus detained by a foe, who with insulting shouts bade them advance, and being exposed to unresisting slaughter, if any of the robbers should climb above and take them in the rear, they determined at once to rush forward in search of the enemy. Hardly had they lost the shelter of the rock, when Lord Ruthven received a shot in the shoulder, which brought him to the ground. Aubrey hastened to his assistance; and, no longer heeding the contest or his own peril, was soon surprised by seeing the robbers' faces around him – his guards having, upon Lord Ruthven's being wounded, immediately thrown up their arms and surrendered.

By promises of great reward, Aubrey soon induced them to convey his wounded friend to a neighbouring cabin; and having agreed upon a ransom, he was no more disturbed by their presence – they being content merely to guard the entrance till their comrade should return with the promised sum, for which he had an order. Lord Ruthven's strength rapidly decreased; in two days mortification ensued, and death seemed advancing with hasty steps. His conduct and appearance had not changed; he seemed as unconscious of pain as he had been of the objects about him: but towards the close of the last evening, his mind became apparently uneasy, and his eye often fixed upon Aubrey, who was induced to offer his assistance with more than usual earnestness – 'Assist me! you may save me – you may do more than that – I mean not my life, I heed the death of my existence as little as that of the passing day; but you may save my honour, your friend's honour.' – 'How? tell me how? I would do any thing,' replied Aubrey. – 'I need but little – my life ebbs apace – I cannot explain the whole but if you would conceal all you know of me, my honour were free from stain in the world's mouth – and if my death were unknown for some time in England – I – I – but life.' – 'It shall not be known.' – 'Swear!' cried the dying man, raising himself with exultant violence, 'Swear by all your soul reveres, by all your nature fears, swear that for a year and a day you will not impart your knowledge of my crimes or death to any living being in any way, whatever may happen, or whatever you may see.' – His eyes seemed bursting from their sockets: 'I swear!' said Aubrey; he sunk laughing upon his pillow, and breathed no more.

Aubrey retired to rest, but did not sleep; the many circumstances attending his acquaintance with this man rose upon his mind, and he knew not why; when he remembered his oath a cold shivering came over him, as if from the presentiment of something horrible awaiting him. Rising early in the morning, he was about to enter the hovel in which he had left the corpse, when a robber met him, and informed him that it was no longer there, having been conveyed by himself and comrades, upon his retiring, to the pinnacle of a neighbouring mount, according to a promise they had given his lordship, that it should be exposed to the first cold ray of the moon that rose after his death. Aubrey astonished, and taking several of the men, determined to go and bury it upon the spot where it lay. But, when he had mounted to the summit he found no trace of either the corpse or the clothes, though the robbers swore they pointed out the identical rock on which they had laid the body. For a time his mind was bewildered in conjectures, but he at last returned, convinced that they had buried the corpse for the sake of the clothes.

Weary of a country in which he had met with such terrible misfortunes, and in which all apparently conspired to heighten that superstitious melancholy that had seized upon his mind, he resolved to leave it, and soon arrived at Smyrna. While waiting for a vessel to convey him to Otranto, or to Naples, he occupied himself in arranging those effects he had with him belonging to Lord Ruthven. Amongst other things there was a case containing several weapons of offence, more or less adapted to ensure the death of the victim. There were several daggers and ataghans. Whilst turning them over, and examining their curious forms, what was his surprise at finding a sheath apparently ornamented in the same style as the dagger discovered in the fatal hut; – he shuddered; – hastening to gain further proof, he found the weapon, and his horror may be imagined when he discovered that it fitted, though peculiarly shaped, the sheath he held in his hand. His eyes seemed to need no further certainty – they seemed gazing to be bound to the dagger; yet still he wished to disbelieve; but the particular form, the same varying tints upon the haft and sheath were alike in splendour on both, and left no room for doubt; there were also drops of blood on each.

He left Smyrna, and on his way home, at Rome, his first inquiries were concerning the lady he had attempted to snatch from Lord Ruthven's seductive arts. Her parents were in distress, their fortune ruined, and she had not been heard of since the departure of his lordship. Aubrey's mind became almost broken under so many repeated horrors; he was afraid that this lady had fallen a victim to the destroyer of Ianthe. He became morose and silent; and his only occupation consisted in urging the speed of the postilions, as if he were going to save the life of some one he held dear. He arrived at Calais; a breeze, which seemed obedient to his will, soon wafted him to the English shores; and he hastened to the mansion of his fathers, and there, for a moment, appeared to lose, in the embraces and caresses of his sister, all memory of the past. If she before, by her infantine caresses, had gained his affection, now that the woman began to appear, she was still more attaching as a companion.

Miss Aubrey had not that winning grace which gains the gaze and applause of the drawing-room assemblies. There was none of that light brilliancy which only exists in the heated atmosphere of a crowded apart-ment. He blue eye was never lit up by the levity of the mind beneath. There was a melancholy charm about it which did not seem to arise from misfortune, but from some feeling within, that appeared to indicate a soul conscious of a brighter realm. Her step was not that light footing, which strays where'er a butterfly or a colour may attract – it was sedate and pensive. When alone, her face was never brightened by the smile of joy;

but when her brother breathed to her his affection, and would in her presence forget those griefs she knew destroyed his rest, who would have exchanged her smile for that of the voluptuary? It seemed as if those eyes, that face were then playing in the light of their own native sphere. She was yet only eighteen, and had not been presented to the world, it having been thought by her guardians more fit that her presentation should be delayed until her brothers' return from the continent, when he might be her protector. It was now, therefore, resolved that the next drawing-room, which was fast approaching, should be the epoch of her entry into the 'busy scene.' Aubrey would rather have remained in the mansion of his fathers, and fed upon the melancholy which overpowered him. He could not feel interest about the frivolities of fashionable strangers, when his mind had been so torn by the events he had witnessed; but he determined to sacrifice his own comfort to the protection of his sister. They soon arrived in town, and prepared for the next day, which had been announced as a drawing-room.

The crowd was excessive – a drawing-room had not been held for a long time, and all who were anxious to bask in the smile of royalty, hastened thither. Aubrey was there with his sister. While he was standing in a corner by himself, heedless of all around him, engaged in the remembrance that the first time he had seen Lord Ruthven was in that very place – he felt himself suddenly seized by the arm, and a voice he recognized too well, sounded in his ear – 'Remember your oath.' He had hardly courage to turn, fearful of seeing a spectre that would blast him, when he perceived, at a little distance, the same figure which had attracted his notice on this spot upon his first entry into society. He gazed till his limbs almost refusing to bear their weight, he was obliged to take the arm of a friend, and forcing a passage through the crowd, he threw himself into his carriage, and was driven home. He paced the room with hurried steps, and fixed his hands upon his head, as if he were afraid his thoughts were bursting from his brain. Lord Ruthven again before him – circumstances started up in dreadful array – the dagger – his oath. – He roused himself, he could not believe it possible – the dead rise again! – He thought his imagination had conjured up the image his mind was resting upon. It was impossible that it could be real – he determined, therefore, to go again into society; for though he attempted to ask concerning Lord Ruthven, the bname hung upon his lips, and he could not succeed in gaining information. He went a few nights after with his sister to the assembly of a near relation. Leaving her under the protection of a matron, he retired into a recess, and there gave himself up to his own devouring thoughts. Perceiving, at last, that many were leaving, he roused himself, and entering another room, found his sister surrounded by several, apparently in earnest conversation; he attempted to pass and get near her, when one, whom he requested to move, turned round, and revealed to him those features he most abhorred. He sprang forward, seized his sister's arm, and, with hurried step, forced her towards the street: at the door he found himself impeded by the crowd of servants who were waiting for their lords; and while he was engaged in passing them, he again heard that voice whisper close to him – 'Remember your oath!' – He did not dare to turn, but, hurrying his sister, soon reached home.

Aubrey became almost distracted. If before his mind had been absorbed by one subject, how much more completely was it engrossed, now that the certainty of the monster's living again pressed upon his thoughts. His sister's attentions were now unheeded, and it was in vain that she intreated him to explain to her what had caused his abrupt conduct. He only uttered a few words, and those terrified her. The more he thought, the more he was bewildered. His oath startled him; – was he then to allow this monster to roam, bearing ruin upon his breath, amidst all he held dear, and not avert its progress? His very sister might have been touched by him. But even if he were to break his oath, and disclose his suspicions, who would believe him? He thought of employing his own hand to free the world from such a wretch; but death, he remembered, had been already mocked. For days he remained in this state; shut up in his room, he saw no one, and ate only when his sister came, who, with eyes streaming with tears, besought him, for her sake, to support nature. At last, no longer capable of bearing stillness and solitude, he left his house, roamed from street to street, anxious to fly that image which haunted him. His dress became neglected, and he wandered, as often exposed to the noon-day sun as to the mid-night damps. He was no longer to be recognized; at first he returned with the evening to the house; but at last he laid him down to rest wherever fatigue overtook him. His sister, anxious for his safety, employed people to follow him; but they were soon distanced by him who fled from a pursuer swifter than any – from thought. His conduct, however, suddenly changed. Struck with the idea that he left by his absence the whole of his friends, with a fiend amongst them, of whose presence they were unconscious, he determined to enter again into society, and watch him closely, anxious to forewarn, in spite of his oath, all whom Lord Ruthven approached with intimacy. But when he entered into a room, his haggard and suspicious looks were so striking, his inward shudderings so visible, that his sister was at last obliged to beg of him to abstain from seeking, for her sake, a society which affected him so strongly. When, however, remonstrance proved unavailing, the guardians thought proper to interpose, and, fearing that his mind was becoming alienated, they thought it high time to resume again that trust which had been before imposed upon them by Aubrey's parents.

Desirous of saving him from the injuries and sufferings he had daily encountered in his wanderings, and of preventing him from exposing to the general eye those marks of what they considered folly, they engaged a physician to reside in the house, and take constant care of him. He hardly appeared to notice it, so completely was his mind absorbed by one terrible subject. His incoherence became at last so great, that he was confined to his chamber. There he would often lie for days, incapable of being roused. He had become emaciated, his eyes had attained a glassy lustre; – the only sign of affection and recollection remaining displayed itself upon the entry of his sister; then he would sometimes start, and, seizing her hands, with looks that severely afflicted her, he would desire her not to touch him. 'Oh, do not touch him – if your love for me is aught, do not go near him!' When, however, she inquired to whom he referred, his only answer was, 'True! true!' and again he sank into a state, whence not even she could rouse him. This lasted many months: gradually, however, as the year was passing, his incoherences became less frequent, and his mind threw off a portion of its gloom, whilst his guardians observed, that several times in the day he would count upon his fingers a definite number, and then smile.

The time had nearly elapsed, when, upon the last day of the year, one of his guardians entering his room, began to converse with his physician upon the melancholy circumstance of Aubrey's being in so awful a situation, when his sister was going next day to be married. Instantly Aubrey's attention was attracted; he asked anxiously to whom. Glad of this mark of returning intellect, of which they feared he had been deprived, they mentioned the name of the Earl of Marsden. Thinking this was a young Earl whom he had met with in society, Aubrey seemed pleased, and astonished them still more by his expressing his intention to be present at the nuptials, and desiring to see his sister. They answered not, but in a few minutes his sister was with him. He was apparently again capable of being affected by the influence of her lovely smile; for he pressed her to his breast, and kissed her cheek, wet with tears, flowing at the thought of her brother's being once more alive to the feelings of affection. He began to speak with all his wonted warmth, and to congratulate her upon her marriage with a person so distinguished for rank and every accomplishment; when he suddenly perceived a locket upon her breast; opening it, what was his surprise at beholding the features of the monster who had so long influenced his life. He seized the portrait in a paroxysm of rage, and trampled it under foot. Upon her asking him why he thus destroyed the resemblance of her future husband, he looked as if he did not understand her; – then seizing her hands, and gazing on her with a frantic expression of countenance, he bade her swear that she would never wed this monster, for he – But he could not advance – it seemed as if that voice again bade him remember his oath – he turned suddenly round, thinking Lord Ruthven was near him but saw no one. In the meantime the guardians and physician, who had heard the whole, and thought this was but a return of his disorder, entered, and forcing him from Miss Aubrey, desired her to leave him. He fell upon his knees to them, he implored, he begged of them to delay but for one day. They, attributing this to the insanity they imagined had taken possession of his mind, endeavoured to pacify him, and retired.

Lord Ruthven had called the morning after the drawing-room, and had been refused with every one else. When he heard of Aubrey's ill health, he readily understood himself to be the cause of it; but when he learned that he was deemed insane, his exultation and pleasure could hardly be concealed from those among whom he had gained this information. He hastened to the house of his former companion, and, by constant attendance, and the pretence of great affection for the brother and interest in his fate, he gradually won the ear of Miss Aubrey. Who could resist his power? His tongue had dangers and toils to recount – could speak of himself as of an individual having no sympathy with any being on the crowded earth, save with her to whom he addressed himself; – could tell how, since he knew her, his existence had begun to seem worthy of preservation, if it were merely that he might listen to her soothing accents; – in fine, he knew so well how to use the serpent's art, or such was the will of fate, that he gained her affections. The title of the elder branch falling at length to him, he obtained an important embassy, which served as an excuse for hastening the marriage (in spite of her brother's deranged state), which was to take place the very day before his departure for the continent.

Aubrey, when he was left by the physician and his guardians, attempted to bribe the servants, but in vain. He asked for pen and paper; it was given him; he wrote a letter to his sister, conjuring her, as she valued her own happiness, her own honour, and the honour of those now in the grave, who once held her in their arms as their hope and the hope of their house, to delay but for a few hours that marriage, on which he denounced the most heavy curses. The servants promised they would deliver it; but giving it to the physician, he thought it better not to harass any more the mind of Miss Aubrey by, what he considered, the ravings of a maniac. Night passed on without rest to the busy inmates of the house; and Aubrey heard, with a horror that may more easily be conceived than described, the notes of busy preparation. Morning came, and the sound of carriages broke upon his ear. Aubrey grew almost frantic. The curiosity of the servants at last overcame their vigilance; they gradually stole away, leaving him in the custody of an helpless old woman. He seized the opportunity, with one bound was out of the room, and in a moment found himself in the apartment where all were nearly assembled. Lord Ruthven was the first to perceive him: he immediately approached, and, taking his arm by force, hurried him from the room, speechless with rage. When on the staircase, Lord Ruthven whispered in his ear – 'Remember your oath, and know, if not my bride to day, your sister is dishonoured. Women are frail!' So saying, he pushed him towards his attendants, who, roused by the old woman, had come in search of him. Aubrey could no longer support himself; his rage not finding vent, had broken a blood-vessel, and he was conveyed to bed. This was not mentioned to his sister, who was not present when he entered, as the physician was afraid of agitating her. The marriage was solemnized, and the bride and bridegroom left London.

Aubrey's weakness increased; the effusion of blood produced symptoms of the near approach of death. He desired his sister's guardians might be called, and when the midnight hour had struck, he related composedly what the reader has perused – he died immediately after.

The guardians hastened to protect Miss Aubrey; but when they arrived, it was too late. Lord Ruthven had disappeared, and Aubrey's sister had glutted the thirst of a VAMPYRE!

Mrs Amworth
E. F. Benson

The village of Maxley, where last summer and autumn, these strange events took place, lies on a heathery and pine-clad upland of Sussex. In all England you could not find a sweeter and saner situation. Should the wind blow from the south, it comes laden with the spices of the sea; to the east high downs protect it from the inclemencies of March; and from the west and north the breezes which reach it travel over miles of aromatic forest and heather. The village itself is insignificant enough in point of population, but rich in amenities and beauty. Half-way down the single street, with its broad road and spacious areas of grass on each side, stands the little Norman Church and the antique graveyard long disused: for the rest there are a dozen small, sedate Georgian houses, red-bricked and long-windowed, each with a square of flower garden in front, and an ampler strip behind; a score of shops, and a couple of score of thatched cottages belonging to labourers on neighbouring estates, complete the entire cluster of its peaceful habitations. The general peace, however, is sadly broken on Saturdays and Sundays, for we lie on one of the main roads between London and Brighton and our quiet street becomes a race-course for flying motor-cars and bicycles. A notice just outside the village begging them to go slowly only seems to encourage them to accelerate their speed, for the road lies open and straight, and there is really no reason why they should do otherwise. By way of protest, there-fore, the ladies of Maxley cover their noses and mouths with their hand-kerchiefs as they see a motor-car approaching, though, as the street is asphalted, they need not really take these precautions against dust. But late on Sunday night the horde of scorchers has passed, and we settle down again to five days of cheerful and leisurely seclusion. Railway strikes which agitate the country so much leave us undisturbed because most of the inhabitants of Maxley never leave it at all.

I am the fortunate possessor of one of these small Georgian houses, and consider myself no less fortunate in having so interesting and stimulating a neighbour as Francis Urcombe, who, the most confirmed of Maxleyites, has not slept away from his house, which stands just opposite to mine in

the village street, for nearly two years, at which date, though still in middle
life he resigned his Physiological Professorship at Cambridge University,
and devoted himself to the study of those occult and curious phenomena
which seem equally to concern the physical and psychical sides of human
nature. Indeed his retirement was not unconnected with his passion for
the strange uncharted places that lie on the confines and borders of
science, the existence of which is so stoutly denied by the more materi-
alistic minds, for he advocated that all medical students should be obliged
to pass some sort of examination in mesmerism, and that one of the tripos
papers should be designed to test their knowledge in such subjects as
appearances at time of death, haunted houses, vampirism, automatic
writing, and possession.

'Of course they wouldn't listen to me,' ran his account of the matter,
'for there is nothing that these seats of learning are so frightened of as
knowledge, and the road to knowledge lies in the study of things like these.
The functions of the human frame are, broadly speaking, known. They
are a country, anyhow, that has been charted and mapped out. But
outside that lie huge tracts of undiscovered country, which certainly exist,
and the real pioneers of knowledge are those who, at the cost of being
derided as credulous and superstitious, want to push on into those misty
and probably perilous places. I felt that I could be of more use by setting
out without compass or knapsack into the mists than by sitting in a cage
like a canary and chirping about what was known. Besides, teaching is
very very bad for a man who knows himself only to be a learner: you only
need to be a self conceited ass to teach.'

Here, then, in Francis Urcombe, was a delightful neighbour to one
who, like myself, has an uneasy and burning curiosity about what he
called the 'misty and perilous places' and this last spring we had a further
and most welcome addition to our pleasant little community, in the person of Mrs Amworth, widow of an Indian civil servant. Her husband had
been a judge in the North-West Provinces, and after his death at Peshawar
she came back to England, and after a year in London found herself
starving for the ampler air and sunshine of the country to take the place of
the fogs and griminess of town. She had, too, a special reason for settling in
Maxley, since her ancestors up till a hundred years ago had long been
native to the place, and in the old churchyard, now disused, are many
gravestones bearing her maiden name of Chaston. Big and energetic, her
vigorous and genial personality speedily woke Maxley up to a higher
degree of sociality than it ever had known. Most of us were bachelors or
spinsters or elderly folk not much inclined to exert ourselves in the
expense and effort of hospitality and hitherto the gaiety of a small tea
party, with bridge afterwards and galoshes (when it was wet) to trip home
in again for a solitary dinner, was about the climax of our festivities. But
Mrs Amworth showed us a more gregarious way, and set an example of

luncheon parties and little dinners, which we began to follow. On other nights when no such hospitality was on foot, a lone man like myself found it pleasant to know that a call on the telephone to Mrs Amworth's house not a hundred yards off, and an inquiry as to whether I might come over after dinner for a game of piquet before bedtime, would probably evoke a response of welcome. There she would be, with comrade-like eagerness for companionship, and there was a glass of port and a cup of coffee and a cigarette and a game of piquet. She played the piano, too, in a free and exuberant manner, and had a charming voice and sang to her own accompaniment; and as the days grew long and the light lingered late, we played our game in her garden, which in the course of a few months she had turned from being a nursery for slugs and snails into a glowing patch of luxuriant blossomings. She was always cheery and jolly; she was interested in everything; and in music, in gardening, in games of all sorts was a competent performer. Everybody (with one exception) liked her, everybody felt her to bring with her the tonic of a sunny day. That one exception was Francis Urcombe; he, though he confessed he did not like her, acknowledged that he was vastly interested in her. This always seemed strange to me, for pleasant and jovial as she was, I could see nothing in her that could call forth conjecture or intrigued surmise, so healthy and unmysterious a figure did she present. But of the genuineness of Urcombe's interest there could be no doubt; one could see him watching and scrutinising her. In matter of age, she frankly volunteered the information that she was forty-five; but her briskness, her activity, her unravaged skin, her coal-black hair, made it difficult to believe that she was not adopting an unusual device and adding ten years on to her age instead of subtracting them.

Often, also, as our quite unsentimental friendship ripened, Mrs Amworth would ring me up and propose her advent. If I was busy writing, I was to give her, so we definitely bargained, a frank negative, and in answer I could hear her jolly laugh and her wishes for a successful evening of work. Sometimes, before her proposal arrived, Urcombe would already have stepped across from his house opposite for a smoke and a chat, and he, hearing who my intended visitor was, always urged me to beg her to come. She and I should play our piquet, said he, and he would look on, if we did not object and learn something of the game. But I doubt whether he paid much attention to it, for nothing could be clearer than that, under that penthouse of forehead and thick eyebrows, his attention was fixed not on the cards, but on one of the players. But he seemed to enjoy an hour spent thus, and often, until one particular evening in July, he would watch her with the air of a man who has some deep problem in front of him. She, enthusiastically keen about our game, seemed not to notice his scrutiny. Then came that evening when, as I see in the light of subsequent events, began the first twitching of the veil that hid the secret horror from my eyes. I did not know it then, though I noticed that there after if she rang up to propose coming round, she always asked not only if I was at leisure, but whether Mr Urcombe was with me. If so, she said, she would not spoil the chat of two old bachelors, and laughingly wished me good-night. Urcombe, on this occasion, had been with me for some half-hour before Mrs Amworth's appearance, and had been talking to me about the medieval beliefs concerning vampirism, one of those border-land subjects which he declared had not been sufficiently studied before it had been consigned by the medical profession to the dustheap of exploded superstitions. There he sat, grim and eager, tracing with that pellucid clearness which had made him in his Cambridge days so admirable a lecturer, the history of those mysterious visitations. In them all there was the same general features; one of those ghoulish spirits took up its abode in a living man or woman, conferring supernatural powers of bat-like flight and glutting itself with nocturnal blood-feasts. When its host died it continued to dwell in the corpse, which remained undecayed. By day it rested, by night it left the grave and went on its awful errands. No European country in the Middle Ages seemed to have escaped them; earlier yet, parallels were to be found in Roman and Greek and in Jewish history.

'It's a large order to set all that evidence aside as being moonshine,' he said. 'Hundreds of totally independent witnesses in many ages have testified to the occurrence of these phenomena, and there's no explanation known to me which covers all the facts. And if you feel inclined to say "Why, then, if these are facts, do we not come across them now?" there are two answers I can make you. One is that there were diseases known in the Middle Ages, such as the black death, which were certainly existent then and which have become extinct since, but for that reason we do not assert that such diseases never existed. Just as the black death visited England and decimated the population of Norfolk, so here in this very district about three hundred years ago there was certainly an outbreak of vampirism, and Maxley was the centre of it. My second answer is even more convincing, for I tell you that vampirism is by no means extinct now. An outbreak of it certainly occurred in India a year or two ago.'

At that moment I heard my knocker plied in the cheerful and peremptory manner in which Mrs Amworth is accustomed to announce her arrival, and I went to the door to open it.

'Come in at once,' I said, 'and save me from having my blood curdled. Mr Urcombe has been trying to alarm me.'

Instantly her vital, voluminous presence seemed to fill the room.

'Ah, but how lovely!' she said. 'I delight in having my blood curdled. Go on with your ghost story, Mr Urcombe. I adore ghost stories.'

I saw that, as his habit was, he was intently observing her.

'It wasn't a ghost story exactly,' said he. 'I was only telling our host how vampirism was not extinct yet. I was saying that there was an outbreak of it in India only a few years ago.'

There was a more than perceptible pause, and I saw that, if Urcombe was observing her, she on her side was observing him with fixed eye and parted mouth. Then her jolly laugh invaded that rather tense silence.

'Oh, what a shame!' she said. 'You're not going to curdle my blood at all. Where did you pick up such a tale, Mr Urcombe? I have lived for years in India and never heard a rumour of such a thing. Some storyteller in the bazaars must have invented it; they are famous at that.'

I could see that Urcombe was on the point of saying something further, but checked himself.

'Ah! very likely that was it,' he said.

But something had disturbed our usual peaceful sociability that night, and something had dampened Mrs Amworth's usual high spirits. She had no gusto for her piquet, and left after a couple of games. Urcombe had been silent too, indeed he hardly spoke again till she departed.

'That was unfortunate,' he said, 'for the outbreak of – of a very mysterious disease, let us call it, took place at Peshawar where she and her husband were. And – '

'Well?' I asked.

'He was one of the victims of it,' said he. 'Naturally I had quite forgotten that when I spoke.'

The summer was unreasonably hot and rainless, and Maxley suffered much from drought, and also from a plague of big black night-flying gnats, the bite of which was very irritating and virulent. They came sailing in of an evening, settling on one's skin so quietly that one perceived nothing till the sharp stab announced that one had been bitten. They did not bite the hands or face, but chose always the neck and throat for their feeding-ground, and most of us, as the poison spread, assumed a temporary goitre. Then about the middle of August appeared the first of those mysterious cases of illness which our local doctor attributed to the long-continued heat coupled with the bite of these venomous insects. The patient was a boy of sixteen or seventeen, the son of Mrs Amworth's gardener, and the symptoms were an anaemic pallor and a languid prostration, accompanied by great drowsiness and an abnormal appetite. He had, too, on his throat two small punctures where, so Dr Ross conjectured, one of these great gnats had bitten him. But the odd thing was that there was no swelling or inflammation round the place where he had been bitten. The heat at this time had begun to abate, but the cooler weather failed to restore him, and the boy, in spite of the quantity of food which he so ravenously swallowed, wasted away to a skinclad skeleton.

I met Dr Ross in the street one afternoon about this time, and in answer to my inquiries about his patient he said that he was afraid the boy was dying. The case, he confessed, completely puzzled him: some obscure form of pernicious anaemia was all he could suggest. But he wondered whether Mr Urcombe would consent to see the boy, on the chance of his being able to throw some new light on the case, and since Urcombe was dining with me that night, I proposed to Dr Ross to join us. He could not do this, but said he would look in later. When he came, Urcombe at once consented to put his skill at the other's disposal, and together they went off at once. Being thus shorn of my sociable evening, I telephoned to Mrs Amworth to know if I might inflict myself on her for an hour. Her answer was a welcoming affirmative, and between piquet and music the hour lengthened itself into two. She spoke of the boy who was lying so desperately and mysteriously ill, and told me that she had often been to see him, taking him nourishing and delicate food. But today – and her kind eyes moistened as she spoke – she was afraid she had paid her last visit. Knowing the antipathy between her and Urcombe, I did not tell her that he had been called into consultation; and when I returned home she accompanied me to the door, for the sake of a breath of night air, and in order to borrow a magazine which contained an article on gardening which she wished to read.

'Ah, this delicious night air,' she said, luxuriously sniffing in the coolness. 'Night air and gardening are the great tonics. There is nothing so stimulating as bare contact with rich mother earth. You are never so fresh as when you have been grubbing in the soil – black hands, black nails, and boots covered with mud.' She gave her great jovial laugh.

'I'm a glutton for air and earth,' she said. 'Positively I look forward to death, for then I shall be buried and have the kind earth all round me. No leaden caskets for me – I have given explicit directions. But what shall I do about air? Well, I suppose one can't have everything. The magazine? A thousand thanks, I will faithfully return it. Good-night: garden and keep your windows open, and you won't have anaemia.'

'I always sleep with my windows open,' said I.

I went straight up to my bedroom, of which one of the windows looks out over the street, and as I undressed I thought I heard voices talking outside not far away. But I paid no particular attention, put out my lights, and falling asleep plunged into the depths of a most horrible dream, distortedly suggested, no doubt, by my last words with Mrs Amworth. I dreamed that I woke, and found that both my bedroom windows were shut. Half-suffocating, I dreamed that I sprang out of bed, and went across to open them. The blind over the first one was drawn down, and pulling it up I saw, with the indescribable horror of incipient nightmare, Mrs Amworth's face suspended close to the pane in the darkness outside, nodding and smiling at me. Pulling down the blind again to keep that terror out, I rushed to the second window on the other side of the room, and there again was Mrs Amworth's face. Then the panic came upon me

in full blast; here was I suffocating in the airless room, and whichever
window I opened Mrs Amworth's face would float in, like those noiseless
black gnats that bit before one was aware. The nightmare rose to screaming point, and with strangled yells I awoke to find my room cool and quiet
with both windows open and blinds up and a half-moon high in its course,
casting an oblong of tranquil light on the floor. But even when I was awake
the horror persisted, and I lay tossing and turning. I must have slept long
before the nightmare seized me, for now it was nearly day, and soon in the
east the drowsy eyelids of morning began to lift.

I was scarcely downstairs next morning – for after the dawn I slept
late – when Urcombe rang up to know if he might see me immediately.
He came in, grim and preoccupied, and I noticed that he was pulling on a
pipe that was not even filled.

'I want your help,' he said, 'and so I must tell you first of all what
happened last night. I went round with the little doctor to see his patient,
and found him just alive, but scarcely more. I instantly diagnosed in my
own mind what this anaemia, unaccountable by any other explanation
meant. The boy is the prey of a vampire.'

He put his empty pipe on the breakfast table, by which I had just sat
down, and folded his arms, looking at me steadily from under his overhanging brows.

'Now about last night,' he said. 'I insisted that he should be moved from
his father's cottage into my house. As we were carrying him on a stretcher,
whom should we meet but Mrs Amworth ? She expressed shocked surprise that we were moving him. Now why do you think she did that?'

With a start of horror, as I remembered my dream that night before, I
felt an idea come into my mind so preposterous and unthinkable that I
instantly turned it out again.

'I haven't the smallest idea,' I said.

'Then listen, while I tell you about what happened later. I put out all light
in the room where the boy lay, and watched. One window was a little open,
for I had forgotten to close it, and about midnight I heard something
outside, trying apparently to push it farther open. I guessed who it was – yes,
it was full twenty feet from the ground – and I peeped round the corner of
the blind. Just outside was the face of Mrs Amworth and her hand was on
the frame of the window. Very softly I crept close, and then banged the
window down, and I think I just caught the tip of one of her fingers.'

'But it's impossible,' I cried. 'How could she be floating in the air like
that? And what had she come for? Don't tell me such – '

Once more, with closer grip, the remembrance of my nightmare seized
me.

'I am telling you what I saw,' said he. 'And all night long, until it was
nearly day, she was fluttering outside like some terrible bat, trying to gain
admittance. Now put together various things I have told you.'

He began checking them off on his fingers.

'Number one,' he said: 'there was an outbreak of disease similar to that which this boy is suffering from at Peshawar, and her husband died of it. Number two: Mrs Amworth protested against my moving the boy to my house. Number three: she, or the demon that inhabits her body, a creature powerful and deadly, tries to gain admittance. And add this, too: in medieval times there was an epidemic of vampirism here at Maxley. The vampire, so the accounts run, was found to be Elizabeth Chaston. ... I see you remember Mrs Amworth's maiden name. Finally, the boy is stronger this morning. He would certainly not have been alive if he had been visited again. And what do you make of it?'

There was a long silence, during which I found this incredible horror assuming the hues of reality.

'I have something to add,' I said, 'which may or may not bear on it. You say that the – spectre went away shortly before dawn?'

'Yes.'

I told him of my dream, and he smiled grimly.

'Yes, you did well to awake,' he said. 'That warning came from your subconscious self, which never wholly slumbers, and cried out to you of deadly danger. For two reasons, then you must help me: one to save others, the second to save yourself.'

'What do you want me to do?' I asked.

'I want you first of all to help me in watching this boy, and ensuring that she does not come near him. Eventually I want you to help me in tracking the thing down, in exposing and destroying it. It is not human: it is an incarnate fiend. What steps we shall have to take I don't know.'

It was now eleven of the forenoon, and presently I went across to his house for a twelve-hour vigil while he slept, to come on duty again that night, so that for the next twenty-four hours either Urcombe or myself was always in the room where the boy, now getting stronger every hour, was lying. The day following was Saturday and a morning of brilliant pellucid weather, and already when I went across to his house to resume my duty the stream of motors down to Brighton had begun. Simultaneously I saw Urcombe with a cheerful face, which boded good news of his patient, coming out of his house, and Mrs Amworth, with a gesture of salutation to me, and a basket in her hand, walking up the broad strip of grass which bordered the road. There we all three met, I noticed (and saw that Urcombe noticed it too) that one finger on her left hand was bandaged.

'Good morning to you both,' said she. 'And I hear your patient is doing well, Mr Urcombe. I have come to bring him a bowl of jelly, and to sit with him for an hour. He and I are great friends. I am overjoyed at his recovery.'

Urcombe paused a moment, as if making up his mind, and then shot out a pointing finger at her.

'I forbid that,' he said. 'You shall not sit with him or see him. And you know the reason as well as I do.'

I have never seen so horribie a change pass over a human face as that which now blanched hers to the colour of grey mist. She put up her hand as if to shield herself from the pointing finger, which drew the sign of the cross in the air, and shrank back cowering on the road. There was a wild hoot from a horn, a grinding of brakes, a shout – too late – from a passing car, and one long scream suddenly cut short. Her body rebounded from the roadway after the first wheel had gone over it, and the second followed it. It lay there, quivering and twitching and was still.

She was buried three days afterwards in the cemetery outside Maxley, in accordance with the wishes she had told me that she had devised about her internment, and the shock which her sudden and awful death had caused to the little community began by degrees to pass off. To two people only, Urcombe and myself, the horror of it was mitigated from the first by the nature of the relief that her death brought; but, naturally enough, we kept our own counsel, and no hint of what greater horror had been thus averted was ever let slip. But, oddly enough, so it seemed to me, he was still not satisfied about something in connnection with her, and would give no answer to my questions on the subject. Then as the days of a tranquil mellow September and the October that followed began to drop away like the leaves of the yellowing trees, his uneasiness relaxed. But before the entry of November the seeming tranquility broke into hurricane.

I had been dining one night at the far end of the village, and about eleven o'clock was walking home again. The moon was of an unusual brilliance, rendering all that it shone on as distinct as in some etching. I had just come opposite the house which Mrs Amworth had occupied, where there was a board up telling that it was to let, when I heard the click of her front gate, and next moment I saw, with a sudden chill and quaking of my very spirit, that she stood there. Her profile vividly illuminated, was turned to me, and I could not be mistaken in my identification of her. She appeared not to see me (indeed the shadow of the yew hedge in front of her garden enveloped me in its blackness) and she went swiftly across the road, and entered the gate of the house directly opposite. There I lost sight of her completely.

My breath was coming in short pants as if I had been running – and now indeed I ran, with fearful backward glances, along the hundred yards that separated me from my house and Urcombe's. It was to his that my flying steps took me, and next minute I was within.

'What have you come to tell me?' he asked. 'Or shall I guess?'

'You can't guess,' said I.

'No; it's no guess. She has come back and you have seen her. Tell me about it.'

I gave my story.

'That's Major Pearsall's house,' he said. 'Come back with me there at once.'

'But what can we do?' I asked.

'I've no idea. That's what we have got to find out.'

A minute later, we were opposite the house. When I had passed it before, it was all dark; now lights gleamed from a couple of windows upstairs. Even as we faced it, the front door opened, and next moment Major Pearsall emerged from the gate. He saw us and stopped.

I'm on my way to Dr Ross, he said quickly. 'My wife has been taken suddenly ill. She had been in bed an hour when I came upstairs, and found her white as a ghost and utterly exhausted. She had been to sleep, it seemed – But you will excuse me.'

'One moment, Major,' said Urcombe. 'Was there any mark on her throat ?'

'How did you guess that?' said he. 'There was; one of those beastly gnats must have bitten her twice there. She was streaming with blood.'

'And there's someone with her?' asked Urcombe.

'Yes, I roused her maid.'

He went off, and Urcombe turned to me. 'I know now what we have to do,' he said. 'Change your clothes, and I'll join you at your house.'

'What is it?' I asked.

'I'll tell you on our way. We're going to the cemetery.'

He carried a pick, a shovel, and a screwdriver when he rejoined me, and wore round his shoulders a long coil of rope. As we walked, he gave me the outlines of the ghastly hour that lay before us.

'What I have to tell you,' he said, 'will seem to you now too fantastic for credence, but before dawn we shall see whether it outstrips reality. By a most fortunate happening, you saw the spectre, the astral body, whatever you choose to call it, of Mrs Amworth going on its grisly business, and therefore, beyound doubt, the vampire spirit which abode in her during life animates her again in death. That is not exceptional – indeed, all these weeks since her death I have been expecting it. If I am right, we shall find her body undecayed and untouched by corruption.'

'But she has been dead nearly two months,' said I.

'If she had been dead two years it would still be so, if the vampire has possession of her. So remember: whatever you see done, it will be done not to her, who in the natural course would now be feeding the grasses above her grave, but to a spirit of untold evil and malignancy, which gives a phantom life to her body.'

'But what shall I see done?' said I.

'I will tell you. We know that now, at this moment, the vampire clad in her mortal semblance is out; dining out. But it must get back before dawn, and it will pass into the material form that lies in her grave. We must wait for that, and then with your help I shall dig up her body. If I am right, you will look on her as she was in life, with the full vigour of the dreadful nutriment she has received pulsing in her veins. And then, when dawn has come, and the vampire cannot leave the lair of her body, I shall strike her with this' – and he pointed to his pick – 'through the heart, and she, who comes to life again only with the animation the fiend gives her, she and her hellish partner will be dead indeed. Then we must bury her again, delivered at last.'

We had come to the cemetery, and in the brightness of the moonshine there was no difficulty in identifying her grave. It lay some twenty yards from the small chapel, in the porch of which, obscured by shadow, we concealed ourselves. From there we had a clear and open sight of the grave, and now we must wait till its infernal visitor returned home. The night was warm and windless, yet even if a freezing wind had been raging I think I should have felt nothing of it, so intense was my preoccupation as to what the night and dawn would bring. There was a bell in the turret of the chapel that struck the quarters of the hour, and it amazed me to find how swiftly the chimes succeeded one another.

The moon had long set, but a twilight of stars shone in a clear sky, when five o'clock of the morning sounded from the turret. A few minutes more passed, and then I felt Urcombe's hand softly nudging me; and looking out in the direction of his pointing finger, I saw that the form of a woman, tall, and large in build, was approaching from the right. Noiselessly, with a motion more of gliding and floating than walking, she moved across the cemetery to the grave which was the centre of our observation. She moved round as if to be certain of its identity, and for a moment stood directly facing us. In the greyness to which now my eyes had grown accustomed, I could easily see her face, and recognise its features.

She drew her hand across her mouth as if wiping it, and broke into a chuckle of such laughter as made my hair stir on my head. Then she leaped onto the grave, holding her hands high above her head, and inch by inch disappeared into the earth. Urcombe's hand was laid on my arm, in an injunction to keep still, but now he removed it.

'Come,' he said.

With pick and shovel and rope we went to the grave. The earth was light and sandy, and soon after six struck we had delved down to the coffin lid. With his pick he loosened the earth around it, and, adjusting the rope through the handles by which it had been lowered, we tried to raise it. This was a long and laborious business, and the light had begun to herald day in the east before we had it out, and lying by the side of the grave. With his screwdriver he loosened the fastenings of the lid, and slid it aside, and standing there we looked on the face of Mrs Amworth. The eyes, once closed in death, were open, the cheeks were flushed with colour – the red, full-lipped mouth seemed to smile.

'One blow and it is all over,' he said. 'You need not look.'

Even as he spoke he took up the pick again, and laying the point of it on her left breast, measured his distance. And though I knew what was coming I could not look away...

He grasped the pick in both hands, raised it an inch or two for the taking of his aim, and then with full force brought it down on her breast. A fountain of blood, though she had been dead so long, spouted high in the air, falling with the thud of a heavy splash over the shroud, and simultaneously from those red lips came one long, appalling cry, swelling up like some hooting siren, and dying away again, With that, instantaneous as a lightning flash, came the touch of corruption on her face, the colour of it faded to ash, the plump cheeks fell in, the mouth dropped.

'Thank God, that's over,' said he, and without pause slipped the coffin lid back into its place.

Day was coming fast now, and, working like men possessed, we lowered the coffin into its place again, and shovelled the earth over it ... The birds were busy with their earliest pipings as we went back to Maxley.

Dracula's Guest
Bram Stoker

When we started for our drive the sun was shining brightly on Munich and the air was full of the joyousness of early summer. Just as we were about to depart, Herr Delbruck (the *maître d'hôtel* of the Quatre Saisons, where I was staying) came down, bareheaded, to the carriage and, after wishing me a pleasant drive, said to the coachman, still holding his hand on the handle of the carriage door: 'Remember you are back by nightfall. The sky looks bright but there is a shiver in the north wind that says there may be a sudden storm. But I am sure you will not be late.' Here he smiled and added, 'for you know what night it is.'

Johann answered with an emphatic, '*Ja, mein Herr,*' and, touching his hat, drove off quickly. When we had cleared the town, I said, after signal-ling to him to stop: 'Tell me, Johann, what is tonight?'

He crossed himself as he answered laconically: 'Walpurgisnacht.' Then he took out his watch, a great, old-fashioned German silver thing as big as a turnip, and looked at it, with his eyebrows gathered together and a little impatient shrug of his shoulders. I realized that this was his way of respectfully protesting against the unnecessary delay and sank back in the carriage, merely motioning him to proceed. He started off rapidly, as if to make up for lost time. Every now and then the horses seemed to throw up their heads and sniffed the air suspiciously. On such occasions I often looked round in alarrn. The road was pretty bleak, for we were traversing a sort of high, wind-swept plateau. As we drove, I saw a road that looked but little used and which seemed to dip through a little, winding valley. It looked so inviting that, even at the risk of offending him, I called Johann to stop and when he had pulled up I told him I would like to drive down that road. He made all sorts of excuses and frequently crossed himself as he spoke. This somewhat piqued my curiosity so I asked him various ques-tions. He answered fencingly and repeatedly looked at his watch in protest. Finally I said: 'Well, Johann, I want to go down this road. I shall not ask you to come unless you like; but tell me why you do not like to go, that is all I ask.' For answer he seemed to throw himself off the box, so quickly did he reach the ground. Then he stretched out his hands appealingly to me and implored me not to go. There was just enough of English mixed with the German for me to understand the drift of his talk. He seemed always just about to tell me something – the very idea of which evidently frightened him, but each time he pulled himself up, saying, as he crossed himself: 'Walpurgisnacht!'

I tried to argue with him, but it was difficult to argue with a man when I did not know his language. The advantage certainly rested with him, for although he began to speak in English, of a very crude and broken kind, he always got excited and broke into his native tongue – and every time he did so he looked at his watch. Then the horses became restless and sniffed the air. At this he grew very pale and, looking around in a frightened way, he suddenly jumped forward, took them by the bridles and led them on some twenty feet. I followed and asked why he had done this. For answer he crossed himself, pointed to the spot we had left and drew his carriage in the direction of the other road, indicating a cross, and said, first in German, then in English: 'Buried him – him what killed themselves.'

I remembered the old custom of burying suicides at cross-roads: 'Ah! I see, a suicide. How interesting!' But for the life of me I could not make out why the horses were frightened.

Whilst we were talking we heard a sort of sound between a yelp and a bark. It was far away, but the horses got very restless and it took Johann all his time to quiet them. He was pale and said, 'It sounds like a wolf – but yet there are no wolves here now.'

'No?' I said, questioning him; 'isn't it long since the wolves were so near the city?'

'Long, long,' he answered, 'in the spring and summer, but with the snow the wolves have been here not so long.'

Whilst he was petting the horses and trying to quiet them, dark clouds drifted rapidly across the sky. The sunshine passed away and a breath of cold wind seemed to drift past us. It was only a breath, however, and more in the nature of a warning than a fact, for the sun came out brightly again. Johann looked under his lifted hand at the horizon and said: 'The storm of snow, he comes before long time.' Then he looked at his watch again and, straightway, holding his reins firmly – for the horses were still pawing the ground restlessly and shaking their heads – he climbed to his box as though the time had come for proceeding on our journey.

I felt a little obstinate and did not at once get into the carriage.

'Tell me,' I said, 'about this place where the road leads,' and I pointed down.

Again he crossed himself and mumbled a prayer before he answered, 'It is unholy.'

'What is unholy?' I enquired.

'The village.'

'Then there is a village?'

'No, no. No one lives there hundreds of years." My curiosity was piqued, 'But you said there was a village.'

'There was.'

'Where is it now?'

Whereupon he burst out into a long story in German and English, so mixed up that I could not quite understand exactly what he said, but roughly I gathered that long ago, hundreds of years, men had died there and been buried in their graves; and sounds were heard under the clay and when the graves were opened, men and women were found rosy with life, and their mouths red with blood. And so, in haste to save their lives (aye, and their souls! – and here he crossed himself) those who were left fled away to other places, where the living lived and the dead were dead and not – not something. He was evidently afraid to speak the last words. As he proceeded with his narration he grew more and more excited. It seemed as if his imagination had got hold of him and he ended in a perfect paroxysm of fear – white-faced, perspiring, trembling and looking round him, as if expecting that some dreadful presence would manifest itself there in the bright sunshine on the open plain. Finally, in an agony of desperation, he cried: 'Walpurgisnacht!' and pointed to the carriage for me to get in. All my English blood rose at this and, standing back, I said: 'You are afraid, Johann – you are afraid. Go home, I shall return alone; the walk will do me good.' The carriage door was open. I took from the seat my oak walking-stick – which I always carry on my holiday excursions – and closed the door, pointing back to Munich, and said, 'Go home, Johann – Walpurgisnacht doesn't concern Englishmen.'

The horses were now more restive than ever and Johann was trying to hold them in, while excitedly imploring me not to do anything so foolish. I pitied the poor fellow, he was deeply in earnest, but all the same I could not help laughing. His English was quite gone now. In his anxiety he had forgotten that his only means of making me understand was to talk my language, so he jabbered away in his native German. It began to be a little tedious. After giving the direction, 'Home!' I turned to go down the cross-road into the valley.

With a despairing gesture, Johann turned his horses towards Munich. I leaned on my stick and looked after him. He went slowly along the road for a while: then there came over the crest of the hill a man tall and thin. I could see so much in the distance. When he drew near the horses, they began to jump and kick about, then to scream with terror. Johann could not hold them in; they bolted down the road, running away madly. I watched them out of sight, then looked for the stranger, but I found that he, too, was gone.

With a light heart I turned down the side road through the deepening valley to which Johann had objected. There was not the slightest reason, that I could see, for his objection, and I daresay I tramped for a couple of hours without thinking of time or distance, and certainly without seeing a person or a house. So far as the place was concerned it was desolation itself. But I did not notice this particularly till, on turning a bend in the road, I came upon a scattered fringe of wood; then I recognized that I had been impressed unconsciously by the desolation of the region through which I had passed.

I sat down to rest myself and began to look around. It struck me that it was considerably colder than it had been at the commencement of my walk – a sort of sighing sound seemed to be around me, with, now and then, high overhead, a sort of muffled roar. Looking upwards I noticed that great thick clouds were drifting rapidly across the sky from north to south at a great height. There were signs of coming storm in some lofty stratum of the air. I was a little chilly and, thinking that it was the sitting still after the exercise of walking, I resumed my journey.

The ground I passed over was now much more picturesque. There were no striking objects that the eye might single out, but in all there was a charm of beauty. I took little heed of time and it was only when the deepening twilight forced itself upon me that I began to think of how I should find my way home. The brightness of the day had gone. The air was cold and the drifting of clouds high overhead was more marked. They were accompanied by a sort of far-away rushing sound, through which seemed to come at intervals that mysterious cry which the driver had said came from a wolf. For a while I hesitated. I had said I would see the deserted village, so on I went and presently came on a wide stretch of open country, shut in by hills all around. Their sides were covered with trees which spread down to the plain, dotting, in clumps, the gentler slopes and hollows which showed here and there. I followed with my eye the winding of the road and saw that it curved close to one of the densest of these clumps and was lost behind it.

As I looked there came a cold shiver in the air and the snow began to fall. I though of the miles and miles of bleak country I had passed and then hurried on to seek the shelter of the wood in front. Darker and darker grew the sky and faster and heavier fell the snow, till the earth before and around me was a glistening white carpet, the father edge of which was lost in misty vagueness. The road was here but crude and when on the level its boundaries were not so marked, as when it passed through the cuttings; and in a little while I found that I must have strayed from it, for I missed underfoot the hard surface and my feet sank deeper in the grass and moss. Then the wind grew strong and blew with ever increasing force, till I was fain to run before it. The air became icy cold and in spite of my exercise I began to suffer. The snow was now falling so thickly and whirling around me in such rapid eddies that I could hardly keep my eyes open. Every now and then the heavens were torn asunder by vivid lightning, and in the flashes I could see ahead of me a great mass of trees, chiefly yew and cypress, all heavily coated with snow.

I was soon amongst the shelter of the trees, and there, in comparative silence, I could hear the rush of the wind high overhead. Presently the blackness of the storm had become merged in the darkness of the night. By and by the storm seemed to be passing away: it now only came in fierce puffs or blasts. At such moments the weird sound of the wolf appeared to be echoed by many similar sounds around me.

Now and again, through the black mass of drifting cloud, came a straggling ray of moonlight, which lit up the expanse and showed me that I was at the edge of a dense mass of cypress and yew trees. As the snow had ceased to fall, I walked out from the shelter and began to investigate more closely. It appeared to me that, amongst so many old foundations as I had passed, there might be still standing a house in which, though in ruins, I could find some sort of shelter for a while. As I skirted the edge of the copse I found that a low wall encircled it, and following this I presently found an opening. Here the cypresses formed an alley leading up to a square mass of some kind of building. Just as I caught sight of this, however, the drifting clouds obscured the moon and I passed up the path in darkness. The wind must have grown colder, for I felt myself shiver as I walked; but there was hope of shelter and I groped my way blindly on.

I stopped, for there was a sudden stillness. The storm had passed and, perhaps in sympathy with nature's silence, my heart seemed to cease to beat. But this was only momentarily, for suddenly the moonlight broke through the clouds, showing me that I was in a graveyard and that the square object before me was a great massive tomb of marble, as white as the snow that lay on and all around it. With the moonlight there came a fierce sigh of the storm, which appeared to resume its course with a long, low howl, as of many dogs or wolves. I was awed and shocked and felt the cold perceptibly grow upon me till it seemed to grip me by the heart. Then, while the flood of moonlight still fell on the marble tomb, the storm gave further evidence of renewing, as though it was returning on its track. Impelled by some sort of fascination I approached the sepulchre to see what it was and why such a thing stood alone in such a place. I walked around it and read, over the Doric door, in German:

COUNTESS DOLINGEN OF GRATZ
IN STYRIA
SOUGHT AND FOUND DEATH
1801

On the top of the tomb, seemingly driven through the solid marble – for the structure was composed of a few vast blocks of stone – was a great iron spike or stake. On going to the back I saw, graven in great Russian letters:

THE DEAD TRAVEL FAST.

There was something so weird and uncanny about the whole thing that it gave me a turn and made me feel quite faint. I began to wish, for the first time, that I had taken Johann's advice. Here a thought struck me, which came under almost mysterious circumstances and with a terrible shock. This was Walpurgis Night!

Walpurgis Night, when, according to the belief of millions of people, the devil was abroad – when the graves were opened and the dead came forth and walked. When evil things of earth and air and water held revel. This very place the driver had specially shunned. This was the depopulated village of centuries ago. This was where the suicide lay; and this was the place where I was alone – unmanned, shivering with cold in a shroud of snow with a wild storm gathering again upon me! It took all my philosophy, all the religion I had been taught, all my courage, not to collapse in a paroxysm of fright.

And now a perfect tornado burst upon me. The ground shook as though thousands of horses thundered across it, and this time the storm bore on its icy wings, not snow, but great hailstones which drove with such violence that they might have come from the thongs of Balearic slingers – hailstones that beat down leaf and branch and made the shelter of the cypresses of no more avail than though their stems were standing corn. At the first I had rushed to the nearest tree, but I was soon fain to leave it and seek the only spot that seemed to afford refuge, the deep Doric doorway of the marble tomb. There, crouching against the massive bronze door, I gained a certain amount of protection from the beating of the hailstones, for now they only drove against me as they ricocheted from the ground and the side of the marble.

As I leaned against the door it moved slightly and opened inwards. The shelter of even a tomb was welcome in that pitiless tempest and I was about to enter it when there came a flash of forked lightning that lit up the whole expanse of the heavens. In the instant, as I am a living man. I saw, as my eyes were turned into the darkness of the tomb, a beautiful woman with rounded cheeks and red lips, seemingly sleeping on a bier. As the thunder broke overhead I was grasped as by the hand of a giant and hurled out into the storm. The whole thing was so sudden that, before I could realize the shock, moral as well as physical, I found the hailstones beating me down. At the same time I had a strange, dominating feeling that I was not alone. I looked towards the tomb. Just then there came another blinding flash, which seemed to strike the iron stake that surmounted the tomb and to pour through to the earth, blasting and crumbling the marble, as in a burst of flame. The dead woman rose for a moment of agony, while she was lapped in the flame, and her bitter scream of pain was drowned in the thundercrash. The last thing I heard was this mingling of dreadful sound, as again I was seized in the giant-grasp and dragged away, while the hailstones beat on me, and the air around seemed reverberant with the howling of wolves. The last sight that I remembered was a vague, white, moving mass, as if all the graves around me had sent out the phantoms of their sheeted dead, and that they were closing in on me through the white cloudiness of the driving hail.

Gradually there came a sort of vague beginning of consciousness, then a sense of weariness that was dreadful. For a time I remembered nothing, but slowly my senses returned. My feet seemed positively racked with pain, yet I could not move them. They seemed to be numbed. There was an icy feeling at the back of my neck and all down my spine, and my ears, like my feet, were dead, yet in torment; but there was in my breast a sense of warmth which was, by comparison, delicious. It was as a nightmare – a physical nightmare, if one may use such an expression – for some heavy weight on my chest made it difficult for me to breathe.

This period of semi-lethargy seemed to remain a long time, and as it faded away I must have slept or swooned. Then came a sort of loathing, like the first stage of sea-sickness, and a wild desire to be free from something – I knew not what. A vast stillness enveloped me, as though all the world were asleep or dead – only broken by the low panting as of some animal close to me. I felt a warm rasping at my throat, then came a consciousness of the awful truth, which chilled me to the heart and sent the blood surging up through my brain. Some great animal was lying on me and now licking my throat. I feared to stir, for some instinct of prudence bade me lie still, but the brute seemed to realize that there was now some change in me, for it raised its head. Through my eyelashes I saw above me the two great flaming eyes of a gigantic wolf. Its sharp white teeth gleamed in the gaping red mouth and I could feel its hot breath fierce and acrid upon me.

For another spell of time I remembered no more. Then I became conscious of a low growl, followed by a yelp, renewed again and again. Then, seemingly very far away, I heard a 'Holloa! holloa!' as of many voices calling in unison. Cautiously I raised my head and looked in the direction whence the sound came, but the cemetery blocked my view. The wolf still continued to yelp in a strange way and a red glare began to move round the grove of cypresses, as though following the sound. As the voices drew closer, the wolf yelped faster and louder. I feared to make either sound or motion. Nearer came the red glow, over the white pall which stretched into the darkness around me. Then all at once from beyond the trees there came at a trot a troop of horsemen bearing torches. The wolf rose from my breast and made for the cemetery. I saw one of the horsemen (soldiers, by their caps and their long military cloaks) raise his carbine and take aim. A companion knocked up his arm, and I heard the ball whizz over my head. He had evidently taken my body for that of the wolf. Another sighted the animal as it slunk away and a shot followed. Then, at a gallop, the troop rode forward – some towards me, others following the wolf as it disappeared amongst the snow-clad cypresses.

As they drew nearer I tried to move, but was powerless, although I could see and hear all that went on around me. Two or three of the soldiers jumped from their horses and knelt beside me. One of them raised my head and placed his hand over my heart.

'Good news, comrades!' he cried. 'His heart still beats!'

Then some brandy was poured down my throat; it put vigour into me and I was able to open my eyes fully and look around. Lights and shadows were moving among the trees and I heard men call to one another. They drew together, uttering frightened exclamations, and the lights flashed as the others came pouring out of the cemetery pell-mell, like men possessed. When the farther ones came close to us, those who were around me asked them eagerly: 'Well, have you found him?'

The reply rang out hurriedly: 'No! no! Come away quick – quick! This is no place to stay, and on this of all nights!'

'What was it?' was the question, asked in all manner of keys. The answer came variously and all indefinitely as though the men were moved by some common impulse to speak, yet were restrained by some common fear from giving their thoughts.

'It – it – indeed!' gibbered one, whose wits had plainly given out for the moment.

'A wolf – and yet not a wolf!' another put in shudderingly.

'No use trying for him without the sacred bullet,' a third remarked in a more ordinary manner.

'Serve us right for coming out on this night! Truly we have earned our thousand marks!' were the ejaculations of a fourth.

'There was blood on the broken marble,' another said after a pause – 'the lightning never brought that there. And for him – is he safe? Look at his throat! See, comrades, the wolf has been lying on him and keeping his blood warm.'

The officer looked at my throat and replied: 'He is all right, the skin is not pierced. What does it all mean? We should never have found him but for the yelping of the wolf.'

'What became of it?' asked the man who was holding up my head and who seemed the least panic stricken of the party, for his hands were steady and without tremor. On his sleeve was the chevron of a petty officer.

'It went to its home,' answered the man, whose long face was pallid and who actually shook with terror as he glanced around him fearfully. 'There are graves enough there in which it may lie. Come, comrades – come quickly! Let us leave this cursed spot.'

The officer raised me to a sitting posture, as he uttered a word of command, then several men placed me upon a horse. He sprang to the saddle behind me, took me in his arms, gave the word to advance and, turning our faces away from the cypresses, we rode away in swift, military order.

As yet my tongue refused its office and I was perforce silent. I must have fallen asleep, for the next thing I remembered was finding myself standing up, supported by a soldier on each side of me. It was almost broad daylight and to the north a red streak of sunlight was reflected, like a path of blood, over the waste of snow. The officer was telling the men to say nothing of what they had seen, except that they found an English stranger, guarded by a large dog.

'Dog! that was no dog,' cut in the man who had exhibited such fear. 'I think I know a wolf when I see one.'

The young officer answered calmly: 'I said a dog.' 'Dog!' reiterated the other ironically. It was evident that his courage was rising with the sun and, pointing to me, he said, 'Look at his throat. Is that the work of a dog, master?'

Instinctively I raised my hand to my throat, and as I touched it I cried out in pain. The men crowded round to look, some stooping down from their saddles, and again there came the calm voice of the young officer: 'A dog, as I said. If aught else were said we should only be laughed at.'

I was then mounted behind a trooper and we rode on into the suburbs of Munich. Here we came across a stray carriage, into which I was lifted, and it was driven off to the Quatre Saisons – the young officer accompanying me, whilst a trooper followed with his horse and the others rode off to their barracks.

When we arrived, Herr Delbrück rushed so quickly down the steps to meet me that it was apparent he had been watching within. Taking me by both hands he solicitously led me in. The officer saluted me and was turning to withdraw when I recognized his purpose, and insisted that he should come to my rooms. Over a glass of wine I warmly thanked him and his brave comrades for saving me. He replied simply that he was more than glad and that Herr Delbrück had at the first taken steps to make all the searching party pleased; at which ambiguous utterance the *maître d'hôtel* smiled, while the officer pleaded duty and withdrew.

'But Herr Delbrück,' I enquired, 'how and why was it that the soldiers searched for me?'

He shrugged his shoulders, as if in depreciation of his own deed, as he replied: 'I was so fortunate as to obtain leave from the commander of the regiment in which I served, to ask for volunteers.'

'But how did you know I was lost?' I asked.

'The driver came hither with the remains of his carriage, which had been upset when the horses ran away.'

'But surely you would not send a search-party of soldiers merely on this account?'

'Oh, no!' he answered, 'but even before the coachman arrived I had this telegram from the Boyar whose guest you are,' and he took from his pocket a telegram which he handed to me, and I read:

Bistritz Be careful of my guest – his safety is most precious to me. Should aught happen to him, or if he be missed, spare nothing to find him and ensure his safety. He is English and therefore adventurous. There are often dangers from snow and wolves and night. Lose not a moment if you suspect harm to him. I answer your zeal with my fortune – *Dracula*.

As I held the telegram in my hand the room seemed to whirl around me, and if the attentive *maître d 'hôtel* had not caught me I think I should have fallen. There was something so strange in all this, something so weird and impossible to imagine, that there grew on me a sense of my being in some way the sport of opposite forces – the mere vague idea of which seemed in a way to paralyze me. I was certainly under some form of mysterious protection. From a distant country had come, in the very nick of time, a message that took me out of the danger of the snow-sleep and the jaws of the wolf.

Good Lady Ducayne
Mary Elizabeth Braddon

I

Bella Rolleston had made up her mind that her only chance of earning her bread and helping her mother to an occasional crust was by going out into the great unknown world as companion to a lady. She was willing to go to any lady rich enough to pay her a salary and so eccentric as to wish for a hired companion. Five shillings told off reluctantly from one of those sovereigns which were so rare with the mother and daughter, and which melted away so quickly, five solid shillings, had been handed to a smartly-dressed lady in an office in Harbeck Street, London, W., in the hope that this very Superior Person would find a situation and a salary for Miss Rolleston. The Superior Person glanced at the two half-crowns as they lay on the table where Bella's hand had placed them, to make sure they were neither of them florins, before she wrote a description of Bella's qualifications and requirements in a formidable-looking ledger.

'Age?' she asked, curtly.

'Eighteen, last July.'

'Any accomplishments?' 'No; I am not at all accomplished. If I were I should want to be a governess – a companion seems the lowest stage.'

'We have some highly accomplished ladies on our books as companions, or chaperon companions.'

'Oh, I know!' babbled Bella, loquacious in her youthful candor. 'But that is quite a different thing. Mother hasn't been able to afford a piano since I was twelve years old, so I'm afraid I've forgotten how to play. And I have had to help mother with her needlework, so there hasn't been much time to study.'

'Please don't waste time upon explaining what you can't do, but kindly tell me anything you can do,' said the Superior Person, crushingly, with her pen poised between delicate fingers waiting to write. 'Can you read aloud for two or three hours at a stretch? Are you active and handy, an early riser, a good walker, sweet tempered, and obliging?'

'I can say yes to all those questions except about the sweetness. I think I have a pretty good temper, and I should be anxious to oblige anybody who paid for my services. I should want them to feel that I was really earning my salary.'

'The kind of ladies who come to me would not care for a talkative companion,' said the Person, severely, having finished writing in her book. 'My connection lies chiefly among the aristocracy, and in that class considerable deference is expected.'

'Oh, of course,' said Bella; 'but it's quite different when I'm talking to you. I want to tell you all about myself once and forever.'

'I am glad it is to be only once!' said the Person, with the edges of her lips.

The Person was of uncertain age, tightly laced in a black silk gown. She had a powdery complexion and a handsome clump of somebody else's hair on the top of her head. It may be that Bella's girlish freshness and vivacity had an irritating effect upon nerves weakened by an eight-hour day in that overheated second floor in Harbeck Street. To Bella the official apartment, with its Brussels carpet, velvet curtains and velvet chairs, and French clock, ticking loud on the marble chimney-piece, suggested the luxury of a palace, as compared with another second floor in Walworth where Mrs Rolleston and her daughter had managed to exist for the last six years.

'Do you think you have anything on your books that would suit me?' faltered Bella, after a pause.

'Oh, dear no; I have nothing in view at present,' answered the Person, who had swept Bella's half-crowns into a drawer, absentmindedly, with the tips of her fingers. 'You see, you are so very unformed – so much too young to be companion to a lady of position. It is a pity you have not enough education for a nursery governess; that would be more in your line.'

'And do you think it will be very long before you can get me a situation?' asked Bella, doubtfully.

'I really cannot say. Have you any particular reason for being so impatient – not a love affair, I hope?'

'A love affair!' cried Bella, with flaming cheeks. 'What utter nonsense. I want a situation because mother is poor, and I hate being a burden to her. I want a salary that I can share with her.'

'There won't be much margin for sharing in the salary you are likely to get at your age – and with your – very – unformed manners,' said the Person, who found Bella's peony cheeks, bright eyes, and unbridled vivacity more and more oppressive.

'Perhaps if you'd be kind enough to give me back the fee I could take it to an agency where the connection isn't quite so aristocratic,' said Bella, who – as she told her mother in her recital of the interview – was determined not to be sat upon.

'You will find no agency that can do more for you than mine,' replied the Person, whose harpy fingers never relinquished coin. 'You will have to wait for your opportunity. Yours is an exceptional case: but I will bear you in mind, and if anything suitable offers I will write to you. I cannot say more than that.'

The half-contemptuous bend of the stately head, weighted with borrowed hair, indicated the end of the interview. Bella went back to Walworth – tramped sturdily every inch of the way in the September afternoon – and 'took off 'the Superior Person for the amusement of her mother and the landlady, who lingered in the shabby little sitting-room after bringing in the tea-tray, to applaud Miss Rolleston's 'taking off.'

'Dear, dear, what a mimic she is!' said the landlady. 'You ought to have let her go on the stage, mum. She might have made her fortune as an actress.

II

Bella waited and hoped, and listened for the postman's knocks which brought such store of letters for the parlors and the first floor, and so few for that humble second floor, where mother and daughter sat sewing with hand and with wheel and treadle, for the greater part of the day. Mrs Rolleston was a lady by birth and education; but it had been her bad fortune to marry a scoundrel; for the last half-dozen years she had been that worst of widows, a wife whose husband had deserted her. Happily, she was courageous, industrious, and a clever needlewoman; and she had been able just to earn a living for herself and her only child, by making mantles and cloaks for a West-end house. It was not a luxurious living. Cheap lodgings in a shabby street off the Walworth Road, scanty dinners, homely food, well-worn raiment, had been the portion of mother and daughter; but they loved each other so dearly, and Nature had made them both so light-hearted, that they had contrived somehow to be happy.

But now this idea of going out into the world as companion to some fine lady had rooted itself into Bella's mind, and although she idolized her mother, and although the parting of mother and daughter must needs tear two loving hearts into shreds, the girl longed for enterprise and change and excitement, as the pages of old longed to be knights, and to start for the Holy Land to break a lance with the infidel.

She grew tired of racing downstairs every time the postman knocked, only to be told 'nothing for you, miss,' by the smudgy-faced drudge who picked up the letters from the passage floor. 'Nothing for you, miss,' grinned the lodging-house drudge, till at last Bella took heart of grace and walked up to Harbeck Street, and asked the Superior Person how it was that no situation had been found for her.

'You are too young,' said the Person, 'and you want a salary.'

'Of course I do,' answered Bella; 'don't other people want salaries?'

'Young ladies of your age generally want a comfortable home.'

'I don't,' snapped Bella: 'I want to help mother.'

'You can call again this day week,' said the Person; 'or, if I hear of anything in the meantime, I will write to you.'

No letter came from the Person, and in exactly a week Bella put on her neatest hat, the one that had been seldomest caught in the rain, and trudged off to Harbeck Street.

It was a dull October afternoon, and there was a greyness in the air which might turn to fog before night. The Walworth Road shops gleamed brightly through that grey atmosphere, and though to a young lady reared in Mayfair or Belgravia such shop-windows would have been unworthy of a glance, they were a snare and temptation for Bella. There were so many things that she longed for, and would never be able to buy.

Harbeck Street is apt to be empty at this dead season of the year, a long, long street, an endless perspective of eminently respectable houses. The Person's office was at the further end, and Bella looked down that long, grey vista almost despairingly, more tired than usual with the trudge from Walworth. As she looked, a carriage passed her, an old-fashioned, yellow chariot, on cee springs, drawn by a pair of high grey horses, with the stateliest of coachmen driving them, and a tall footman sitting by his side.

'It looks like the fairy godmother's coach,' thought Bella. 'I shouldn't wonder if it began by being a pumpkin.'

It was a surprise when she reached the Person's door to find the yellow chariot standing before it, and the tall footman waiting near the doorstep. She was almost afraid to go in and meet the owner of that splendid carriage. She had caught only a glimpse of its occupant as the chariot rolled by, a plumed bonnet, a patch of ermine.

The Person's smart page ushered her upstairs and knocked at the official door. 'Miss Rolleston,' he announced, apologetically, while Bella waited outside.

'Show her in,' said the Person, quickly; and then Bella heard her murmuring something in a low voice to her client.

Bella went in fresh, blooming, a living image of youth and hope, and before she looked at the Person her gaze was riveted by the owner of the chariot.

Never had she seen anyone as old as the old lady sitting by the Person's fire: a little old figure, wrapped from chin to feet in an ermine mantle; a withered, old face under a plumed bonnet – a face so wasted by age that it seemed only a pair of eyes and a peaked chin. The nose was peaked, too, but between the sharply pointed chin and the great, shining eyes, the small, aquiline nose was hardly visible.

'This is Miss Rolleston, Lady Ducayne.'

Claw-like fingers, flashing with jewels, lifted a double eyeglass to Lady

Ducayne's shining black eyes, and through the glasses Bella saw those unnaturally bright eyes magnified to a gigantic size, and glaring at her awfully.

'Miss Torpinter has told me all about you,' said the old voice that belonged to the eyes. 'Have you good health? Are you strong and active, able to eat well, sleep well, walk well, able to enjoy all that there is good in life?'

'I have never known what it is to be ill, or idle,' answered Bella.

'Then I think you will do for me.'

'Of course, in the event of references being perfectly satisfactory,' put in the Person.

'I don't want references. The young woman looks frank and innocent. I'll take her on trust.'

'So like you, dear Lady Ducayne,' murmured Miss Torpinter.

'I want a strong young woman whose health will give me no trouble.'

'You have been so unfortunate in that respect,' cooed the Person, whose voice and manner were subdued to a melting sweetness by the old woman's presence.

'Yes, I've been rather unlucky,' grunted Lady Ducayne.

'But I am sure Miss Rolleston will not disappoint you, though certainly after your unpleasant experience with Miss Tomson, who looked the picture of health – and Miss Blandy, who said she had never seen a doctor since she was vaccinated – '

'Lies, no doubt,' muttered Lady Ducayne, and then turning to Bella, she asked, curtly, 'You don't mind spending the winter in Italy, I suppose?'

In Italy! The very word was magical. Bella's fair young face flushed crimson.

'It has been the dream of my life to see Italy,' she gasped.

Fromng Walworth to Italy! How far, how impossible such a journey had seemed to that romantic dreamer.

'Well, your dream will be realized. Get yourself ready to leave Charing Cross by the train deluxe this day week at eleven. Be sure you are at the station a quarter before the hour. My people will look after you and your luggage.'

Lady Ducayne rose from her chair, assisted by her crutch-stick, and Miss Torpinter escorted her to the door.

'And with regard to salary?' questioned the Person on the way.

'Salary, oh, the same as usual – and if the young woman wants a quarter's pay in advance you can write to me for a check,' Lady Ducayne answered, carelessly.

Miss Torpinter went all the way downstairs with her client, and waited to see her seated in the yellow chariot. When she came upstairs again she was slightly out of breath, and she had resumed that superior manner which Bella had found so crushing.

'You may think yourself uncommonly lucky, Miss Rolleston,' she said. 'I have dozens of young ladies on my books whom I might have recommended for this situation – but I remembered having told you to call this afternoon – and I thought I would give you a chance. Old Lady Ducayne is one of the best people on my books. She gives her companion a hundred a year, and pays all travelling expenses. You will live in the lap of luxury.'

'A hundred a year! How too lovely! Shall I have to dress very grandly? Does Lady Ducayne keep much company?'

'At her age! No, she lives in seclusion – in her own apartments – her French maid, her footman, her medical attendant, her courier.'

'Why did those other companions leave her?' asked Bella.

'Their health broke down!'

'Poor things, and so they had to leave?'

'Yes, they had to leave. I suppose you would like a quarter's salary in advance?'

'Oh, yes, please. I shall have things to buy.'

'Very well, I will write for Lady Ducayne's check, and I will send you the balance after deducting my commission for the year.'

'To be sure, I had forgotten the commission.'

'You don't suppose I keep this office for pleasure.'

'Of course not,' murmured Bella, remembering the five shillings entrance fee; but nobody could expect a hundred a year and a winter in Italy for five shillings.

III

'From Miss Rolleston, at Cap Ferrino, to Mrs Rolleston, in Beresford Street, Walworth, London.

'How I wish you could see this place, dearest; the blue sky, the olive woods, the orange and lemon orchards between the cliffs and the sea – sheltering in the hollow of the great hills – and with summer waves dancing up to the narrow ridge of pebbles and weeds which is the Italian idea of a beach! Oh, how I wish you could see it all, mother dear, and bask in this sunshine, that makes it so difficult to believe the date at the head of this paper. November! The air is like an English June – the sun is so hot that I can't walk a few yards without an umbrella. And to think of you at Walworth while I am here! I could cry at the thought that perhaps you will never see this lovely coast, this wonderful sea, these summer flowers that bloom in winter. There is a hedge of pink geraniums under my window, mother – a thick rank hedge, as if the flowers grew wild – and there are Dijon roses climbing over arches and palisades all along the terrace – a rose garden full of bloom in November! Just picture it all! You could never imagine the luxury of this hotel. It is nearly new, and has been built and decorated regardless of expense. Our rooms are upholstered in pale blue satin, which shows up Lady Ducayne's parchment complexion; but as she sits all day in a corner of the

balcony basking in the sun, except when she is in her carriage, and all the evening in her armchair close to the fire, and never sees anyone but her own people, her complexion matters very little.

'*She has the handsomest suite of rooms in the hotel. My bedroom is inside hers, the sweetest room – all blue satin and white lace – white enamelled furniture, looking-glasses on every wall, till I know my pert little profile as I never knew it before. The room was really meant for Lady Ducayne's dressing-room, but she ordered one of the blue satin couches to be arranged as a bed for me – the prettiest little bed, which I can wheel near the window on sunny mornings, as it is on castors and easily moved about. I feel as if Lady Ducayne were a funny old grandmother, who had suddenly appeared in my life, very, very rich, and very, very kind.*

'*She is not at all exacting. I read aloud to her a good deal, and she dozes and nods while I read. Sometimes I hear her moaning in her sleep – as if she had troublesome dreams. When she is tired of my reading she orders Francine, her maid, to read a French novel to her, and I hear her chuckle and groan now and then, as if she were more interested in those books than in Dickens or Scott. My French is not good enough to follow Francine, who reads very quickly. I have a great deal of liberty, for Lady Ducayne often tells me to run away and amuse myself; I roam about the hills for hours. Everything is so lovely. I lose myself in olive woods, always climbing up and up towards the pine woods above – and above the pines there are the snow mountains that just show their white peaks above the dark hills. Oh, you poor dear, how can I ever make you understand what this place is like – you, whose poor, tired eyes have only the opposite side of Beresford Street? Sometimes I go no farther than the terrace in front of the hotel, which is a favorite lounging-place with everybody. The gardens lie below, and the tennis courts where I sometimes play with a very nice girl, the only person in the hotel with whom I have made friends. She is a year older than I, and has come to Cap Ferrino with her brother, a doctor – or a medical student, who is going to be a doctor. He passed his M.B. exam, at Edinburgh just before they left home, Lotta told me. He came to Italy entirely on his sister's account. She had a troublesome chest attack last summer and was ordered to winter abroad. They are orphans, quite alone in the world, and so fond of each other. It is very nice for me to have such a friend as Lotta. She is so thoroughly respectable. I can't help using that word, for some of the girls in this hotel go on in a way that I know you would shudder at. Lotta was brought up by an aunt, deep down in the country, and knows hardly anything about life. Her brother won't allow her to read a novel, French or English, that he has not read and approved.*

'*He treats me like a child,*' she told me, '*but I don't mind, for it's nice to know somebody loves me, and cares about what I do, and even about my thoughts.*'

'*Perhaps this is what makes some girls so eager to marry – the want of someone strong and brave and honest and true to care for them and order them about. I want no one, mother darling, for I have you, and you are all the world to me. No husband could ever come between us two. If I ever were to marry he would have only the second place in my heart. But I don't suppose I ever shall marry, or even know what it is like to have an offer of marriage. No young man can afford to marry a penniless girl nowadays. Life is too expensive.*

'Mr Stafford. Lotta's brother, is very clever, and very kind. He thinks it is rather hard for me to have to live with such an old woman as Lady Ducayne, but then he does not know how poor we are – you and I – and what a wonderful life this seems to me in this lovely place. I feel a selfish wretch for enjoying all my luxuries, while you, who want them so much more than I, have none of them – hardly know what they are like – do you, dearest? – for my scamp of a father began to go to the dogs soon after you were married, and since then life has been all trouble and care and struggle for you.'

This letter was written when Bella had been less than a month at Cap Ferrino, before the novelty had worn off the landscape, and before the pleasure of luxurious surroundings had begun to cloy. She wrote to her mother every week, such long letters as girls who have lived in closest companionship with a mother alone can write; letters that are like a diary of heart and mind. She wrote gaily always; but when the new year began Mrs Rolleston thought she detected a note of melancholy under all those lively details about the place and the people.

'My poor girl is getting homesick,' she thought. 'Her heart is in Beresford Street.'

It might be that she missed her new friend and companion, Lotta Stafford, who had gone with her brother for a little tour to Genoa and Spezia, and as far as Pisa. They were to return before February; but in the meantime Bella might naturally feel very solitary among all those strangers, whose manners and doings she described so well.

The mother's instinct had been true. Bella was not so happy as she had been in that first flush of wonder and delight which followed the change from Walworth to the Riviera. Somehow, she knew not how, lassitude had crept upon her. She no longer loved to climb the hills, no longer flourished her orange stick in sheer gladness of heart as her light feet skipped over the rough ground and the coarse grass on the mountain side. The odor of rosemary and thyme, the fresh breath of the sea, no longer filled her with rapture. She thought of Beresford Street and her mother's face with a sick longing. They were so far – so far away! And then she thought of Lady Ducayne, sitting by the heaped-up olive logs in the overheated salon – thought of that wizened-nutcracker profile, and those gleaming eyes, with an invincible horror.

Visitors at the hotel had told her that the air of Cap Ferrino was relaxing – better suited to age than to youth, to sickness than to health. No doubt it was so. She was not so well as she had been at Walworth; but she told herself that she was suffering only from the pain of separation from the dear companion of her girlhood, the mother who had been nurse, sister, friend, flatterer, all things in this world to her. She had shed many tears over that parting, had spent many a melancholy hour on the marble terrace with yearning eyes looking westward, and with her heart's desire a thousand miles away.

She was sitting in her favorite spot, an angle at the eastern end of the terrace, a quiet little nook sheltered by orange trees, when she heard a couple of Riviera habitués talking in the garden below. They were sitting on a bench against the terrace wall.

She had no idea of listening to their talk, till the sound of Lady Ducayne's name attracted her, and then she listened without any thought of wrong-doing. They were talking no secrets – just casually discussing a hotel acquaintance.

They were two elderly people whom Bella only knew by sight. An English clergyman who had wintered abroad for half his lifetime; a stout, comfortable, well-to-do spinster, whose chronic bronchitis obliged her to migrate annually.

'I have met her about Italy for the last ten years,' said the lady; 'but have never found out her real age.'

'I put her down at a hundred – not a year less,' replied the parson. 'Her reminiscences all go back to the Regency. She was evidently then in her zenith; and I have heard her say things that showed she was in Parisian society when the First Empire was at its best – before Josephine was divorced.'

'She doesn't talk much now.'

'No; there's not much life left in her. She is wise in keeping herself secluded. I only wonder that wicked old quack, her Italian doctor, didn't finish her off years ago.'

'I should think it must be the other way, and that he keeps her alive.'

'My dear Miss Manders, do you think foreign quackery ever kept anybody alive?'

'Well, there she is – and she never goes anywhere without him. He certainly has an unpleasant countenance.'

'Unpleasant,' echoed the parson, 'I don't believe the foul fiend himself can beat him in ugliness. I pity that poor young woman who has to live between old Lady Ducayne and Dr Parravicini.'

'But the old lady is very good to her companions.'

'No doubt. She is very free with her cash; the servants call her good Lady Ducayne. She is a withered old female Croesus, and knows she'll never be able to get through her money, and doesn't relish the idea of other people enjoying it when she's in her coffin. People who live to be as old as she is become slavishly attached to life. I daresay she's generous to those poor girls – but she can't make them happy. They die in her service.'

'Don't say they, Mr Carton; I know that one poor girl died at Mentone last spring.'

'Yes, and another poor girl died in Rome three years ago. I was there at the time. Good Lady Ducayne left her there in an English family. The girl had every comfort. The old woman was very liberal to her – but she died.

I tell you, Miss Manders, it is not good for any young woman to live with two such horrors as Lady Ducayne and Parravicini.'

They talked of other things – but Bella hardly heard them. She sat motionless, and a cold wind seemed to come down upon her from the mountains and to creep up to her from the sea, till she shivered as she sat there in the sunshine, in the shelter of the orange trees in the midst of all that beauty and brightness.

Yes, they were uncanny, certainly, the pair of them – she so like an aristocratic witch in her withered old age; he of no particular age, with a face that was more like a waxen mask than any human countenance Bella had ever seen. What did it matter? Old age is venerable, and worthy of all reverence; and Lady Ducayne had been very kind to her. Dr Parravicini was a harmless, inoffensive student, who seldom looked up from the book he was reading. He had his private sitting-room, where he made experiments in chemistry and natural science – perhaps in alchemy. What could it matter to Bella? He had always been polite to her, in his far-off way. She could not be more happily placed than she was – in his palatial hotel, with this rich old lady.

No doubt she missed the young English girl who had been so friendly, and it might be that she missed the girl's brother, for Mr Stafford had talked to her a good deal – had interested himself in the books she was reading, and her manner of amusing herself when she was not on duty.

'You must come to our little salon when you are "off," as the hospital nurses call it, and we can have some music. No doubt you play and sing?' Upon which Bella had to own with a blush of shame that she had forgotten how to play the piano ages ago.

'Mother and I used to sing duets sometimes between the lights, without accompaniment,' she said, and the tears came into her eyes as she thought of the humble room, the half-hour's respite from work, the sewing machine standing where a piano ought to have been, and her mother's plaintive voice, so sweet, so true, so dear.

Sometimes she found herself wondering whether she would ever see that beloved mother again. Strange forebodings came into her mind. She was angry with herself for giving way to melancholy thoughts.

One day she questioned Lady Ducayne's French maid about those two companions who had died within three years.

'They were poor, feeble creatures,' Francine told her. 'They looked fresh and bright enough when they came to Miladi; but they ate too much, and they were lazy. They died of luxury and idleness. Miladi was too kind to them. They had nothing to do; and so they took to fancying things; fancying the air didn't suit them, that they couldn't sleep.'

'I sleep well enough, but I have had a strange dream several times since I have been in Italy.'

'Ah, you had better not begin to think about dreams, or you will be like those other girls. They were dreamers – and they dreamt themselves into the cemetery.'

The dream troubled her a little, not because it was a ghastly or frightening dream, but on account of sensations which she had never felt before in sleep – a whirring of wheels that went round in her brain, a great noise like a whirlwind, but rhythmical like the ticking of a gigantic clock: and then in the midst of this uproar as of winds and waves she seemed to sink into a gulf of unconsciousness, out of sleep into far deeper sleep – total extinction. And then, after that black interval, there had come the sound of voices, and then again the whirr of wheels, louder and louder – and again the black – and then she awoke, feeling languid and oppressed.

She told Dr Parravicini of her dream one day, on the only occasion when she wanted his professional advice. She had suffered rather severely from the mosquitoes before Christmas – and had been almost frightened at finding a wound upon her arm which she could only attribute to the venomous sting of one of these torturers. Parravicini put on his glasses, and scrutinized the angry mark on the round, white arm as Bella stood before him and Lady Ducayne with her sleeve rolled up above her elbow.

'Yes, that's rather more than a joke,' he said; 'he has caught you on the top of a vein. What a vampire! But there's no harm done, signorina, nothing that a little dressing of mine won't heal. You must always show me any bite of this nature. It might be dangerous if neglected. These creatures feed on poison and disseminate it.'

'And to think that such tiny creatures can bite like this,' said Bella; 'my arm looks as if it had been cut by a knife.'

'If I were to show you a mosquito's sting under my microscope you wouldn't be surprised at that,' replied Parravicini.

Bella had to put up with the mosquito bites, even when they came on the top of a vein, and produced that ugly wound. The wound recurred now and then at longish intervals, and Bella found Dr Parravicini's dressing a speedy cure. If he were the quack his enemies called him, he had at least a light hand and a delicate touch in performing this small operation.

'Bella Rolleston to Mrs Rolleston – April 14th.

'EVER DEAREST,

Behold the check for my second quarter's salary – five and twenty pounds. There is no one to pinch off a whole tenner for a year's commission as there was last time, so it is all for you, mother, dear. I have plenty of pocket-money in hand from the cash I brought away with me, when you insisted on my keeping more than I wanted. It isn't possible to spend money here – except on occasional tips to servants, or sous to beggars and children – unless one had lots to spend, for everything one would like to buy – tortoise-shell, coral, lace – is so ridiculously dear that only a millionaire ought to look at it. Italy is a dream of beauty: but for shopping, give me Newington Causeway.

'You ask me so earnestly if I am quite well that I fear my letters must have been very dull lately. Yes, dear, I am well – but I am not quite so strong as I was when I used to trudge to the West-end to buy half a pound of tea – just for a constitutional walk – or to Dulwich to look at the pictures. Italy is relaxing; and I feel what the people here call "slack." But I fancy I can see your dear face looking worried as you read this. Indeed, and indeed, I am not ill. I am only a little tired of this lovely scene – as I suppose one might get tired of looking at one of Turner's pictures if it hung on a wall that was always opposite one. I think of you every hour in every day – think of you and our homely little room – our dear little shabby parlor, with the armchairs from the wreck of your old home, and Dick singing in his cage over the sewing machine. Dear, shrill, maddening Dick, who, we flattered ourselves, was so passionately fond of us. Do tell me in your next letter that he is well.

'My friend Lotta and her brother never came back after all. They went from Pisa to Rome. Happy mortals! And they are to be on the Italian lakes in May; which lake was not decided when Lotta last wrote to me. She has been a charming correspondent, and has confided all her little flirtations to me. We are all to go to Bellaggio next week – by Genoa and Milan. Isn't that lovely? Lady Ducayne travels by the easiest stages – except when she is bottled up in the train deluxe. We shall stop two days at Genoa and one at Milan. What a bore I shall be to you with my talk about Italy when I come home.

'Love and love – and ever more love from your adoring, BELLA.'

IV

Herbert Stafford and his sister had often talked of the pretty English girl with her fresh complexion, which made such a pleasant touch of rosy color among all those sallow faces at the Grand Hotel. The young doctor thought of her with a compassionate tenderness – her utter loneliness in that great hotel where there were so many people, her bondage to that old, old woman, where everybody else was free to think of nothing but enjoying life. It was a hard fate; and the poor child was evidently devoted to her mother, and felt the pain of separation – 'only two of them, and very poor, and all the world to each other,' he thought.

Lotta told him one morning that they were to meet again at Bellaggio. 'The old thing and her court are to be there before we are,' she said. 'I shall be charmed to have Bella again. She is so bright and gay – in spite of an occasional touch of homesickness. I never took to a girl on a short acquaintance as I did to her.'

'I like her best when she is homesick,' said Herbert; 'for then I am sure she has a heart.'

'What have you to do with hearts, except for dissection? Don't forget that Bella is an absolute pauper. She told me in confidence that her mother makes mantles for a West-end shop. You can hardly have a lower depth than that.'

'I shouldn't think any less of her if her mother made matchboxes.'

'Not in the abstract – of course not. Matchboxes are honest labor. But you couldn't marry a girl whose mother makes mantles.'

'We haven't come to the consideration of that question yet,' answered Herbert, who liked to provoke his sister.

In two years' hospital practice he had seen too much of the grim realities of life to retain any prejudices about rank. Cancer, phthisis, gangrene, leave a man with little respect for the humanity. The kernel is always the same – fearfully and wonderfully made – a subject for pity and terror.

Mr Stafford and his sister arrived at Bellaggio in a fair May evening. The sun was going down as the steamer approached the pier; and all that glory of purple bloom which curtains every wall at this season of the year flushed and deepened in the glowing light. A group of ladies were standing on the pier watching the arrivals, and among them Herbert saw a pale face that startled him out of his wonted composure.

'There she is,' murmured Lotta, at his elbow, 'but how dreadfully changed. She looks a wreck.'

They were shaking hands with her a few minutes later, and a flush had lighted up her poor pinched face in the pleasure of meeting.

'I thought you might come this evening,' she said. 'We have been here a week.'

She did not add that she had been there every evening to watch the boat in, and a good many times during the day. The Grand Bretagne was close by, and it had been easy for her to creep to the pier when the boat bell rang. She felt a joy in meeting these people again; a sense of being with friends; a confidence which Lady Ducayne's goodness had never inspired in her.

'Oh, you poor darling, how awfully ill you must have been,' exclaimed Lotta, as the two girls embraced.

Bella tried to answer, but her voice was choked with tears.

'What has been the matter, dear? That horrid influenza, I suppose?'

'No, no, I have not been ill – I have only felt a little weaker than I used to be. I don't think the air of Cap Ferrino quite agreed with me.'

'It must have disagreed with you abominably. I never saw such a change in anyone. Do let Herbert doctor you. He is fully qualified, you know. He prescribed for ever so many influenza patients at the Londres. They were glad to get advice from an English doctor in a friendly way.'

'I am sure he must be very clever!' faltered Bella, 'but there is really nothing the matter. I am not ill, and if I were ill, Lady Ducayne's physician – '

'That dreadful man with the yellow face? I would as soon one of the Borgias prescribed for me. I hope you haven't been taking any of his medicines.'

'No, dear, I have taken nothing. I have never complained of being ill.'

This was said while they were all three walking to the hotel. The Staffords' rooms had been secured in advance, pretty ground-floor rooms, opening into the garden. Lady Ducayne's statelier apartments were on the floor above.

'I believe these rooms are just under ours,' said Bella.

'Then it will be all the easier for you to run down to us,' replied Lotta, which was not really the case, as the grand staircase was in the center of the hotel.

'Oh, I shall find it easy enough,' said Bella. 'I'm afraid you'll have too much of my society. Lady Ducayne sleeps away half the day in this warm weather, so I have a good deal of idle time; and I get awfully moped thinking of mother and home.'

Her voice broke upon the last word. She could not have thought of that poor lodging which went by the name of home more tenderly had it been the most beautiful that art and wealth ever created. She moped and pined in this lovely garden, with the sunlit lake and the romantic hills spreading out their beauty before her. She was homesick and she had dreams; or, rather, an occasional recurrence of that one bad dream with all its strange sensations – it was more like a hallucination than dreaming – the whirring of wheels, the sinking into an abyss, the struggling back to consciousness. She had the dream shortly before she left Cap Ferrino, but not since she had come to Bellaggio, and she began to hope the air in this lake district suited her better, and that those strange sensations would never return.

Mr Stafford wrote a prescription and had it made up at the chemist's near the hotel. It was a powerful tonic, and after two bottles, and a row or two on the lake, and some rambling over the hills and in the meadows where the spring flowers made earth seem paradise, Bella's spirits and looks improved as if by magic.

'It is a wonderful tonic,' she said, but perhaps in her heart of hearts she knew that the doctor's kind voice, and the friendly hand that helped her in and out of the boat, and the lake, had something to do with her cure.

'I hope you don't forget that her mother makes mantles,' Lotta said warningly.

'Or matchboxes; it is just the same thing, so far as I am concerned.'

'You mean that in no circumstances could you think of marrying her?'

'I mean that if ever I love a woman well enough to think of marrying her, riches or rank will count for nothing with me. But I fear – I fear your poor friend may not live to be any man's wife.'

'Do you think her so very ill?'

He sighed, and left the question unanswered.

One day, while they were gathering wild hyacinths in an upland meadow, Bella told Mr Stafford about her bad dream.

'It is curious only because it is hardly like a dream,' she said. 'I daresay you could find some commonsense reason for it. The position of my head on my pillow, or the atmosphere, or something.'

And then she described her sensations; how in the midst of sleep there came a sudden sense of suffocation; and then those whirring wheels, so loud, so terrible; and then a blank, and then a coming back to waking consciousness.

'Have you ever had chloroform given you – by a dentist, for instance?'

'Never – Dr Parravicini asked me that question one day.'

'Lately?'

'No, long ago, when we were in the train deluxe.'

'Has Dr Parravicini prescribed for you since you began to feel weak and ill?'

'Oh, he has given me a tonic from time to time, but I hate medicine, and took very little of the stuff. And then I am not ill, only weaker than I used to be. I was ridiculously strong and well when I lived at Walworth, and used to take long walks every day. Mother made me take those tramps to Dulwich or Norwood, for fear I should suffer from too much sewing machine; sometimes – but very seldom – she went with me. She was generally toiling at home while I was enjoying fresh air and exercise. And she was very careful about our food – that, however plain it was, it should be always nourishing and ample. I owe it to her care that I grew up such a great, strong creature.'

'You don't look great or strong now, you poor dear,' said Lotta.

'I'm afraid Italy doesn't agree with me.'

'Perhaps it is not Italy, but being cooped up with Lady Ducayne that has made you ill.'

'But I am never cooped up. Lady Ducayne is absurdly kind, and lets me roam about or sit in the balcony all day if I like. I have read more novels since I have been with her than in all the rest of my life.'

'Then she is very different from the average old lady, who is usually a slave driver,' said Stafford. 'I wonder why she carries a companion about with her if she has so little need of society.'

'Oh, I am only part of her state. She is inordinately rich – and the salary she gives me doesn't count. Apropos of Dr Parravicini, I know he is a clever doctor, for he cures my horrid mosquito bites.'

'A little ammonia would do that, in the early stage of the mischief. But there are no mosquitoes to trouble you now.'

'Oh, yes, there are; I had a bite just before we left Cap Ferrino.' She pushed up her loose lawn sleeve, and exhibited a scar, which he scrutinized intently, with a surprised and puzzled look.

'This is no mosquito bite,' he said.

'Oh, yes it is – unless there are snakes or adders at Cap Ferrino.'

'It is not a bite at all. You are trifling with me. Miss Rolleston – you have allowed that wretched Italian quack to bleed you. They killed the greatest man in modern Europe that way, remember. How very foolish of you.'

'I was never bled in my life, Mr Stafford.'

'Nonsense! Let me look at your other arm. Are there any more mosquito bites?'

'Yes; Dr Parravicini says I have a bad skin for healing, and that the poison acts more virulently with me than with most people.'

Stafford examined both her arms in the broad sunlight, scars new and old.

'You have been very badly bitten, Miss Rolleston,' he said, 'and if ever I find the mosquito I shall make him smart. But, now tell me, my dear girl, on your word of honor, tell me as you would tell a friend who is sincerely anxious for your health and happiness – as you would tell your mother if she were here to question you – have you no knowledge of any cause for these scars except mosquito bites – no suspicion even?'

'No, indeed! No, upon my honor! I have never seen a mosquito biting my arm. One never does see the horrid little fiends. But I have heard them trumpeting under the curtains and I know that I have often had one of the pestilent wretches buzzing about me.'

Later in the day Bella and her friends were sitting at tea in the garden, while Lady Ducayne took her afternoon drive with her doctor.

'How long do you mean to stop with Lady Ducayne, Miss Rolleston?' Herbert Stafford asked, after a thoughtful silence, breaking suddenly upon the trivial talk of the two girls.

'As long as she will go on paying me twenty-five pounds a quarter.'

'Even if you feel your health breaking down in her service?'

'It is not the service that has injured my health. You can see that I have really nothing to do – to read aloud for an hour or so once or twice a week; to write a letter once in a while to a London tradesman. I shall never have such an easy time with anybody. And nobody else would give me a hundred a year.'

'Then you mean to go on till you break down; to die at your post?'

'Like the other two companions? No! If ever I feel seriously ill – really ill – I shall put myself in a train and go back to Walworth without stopping.'

'What about the other two companions?'

'They both died. It was very unlucky for Lady Ducayne. That's why she engaged me; she chose me because I was ruddy and robust. She must feel rather disgusted at my having grown white and weak. By-the-bye, when I told her about the good your tonic had done me, she said she would like to see you and have a little talk with you about her own case.'

'And I should like to see Lady Ducayne. When did she say this?'

'The day before yesterday.'

'Will you ask her if she will see me this evening?'

'With pleasure! I wonder what you will think of her? She looks rather terrible to a stranger; but Dr Parravicini says she was once a famous beauty.'

It was nearly ten o'clock when Mr Stafford was summoned by message from Lady Ducayne, whose courier came to conduct him to her ladyship's salon. Bella was reading aloud when the visitor was admitted; and he noticed the languor in the low, sweet tones, the evident effort.

'Shut up the book,' said the querulous old voice. 'You are beginning to drawl like Miss Blandy.'

Stafford saw a small, bent figure crouching over the piled up olive logs; a shrunken old figure in a gorgeous garment of black and crimson brocade, a skinny throat emerging from a mass of old Venetian lace, clasped with diamonds that flashed like fireflies as the trembling old head turned towards him.

The eyes that looked at him out of the face were almost as bright as the diamonds – the only living feature in that narrow parchment mask. He had seen terrible faces in the hospital – faces on which disease had set dreadful marks but he had never seen a face that impressed him so painfully as this withered countenance, with its indescribable horror of death outlived, a face that should have been hidden under a coffin-lid years and years ago.

The Italian physician was standing on the other side of the fireplace, smoking a cigarette, and looking down at the little old woman brooding over the hearth as if he were proud of her.

'Good evening, Mr Stafford; you can go to your room, Bella, and write your everlasting letter to your mother at Walworth,' said Lady Ducayne. 'I believe she writes a page about every wild flower she discovers in the woods and meadows. I don't know what else she can find to write about,' she added, as Bella quietly withdrew to the pretty little bedroom opening out of Lady Ducayne's spacious apartment. Here, as at Cap Ferrino, she slept in a room adjoining the old lady's.

'You are a medical man, I understand, Mr Stafford.'

'I am a qualified practitioner, but I have not begun to practice.'

'You have begun upon my companion, she tells me.'

'I have prescribed for her, certainly, and I am happy to find my prescription has done her good; but I look upon that improvement as temporary. Her case will require more drastic treatment.'

'Never mind her case. There is nothing the matter with the girl – absolutely nothing – except girlish nonsense; too much liberty and not enough work.'

'I understand that two of your ladyship's previous companions died of

the same disease,' said Stafford, looking first at Lady Ducayne, who gave
her tremulous old head an impatient jerk, and then at Parravicini, whose
yellow complexion had paled a little under Stafford's scrutiny.

'Don't bother me about my companions, sir,' said Lady Ducayne. 'I
sent for you to consult you about myself – not about a parcel of anemic
girls. You are young, and medicine is a progressive science, the newspapers tell me. Where have you studied?'

'In Edinburgh – and in Paris.'

'Two good schools. And know all the new-fangled theories, the modern
discoveries – that remind one of the medieval witchcraft, of Albertus
Magnus, and George Ripley; you have studied hypnotism – eletricity?'

'And the transfusion of blood,' said Stafford, very slowly, looking at
Parravicini.

'Have you made any discovery that teaches you to prolong human
life – any elixir – any mode of treatment? I want my life prolonged, young
man. That man there has been my physician for thirty years. He does all
he can to keep me alive – after his lights. He studies all the new theories of
all the scientists – but he is old; he gets older every day – his brain-power
is going – he is bigoted – prejudiced – can't receive new ideas – can't
grapple with new systems. He will let me die if I am not on my guard
against him.'

'You are of an unbelievable ingratitude, Ecclenza,' said Parravicini.

'Oh, you needn't complain. I have paid you thousands to keep me alive.
Every year of my life has swollen your hoards; you know there is nothing
to come to you when I am gone. My whole fortune is left to endow a home
for indigent women of quality who have reached their ninetieth year.
Come, Mr Stafford, I am a rich woman. Give me a few years more in the
sunshine, a few years more above ground, and I will give you the price of a
fashionable London practice – I will set you up at the West-end.'

'How old are you, Lady Ducayne?'

'I was born the day Louis XVI was guillotined.'

'Then I think you have had your share of the sunshine and the pleasures of the earth, and that you should spend your few remaining days in
repenting your sins and trying to make atonement for the young lives that
have been sacrificed to your love of life.'

'What do you mean by that, sir?'

'Oh, Lady Ducayne, need I put your wickedness and your physician's
still greater wickedness in plain words? The poor girl who is now in your
employment has been reduced from robust health to a condition of absolute danger by Dr Parravicini's experimental surgery; and I have no
doubt those other two young women who broke down in your service
werloe treated by him in the same manner. I could take upon myself to
demonstrate – by most convincing evidence, to a jury of medical men –
that Dr Parravicini has been bleeding Miss Rolleston after putting her

under chloroform, at intervals, ever since she has been in your service. The deterioration in the girl's health speaks for itself; the lancet marks upon the girl's arms are unmistakable; and her description of a series of sensations, which she calls a dream, points unmistakably to the administration of chloroform while she was sleeping. A practice so nefarious, so murderous, must, if exposed, result in a sentence only less severe than the punishment of murder.'

'I laugh,' said Parravicini, with an airy motion of his skinny fingers; 'I laugh at once at your theories and at your threats. I, Parravicini Leopold, have no fear that the law can question anything I have done.'

'Take the girl away, and let me hear no more of her,' cried Lady Ducayne, in the thin, old voice, which so poorly matched the energy and fire of the wicked old brain that guided its utterances. 'Let her go back to her mother – I want no more girls to die in my service. There are girls enough and to spare in the world, God knows.'

'If you ever engage another companion – or take another English girl into your service, Lady Ducayne, I will make all England ring with the story of your wickedness.'

'I want no more girls. I don't believe in his experiments. They have been full of danger for me as well as for the girl – an air bubble, and I should be gone. I'll have no more of his dangerous quackery. I'll find some new man – a better man than you, sir, a discoverer like Pasteur, or Virchow, a genius – to keep me alive. Take your girl away, young man. Marry her if you like. I'll write a check for a thousand pounds, and let her go and live on beef and beer, and get strong and plump again. I'll have no more such experiments. Do you hear, Parravicini?' she screamed, vindictively, the yellow, wrinkled face distorted with fury, the eyes glaring at him.

The Staffords carried Bella Rolleston off to Varese next day, she very loath to leave Lady Ducayne, whose liberal salary afforded such help for the dear mother. Herbert Stafford insisted, however, treating Bella as coolly as if he had been the family physician, and she had been given over wholly to his care.

'Do you suppose your mother would let you stop here to die?' he asked. 'If Mrs Rolleston knew how ill you are, she would come post haste to fetch you.'

'I shall never be well again till I get back to Walworth,' answered Bella, who was low-spirited and inclined to tears this morning, a reaction after her good spirits of yesterday.

'We'll try a week or two at Varese first,' said Stafford. 'When you can walk halfway up Monte Generoso without palpitation of the heart, you shall go back to Walworth.'

'Poor mother, how glad she will be to see me, and how sorry that I've lost such a good place.'

This conversation took place on the boat when they were leaving Bellaggio. Lotta had gone to her friend's room at seven o'clock that morning, long before Lady Ducayne's withered eyelids had opened to the daylight, before even Francine, the French maid, was astir, and had helped to pack a Gladstone bag with essentials, and hustled Bella downstairs and out of doors before she could make any strenuous resistance.

'It's all right,' Lotta assured her. 'Herbert had a good talk with Lady Ducayne last night, and it was settled for you to leave this morning. She doesn't like invalids, you see.'

'No,' sighed Bella, 'she doesn't like invalids. It was very unlucky that I should break down, just like Miss Tomson and Miss Blandy.'

'At any rate, you are not dead, like them,' answered Lotta, 'and my brother says you are not going to die.'

It seemed rather a dreadful thing to be dismissed in that offhand way, without a word of farewell from her employer.

'I wonder what Miss Torpinter will say when I go to her for another situation,' Bella speculated, ruefully, while she and her friends were breakfasting on board the steamer.

'Perhaps you may never want another situation,' said Stafford.

'You mean that I may never be well enough to be useful to anybody?'

'No, I don't mean anything of the kind.'

It was after dinner at Varese, when Bella had been induced to take a hwhole glass of Chianti, and quite sparkled after that unaccustomed stimulant, that Mr Stafford produced a letter from his pocket.

'I forgot to give you Lady Ducayne's letter of adieu!' he said.

'What, did she write to me? I am so glad – I hated to leave her in such a cool way; for after all she was very kind to me, and if I didn't like her it was only because she was too dreadfully old.'

She tore open the envelope. The letter was short and to the point: –

'Goodbye, child. Go and marry your doctor. I enclose a farewell gift for your trousseau.

—ADELINE DUCAYNE

'A hundred pounds, a whole year's salary – no – why, it's for a – A check for a thousand!' cried Bella. 'What a generous old soul! She really is the dearest old thing.'

'She just missed being very dear to you, Bella,' said Stafford.

He had dropped into the use of her Christian name while they were on board the boat. It seemed natural now that she was to be in his charge till they all three went back to England.

'I shall take upon myself the privileges of an elder brother till we land at Dover,' he said; 'after that – well, it must be as you please.'

The question of their future relations must have been satisfactorily settled before they crossed the Channel, for Bella's next letter to her mother communicated three startling facts.

First, that the inclosed check for £1,000 was to be invested in debenture stock in Mrs Rolleston's name, and was to be her very own, income and principal, for the rest of her life.

Next, that Bella was going home to Walworth immediately.

And last, that she was going to be married to Mr Herbert Stafford in the following autumn.

'And I am sure you will adore him, mother, as much as I do,' wrote Bella.

'It is all good Lady Ducayne's doing. I never could have married if I had not secured that little nest-egg for you. Herbert says we shall be able to add to it as the years go by, and that wherever we live there shall be always a room in our house for you. The word "mother-in-law" has no terrors for him.'

The Mindworm
C. M. Kornbluth

The handsome j. g. and the pretty nurse held out against it as long as they reasonably could, but blue Pacific water, languid tropical nights, the low atoll dreaming on the horizon – and the complete absence of any other nice young people for company on the small, uncomfortable parts boat – did their work. On June 30th they watched through dark glasses as the dazzling thing burst over the fleet and the atoll. Her manicured hand gripped his arm in excitement and terror. Unfelt radiation sleeted through their loins.

A storekeeper-third-class named Bielaski watched the young couple with more interest than he showed in Test Able. After all, he had twenty-five dollars riding on the nurse. That night he lost it to a chief bosun's mate who had backed the j. g.

In the course of time, the careless nurse was discharged under conditions other than honorable. The j. g., who didn't like to put things in writing, phoned her all the way from Manila to say it was a damned shame. When her gratitude gave way to specific inquiry, their overseas connection went bad and he had to hang up.

She had a child, a boy, turned it over to a foundling home, and vanished from his life into a series of good jobs and finally marriage.

The boy grew up stupid, puny and stubborn, greedy and miserable. To the home's hilarious young athletics director he suddenly said: 'You hate me. You think I make the rest of the boys look bad.'

The athletics director blustered and laughed, and later told the doctor over coffee: 'I watch myself around the kids. They're sharp – they catch a look or a gesture and it's like a blow in the face to them, I know that, so I watch myself. So how did he know?'

The doctor told the boy: 'Three pounds more this month isn't bad, but how about you pitch in and clean up your plate *every* day? Can't live on meat and water; those vegetables make you big and strong.'

The boy said: 'What's "neurasthenic" mean?'

The doctor later said to the director: 'It made my flesh creep. I was looking at his little spindling body and dishing out the old pep talk about growing big and strong, and inside my head I was thinking "we'd call him neurasthenic in the old days" and then out he popped with it. What should we do? Should we do anything? Maybe it'll go away. I don't know anything about these things. I don't know whether anybody does.'

'Reads minds, does he?' asked the director. *Be damned if he's going to read my mind about Shultz Meat Market's ten percent.* 'Doctor, I think I'm going to take my vacation a little early this year. Has anybody shown any interest in adopting the child?'

'Not him. He wasn't a baby doll when we got him, and at present he's an exceptionally unattractive-looking kid. You know how people don't give a damn about anything but their looks.'

'*Some* couples would take anything, or so they tell me.'

'Unapproved for foster-parenthood, you mean?'

'Red tape and arbitrary classifications sometimes limit us too severely in our adoptions.'

'If you're going to wish him on some screwball couple that the courts turned down as unfit, I want no part of it.'

'You don't have to have any part of it, doctor. By the way, which dorm does he sleep in?'

'West,' grunted the doctor, leaving the office.

The director called a few friends – a judge, a couple the judge referred him to, a court clerk. Then he left by way of the east wing of the building.

The boy survived three months with the Berrymans. Hard-drinking Mimi alternately caressed and shrieked at him; Edward W., tried to be a good scout and just gradually lost interest, looking clean through him. He hit the road in June and got by with it for a while. He wore a Boy Scout uniform, and Boy Scouts can turn up anywhere, any time. The money he had taken with him lasted a month. When the last penny of the last dollar was three days spent, he was adrift on a Nebraska prairie. He had walked out of the last small town because the constable was beginning to wonder what on earth he was hanging around for and who he belonged to. The m town was miles behind on the two-lane highway; the infrequent cars did not stop.

One of Nebraska's 'rivers,' a dry bed at this time of year, lay ahead, spanned by a railroad culvert. There were some men in its shade, and he was hungry.

They were ugly, dirty men, and their thoughts were muddled and stupid. They called him 'Shorty' and gave him a little dirty bread and some stinking sardines from a can. The thoughts of one of them became less muddled and uglier. He talked to the rest out of the boy's hearing, and they whooped with laughter. The boy got ready to run, but his legs wouldn't hold him up.

He could read the thoughts of the men quite clearly as they headed for him. Outrage, fear, and disgust blended in him and somehow turned inside-out and one of the men was dead on the dry ground, grasshoppers vaulting onto his flannel shirt, the others backing away, frightened now, not frightening.

He wasn't hungry any more; he felt quite comfortable and satisfied. He got up and headed for the other men, who ran. The rearmost of them was thinking *Jeez he folded up the evil eye we was only gonna –*

Again the boy let the thoughts flow into his head and again he flipped his own thoughts around them; it was quite easy to do. It was different – this man's terror from the other's lustful anticipation. But both had their points ...

At his leisure, he robbed the bodies of three dollars and twenty four cents.

Thereafter his fame preceded him like a death wind. Two years on the road and he had his growth and his fill of the dull and stupid minds he met there. He moved to northern cities, a year here, a year there, quiet, unobtrusive, prudent, an epicure.

Sebastian Long woke suddenly, with something on his mind. As night fog cleared away he remembered, happily. Today he started the Demeter Bowl! At last there was time, at last there was money – six hundred and twenty-three dollars in the bank. He had packed and shipped the three dozen cocktail glasses last night, engraved with Mrs Klausman's initials – his last commercial order for as many months as the Bowl would take.

He shifted from nightshirt to denims, gulped coffee, boiled an egg but was too excited to eat it. He went to the front of his shop-workroom-apartment, checked the lock, waved at neighbors' children on their way to school, and ceremoniously set a sign in the cluttered window.

It said: 'NO COMMERCIAL ORDERS TAKEN UNTIL FUR-THER NOTICE.'

From a closet he tenderly carried a shrouded object that made a double armful and laid it on his workbench. Unshrouded, it was a glass bowl – what a glass bowl! The clearest Swedish lead glass, the purest lines he had ever seen, his secret treasure since the crazy day he had bought it, long ago, for six months' earnings. His wife had given him hell for that until the day she died. From the closet he brought a portfolio filled with sketches and designs dating back to the day he had bought the bowl. He smiled over the first, excitedly scrawled – a florid, rococo conception, unsuited to the classicism of the lines and the serenity of the perfect glass.

Through many years and hundreds of sketches he had refined his conception to the point where it was, he humbly felt, not unsuited to the medium. A strongly-molded Demeter was to dominate the piece, a matron as serene as the glass, and all the fruits of the earth would flow from her gravely outstretched arms.

Suddenly and surely, he began to work. With a candle he thinly smoked an oval area on the outside of the bowl. Two steady fingers clipped the

Demeter drawing against the carbon black; a hair-fine needle in his other hand traced her lines. When the transfer of the design was done, Sebastian Long readied his lathe. He fitted a small copper wheel, slightly worn as he liked them, into the chuck and with his fingers charged it with the finest rouge from Rouen. He took an ashtray cracked in delivery and held it against the spinning disk. It bit in smoothly, with the *wiping* feel to it that was exactly right.

Holding out his hands, seeing that the fingers did not tremble with excitement, he eased the great bowl to the lathe and was about to make the first tiny cut of the millions that would go into the masterpiece.

Somebody knocked on his door and rattled the doorknob.

Sebastian Long did not move or look toward the door. Soon the busybody would read the sign and go away. But the pounding and the rattling of the knob went on. He eased down the bowl and angrily went to the window, picked up the sign, and shook it at whoever it was – he couldn't make out the face very well. But the idiot wouldn't go away.

The engraver unlocked the door, opened it a bit, and snapped: 'The shop is closed. I shall not be taking any orders for several months. Please don't bother me now.'

'It's about the Demeter Bowl,' said the intruder.

Sebastian Long stared at him. 'What the devil do you know about my Demeter Bowl?' He saw the man was a stranger, undersized by a little, middle-aged ...

'Just let me in please,' urged the man. 'It's important. Please!'

'I don't know what you're talking about,' said the engraver. 'But what do you know about my Demeter Bowl?' He hooked his thumbs pugnaciously over the waistband of his denims and glowered at the stranger. The stranger promptly took advantage of his hand being removed from the door and glided in.

Sebastian Long thought briefly that it might be a nightmare as the man darted quickly about his shop, picking up a graver and throwing it down, picking up a wire scratch-wheel and throwing it down. 'Here, you!' he roared, as the stranger picked up a crescent wrench which he did not throw down.

As Long started for him, the stranger darted to the workbench and brought the crescent wrench down shatteringly on the bowl.

Sebastian Long's heart was bursting with sorrow and rage; such a storm of emotions as he never had known thundered through him. Paralyzed, he saw the stranger smile with anticipation.

The engraver's legs folded under him and he fell to the floor, drained and dead.

The Mindworm, locked in the bedroom of his brownstone front, smiled again reminiscently.

Smiling, he checked the day on a wall calender.

'Dolores!' yelled her mother in Spanish. 'Are you going to pass the whole day in there?'

She had been practicing low-lidded, sexy half-smiles like Lauren Bacall in the bathroom mirror. She stormed out and yelled in English: 'I don't know how many times I tell you not to call me that Spick name no more!'

'Dolly!' sneered her mother. 'Dah-lee! When was there a Saint Dah-lee that you call yourself after, eh?'

The girl snarled a Spanish obscenity at her mother and ran down the tenement stairs. Jeez, she was gonna be late for sure!

Held up by a stream of traffic between her and her streetcar, she danced with impatience. Then the miracle happened. Just like in the movies, a big convertible pulled up before her and its lounging driver said, opening the door: 'You seem to be in a hurry. Could I drop you somewhere?'

Dazed at the sudden realization of a hundred daydreams, she did not fail to give the driver a low-lidded, sexy smile as she said: 'Why, *thanks!*' and climbed in. He wasn't no Cary Grant, but he had all his hair . . kind of small, but so was she . . and jeez, the convertible had *leopard-skin seat covers!*

The car was in the stream of traffic, purring down the avenue. 'It's a lovely day." she said. 'Really too nice to work.'

The driver smiled shyly, kind of like Jimmy Stewart but of course not so tall, and said: 'I feel like playing hooky myself. How would you like a spin down Long Island?'

'Be wonderful!' The convertible cut left on an odd-numbered street.

'Play hooky, you said. What do you do?'

"Advertising.'

Advertising! Dolly wanted to kick herself for ever having doubted, for ever having thought in low, self-loathing moments that it wouldn't work out, that she'd marry a grocer or a mechanic and live forever after in a smelly tenement and grow old and sick and stooped. She felt vaguely in her happy daze that it might have been cuter, she might have accidentally pushed him into a pond or something, but this was cute enough. An advertising man, leopard-skin seat covers . . . what more could a girl with a sexy smile and a nice little figure want?

Speeding down the South Shore she learned that his name was Michael Brent, exactly as it ought to be. She wished she could tell him she was Jennifer Brown or one of those real cute names they had nowadays, but was reassured when he told her he thought Dolly Gonzalez was a beautiful name. He didn't, and she noticed the omission, add: 'It's the most beautiful name I ever heard!' That, she comfortably thought as she settled herself against the cushions, would come later.

They stopped at Medford for lunch, a wonderful lunch in a little restaurant where you went down some steps and there were candles on the table. She called him 'Michael' and he called her 'Dolly.' She learned that he liked dark girls and thought the stories in *True Story* really were true, and that he thought she was just tall enough, and that Greer Garson was wonderful, but not the way she was, and that he thought her dress was just wonderful.

They drove slowly after Medford, and Michael Brent did most of the talking. He had traveled all over the world. He had been in the war and wounded – just a flesh wound. He was thirty-eight, and had been married once, but she died. There were no children. He was alone in the world. He had nobody to share his town house in the 50's, his country place in Westchester, his lodge in the Maine woods. Every word sent the girl floating higher and higher on a tide of happiness; the signs were unmistakable.

When they reached Montauk Point, the last sandy bit of the continent before blue water and Europe, it was sunset, with a great wrinkled sheet of purple and rose stretching half across the sky and the first stars appearing above the dark horizon of the water.

The two of them walked from the parked car out onto the sand, alone, bathed in glorious Technicolor. Her heart was nearly bursting with joy as she heard Michael Brent say, his arms tightening around her: 'Darling, will you marry me?'

'Oh, *yes*, Michael!' she breathed, dying.

The Mindworm, drowsing, suddenly felt the sharp sting of danger. He cast out through the great city, dragging tentacles of thought:

'... die if she don't let me ...'

'... six an' six is twelve an' carry one an' three is four ...'

'... gobblegobble madre de dios pero soy gobblegobble ...'

'... parlay Domino an' Missab and shoot the roll on Duchess Peg in the feature ...'

'... melt resin add the silver chloride and dissolve in oil of lavender stand and decant and fire to cone zero twelve give you shimmering streaks of luster down the walls ...'

'... moiderin' square-headed gobblegobble tried ta poke his eye out wassamatta witta ref ...'

'... O God I am most heartily sorry I have offended thee in ...'

'... talk like a commie ...'

'... gobblegobblegobble two dolla twenny-fi' sense gobble ...'

'... just a nip and fill it up with water and brush my teeth ...'

'... really know I'm God but fear to confess their sins ...'

'... dirty lousy rock-headed claw-handed paddle-footed goggle-eyed snot-nosed hunch-backed feeble-minded pot-bellied son of ...'

... write on the wall alfie is a stunkur and then ...'

'... thinks I believe it's a television set but I know he's got a bomb in there but who can I tell who can help so alone ...'

'... gabble was ich weiss nicht gabble geh bei Broadvay gabble ...'
'... habt mein daughter Rosie such a fella gobblegobble ...'
'... wonder if that's one didn't look back ...'
'... seen with her in the Medford restaurant ...'
The Mindworm struck into that thought.
'... not a mark on her but the M. E.'s have been wrong before and heart failure don't mean a thing anyway try to talk to her old lady authorize an autopsy get Pancho little guy talks Spanish be best ...'
The Mindworm knew he would have to be moving again – soon. He was sorry; some of the thoughts he had tapped indicated good ... hunting?
Regretfully, he again dragged his net:
'... with chartreuse drinks I mean drapes could use a drink come to think of it ...'
'... reep-beep-reep-beep reepiddy-beepiddy-beep bop man wadda beat ...'

$$\text{`}\sum_{r=l+1}^{n} \phi\,(\alpha_x, \alpha_r) - \sum_{s=1}^{\prime} \phi\,(\alpha_x, \alpha_r). \quad \textit{What the Hell was that?'}$$

The Mindworm withdrew, in frantic haste. The intelligence was massive, its overtones those of a vigorous adult. He had learned from certain dangerous children that there was peril of a leveling flow. Shaken and scared, he contemplated traveling. He would need more than that wretched girl had supplied, and it would not be epicurean. There would be no time to find individuals at a ripe emotional crisis, or goad them to one. It would be plain – munching. The Mindworm drank a glass of water, also necessary to his metabolism.

EIGHT FOUND DEAD
IN UPTOWN MOVIE;
'MOLESTER' SOUGHT

Eight persons, including three women, were found dead Wednesday night of unknown causes in widely separated seats in the balcony of the Odeon Theater at 117th St. and Broadway. Police are seeking a man described by the balcony usher, Michael Fenelly, 18, as 'acting like a woman-molester.'
Fenelly discovered the first of the fatalities after seeing the man 'moving from one empty seat to another several times.' He went to ask a woman in a seat next to one the man had just vacated whether he had annoyed her. She was dead.
Almost at once, a scream rang out. In another part of the balcony Mrs Sadie Rabinowitz, 40, uttered the cry when another victim toppled from his seat next to her.

Theater manager I. J. Marcusohn stopped the show and turned on the house lights. He tried to instruct his staff to keep the audience from leaving before the police arrived. He failed to get word to them in time, however, and most of the audience was gone when a detail from the 24th Pct, and an ambulance from Harlem Hospital took over at the scene of the tragedy.

The Medical Examiner's office has not yet made a report as to the causes of death. A spokesman said the victims showed no signs of poisoning or violence. He added that it 'was inconceivable that it could be a coincidence.'

Lt John Braidwood of the 24th Pct. said of the alleged molester: 'We got a fair description of him and naturally we will try to bring him in for questioning.'

Clickety-click, clickety-click, clickety-click sang the rails as the Mindworm drowsed in his coach seat.

Some people were walking forward from the diner. One was thinking: 'Different-looking fellow. (a) he's aberrant. (b) he's nonaberrant and ill. Cancel (b)-respiration normal, skin smooth and healthy, no tremor of limbs, well-groomed. Is aberrant (1) trivially. (2) significantly. Cancel (I)-displayed no involuntary interest when . . , odd! *Running* for the wash-room! Unexpected because (a) neat grooming indicates amour propre inconsistent with amusing others; (b) evident health inconsistent with . . .' It had taken one second, was fully detailed.

The Mindworm, locked in the toilet of the coach, wondered what the next stop was. He was getting off at it – not frightened, just careful. Dodge them, keep dodging them and everything would be all right. Send out no mental taps until the train was far away and everything would be all right.

He got off at a West Virginia coal and iron town surrounded by ruined mountains and filled with the offscourings of Eastern Europe. Serbs, Albanians, Croats, Hungarians, Slovenes, Bulgarians, and all possible combinations and permutations thereof. He walked slowly from the smoke-stained, brownstone passenger station. The train had roared on its way.

'. . . ain' no gemmum that's fo sho', fi-cen'tip fo' a good shine lak ah give um . . .'

'. . . dumb bassar don't know how to make out a billa lading yet he ain't never gonna know so fire him get it over with . . .'

'. . . gabblegabblegabble . . .' Not a word he recognized in it.

'. . . gobblegobble dat tam vooman I brek she nack . . .'

'. . . gobble trink visky chin glassabeer gobblegobblegobble . . .'

'. . . gabblegabblegabble . . .'

'. . . makes me so gobblegobble mad little no-good tramp no she ain' but I don' like no standup from no dame . . .'

A blond, square-headed boy fuming under a street light.

'... out wit' Casey Oswiak I could kill that dumb bohunk alla time trine ta paw her ...'

It was a possibility. The Mindworm drew near.

'... stand me up for that gobblegobble bohunk I oughtta slap her inna mush like my ole man says ...'

'Hello,' said the Mindworm.

'Waddaya wan'?'

'Casey Oswiak told me to tell you not to wait up for your girl. He's taking her out tonight.'

The blond boy's rage boiled into his face and shot from his eyes. He was about to swing when the Mindworm began to feed. It was like pheasant after chicken, venison after beef. The coarseness of the environment, or the ancient strain? The Mindworm wondered as he strolled down the street. A girl passed him:

'... oh but he's gonna be mad like last time wish I came right away so jealous kinda nice but he might bust me one some day be nice to him tonight there he is lam'post leaning on it looks kinda funny gawd I hope he ain't drunk looks kinda funny sleeping sick or bozhe moi gabblegabblegab-ble ...'

Her thoughts trailed into a foreign language of which the Mindworm knew not a word. After hysteria had gone she recalled, in the foreign language, that she had passed him.

The Mindworm, stimulated by the unfamiliar quality of the last feeding, determined to stay for some days. He checked in at a Main Street hotel.

Musing, he dragged his net:

'... gobblegobblewhompyeargobblecheskygobblegabblechyesh ...'

'... take him down cellar beat the can off the damn chesky thief put the fear of god into him teach him can't bust into no boxcars in *mah* parta the caounty ...'

'... gabblegabble. . .'

'... phone ole Mister Ryan in She-cawgo and he'll tell them three-card monte grifters who got the horse-room rights in this necka the woods by damn don't pay protection money for no protection ...'

The Mindworm followed that one further; it sounded as though it could lead to some money if he wanted to stay in the town long enough.

The Eastern Europeans of the town, he mistakenly thought, were like the tramps and bums he had known and fed on during his years on the road – stupid and safe, safe and stupid, quite the same thing.

In the morning he found no mention of the square-headed boy's death in the town's paper and thought it had gone practically unnoticed. It had – by the paper, which was of, by, and for the coal and iron company and its native-American bosses and straw bosses. The other town, the one without a charter or police force, with only an imported weekly newspaper or two from the nearest city, noticed it. The other town had roots more than two thousand years deep, which are hard to pull up. But the Mindworm didn't know it was there.

He fed again that night, on a giddy young streetwalker in her room. He had astounded and delighted her with a fistful of ten-dollar bills before he began to gorge. Again the delightful difference from citybred folk was there....

Again in the morning he had been unnoticed, he thought. The chartered town, unwilling to admit that there were streetwalkers or that they were found dead, wiped the slate clean; its only member who really cared was the native-American cop on the beat who had collected weekly from the dead girl.

The other town, unknown to the Mindworm, buzzed with it. A delegation went to the other town's only public officer. Unfortunately he was young, American-trained, perhaps even ignorant about some important things. For what he told them was: 'My children, that is a foolish superstition. Go home.'

'The Mindworm, through the day, roiled the surface of the town proper by allowing himself to be roped into a poker game in a parlor of the hotel. He wasn't good at it, he didn't like it, and he quit with relief when he had cleaned six shifty-eyed, hard-drinking loafers out of about three hundred dollars. One of them went straight to the police station and accused the unknown of being a sharper. A humorous sergeant, the Mindworm was pleased to note, joshed the loafer out of his temper.

Nightfall again, hunger again ...

He walked the streets of the town and found them empty. It was strange. The native-American citizens were out, tending bar, walking their beats, locking up their newspaper on the stones, collecting their rents, managing their movies – but where were the others? He cast his net:

'... gobblegobblegobble whomp year gobble ...'

'... crazy old pollack mama of mine try to lock me in with Errol Flynn at the Majestic never know the difference if I sneak out the back ...'

That was near. He crossed the street and it was nearer. He homed on the thought:

'... jeez he's a hunka man like Stanley but he never looks at me that Vera Kowalik I'd like to kick her just once in the gobblegobblegobble crazy old mama won't be American so ashamed ...'

It was half a block, no more, down a side street. Brick houses, two stories, with back yards on an alley. She was going out the back way.

How strangely quiet it was in the alley.

'... ea-sy down them steps fix that damn board that's how she caught me last time what the hell are they all so scared of went to see Father Drugas won't talk bet somebody got it again that Vera Kowalik and her big ...'

'... gobble bozhe gobble whomp year gobble ...'

She was closer; she was closer.

'All think I'm a kid show them who's a kid bet if Stanley caught me alone out here in the alley dark and all he wouldn't think I was a kid that damn Vera Kowalik her folks don't think she's a kid ...'

For all her bravado she was stark terrified when he said: 'Hello.'

'Who – who – who – ?' she stammered.

Quick, before she screamed. Her terror was delightful.

Not too replete to be alert, he cast about, questing.

'... gobblegobblegobble whomp year.'

The countless eyes of the other town, with more than two thousand years of experience in such things, had been following him. What he had sensed as a meaningless hash of noise was actually an impassioned outburst in a nearby darkened house.

'Fools! fools! Now he has taken a virgin! I said not to wait. What will we say to her mother?'

An old man with handlebar mustache and, in spite of the heat, his shirt sleeves decently rolled down and buttoned at the cuffs, evenly replied: My heart in me died with hers, Casimir, but one must be sure. It would be a terrible thing to make a mistake in such an affair.'

The weight of conservative elder opinion was with him. Other old men with mustaches, some perhaps remembering mistakes long ago, nodded and said: 'A terrible thing. A terrible thing.'

The Mindworm strolled back to his hotel and napped on the made bed briefly. A tingle of danger awakened him. Instantly he cast out:

'... gobblegobble whompyear.'

'... whampyir.'

'WAMPYIR!'

Close! Close and deadly!

The door of his room burst open, and mustached old men with their shirt sleeves rolled down and decently buttoned at the cuffs unhesitatingly marched in, their thoughts a turmoil of alien noises, foreign gibberish that he could not wrap his mind around, disconcerting, from every direction.

The sharpened stake was through his heart and the scythe blade through his throat before he could realize that he had not been the first of his kind; and that what clever people have not yet learned, some quite ordinary people have not yet entirely forgotten.

Luella Miller
Mary E. Wilkins-Freeman

Close to the village street stood the one-story house in which Luella
Miller, who had an evil name in the village, had dwelt. She had been dead
for years, yet there were those in the village who, in spite of the clearer
light which comes on a vantage-point from a long-past danger, half
believed in the tale which they had heard from their childhood. In their
hearts, although they scarcely would have owned it, was a survival of the
wild horror and frenzied fear of their ancestors who had dwelt in the same
age with Luella Miller. Young people even would stare with a shudder at
the old house as they passed, and children never played around it as was
their wont around an untenanted building. Not a window in the old
Miller house was broken: the panes reflected the morning sunlight in
patches of emerald and blue, and the latch of the sagging front door was
never lifted, although no bolt secured it. Since Luella Miller had been
carried out of it, the house had had no tenant except one friendless old
soul who had no choice between that and the far-off shelter of the open
sky. This old woman, who had survived her kindred and friends, lived in
the house one week, then one morning no smoke came out of the
chimney, and a body of neighbours, a score strong, entered and found her
dead in her bed. There were dark whispers as to the cause of her death,
and there were those who testified to an expression of fear so exalted that
it showed forth the state of the departing soul upon the dead face. The old
woman had been hale and hearty when she entered the house, and in
seven days she was dead; it seemed that she had fallen a victim to some
uncanny power. The minister talked in the pulpit with covert severity
against the sin of superstition; still the belief prevailed. Not a soul in the
village but would have chosen the almshouse rather than that dwelling.
No vagrant, if he heard the tale, would seek shelter beneath that old roof,
unhallowed by nearly half a century of superstitious fear.

There was only one person in the village who had actually known
Luella Miller. That person was a woman well over eighty, but a marvel of
vitality and unextinct youth. Straight as an arrow, with the spring of one
recently let loose from the bow of life, she moved about the streets, and she

always went to church, rain or shine. She had never married, and had lived alone for years in a house across the road from Luella Miller's.

This woman had none of the garrulousness of age, but never in all her life had she ever held her tongue for any will save her own, and she never spared the truth when she essayed to present it. She it was who bore testimony to the life, evil, though possibly wittingly or designedly so, of Luella Miller, and to her personal appearance. When this old woman spoke – and she had the gift of description, although her thoughts were clothed in the rude vernacular of her native village – one could seem to see Luella Miller as she had really looked. According to this woman, Lydia Anderson by name, Luella Miller had been a beauty of a type rather unusual in New England. She had been a slight, pliant sort of creature, as ready with a strong yielding to fate and as unbreakable as a willow. She had glimmering lengths of straight, fair hair, which she wore softly looped round a long, lovely face. She had blue eyes full of soft pleading, little slender, clinging hands, and a wonderful grace of motion and attitude.

'Luella Miller used to sit in a way nobody else could if they sat up and studied a week of Sundays,' said Lydia Anderson, 'and it was a sight to see her walk. If one of them willows over there on the edge of the brook could start up and get its roots free of the ground, and move off, it would go just the way Luella Miller used to. She had a green shot silk she used to wear, too, and a hat with green ribbon streamers, and a lace veil blowing across her face and out sideways, and a green ribbon flyin' from her waist. That was what she came out bride in when she married Erastus Miller. Her name before she was married was Hill. There was always a sight of 'l's' in her name, married or single. Erastus Miller was good lookin', too, better lookin' than Luella. Sometimes I used to think that Luella wa'n't so handsome after all. Erastus just about worshiped her. I used to know him pretty well. He lived next door to me, and we went to school together. Folks used to say he was waitin' on me, but he wa'n't. I never thought he was except once or twice when he said things that some girls might have suspected meant somethin'. That was before Luella came here to teach the district school. It was funny how she came to get it, for folks said she hadn't any education, and that one of the big girls, Lottie Henderson, used to do all the teachin' for her, while she sat back and did embroidery work on a cambric pocket-handkerchief. Lottie Henderson was a real smart girl, a splendid scholar, and she just set her eyes by Luella, as all the girls did. Lottie would have made a real smart woman, but she died when Luella had been here about a year – just faded away and died: nobody knew what ailed her. She dragged herself to that schoolhouse and helped Luella teach till the very last minute. The committee all knew how Luella didn't do much of the work herself, but they winked at it. It wa'n't long after Lottie died that Erastus married her. I always thought he hurried it up because she wa'n't fit to teach. One of the big boys used to help her after Lottie died, but he hadn't much government, and the school didn't do very well, and Luella might have had to give it up, for the committee couldn't have shut their eyes to things much longer. The boy that helped her was a real honest, innocent sort of fellow, and he was a good scholar, too. Folks said he overstudied, and that was the reason he was took crazy the year after Luella married, but I don't know. And I don't know what made Erastus Miller go into consumption of the blood the year after he was married: consumption wa'n't in his family. He just grew weaker and weaker, and went almost bent double when he tried to wait on Luella, and he spoke feeble, like an old man. He worked terrible hard till the last trying to save up a little to leave Luella. I've seen him out in the worst storms on a wood-sled – he used to cut and sell wood – and he was hunched up on top lookin' more dead than alive. Once I couldn't stand it: I went over and helped him pitch some wood on the cart – I was always strong in my arms. I wouldn't stop for all he told me to, and I guess he was glad enough for the help. That was only a week before he died. He fell on the kitchen floor while he was gettin' breakfast. He always got the breakfast and let Luella lay abed. He did all the sweepin' and the washin' and the ironin' and most of the cookin'. He couldn't bear to have Luella lift her finger, and she let him do for her. She lived like a queen for all the work she did. She didn't even do her sewin'. She said it made her shoulder ache to sew, and poor Erastus's sister Lily used to do all her sewin'. She wa'n't able to, either; she was never strong in her back, but she did it beautifully. She had to, to suit Luella, she was so dreadful particular. I never saw anythin' like the fagottin' and hemstitchin' that Lily Miller did for Luella. She made all Luella's weddin' outfit, and that green silk dress, after Maria Babbit cut it. Maria she cut it for nothin', and she did a lot more cuttin' and fittin' for nothin' for Luella, too. Lily Miller went to live with Luella after Erastus died. She gave up her home, though she was real attached to it and wa'n't a mite afraid to stay alone. She rented it and she went to live with Luella right away after the funeral.'

Then this old woman, Lydia Anderson, who remembered Luella Miller, would go on to relate the story of Lily Miller. It seemed that on the removal of Lily Miller to the house of her dead brother, to live with his widow, the village people first began to talk. This Lily Miller had been hardly past her first youth, and a most robust and blooming woman, rosy-cheeked, with curls of strong, black hair overshadowing round, candid temples and bright dark eyes. It was not six months after she had taken up her residence with her sister-in-law that her rosy colour faded and her pretty curves become wan hollows. White shadows began to show in the black rings of her hair, and the light died out of her eyes, her features sharpened, and there were pathetic lines at her mouth, which yet wore always an expression of utter sweetness and even happiness. She was devoted to her sister; there was no doubt that she loved her with her whole heart, and was perfectly content in her service. It was her sole anxiety lest she should die and leave her alone.

'The way Lily Miller used to talk about Luella was enough to make you mad and enough to make you cry,' said Lydia Anderson. 'I've been in there sometimes toward the last when she was too feeble to cook and carried her some blanc-mange or custard – somethin' I thought she might relish, and she'd thank me, and when I asked her how she was, say she felt better than she did yesterday, and asked me if I didn't think she looked better, dreadful pitiful, and say poor Luella had an awful time takin' care of her and doin' the work she wa'n't strong enough to do anythin' – when all the time Luella wa'n't liftin' her finger and poor Lily didn't get any care except what the neighbours gave her, and Luella eat up everythin' that was carried in for Lily. I had it real straight that she did. Luella used to just sit and cry and do nothin'. She did act real fond of Lily, and she pined away considerable, too. There was those that thought she'd go into a decline herself. But after Lily died, her Aunt Abby Mixter came, and then Luella picked up and grew as fat and rosy as ever. But poor Aunt Abby begun to droop just the way Lily had, and I guess somebody wrote to her married daughter, Mrs Sam Abbot, who lived in Barre, for she wrote her mother that she must leave right away and come and make her a visit, but Aunt Abby wouldn't go. I can see her now. She was a real good-lookin' woman, tall and large, with a big, square face and a high forehead that looked of itself kind of benevolent and good. She just tended out on Luella as if she had been a baby, and when her married daughter sent for her she wouldn't stir one inch. She'd always thought a lot of her daughter, too, but she said Luella needed her and her married daughter didn't. Her daughter kept writin' and writin', but it didn't do any good. Finally she came, and when she saw how bad her mother looked, she broke down and cried and all but went on her knees to have her come away. She spoke her mind out to Luella, too. She told her that she'd killed her husband and everybody that had anythin' to do with her, and she'd thank her to leave her mother alone. Luella went into hysterics, and Aunt Abby was so frightened that she called me after her daughter went. Mrs Sam Abbot she went away fairly cryin' out loud in the buggy, the neighbours heard her, and well she might, for she never saw her mother again alive. I went in that night when Aunt Abby called for me, standin' in the door with her little green-checked shawl over her head. I can see her now. "Do come over here, Miss Anderson," she sung out, kind of gasping for breath. I didn't stop for anythin'. I put over as fast as I could, and when I got there, there was Luella laughin' and cryin' all together, and Aunt Abby trying to hush her, and all the time she herself was white as a sheet and shakin' so she could hardly stand. 'For the land sakes, Mrs Mixter,' says I, 'you look worse than she does. You ain't fit to be up out of your bed.'

'"Oh, there ain't anythin' the matter with me," says she. Then she went on talkin' to Luella. "There, there, don't, don't, poor little lamb," says she. Aunt Abby is here. She ain't goin' away and leave you. Don't, poor little lamb.'

'"Do leave her with me, Mrs Mixter, and you get back to bed," says I, for Aunt Abby had been layin' down considerable lately, though somehow she contrived to do the work.'

'"I'm well enough," says she. "Don't you think she had better have the doctor, Miss Anderson?"'

'"The doctor," says I. "I think you had better have the doctor. I think you need him much worse than some folks I could mention." And I looked right straight at Luella Miller laughin' and cryin' and goin' on as if she was the centre of all creation. All the time she was actin' so – seemed as if she was too sick to sense anythin' – she was keepin' a sharp lookout as to how we took it out of the corner of one eye. I see her. You could never cheat me about Luella Miller. Finally I got real mad and I ran home and I got a bottle of valerian I had, and I poured some boilin' hot water on a handful of catnip, and I mixed up that catnip tea with most half a wineglass of valerian, and I went with it over to Luella's. I marched right up to Luella, a-holdin' out of that cup, all smokin'. "Now," says I, "Luella Miller, *you swaller this*!"

'What is – what is it, oh, what is it?' she sort of screeches out. Then she goes off a-laughin' enough to kill.

'Poor lamb, poor little lamb,' says Aunt Abby, standin' over her, all kind of tottery, and tryin' to bathe her head with camphor.

'"*You swaller this right down*," says I. And I didn't waste any ceremony. I just took hold of Luella Miller's chin and I tipped her head back, and I caught her mouth open with laughin', and I clapped that cup to her lips and I fairly hollered at her: "Swaller, swaller, swaller!" and she gulped it right down. She had to, and I guess it did her good. Anyhow, she stopped cryin' and laughin' and let me put her to bed, and she went to sleep like a baby inside of half an hour. That was more than poor Aunt Abby did. She lay awake all that night and I stayed with her, though she tried not to have me; said she wa'n't sick enough for watchers. But I stayed, and I made some good cornmeal gruel and I fed her a teaspoon every little while all night long. It seemed to me as if she was jest dyin' from bein' all wore out. In the mornin' as soon as it was light I run over to the Bisbees and sent Johnny Bisbee for the doctor. I told him to tell the doctor to hurry, and he come pretty quick. Poor Aunt Abby didn't seem to know much of anythin' when he got there. You couldn't hardly tell she breathed, she was so used up. When the doctor had gone, Luella came into the room lookin' like a baby in her ruffled nightgown. I can see her now. Her eyes were as blue and her face all pink and white like a blossom, and she looked at Aunt Abby in the bed sort of innocent and surprised. "Why," says she, "Aunt Abby ain't got up yet?"

' "No, she ain't," says I, pretty short.

' "I thought I didn't smell the coffee," says Luella. "Coffee," says I. "I guess if you have coffee this mornin' you'll make it yourself."

' "I never made the coffee in all my life," says she, dreadful astonished. Erastus always made the coffee as long as he lived, and then Lily she made it, and then Aunt Abby made it. I don't believe I *can* make the coffee, Miss Anderson."

' "You can make it or go without, jest as you please," says I.

' "Ain't Aunt Abby goin' to get up?" says she.

' "I guess she won't get up,' says I, 'sick as she is." I was gettin' madder and madder. There was somethin' about that little pink-and-white thing standin' there and talkin' about coffee, when she had killed so many better folks than she was, and had jest killed another, that made me feel most as if I wished somebody would up and kill her before she had a chance to do any more harm.

' "Is Aunt Abby sick?" says Luella, as if she was sort of aggrieved and injured.

' "Yes," says I, "she's sick, and she's goin' to die, and then you'll be left alone, and you'll have to do for yourself and wait on yourself, or do without things." I don't know but I was sort of hard, but it was the truth, and if I was any harder than Luella Miller had been I'll give up. I ain't never been sorry that I said it. Well, Luella, she up and had hysterics again at that, and I jest let her have 'em. All I did was to bundle her into the room on the other side of the entry where Aunt Abby couldn't hear her, if she wa'n't past it – I don't know but she was – and set her down hard in a chair and told her not to come back into the other room, and she minded. She had her hysterics in there till she got tired. When she found out that nobody was comin' to coddle her and do for her she stopped. At least I suppose she did. I had all I could do with poor Aunt Abby tryin' to keep the breath of life in her. The doctor had told me that she was dreadful low, and give me some very strong medicine to give to her in drops real often, and told me real particular about the nourishment. Well, I did as he told me real faithful till she wa'n't able to swaller any longer. Then I had her daughter sent for. I had begun to realize that she wouldn't last any time at all. I hadn't realized it before, though I spoke to Luella the way I did. The doctor he came, and Mrs Sam Abbot, but when she got there it was too late; her mother was dead. Aunt Abby's daughter just give one look at her mother layin' there, then she turned sort of sharp and sudden and looked at me.

' "Where is she?" says she, and I knew she meant Luella.

' "She's out in the kitchen," says I. "She's too nervous to see folks die. She's afraid it will make her sick."

'The Doctor he speaks up then. He was a young man. Old Doctor Park had died the year before, and this was a young fellow just out of college.

"Mrs Miller is not strong," says he, kind of severe, "and she is quite right in not agitating herself."

'"You are another, young man; she's got her pretty claw on you," thinks I, but I didn't say anything to him. "I just said over to Mrs Sam Abbot that Luella was in the kitchen, and Mrs Sam Abbot she went out there, and I went, too, and I never heard anythin' like the way she talked to Luella Miller. I felt pretty hard to Luella myself, but this was more than I ever would have dared to say. Luella she was too scared to go into hysterics. She jest flopped. She seemed to jest shrink away to nothin' in that kitchen chair, with Mrs Sam Abbot standin' over her and talkin' and tellin' her the truth. I guess the truth was most too much for her and no mistake, because Luella presently actually did faint away, and there wa'n't any sham about it, the way I always suspected there was about them hysterics. She fainted dead away and we had to lay her flat on the floor, and the Doctor he came runnin' out and he said somethin' about a weak heart dreadful fierce to Mrs Sam Abbot, but she wa'n't a mite scared. She faced him jest as white as even Luella was layin' there lookin' like death and the Doctor feelin' of her pulse.

"Weak heart," says she, "weak heart; weak fiddlesticks! There ain't nothin' weak about that woman. She's got strength enough to hang onto other folks till she kills 'em. Weak? It was my poor mother that was weak: this woman killed her as sure as if she had taken a knife to her."

'But the Doctor he didn't pay much attention. He was bendin' over Luella layin' there with her yellow hair all streamin' and her pretty pink-and-white face all pale, and her blue eyes like stars gone out, and he was holdin' onto her hand and smoothin' her forehead, and tellin' me to get the brandy in Aunt Abby's room, and I was sure as I wanted to be that Luella had got somebody else to hang onto, now Aunt Abby was gone, and I thought of poor Erastus Miller, and I sort of pitied the poor young Doctor, led away by a pretty face, and I made up my mind I'd see what I could do.

'I waited till Aunt Abby had been dead and buried about a month, and the Doctor was goin' to see Luella steady and folks were beginnin' to talk; then one evenin', when I knew the Doctor had been called out of town and wouldn't be round, I went over to Luella's. I found her all dressed up in a blue muslin with white polka dots on it, and her hair curled jest as pretty, and there wa'n't a young girl in the place could compare with her. There was somethin' about Luella Miller seemed to draw the heart right out of you, but she didn't draw it out of *me*. She was settin' rocking in the chair by her sittin'-room window, and Maria Brown had gone home. Maria Brown had been in to help her, or rather to do the work, for Luella wa'n't helped when she didn't do anything'. Maria Brown was real capable and she didn't have any ties; she wa'n't married, and lived alone, so she'd offered. I couldn't see why she should do the work any more than

Luella; she wa'n't any too strong; but she seemed to think she could and Luella seemed to think so, too, so she went over and did all the work – washed, and ironed, and baked, while Luella sat and rocked. Maria didn't live long afterward. She began to fade away just the same fashion the others had. Well, she was warned, but she acted real mad when folks said anythin': said Luella was a poor, abused woman, too delicate to help herself, and they'd ought to be ashamed, and if she died helpin' them that couldn't help themselves she would – and she did.

'"I s'pose Maria has gone home," says I to Luella, when I had gone in and sat down opposite her.

'"Yes, Maria went half an hour ago, after she had got supper and washed the dishes," says Luella, in her pretty way.

'"I suppose she has got a lot of work to do in her own house tonight," says I, kind of bitter, but that was all thrown away on Luella Miller. It seemed to her right that other folks that wa'n't any better able than she was herself should wait on her, and she couldn't get it through her head that anybody should think it *wa'n't* right.

'"Yes," says Luella, real sweet and pretty, "yes, she said she had to do her washin to-night. She has let it go for a fortnight along of comin' over here."

'Why don't she stay home and do her washin' instead of comin' over here and doin' *your* work, when you are just as well able, and enough sight more so, than she is to do it?' says I.

'Then Luella she looked at me like a baby who has a rattle shook at it. She sort of laughed as innocent as you please. 'Oh, I can't do the work myself, Miss Anderson,' says she. 'I never did. Maria *has* to do it.'

'Then I spoke out: "Has to do it!" says I. "Has to do it! She don't have to do it, either. Maria Brown has her own home and enough to live on. She ain't beholden to you to come over here and slave for you and kill herself."

'Luella she jest set and stared at me for all the world like a doll-baby that was so abused that it was comin' to life.

'"Yes," says I, "she's killin' herself. She's goin' to die just the way Erastus did, and Lily, and your Aunt Abby. You're killin' her jest as you did them. I don't know what there is about you, but you seem to bring a curse," says I. "You kill everybody that is fool enough to care anythin' about you and do for you."

'She stared at me and she was pretty pale.

'"And Maria ain't the only one you're goin' to kill," says I. "You're goin' to kill Doctor Malcom before you're done with him."

'Then a red colour came flamin' all over her face. "I ain't goin' to kill him, either," says she, and she begun to cry.

'"Yes, you *be!*" says I. Then I spoke as I had never spoke before. You see, I felt it on account of Erastus. I told her that she hadn't any business to think of another man after she'd been married to one that had died for her: that she was a dreadful woman; and she was, that's true enough, but sometimes I have wondered lately if she knew it – if she wa'n't like a baby with scissors in its hand cuttin' everybody without knowin' what it was doin'.

'Luella she kept gettin' paler and paler, and she never took her eyes off my face. There was somethin' awful about the way she looked at me and never spoke one word. After awhile I quit talkin' and I went home. I watched that night, but her lamp went out before nine o'clock, and when Doctor Malcom came drivin' past and sort of slowed up he see there wa'n't any light and he drove along. I saw her sort of shy out of meetin' the next Sunday, too, so he shouldn't go home with her, and I begun to think mebbe she did have some conscience after all. It was only a week after that that Maria Brown died – sort of sudden at the last, though everybody had seen it was comin'. Well, then there was a good deal of feelin' and pretty dark whispers. Folks said the days of witchcraft had come again, and they were pretty shy of Luella. She acted sort of offish to the Doctor and he didn't go there, and there wa'n't anybody to do anythin' for her. I don't know how she *did* get along. I wouldn't go in there and offer to help her – not because I was afraid of dyin' like the rest but I thought she was just as well able to do her own work as I was to do it for her, and I thought it was about time that she did it and stopped killin' other folks. But it wa'n't very long before folks began to say that Luella herself was goin' into a decline jest the way her husband, and Lily, and Aunt Abby and the others had, and I saw myself that she looked pretty bad. I used to see her goin' past from the store with a bundle as if she could hardly crawl, but I remembered how Erastus used to wait and 'tend when he couldn't hardly put one foot before the other, and I didn't go out to help her.

'But at last one afternoon I saw the Doctor come drivin' up like mad with his medicine chest, and Mrs Babbit came in after supper and said that Luella was real sick.

' "I'd offer to go in and nurse her," says she, "but I've got my children to consider, and mebbe it ain't true what they say, but it's queer how many folks that have done for her have died."

'I didn't say anythin', but I considered how she had been Erastus's wife and how he had set his eyes by her, and I made up my mind to go in the next mornin', unless she was better, and see what I could do; but the next mornin' I see her at the window, and pretty soon she came steppin' out as spry as you please, and a little while afterward Mrs Babbit came in and told me that the Doctor had got a girl from out of town, a Sarah Jones, to come there, and she said she was pretty sure that the Doctor was goin' to marry Luella.

'I saw him kiss her in the door that night myself, and I knew it was true. The woman came that afternoon, and the way she flew around was a caution. I don't believe Luella had swept since Maria died. She swept and dusted, and washed and ironed; wet 'clothes and dusters and carpets were flyin' over there all day, and every time Luella set her foot out when the Doctor wa'n't there there was that Sarah Jones helpin' of her up and down the steps, as if she hadn't learned to walk.

'Well, everybody knew that Luella and the Doctor were goin' to be married, but it wa'n't long before they began to talk about his lookin' so poorly, jest as they had about the others; and they talked about Sarah Jones, too.

'Well, the Doctor did die, and he wanted to be married first, so as to leave what little he had to Luella, but he died before the minister could get there, and Sarah Jones died a week afterward.

'Well, that wound up everything for Luella Miller. Not another soul in the whole town would lift a finger for her. There got to be a sort of panic. Then she began to droop in good earnest. She used to have to go to the store herself, for Mrs Babbit was afraid to let Tommy go for her, and I've seen her goin' past and stoppin' every two or three steps to rest. Well, I stood it as long as I could, but one day I see her comin' with her arms full and stoppin' to lean against the Babbit fence, and I run out and took her bundles and carried them to her house. Then I went home and never spoke one word to her though she called after me dreadful kind of pitiful. Well, that night I was taken sick with a chill, and I was sick as I wanted to be for two weeks. Mrs Babbit had seen me run out to help Luella and she came in and told me I was goin' to die on account of it. I didn't know whether I was or not, but I considered I had done right by Erastus's wife.

'That last two weeks Luella, she had a dreadful hard time, I guess. She was pretty sick, and as near as I could make out nobody dared go near her. I don't know as she was really needin' anythin' very much, for there was enough to eat in her house and it was warm weather, and she made out to cook a little flour gruel every day, I know, but I guess she had a hard time, she that had been so petted and done for all her life.

'When I got so I could go out, I went over there one morning. Mrs Babbit had just come in to say she hadn't seen any smoke and she didn't know but what it was somebody's duty to go in, but she couldn't help thinkin' of her children, and I got right up, though I hadn't been out of the house for two weeks, and I went in there, and Luella she was layin' on the bed, and she was dyin'.

'She lasted all that day and into the night. But I sat there after the new doctor had gone away. Nobody else dared to go there. It was about midnight that I left her for a minute to run home and get some medicine I had been takin', for I begun to feel rather bad.

'It was a full moon that night, and just as I started out of my door to cross the street back to Luella's, I stopped short, for I saw something.'

Lydia Anderson at this juncture always said with a certain defiance that she did not expect to be believed, and then proceeded in a hushed voice:

'I saw what I saw, and I know I saw it, and I will swear on my death bed that I saw it. I saw Luella Miller and Erastus Miller, and Lily, and Aunt Abby, and Maria, and the Doctor, and Sarah, all goin' out of her door, and all but Luella shone white in the moonlight, and they were all helpin' her along till she seemed to fairly fly in the midst of them. Then it all disappeared. I stood a minute with my heart poundin', then I went over there. I thought of goin' for Mrs Babbit, but I thought she'd be afraid. So I went alone, though I knew what had happened. Luella was layin' real peaceful, dead on her bed.'

This was the story that the old woman, Lydia Anderson, told, but the sequel was told by the people who survived her, and this is the tale which has become folklore in the village.

Lydia Anderson died when she was eighty-seven. She had continued wonderfully hale and hearty for one of her years until about two weeks before her death.

One bright moonlight evening she was sitting beside a window in her parlour when she made a sudden exclamation, and was out of the house and across the street before the neighbour who was taking care of her could stop her. She followed as fast as possible and found Lydia Anderson stretched on the ground before the door of Luella Miller's deserted house, and she was quite dead.

The next night there was a red gleam of fire athwart the moonlight and the old house of Luella Miller was burned to the ground. Nothing is now left of it except a few old cellar stones and a lilac bush, and in summer a helpless trail of morning glories among the weeds, which might be considered emblematic of Luella herself.

The Drifting Snow
August Derleth

Aunt Mary's advancing footsteps halted suddenly, short of the table, and Clodetta turned to see what was keeping her. She was standing very rigidly, her eyes fixed upon the French windows just opposite the door through which she had entered, her cane held stiffly before her.

Clodetta shot a quick glance across the table toward her husband, whose attention had also been drawn to his aunt; his face vouchsafed her nothing. She turned again to find that the old lady had transferred her gaze to her, regarding her stonily and in silence. Clodetta felt uncomfortable.

'Who withdrew the curtains from the west windows?'

Clodetta flushed, remembering. 'I did, Aunt. I'm sorry. I forgot about your not wanting them drawn away.'

The old lady made an odd, grunting sound, shifting her gaze once again to the French windows. She made a barely perceptible movement, and Lisa ran forward from the shadow of the hall, where she had been regarding the two at table with stern disapproval. The servant went directly to the west windows and drew the curtains.

Aunt Mary came slowly to the table and took her place at its head. She put her cane against the side of her chair, pulled at the chain about her neck so that her lorgnette lay in her lap, and looked from Clodetta to her nephew, Ernest.

Then she fixed her gaze on the empty chair at the foot of the table, and spoke without seeming to see the two beside her.

'I told both of you that none of the curtains over the west windows was to be withdrawn after sundown, and you must have noticed that none of those windows has been for one instant uncovered at night. I took especial care to put you in rooms facing east, and the sitting-room is also in the east.'

'I'm sure Clodetta didn't mean to go against your wishes, Aunt Mary,' said Ernest abruptly.

'No, of course not, Aunt.'

The old lady raised her eyebrows, and went on impassively. 'I didn't think it wise to explain why I made such a request. I'm not going to explain. But I do want to say that there is a very definite danger in drawing away the curtains. Ernest has heard that before, but you, Clodetta, have not.'

Clodetta shot a startled glance at her husband. The old lady caught it, and said, 'It's all very well to believe that my mind's wandering or that I'm getting eccentric, but I shouldn't advise you to be satisfied with that.'

A young man came suddenly into the room and made for the seat at the foot of the table, into which he flung himself with an almost inaudible greeting to the other three.

'Late again, Henry,' said the old lady.

Henry mumbled something and began hurriedly to eat. The old lady sighed, and began presently to eat also, whereupon Clodetta and Ernest did likewise. The old servant, who had continued to linger behind Aunt Mary's chair, now withdrew, not without a scornful glance at Henry.

Clodetta looked up after a while and ventured to speak. 'You aren't as isolated as I thought you might be up here, Aunt Mary.'

'We aren't, my dear, what with telephones and cars and all. But only twenty years ago it was quite a different thing, I can tell you.' She smiled reminiscently and looked at Ernest. 'Your grandfather was living then, and many's the time he was snowbound with no way to let anybody know.'

'Down in Chicago when they speak of "up north" or the "Wisconsin woods" it seems very far away,' said Clodetta.

Well it *is* far away,' put in Henry, abruptly. 'And, Aunt, I hope you've made some provision in case we're locked in here for a day or two. It looks like snow outside, and the radio says a blizzard's coming.'

The old lady grunted and looked at him. 'Ha, Henry – you're overly concerned, it seems to me. I'm afraid you've been regretting this trip ever since you set foot in my house. If you're worrying about a snowstorm, I can have Sam drive you down to Wausau, and you can be in Chicago tomorrow.'

'Of course not.'

Silence fell, and presently the old lady called gently, 'Lisa,' and the servant came into the room to help her from her chair, though, as Clodetta had previously said to her husband, 'She didn't need help.'

From the doorway, Aunt Mary bade them all good-night, looking impressively formidable with her cane in one hand and her unopened lorgnette in the other, and vanished into the dusk of the hall, from which her receding footsteps sounded together with those of the servant, who was seldom seen away from her. These two were alone in the house most of the time, and only very brief periods when the old lady had up her nephew Ernest, 'dear John's boy,' or Henry, of whose father the old lady never spoke, helped to relieve the pleasant somnolence of their quiet lives. Sam, who usually slept in the garage, did not count.

Clodetta looked nervously at her husband, but it was Henry who said what was uppermost in their thoughts.

'I think she's losing her mind,' he declared matter-of-factly. Cutting off Clodetta's protest on her lips, he got up and went into the sitting-room, from which came presently the strains of music from the radio.

Clodetta fingered her spoon idly and finally said, 'I do think she is a little queer, Ernest.'

Ernest smiled tolerantly. 'No, I don't think so. I've an idea why she keeps the west windows covered. My grandfather died out there – he was overcome by the cold one night, and froze on the slope of the hill. I don't rightly know how it happened – I was away at the time. I suppose she doesn't like to be reminded of it.'

'But where's the danger she spoke of, then?'

He shrugged. 'Perhaps it lies in her – she might be affected and affect us in turn.' He paused for an instant, and finally added, 'I suppose she *does* seem a little strange to you – but she was like that as long as I can remember; next time you come, you'll be used to it.'

Clodetta looked at her husband for a moment before replying. At last she said, 'I don't think I like the house, Ernest.'

'Oh, nonsense, darling.' He started to get up, but Clodetta stopped him.

'Listen Ernest. I remembered perfectly well Aunt Mary's not wanting those curtains drawn away – but I just felt I had to do it. I didn't want to, but – *something made me do it.*' Her voice was unsteady.

'Why, Clodetta,' he said, faintly alarmed. 'Why didn't you tell me before?'

She shrugged. 'Aunt Mary might have thought I'd gone wool-gathering.'

'Well, it's nothing serious, but you've let it bother you a little and that isn't good for you. Forget it; think of something else. Come and listen to the radio.'

They rose and moved toward the sitting-room together. At the door Henry met them. He stepped aside a little, saying, 'I might have known we'd be marooned up here,' and adding, as Clodetta began to protest, 'We're going to be all right. There's a wind coming up and it's beginning to snow, and I know what that means.' He passed them and went into the deserted dining-room, where he stood a moment looking at the too long table. Then he turned aside and went over to the French windows, from which he drew away the curtains and stood there peering out into the darkness. Ernest saw him standing at the window, and protested from the sitting-room.

'Aunt Mary doesn't like those windows uncovered, Henry.'

Henry half turned and replied, 'Well, *she* may think it's dangerous, but I can risk it.'

Clodetta, who had been staring beyond Henry into the night through the French windows, said suddenly, 'Why, there's someone out there!'

Henry looked quickly through the glass and replied, 'No, that's the snow; it's coming down heavily, and the wind's drifting it this way and that.' He dropped the curtains and came away from the windows.

Clodetta said uncertainly, 'Why, I could have sworn I saw someone out there, walking past the window.'

'I suppose it does look that way from here,' offered Henry, who had come back into the sitting-room. 'But personally, I think you've let Aunt Mary's eccentricities impress you too much.'

Ernest made an impatient gesture at this, and Clodetta did not answer. Henry sat down before the radio and began to move the dial slowly. Ernest had found himself a book, and was becoming interested, but Clodetta continued to sit with her eyes fixed upon the still slowly moving curtains cutting off the French windows. Presently she got up and left the room, going down the long hall into the east wing, where she tapped gently upon Aunt Mary's door.

'Come in,' called the old lady.

Clodetta opened the door and stepped into the room where Aunt Mary sat in her dressing-robe, her dignity, in the shape of her lorgnette and cane, resting respectively on her bureau and in the corner. She looked surprisingly benign, as Clodetta at once confessed.

'Ha, thought I was an ogre in disguise, did you?' said the old lady, smiling in spite of herself. 'I'm really not, you see, but I am a sort of bogy about the west windows, as you have seen.'

'I wanted to tell you something about those windows, Aunt Mary,' said Clodetta. She stopped suddenly. The expression on the old lady's face had given way to a curiously dismaying one. It was not anger, not distaste – it was a lurking suspense. Why, the old lady was afraid!

'What?' she asked Clodetta shortly.

'I was looking out – just for a moment or so – and I thought I saw someone out there.'

'Of course, you didn't, Clodetta. Your imagination, perhaps, or the drifting snow.'

'My imagination? Maybe. But there was no wind to drift the snow, though one has come up since.'

'I've often been fooled that way, my dear. Sometimes I've gone out in the morning to look for footprints – there weren't any, ever. We're pretty far away from civilization in a snowstorm, despite our telephones and radios. Our nearest neighbor is at the foot of the long, sloping rise – over three miles away – and all wooded land between. There's no highway nearer than that.'

'It was so clear, I could have sworn to it.'

'Do you want to go out in the morning and look?' asked the old lady shortly.

'Of course not.'

'Then you didn't see anything?'

It was half question, half demand. Clodetta said, 'Oh, Aunt Mary, you're making an issue of it now.'

'Did you or didn't you in your own mind see anything, Clodetta?'

'I guess I didn't, Aunt Mary.'

'Very well. And now do you think we might talk about something more pleasant?'

'Why, I'm sure – I'm sorry, Aunt. I didn't know that Ernest's grandfather had died out there.'

'Ha, he's told you that, has he? Well?'

'Yes, he said that was why you didn't like the slope after sunset – that you didn't like to be reminded of his death.'

The old lady looked at Clodetta impassively. 'Perhaps he'll never know how near right he was.'

'What do you mean, Aunt Mary?'

'Nothing for you to know, my dear.' She smiled again, her sternness dropping from her. 'And now I think you'd better go, Clodetta; I'm tired.'

Clodetta rose obediently and made for the door, where the old lady stopped her. 'How's the weather?'

'It's snowing – hard, Henry says – and blowing.'

The old lady's face showed her distaste at the news. 'I don't like to hear that, not at all. Suppose someone should look down that slope tonight?' She was speaking to herself, having forgotten Clodetta at the door. Seeing her again abruptly, she said, 'But you don't know, Clodetta. Goodnight.'

Clodetta stood with her back against the closed door, wondering what the old lady could have meant. *But you don't know, Clodetta.* That was curious. For a moment or two the old lady had completely forgotten her.

She moved away from the door, and came upon Ernest just turning into the east wing.

'Oh, there you are,' he said. 'I wondered where you had gone.'

'I was talking a bit with Aunt Mary.'

'Henry's been at the west windows again – and now *he* thinks there's someone out there.'

Clodetta stopped short. 'Does he really think so?'

Ernest nodded gravely. 'But the snow's drifting frightfully, and I can imagine how that suggestion of yours worked on his mind.'

Clodetta turned and went back along the hall. 'I'm going to tell Aunt Mary.'

He started to protest, but to no avail, for she was already tapping on the old lady's door, and indeed opening the door and entering the room before he could frame an adequate protest.

'Aunt Mary,' she said, 'I didn't want to disturb you again, but Henry's been at the French windows in the dining-room, and he says he's seen someone out there.'

The effect on the old lady was magical. 'He's seen them!' she exclaimed. Then she was on her feet, coming rapidly over to Clodetta. 'How long ago?' she demanded, seizing her almost roughly by the arms. 'Tell me, quickly. How long ago did he see them?'

Clodetta's amazement kept her silent for a moment, but at last she spoke, feeling the old lady's keen eyes staring at her. 'It was some time ago, Aunt Mary, after supper.'

The old lady's hands relaxed, and with it her tension. 'Oh,' she said, and turned and went back slowly to her chair, taking her cane from the corner where she had put it for the night.

'Then there *is* someone out there?' challenged Clodetta, when the old lady had reached her chair.

For a long time, it seemed to Clodetta, there was no answer. Then presently the old lady began to nod gently, and a barely audible 'Yes' escaped her lips.

'Then we had better take them in, Aunt Mary.'

The old lady looked at Clodetta earnestly for a moment; then she replied, her voice firm and low, her eyes fixed upon the wall beyond. 'We can't take them in, Clodetta – because they're not alive.'

At once Henry's words came flashing into Clodetta's memory – 'She's losing her mind' – and her involuntary start betrayed her thought.

'I'm afraid I'm not mad, my dear – I hoped at first I might be, but I wasn't. I'm not, now. There was only one of them out there at first – the girl; Father is the other. Quite long ago, when I was young, my father did something which he regretted all his days. He had a too strong temper, and it maddened him. One night he found out that one of my brothers – Henry's father – had been very familiar with one of the servants, a very pretty girl, older than I was. He thought she was to blame, though she wasn't, and he didn't find it out until too late. He drove her from the house, then and there. Winter had not yet set in, but it was quite cold, and she had some five miles to go to her home. We begged Father not to send her away – though we didn't know what was wrong then – but he paid no attention to us. The girl had to go.

'Not long after she had gone, a biting wind came up, and close upon it a fierce storm. Father had already repented his hasty action, and sent some of the men to look for the girl. They didn't find her, but in the morning she was found frozen to death on the long slope of the hill to the west.'

The old lady sighed, paused a moment, and went on. 'Years later – she came back. She came in a snowstorm, as she went; but she had become a vampire. We all saw her. We were at supper table, and Father saw her first. The boys had already gone upstairs, and Father and the two of us girls, my sister and I, did not recognize her. She was just a dim shape floundering about in the drifting snow beyond the French windows. Father ran out to her, calling to us to send the boys after him. We never saw him alive again. In the morning we found him in the same spot where years before the girl had been found. He, too, had died of exposure.

'Then, a few years after – she returned with the snow, and she brought him along; he, too, had become a vampire. They stayed until the last snow, always trying to lure someone out there. After that, I knew, and had the windows covered during the winter nights, from sunset to dawn, because they never went beyond the west slope.

'Now you know, Clodetta.'

Whatever Clodetta was going to say was cut short by running footsteps in the hall, a hasty rap, and Ernest's head appearing suddenly in the open doorway.

'Come on, you two,' he said, almost gayly, 'there *are* people out on the west slope – a girl and an old man – and Henry's gone out to fetch them in!'

Then, triumphant, he was off. Clodetta came to her feet, but the old lady was before her, passing her and almost running down the hall, calling loudly for Lisa, who presently appeared in nightcap and gown from her room.

'Call Sam, Lisa,' said the old lady, 'and send him to me in the dining-room.'

She ran on into the dining-room, Clodetta close on her heels. The French windows were open, and Ernest stood on the snow-covered terrace beyond, calling his cousin. The old lady went directly over to him, even striding into the snow to his side, though the wind drove the snow against her with great force. The wooded western slope was lost in a snow-fog; the nearest trees were barely discernible.

'Where could they have gone?' Ernest said, turning to the old lady, whom he had thought to be Clodetta. Then, seeing that it was the old lady, he said, 'Why, Aunt Mary – and so little on, too! You'll catch your death of cold.'

'Never mind, Ernest.' said the old lady. 'I'm all right. I've had Sam get up to help you look for Henry – but I'm afraid you won't find him."

'He can't be far; he just now went out.'

'He went before you saw where; he's far enough gone.'

Sam came running into the blowing snow from the dining-room, muffled in a greatcoat. He was considerably older than Ernest, almost the old lady's age. He shot a questioning glance at her and asked, 'Have they come again?'

Aunt Mary nodded. "You'll have to look for Henry. Ernest will help you. And remember, don't separate. And don't go far from the house.'

Clodetta came with Ernest's overcoat, and together the two women stood there, watching them until they were swallowed up in the wall of driven snow. Then they turned slowly and went back into the house.

The old lady sank into a chair facing the windows. She was pale and drawn, and looked, as Clodetta said afterward, 'as if she'd fallen together.' For a long time she said nothing. Then, with a gentle little sigh, she turned to Clodetta and spoke.

'Now there'll be three of them out there.'

Then, so suddenly that no one knew how it happened, Ernest and Sam appeared beyond the windows, and between them they dragged Henry. The old lady flew to open the windows, and the three of them, cloaked in snow, came into the room.

'We found him – but the cold's hit him pretty hard, I'm afraid,' said Ernest.

The old lady sent Lisa for cold water, and Ernest ran to get himself other clothes. Clodetta went with him, and in their rooms told him what the old lady had related to her.

Ernest laughed. 'I think you believed that, didn't you, Clodetta? Sam and Lisa do, I know, because Sam told me the story long ago. I think the shock of Grandfather's death was too much for all three of them.'

'But the story of the girl, and then –'

'That part's true, I'm afraid. A nasty story, but it did happen.'

'But those people Henry and I saw!' protested Clodetta weakly.

Ernest stood without movement. 'That's so,' he said, 'I saw them, too. Then they're out there yet, and we'll have to find them!' He took up his overcoat again, and went from the room, Clodetta protesting in a shrill unnatural voice. The old lady met him at the door of the dining-room, having overheard Clodetta pleading with him.

'No, Ernest – you can't go out there again,' she said. 'There's no one there.'

He pushed gently into the room and called to Sam, 'Coming Sam? There're still two of them out there – we almost forgot them.'

Sam looked at him strangely. 'What do you mean?' he demanded roughly. He looked challengingly at the old lady, who shook her head.

'The girl and the old man, Sam. We've got to get them, too.'

'*Oh, them.*' said Sam. 'They're dead!'

'Then I'll go out alone,' said Ernest.

Henry came to his feet suddenly, looking dazed. He walked forward a few steps, his eyes traveling from one to the other of them, yet apparently not seeing them. He began to speak abruptly, in an unnatural child-like voice.

'*The snow,*' he murmured, '*the snow – the beautiful hands, so little, so lovely her beautiful hands – and the snow, the beautiful, lovely snow, drifting and falling about her. . . .'*

He turned slowly and looked toward the French windows, the others following his gaze. Beyond was a wall of white, where the snow was drifting against the house. For a moment Henry stood quietly watching; then suddenly a white figure came forward from the snow – a young girl, cloaked in long snow-whips, her glistening eyes strangely fascinating.

The old lady flung herself forward, her arms outstretched to cling to Henry, but she was too late. Henry had run toward the windows, had opened them, and even as Clodetta cried out had vanished into the wall of snow beyond.

Then Ernest ran forward, but the old lady threw her arms around him and held him tightly, murmuring, 'You shall not go! Henry is gone beyond our help!'

Clodetta came to help her, and Sam stood menacingly at the French windows, now closed against the wind and the sinister snow. So they held him, and would not let him go.

'And tomorrow,' said the old lady in a harsh whisper, 'we must go to their graves and stake them down. We should have gone before.'

In the morning they found Henry's body crouched against the bole of an ancient oak, where two others had been found years before. There were almost obliterated marks of where something had dragged him, a long, uneven swath in the snow, and yet no footprints, only strange, hollowed places along the way, as if the wind had whirled the snow away, and only the wind.

But on his skin were signs of the snow vampire – the delicate small prints of a young girl's hands.

The Living Dead
Robert Bloch

All day long he rested, while the guns thundered in the village below. Then, in the slanting shadows of the late afternoon, the rumbling echoes faded into the distance and he knew it was over. The American advance had crossed the river. They were gone at last, and it was safe once more.

Above the village, in the crumbling ruins of the great château atop the wooded hillside, Count Barsac emerged from the crypt.

The Count was tall and thin – cadaverously thin, in a manner most hideously appropriate. His face and hands had a waxen pallor; his hair was dark, but not as dark as his eyes and the hollows beneath them. His cloak was black, and the sole touch of color about his person was the vivid redness of his lips when they curled in a smile.

He was smiling now, in the twilight, for it was time to play the game.

The name of the game was Death, and the Count had played it many times.

He had played it in Paris on the stage of the Grand Guignol; his name had been plain Eric Karon then, but still he'd won a certain renown for his interpretation of bizarre roles. Then the war had come and, with it, his opportunity.

Long before the Germans took Paris, he'd joined their Underground, working long and well. As an actor he'd been invaluable.

And this, of course, was his ultimate reward – to play the supreme role, not on the stage, but in real life. To play without the artifice of spotlights, in true darkness; this was the actor's dream come true. He had even helped to fashion the plot.

'Simplicity itself,' he told his German superiors. 'Château Barsac has been deserted since the Revolution. None of the peasants from the village dare to venture near it, even in daylight, because of the legend. It is said, you see, that the last Count Barsac was a vampire.'

And so it was arranged. The shortwave transmitter had been set up in the large crypt beneath the château, with three skilled operators in attendance, working in shifts. And he, 'Count Barsac,' in charge of the entire operation, as guardian angel. Rather, as guardian demon.

'There is a graveyard on the hillside below.' he informed them. 'A humble resting place for poor and ignorant people. It contains a single imposing crypt – the ancestral tomb of the Barsacs. We shall open that crypt, remove the remains of the last Count, and allow the villagers to discover that the coffin is empty. They will never dare come near the spot or the château again, because this will prove that the legend is true – Count Barsac is a vampire, and walks once more.'

The question came then. 'What if there are sceptics? What if someone does not believe?'

And he had his answer ready. 'They will believe. For at night I shall walk – I, Count Barsac.'

After they saw him in the makeup, wearing the black cloak, there were no more questions. The role was his.

The role was his, and he'd played it well. The Count nodded to himself as he climbed the stairs and entered the roofless foyer of the château, where only a configuration of cobwebs veiled the radiance of the rising moon.

Now, of course, the curtain must come down. If the American advance had swept past the village below, it was time to make one's bow and exit. And that too had been well arranged.

During the German withdrawal another advantageous use had been made of the tomb in the graveyard. A cache of Air Marshal Goering's art treasures now rested safely and undisturbed within the crypt. A truck had been placed in the chateau. Even now the three wireless operators would be playing new parts – driving the truck down the hillside to the tomb, placing the *objets d'art* in it.

By the time the Count arrived there, everything would be packed. They would then don the stolen American Army uniforms, carry the forged identifications and permits, drive through the lines across the river, and rejoin the German forces at a predesignated spot. Nothing had been left to chance. Someday, when he wrote his memoirs ...

But there was not time to consider that now. The Count glanced up through the gaping aperture in the ruined roof. The moon was high. It was time to leave.

In a way he hated to go. Where others saw only dust and cobwebs he saw a stage – the setting of his finest performance. Playing a vampire's role had not addicted him to the taste of blood – but as an actor he enjoyed the taste of triumph. And he had triumphed here.

'Parting is such sweet sorrow.' Shakespeare's line. Shakespeare, who had written of ghosts and witches, of bloody apparitions. Because Shakespeare knew that his audiences, the stupid masses, believed in such things – just as they still believed today. A great actor could always make them believe.

The Count moved into the shadowy darkness outside the entrance of the château. He started down the pathway toward the beckoning trees.

It was here, amid the trees, that he had come upon Raymond, one evening weeks ago. Raymond had been his most appreciative audience – a stern, dignified, white-haired elderly man, mayor of the village of Barsac. But there had been nothing dignified about the old fool when he'd caught sight of the Count looming up before him out of the night. He'd screamed like a woman and run.

Probably Raymond had been prowling around, intent on poaching, but all that had been forgotten after his encounter in the woods. The mayor was the one to thank for spreading the rumors that the Count was again abroad. He and Clodez, the oafish miller, had then led an armed band to the graveyard and entered the Barsac tomb. What a fright they got when they discovered the Count's coffin open and empty!

The coffin had contained only dust that had been scattered to the winds, but they could not know that. Nor could they know about what had happened to Suzanne.

The Count was passing the banks of the small stream now. Here, on another evening, he'd found the girl – Raymond's daughter, as luck would have it – in an embrace with young Antoine LeFevre, her lover.

Antoine's shattered leg had invalided him out of the army, but he ran like a deer when he glimpsed the cloaked and grinning Count. Suzanne had been left behind and that was unfortunate, because it was necessary to dispose of her. Her body had been buried in the woods, beneath great stones, and there was no question of discovery; still, it was a regrettable incident.

In the end, however, everything was for the best. Now silly superstitious Raymond was doubly convinced that the vampire walked. He had seen the creature himself, had seen the empty tomb and the open coffin; his own daughter had disappeared. At his command none dared venture near the graveyard, the woods, or the château beyond.

Poor Raymond! He was not even a mayor any more – his village had been destroyed in the bombardment. Just an ignorant, broken old man, mumbling his idiotic nonsense about the 'living dead.'

The Count smiled and walked on, his cloak fluttering in the breeze, casting a batlike shadow on the pathway before him. He could see the graveyard now, the tilted tombstones rising from the earth like leprous fingers rotting in the moonlight. His smile faded; he did not like such thoughts. Perhaps the greatest tribute to his talent as an actor lay in his actual aversion to death, to darkness and what lurked in the night. He hated the sight of blood, had developed within himself an almost claustrophobic dread of the confinement of the crypt.

Yes, it had been a great role, but he was thankful it was ending. It would be good to play the man once more, and cast off the creature he had created.

As he approached the crypt he saw the truck waiting in the shadows.

The entrance to the tomb was open, but no sounds issued from it. That meant his colleagues had completed their task of loading and were ready to go. All that remained now was to change his clothing, remove the makeup and depart.

The Count moved to the darkened truck. And then ...

Then they were upon him, and he felt the tines of the pitchfork bite into his back, and as the flash of lanterns dazzled his eyes he heard the stern command. 'Don't move!'

He didn't move. He could only stare as they surrounded him – Antoine, Clodez, Raymond, and the others, a dozen peasants from the village. A dozen armed peasants, glaring at him in mingled rage and fear, holding him at bay.

But how could they dare?

The American corporal stepped forward. That was the answer, of course – the American corporal and another man in uniform, armed with a sniper's rifle. They were responsible. He didn't even have to see the riddled corpses of the three shortwave operators piled in the back of the truck to understand what had happened. They'd stumbled on his men while they worked, shot them down, then summoned the villagers.

Now they were jabbering questions at him, in English, of course. He understood English, but he knew better than to reply. 'Who are you? Were these men working under your orders? Where were you going with this truck?'

The Count smiled and shook his head. After a while they stopped, as he knew they would.

The corporal turned to his companion. 'Okay,' he said. 'Let's go.' The other man nodded and climbed into the cab of the truck as the motor coughed into life. The corporal moved to join him, then turned to Raymond.

'We're taking this across the river,' he said. 'Hang on to our friend here – they'll be sending a guard detail for him within an hour.'

Raymond nodded.

The truck drove off into the darkness.

And as it was dark now – the moon had vanished behind a cloud. The Count's smile vanished, too, as he glanced around at his captors. A rabble of stupid clods, surly and ignorant. But armed. No chance of escaping. And they kept staring at him, and mumbling.

'Take him into the tomb.'

It was Raymond who spoke, and they obeyed, prodding their captive forward with pitchforks. That was when the Count recognized the first faint ray of hope. For they prodded him most gingerly, no man coming close, and when he glared at them their eyes dropped.

They were putting him in the crypt because they were afraid of him. Now the Americans were gone, they feared him once more – feared his presence and his power. After all, in their eyes he was a vampire – he might turn into a bat and vanish entirely. So they wanted him in the tomb for safekeeping.

The Count shrugged, smiled his most sinister smile, and bared his teeth. They shrank back as he entered the doorway. He turned and, on impulse, furled his cape. It was an instinctive final gesture, in keeping with his role – and it provoked the appropriate response. They moaned, and old Raymond crossed himself. It was better, in a way, than any applause.

In the darkness of the crypt the Count permitted himself to relax a trifle. He was offstage now. A pity he'd not been able to make his exit the way he'd planned, but such were the fortunes of war. Soon he'd be taken to the American headquarters and interrogated. Undoubtedly there would be some unpleasant moments, but the worst that could befall him was a few months in a prison camp. And even the Americans must bow to him in appreciation when they heard the story of his masterful deception.

It was dark in the crypt, and musty. The Count moved about restlessly. His knee grazed the edge of the empty coffin set on a trestle in the tomb. He shuddered involuntarily, loosening his cape at the throat. It would be good to remove it, good to be out of here, good to shed the role of vampire forever. He'd played it well, but now he was anxious to be gone.

There was a mumbling audible from outside, mingled with another and less identifiable noise – a scraping sound. The Count moved to the closed door of the crypt and listened intently; but now there was only silence.

What were the fools doing out there? He wished the Americans would hurry back. It was too hot in here. And why the sudden silence?

Perhaps they'd gone.

Yes. That was it. The Americans had told them to wait and guard him, but they were afraid. They really believed he was a vampire – old Raymond had convinced them of that. So they'd run off. They'd run off, and he was free, he could escape now . . .

So the Count opened the door.

And he saw them then, saw them standing and waiting, old Raymond staring sternly for a moment before he moved forward. He was holding something in his hand, and the Count recognized it, remembering the scraping sound that he'd heard.

It was a long wooden stake with a sharp point.

Then he opened his mouth to scream, telling them it was only a trick, he was no vampire, they were a pack of superstitious fools . . .

But all the while they bore him back into the crypt, lifting him up and thrusting him into the open coffin, holding him there as the grim-faced Raymond raised the pointed stake above his heart.

It was only when the stake came down that he realized there's such a thing as playing a role too well.

Ringing the Changes
Robert Aickman

He had never been among those many who deeply dislike church bells, but the ringing that evening at Holihaven changed his view. Bells could certainly get on one's nerves he felt, although he had only just arrived in the town.

*　　*　　*

He had been too well aware of the perils attendant upon marrying a girl twenty-four years younger than himself to add to them by a conventional honeymoon. The strange force of Phrynne's love had borne both of them away from their previous selves; in him a formerly haphazard and easy-going approach to life had been replaced by much deep planning to wall in happiness; and she, though once thought cold and choosy, would now agree to anything as long as she was with him. He had said that if they were to marry in June, it would be at the cost of not being able to honeymoon until October. Had they been courting longer, he had explained, gravely smiling, special arrangements could have been made; but, as it was, business claimed him. This, indeed, was true; because his business position was less influential than he had led Phrynne to believe. Finally, it would have been impossible for them to have courted longer, because they had courted from the day they met, which was less than six weeks before the day they married.

'"A village",' he had quoted as they entered the branch line train at the junction (itself sufficiently remote), '"from which (it was said) persons of sufficient longevity might hope to reach Liverpool Street".' By now he was able to make jokes about age, although perhaps he did so rather too often.

'Who said that?'

'Bertrand Russell.'

She had looked at him with her big eyes in her tiny face.

'Really.' He had smiled confirmation.

'I'm not arguing.' She had still been looking at him. The romantic gas light in the charming period compartment had left him uncertain whether she was smiling back or not. He had given himself the benefit of the doubt, and kissed her.

The guard had blown his whistle and they had rumbled out into the darkness. The branch line swung so sharply away from the main line that Phrynne had been almost toppled from her seat.

'Why do we go so slowly when it's so flat?'

'Because the engineer laid the line up and down the hills and valleys such as they are, instead of cutting through and embanking over them.' He liked being able to inform her.

'How do you know? Gerald! You said you hadn't been to Holihaven before.'

'It applies to most of the railways in East Anglia.'

'So that even though it's flatter, it's slower?'

'Time matters less.'

'I should have hated going to a place where time mattered or that you'd been to before. You'd have had nothing to remember me by.'

He hadn't been quite sure that her words exactly expressed her thoughts, but the thought had lightened his heart.

*   *   *

Holihaven station could hardly have been built in the days of the town's magnificence, for they were in the Middle Ages; but it still implied grander functions than came its way now. The platforms were long enough for visiting London expresses, which had since gone elsewhere; and the architecture of the waiting rooms would have been not insufficient for occasional use by foreign royalty. Oil lamps on perches like those occupied by macaws, lightened the uniformed staff, who numbered two and, together with every native of Holihaven, looked like storm-habituated mariners.

The station-master and porter, as Gerald took them to be, watched him approach down the platform with a heavy suitcase in each hand and Phrynne walking deliciously by his side. He saw one of them address a remark to the other, but neither offered to help. Gerald had to put down the cases in order to give up their tickets. The other passengers had already disappeared.

'Where's the Bell?'

Gerald had found the hotel in a reference book. It was the only one allotted to Holihaven. But as Gerald spoke, and before the ticket-collector could answer, the sudden deep note of an actual bell rang through the darkness. Phrynne caught hold of Gerald's sleeve.

Ignoring Gerald, the station-master, if such he was, turned to his colleague. 'They're starting early.'

'Every reason to be in good time,' said the other man.

The station-master nodded, and put Gerald's tickets indifferently in his jacket pocket.

'Can you please tell me how I get to the Bell Hotel?'

The station-master's attention returned to him. 'Have you a room booked?'

'Certainly.'

'Tonight?' The station-master looked inappropriately suspicious.

'Of course.'

Again the station-master looked at the other man.

'It's them Pascoes.'

'Yes,' said Gerald. 'That's the name. Pascoe.'

'We don't use the Bell,' explained the station-master. 'But you'll find it in Wrack Street.' He gesticulated vaguely and unhelpfully. 'Straight ahead. Down Station Road. Then down Wrack Street. You can't miss it.'

'Thank you.'

As soon as they entered the town, the big bell began to boom regularly.

'What narrow streets!' said Phrynne.

'They follow the lines of the medieval city. Before the river silted up, Holihaven was one of the most important seaports in Great Britain.'

'Where's everybody got to?'

Although it was only six o'clock, the place certainly seemed deserted.

'Where's the hotel got to?' rejoined Gerald.

'Poor Gerald! Let me help.' She laid her hand beside his on the handle of the suitcase nearest to her, but as she was about fifteen inches shorter than he, she could be of little assistance. They must already have gone more than a quarter of a mile. 'Do you think we're in the right street?'

'Most unlikely, I should say. But there's no one to ask.'

'Must be early closing day.'

The single deep notes of the bell were now coming more frequently.

'Why are they ringing that bell? Is it a funeral?'

'Bit late for a funeral.'

She looked at him a little anxiously.

'Anyway it's not cold.'

'Considering we're on the east coast it's quite astonishingly warm.'

'Not that I care.'

'I hope that bell isn't going to ring all night.'

She pulled on the suitcase. His arms were in any case almost parting from his body. 'Look! We've passed it.'

They stopped, and he looked back. 'How could we have done that?'

'Well, we have.'

She was right. He could see a big ornamental bell hanging from a bracket attached to a house about a hundred yards behind them.

They retraced their steps and entered the hotel. A woman dressed in a navy blue coat and skirt, with a good figure but dyed red hair and a face ridged with make-up, advanced upon them.

'Mr and Mrs Banstead? I'm Hilda Pascoe. Don, my husband, isn't very well.'

Gerald felt full of doubts. His arrangements were not going as they should. Never rely on guide-book recommendations. The trouble lay partly in Phrynne's insistence that they go somewhere he did not know. 'I'm sorry to hear that,' he said.

'You know what men are like when they're ill?' Mrs Pascoe spoke understandingly to Phrynne.

'Impossible,' said Phrynne. 'Or very difficult.'

'Talk about "Woman in our hours of ease".'

'Yes,' said Phrynne. 'What's the trouble?'

'It's always been the same trouble with Don,' said Mrs Pascoe; then checked herself. 'It's his stomach,' she said. 'Ever since he was a kid, Don's had trouble with the lining of his stomach.'

Gerald interrupted. 'I wonder if we could see our rooms?'

'So sorry,' said Mrs Pascoe. 'Will you register first?' She produced a battered volume bound in peeling imitation leather. 'Just the name and address.' She spoke as if Gerald might contribute a résumé of his life.

It was the first time he and Phrynne had ever registered in an hotel; but his confidence in the place was not increased by the long period which had passed since the registration above.

'We're always quiet in October,' remarked Mrs Pascoe, her eyes upon him. Gerald noticed that her eyes were slightly bloodshot. 'Except sometimes for the bars, of course.'

'We wanted to come out of the season,' said Phrynne soothingly.

'Quite,' said Mrs Pascoe.

'Are we alone in the house?' enquired Gerald. After all the woman was probably doing her best.

'Except for Commandant Shotcroft. You won't mind him, will you? He's a regular.'

'I'm sure we shan't,' said Phrynne.

'People say the house wouldn't be the same without Commandant Shotcroft.'

'I see.'

'What's that bell?' asked Gerald. Apart from anything else, it really was much too near.

Mrs Pascoe looked away. He thought she looked shifty under her entrenched make-up. But she only said 'Practice.'

'Do you mean there will be more of them later?'

She nodded. 'But never mind,' she said encouragingly. 'Let me show you to your room. Sorry there's no porter.'

Before they had reached the bedroom, the whole peal had commenced.

'Is this the quietest room you have?' enquired Gerald. 'What about the other side of the house?'

'This *is* the other side of the house. Saint Guthlac's is over there.' She pointed out through the bedroom door.

'Darling,' said Phrynne, her hand on Gerald's arm, 'they'll soon stop. They're only practising.'

Mrs Pascoe said nothing. Her expression indicated that she was one of those people whose friendliness has a precise and never exceeded limit.

'If *you* don't mind,' said Gerald to Phrynne, hesitating.

'They have ways of their own in Holihaven,' said Mrs Pascoe. Her undertone of militancy implied, among other things, that if Gerald and Phrynne chose to leave, they were at liberty to do so. Gerald did not care for that either: her attitude would have been different, he felt, had there been anywhere else for them to go. The bells were making him touchy and irritable.

'It's a very pretty room,' said Phrynne. 'I adore four-posters.'

'Thank you,' said Gerald to Mrs Pascoe. 'What time's dinner?'

'Seven-thirty. You've time for a drink in the bar first.'

She went.

'We certainly have,' said Gerald when the door was shut. 'It's only just six.'

'Actually,' said Phrynne, who was standing by the window looking down into the street, 'I *like* church bells.'

'All very well,' said Gerald, 'but on one's honeymoon they distract the attention.'

'Not mine,' said Phrynne simply. Then she added, 'There's still no one about.'

'I expect they're all in the bar.'

'I don't want a drink. I want to explore the town.'

'As you wish. But hadn't you better unpack?'

'I ought to, but I'm not going to. Not until after I've seen the sea.' Such small shows of independence in her enchanted Gerald.

Mrs Pascoe was not about when they passed through the lounge, nor was there any sound of activity in the establishment.

Outside, the bells seemed to be booming and bounding immediately over their heads.

'It's like warriors fighting in the sky,' shouted Phrynne. 'Do you think the sea's down there?' She indicated the direction from which they had previously retraced their steps.

'I imagine so. The street seems to end in nothing. That would be the sea.'

'Come on. Let's run.' She was off, before he could even think about it. Then there was nothing to do but run after her. He hoped there were not eyes behind blinds.

She stopped, and held wide her arms to catch him. The top of her head hardly came up to his chin. He knew she was silently indicating that his failure to keep up with her was not a matter for self-consciousness.

'Isn't it beautiful?'

'The sea?' There was no moon; and little was discernible beyond the end of the street.

'Not only.'

'Everything but the sea. The sea's invisible.'

'You can smell it.'

'I certainly can't hear it.'

She slackened her embrace and cocked her head away from him.

'The bells echo so much, it's as if there were two churches.'

'I'm sure there are more than that. There always are in old towns like this.' Suddenly he was struck by the significance of his words in relation to what she had said. He shrank into himself, tautly listening.

'Yes,' cried Phrynne delightedly. 'It *is* another church.'

'Impossible,' said Gerald. 'Two churches wouldn't have practice ringing on the same night.'

'I'm quite sure. I can hear one lot of bells with my left ear, and another lot with my right.'

They had still seen no one. The sparse gas lights fell on the furnishings of a stone quay, small but plainly in regular use.

'The whole population must be ringing the bells.' His own remark discomfited Gerald.

'Good for them,' she took his hand. 'Let's go down on the beach and look for the sea.'

They descended a flight of stone steps at which the sea had sucked and bitten. The beach was as stony as the steps, but lumpier.

'We'll just go straight on,' said Phrynne. 'Until we find it.'

Left to himself, Gerald would have been less keen. The stones were very large and very slippery, and his eyes did not seem to be becoming accustomed to the dark.

'You're right, Phrynne, about the smell.'

'Honest sea smell.'

'Just as you say.' He took it rather to be the smell of dense rotting weed; across which he supposed they must be slithering. It was not a smell he had previously encountered in such strength.

Energy could hardly be spared for thinking, and advancing hand in hand was impossible.

After various random remarks on both sides and the lapse of what seemed a very long time, Phrynne spoke again. 'Gerald, where is it? What sort of seaport is it that has no sea?'

She continued onwards, but Gerald stopped and looked back. He had thought the distance they had gone overlong, but was startled to see how great it was. The darkness was doubtless deceitful, but the few lights on the quay appeared as on a distant horizon.

The far glimmering specks still in his eyes, he turned and looked after Phrynne. He could barely see her. Perhaps she was progressing faster without him.

'Phrynne! Darling!'

Unexpectedly she gave a sharp cry.

'Phrynne!'

She did not answer.

'Phrynne!'

Then she spoke more or less calmly. 'Panic over. Sorry, darling. I stood on something.'

He realized that a panic it had indeed been; at least in him.

'You're all right?'

'Think so.'

He struggled up to her. 'The smell's worse than ever.' It was overpowering.

'I think it's coming from what I stepped on. My foot went right in, and then there was the smell.'

'I've never known anything like it.'

'Sorry darling,' she said gently mocking him. 'Let's go away.'

'Let's go back. Don't you think?'

'Yes,' said Phrynne. 'But I must warn you I'm very disappointed. I think that seaside attractions should include the sea.'

He noticed that as they retreated, she was scraping the sides of one shoe against the stones, as if trying to clean it.

'I think the whole place is a disappointment,' he said. 'I really must apologize. We'll go somewhere else.'

'I like the bells,' she replied, making a careful reservation.

Gerald said nothing.

'I don't want to go somewhere where you've been before.'

The bells rang out over the desolate unattractive beach. Now the sound seemed to be coming from every point along the shore.

'I suppose all the churches practise on the same night in order to get it over with,' said Gerald.

'They do it in order to see which can ring the loudest,' said Phrynne.

'Take care you don't twist your ankle.'

The din as they reached the rough little quay was such as to suggest that Phrynne's idea was literally true.

*   *   *

The Coffee Room was so low that Gerald had to dip beneath a sequence of thick beams.

'Why "Coffee Room"?' asked Phrynne, looking at the words on the door. 'I saw a notice that coffee will only be served in the lounge.'

'It's the *lucus a non lucendo* principle.'

'That explains everything. I wonder where we sit.' A single electric lantern, mass produced in an antique pattern, had been turned on. The bulb was of that limited wattage which is peculiar to hotels. It did little to penetrate the shadows.

'The *lucus a non lucendo* principle is the principle of calling white black.'

'Not at all,' said a voice from the darkness. 'On the contrary. The word black comes from an ancient root which means "to bleach".'

They had thought themselves alone, but now saw a small man seated by himself at an unlighted corner table. In the darkness he looked like a monkey.

'I stand corrected,' said Gerald.

They sat at the table under the lantern.

The man in the corner spoke again. 'Why are you here at all?'

Phrynne looked frightened, but Gerald replied quietly. 'We're on holiday. We prefer it out of the season. I presume you are Commandant Shotcroft?'

'No need to presume.' Unexpectedly the Commandant switched on the antique lantern which was nearest to him. His table was littered with a finished meal. It struck Gerald that he must have switched off the light when he heard them approach the Coffee Room. 'I'm going anyway.'

'Are we late?' asked Phrynne, always the assuager of situations.

'No, you're not late,' called the Commandant in a deep moody voice. 'My meals are prepared half an hour before the time the rest come in. I don't like eating in company.' He had risen to his feet. 'So perhaps you'll excuse me.'

Without troubling about an answer, he stepped quickly out of the Coffee Room. He had cropped white hair; tragic, heavy-lidded eyes; and a round face which was yellow and lined.

A second later his head reappeared round the door.

'Ring,' he said; and again withdrew.

'Too many other people ringing,' said Gerald. 'But I don't see what else we can do.'

The Coffee Room bell, however, made a noise like a fire alarm.

Mrs Pascoe appeared. She looked considerably the worse for drink.

'Didn't see you in the bar.'

'Must have missed us in the crowd,' said Gerald amiably.

'Crowd?' enquired Mrs Pascoe drunkenly. Then, after a difficult pause, she offered them a hand-written menu.

They ordered; and Mrs Pascoe served them throughout. Gerald was apprehensive lest her indisposition increase during the course of the meal; but her insobriety, like her affability, seemed to have an exact and definite limit.

'All things considered, the food might be worse,' remarked Gerald, towards the end. It was a relief that something was going reasonably well. 'Not much of it, but at least the dishes are hot.'

When Phrynne translated this into a compliment to the cook, Mrs Pascoe said, 'I cooked it all myself, although I shouldn't be the one to say so.'

Gerald felt really surprised that she was in a condition to have accomplished this. Possibly, he reflected with alarm, she had had much practice under similar conditions.

'Coffee is served in the lounge,' said Mrs Pascoe.

They withdrew. In a corner of the lounge was a screen decorated with winning Elizabethan ladies in ruffs and hoops. From behind it, projected a pair of small black boots. Phrynne nudged Gerald and pointed to them. Gerald nodded. They felt constrained to talk about things which bored them.

The hotel was old and its walls thick. In the empty lounge the noise of the bells would not prevent conversation being overheard, but still came from all around, as if the hotel were a fortress beleaguered by surrounding artillery.

After their second cups of coffee, Gerald suddenly said he couldn't stand it.

'Darling, it's not doing us any harm. I think it's rather cosy.' Phrynne subsided in the wooden chair with its sloping back and long mud-coloured mock-velvet cushions; and opened her pretty legs to the fire.

'Every church in the town must be ringing its bells. It's been going on for two and a half hours and they never seem to take the usual breathers.'

'We wouldn't hear. Because of all the other bells ringing. I think it's nice of them to ring the bells for us.'

Nothing further was said for several minutes. Gerald was beginning to realize that they had yet to evolve a holiday routine.

'I'll get you a drink. What shall it be?'

'Anything you like. Whatever *you* have.' Phrynne was immersed in female enjoyment of the fire's radiance on her body.

Gerald missed this, and said 'I don't quite see why they have to keep the place like a hothouse. When I come back, we'll sit somewhere else.'

'Men wear too many clothes, darling,' said Phrynne drowsily.

Contrary to his assumption, Gerald found the lounge bar as empty as everywhere else in the hotel and the town. There was not even a person to dispense.

Somewhat irritably Gerald struck a brass bell which stood on the counter. It rang out sharply as a pistol shot.

Mrs Pascoe appeared at a door among the shelves. She had taken off her jacket, and her make-up had begun to run.

'A cognac, please. Double. And a Kummel.'

Mrs Pascoe's hands were shaking so much that she could not get the cork out of the brandy bottle.

'Allow me.' Gerald stretched his arm across the bar.

Mrs Pascoe stared at him blearily. 'O.K. But I must pour it.'

Gerald extracted the cork and returned the bottle. Mrs Pascoe slopped a far from precise dose into a balloon.

Catastrophe followed. Unable to return the bottle to the high shelf where it resided. Mrs Pascoe placed it on a waist-level ledge. Reaching for the alembic of Kummel, she swept the three-quarters full brandy bottle onto the tiled floor. The stuffy air became fogged with the fumes of brandy from behind the bar.

At the door from which Mrs Pascoe had emerged appeared a man from the inner room. Though still youngish, he was puce and puffy, and in his braces, with no collar. Streaks of sandy hair laced his vast red scalp. Liquor oozed all over him, as if from a perished gourd. Gerald took it that this was Don.

The man was too drunk to articulate. He stood in the doorway, clinging with each red hand to the ledge, and savagely struggling to flay his wife with imprecations.

'How much?' said Gerald to Mrs Pascoe. It seemed useless to try for the Kummel. The hotel must have another bar.

'Three and six,' said Mrs Pascoe, quite lucidly; but Gerald saw that she was about to weep.

He had the exact sum. She turned her back on him and flicked the cash register. As she returned from it, he heard the fragmentation of glass as she stepped on a piece of the broken bottle. Gerald looked at her husband out of the corner of his eye. The sagging, loose-mouthed figure made him shudder. Something moved him.

'I'm sorry about the accident,' he said to Mrs Pascoe. He held the balloon in one hand, and was just going.

Mrs Pascoe looked at him. The slow tears of desperation were edging down her face, but she now seemed quite sober. 'Mr Banstead,' she said in a flat, hurried voice. 'May I come and sit with you and your wife in the lounge? Just for a few minutes.'

'Of course.' It was certainly not what he wanted, and he wondered what would become of the bar, but he felt unexpectedly sorry for her, and it was impossible to say no.

To reach the flap of the bar, she had to pass her husband. Gerald saw her hesitate for a second; then she advanced resolutely and steadily, and looking straight before her. If the man had let go with his hands, he would have fallen; but as she passed him, he released a great gob of spit. He was far too incapable to aim, and it fell on the side of his own trousers. Gerald lifted the flap for Mrs Pascoe and stood back to let her precede him from the bar. As he followed her, he heard her husband maundering off into unintelligible inward searchings.

'The Kummel!' said Mrs Pascoe, remembering in the doorway.

'Never mind,' said Gerald. 'Perhaps I could try one of the other bars?'

'Not tonight. They're shut. I'd better go back.'

'No. We'll think of something else.' It was not yet nine o'clock, and Gerald wondered about the Licensing Justices.

But in the lounge was another unexpected scene. Mrs Pascoe stopped as soon as they entered, and Gerald, caught between two imitation-leather armchairs, looked over her shoulder.

Phrynne had fallen asleep. Her head was slightly on one side, but her mouth was shut, and her body no more than gracefully relaxed, so that she looked most beautiful, and, Gerald thought, a trifle unearthly, like a dead girl in an early picture by Millais.

The quality of her beauty seemed also to have impressed Commandant Shotcroft; for he was standing silently behind her and looking down at her, his sad face transfigured. Gerald noticed that a leaf of the pseudo-Elizabethan screen had been folded back, revealing a small cretonne-covered chair, with an open tome face downward in its seat.

'Won't you join us?' said Gerald boldly. There was that in the Commandant's face which boded no hurt. 'Can I get you a drink?'

The Commandant did not turn his head, and for a moment seemed unable to speak. Then in a low voice he said, 'For a moment only.'

'Good,' said Gerald. 'Sit down. And you, Mrs Pascoe.' Mrs Pascoe was dabbing at her face. Gerald addressed the Commandant. 'What shall it be?'

'Nothing to drink,' said the Commandant in the same low mutter. It occurred to Gerald that if Phrynne awoke, the Commandant would go.

'What about you?' Gerald looked at Mrs Pascoe, earnestly hoping she would decline.

'No thanks.' She was glancing at the Commandant. Clearly she had not expected him to be there.

Phrynne being asleep, Gerald sat down too. He sipped his brandy. It was impossible to romanticize the action with a toast.

The events in the bar had made him forget about the bells. Now, as they sat silently round the sleeping Phrynne, the tide of sound swept over him once more.

'You mustn't think,' said Mrs Pascoe, 'that he's always like that.' They all spoke in hushed voices. All of them seemed to have reason to do so. The Commandant was again gazing sombrely at Phrynne's beauty.

'Of course not.' But it was hard to believe.

'The licensed business puts temptations in a man's way.'

'It must be very difficult.'

'We ought never to have come here. We were happy in South Norwood.'

'You must do good business during the season.'

'Two months,' said Mrs Pascoe bitterly, but still softly. 'Two and a half at the very most. The people who come during the season have no idea what goes on out of it.'

'What made you leave South Norwood?'

'Don's stomach. The doctor said the air would do him good.'

'Speaking of that, doesn't the sea go too far out? We went down on the beach before dinner, but couldn't see it anywhere.'

On the other side of the fire, the Commandant turned his eyes from Phrynne and looked at Gerald.

'I wouldn't know,' said Mrs Pascoe. 'I never have time to look from one year's end to the other.' It was a customary enough answer, but Gerald felt that it did not disclose the whole truth. He noticed that Mrs Pascoe glanced uneasily at the Commandant, who by now was staring neither at Phrynne nor at Gerald but at the toppling citadels in the fire.

'And now I must get on with my work,' continued Mrs Pascoe, 'I only came in for a minute.' She looked Gerald in the face. 'Thank you,' she said, and rose.

'Please stay a little longer,' said Gerald, 'Wait till my wife wakes up.' As he spoke, Phrynne slightly shifted.

'Can't be done,' said Mrs Pascoe, her lips smiling. Gerald noticed that all the time she was watching the Commandant from under her lids, and she knew that were he not there, she would have stayed.

As it was, she went. 'I'll probably see you later to say goodnight. Sorry the water's not very hot. It's having no porter.'

The bells showed no sign of flagging.

When Mrs Pascoe had closed the door, the Commandant spoke.

'He was a fine man once. Don't think otherwise.'

'You mean Pascoe?'

The Commandant nodded seriously.

'Not my type,' said Gerald.

'D.S.O. and bar. D.F.C. and bar.'

'And now bar only. Why?'

'You heard what she said. It was a lie. They didn't leave South Norwood for the sea air.'

'So I supposed.'

'He got into trouble. He was fixed. He wasn't the kind of man to know about human nature and all its rottenness.'

'A pity,' said Gerald. 'But perhaps, even so, this isn't the best place for him?'

'It's the worst,' said the Commandant, a dark flame in his eyes. 'For him or anyone else.'

Again Phrynne shifted in her sleep: this time more convulsively, so that she nearly woke. For some reason the two men remained speechless and motionless until she was again breathing steadily. Against the silence within, the bells sounded louder than ever. It was as if the tumult were tearing holes in the roof.

'It's certainly a very noisy place,' said Gerald, still in an undertone.

'Why did you have to come tonight of all nights?' The Commandant spoke in the same undertone, but his vehemence was extreme.

'This doesn't happen often?'

'Once every year.'

'They should have told us.'

'They don't usually accept bookings. They've no right to accept them. When Pascoe was in charge they never did.'

'I expect that Mrs Pascoe felt they were in no position to turn away business.'

'It's not a matter that should be left to a woman.'

'Not much alternative surely?'

'At heart, women are creatures of darkness all the time.' The Commandant's seriousness and bitterness left Gerald without a reply.

'My wife doesn't mind the bells,' he said after a moment. 'In fact she rather likes them.' The Commandant really was converting a nuisance, though an acute one, into a melodrama.

The Commandant turned and gazed at him. It struck Gerald that what he had just said in some way, for the Commandant, placed Phrynne also in a category of the lost.

'Take her away, man,' said the Commandant, with scornful ferocity.

'In a day or two perhaps,' said Gerald, patiently polite. 'I admit that we are disappointed with Holihaven.'

'Now. While there's still time. This *instant*.'

There was an intensity of conviction about the Commandant which was alarming.

Gerald considered. Even the empty lounge, with its dreary decorations and commonplace furniture, seemed inimical. 'They can hardly go on practising all night,' he said. But now it was fear that hushed his voice.

'Practising!' The Commandant's scorn flickered coldly through the overheated room.

'What else?'

'They're ringing to wake the dead.'

A tremor of wind in the flue momentarily drew on the already roaring fire. Gerald had turned very pale.

'That's a figure of speech,' he said, hardly to be heard.

'Not in Holihaven.' The Commandant's gaze had returned to the fire.

Gerald looked at Phrynne. She was breathing less heavily. His voice dropped to a whisper. 'What happens?'

The Commandant also was nearly whispering. 'No one can tell how long they have to go on ringing. It varies from year to year. I don't know why. You should be all right up to midnight. Probably for some while after. In the end the dead awake. First one or two, then all of them. Tonight even the sea draws back. You have seen that for yourself. In a place like this there are always several drowned each year. This year there've been more than several. But even so that's only a few. Most of them come not from the water but from the earth. It is not a pretty sight.'

'Where do they go?'

'I've never followed them to see. I'm not stark staring mad.' The red of the fire reflected in the Commandant's eyes. There was a long pause.

'I don't believe in the resurrection of the body,' said Gerald. As the hour grew later, the bells grew louder. 'Not of the body.'

'What other kind of resurrection is possible? Everything else is only theory. You can't even imagine it. No one can.'

Gerald had not argued such a thing for twenty years. 'So,' he said, 'you advise me to go. Where?'

'Where doesn't matter.'

'I have no car.'

'Then you'd better walk.'

'With her?' He indicated Phrynne only with his eyes.

'She's young and strong.' A forlorn tenderness lay within the Commandant's words. 'She's twenty years younger than you and therefore twenty years more important.'

'Yes,' said Gerald. 'I agree . . . What about you? What will you do?'

'I've lived here some time now. I know what to do.'

'And the Pascoes?'

'He's drunk. There is nothing in the world to fear if you're thoroughly drunk. D.S.O. and bar. D.F.C. and bar.'

'But you're not drinking yourself?'

'Not since I came to Holihaven. I lost the knack.'

Suddenly Phrynne sat up. 'Hallo,' she said to the Commandant; not yet fully awake. Then she said, 'What fun! The bells are still ringing.'

The Commandant rose, his eyes averted. 'I don't think there's anything more to say,' he remarked, addressing Gerald. 'You've still got time.' He nodded slightly to Phrynne, and walked out of the lounge.

'What have you still got time for?' asked Phrynne, stretching. 'Was he trying to convert you? I'm sure he's an Anabaptist.'

'Something like that,' said Gerald, trying to think.

'Shall we go to bed? Sorry, I'm so sleepy.'

'Nothing to be sorry about.'

'Or shall we go for another walk? That would wake me up. Besides the tide might have come in.'

Gerald, although he half-despised himself for it, found it impossible to explain to her that they should leave at once; without transport or a destination; walk all night if necessary. He said to himself that probably he would not go even were he alone.

'If you're sleepy, it's probably a *good* thing.'

'Darling!'

'I mean with these bells. God knows when they will stop.' Instantly he felt a new pang of fear at what he had said.

Mrs Pascoe had appeared at the door leading to the bar, and opposite to that from which the Commandant had departed. She bore two steaming glasses on a tray. She looked about, possibly to confirm that the Commandant had really gone.

'I thought you might both like a nightcap. Ovaltine, with something in it.'

'Thank you,' said Phrynne. 'I can't think of anything nicer.'

Gerald set the glasses on a wicker table, and quickly finished his cognac.

Mrs Pascoe began to move chairs and slap cushions. She looked very haggard.

'Is the Commandant an Anabaptist?' asked Phrynne over her shoulder. She was proud of her ability to outdistance Gerald in beginning to consume a hot drink.

Mrs Pascoe stopped slapping for a moment. 'I don't know what that is,' she said.

'He's left his book,' said Phrynne, on a new tack.

'I wonder what he's reading,' continued Phrynne. 'Foxe's *Lives of the Martyrs,* I expect.' A small unusual devil seemed to have entered into her.

But Mrs Pascoe knew the answer. 'It's always the same,' she said contemptuously. 'He only reads one. It's called *Fifteen Decisive Battles of the World.* He's been reading it ever since he came here. When he gets to the end, he starts again.'

'Should I take it up to him?' asked Gerald. It was neither courtesy nor inclination, but rather a fear lest the Commandant return to the lounge: a desire, after those few minutes of reflection, to cross-examine.

'Thanks very much,' said Mrs Pascoe, as if relieved of a similar apprehension. 'Room One. Next to the suit of Japanese armour.' She went on tipping and banging. To Gerald's inflamed nerves, her behaviour seemed too consciously normal.

He collected the book and made his way upstairs. The volume was bound in real leather, and the top of its pages were gilded: apparently a presentation copy. Outside the lounge, Gerald looked at the fly-leaf: in a very large hand was written 'To my dear Son, Raglan, on his being honoured by the Queen. From his proud Father, B. Shotcroft, Major-General.' Beneath the inscription a very ugly military crest had been appended by a stamper of primitive type.

The suit of Japanese armour lurked in a dark corner as the Commandant himself had done when Gerald had first encountered him. The wide brim of the helmet concealed the black eyeholes in the headpiece; the moustache bristled realistically. It was exactly as if the figure stood guard over the door behind it. On this door was no number, but, there being no other in sight, Gerald took it to be the door of Number One. A short way down the dim empty passage was a window, the ancient sashes of which shook in the din and blast of the bells. Gerald knocked sharply.

It there was a reply, the bells drowned it; and he knocked again. When to the third knocking there was still no answer, he gently opened the door. He really had to know whether all would, or could be well if Phrynne, and doubtless he also, were at all costs to remain in their room until it was dawn. He looked into the room and caught his breath.

There was no artificial light, but the curtains, if there were any, had been drawn back from the single window, and the bottom sash forced up as far as it would go. On the floor by the dusky void, a maelstrom of sound, knelt the Commandant, his cropped white hair faintly catching the moonless glimmer, as his head lay on the sill, like that of a man about to be guillotined. His face was in his hands, but slightly sideways, so that Gerald received a shadowy distorted idea of his expression. Some might have called it ecstatic, but Gerald found it agonized. It frightened him more than anything which had yet happened. Inside the room the bells were like plunging roaring lions.

He stood for some considerable time quite unable to move. He could not determine whether or not the Commandant knew he was there. The Commandant gave no direct sign of it, but more than once he writhed and shuddered in Gerald's direction, like an unquiet sleeper made more unquiet by an interloper. It was a matter of doubt whether Gerald should leave the book; and he decided to do so mainly because the thought of further contact with it displeased him. He crept into the room and softly laid it on a hardly visible wooden trunk at the foot of the plain metal bedstead. There seemed no other furniture in the room. Outside the door, the hanging mailed fingers of the Japanese figure touched his wrist.

He had not been away from the lounge for long, but it was long enough for Mrs Pascoe to have begun to drink again. She had left the tidying up half completed, or rather the room half disarranged; and was leaning against the over-mantel, drawing heavily on a dark tumbler of whisky. Phrynne had not yet finished her Ovaltine.

'How long before the bells stop?' asked Gerald as soon as he opened the lounge door. Now he was resolved that, come what might, they must go. The impossibility of sleep should serve as an excuse.

'I don't expect Mrs Pascoe can know any more than we can,' said Phrynne.

'You should have told us about this – this annual event before accepting our booking.'

Mrs Pascoe drank some more whisky. Gerald suspected that it was neat. 'It's not always the same night,' she said throatily, looking at the floor.

'We're not staying,' said Gerald wildly.

'Darling!' Phrynne caught him by the arm.

'Leave this to me, Phrynne.' He addressed Mrs Pascoe. 'We'll pay for the room, of course. Please order me a car.'

Mrs Pascoe was now regarding him stonily. When he asked for a car, she gave a very short laugh. Then her face changed, she made an effort, and she said, 'You mustn't take the Commandant so seriously, you know.'

Phrynne glanced quickly at her husband.

The whisky was finished. Mrs Pascoe placed the empty glass on the plastic over-mantel with too much of a thud. 'No one takes Commandant Shotcroft seriously,' she said. 'Not even his nearest and dearest.'

'Has he any?' asked Phrynne. 'He seemed so lonely and pathetic.'

'He's Don and I's mascot,' she said, the drink interfering with her grammar. But not even the drink could leave any doubt about her rancour.

'I thought he had personality,' said Phrynne.

'That and a lot more no doubt,' said Mrs Pascoe. 'But they pushed him out, all the same.'

'Out of what?'

'Cashiered, court-martialled, badges of rank stripped off, sword broken in half, muffled drums, the works.'

'Poor old man. I'm sure it was a miscarriage of justice.'

'That's because you don't know him.'

Mrs Pascoe looked as if she were waiting for Gerald to offer her another whisky.

'It's a thing he could never live down,' said Phrynne, brooding to herself, and tucking her legs beneath her. 'No wonder he's so queer if all the time it was a mistake.'

'I just told you it was not a mistake,' said Mrs Pascoe insolently.

'How can we possibly know?'

'*You* can't. *I* can. No one better.' She was at once aggressive and tearful.

'If you want to be paid,' cried Gerald, forcing himself in, 'make out your bill. Phrynne, come upstairs and pack.' If only he hadn't made her unpack between their walk and dinner.

Slowly Phrynne uncoiled and rose to her feet. She had no intention of either packing or departing, but nor was she going to argue, 'I shall need your help,' she said, softly. 'If I'm going to pack.'

In Mrs Pascoe there was another change. Now she looked terrified. 'Don't go. Please don't go. Not now. It's too late.'

Gerald confronted her. 'Too late for what?' he asked harshly.

Mrs Pascoe looked paler than ever. 'You said you wanted a car,' she faltered. 'You're too late.' Her voice trailed away.

Gerald took Phrynne by the arm. 'Come on up.'

Before they reached the door, Mrs Pascoe made a further attempt. 'You'll be all right if you stay. Really you will.' Her voice, normally somewhat strident, was so feeble that the bells obliterated it. Gerald observed that from somewhere she had produced the whisky bottle and was refilling her tumbler.

With Phrynne on his arm he went first to the stout front door. To his surprise it was neither locked nor bolted, but opened at a half-turn of the handle. Outside the building the whole sky was full of bells, the air an inferno of ringing.

He thought that for the first time Phrynne's face also seemed strained and crestfallen. 'They've been ringing too long,' she said, drawing close to him. 'I wish they'd stop.'

'We're packing and going. I needed to know whether we could get out this way. We must shut the door quietly.'

It creaked a bit on its hinges, and he hesitated with it half shut, uncertain whether to rush the creak or to ease it. Suddenly, something dark and shapeless, with its arm seeming to hold a black vesture over its head, flitted, all sharp angles, like a bat, down the narrow ill-lighted street, the sound of its passage audible to none. It was the first being that either of them had seen in the streets of Holihaven; and Gerald was acutely relieved that he alone had set eyes upon it. With his hand trembling, he shut the door much too sharply.

But no one could possibly have heard, although he stopped for a second outside the lounge. He could hear Mrs Pascoe now weeping hysterically; and again was glad that Phrynne was a step or two ahead of him. Upstairs the Commandant's door lay straight before them. They had to pass close beside the Japanese figure, in order to take the passage to the left of it.

But soon they were in their room, with the key turned in the big rim lock.

'Oh God,' cried Gerald, sinking on the double bed. 'It's pandemonium.' Not for the first time that evening he was instantly more frightened than ever by the unintended appositeness of his own words.

'It's pandemonium all right,' said Phrynne, almost calmly. 'And we're not going out in it.'

He was at a loss to divine how much she knew, guessed, or imagined; and any word of enlightenment from him might be inconceivably dangerous. But he was conscious of the strength of her resistance, and lacked the reserves to battle with it.

She was looking out of the window into the main street. 'We might *will* them to stop,' she suggested wearily.

Gerald was now far less frightened of the bells continuing than of their ceasing. But that they should go on ringing until day broke seemed hopelessly impossible.

Then one peal stopped. There could be no other explanation for the obvious diminution in sound.

'You see!' said Phrynne.

Gerald sat up straight on the side of the bed.

Almost at once further sections of sound subsided, quickly one after the other, until only a single peal was left, that which had begun the ringing. Then the single peal tapered off into a single bell. The single bell tolled on its own, disjointedly, five or six or seven times. Then it stopped, and there was nothing.

Gerald's head was a cave of echoes, mountingly muffled by the noisy current of his blood.

'Oh goodness,' said Phrynne, turning from the window and stretching her arms above her head. 'Let's go somewhere else tomorrow.' She began to take off her dress.

Sooner than usual they were in bed, and in one another's arms. Gerald had carefully not looked out of the window, and neither of them suggested that it should be opened, as they usually did.

'As it's a four-poster, shouldn't we draw the curtains?' asked Phrynne. 'And be really snug? After those damned bells?'

'We should suffocate.'

'They only drew the curtains when people were likely to pass through the room.'

'Darling, you're shivering. I think we *should* draw them.''

'Lie still instead, and love me.'

But all his nerves were straining out into the silence. There was no sound of any kind, beyond the hotel or within it; not a creaking floorboard or a prowling cat or a distant owl. He had been afraid to look at his watch when the bells stopped, or since; the number of the dark hours before they could leave Holihaven weighed on him. The vision of the Commandant kneeling in the dark window was clear before his eyes, as if the intervening panelled walls were made of stage gauze; and the thing he had seen in the street darted on its angular way back and forth through memory.

Then passion began to open its petals within him, layer upon slow layer; like an illusionist's red flower which, without soil or sun or sap, grows as it is watched. The languor of tenderness began to fill the musty room with its texture and perfume. The transparent walls became again opaque, the old man's vaticinations mere obsession. The street must have been empty, as it was now; the eye deceived.

But perhaps rather it was the boundless sequacity of love that deceived, and most of all in the matter of the time which had passed since the bells stopped ringing; for suddenly Phrynne drew very close to him, and he heard steps in the thoroughfare outside, and a voice calling. These were loud steps, audible from afar even through the shut window; and the voice had the possessed stridency of the street evangelist.

'The dead are awake!'

Not even the thick bucolic accent, the guttural vibrato of emotion, could twist or mask the meaning. At first Gerald lay listening with all his body, and concentrating the more as the noise grew; then he sprang from the bed and ran to the window.

A burly, long-limbed man in a seaman's jersey was running down the street, coming clearly into view for a second at each lamp, and between them lapsing into a swaying lumpy wraith. As he shouted his joyous message, he crossed from side to side and waved his arms like a negro. By flashes, Gerald could see that his weatherworn face was transfigured.

'The dead are awake!'

Already, behind him, people were coming out of their houses, and descending from the rooms above shops. There were men, women, and children. Most of them were fully dressed, and must have been waiting in silence and darkness for the call; but a few were dishevelled in night attire or the first garments which had come to hand. Some formed themselves into groups, and advanced arm in arm, as if towards the conclusion of a Blackpool beano. More came singly, ecstatic and waving their arms above their heads, as the first man had done. All cried out, again and again, with no cohesion or harmony. 'The dead are awake! The dead are awake!'

Gerald became aware that Phrynne was standing behind him.

'The Commandant warned me,' he said brokenly. 'We should have gone.'

Phrynne shook her head and took his arm. 'Nowhere to go,' she said. But her voice was soft with fear, and her eyes blank. 'I don't expect they'll trouble *us*.'

Swiftly Gerald drew the thick plush curtains, leaving them in complete darkness. 'We'll sit it out,' he said, slightly histrionic in his fear. 'No matter what happens.'

He scrambled across to the switch. But when he pressed it, light did not come. 'The current's gone. We must get back into bed.'

'Gerald! Come and help me.' He remembered that she was curiously vulnerable in the dark. He found his way to her, and guided her to the bed.

'No more love,' she said ruefully and affectionately, her teeth chattering.

He kissed her lips with what gentleness the total night made possible.

'They were going towards the sea,' she said timidly.

'We must think of something else.'

But the noise was still growing. The whole community seemed to be passing down the street, yelling the same dreadful words again and again.

'Do you think we can?'

'Yes,' said Gerald. 'It's only until tomorrow.'

'They can't be actually dangerous,' said Phrynne. 'Or it would be stopped.'

'Yes, of course.'

By now, as always happens, the crowd had amalgamated their utterances and were beginning to shout in unison. They were like agitators bawling a slogan, or massed trouble-makers at a football match. But at the same time the noise was beginning to draw away. Gerald suspected that the entire population of the place was on the march.

Soon it was apparent that a processional route was being followed. The tumult could be heard winding about from quarter to quarter; sometimes drawing near, so that Gerald and Phrynne were once more seized by the first chill of panic, then again almost fading away. It was possibly this great variability in the volume of the sound which led Gerald to believe that there were distinct pauses in the massed shouting; periods when it was superseded by far, disorderly cheering. Certainly it began also to seem that the thing shouted had changed; but he could not make out the new cry, although unwillingly he strained to do so.

'It's extraordinary how frightened one can be,' said Phrynne, 'even

when one is not directly menaced. It must prove that we all belong to
one another, or whatever it is, after all.'

In many similar remarks they discussed the thing at one remove.
Experience showed that this was better than not discussing it at all.

In the end there could be no doubt that the shouting had stopped,
and that now the crowd was singing. It was no song that Gerald had ever
heard, but something about the way it was sung convinced him that it
was a hymn or psalm set to an out of date popular tune. Once more the
crowd was approaching; this time steadily, but with strange, intermin-
able slowness.

'What the hell are they doing now?' asked Gerald of the blackness,
his nerves wound so tight that the foolish question was forced out of
them.

Palpably the crowd had completed its peregrination, and was
returning up the main street from the sea. The singers seemed to gasp
and fluctuate, as if worn out with gay exercise, like children at a party.
There was a steady undertow of scraping and scuffling. Time passed and
more time.

Phrynne spoke. 'I believe they're *dancing*.'

She moved slightly, as if she thought of going to see.

'No, no,' said Gerald, and clutched her fiercely.

There was a tremendous concussion on the ground floor below them.
The front door had been violently thrown back. They could hear the
hotel filling with a stamping, singing mob.

Doors banged everywhere, and furniture was overturned, as the
beatic throng surged and stumbled through the involved darkness of the
old building. Glasses went and china and Birmingham brass warming
pans. In a moment, Gerald heard the Japanese armour crash to the
boards. Phrynne screamed. Then a mighty shoulder, made strong by the
sea's assault, rammed at the panelling and their door was down.

'*The living and the dead dance together.*
Now's the time. Now's the place. Now's the weather.'

At last Gerald could make out the words.

The stresses in the song were heavily beaten down by much
repetition.

Hand in hand, through the dim grey gap of the doorway, the dancers
lumbered and shambled in, singing frenziedly and brokenly; ecstatic but
exhausted. Through the stuffy blackness they swayed and shambled,
more and more of them, until the room must have been packed tight
with them.

Phrynne screamed again. 'The smell. Oh, God, the smell.'

It was the smell they had encountered on the beach; in the congested
room, no longer merely offensive, but obscene, unspeakable.

Phrynne was hysterical. All self-control gone, she was scratching and

tearing, and screaming again and again. Gerald tried to hold her, but
one of the dancers struck him so hard in the darkness that she was jolted
out of his arms. Instantly it seemed that she was no longer there at all.

The dancers were thronging everywhere, their limbs whirling, their
lungs bursting with the rhythm of the song. It was difficult for Gerald
even to call out. He tried to struggle after Phrynne, but immediately a
blow from a massive elbow knocked him to the floor, an abyss of invisible
trampling feet.

But soon the dancers were going again: not only from the room, but,
it seemed, from the building also. Crushed and tormented though he
was, Gerald could hear the song being resumed in the street, as the
various frenzied groups debouched and reunited. Within, before long
there was nothing but the chaos, the darkness, and the putrescent odour.
Gerald felt so sick that he had to battle with unconsciousness. He could
not think or move, despite the desperate need.

Then he struggled into a sitting position, and sank his head on the
torn sheets of the bed. For an uncertain period he was insensible to
everything: but in the end he heard steps approaching down the dark
passage. His door was pushed back, and the Commandant entered
gripping a lighted candle. He seemed to disregard the flow of hot wax
which had already congealed on much of his knotted hand.

'She's safe. Small thanks to you.'

The Commandant stared icily at Gerald's undignified figure. Gerald
tried to stand. He was terribly bruised, and so giddy that he wondered if
this could be concussion. But relief rallied him.

'Is it thanks to *you*?'

'She was caught up in it. Dancing with the rest.' The Commandant's
eyes glowed in the candlelight. The singing and the dancing had almost
died away.

Still Gerald could do no more than sit upon the bed. His voice was
low and indistinct, as if coming from outside his body. 'Were
they ... were some of them ...'

The Commandant replied, more scornful than ever of his weakness.
'She was between two of them. Each had one of her hands.'

Gerald could not look at him. 'What did you do?' he asked in the
same remote voice.

'I did what had to be done. I hope I was in time.' After the slightest
possible pause he continued. 'You'll find her downstairs.'

'I'm grateful. Such a silly thing to say, but what else is there?'

'Can you walk?'

'I think so.'

'I'll light you down.' The Commandant's tone was as uncompromis-
ing as always.

There were two more candles in the lounge, and Phrynne, wearing a woman's belted overcoat which was not hers, sat between them, drinking. Mrs Pascoe, fully dressed but with eyes averted, pottered about the wreckage. It seemed hardly more than as if she were completing the task which earlier she had left unfinished.

'Darling, look at you!' Phrynne's words were still hysterical, but her voice was as gentle as it usually was.

Gerald, bruises and thoughts of concussion forgotten, dragged her into his arms. They embraced silently for a long time; then he looked into her eyes.

'Here I am,' she said, and looked away. 'Not to worry.'

Silently and unnoticed, the Commandant had already retreated.

Without returning his gaze, Phrynne finished her drink as she stood there. Gerald supposed that it was one of Mrs Pascoe's concoctions.

It was so dark where Mrs Pascoe was working that her labours could have been achieving little; but she said nothing to her visitors, nor they to her. At the door Phrynne unexpectedly stripped off the overcoat and threw it on a chair. Her nightdress was so torn that she stood almost naked. Dark though it was, Gerald saw Mrs Pascoe regarding Phrynne's pretty body with a stare of animosity.

'May we take one of the candles?' he said, normal standards reasserting themselves in him.

But Mrs Pascoe continued to stand silently staring; and they lighted themselves through the wilderness of broken furniture to the ruins of their bedroom. The Japanese figure was still prostrate, and the Commandant's door shut. And the smell had almost gone.

*   *   *

Even by seven o'clock the next morning surprisingly much had been done to restore order. But no one seemed to be about, and Gerald and Phrynne departed without a word.

In Wrack Street a milkman was delivering, but Gerald noticed that his cart bore the name of another town. A minute boy whom they encountered later on an obscure purposeful errand might, however, have been indigenous; and when they reached Station Road, they saw a small plot of land on which already men were silently at work with spades in their hands. They were as thick as flies on a wound, and as black. In the darkness of the previous evening, Gerald and Phrynne had missed the place. A board named it the New Municipal Cemetery.

In the mild light of an autumn morning the sight of the black and silent toilers was horrible; but Phrynne did not seem to find it so. On the contrary, her cheeks reddened and her soft mouth became fleetingly more voluptuous still.

She seemed to have forgotten Gerald, so that he was able to examine her closely for a moment. It was the first time he had done so since the night before. Then, once more, she became herself. In those previous seconds Gerald had become aware of something dividing them which neither of them would ever mention or ever forget.

My Adventure in Norfolk
A. J. Alan

I don't know how it is with you, but during February *my* wife generally says to me: 'Have you thought at all about what we are going to do for August?' And, of course, I say 'No,' and then she begins looking through the advertisements of bungalows to let.

Well, this happened last year, as usual, and she eventually produced one that looked possible. It said: 'Norfolk – Hickling Broad – Furnished Bungalow – Garden – Garage, Boathouse,' and all the rest of it—— Oh – *and* plate and linen. It also mentioned an exorbitant rent. I pointed out the bit about the rent, but my wife said: 'Yes, you'll have to go down and see the landlord, and get him to come down. They always do.' As a matter of fact, they always don't, but that's a detail.

Anyway, I wrote off to the landlord and asked if he could arrange for me to stay the night in the place to see what it was really like. He wrote back and said: 'Certainly,' and that he was engaging Mrs So-and-so to come in and 'oblige me', and make up the beds and so forth.

I tell you, we do things thoroughly in our family – I have to sleep in all the beds, and when I come home my wife counts the bruises and decides whether they will do or not.

At any rate, I arrived, in a blinding snowstorm, at about *the* most desolate spot on God's earth. I'd come to Potter Heigham by train, and been driven on – (it was a good five miles from the station). Fortunately, Mrs Selston, the old lady who was going to 'do' for me, was there, and she'd lighted a fire, and cooked me a steak, for which I was truly thankful.

I somehow think the cow, or whatever they get steaks off, had only died that morning. It was very – er – obstinate. While I dined, she talked to me. She *would* tell me all about an operation her husband had just had. *All* about it. It was almost a lecture on surgery. The steak was rather underdone, and it sort of made me feel I was illustrating her lecture. Anyway, she put me clean off my dinner, and then departed for the night.

I explored the bungalow and just had a look outside. It was, of course, very dark, but not snowing quite so hard. The garage stood about fifteen yards from the back door. I walked round it but didn't go in. I also went down to the edge of the broad, and verified the boathouse. The whole place looked as though it might be all right in the summertime, but just then it made one wonder why people ever wanted to go to the North Pole.

Anyhow, I went indoors, and settled down by the fire. You've no idea how quiet it was; even the water-fowl had taken a night off – at least, they weren't working.

At a few minutes to eleven I heard the first noise there'd been since Mrs What's-her-name – Selston – had cleared out. It was the sound of a car. If it had gone straight by I probably shouldn't have noticed it at all, only it didn't go straight by; it seemed to stop farther up the road, before it got to the house. Even that didn't made much impression. After all, cars *do* stop.

It must have been five or ten minutes before it was borne in on me that it hadn't gone on again. So I got up and looked out of the window. It had left off snowing, and there was a glare through the gate that showed that there were headlamps somewhere just out of sight. I thought I might as well stroll out and investigate.

I found a fair-sized limousine pulled up in the middle of the road about twenty yards short of my gate. The light was rather blinding, but when I got close to it I found a girl with the bonnet open, tinkering with the engine. Quite an attractive young female, from what one could see, but she was so muffled up in furs that it was rather hard to tell.

I said:

'Er – good evening – anything I can do?'

She said she didn't know what was the matter. The engine had just stopped, and wouldn't start again. And it *had*! It wouldn't even turn, either with the self-starter or the handle. The whole thing was awfully hot, and I asked her whether there was any water in the radiator. She didn't see why there shouldn't be, there always had been. This didn't strike me as entirely conclusive. I said, we'd better put some in, and see what happened. She said, why not use snow? But I thought not. There was an idea at the back of my mind that there was some reason why it was unwise to use melted snow, and it wasn't until I arrived with a bucketful that I remembered what it was. Of course – goitre.

When I got back to her she'd got the radiator cap off, and inserted what a Danish friend of mine calls a 'funeral'. We poured a little water in . . . Luckily I'd warned her to stand clear. The first tablespoonful that went in came straight out again, red-hot, and blew the 'funeral' sky-high. We waited a few minutes until things had cooled down a bit, but it was no go. As fast as we poured water in it simply ran out again into the road underneath. It was quite evident that she'd been driving with the radiator bone dry, and that her engine had seized right up.

I told her so. She said:

'Does that mean I've got to stop here all night?'

I explained that it wasn't as bad as all that; that is, if she cared to accept the hospitality of my poor roof (and it *was* a poor roof – it let the wet in). But she wouldn't hear of it. By the by, she didn't know the – er – circumstances, so it wasn't that. No, she wanted to leave the car where it was and go on on foot.

I said:

'Don't be silly, it's miles to anywhere.'

However, at that moment we heard a car coming along the road, the same way as she'd come. We could see its lights, too, although it was a very long way off. You know how flat Norfolk is – you can see a terrific distance.

I said:

'There's the way out of all your troubles. This thing, whatever it is, will give you a tow to the nearest garage, or at any rate a lift to some hotel.'

One would have expected her to show some relief, but she didn't. I began to wonder what she jolly well *did* want. She wouldn't let me help her to stop where she was, and she didn't seem anxious for anyone to help her to go anywhere else.

She was quite peculiar about it. She gripped hold of my arm, and said:

'What do you think this is that's coming?'

I said:

'I'm sure I don't know, being a stranger in these parts, but it sounds like a lorry full of milk cans.'

I offered to lay her sixpence about it (this was before the betting tax came in). She'd have had to pay, too, because it *was* a lorry full of milk cans. The driver had to pull up because there wasn't room to get by.

He got down and asked if there was anything he could do to help. We explained the situation. He said he was going to Norwich, and was quite ready to give her a tow if she wanted it. However, she wouldn't do that, and it was finally decided to shove her car into my garage for the night, to be sent for next day, and the lorry was to take her along to Norwich.

Well, I managed to find the key of the garage, and the lorry-driver – Williams, his name was – and I ran the car in and locked the door. This having been done – (ablative absolute) – I suggested that it was a very cold night. Williams agreed, and said he didn't mind if he did. So I took them both indoors and mixed them a stiff whisky and water each. There wasn't any soda. And, naturally, the whole thing had left *me* very cold, too. I hadn't an overcoat on.

Up to now I hadn't seriously considered the young woman. For one thing it had been dark, *and* there had been a seized engine to look at. Er – I'm afraid that's not a very gallant remark. What I mean is that to anyone with a mechanical mind a motor car in that condition is much more interesting than – er – well, it *is* very interesting – but why labour the point? However, in the sitting-room, in the lamplight, it was possible to get more of an idea. She was a little older than I'd thought, and her eyes were too close together.

Of course, she wasn't a – how shall I put it? Her manners weren't quite easy and she was careful with her English. *You* know. But that wasn't it. She treated us with a lack of friendliness which was – well, we'd done nothing to deserve it. There was a sort of vague hostility and suspicion, which seemed rather hard lines, considering. Also, she was so anxious to keep in the shadow that if I hadn't moved the lamp away she'd never have got near the fire at all.

And the way she hurried the wretched Williams over his drink was quite distressing; and foolish, too, as *he* was going to drive, but that was her – funnel. When he'd gone out to start up his engine I asked her if she was all right for money, and she apparently was. Then they started off, and I shut up the place and went upstairs.

There happened to be a local guide-book in my bedroom, with maps in it. I looked at these and couldn't help wondering where the girl in the car had come from; I mean my road seemed so very unimportant. The sort of road one might use if one wanted to avoid people. If one were driving a stolen car, for instance. This was quite a thrilling idea. I thought it might be worth while having another look at the car. So I once more unhooked the key from the kitchen dresser and sallied forth into the snow. It was as black as pitch, and so still that my candle hardly flickered. It wasn't a large garage, and the car nearly filled it. By the by, we'd backed it in so as to make it easier to tow it out again.

The engine I'd already seen, so I squeezed past along the wall and opened the door in the body part of the car. At least, I only turned the handle, and the door was pushed open from the inside and – something – fell out on me. It pushed me quite hard, and wedged me against the wall. It also knocked the candle out of my hand and left me in the dark – which was a bit of a nuisance. I wondered what on earth the thing was – barging into me like that – so I felt it, rather gingerly, and found it was a man – a dead man – with a moustache. He'd evidently been sitting propped up against the door. I managed to put him back, as decorously as possible, and shut the door again.

After a lot of grovelling about under the car I found the candle and lighted it, and opened the opposite door and switched on the little lamp in the roof – and then – oo-er!

Of course, I had to make some sort of examination. He was an extremely tall and thin individual. He must have been well over six feet three. He was dark and very cadaverous looking. In fact, I don't suppose he'd ever looked so cadaverous in his life. He was wearing a trench coat.

It wasn't difficult to tell what he'd died of. He'd been shot through the back. I found the hole just under the right scrofula, or scalpel – what is shoulder-blade, anyway? Oh, clavicle – stupid of me – well, that's where it was, and the bullet had evidently gone through into the lung. I say 'evidently', and leave it at that.

There were no papers in his pockets, and no tailor's name on his clothes, but there was a note-case, with nine pounds in it. Altogether a most unpleasant business. Of course, it doesn't do to question the workings of Providence, but one couldn't help wishing it hadn't happened. It was just a little mysterious, too – er – who had killed him? It wasn't likely that the girl had or she wouldn't have been joy-riding about the country with him; and if someone else had murdered him why hadn't she mentioned it? Anyway, she hadn't and she'd gone, so one couldn't do anything for the time being. No telephone, of course. I just locked up the garage and went to bed. That was two o'clock.

Next morning I woke early, for some reason or other, and it occurred to me as a good idea to go and have a look at things – by daylight, and before Mrs Selston turned up. So I did. The first thing that struck me was that it had snowed heavily during the night, because there were no wheel tracks or footprints, and the second was that I'd left the key in the garage door. I opened it and went in. The place was completely empty. No car, no body, no nothing. There was a patch of grease on the floor where I'd dropped the candle, otherwise there was nothing to show I'd been there before. One of two things must have happened: either some people had come along during the night and taken the car away, or else I'd fallen asleep in front of the fire and dreamt the whole thing.

Then I remembered the whisky glasses.

They should still be in the sitting-room. I went back to look, and they were, all three of them. So it *hadn't* been a dream and the car *had* been fetched away, but they must have been jolly quiet over it.

The girl had left her glass on the mantelpiece, and it showed several very clearly defined finger-marks. Some were mine, naturally, because I'd fetched the glass from the kitchen and poured out the drink for her, but hers, her finger-marks, were clean, and mine were oily, so it was quite easy to tell them apart. It isn't necessary to point out that this glass was very important. There'd evidently been a murder, or something of that kind, and the girl must have known all about it, even if she hadn't actually done it herself, so anything she had left in the way of evidence ought to be handed over to the police; and this was all she *had* left. So I packed it up with meticulous care in an old biscuit box out of the larder.

When Mrs Selston came, I settled up with her and came back to town. Oh, I called on the landlord on the way and told him I'd 'let him know' about the bungalow. Then I caught my train, and in due course drove straight to Scotland Yard. I went up and saw my friend there. I produced the glass and asked him if his people could identify the marks. He said, 'Probably not,' but he sent it down to the fingerprint department and asked me where it came from. I said: 'Never you mind; let's have the identification first.' He said: 'All right.'

They're awfully quick, these people – the clerk was back in three minutes with a file of papers. They knew the girl all right. They told me her name and showed me her photograph; not flattering. Quite an adventurous lady, from all accounts. In the early part of her career she'd done time twice for shoplifting, chiefly in the book department. Then she'd what they call 'taken up with' a member of one of those race gangs one sometimes hears about.

My pal went on to say that there'd been a fight between two of these gangs, in the course of which her friend had got shot. She'd managed to get him away in a car, but it had broken down somewhere in Norfolk. So she'd left it and the dead man in someone's garage, and had started off for Norwich in a lorry. Only she never got there. On the way the lorry had skidded, and both she and the driver – a fellow called Williams – had been thrown out, and they'd rammed their heads against a brick wall, which everyone knows is a fatal thing to do. At least, it was in their case.

I said: 'Look here, it's all very well, but you simply can't know all this; there hasn't been time – it only happened last night.'

He said: 'Last night be blowed! It all happened in February 1919. The people you've described have been dead for years.'

I said: 'Oh!'

And to think that I might have stuck to that nine pounds!

The Leaden Ring
S. Baring-Gould

'It is not possible, Julia. I cannot conceive how the idea of attending the
county ball can have entered your head after what has happened. Poor
young Hattersley's dreadful death suffices to stop that.'

'But, Aunt, Mr Hattersley is no relation of ours.'

'No relation – but you know that the poor fellow would not have
shot himself if it had not been for you.'

'Oh, Aunt Elizabeth, how can you say so, when the verdict was that
he committed suicide when in an unsound condition of mind? How
could I help his blowing out his brains, when those brains were
deranged?'

'Julia, do not talk like this. If he did go off his head, it was you who
upset him by first drawing him on, leading him to believe that you liked
him, and then throwing him over as soon as the Hon. James Lawlor
appeared on the *tapis*. Consider: what will people say if you go to the
assembly?'

'What will they say if I do not go? They will immediately set it down
to my caring deeply for James Hattersley, and they will think that there
was some sort of engagement.'

'They are not likely to suppose that. But really, Julia, you were for a
while all smiles and encouragement. Tell me, now, did Mr Hattersley
propose to you?'

'Well – yes, he did, and I refused him.'

'And then he went and shot himself in despair. Julia, you cannot
with any face go to the ball.'

'Nobody knows that he proposed. And precisely because I do go
everyone will conclude that he did not propose. I do not wish it to be
supposed that he did.'

'His family, of course, must have been aware. They will see your
name among those present at the assembly.'

'Aunt, they are in too great trouble to look at the paper to see who
were at the dance.'

'His terrible death lies at your door. How you can have the heart, Julia ...'

'I don't see it. Of course, I feel it. I am awfully sorry, and awfully sorry for his father, the admiral. I cannot bring him to life again. I wish that when I rejected him he had gone and done as did Joe Pomeroy, marry one of his landlady's daughters.'

'There, Julia, is another of your deliquencies. You lured on young Pomeroy till he proposed, then you refused him, and in a fit of vexation and mortified vanity he married a girl greatly beneath him in social position. If the *ménage* proves a failure you will have it on your conscience that you have wrecked his life and perhaps hers as well.'

'I cannot throw myself away as a charity to save this man or that from doing a foolish thing.'

'What I complain of, Julia, is that you encouraged young Mr Pomeroy till Mr Hattersley appeared, whom you thought more eligible, and then you tossed him aside; and you did precisely the same with James Hattersley as soon as you came to know Mr Lawlor. After all, Julia, I am not so sure that Mr Pomeroy has not chosen the better part. The girl, I dare say, is simple, fresh, and affectionate.'

'Your implication is not complimentary, Aunt Elizabeth.'

'My dear, I have no patience with the young lady of the present day, who is shallow, self-willed, and indifferent to the feelings and happiness of others, who craves excitement and pleasures, and desires nothing that is useful and good. Where now will you see a girl like Viola's sister, who let concealment, like a worm i' the bud, feed on her damask cheek? Nowadays a girl lays herself at the feet of a man if she likes him, turns herself inside out to let him and all the world read her heart.'

'I have no relish to be like Viola's sister, and have my story – a blank. I never grovelled at the feet of Joe Pomeroy or James Hattersley.'

'No, but you led each to consider himself the favoured one till he proposed, and then you refused him. It was like smiling at a man and then stabbing him to the heart.'

'Well – I don't want people to think that James Hattersley cared for me – I certainly never cared for him – nor that he proposed; so I shall go to the ball.'

Julia Demant was an orphan. She had been kept at school till she was eighteen, and then had been removed just at the age when a girl begins to take an interest in her studies, and not to regard them as drudgery. On her removal she had cast away all that she had acquired, and had been plunged into the whirl of Society. Then suddenly her father died – she had lost her mother some years before – and she went to live with her aunt, Miss Flemming. Julia had inherited a sum of about five hundred pounds a year, and would probably come in for a good estate and funds as well on the death of her aunt. She had been

flattered as a girl at home, and at school as a beauty, and she certainly
thought no small bones of herself.

Miss Flemming was an elderly lady with a sharp tongue, very
outspoken, and very decided in her opinions; but her action was weak,
and Julia soon discovered that she could bend the aunt to do anything
she willed, though she could not modify or alter her opinions.

In the matter of Joe Pomeroy and James Hattersley, it was as Miss
Flemming had said. Julia had encouraged Mr Pomeroy, and had only
cast him off because she thought better of the suit of Mr Hattersley, son
of an admiral of that name. She had seen a good deal of young
Hattersley, had given him every encouragement, had so entangled him,
that he was madly in love with her; and then, when she came to know
the Hon. James Lawlor, and saw that he was fascinated, she rejected
Hattersley with the consequences alluded to in the conversation above
given.

Julia was particularly anxious to be present at the county ball, for
she had been already booked by Mr Lawlor for several dances, and she
was quite resolved to make an attempt to bring him to a declaration.

On the evening of the ball Miss Flemming and Julia entered the
carriage. The aunt had given way, as was her wont, but under protest.

For about ten minutes neither spoke, and then Miss Flemming said,
'Well, you know my feelings about this dance. I do not approve. I
distinctly disapprove. I do not consider your going to the ball in good
taste, or, as you would put it, in good form. Poor young Hattersley . . .'

'Oh, dear Aunt, do let us put young Hattersley aside. He was buried
with the regular forms, I suppose?'

'Yes, Julia.'

'Then the rector accepted the verdict of the jury at the inquest. Why
should not we? A man who is unsound in his mind is not responsible for
his actions.'

'I suppose not.'

'Much less, then, I who live ten miles away.'

'I do not say that you are responsible for his death, but for the
condition of mind that led him to do the dreadful deed. Really, Julia,
you are one of those into whose head or heart only by a surgical
operation could the thought be introduced that you could be in the
wrong. A hypodermic syringe would be too weak an instrument to effect
such a radical change in you. Everyone else may be in the wrong, you –
never. As for me, I cannot get young Hattersley out of my head.'

'And I,' retorted Julia with asperity, for her aunt's words had stung
her – 'I, for my part, do not give him a thought.'

She had hardly spoken the words before a chill wind began to pass
round her. She drew the Barege shawl that was over her bare shoulders
closer about her, and said, 'Auntie! is the glass down on your side?'

'No, Julia; why do you ask?'

'There is such a draught.'

'Draught! – I do not feel one; perhaps the window on your side hitches.'

'Indeed, that is all right. It is blowing harder and is deadly cold. Can one of the front panes be broken?'

'No. Rogers would have told me had that been the case. Besides, I can see that they are sound.'

The wind of which Julia complained swirled and whistled about her. It increased in force; it plucked at her shawl and slewed it about her throat; it tore at the lace on her dress. It snatched at her hair, it wrenched it away from the pins, the combs that held it in place; one long tress was lashed across the face of Miss Flemming. Then the hair, completely released, eddied up above the girl's head, and the next moment was carried as a drift before her, blinding her. Then – a sudden explosion, as though a gun had been fired into her ear; and with a scream of terror she sank back among the cushions. Miss Flemming, in great alarm, pulled the check-string, and the carriage stopped. The footman descended from the box and came to the side. The old lady drew down the window and said: 'Oh! Phillips, bring the lamp. Something has happened to Miss Demant.'

The man obeyed, and sent a flood of light into the carriage. Julia was lying back, white and senseless. Her hair was scattered over her face, neck, and shoulders; the flowers that had been stuck in it, the pins that had fastened it in place, the pads that had given shape to the convolutions lay strewn, some on her lap, some in the rug at the bottom of the carriage.

'Phillips!' ordered the old lady in great agitation, 'tell Rogers to turn the horses and drive home at once; and you run as fast you can for Dr Crate.'

A few minutes after the carriage was again in motion, Julia revived. Her aunt was chafing her hand.

'Oh, Aunt!' she said, 'are all the glasses broken?'

'Broken – what glasses?'

'Those of the carriage – with the explosion.'

'Explosion, my dear!'

'Yes. That gun which was discharged. It stunned me. Were you hurt?'

'I heard no gun – no explosion.'

'But I did. It was as though a bullet had been discharged into my brain. I wonder that I escaped. Who can have fired at us?'

'My dear, no one fired. I heard nothing. I know what it was. I had the same experience many years ago. I slept in a damp bed, and awoke stone deaf in my right ear. I remained so for three weeks. But one night when I was at a ball and was dancing, all at once I heard a report as of a pistol in my right ear, and immediately heard quite clearly again. It was wax.'

'But, Aunt Elizabeth, I have not been deaf.'

'You have not noticed that you were deaf.'

'Oh! but look at my hair; it was that wind that blew it about.'

'You are labouring under a delusion, Julia. There was no wind.'

'But look – feel how my hair is down.'

'That has been done by the motion of the carriage. There are many ruts in the road.'

They reached home, and Julia, feeling sick, frightened and bewildered, retired to bed. Dr Crate arrived, said that she was hysterical, and ordered something to soothe her nerves. Julia was not convinced. The explanation offered by Miss Flemming did not satisfy her. That she was a victim to hysteria she did not in the least believe. Neither her aunt, nor the coachman, nor Phillips had heard the discharge of a gun. As to the rushing wind, Julia was satisfied that she had experienced it. The lace was ripped, as by a hand, from her dress, and the shawl was twisted about her throat; besides, her hair had not been so slightly arranged that the jolting of the carriage would completely disarrange it. She was vastly perplexed over what she had undergone. She thought and thought, but could get no nearer to a solution of the mystery.

Next day, as she was almost herself again, she rose and went about as usual.

In the afternoon the Hon. James Lawlor called and asked after Miss Flemming. The butler replied that his mistress was out making calls, but that Miss Demant was at home, and he believed was on the terrace. Mr Lawlor at once asked to see her.

He did not find Julia in the parlour or on the terrace, but in a lower garden to which she had descended to feed the goldfish in the pond.

'Oh! Miss Demant,' said he, 'I was so disappointed not to see you at the ball last night.'

'I was very unwell; I had a fainting fit and could not go.'

'It threw a damp on our spirits – that is to say, on mine. I had you booked for several dances.'

'You were able to give them to others.'

'But that was not the same to me. I did an act of charity and self-denial. I danced instead with the ugly Miss Burgons and with Miss Pounding, and that was like dragging about a sack of potatoes. I believe it would have been a jolly evening, but for that shocking affair of young Hattersley which kept some of the better sort away. I mean those who knew the Hattersleys. Of course, for me that did not matter, we were not acquainted. I never even spoke with the fellow. You knew him, I believe? I heard some people say so, and that you had not come because of him. The supper, for a subscription ball, was not atrociously bad.'

'What did they say of me?'

'Oh! – if you will know – that you did not attend the ball because you liked him very much, and were awfully cut up.'

'I – I! What a shame that people should talk! I never cared a rush for him. He was nice enough in his way, not a bounder, but tolerable as young men go.'

Mr Lawlor laughed. 'I should not relish to have such a qualified estimate made of me.'

'Nor need you. You are interesting. He became so only when he had shot himself. It will be by this alone that he will be remembered.'

'But there is no smoke without fire. Did he like you – much?'

'Dear Mr Lawlor, I am not a clairvoyante, and never was able to see into the brains or hearts of people – least of all of young men. Perhaps it is fortunate for me that I cannot.'

'One lady told me that he had proposed to you.'

'Who was that? The potato-sack?'

'I will not give her name. Is there any truth in it? Did he?'

'No.'

At the moment she spoke there sounded in her ear a whistle of wind, and she felt a current like a cord of ice creep round her throat, increasing in force and compression; her hat was blown off, and next instant a detonation rang through her head as though a gun had been fired into her ear. She uttered a cry and sank upon the ground.

James Lawlor was bewildered. His first impulse was to run to the house for assistance; then he considered that he could not leave her lying on the wet soil, and he stooped to raise her in his arms and to carry her within. In novels young men perform such a feat without difficulty; but in fact they are not able to do it, especially when the girl is tall and big-boned. Moreover, one in a faint is a dead weight. Lawlor staggered under his burden to the steps. It was as much as he could perform to carry her up to the terrace, and there he placed her on a seat. Panting, and with his muscles quivering after the strain, he hastened to the drawing-room, rang the bell, and when the butler appeared, he gasped: 'Miss Demant has fainted; you and I and the footman must carry her within.'

'She fainted last night in the carriage,' said the butler.

When Julia came to her senses, she was in bed attended by the housekeeper and her maid. A few moments later Miss Flemming arrived.

'Oh, Aunt! I have heard it again.'

'Heard what, dear?'

'The discharge of a gun.'

'It is nothing but wax,' said the old lady. 'I will drop a little sweet-oil into your ear, and then have it syringed with warm water.'

'I want to tell you something – in private.'

Miss Flemming signed to the servants to withdraw.

'Aunt,' said the girl, 'I must say something. This is the second time that this has happened. I am sure it is significant. James Lawlor was with me in the sunken garden, and he began to speak about James Hattersley. You know it was when we were talking about him last night that I heard that awful noise. It was precisely as if a gun had been discharged into my ear. I felt as if all the nerves and tissues of my head were being torn, and all the bones of my skull shattered – just what Mr Hattersley must have undergone when he pulled the trigger. It was an agony for a moment perhaps, but it felt as if it lasted an hour. Mr Lawlor had asked me point blank if James Hattersley had proposed to me, and I said, "No." I was perfectly justified in so answering, because he had no right to ask me such a question. It was an impertinence on his part, and I answered him shortly and sharply with a negative.

'But actually James Hattersley proposed twice to me. He would not accept a first refusal, but came next day bothering me again, and I was pretty curt with him. He made some remarks that were rude about how I had treated him, and which I will not repeat, and as he left, in a state of great agitation, he said, "Julia, I vow that you shall not forget this, and you shall belong to no one but me, alive or dead." I considered this great nonsense, and did not accord it another thought. But, really, these terrible annoyances, this wind and the bursts of noise, do seem to me to come from him. It is just as though he felt a malignant delight in distressing me, now that he is dead. I should like to defy him, and I will do it if I can, but I cannot bear more of these experiences – they will kill me.'

Several days elapsed.

Mr Lawlor called repeatedly to enquire, but a week passed before Julia was sufficiently recovered to receive him, and then the visit was one of courtesy and of sympathy, and the conversation turned upon her health, and on indifferent themes.

But some few days later it was otherwise. She was in the conservatory alone, pretty much herself again, when Mr Lawlor was announced.

Physically she had recovered, or believed that she had, but her nerves had actually received a severe shock. She had made up her mind that the phenomena of the circling wind and the explosion were in some mysterious manner connected with Hattersley.

She bitterly resented this, but she was in mortal terror of a recurrence; and she felt no compunction for her treatment of the unfortunate young man, but rather a sense of deep resentment against him. If he were dead, why did he not lie quiet and cease from vexing her?

To be a martyr was to her no gratification, for hers was not a martyrdom that provoked sympathy, and which could make her interesting.

She had hitherto supposed that when a man died there was an end of him; his condition was determined for good or for ill. But that a disembodied spirit should hover about and make itself a nuisance to the living, had never entered into her calculations.

'Julia – if I may be allowed so to call you——' began Mr Lawlor, 'I have brought you a bouquet of flowers. Will you accept them?'

'Oh!' she said, as he handed the bunch to her, 'how kind of you. At this time of the year they are so rare, and Aunt's gardener is so miserly that he will spare me none for my room but some miserable bits of geranium. It is too bad of you wasting your money like this upon me.'

'It is no waste, if it affords you pleasure.'

'It is a pleasure. I dearly love flowers.'

'To give you pleasure,' said Mr Lawlor, 'is the great object of my life. If I could assure you happiness – if you would allow me to hope – to seize this opportunity, now that we are alone together ...'

He drew near and caught her hand. His features were agitated, his lips trembled, there was earnestness in his eyes.

At once a cold blast touched Julia and began to circle about her and to flutter her hair. She trembled and drew back. That paralysing experience was about to be renewed. She turned deadly white, and put her hand to her right ear. 'Oh, James! James!' she gasped. 'Do not, pray do not speak what you want to say, or I shall faint. It is coming on. I am not yet well enough to hear it. Write to me and I will answer. For pity's sake do not speak it.' Then she sank upon a seat – and at that moment her aunt entered the conservatory.

On the following day a note was put into her hand, containing a formal proposal from the Hon. James Lawlor; and by return of post Julia answered with an acceptance.

There was no reason whatever why the engagement should be long; and the only alternative mooted was whether the wedding should take place before or after Easter. Finally, it was settled that it should be celebrated on Shrove Tuesday. This left a short time for the necessary preparations, Miss Flemming would have to go to town with her niece concerning a trousseau, and a trousseau is not turned out rapidly any more than an armed cruiser.

There is usually a certain period allowed to young people who have become engaged to see much of each other, to get better acquainted with one another, to build their castles in the air, and to indulge in little passages of affection, vulgarly called 'spooning'. But in this case the spooning had to be curtailed and postponed.

At the outset, when alone with James, Julia was nervous. She feared a recurrence of those phenomena that so affected her. But, although every now and then the wind curled and soughed about her, it was not violent, nor was it chilling; and she came to regard it as a wail of discomfiture. Moreover, there was no recurrence of the detonation, and she fondly hoped that with her marriage the vexation would completely cease.

In her heart was deep down a sense of exultation. She was defying James Hattersley and setting his prediction at naught. She was not in love with Mr Lawlor; she liked him, in her cold manner, and was not insensible to the social advantage that would be hers when she became the Honourable Mrs Lawlor.

The day of the wedding arrived. Happily it was fine. 'Blessed is the bride the sun shines on,' said the cheery Miss Flemming; 'an omen, I trust, of a bright and unruffled life in your new condition.'

All the neighbourhood was present at the church. Miss Flemming had many friends. Mr Lawlor had fewer present, as he belonged to a distant county. The church path had been laid with red cloth, the church decorated with flowers, and a choir was present to twitter 'The voice that breathed o'er Eden'.

The rector stood by the altar, and two cushions had been laid at the chancel steps. The rector was to be assisted by an uncle of the bridegroom who was in Holy orders; the rector, being old-fashioned, had drawn on pale grey kid gloves.

First arrived the bridegroom with his best man, and stood in a nervous condition balancing himself first on one foot, then on the other, waiting, observed by all eyes.

Next entered the procession of the bride, attended by her maids, to the 'Wedding March' in *Lohengrin*, on a wheezy organ. Then Julia and her intended took their places at the chancel step for the performance of the first portion of the ceremony, and the two clergy descended to them from the altar.

'Wilt thou have this woman to thy wedded wife?'

'I will.'

'Wilt thou have this man to thy wedded husband?'

'I will.'

'I, James, take thee, Julia, to my wedded wife, to have and to hold ...' and so on.

As the words were being spoken, a cold rush of air passed over the clasped hands, numbing them, and began to creep round the bride, and to flutter her veil. She set her lips and knitted her brows. In a few moments she would be beyond the reach of these manifestations.

When it came to her turn to speak, she began firmly: 'I, Julia, take thee, James ...' but as she proceeded the wind became fierce; it raged about her, it caught her veil on one side and buffeted her cheek, it switched the veil about her throat, as though strangling her with a drift of snow contracting into ice. But she persevered to the end.

Then James Lawlor produced the ring, and was about to place it on her finger with the prescribed words: 'With this ring I thee wed ...' when a report rang in her ear, followed by a heaving of her skull, as though the bones were being burst asunder, and she sank unconscious on the chancel step.

In the midst of profound commotion, she was raised and conveyed to the vestry, followed by James Lawlor, trembling and pale. He had slipped the ring back into his waistcoat pocket. Dr Crate, who was present, hastened to offer his professional assistance.

In the vestry Julia rested in a Glastonbury chair, white and still, with her hands resting in her lap. And to the amazement of those present, it was seen that on the third finger of her left hand was a leaden ring, rude and solid as though fashioned out of a bullet. Restoratives were applied, but fully a quarter of an hour elapsed before Julia opened her eyes, and a little colour returned to her lips and cheek. But, as she raised her hands to her brow to wipe away the damp that had formed on it, her eye caught sight of the leaden ring, and with a cry of horror she sank again into insensibility.

The congregation slowly left the church, awestruck, whispering, asking questions, receiving no satisfactory answers, forming surmises all incorrect.

'I am very much afraid, Mr Lawlor,' said the rector, 'that it will be impossible to proceed with the service today; it must be postponed till Miss Demant is in a condition to conclude her part, and to sign the register. I do not see how it can be gone on with today. She is quite unequal to the effort.'

The carriage which was to have conveyed the couple to Miss Flemming's house, and then, later, to have taken them to the station for their honeymoon, the horses decorated with white rosettes, the whip adorned with a white bow, had now to convey Julia, hardly conscious, supported by her aunt, to her home.

No rice could be thrown. The bell-ringers, prepared to give a joyous peal, were constrained to depart.

The reception at Miss Flemming's was postponed. No one thought of attending. The cakes, the ices, were consumed in the kitchen.

The bridegroom, bewildered, almost frantic, ran hither and thither, not knowing what to do, what to say.

Julia lay as a stone for fully two hours; and when she came to herself could not speak. When conscious, she raised her left hand, looked on the leaden ring, and sank back into senselessness.

Not till late in the evening was she sufficiently recovered to speak, and then she begged her aunt, who had remained by her bed without stirring, to dismiss attendants. She desired to speak with her alone. When no one was in the room with her, save Miss Flemming, she said in a whisper: 'Oh, Aunt Elizabeth! Oh, Auntie! Such an awful thing has happened. I can never marry Mr Lawlor, never. I have married James Hattersley; I am a dead man's wife. At the time that James Lawlor was making the responses, I heard a piping voice in my ear, an unearthly voice, saying the same words. When I said: "I, Julia, take you, James, to my wedded husband" – you know Mr Hattersley is James as well as Mr Lawlor – then the words applied to him as much or as well as to the other. And then, when it came to the giving of the ring, there was the explosion in my ear, as before – and the leaden ring was forced on to my finger, and not James Lawlor's golden ring. It is of no use my resisting any more. I am a dead man's wife, and I cannot marry James Lawlor.'

Some years have elapsed since that disastrous day and that incomplete marriage.

Miss Demant is Miss Demant still, and she has never been able to remove the leaden ring from the third finger of her left hand. Whenever the attempt has been made, either to disengage it by drawing it off or by cutting through it, there has ensued that terrifying discharge as of a gun into her ear, causing insensibility. The prostration that has followed, the terror it has inspired, have so affected her nerves, that she has desisted from every attempt to rid herself of the ring.

She invariably wears a glove on her left hand, and it is bulged over the third finger, where lies the leaden ring.

She is not a happy woman, although her aunt is dead and has left her a handsome estate. She has not got many acquaintances. She has no friends; for her temper is unamiable, and her tongue is bitter. She supposes that the world, as far as she knows it, is in league against her.

Towards the memory of James Hattersley she entertains a deadly hate. If an incantation could lay his spirit, if prayer could give him repose, she would have recourse to none of these expedients, even though they might relieve her, so bitter is her resentment. And she harbours a silent wrath against Providence for allowing the dead to walk and to molest the living.

The Middle Toe of the Right Foot
Ambrose Bierce

It is well known that the old Manton house is haunted. In all the rural district near about, and even in the town of Marshall, a mile away, not one person of unbiased mind entertains a doubt of it; incredulity is confined to those opinionated people who will be called 'cranks' as soon as the useful word shall have penetrated the intellectual demesne of the Marshall *Advance*. The evidence that the house is haunted is of two kinds: the testimony of disinterested witnesses who have had ocular proof, and that of the house itself. The former may be disregarded and ruled out on any of the various grounds of objection which may be urged against it by the ingenious; but facts within the observation of all are fundamental and controlling.

In the first place, the Manton house has been unoccupied by mortals for more than ten years, and with its outbuildings is slowly falling into decay – a circumstance which in itself the judicious will hardly venture to ignore. It stands a little way off the loneliest reach of the Marshall and Harriston road, in an opening which was once a farm and is still disfigured with strips of rotting fence and half covered with brambles overrunning a stony and sterile soil long unacquainted with the plough. The house itself is in tolerably good condition, though badly weather-stained and in dire need of attention from the glazier, the smaller male population of the region having attested in the manner of its kind its disapproval of dwellings without dwellers. The house is two stories in height, nearly square, its front pierced by a single doorway flanked on each side by a window boarded up to the very top. Corresponding windows above, not protected, serve to admit light and rain to the rooms of the upper floors. Grass and weeds grow pretty rankly all about, and a few shade trees, somewhat the worse for wind and leaning all in one direction, seem to be making a concerted effort to run away. In short, as the Marshall town humourist explained in the columns of the *Advance*, 'the proposition that the Manton house is badly haunted is the only logical conclusion from the premises.' The fact that in this dwelling Mr Manton thought it expedient one night some ten years ago to rise and cut the throats of his wife and two small children, removing at once to another part of the country, has no doubt done its share in directing public attention to the fitness of the place for supernatural phenomena.

To this house, one summer evening, came four men in a waggon. Three of them promptly alighted, and the one who had been driving hitched the team to the only remaining post of what had been a fence. The fourth remained seated in the waggon. 'Come,' said one of his companions, approaching him, while the others moved away in the direction of the dwelling – 'this is the place.'

The man addressed was deathly pale and trembled visibly. 'By God!' he said harshly, 'this is a trick, and it looks to me as if you were in it.'

'Perhaps I am,' the other said, looking him straight in the face and speaking in a tone which had something of contempt in it. 'You will remember, however, that the choice of place was, with your own assent, left to the other side. Of course if you are afraid of spooks——'

'I am afraid of nothing,' the man interrupted with another oath, and sprang to the ground. The two of them joined the others at the door, which one of them had already opened with some difficulty, caused by rust of lock and hinge. All entered. Inside it was dark, but the man who had unlocked the door produced a candle and matches and made a light. He then unlocked a door on their right as they stood in the passage. This gave them entrance to a large, square room, which the candle but dimly lighted. The floor had a thick carpeting of dust, which partly muffled their footfalls. Cobwebs were in the angles of the walls and depended from the ceiling like strips of rotting lace, making undulatory movements in the disturbed air. The room had two windows in adjoining sides, but from neither could anything be seen except the rough inner surfaces of boards a few inches from the glass. There was no fireplace, no furniture; there was nothing. Besides the cobwebs and the dust, the four men were the only objects there which were not a part of the architecture. Strange enough they looked in the yellow light of the candle. The one who had so reluctantly alighted was especially 'spectacular' – he might have been called sensational. He was of middle age, heavily built, deep-chested and broad-shouldered. Looking at his figure, one would have said that he had a giant's strength; at his face, that he would use it like a giant. He was clean shaven, his hair rather closely cropped and grey. His low forehead was seamed with wrinkles above the eyes, and over the nose these became vertical. The heavy black brows followed the same law, saved from meeting only by an upward turn at what would otherwise have been the point of contact. Deeply sunken beneath these, glowed in the obscure light a pair of eyes of uncertain colour, but, obviously enough, too small. There was something forbidding in their expression, which was not bettered by the cruel mouth and wide jaw. The nose was well enough, as noses go; one does not expect much of noses. All that was sinister in the man's face seemed accentuated by an unnatural pallor – he appeared altogether bloodless.

The appearance of the other men was sufficiently commonplace: they were such persons as one meets and forgets that one met. All were younger than the man described, between whom and the eldest of the others, who stood apart, there was apparently no kindly feeling. They avoided looking at one another.

'Gentlemen,' said the man holding the candle and keys, 'I believe everything is right. Are you ready, Mr Rosser?'

The man standing apart from the group bowed and smiled.

'And you, Mr Grossmith?'

The heavy man bowed and scowled.

'You will please remove your outer clothing.'

Their hats, coats, waistcoats and neckwear were soon removed and thrown outside the door, in the passage. The man with the candle now nodded, and the fourth man – he who had urged Mr Grossmith to leave the waggon – produced from the pocket of his overcoat two long, murderous-looking bowie knives, which he drew from the scabbards.

'They are exactly alike,' he said, presenting one to each of the two principals – for by this time the dullest observer would have understood the nature of this meeting. It was to be a duel to the death.

Each combatant took a knife, examined it critically near the candle and tested the strength of blade and handle across his lifted knee. Their persons were then searched in turn, each by the second of the other.

'If it is agreeable to you, Mr Grossmith,' said the man holding the light, 'you will place yourself in that corner.'

He indicated the angle of the room farthest from the door, to which Grossmith retired, his second parting from him with a grasp of the hand which had nothing of cordiality in it. In the angle nearest the door Mr Rosser stationed himself and, after a whispered consultation, his second left him, joining the other near the door. At that moment the candle was suddenly extinguished, leaving all in profound darkness. This may have been done by a draught from the open door; whatever the cause, the effect was appalling!

'Gentlemen,' said a voice which sounded strangely unfamiliar in the altered condition affecting the relations of the senses, 'gentlemen, you will not move until you hear the closing of the outer door.'

A sound of trampling ensued, the closing of the inner door, and finally the outer one closed with a concussion which shook the entire building.

A few minutes later a belated farmer's boy met a waggon which was being driven furiously towards the town of Marshall. He declared that behind the two figures on the front seat stood a third with its hands upon

the bowed shoulders of the others, who appeared to struggle vainly to
free themselves from its grasp. This figure, unlike the others, was clad in
white, and had undoubtedly boarded the waggon as it passed the
haunted house. As the lad could boast a considerable former experience
with the supernatural thereabout, his word had the weight justly due to
the testimony of an expert. The story eventually appeared in the *Advance*,
with some slight literary embellishments and a concluding intimation
that the gentlemen referred to would be allowed the use of the paper's
columns for their version of the night's adventure. But the privilege
remained without a claimant.

*   *   *

The events which led up to this 'duel in the dark' were simple enough.
One evening three young men of the town of Marshall were sitting in a
quiet corner of the porch of the village hotel, smoking and discussing
such matters as three educated young men of a Southern village would
naturally find interesting. Their names were King, Sancher and Rosser.
At a little distance, within easy hearing but taking no part in the
conversation, sat a fourth. He was a stranger to the others. They merely
knew that on his arrival by the stage coach that afternoon he had written
in the hotel register the name Robert Grossmith. He had not been
observed to speak to anyone except the hotel clerk. He seemed, indeed,
singularly fond of his own company – or, as the *personnel* of the *Advance*
expressed it, 'grossly addicted to evil associations.' But then it should be
said in justice to the stranger that the *personnel* was himself of a too
convivial disposition fairly to judge one differently gifted, and had,
moreover, experienced a slight rebuff in an effort at an 'interview'.

   'I hate any kind of deformity in a woman,' said King, 'whether
natural or – or acquired. I have a theory that any physical defect has its
correlative mental and moral defect.'

   'I infer, then,' said Rosser, gravely, 'that a lady lacking the
advantage of a nose would find the struggle to become Mrs King an
arduous enterprise.'

   'Of course you may put it that way,' was the reply; 'but, seriously, I
once threw over a most charming girl on learning, quite accidentally,
that she had suffered amputation of a toe. My conduct was brutal, if you
like, but if I had married that girl I should have been miserable and
should have made her so.'

   'Whereas,' said Sancher, with a light laugh, 'by marrying a
gentleman of more liberal views she escaped with a cut throat.'

   'Ah, you know to whom I refer! Yes, she married Manton, but I
don't know about his liberality; I'm not sure but he cut her throat
because he discovered that she lacked that excellent thing in woman, the
middle toe of the right foot.'

'Look at that chap!' said Rosser in a low voice, his eyes fixed upon the stranger.

That person was obviously listening intently to the conversation.

'That's an easy one,' Rosser replied, rising. 'Sir,' he continued, addressing the stranger, 'I think it would be better if you would remove your chair to the other end of the verandah. The presence of gentlemen is evidently an unfamiliar situation to you.'

The man sprang to his feet and strode forward with clenched hands, his face white with rage. All were now standing. Sancher stepped between the belligerents.

'You are hasty and unjust,' he said to Rosser; 'this gentleman has done nothing to deserve such language.'

But Rosser would not withdraw a word. By the custom of the country and the time, there could be but one outcome to the quarrel.

'I demand the satisfaction due to a gentleman,' said the stranger, who had become more calm. 'I have not an acquaintance in this region. Perhaps you, sir,' bowing to Sancher, 'will be kind enough to represent me in this matter.'

Sancher accepted the trust – somewhat reluctantly, it must be confessed, for the man's appearance and manner were not at all to his liking. King, who during the colloquy had hardly removed his eyes from the stranger's face, and had not spoken a word, consented with a nod to act for Rosser, and the upshot of it was that, the principals having retired, a meeting was arranged for the next evening. The nature of the arrangements has been already disclosed. The duel with knives in a dark room was once a commoner feature of South-western life than it is likely to be again. How thin a veneering of 'chivalry' covered the essential brutality of the code under which such encounters were possible, we shall see.

* * *

In the blaze of a midsummer noonday, the old Manton house was hardly true to its traditions. It was of the earth, earthy. The sunshine caressed it warmly and affectionately, with evident unconsciousness of its bad reputation. The grass greening all the expanse in its front seemed to grow, not rankly, but with a natural and joyous exuberance, and the weeds blossomed quite like plants. Full of charming lights and shadows, and populous with pleasant-voiced birds, the neglected shade trees no longer struggled to run away, but bent reverently beneath their burdens of sun and song. Even in the glassless upper windows was an expression of peace and contentment, due to the light within. Over the stony fields the visible heat danced with a lively tremor incompatible with the gravity which is an attribute of the supernatural.

Such was the aspect under which the place presented itself to Sheriff Adams and the two other men who had come out from Marshall to look at it. One of these men was Mr King, the sheriff's deputy; the other, whose name was Brewer, was a brother of the late Mrs Manton. Under a beneficent law of the State relating to property which has been for a certain period abandoned by its owner, whose residence cannot be ascertained, the sheriff was the legal custodian of the Manton farm and the appurtenances thereunto belonging. His present visit was in mere perfunctory compliance with some order of a court in which Mr Brewer had an action to get possession of the property as heir to his deceased sister. By a mere coincidence the visit was made on the day after the night that Deputy King had unlocked the house for another and very different purpose. His presence now was not of his own choosing: he had been ordered to accompany his superior, and at the moment could think of nothing more prudent than simulated alacrity in obedience. He had intended going anyhow, but in other company.

Carelessly opening the front door, which to his surprise was not locked, the sheriff was amazed to see, lying on the floor of the passage into which it opened, a confused heap of men's apparel. Examination showed it to consist of two hats, and the same number of coats, waistcoats and scarves, all in a remarkably good state of preservation, albeit somewhat defiled by the dust in which they lay. Mr Brewer was equally astonished, but Mr King's emotion is not on record. With a new and lively interest in his own actions, the sheriff now unlatched and pushed open a door on the right, and the three entered. The room was apparently vacant – no; as their eyes became accustomed to the dimmer light, something was visible in the farthest angle of the wall. It was a human figure – that of a man crouching close in the corner. Something in the attitude made the intruders halt when they had barely passed the threshold. The figure more and more clearly defined itself. The man was on one knee, his back in the angle of the wall, his shoulders elevated to the level of his ears, his hands before his face, palms outward, the fingers spread and crooked like claws; the white face turned upward on the retracted neck had an expression of unutterable fright, the mouth half open, the eyes incredibly expanded. He was stone dead – dead of terror! Yet, with the exception of a knife, which had evidently fallen from his own hand, not another object was in the room.

In the thick dust which covered the floor were some confused footprints near the door and along the wall through which it opened. Along one of the adjoining walls, too, past the boarded-up windows, was the trail made by the man himself in reaching his corner. Instinctively in approaching the body the three men now followed that trail. The sheriff grasped one of the out-thrown arms; it was as rigid as iron, and the application of a gentle force rocked the entire body without altering the relation of its parts. Brewer, pale with terror, gazed intently into the distorted face. 'God of mercy!' he suddenly cried, 'it is Manton!'

'You are right,' said King, with an evident attempt at calmness: 'I knew Manton. He then wore a full beard and his hair long, but this is he.'

He might have added: 'I recognized him when he challenged Rosser. I told Rosser and Sancher who he was before we played him this horrible trick. When Rosser left this dark room at our heels, forgetting his clothes in the excitement, and driving away with us in his shirt – all through the discreditable proceedings we knew whom we were dealing with, murderer and coward that he was!'

But nothing of this did Mr King say. With his better light he was trying to penetrate the mystery of the man's death. That he had not once moved from the corner where he had been stationed, that his posture was that of neither attack nor defence, that he had dropped his weapon, that he had obviously perished of sheer terror of something that he *saw* – these were circumstances which Mr King's disturbed intelligence could not rightly comprehend.

Groping in intellectual darkness for a clue to his maze of doubt, his gaze directed mechanically downward, as is the way of one who ponders momentous matters, fell upon something which, there, in the light of day, and in the presence of living companions, struck him with an invincible terror. In the dust of years that lay thick upon the floor – leading from the door by which they had entered, straight across the room to within a yard of Manton's crouching corpse – were three parallel lines of footprints – light but definite impressions of bare feet, the outer ones those of small children, the inner a woman's. From the point at which they ended they did not return; they pointed all one way. Brewer, who had observed them at the same moment, was leaning forward in an attitude of rapt attention, horribly pale.

'Look at that!' he cried, pointing with both hands at the nearest print of the woman's right foot, where she had apparently stopped and stood. 'The middle toe is missing – it was Gertrude!'

Gertrude was the late Mrs Manton, sister to Mr Brewer.

Keeping His Promise
Algernon Blackwood

It was eleven o'clock at night, and young Marriott was locked into his room, cramming as hard as he could cram. He was a Fourth Year Man at Edinburgh University and he had been ploughed for this particular examination so often that his parents had positively declared they could no longer supply the funds to keep him there.

His rooms were cheap and dingy, but it was the lecture fees that took the money. So Marriott pulled himself together at last and definitely made up his mind that he would pass or die in the attempt, and for some weeks now he had been reading as hard as mortal man can read. He was trying to make up for lost time and money in a way that showed conclusively he did not understand the value of either. For no ordinary man – and Marriott was in every sense an ordinary man – can afford to drive the mind as he had lately been driving his, without sooner or later paying the cost.

Among the students he had few friends or acquaintances, and these few had promised not to disturb him at night, knowing he was at last reading in earnest. It was, therefore, with feelings a good deal stronger than mere surprise that he heard his doorbell ring on this particular night and realized that he was to have a visitor. Some men would simply have muffled the bell and gone on quietly with their work. But Marriott was not this sort. He was nervous. It would have bothered and pecked at his mind all night long not to know who the visitor was and what he wanted. The only thing to do, therefore, was to let him in – and out again – as quickly as possible.

The landlady went to bed at ten o'clock punctually, after which hour nothing would induce her to pretend she heard the bell, so Marriott jumped up from his books with an exclamation that augured ill for the reception of his caller, and prepared to let him in with his own hand.

The streets of Edinburgh town were very still at this late hour – it was late for Edinburgh – and in the quiet neighbourhood of F—— Street, where Marriott lived on the third floor, scarcely a sound broke the silence. As he crossed the floor, the bell rang a second time, with unnecessary clamour, and he unlocked the door and passed into the little hall-way with considerable wrath and annoyance in his heart at the insolence of the double interruption.

'The fellows all know I'm reading for this exam. Why in the world do they come to bother me at such an unearthly hour?'

The inhabitants of the building, with himself, were medical students, general students, poor Writers to the Signet, and some others whose vocations were perhaps not so obvious. The stone staircase, dimly lighted at each floor by a gas jet that would not turn above a certain height, wound down to the level of the street with no pretence at carpet or railing. At some levels it was cleaner than at others. It depended on the landlady of the particular level.

The acoustic properties of a spiral staircase seem to be peculiar. Marriott, standing by the open door, book in hand, thought every moment the owner of the footsteps would come into view. The sound of the boots was so close and so loud that they seemed to travel disproportionately in advance of their cause. Wondering who it could be, he stood ready with all manner of sharp greetings for the man who dared thus to disturb his work. But the man did not appear. The steps sounded almost under his nose, yet no one was visible.

A sudden queer sensation of fear passed over him – a faintness and a shiver down the back. It went, however, almost as soon as it came, and he was just debating whether he would call aloud to his invisible visitor, or slam the door and return to his books, when the cause of the disturbance turned the corner very slowly and came into view.

It was a stranger. He saw a youngish man, short of figure and very broad. His face was the colour of a piece of chalk, and the eyes, which were very bright, had heavy lines underneath them. Though the cheeks and chin were unshaven and the general appearance unkempt, the man was evidently a gentleman, for he was well dressed and bore himself with a certain air. But, strangest of all, he wore no hat, and carried none in his hand, and although rain had been falling steadily all the evening, he appeared to have neither overcoat nor umbrella.

A hundred questions sprang up in Marriott's mind and rushed to his lips, chief among which was something like 'Who in the world are you?' and 'What in the name of Heaven do you come to me for?' But none of these questions found time to express themselves in words, for almost at once the caller turned his head a little so that the gaslight in the hall fell upon his features from a new angle. Then in a flash Marriott recognized him.

'Field! Man alive! Is it you?' he gasped.

The Fourth Year Man was not lacking in intuition, and he perceived at once that here was a case for delicate treatment. He divined, without any actual process of thought, that the catastrophe often predicted had come at last, and that this man's father had turned him out of the house. They had been at a private school together years before, and though they had hardly met once since, the news had not failed to reach him from time to time with considerable detail, for the family lived near his own, and between certain of the sisters there was great intimacy. Young Field had gone wild later, he remembered hearing about it all – drink, a woman, opium, or something of the sort – he could not exactly call to mind.

'Come in,' he said at once, his anger vanishing. 'There's been something wrong, I can see. Come in, and tell me all about it and perhaps I can help——' He hardly knew what to say, and stammered a lot more besides. The dark side of life, and the horror of it, belonged to a world that lay remote from his own select little atmosphere of books and dreamings. But he had a man's heart for all that.

He led the way across the hall, shutting the front door carefully behind him, and noticed as he did so that the other, though certainly sober, was unsteady on his legs, and evidently much exhausted. Marriott might not be able to pass his examinations, but he at least knew the symptoms of starvation – acute starvation, unless he was much mistaken – when they stared him in the face.

'Come along,' he said cheerfully, and with genuine sympathy in his voice. 'I'm glad to see you. I was going to have a bite of something to eat, and you're just in time to join me.'

The other made no audible reply, and shuffled so feebly with his feet that Marriott took his arm by way of support. He noticed for the first time that the clothes hung on him with pitiful looseness. The broad frame was literally hardly more than a frame. He was as thin as a skeleton. But, as he touched him, the sensation of faintness and dread returned. It only lasted a moment, and then passed off, and he ascribed it not unnaturally to the distress and shock of seeing a former friend in such a pitiful plight.

'Better let me guide you. It's shamefully dark – this hall. I'm always complaining,' he said lightly, recognizing by the weight upon his arm that the guidance was sorely needed, 'but the old cat never does anything except promise.' He led him to the sofa, wondering all the time where he had come from and how he had found out the address. It must be at least seven years since those days at the private school when they used to be such close friends.

'Now, if you'll forgive me for a minute,' he said, 'I'll get supper ready – such as it is. And don't bother to talk. Just take it easy on the sofa. I see you're dead tired. You can tell me about it afterwards, and we'll make plans.'

The other sat down on the edge of the sofa and stared in silence, while Marriott got out the brown loaf, scones and a huge pot of marmalade that Edinburgh students always keep in their cupboards. His eyes shone with a brightness that suggested drugs, Marriott thought, stealing a glance at him from behind the cupboard door. He did not like yet to take a full square look. The fellow was in a bad way, and it would have been so like an examination to stare and wait for explanations. Besides, he was evidently almost too exhausted to speak. So, for reasons of delicacy – and for another reason as well which he could not exactly formulate to himself – he let his visitor rest apparently unnoticed, while he busied himself with the supper. He lit the spirit-lamp to make cocoa, and when the water was boiling he drew up the table with the good things to the sofa, so that Field need not have even the trouble of moving to a chair.

'Now, let's tuck in,' he said, 'and afterwards we'll have a pipe and a chat. I'm reading for an exam, you know, and I always have something about this time. It's jolly to have a companion.'

He looked up and caught his guest's eyes directed straight upon his own. An involuntary shudder ran through him from head to foot. The face opposite him was deadly white and wore a dreadful expression of pain and mental suffering.

'By gad!' he said, jumping up, 'I quite forgot. I've got some whisky somewhere. What an ass I am. I never touch it myself when I'm working like this.'

He went to the cupboard and poured out a stiff glass which the other swallowed at a single gulp and without any water. Marriott watched him while he drank it, and at the same time noticed something else as well – Field's coat was all over dust, and on one shoulder was a bit of cobweb. It was perfectly dry; Field arrived on a soaking wet night without hat, umbrella or overcoat, and yet perfectly dry, even dusty. Therefore he had been under cover. What did it all mean? Had he been hiding in the building? . . .

It was very strange. Yet he volunteered nothing; and Marriott had pretty well made up his mind by this time that he would not ask any questions until he had eaten and slept. Food and sleep were obviously what the poor devil needed most and first – he was pleased with his powers of ready diagnosis – and it would not be fair to press him till he had recovered a bit.

They ate their supper together while the host carried on a running one-sided conversation, chiefly about himself and his exams and his 'old cat' of a landlady, so that the guest need not utter a single word unless he really wished to – which he evidently did not! But, while he toyed with his food, feeling no desire to eat, the other ate voraciously. To see a hungry man devour cold scones, stale oatcake, and brown bread laden with marmalade was a revelation to this inexperienced student who had never known what it was to be without at least three meals a day. He watched in spite of himself, wondering why the fellow did not choke in the process.

But Field seemed to be as sleepy as he was hungry. More than once his head dropped and he ceased to masticate the food in his mouth. Marriott had positively to shake him before he would go on with his meal. A stronger emotion will overcome a weaker, but this struggle between the sting of real hunger and the magical opiate of overpowering sleep was a curious sight to the student, who watched it with mingled astonishment and alarm. He had heard of the pleasure it was to feed hungry men, and watch them eat, but he had never actually witnessed it, and he had no idea it was like this. Field ate like an animal – gobbled, stuffed, gorged. Marriott forgot his reading, and began to feel something very much like a lump in his throat.

'Afraid there's been awfully little to offer you, old man,' he managed to blurt out when at length the last scone had disappeared, and the rapid, one-sided meal was at an end. Field still made no reply, for he was almost asleep in his seat. He merely looked up wearily and gratefully.

'Now you must have some sleep, you know,' he continued, 'or you'll go to pieces. I shall be up all night reading for this blessed exam. You're more than welcome to my bed. Tomorrow we'll have a late breakfast and – and see what can be done – and make plans – I'm awfully good at making plans, you know,' he added with an attempt at lightness.

Field maintained his 'dead sleepy' silence, but appeared to acquiesce, and the other led the way into the bedroom, apologizing as he did so to this half-starved son of a baronet – whose own home was almost a palace – for the size of the room. The weary guest, however, made no pretence of thanks or politeness. He merely steadied himself on his friend's arm as he staggered across the room, and then, with all his clothes on, dropped his exhausted body on the bed. In less than a minute he was to all appearances sound asleep.

For several minutes Marriott stood in the open door and watched him; praying devoutly that he might never find himself in a like predicament, and then fell to wondering what he would do with his unbidden guest on the morrow. But he did not stop long to think, for the call of his books was imperative, and happen what might, he must see to it that he passed that examination.

Having again locked the door into the hall, he sat down to his books and resumed his notes on *materia medica* where he had left off when the bell rang. But it was difficult for some time to concentrate his mind on the subject. His thoughts kept wandering to the picture of that white-faced, strange-eyed fellow, starved and dirty, lying in his clothes and boots on the bed. He recalled their schooldays together before they had drifted apart, and how they had vowed eternal friendship – and all the rest of it. And now! What horrible straits to be in. How could any man let the love of dissipation take such hold upon him?

But one of their vows together Marriott, it seemed, had completely forgotten. Just now, at any rate, it lay too far in the background of his memory to be recalled.

Through the half-open door – the bedroom led out of the sitting-room and had no other door – came the sound of deep, long-drawn breathing, the regular steady breathing of a tired man, so tired that even to listen to it made Marriott almost want to go to sleep himself.

'He needed it,' reflected the student, 'and perhaps it came only just in time!'

Perhaps so; for outside the bitter wind from across the Forth howled cruelly and drove the rain in cold streams against the window-panes, and down the deserted streets. Long before Marriott settled down again properly to his reading, he heard distinctly, as it were, through the sentences of the book, the heavy, deep breathing of the sleeper in the next room.

A couple of hours later, when he yawned and changed his books, he still heard the breathing, and went cautiously up to the door to look round.

At first the darkness of the room must have deceived him, or else his eyes were confused and dazzled by the recent glare of the reading-lamp. For a minute or two he could make out nothing at all but dark lumps of furniture, the mass of the chest of drawers by the wall, and the white patch where his bath stood in the centre of the floor.

Then the bed came slowly into view. And on it he saw the outline of the sleeping body gradually take shape before his eyes, growing up strangely into the darkness, till it stood out in marked relief – the long black form against the white counterpane.

He could hardly help smiling. Field had not moved an inch. He watched him a moment or two and then returned to his books. The night was full of the singing voices of the wind and rain. There was no sound of traffic; no hansoms clattered over the cobbles, and it was still too early for the milk-carts. He worked on steadily and conscientiously, only stopping now and again to change a book, or to sip some of the poisonous stuff that kept him awake and made his brain so active, and on these occasions Field's breathing was always distinctly audible in the room. Outside, the storm continued to howl, but inside the house all was stillness. The shade of the reading-lamp threw all the light upon the littered table, leaving the other end of the room in comparative darkness. The bedroom door was exactly opposite him where he sat. There was nothing to disturb the worker, nothing but an occasional rush of wind against the windows, and a slight pain in his arm.

This pain, however, which he was unable to account for, grew once or twice very acute. It bothered him; and he tried to remember how, and when, he could have bruised himself so severely, but without success.

At length the page before him turned from yellow to grey, and there were sounds of wheels in the street below. It was four o'clock. Marriott leaned back and yawned prodigiously. Then he drew back the curtains. The storm had subsided and the Castle Rock was shrouded in mist. With another yawn he turned away from the dreary outlook and prepared to sleep the remaining few hours till breakfast on the sofa. Field was still breathing heavily in the next room, and he first tiptoed across the floor to take another look at him.

Peering cautiously round the half-opened door his first glance fell upon the bed now plainly discernible in the grey light of morning. He stared hard. Then he rubbed his eyes. Then he rubbed his eyes again and thrust his head farther round the edge of the door. With fixed eyes, he stared harder still, and harder.

But it made no difference at all. He was staring into an empty room.

The sensation of fear he had felt when Field first appeared upon the scene returned suddenly, but with much greater force. He became conscious, too, that his left arm was throbbing violently and causing him great pain. He stood wondering, and staring, and trying to collect his thoughts. He was trembling from head to foot.

By a great effort of the will he left the support of the door and walked forward boldly into the room.

There, upon the bed, was the impress of a body, where Field had lain and slept. There was the mark of the head on the pillow, and the slight indentation at the foot of the bed where the boots had rested on the counterpane. And there, plainer than ever – for he was closer to it – was *the breathing*!

Marriott tried to pull himself together. With a great effort he found his voice and called his friend aloud by name!

'Field! Is that you? Where are you?'

There was no reply; but the breathing continued without interruption, coming directly from the bed. His voice had such an unfamiliar sound that Marriott did not care to repeat his questions, but he went down on his knees and examined the bed above and below, pulling the mattress off finally, and taking the coverings away separately one by one. But though the sounds continued there was no visible sign of Field, nor was there any space in which a human being, however small, could have concealed itself. He pulled the bed out from the wall, but the sound *stayed where it was*. It did not move with the bed.

Marriott, finding self-control a little difficult in his weary condition, at once set about a thorough search of the room. He went through the cupboard, the chest of drawers, the little alcove where the clothes hung – everything. But there was no sign of anyone. The small window near the ceiling was closed; and, anyhow, was not large enough to let a cat pass. The sitting-room door was locked on the inside; he could not have got out that way. Curious thoughts began to trouble Marriott's mind, bringing in their train unwelcome sensations. He grew more and more excited; he searched the bed again till it resembled the scene of a pillow fight; he searched both rooms, knowing all the time it was useless – and then he searched again. A cold perspiration broke out all over his body; and the sound of heavy breathing, all this time, never ceased to come from the corner where Field had lain down to sleep.

Then he tried something else. He pushed the bed back exactly into its original position – and himself lay down upon it just where his guest had lain. But the same instant he sprang up again in a single bound. The breathing was close beside him, almost on his cheek, and between him and the wall! Not even a child could have squeezed into the space.

He went back into his sitting-room, opened the windows, welcoming all the light and air possible, and tried to think the whole matter over quietly and clearly. Men who read too hard, and slept too little, he knew, were sometimes troubled with very vivid hallucinations. Again he calmly reviewed every incident of the night: his accurate sensations; the vivid details; the emotions stirred in him; the dreadful feast – no single hallucination could ever combine all these and cover so long a period of time. But with less satisfaction he thought of the recurring faintness, and curious sense of horror that had once or twice come over him, and then of the violent pains in his arm. These were quite unaccountable.

Moreover, now that he began to analyse and examine, there was one other thing that fell upon him like a sudden revelation: *during the whole time Field had not actually uttered a single word!* Yet, as though in mockery upon his reflections, there came ever from that inner room the sound of the breathing, long-drawn, deep and regular. The thing was incredible. It was absurd.

Haunted by visions of brain fever and insanity, Marriott put on his cap and mackintosh and left the house. The morning air on Arthur's Seat would blow the cobwebs from his brain; the scent of the heather, and above all, the sight of the sea. He roamed over the wet slopes above Holyrood for a couple of hours, and did not return until the exercise had shaken some of the horror out of his bones, and given him a ravening appetite into the bargain.

As he entered he saw that there was another man in the room, standing against the window with his back to the light. He recognized his fellow-student, Greene, who was reading for the same examination.

'Read hard all night, Marriott,' he said, 'and thought I'd drop in here to compare notes and have some breakfast. You're out early?' he added, by way of a question. Marriott said he had a headache and a walk had helped it, and Greene nodded and said, 'Ah!' But when the girl had set the steaming porridge on the table and gone out again, he went on with rather a forced tone, 'Didn't know you had any friends who drank, Marriott?'

This was obviously tentative, and Marriott replied dryly that he did not know it either.

'Sounds just as if some chap were "sleeping it off" in there, doesn't it, though?' persisted the other, with a nod in the direction of the bedroom, and looking curiously at his friend. The two men stared steadily at each other for several seconds, and then Marriott said earnestly:

'Then you hear it too, thank God!'

'Of course I hear it. The door's open. Sorry if I wasn't meant to.'

'Oh, I don't mean that,' said Marriott, lowering his voice. 'But I'm awfully relieved. Let me explain. Of course, if you hear it too, then it's all right; but really it frightened me more than I can tell you. I thought I was going to have brain fever, or something, and you know what a lot depends on this exam. It always begins with sounds, or visions, or some sort of beastly hallucination, and I——'

'Rot!' ejaculated the other impatiently. 'What *are* you talking about?'

'Now, listen to me, Greene,' said Marriott, as calmly as he could, for the breathing man was still plainly audible, 'and I'll tell you what I mean, only don't interrupt.' And thereupon he related exactly what had happened during the night, telling everything, even down to the pain in his arm. When it was over he got up from the table and crossed the room.

'You hear the breathing now plainly, don't you?' he said. Greene said he did. 'Well, come with me, and we'll search the room together.' The other, however, did not move from his chair.

'I've been in already,' he said sheepishly; 'I heard the sounds and thought it was you. The door was ajar – so I went in.'

Marriott made no comment, but pushed the door open as wide as it would go. As it opened, the sound of breathing grew more and more distinct.

'*Someone* must be in there,' said Greene under his breath.

'*Someone* is in there, but *where?*' said Marriott. Again he urged his friend to go in with him. But Greene refused point-blank; said he had been in once and had searched the room and there was nothing there. He would not go in again for a good deal.

They shut the door and retired into the other room to talk it all over with many pipes. Greene questioned his friend very closely, but without illuminating result, since questions cannot alter facts.

'The only thing that ought to have a proper, logical explanation is the pain in my arm,' said Marriott, rubbing that member with an attempt at a smile. 'It hurts so infernally and aches all the way up. I can't remember bruising it, though.'

'Let me examine it for you,' said Greene. 'I'm awfully good at bones in spite of the examiners' opinion to the contrary.' It was a relief to play the fool a bit and Marriott took his coat off and rolled up his sleeve.

'By George, though, I'm bleeding!' he exclaimed. 'Look here! What on earth is this?'

On the forearm, quite close to the wrist, was a thin red line. There was a tiny drop of apparently fresh blood on it. Greene came over and looked closely at it for some minutes. Then he sat back in his chair, looking curiously at his friend's face.

'You've scratched yourself without knowing it,' he said presently.

'There's no sign of a bruise. It must be something else that made the arm ache.'

Marriott sat very still, staring silently at his arm as though the solution of the whole mystery lay there actually written upon the skin.

'What's the matter? I see nothing very strange about a scratch,' said Greene, in an unconvincing sort of voice. 'It was your cuff-links probably. Last night in your excitement——'

But Marriott, white to the very lips, was trying to speak. The sweat stood in great beads on his forehead. At last he leaned forward close to his friend's face.

'Look,' he said, in a low voice that shook a little. 'Do you see that red mark? I mean *underneath* what you call the scratch?'

Greene admitted he saw something or other, and Marriott wiped the place clean with his handkerchief and told him to look again more closely.

'Yes, I see,' returned the other lifting his head after a moment's careful inspection. 'It looks like an old scar.'

'It *is* an old scar,' whispered Marriott, his lips trembling. '*Now* it all comes back to me.'

'All what?' Greene fidgeted on his chair. He tried to laugh, but without success. His friend seemed bordering on collapse.

'Hush! Be quiet, and – I'll tell you,' he said. '*Field made that scar.*'

For a whole minute the two men looked each other full in the face without speaking.

'Field made that scar!' repeated Marriott at length in a louder voice.

'Field! You mean – last night?'

'No, not last night. Years ago – at school, with his knife. And I made a scar in his arm with mine.' Marriott was talking rapidly now.

'We exchanged drops of blood in each other's cuts. He put a drop into my arm and I put one into his——'

'In the name of heaven, what for?'

'It was a boys' compact. We made a sacred pledge, a bargain. I remember it all perfectly now. We had been reading some dreadful book and we swore to appear to one another – I mean, whoever died first swore to show himself to the other. And we sealed the compact with each other's blood. I remember it all so well – the hot summer afternoon in the playground, seven years ago – and one of the masters caught us and confiscated the knives – and I have never thought of it again to this day——'

'And you mean——' stammered Greene.

But Marriott made no answer. He got up and crossed the room and law down wearily upon the sofa, hiding his face in his hands.

Greene himself was a bit nonplussed. He left his friend alone for a little while, thinking it all over again. Suddenly an idea seemed to strike him. He went over to where Marriott still lay motionless on the sofa and roused him. In any case it was better to face the matter, whether there was an explanation or not. Giving in was always the silly exit.

'I say, Marriott,' he began, as the other turned his white face up to him. 'There's no good being so upset about it. I mean – if it's all a hallucination we know what to do. And if it isn't – well, we know what to think, don't we?'

'I suppose so. But it frightens me horribly for some reason,' returned his friend in a hushed voice. 'And that poor devil——'

'But, after all, if the worst is true and – and that chap *has* kept his promise – well, he has; that's all, isn't it?'

Marriott nodded.

'There's only one thing that occurs to me,' Greene went on, 'and that is, are you quite sure that – that he really ate like that – I mean that he actually *ate anything at all?*' he finished, blurting out all his thought.

Marriott stared at him for a moment and then said he could easily make certain. He spoke quietly. After the main shock no lesser surprise could affect him.

'I put the things away myself,' he said, 'after we had finished. They are on the third shelf in that cupboard. No one's touched 'em since.'

He pointed without getting up, and Greene took the hint and went over to look.

'Exactly,' he said, after a brief examination; 'just as I thought. It was partly hallucination, at any rate. The things haven't been touched. Come and see for yourself.'

Together they examined the shelf. There was the brown loaf, the plate of stale scones, the oatcake, all untouched. Even the glass of whisky Marriott had poured out stood there with the whisky still in it.

'You were feeding – no one,' said Greene. 'Field ate and drank nothing. He was not there at all!'

'But the breathing?' urged the other in a low voice, staring with a dazed expression on his face.

Greene did not answer. He walked over to the bedroom, while Marriott followed him with his eyes. He opened the door, and listened.

There was no need for words. The sound of deep, regular breathing came floating through the air. There was no hallucination about that, at any rate. Marriott could hear it where he stood on the other side of the room.

Greene closed the door and came back. 'There's only one thing to do,' he declared with decision. 'Write home and find out about him, and meanwhile come and finish your reading in my rooms. I've got an extra bed.'

'Agreed,' returned the Fourth Year Man; 'there's no hallucination about that exam; I must pass that whatever happens.'

And this was what they did.

It was about a week later when Marriott got the answer from his sister. Part of it he read out to Greene:

'It is curious,' she wrote, 'that in your letter you should have enquired after Field. It seems a terrible thing, but you know only a short while ago Sir John's patience became exhausted, and he turned him out of the house, they say without a penny. Well, what do you think? He has killed himself. At least, it looks like a suicide. Instead of leaving the house, he went down into the cellar and simply starved himself to death... They're trying to suppress it, of course, but I heard it all from my maid, who got it from their footman... They found the body on the 14th, and the doctor said he had died about twelve hours before... He was dreadfully thin...'

'Then he died on the 13th,' said Greene.

Marriott nodded.

'That's the very night he came to see you.'

Marriott nodded again.

Couching at the Door
D. K. Broster

The first inkling which Augustine Marchant had of the matter was on one fine summer morning about three weeks after his visit to Prague, that is to say, in June 1898. In his library at Abbot's Medding he was reclining, as his custom was when writing his poetry, on the very comfortable sofa near the french windows, one of which was open to the garden. Pausing for inspiration – he was nearly at the end of his poem, *Salutation to All Unbeliefs* – he let his eyes wander round the beautifully appointed room, with its cloisonné and Satsuma, Buhl and first editions, and then allowed them to stray towards the sunlight outside. And so, between the edge of the costly Herat carpet and the sill of the open window, across the strip of polished oak flooring, he observed what he took to be a small piece of dark fluff blowing in the draught; and instantly made a note to speak to his housekeeper about the parlour-maid. There was slackness somewhere; and in Augustine Marchant's house no one was allowed to slack but himself.

There had been a time when the poet would not for a moment have been received, as he was now, in country and even county society – those days, even before the advent of *The Yellow Book* and *The Savoy*, when he had lived in London, writing the plays and poems which had so startled and shocked all but the 'decadent' and the 'advanced', *Pomegranates of Sin, Queen Theodora and Queen Marozia, The Nights of the Tour de Nesle, Amor Cypriacus* and the rest. But when, as the 'nineties began to wane, he inherited Abbot's Medding from a distant cousin and came to live there, being then at the height of an almost international reputation, Wiltshire society at first tolerated him for his kinship with the late Lord Medding, and then, placated by the excellence of his dinners and further mollified by the patent staidness of his private life, decided that, in his personal conduct at any rate, he must have turned over a new leaf. Perhaps indeed he had never been as bad as he was painted, and if his writings continued to be no less scandalously free-thinking than before, and needed to be just as rigidly

kept out of the hands of daughters, well, no country gentleman in the
neighbourhood was obliged to read them!

And indeed Augustine Marchant in his fifty-first year was too keenly
alive to the value of the good opinion of county society to risk shocking
it by any overt doings of his. He kept his licence for his pen. When he
went abroad, as he did at least twice a year – but that was another
matter altogether. The nose of Mrs Grundy was not sharp enough to
smell out his occupations in Warsaw or Berlin or Naples, nor her eyes
long-sighted enough to discern what kind of society he frequented
even so near home as Paris. At Abbot's Medding his reputation for
being 'wicked' was fast declining into just enough of a sensation to
titillate a croquet party. He had charming manners, could be witty at
moments (though he could not keep it up), still retained his hyacinthine
locks (by means of hair restorers), wore his excellently cut velvet coats
and flowing ties with just the right air – half poet, half man of the
world – and really had, at Abbot's Medding, no dark secret to hide
beyond the fact, sedulously concealed by him for five-and-twenty years,
that he had never been christened Augustine. Between Augustus and
Augustine, what a gulf! But he had crossed it, and his French poems
(which had to be smuggled into his native land) were signed *Augustin*
– Augustin Lemarchant.

Removing his gaze from the objectionable evidence of domestic
carelessness upon the floor, Mr Marchant now fixed it meditatively
upon the ruby-set end of the gold pencil which he was using. Rossell
& Ward, his publishers, were about to bring out an édition de luxe of
Queen Theodora and Queen Marozia with illustrations by a hitherto unknown young artist – if they were not too daring. It would be a
sumptuous affair in a limited edition. And as he thought of this the
remembrance of his recent stay in Prague returned to the poet. He
smiled to himself, as a man smiles when he looks at a rare wine,
and thought, *Yes, if these blunt-witted Pharisees round Abbot's Medding*
only knew! It was a good thing that the upholders of British petty
morality were seldom great travellers; a dispensation of – ahem,
Providence!

Twiddling his gold pencil between plump fingers, Augustine
Marchant returned to his ode, weighing one epithet against another.
Except in summer he was no advocate of open windows, and even in
summer he considered that to get the most out of that delicate and
precious instrument, his brain, his feet must always be kept thoroughly
warm; he had therefore cast over them, before settling into his semi-
reclining position, a beautiful rose-coloured Indian *sari* of the purest and
thickest silk, leaving the ends trailing on the floor. And he became
aware, with surprise and annoyance, that the piece of brown fluff or
whatever it was down there, travelling in the draught from the window,

had reached the nearest end of the *sari* and was now, impelled by the same current, travelling up it.

The master of Abbot's Medding reached out for the silver handbell on the table by his side. There must be more breeze coming in than he had realized, and he might take cold, a catastrophe against which he guarded himself as against the plague. Then he saw that the upward progress of the dark blot – it was about the size of a farthing – could not by any possibility be assigned to any other agency than its own. It was *climbing* up – some horrible insect, plainly, some disgusting kind of almost legless and very hairy spider, round and vague in outline. The poet sat up and shook the *sari* violently. When he looked again the invader was gone. He had obviously shaken it onto the floor, and on the floor somewhere it must still be. The idea perturbed him, and he decided to take his writing out to the summerhouse, and give orders later that the library was to be thoroughly swept out.

Ah! it was good to be out of doors and in a pleasance so delightfully laid out, so exquisitely kept, as his! In the basin of the fountain the sea-nymphs of rosy-veined marble clustered round a Thetis as beautiful as Aphrodite herself; the lightest and featheriest of acacia trees swayed near. And as the owner of all this went past over the weedless turf he repeated snatches of Verlaine to himself about '*sveltes jets d'eau*' and '*sanglots d'extase.*'

Then turning his head to look back at the fountain, he became aware of a little dark brown object about the size of a halfpenny running towards him over the velvet-smooth sward ...

He believed afterwards that he must first have had a glimpse of the truth at that instant in the garden, or he would not have acted so instinctively as he did and so promptly. For, a moment later, he was standing at the edge of the basin of Thetis, his face blanched in the sunshine, his hand firmly clenched. Inside that closed hand something feather-soft pulsated ... Holding back as best he could the disgust and the something more which clutched at him, Augustine Marchant stooped and plunged his whole fist into the bubbling water, and let the stream of the fountain whirl away what he had picked up. Then with uncertain steps he went and sat down on the nearest seat and shut his eyes. After a while he took out his lawn handkerchief and carefully dried his hand with the intaglio ring, dried it, and then looked curiously at the palm. *I did not know I had so much courage*, he was thinking; *so much courage and good sense!* ... I would doubtless drown very quickly.

Burrows, his butler, was coming over the lawn. 'Mr and Mrs Morrison have arrived, sir.'

'Ah, yes; I had forgotten for the moment.' Augustine Marchant got up and walked towards the house and his guests, throwing back his

shoulders and practising his famous enigmatic smile, for Mrs Morrison
was a woman worth impressing.

(But what had it been exactly? Why, just what it had looked – a
tuft of fur blowing over the grass, a tuft of fur! Sheer imagination that
it had moved in his closed hand with a life of its own ... Then why
had he shut his eyes as he stooped and made a grab at it? Thank God,
thank God, it was nothing now but a drenched smear swirling round
the nymphs of Thetis!)

'Ah, dear lady, you must forgive me! Unpardonable of me not to be
in to receive you!' He was in the drawing-room now, fragrant with its
banks of hothouse flowers, bending over the hand of the fashionably
attired guest on the sofa, in her tight bodice and voluminous sleeves,
with a fly-away hat perched at a rakish angle on her gold-brown hair.

'Your man told us that you were writing in the garden,' said her
goggle-eyed husband reverentially.

'*Cher maître*, it is we who ought not to be interrupting your
rendezvous with the Muse,' returned Mrs Morrison in her sweet, high
voice. 'Terrible to bring you from such company into that of mere
visitors!'

Running his hand through his carefully tended locks the *cher maître*
replied, 'Between a visit from the Muse and one from beauty's self no
true poet would hesitate! – Moreover, luncheon awaits us, and I trust
it is a good one.'

He liked faintly to shock fair admirers by admitting that he cared
for the pleasures of the table; it was quite safe to do so, since none of
them had sufficient acumen to see that it was true.

The luncheon was excellent, for Augustine kept an admirable cook.
Afterwards he showed his guests over the library – yes, even though it
had not received the sweeping which would not be necessary now – and
round the garden; and in the summerhouse was prevailed upon to read
some of *Amor Cypriacus* aloud. And Mrs Frances (nowadays Francesca)
Morrison was thereafter able to recount to envious friends how the Poet
himself had read her stanza after stanza from that most *daring* poem of
his; and how poor Fred, fanning himself meanwhile with his straw hat
– not from the torridity of the verse but because of the afternoon heat
– said afterwards that he had not understood a single word. A good
thing, perhaps ...

When they had gone Augustine Marchant reflected rather cynically,
All that was just so much bunkum when I wrote it. For, ten years ago, in spite of
those audacious, glowing verses, he was an ignorant neophyte. Of
course, since then ... He smiled, a private, sly, self-satisfied smile. It
was certainly pleasant to know oneself no longer a fraud!

Returning to the summerhouse to fetch his poems he saw what he
took to be Mrs Morrison's fur boa lying on the floor just by the basket

chair which she had occupied. Odd of her not to have missed it on departure – a tribute to his verses perhaps. His housekeeper must send it after her by post. But just at that moment his head gardener approached, desiring some instructions, and when the matter was settled, and Augustine Marchant turned once more to enter the summerhouse, he found that he had been mistaken about the dropped boa, for there was nothing on the floor.

Besides, he remembered now that Mrs Morrison's boa had been a rope of grey feathers, not of dark fur. As he took up *Amor Cypriacus* he asked himself lazily what could have led him to imagine a woman's boa there at all, much less a fur one.

Suddenly he knew why. A lattice in the house of memory had opened, and he remained rigid, staring out at the jets of the fountain rising and falling in the afternoon sun. Yes; of that glamorous, wonderful, abominable night in Prague, the part he least wished to recall was connected – incidentally but undeniably – with a fur boa – a long boa of dark fur . . .

He had to go up to town next day to a dinner in his honour. There and then he decided to go up that same night by a late train, a most unusual proceeding, and most disturbing to his valet, who knew that it was doubtful whether he could at such short notice procure him a first-class carriage to himself. However, Augustine Marchant went, and even, to the man's amazement, deliberately chose a compartment with another occupant when he might, after all, have had an empty one.

The dinner was brilliant: Augustine had never spoken better. Next day he went round to the little street not far from the British Museum where he found Lawrence Storey, his new illustrator, working feverishly at his drawings for *Queen Theodora and Queen Marozia*, and quite overwhelmed at the honour of a personal visit. Augustine was very kind to him, and, while offering a few criticisms, highly praised his delineation of those two Messalinas of tenth-century Rome, their long supple hands, their heavy eyes, their full, almost repellent mouths. Storey had followed the same type for mother and daughter, but with a subtle difference.

'They were certainly two most evil women, especially the younger.' he observed ingenuously. 'But I suppose that, from an artistic point of view, that doesn't matter nowadays!'

Augustine, smoking one of his special cigarettes, made a delicate little gesture. 'My dear fellow, Art has nothing whatever to do with what is called "morality"; happily we know that at last! Show me how you thought of depicting the scene where Marozia orders the execution of her mother's papal paramour. Good, very good! Yes; the lines there, even the fall of that loose sleeve from the extended arm, express with clarity what I had in mind. You have great gifts!'

'I have tried to make her look wicked,' said the young man, red-

dening with pleasure. 'But,' he added deprecatingly, 'it is very hard for
a ridiculously inexperienced person like myself to have the right artistic
vision. For to you, Mr Marchant, who have penetrated into such
wonderful arcana of the forbidden, it would be foolish to pretend to
be other than I am.'

'How do you know that I have penetrated into any such arcana?'
enquired the poet, half shutting his eyes and looking (though not to the
almost worshipping gaze of young Storey) like a great cat being stroked.

'Why, one has only to read you!'

'You must come down and stay with me soon,' were Augustine
Marchant's parting words. (He would give the boy a few days' good
living, for which he would be none the worse; let him drink some decent
wine.) 'How soon do you think you will be able to finish the rough
sketches for the rest, and the designs for the *culs de lampe*? A fortnight
or three weeks? Good; I shall look to see you then. Goodbye, my dear
fellow; I am very, very much pleased with what you have shown
me!'

The worst of going up to London from the country was that one was
apt to catch a cold in town. When he got back Augustine Marchant
almost sure that this misfortune had befallen him, so he ordered a fire in
his bedroom, despite the season, and consumed a *recherché* little supper
in seclusion. And, as the cold turned out to have been imaginary, he was
very comfortable, sitting there in his silken dressing-gown, toasting his
toes and holding up a glass of golden Tokay to the flames. Really
Theodora and Marozia would make as much sensation when it came out
with these illustrations as when it first appeared!

All at once he set down his glass. Not far away on his left stood
a big cheval mirror, like a woman's, in which a good portion of the bed
behind him was reflected. And, in this mirror, he had just seen the
valance of the bed move. There could be no draught to speak of in this
warm room, he never allowed a cat in the house, and it was quite
impossible that there should be a rat about. If after all some stray cat
should have got in it must be ejected at once. Augustine hitched round
in his chair to look at the actual bedhanging.

Yes, the topaz-hued silk valance again swung very slightly outward
as though it were being pushed. Augustine bent forward to the bellpull
to summon his valet. Then the flask of Tokay rolled over on the table
as he leaped from his chair instead. Something like a huge, dark
caterpillar was emerging very slowly from under his bed, moving as a
caterpillar moves, with undulations running over it. Where its head
should have been was merely a tapering end smaller than the rest of
it, but of like substance. It was a dark fur boa.

Augustine Marchant felt that he screamed, but he could not have
done so, for his tongue clave to the roof of his mouth. He merely stood

staring, staring, all the blood gone from his heart. Still very slowly, the thing continued to creep out from under the valance, waving that eyeless, tapering end to and fro, as though uncertain where to proceed. *I am going mad, mad, mad!* thought Augustine, and then, with a revulsion, *No, it can't be! It's a real snake of some kind!*

That could be dealt with. He snatched up the poker as the boa-thing, still swaying the head which was no head, kept pouring steadily out from under the lifted yellow frill, until quite three feet were clear of the bed. Then he fell upon it furiously, with blow after blow.

But they had no effect on the furry, spineless thing; it merely gave under them and rippled up in another place. Augustine hit the bed, the floor; at last, really screaming, he threw down his weapon and fell upon the thick, hairy rope with both hands, crushing it together into a mass – there was little if any resistance in it – and hurled it into the fire and, panting, kept it down with shovel and tongs. The flames licked up instantly and, with a roar, made short work of it, though there seemed to be some slight effort to escape, which was perhaps only the effect of the heat. A moment later there was a very strong smell of burned hair, and that was all.

Augustine Marchant seized the fallen flask of Tokay and drained from its mouth what little was left in the bottom ere, staggering to the bed, he flung himself upon it and buried his face in the pillows, even heaping them over his head as if he could thus stifle the memory of what he had seen.

He kept his bed next morning; the supposed cold afforded a good pretext. Long before the maid came in to re-lay the fire he had crawled out to make sure that there were no traces left of – what he had burned there. There were none. A nightmare could not have left a trace, he told himself. But well he knew that it was not a nightmare.

And now he could think of nothing but that room in Prague and the long fur boa of the woman. Some department of his mind (he supposed) must have projected that thing, scarcely noticed at the time, scarcely remembered, into the present and the here. It was terrible to think that one's mind possessed such dark, unknown powers. But not so terrible as if the – apparition – had been endowed with an entirely separate objective existence. In a day or two he would consult his doctor and ask him to give him a tonic.

But, expostulated an uncomfortably lucid part of his brain, you are trying to run with the hare and hunt with the hounds. Is it not better to believe that the thing *had* an objective existence, for you have burned it to nothing? Well and good! But if it is merely a projection from your own mind, what is to prevent it from reappearing, like the phoenix, from the ashes?

There seemed no answer to that, save in an attempt to persuade himself that he had been feverish last night. Work was the best antidote. So Augustine Marchant rose, and was surprised and delighted to find the atmosphere of his study unusually soothing and inspiring, and that day, against all expectation, *Salutation to All Unbeliefs* was completed by some stanzas with which he was not too ill-pleased. Realizing nevertheless that he should be glad of company that evening, he had earlier sent round a note to the local solicitor, a good fellow, to come and dine with him; played a game of billiards with the lawyer afterwards and retired to bed after some vintage port and a good stiff whisky and soda with scarcely a thought of the visitant of the previous night.

He woke at that hour when the thrushes in early summer punctually greet the new day – three o'clock. They were greeting it even vociferously, and Augustine Marchant was annoyed with their enthusiasm. His golden damask window-curtains kept out all but a glimmer of the new day, yet as, lying upon his back, the poet opened his eyes for a moment, his only half-awakened sense of vision reported something swinging to and fro in the dimness like a pendulum of rope. It was indistinct but seemed to be hanging from the tester of the bed. And, wide awake in an instant, with an unspeakable anguish of premonition tearing through him, he felt, next moment, a light thud on the coverlet about the level of his knees. Something had arrived on the bed . . .

And Augustine Marchant neither shrieked nor leaped from his bed; he could not. Yet, now that his eyes were grown used to the twilight of the room, he saw it clearly, the fur rope which he had burned to extinction two nights ago, dark and shining as before, rippling with a gentle movement as it coiled itself neatly together in the place where it had struck the bed, and subsided there in a symmetrical round, with only that tapering end a little raised and, as it were, looking at him – only, eyeless and featureless, it could not look. One thought of disgusted relief, that it was not at any rate going to attack him, and Augustine Marchant fainted.

Yet his swoon must have merged into sleep, for he woke in a more or less ordinary fashion to find his man placing his early tea-tray beside him and enquiring when he should draw his bath. There was nothing on the bed.

I shall change my bedroom, thought Augustine to himself, looking at the haggard, fallen-eyed man who faced him in the mirror as he shaved. *No, better still, I will go away for a change. Then I shall not have these – dreams. I'll go to old Edgar Fortescue for a few days; he begged me again not long ago to come any time.*

So to the house of that old Maecenas he went. He was much too great a man now to be in need of Sir Edgar's patronage. It was homage which he received there, both from host and guests. The stay did much

to soothe his scarified nerves. Unfortunately the last day undid the good
of all the foregoing ones.

Sir Edgar possessed a pretty young wife – his third – and, among
other charms of his place in Somerset, an apple orchard underplanted
with flowers. And in the cool of the evening Augustine walked there
with his host and hostess almost as if he were the Almighty with the
dwellers in Eden. Presently they sat down upon a rustic seat (but a
very comfortable one) under the shade of the apple boughs, amid the
incongruous but pleasant parterres.

'You have come at the wrong season for these apple trees,
Marchant,' observed Sir Edgar after a while, taking out his cigar.
'Blossom-time or apple-time – they are showy at either, in spite of the
underplanting. What is attracting you on that tree – a titmouse? We
have all kinds here, pretty, destructive little beggars!'

'I did not know that I was looking – it's nothing – thinking of
something else,' stammered the poet. Surely, surely he had been mistaken in thinking that he had seen a sinuous, dark furry thing undulat-
ing like a caterpillar down the stem of that particular apple tree at a
few yards' distance?

Talk went on, even his; there was safety in it. It was only the
breeze which faintly rustled that bed of heliotrope behind the seat.
Augustine wanted desperately to get up and leave the orchard, but
neither Sir Edgar not his wife seemed disposed to move, and so the
poet remained at his end of the seat, his left hand playing nervously
with a long bent of grass which had escaped the scythe.

All at once he felt a tickling sensation on the back of his hand,
looked down and saw that featureless snout of fur protruding upward
from underneath the rustic bench and sweeping itself backward and
forward against his hand with a movement which was almost caressing.
he was on his feet in a flash.

'Do you mind if I go in?' he asked abruptly. 'I'm not – feeling very
well.'

*   *   *

If the thing could follow him it was of no use to go away. He returned
to Abbot's Medding looking so much the worse for his change of air
that Burrows expressed a respectful hope that he was not indisposed.
And almost the first thing that occurred, when Augustine sat down at
his writing-table to attend to his correspondence, was the unwinding of
itself from one of its curved legs, of a soft, brown, oscillating serpent
which slowly waved an end at him as if in welcome ...

In welcome, yes, that was it! The creature, incredible though it was,
the creature seemed glad to see him! Standing at the other end of the

room, his hands pressed over his eyes – for what was the use of attempting to hurt or destroy it – Augustine Marchant thought shudderingly that, like a witch's cat, a 'familiar' would not, presumably, be ill-disposed towards its master. Its master! Oh, God!

The hysteria which he had been trying to keep down began to mount uncontrollably when, removing his hand, Augustine glanced again towards his writing-table and saw that the boa had coiled itself in his chair and was sweeping its end to and fro over the back, somewhat in the way that a cat, purring meanwhile, rubs itself against furniture or a human leg in real or simulated affection.

'Oh, go away from there!' he suddenly screamed at it, advancing with outstretched hand. 'In the devil's name, get out.'

To his utter amazement, he was obeyed. The rhythmic movements ceased, the fur snake poured itself down out of the chair and writhed towards the door. Venturing back to his writing-table after a moment Augustine saw it coiled on the threshold, the blind end turned towards him as usual, as though watching. And he began to laugh. What would happen if he rang and someone came; would the opening door scrape it aside – would it vanish? Had it, in short, an existence for anyone else but himself?

But he dared not make the experiment. He left the room by the french window, feeling that he could never enter the house again. And perhaps, had it not been for the horrible knowledge just acquired that it could follow him, he might easily have gone away for good from Abbot's Medding and all his treasures and comforts. But of what use would that be – and how should he account for so extraordinary an action? No; he must think and plan while he yet remained sane.

To what, then, could he have recourse? The black magic in which he had dabbled with such disastrous consequences might possibly help him. Left to himself he was but an amateur, but he had a number of books . . . There was also that other realm whose boundaries sometimes marched side by side with magic – religion. But how could he pray to a Deity in whom he did not believe? Rather pray to the Evil which had sent this curse upon him, to show him how to banish it. Yet since he had deliberately followed what religion stigmatized as sin, what even the world would label as lust and necromancy, supplication to the dark powers was not likely to deliver him from them. They must somehow be outwitted.

He kept his *grimoires* and books of the kind in a locked bookcase in another room, not in his study; in that room he sat up till midnight. But the spells which he read were useless; moreover, he did not really believe in them. The irony of the situation was that, in a sense, he had only played at sorcery; it had but lent a spice to sensuality. He wandered wretchedly about the room dreading at any moment to see his

'familiar' wreathed round some object in it. At last he stopped at a
small bookcase which held some old forgotten books of his mother's –
Longfellow and Mrs Hemans, *John Halifax, Gentleman*, and a good many
volumes of sermons and mild essays. And when he looked at that
blameless assembly a cloud seemed to pass over Augustine Marchant's
vision, and he saw his mother, gentle and lace-capped as years and years
ago she used to sit, hearing his lessons, in an antimacassared chair. She
had been everything to him then, the little boy whose soul was not
smirched. He called silently to her now, 'Mamma, Mamma, can't you
help me? Can't you send this thing away?'

When the cloud had passed he found that he had stretched out his
hand and removed a big book. Looking at it he saw that it was her
Bible, with *Sarah Amelia Marchant* on the faded yellow flyleaf. Her spirit
was going to help him! He turned over a page or two, and out of the
largish print there sprang instantly at him: *Now the serpent was more subtle
than any beast in the field.* Augustine shuddered and almost put the Bible
back, but the conviction that there was help there urged him to go on.
He turned a few more pages of Genesis and his eyes were caught by this
verse, which he had never seen before in his life:

*And if thou doest well, shalt thou not be accepted? And if thou doest not well,
sin lieth at the door. And unto thee shall be his desire, and thou shalt rule
over him.*

What strange words! What could they possibly mean? Was there
light for him in them? *Unto thee shall be his desire.* That Thing, the loathsome semblance of affection which hung about it ... *Thou shalt rule over
him.* It *had* obeyed him, up to a point ... Was this Book, of all others,
showing him the way to be free? But the meaning of the verse was so
obscure! He had not, naturally, such a thing as a commentary in the
house. Yet, when he came to think of it, he remembered that some pious
and anonymous person, soon after the publication of *Pomegranates of Sin*,
had sent him a Bible in the Revised Version, with an inscription
recommending him to read it. He had it somewhere, though he had
always meant to get rid of it.

After twenty minutes' search through the sleeping house he found it
in one of the spare bedrooms. But it gave him little enlightenment, for
there was scant difference in the rendering, save that for *lieth at the door*,
this version had *coucheth*, and that the margin held an alternative
translation for the end of the verse: *And unto thee is its desire, but thou
shouldst rule over it.*

Nevertheless, Augustine Marchant stood after midnight in this
silent, sheeted guest-chamber repeating, '*But thou shouldst rule over it.*'

And all at once he thought of a way of escape.

*   *   *

It was going to be a marvellous experience, staying with Augustine Marchant. Sometimes Lawrence Storey hoped there would be no other guests at Abbot's Medding; at other times he hoped there would be. A *tête-à-tête* of four days with the great poet – could he sustain his share worthily? For Lawrence, despite the remarkable artistic gifts which were finding their first real flowering in these illustrations to Augustine's poem, was still unspoiled, still capable of wonder and admiration, still humble and almost naïve. It was still astonishing to him that he, an architect's assistant, should have been snatched away, as Ganymede by the eagle, from the lower world of elevations and drains to serve on Olympus. It was not, indeed, Augustine Marchant who had first discovered him, but it was Augustine Marchant who was going to make him famous.

The telegraph poles flitted past the second-class carriage window, and more than one traveller glanced with a certain envy and admiration at the fair, good-looking young man who diffused such an impression of happiness and candour, and had such a charming smile on his boyish lips. He carried with him a portfolio which he never let out of reach of his hand; the oldish couple opposite, speculating upon its contents, might have changed their opinion of him had they seen them.

But no shadow of the dark weariness of things unlawful rested on Lawrence Storey; to know Augustine Marchant, to be illustrating his great poem, to have learned from him that art and morality had no kinship, this was to plunge into a new realm of freedom and enlarging experience. Augustine Marchant's poetry, he felt, had already taught his hand what his brain and heart knew nothing of.

There was a dogcart to meet him at the station, and in the scented June evening he was driven with a beating heart past meadows and hayfields to his destination.

Mr Marchant, awaiting him in the hall, was at his most charming. 'My dear fellow, are those the drawings? Come, let us lock them away at once in my safe! If you had brought me diamonds I should not be one quarter so concerned about thieves. And did you have a comfortable journey? I have had you put in the orange room; it is next to mine. There is no one else staying here, but there are a few people coming to dinner to meet you.'

There was only just time to dress for dinner, so that Lawrence did not get an opportunity to study his host until he saw him seated at the head of the table. Then he was immediately struck by the fact that he looked curiously ill. His face – ordinarily by no means attenuated – seemed to have fallen in, there were dark circles under his eyes, and the perturbed Lawrence, observing him as the meal progressed, thought that his manner too seemed strange and once or twice quite absent-minded. And there was one moment when, though the lady on his right was addressing him, he sharply turned his head away and looked down at the side of his chair just as if he saw something on the floor. Then he apologized, saying that he had a horror of cats, and that sometimes the tiresome animal from the stables ... But after that he continued to entertain his guests in his own inimitable way, and, even to the shy Lawrence, the evening proved very pleasant.

The ensuing three days were wonderful and exciting to the young artist – days of uninterrupted contact with a master mind which acknowledged, as the poet himself admitted, none of the petty barriers which man, for his own convenience, had set up between alleged right and wrong. Lawrence had learned why his host did not look well; it was loss of sleep, the price exacted by inspiration. He had a new poetic drama shaping in his mind which would scale heights that he had not yet attempted.

There was almost a touch of fever in the young man's dreams tonight – his last night but one. He had several. First he was standing by the edge of a sort of mere, inexpressibly desolate and unfriendly, a place he had never seen in his life, which yet seemed in some way familiar; and something said to him, 'You will never go away from here!' He was alarmed, and woke, but went to sleep again almost immediately, and this time was back, oddly enough, in the church where in his earliest years he had been taken to service by the aunt who had brought him up – a large church full of pitch-pine pews with narrow ledges for hymn-books, which ledges he used surreptitiously to lick during the long dull periods of occultation upon his knees. But most of all he remembered the window with Adam and Eve in the Garden of Eden, on either side of an apple tree round whose trunk was coiled a monstrous snake with a semi-human head. Lawrence had hated and dreaded that window, and because of it he would never go near an orchard and had no temptation to steal apples ... Now he was back in that church again, staring at the window, lit up with some infernal glow from behind. He woke again, little short of terrified – he, a grown man! But again he went to sleep quite quickly.

His third dream had for background, as sometimes happens in nightmares, the very room in which he lay. He dreamed that a door opened in the wall, and in the doorway, quite plain against the light from another room behind him, stood Augustine Marchant in his dressing-gown. He was looking down at something on the ground which Lawrence did not see, but his hand was pointing at Lawrence in the bed, and he was saying in a voice of command, 'Go to him, do you hear? Go to him! Go to *him*! Am I not your master?'

And Lawrence, who could neither move nor utter a syllable, wondered uneasily what this could be which was thus commanded, but his attention was chiefly focused on Augustine Marchant's face. After he

had said these words several times, and apparently without result, a
dreadful change came upon it, a look of the most unutterable despair.
It seemed visibly to age and wither; he said, in a loud, penetrating
whisper, 'Is there no escape then?' covered his ravaged face a moment
with his hands, and then went back and softly closed the door. At that
Lawrence woke; but in the morning he had forgotten all three dreams.

The *tête-à-tête* dinner on the last night of his stay
would have lingered in a gourmet's memory, so that it was a pity the
young man did not know in the least what he was eating. At last there
was happening what he had scarcely dared hope for; the great poet of
the sensuous was revealing to him some of the unimaginably strange and
secret sources of his inspiration. In the shaded rosy candlelight, his
elbows on the table among trails of flowers he, who was not even a
neophyte, listened like a man learning for the first time of some spell
or spring which will make him more than mortal.

'Yes,' said Augustine Marchant, after a long pause, 'yes, it was a
marvellous, an undying experience – one that is not given to many.
It opened doors, it – but I despair of doing it justice in mere words.'
His look was transfigured, almost dreamy.

'But she – the woman – how did you——?' asked Lawrence Storey
in a hushed voice.

'Oh, the woman?' said Augustine, suddenly finishing off his wine.
'The woman was only a common streetwalker.'

A moment or two later Lawrence was looking at his host wonder-
ingly and wistfully. 'But this was in Prague. Prague is a long way
off.'

'One does not need to go so far, in reality. Even in Paris——'

'One could – have that experience in Paris?'

'If you knew where to go. And of course, it is necessary to have
credentials. I mean that – like all such enlightenments – it has to be
kept secret, most secret, from the vulgar minds who lay their restrictions
on the finer. That is self-evident.'

'Of course,' said the young man, and sighed deeply.

His host looked at him affectionately. 'You, my dear Lawrence – I
may call you Lawrence? – want just that touch of – what shall I call
them – *les choses cachées* – to liberate your immense artistic gifts from the
shackles which still bind them. Through that gateway you would find
the possibility of their full fruition! It would fertilize your genius to a
still finer blossoming . . . But you would have scruples – and you are very
young.'

'You know,' said Lawrence in a low and trembling tone, 'what I feel
about your poetry. You know how I ache to lay the best that is in me
at your feet. If only I could make my drawings for the Two Queens
more worthy – already it is an honour which overwhelms me that you

should have selected me to do them – but they are not what they should be. I am *not* sufficiently liberated . . .'

Augustine leaned forward on the flower-decked table. His eyes were glowing. 'Do you truly desire to be?'

The young man nodded, too full of emotion to find his voice.

The poet got up, went over to a cabinet in a corner and unlocked it. Lawrence watched his fine figure in a sort of trance. Then he half rose with an exclamation.

'What is it?' asked Augustine very sharply, facing round.

'Oh, nothing, sir – only I believe you hate cats, and I thought I saw one, or rather its tail, disappearing into that corner.'

'There's no cat here,' said Augustine quickly. His face had become all shiny and mottled, but Lawrence did not notice it. The poet stood a moment looking at the carpet; one might almost have thought that he was gathering resolution to cross it; then he came swiftly back to the table.

'Sit down again,' he commanded. 'Have you a pocket-book with you, a pocket-book which you never leave about? Good! Then write *this* in one place; and *this* on another page – write it small – among other entries is best – not on a blank page – write it in Greek characters if you know them . . .'

'What – what is it?' asked Lawrence, all at once intolerably excited, his eyes fixed on the piece of paper in Augustine's hand.

'The two halves of the address in Paris.'

* * *

Augustine Marchant kept a diary in those days, a locked diary, written in cipher. And for more than a month after Lawrence Storey's visit the tenor of the entries there was almost identical:

> *No change . . . always with me . . . How much longer can I endure it? The alteration in my looks is being remarked upon to my face. I shall have to get rid of Thornton* [his man] *on some pretext or other, for I begin to think that he has seen It. No wonder, since It follows me about like a dog. When It is visible to everyone it will be the end . . . I found It in bed with me this morning, pressed up against me as if for warmth . . .*

But there was a different class of entry also, appearing at intervals with an ever-increasing note of impatience:

> *Will L.S. go there? . . . When shall I hear from L.S.? . . . Will the experiment do what I think? It is my last hope.*

Then, suddenly, after five weeks had elapsed, an entry in a trembling hand:

For twenty-four hours I have seen no sign of It! Can it be possible?

And next day:

Still nothing. I begin to live again. – This evening has just come an ecstatic letter from L.S., from Paris, telling me that he had 'presented his credentials' and was to have the experience next day. He has had it by now – by yesterday, in fact. Have I really freed myself? It looks like it!

In one week from the date of that last entry it was remarked in Abbot's Medding how much better Mr Marchant was looking again. Of late he had not seemed at all himself; his cheeks had fallen in, his clothes seemed to hang loosely upon him, who had generally filled them so well, and he appeared nervous. Now he was as before, cheery, courtly, debonair. And last Sunday, will you believe it, he went to church! The rector was so astonished when he first became aware of him from the pulpit that he nearly forgot to give out his text. And the poet joined in the hymns, too! Several observed this amazing phenomenon.

It was the day after this unwonted appearance at St Peter's. Augustine was strolling in his garden. The air had a new savour, the sun a new light; he could look again with pleasure at Thetis and her nymphs of the fountain, could work undisturbed in the summerhouse. Free, free! All the world was good to the senses once again, and the hues and scents of early autumn better, in truth, than the brilliance of that summer month which had seen his curse descend upon him.

The butler brought him out a letter with a French stamp. From Lawrence Storey, of course; to tell him – what? Where had he caught his first glimpse of it? In one of those oppressively furnished French bedrooms? And how had he taken it?

At first, however, Augustine was not sure that the letter was from Storey. The writing was very different, cramped instead of flowing, and, in places, spluttering, the pen having dug into the paper as if the hand which held it had not been entirely under control – almost, thought Augustine, his eyes shining with excitement, almost as though something had been twined, liana-like, round the wrist. (He had a sudden sick recollection of a day when that had happened to him, quickly submerged in a gush of eager anticipation.) Sitting down upon the edge of the fountain he read – not quite what he had looked for:

I don't know what is happening to me, began the letter without other opening. *Yesterday I was in a café by myself, and had just ordered some absinthe – though I do not like it. And quite suddenly, although I knew that I was in the café, I realized that I was also back in that room. I could see every feature of it, but I could see the café too, with all the people in it; the one was, as it were, superimposed upon the other, the room, which was a good deal smaller than the café, being inside the latter, as a box may be within a larger box. And all the*

*while the room was growing clearer, the cafe jading. I saw the glass of absinthe
suddenly standing on nothing, as it were. All the furniture of the room, all the
accessories you know of, were mixed up with the chairs and tables of the café. I
do not know how I managed to find my way back to the* comptoir, *pay and get
out. I took a fiacre back to my hotel. By the time I arrived there I was all right.
I suppose that it was only the after-effects of a very strange and violent emotional
experience. But I hope to God that it will not recur!*

'How interesting!' said Augustine Marchant, dabbling his hand
in the swirling water where he had once drowned a piece of dark fluff.
'And why indeed should I have expected that It would couch at his
door in the same form as at mine?'

Four days more of new-found peace and he was reading this:

*In God's name – or the Devil's – come over and help me! I have hardly an
hour now by night or day when I am sure of my whereabouts. I could not risk
the journey back to England alone. It is like being imprisoned in some kind of
infernal half-transparent box, always growing a little smaller. Whereever I go
now I carry it about with me; when I am in the street I hardly know which is the
pavement and which is the roadway, because I am always treading on that black
carpet with the cabalistic designs; if I speak to anyone they may suddenly
disappear from sight. To attempt to work is naturally useless. I would consult a
doctor, but that would mean telling him everything . . .*

'I hope to God he won't do that!' muttered Augustine uneasily.
'He can't – he swore to absolute secrecy. I hadn't bargained, however,
for his ceasing work. Suppose he finds himself unable to complete the
designs for *Theodora and Marozia!* That would be serious . . . However,
to have freed myself is worth *any* sacrifice . . . But Storey cannot,
obviously, go on living indefinitely on two planes at once . . . Artistically,
though, it might inspire him to something quite unprecedented. I'll
write to him and point that out; it might encourage him. But go near
him in person – is it likely!'

The next day was one of great literary activity. Augustine was so
deeply immersed in his new poetical drama that he neglected his
correspondence and almost his meals – except his dinner, which seemed
that evening to be shared most agreeably and excitingly by these new
creations of his brain. Such, in fact, was his preoccupation with them
that it was not until he had finished the savoury and poured out a
glass of his superlative port that he remembered a telegram which had
been handed to him as he came in to dinner. It still lay unopened by
his plate. Now, tearing apart the envelope, he read with growing
bewilderment these words above his publishers' names:

Please inform us immediately what steps to take are prepared send to France recover drawings if possible what suggestions can you make as to successor Rossell and Ward.

Augustine was more than bewildered; he was stupefied. Had some accident befallen Lawrence Storey of which he knew nothing? But he had opened all his letters this morning though he had not answered any. A prey to a sudden very nasty anxiety he got up and rang the bell.

'Burrows, bring me *The Times* from the library.'

The newspaper came, unopened. Augustine, now in a frenzy of uneasiness, scanned the pages rapidly. But it was some seconds before he came upon the headline: TRAGIC DEATH OF A YOUNG ENGLISH ARTIST, and read the following, furnished by the Paris correspondent:

Connoisseurs who were looking forward to the appearance of the superb illustrated edition of Mr Augustine Marchant's Queen Theodora and Queen Marozia *will learn with great regret of the death by drowning of the gifted young artist, Mr Lawrence Storey, who was engaged upon the designs for it. Mr Storey had recently been staying in Paris, but left one day last week for a remote spot in Brittany, it was supposed in pursuance of his work. On Friday last his body was discovered floating in a lonely pool near Carhaix. It is hard to see how Mr Storey could have fallen in, since this piece of water – the Mare de Plougouven – has a completely level shore surrounded by reeds, and is not in itself very deep, nor is there any boat upon it. It is said the unfortunate young Englishman had been somewhat strange in his manner recently and complained of hallucinations; it is therefore possible that under their influence he deliberately waded out into the Mare de Plougouven. A strange feature of the case is that he had fastened round him under his coat the finished drawings for Mr Marchant's book, which were of course completely spoiled by the water before the body was found. It is to be hoped that they were not the only——*

Augustine threw *The Times* furiously from him and struck the dinner table with his clenched fist.

'Upon my soul, that is too much! It is criminal! My property – and I who had done so much for him! Fastened them round himself – he must have been crazy!'

But had he been so crazy? When his wrath had subsided a little Augustine could not but ask himself whether the young artist had not in some awful moment of insight guessed the truth, or part of it – that his patron had deliberately corrupted him? It looked almost like it. But, if he had really taken all the finished drawings with him to this place in Brittany, what an unspeakably mean trick of revenge thus to destroy them! ... yet, even if it were so, he must regard their loss as the price of his own deliverance, since, from his point of view, the desperate expedient of passing on his 'familiar' had been a complete success. By getting someone else to plunge even deeper than he had done into the unlawful (for he had seen to it that Lawrence Storey should do that) he had proved, as that verse in Genesis said, that he *had* ruled over – what had pursued him in tangible form as a consequence of his own night in Prague. He could not be too thankful. The literary world might well be thankful too. For his own art was of infinitely more importance than the subservient, the parasitic art of an illustrator. He could with a little search find half a dozen just as gifted as that poor hallucination-ridden Storey to finish *Theodora and Marozia* – even, if necessary, to begin an entirely fresh set of drawings. And meanwhile, in the new lease of creative energy which this unfortunate but necessary sacrifice had made possible for him, he would begin to put on paper the masterpiece which was now taking brilliant shape in his liberated mind. A final glass, and then an evening in the workshop!

Augustine poured out some port, and was raising the glass, prepared to drink to his own success, when he thought he heard a sound near the door. He looked over his shoulder. Next instant the stem of the wine-glass had snapped in his hand and he had sprung back to the farthest limit of the room.

Reared up for quite five feet against the door, huge, dark, sleeked with wet and flecked with bits of green waterweed, was something half python, half gigantic cobra, its head drawn back as if to strike – its head, for in its former featureless tapering end were now two reddish eyes, such as furriers put into the heads of stuffed creatures. And they were fixed in an unwavering and malevolent glare upon him, as he cowered there clutching the bowl of the broken wineglass, the crumpled copy of *The Times* lying at his feet.

Don't You Dare
John Burke

She had always prophesied contemptuously that he would die before she did. He wouldn't reach fifty, she said. She would be young enough and attractive enough to marry again, and next time it would be someone she could respect. A real man, next time.

Once he tried to stem the flow of her derision by asking what she wanted him to do if she should happen to go first. She might be involved in an accident. It was only practical to make plans for the children. Michael showed signs of being able to take pretty good care of himself but Candida, at twelve, was sly and difficult, pruriently addicted to reading dubious American thrillers from the public library or even more dubious paperbacks which she bought with her pocket money in spite of being forbidden to do so. It was her father who had forbidden this. Her mother laughed and told him not to be so stuffy.

'I used to read them by the dozen when I was her age,' she said. 'Everything I could get my hands on. It did me good.'

'Did it?' he rashly said. It was the excuse for her to launch another of her scathing attacks on him.

Candida read half surreptitiously, half defiantly. She thought strange thoughts. She came out with outrageous remarks and then had long spells of mysterious silence. Her mother alternately doted on her and raged at her. She would goad Candida into a tantrum and then hit her across the side of the head and scream at her; and then, just as Robert was sickening with the savagery of it, the two of them would be crying and wrapping their arms round each other. Laura was a great believer in the richness of impetuous swings from one emotion to another, declaring that children loved you more this way than if you were nasty and cold and rational; that everyone, in fact, loved you more this way.

But if there was a sudden end to it, if she was no longer there to sneer and rage and coo, to run things her way because there was no other conceivable way – what then?

'I'd be the one who'd have to marry again,' he said, trying to keep it casual and light-hearted.

'You think anyone would have you?'

'Wouldn't be surprised.'

'You're trying to tell me you've already got someone lined up?'

She would have loved such an excuse to pile even further abuse on him. He was perversely tempted to give her this opportunity: the insults would at any rate be in a different vein from the usual ones. But the whole thing was absurd. He said:

'Of course not. There's nobody.'

'I didn't really imagine there would be.'

'But if I *were* left with the kids ...'

'Don't you dare,' she said. 'Marry again? Don't you dare.'

He ought to have known that such a discussion would get nowhere. None of their arguments ever did. And, after all, it was stupid to talk about dying. You didn't plan for death when you were still only in your late thirties.

'In any case,' Laura summed up, 'it won't happen.' Again she trotted out her happy prediction: 'You'll die before I do.'

Yet she was the first to go. On her fortieth birthday she was dead and he was left with Michael and Candida.

Don't you dare ...

But he dared.

He married Janet within the year. The quivering tension which Laura had maintained in the house was followed, after her death, by numbness. Now there came warmth and relaxation, a gradual stretching of the limbs and the mind.

Laura had been tall and fair. No matter what the current fashion, she kept her hair long – a beautiful silky mane of which she was swaggeringly proud. Between her shoulder blades she had a streak of faint golden down. She talked about it to friends and even to strangers, and lost no opportunity of exhibiting it. In a swimming costume she would turn her back to the sun and writhe gently so that the light could play on this glimmering fur. She implied that there was something very specially, madly sexy about it.

'Robert' – she would wave her hand at her husband with tolerant despair – 'has hardly any hair anywhere. But *anywhere*, my dears.'

She had married Robert in order to escape from a plump, slack, pathetically ignorant mother whom she despised; but after her mother's death she began to talk of her with growing affection. In no time at all she persuaded herself that they had been an ideal mother and daughter and that she ought to have listened more attentively to her mother's shrewd advice.

'I married too young, of course. Not that I blame Robert for that.

But I didn't have the chance of doing any of the things I really ought to have done.'

She ought to have been taken up by an international playboy, ought to have gone round the world, ought to have taken up skiing and surfing. She would have been so good: she could sense just how good she would have been. She could have become a tennis champion if Robert hadn't come along and penned her in physically and emotionally, and given her two children. They had nothing in common: it was tragic that she should have discovered this too late.

Next time it would be a real man.

'Given my time over again,' she would laugh to her friends, not finishing the sentence but promising them and Robert and herself that she would, before it was too late, somehow have her time over again.

Her interests waxed and waned. Some were taken up merely to spite Robert and in due course were dropped. Others became obsessions. Whatever Laura discovered was indeed a discovery: nobody had ever known it as she knew it, nobody could understand it as she immediately, intuitively understood it.

Swimming was her greatest passion. It was because of this that Robert slaved to buy the house on the river. Then there was more expense because Laura wanted to have people dropping in from the other houses and from the island and from the plushy cabin cruisers, and they all needed drinks and lots of drinks; and she wanted new clothes so that they could go over and drop in on the houses and the island and the cabin cruisers for drinks and lots of drinks. She nagged him about buying a boat. While he worked, she lounged in a bikini on the lawn which sloped down into the river, or swam across to say hello to her friends who weren't ever his friends or swam along the river and communed with herself and came back reinvigorated, ready to sneer at him yet again.

The river became her personal property. No matter how many boats came and went, no matter how many other people plunged into the water, it was her river. She had used it, so it was hers. She loved it – loved to succumb to it and then to dominate it. She flouted the current by surrendering herself and allowing herself to be pulled towards the weir, knowing the exact moment when she could beat it and escape.

Some evenings in moonlight or pitch darkness she walked down the lawn and into the water and swam across to the lawn on the far side. The Major who lived alone across there was always glad to offer her a drink. Between them she and Robert never referred to him as anything other than the Major. At first it had been a joke. Then Laura started to talk less jokingly about him and to indicate that he was nice, a sweetie, rather a pet. A real man.

She went over to the Major naked but for those two strips of nylon and invariably stayed for a long time and came back dripping and laughing.

Sometimes Robert knew, but never dared to raise it as a matter of discipline, that Candida was watching from an upper window. Long after she ought to have been asleep she would watch, wide-eyed and attentive until her mother came out of the water and shook herself and walked arrogantly up the lawn with her hands playing a gentle little tattoo on her scarcely veiled breasts.

On one occasion Laura was prosecuted under some complex waterways by-law. She paid the fine and laughed and made her friends laugh with her. The friends said that one day she would take too big a risk and be swept over the weir on to the harsh, jutting stakes of the breakwater below; but they said it adoringly and didn't really believe it.

Until she went over.

Dead and gone. It was impossible to believe that her vicious, humiliating voice had at last been drowned in the roar of the weir.

'I suppose all marriages go this way.' Robert could not forget it, resonant and repetitive, chattering so lightly and yet so purposefully to as large an audience as she could muster. 'Men! First they leap on you with a glad cry – and then it sort of softens off to a reluctant groan. I suppose it's the same for everyone.'

But she didn't really suppose any such thing. She was sure that somewhere there was a man who could satisfy her. Her hatred was reserved for Robert only, directed tirelessly against Robert.

She was dead. Her hatred must have died with her.

Disconcertingly it didn't feel like that. She had lived on her resentments and it was inconceivable that their power should have ebbed so swiftly. Her vindictiveness had become a living, physical force stronger than herself. Robert had braced himself against it, his head bowed against it, like a man learning to live with a remorseless prevailing wind. He was not ready to adjust to the fact that the wind had dropped.

If he had died before she did, would she have found it possible to fulfil all those threats she had made to him, all the promises she had made to herself? Without the goad of his presence would she have found any of it worth while?

Robert found it easier now to be sympathetic towards her. He could afford to be detached and tolerant. It was easier to assess, to find psychological phrases, to nod understandingly over her disappointments and her knotted agonies. She had made his life hell, but even without him there to storm against could she ever have been happy?

She was gone. He kept telling himself that she was gone.

Janet was small and dark and softly spoken. She could not have been more different from Laura. Robert had not consciously chosen her because of this but he wryly admitted to himself that it would not have worked out so rightly and inevitably if she had not been such a complete contrast. He could not help making comparisons; but he did not pass these onto Janet.

She was more interested in her home than Laura had ever been. She found reasons for liking things rather than for disliking them. Ashtrays were emptied, the place was cleaned, towels were not thrown in a heap on the bathroom floor, lights weren't left on and doors weren't left banging. She was tidy without being fussy. The place had a new smell about it, a new glow, a new comfort.

Janet was thirty-five and had not been married before because of a chain of circumstances not one of which was significant in itself but which, one after the other, had somehow prevented her from settling down. Her parents had gone through various emotional upsets and had both relied on her. Then her father had had a long illness. A job in Wales had been interrupted by the need to look after her brother when he was badly injured in an accident. She spent an unsatisfactory year in Canada. For three years she was involved with a married man and then quietly, resolutely walked out on the situation. If she had been hurt she did not scratch the scars.

After so many years of independence she might well have been diffident and awkward in marriage. Instead, she was graceful and appreciative. Pleasure came to them without having to be desperately pursued.

Laura's body had been magnificent. At forty she had been as sleek and glossy and splendid as a girl of eighteen. In spite of her repeated lamentations she had not suffered from the bearing of two children. Yet for all that flawless beauty she had been cold and brittle and somehow unrewarding.

Janet was ... oh, he had to say it: Janet was cuddly. Ludicrous word. He thought how Laura would have shrieked with laughter. *Cuddly!* but why not? What was so wrong with that? He didn't have to worry ever again about what Laura would say, because Laura could say nothing.

Still it was hard not to listen, not to wait for that harsh laugh. The echoes were taking a long time to die.

One evening he was late leaving the office and was stuck for twenty minutes in a traffic jam. He began to frame excuses. He would be as reasonable as possible until the row started; then he would have to have a few phrases ready, a few parries.

'Nobody's asking you to apologize' – he could hear Laura saying it – 'for not wanting to come home to me. If you want to stop for a drink, at least have the guts to say so.'

'I didn't stop for a drink. I had a call from Paris.'

'As if it matters. Though you *might* have remembered that Harry and Josie were coming in for a chat. I had to let them go, of course.'

'They could have waited.'

'Until you condescended to arrive? A phone call wouldn't have hurt. A little courtesy ...'

'I rang before I left but you must have been out.'

'Liar.'

'I tell you ...'

'I don't want you to tell me anything. It's really not worth the fuss. I don't know why you have to make such a pathetic fuss. Do grow up, Robert, dear.'

He rehearsed it, lived through it before it was even begun. And then, as he swung the car down the slope and saw the river curling below him, he realized that he didn't have to practise the scene, didn't have to anticipate every snarled word and impatient twitch of the shoulders: Laura wasn't there; it was Janet now, and Janet wouldn't want to start a petty argument.

He had thought Janet might be intimidated by the children but she was perfectly at ease. She treated Michael as an equal and was wary yet decisive with Candida.

Michael was in his first year at Sussex University. He had acquired some odd mannerisms but Janet took them as they came and did not make exaggerated faces as Laura would have done, or grow sweetly patronizing as Laura would have done. Michael let it be known that he would eventually become something in television. It was a phrase much used by his friends. He was not sure, any more than they were, of quite what that something was to be; but he wore a pink shirt and a sandy beard in readiness for the day when he was discovered. He spent a holiday in Greece and discovered an island which could be fully appreciated only by himself and two chosen friends. His favourite word during the first few weeks of this Easter vacation, when he and Janet got to know each other, was 'plasticity'. Last year it had been 'conceptual'. Robert felt that he was a nice healthy boy at heart.

Candida, at the local school, was a heavier responsibility. She lived at home and sulked, brooded, sniggered and grew ecstatic or despairing as she had always done, though with added emphasis, as though to challenge Janet and learn how far she dared go.

Janet coped. She was not domineering and she was not prissy. She did not spy, but she contrived to keep the wrong sort of book out of Candida's hands. She didn't force the pace: she was steady, humorous and unfaltering.

'I don't believe it,' said Robert one Sunday.

'Don't believe what?'

'The ... well ...' Again he was thinking something naïve – and enjoying it. 'The happiness,' he said. 'That's all – just happiness, just like that.'

She blushed and gave a little pout, shyly repudiating the idea yet loving it.

She said: 'You're so sweet.'

Every word they said to each other was true and uncomplicated. *Don't you dare ...*

He had dared and he was happy.

'You're looking well,' his business acquaintances said.

The weeks of summer rolled past and at last he began to accept – really to accept – that Laura was dead. He didn't have to keep saying it to himself any more: it was all right and it didn't need repeating.

For some time he had kept neighbours at arm's length. Then Janet got to know one or two of them. Characteristically, he thought, she picked on the nicer ones and somehow just didn't get round to meeting the rowdier ones.

One Saturday afternoon the Major came over for a drink.

'You're looking pretty fit, old boy,' he observed.

He did not gloat over Janet as he had shamelessly gloated over Laura. He spoke to her with genuine warmth and respect, and for the first time began to treat Robert also with respect.

Lulled into ease and near-complacency, Robert was taken off guard when Laura once again smiled her old, evil smile at him.

He should have been ready. He should have known that the contentment wouldn't last.

Laura was back. Laura was smiling.

It was a hot afternoon. In slacks and a white shirt Janet sat in the shade of the cherry tree, reading desultorily. Michael sprawled on the grass a few feet away. Every now and then he murmured something to himself or to Janet – from where Robert was working at the water's edge, clearing away some flotsam which had piled up against the bank, it was difficult to tell which. A small aeroplane buzzed drowsily overhead. The weir roared a faint, undisturbing roar.

Suddenly Michael and Janet began to laugh. Michael pushed himself up on to his knees and leaned towards Janet. He said something quickly, and they laughed again. Their heads turned momentarily towards Robert and then turned away again.

He straightened up and sauntered along the lawn up the slope to the shade of the tree.

'What are you two plotting?' he asked affectionately.

And there was Laura, gleaming her malice at him. Just one swift, savage gleam of a smile. It took his breath away. He stopped where he was, swaying. He closed his eyes and opened them again. Laura's face had disappeared. It could never have been there; couldn't possibly have been there.

Michael had Laura's eyes. Just for a moment, just in a trick of the light and the dappled shade, Michael's eyes and mouth must have fooled him.

But it hadn't been like that. He knew it hadn't. The brief glimpse had not been of Michael's face. Laura had looked at him and jeered at him not out of her son but out of Janet.

'What's the matter, Robert?'

Janet's voice was soft and concerned. She began to get up from her chair. As she emerged into the full blaze of the sun she was his dark, sweet Janet.

An illusion. Nothing more than that. It wouldn't happen again.

Two days later he walked past the open door of Candida's bedroom and saw her sprawled on the bed, reading. He went casually in.

'Not swotting for next term already?'

She drew the edge of the coverlet slowly over the book. The gesture was languid and almost indifferent. She couldn't really be bothered to hide it from him.

'Candida,' he said reproachfully.

She rolled to one side so that he could pull the coverlet back and see the gaudy cover of the book.

It was a paperback showing the photographed back view of a girl wearing only a bra. A man bent over her with a whip in his hand, and there was a streak of blood across her right shoulder. It was crude, yet not as crude as paperbacks had once been: it was too glossy and looked photographically, colourfully real.

'What's wrong?'

Janet had come along the passage and was standing in the open doorway. Robert prodded the book. 'I thought we'd got over this kind of thing. Honestly, Candida, it's stupid – can't you tell that when you read it?'

'I wouldn't know how stupid it was till I'd had a chance of reading it, would I?' she said pertly.

Robert picked it up.

Janet said: 'Do we have to make a big scene about it?'

He froze. There was a crackle in her voice which he recognized. And he saw that this time it wasn't just his imagination. Candida recognized it, too. Candida stared past him, incredulous, and then began to smile, almost hugging herself with glee.

Very carefully he said: 'I thought we'd agreed there would be no more of this nonsense. Janet ...'

'It's nonsense,' she agreed crisply, 'and what harm can it possibly do her?'

'I suppose you used to read them by the dozen when you were her age?'

'Why do you say that?'

'Oh ... never mind. Never mind.'

Janet shrugged. 'Let her get it out of her system.'

Candida went on staring at her and now held out her hand. Janet took the book from Robert and tossed it back onto the bed.

He wanted to talk to Janet. It was imperative that he should talk to her. This whole thing had to be settled today, before trouble overtook them. Yet he found he could not speak. He watched her walk off ahead of him and he couldn't make a move. He wanted to go after her and put his arm round her shoulders and start talking reasonably, as they had always talked until now. But he was afraid. In his fingertips he could already feel how she would shrug him off.

By evening he began to feel safe again. They sat by the open window in companionable silence. The haze from the river made a silvery dusk, softening the outlines of trees and houses on the far bank. Candida was with friends whose parents would drive her home about half an hour from now. Michael was out on one of his meditative rambles. There was peace.

Robert said: 'Darling ...'

'Mm?'

'About Candida.'

'Yes. That business earlier today.' Janet put her head on one side as though to catch a puzzling echo. 'You know, I don't quite ...'

There was the slam of the front door. Michael came in. He flapped a hand amiably at his father and went towards an armchair in the shadows at the end of the room.

Janet said: 'Don't I get a kiss?'

Michael slowly approached the window. Robert tried not to look. He fixed his gaze resolutely on his hands, clasped on his knees. But such resolution could not be sustained. He looked up, looked across at Janet's profile as she turned towards Michael. The silvery twilight blurred even her dark hair. For one dazzling fraction of a second he saw her face and hands and hair bleached fairer and whiter than death.

Michael bent and kissed her.

'Mm,' said Janet throatily. 'It *is* nice to have a man about the house.'

Robert got up and reached for the nearest switch. Light flooded from the squat, wide-shaded lamp by the hearth.

'Since you're up,' said Janet, 'you could pour me a drink. Pour us all a drink.'

Robert's hand shook as he got out the glasses. He poured slowly so that there would be time for everything to become normal again. And on the face of it, when they drank, things were normal enough. Janet asked Michael where he had been and Michael muttered in his usual vague way. But there was a strange sense of communication between them: odd references and unfinished sentences which meant nothing to Robert somehow made sense to Janet; a brief little conspiratorial smile flickered to and fro.

Candida was late getting home. The man who brought her apologized, explaining that there had been difficulty getting the car started and that he had stupidly taken a wrong turning and gone miles out of his way. He accepted a drink and left.

Janet swung round upon Candida with her hand raised.

'I told you what time to be back. I told you to make them bring you back in good time.'

'But it wasn't my fault. He's just told you ...'

'He's covering up for you. I know your little game. You spin things out as long as you can, and then blame other people.'

She struck Candida full across the face. Before Robert could protest, Candida ran from the room. Janet went after her as though to strike her again.

'Janet – stop!'

Robert followed. Janet caught up with the girl at the foot of the stairs and seized her arm. Each of them had a foot on the lowest step. Candida suddenly sagged against Janet. They put their arms round each other and laughed and sobbed weakly.

Above Candida's head, Janet said: 'Let's not have one of your nasty, cold, rational lectures, Robert. You just don't understand girls at all. Girls of any age.'

That night he tried to make love to her. He simply had to restore things to what they had so recently been. But her body had an unyielding softness – a contradiction in terms, an impossibility that was nevertheless a humiliating reality. In the darkness she chuckled. When he fell despairingly away from her she said mockingly: 'Never mind, Robert, dear. Never mind.'

He was glad of the hours he could spend in his office. With staff away on summer holidays, there was a pile-up of work. He welcomed it. It kept him late and he was not sorry to be late. It was not until he was driving home that he began to face up to what lay in wait for him.

Arguments shaped up in his head. He had to work for their living, didn't he? If he stayed late and got home late it was because there was a lot to be done and someone had to do it and he was that someone.

No. No need for arguments. Of course not. Janet was there. Janet would be Janet and nobody else. She would meet him at the door and she would be Janet again.

The arguments seethed over one another, tumbling and twisting.

She would be waiting for him. He kept telling himself that. The old Janet. The only Janet.

When he went into the house there was silence. It was a hot evening, and down here in the river valley it was even more difficult to breathe than it had been in the city.

'Janet?' he called.

There was no reply.

The windows were open on to the garden. Robert went out on to the lawn.

The Major was stretched out in a deck-chair on the other side of the river. He waved. And Laura came swimming back across the river as she had so often done. Robert watched, terrified. How could he stop her coming up out of the water, on to the lawn, savage and vengeful?

But it wasn't Laura. It was Janet. She swam noisily and badly. She was floundering as she reached the bank, having to fight the last few yards of the way against the treacherous snatching of the current.

Robert ran to meet her.

'What are you up to? Don't you know how close we are to the weir?'

She stood up, trim and self-possessed in her one-piece black costume. She was breathing hard but she managed to say:

'Pity to have the river here and not use it.'

'But you oughtn't to risk it. You're not a good swimmer – are you?'

'I will be.'

'But ...'

'Nobody's asking you to come in with me,' Janet snapped. She looked him up and down, then put her hands behind her head and swung languidly round in the evening sunshine. The Major waved as she spun to face him. When she had made the full circuit she appraised Robert again. 'The water too cold for you?' she said, and walked past him and into the house.

The house was haunted. The house ... or perhaps the family. Now he knew it. Haunted not by a separate ghost, an entity, a wandering phantom apart from them, but by a creature indistinguishable from Janet, from Candida, from Michael. They were possessed. This was no mournful shadow waiting in dark corners: it was with them and in them in broad daylight, growing stronger as it fed on them.

Janet took fiercely and repeatedly to the river. One night when Michael and Candida had gone to bed and Robert was yawning, about to comment that it was gone eleven o'clock, Janet abruptly said that she wanted to go out. Just for a little while, to clear her head. Before he could question her, she went up to their room. When she came down she was wearing a wispy bikini. It did not suit her as it had suited Laura: she was an inch or two wrong, slightly too plump, not quite tall enough. But

she walked as Laura walked. When she went out down the garden to the
darkness of the water, she was Laura.

Robert hurried after her down the lawn.

'You can't. It's mad. At this time of night . . .'

'You can stand by with a lifebelt if it worries you.'

Janet plunged in.

He stood there, helpless. Across the river, lights burned in the
windows of the Major's house and made a glowing, rippling pool below
the bank. Janet swam strongly though clumsily towards it.

Robert turned and looked back at his own house.

Michael's bedroom was at one end, Candida's at the other. Their
curtains were drawn back. In each window there was a pale, watching
face.

Janet was away for over an hour. When she came back she was
breathing hard but laughing at the same time. She cupped her hands
over her breasts and her fingers beat out a joyful tattoo on her wet flesh.

She said: 'I've invited the Major over to our party next
Wednesday.'

'I didn't know we were having a party next Wednesday.'

'Well, we are. I've just decided.'

Among the people she invited were several Robert had not seen for
some months. He hadn't known that Janet had even met them. There
were the two alcoholics from the island who had always squealed
ecstatically over Laura's jokes and then quarrelled at the end of every
evening and had to be taken home. There was the old harpy from one of
the boats, and a limp young man whom Michael had once claimed to
despise but whom he now greeted as a long-lost friend. And there was
the couple who lived in sin on the seediest of the nearby boats and made
a point of letting everyone know that they were living in sin as though to
proclaim their superiority over duller mortals.

Janet had been to have her hair done for the occasion. She had had
it dyed blonde. The black softness of it had been converted to a harsh
golden helmet.

Robert stared. She did not bother to ask him what he thought about
it.

When the Major arrived, he, too, stared.

'Like it?' said Janet.

He studied the hair again, then looked her up and down and
smacked his lips with exaggerated relish.

'Robert,' said Janet in a tone of patient suffering, 'do keep an eye on
the drinks, won't you? Do pretend to be a perfect host.'

It was a long time since he had heard this range and volume of
voices. It was the first time for months that glass was trodden into the
carpet once more. And the Major was touching Janet's arm and

gloating, and the couple from the boat were pawing each other and making sure that everyone saw it.

'It's love,' said Janet suddenly. She swayed above them with her glass slopping gin over the side. 'I mean, don't you think it's so pretty to watch?' She waved her free arm towards Robert. 'You know, Robert, perhaps we ought never to have got married. Don't you think marriage spoils things?' Now she addressed the assembly, raising her voice and talking them all down. 'You don't get the same kick when it's all been legalized, do you? At least, men don't seem to. Bags of enthusiasm at first, and then all they want is food and someone to sweep the place up. In no time at all they've given up leaping on you with a glad cry and ...'

'No,' said Robert. 'Don't say it.'

Janet's eyes widened. They looked at him as they had looked at him year after year, year after terrible year. 'Goodness me, we're on edge this evening, aren't we?'

He tried to get close to her and make a last appeal. But she brushed past him and stood above the Major. His arm lay along the arm of his chair. Hair on his wrist was tangled under his watch strap. Janet meditatively stroked the hair up and then smoothed it down again.

She looked at Robert. 'Funny, isn't it? Now, Robert hasn't ...'

'Stop it.'

'Stop what, Robert, dear.'

The way in which the word 'dear' was wrenched out of her mouth was all too familiar. Her eyes were pools of poison. 'Given my time over again ...' Laura had said it but never completed the sentence. She had been given her time over again; and she was just the same, she could do no better than before.

She must not be allowed to do worse.

He said: 'Remember what happened last time.'

Janet said: 'Don't you dare.'

In front of them all he went through it again. They didn't know what he was going to do, so they made no move to stop him; Laura knew, but she wasn't fast enough.

He grabbed the heavy marble ashtray, scattering ash as he swung it. The gilded head ducked and someone screamed – Laura or Janet, he couldn't tell which. Then he slammed the stone edge into the side of that head. The force almost carried him over, but he staggered, gripped the edge of the ashtray, and brought it down again as the head sagged and the body crumpled at his feet. Twice and then three times he was able to lift it and smack it down. Then they were dragging him back.

They didn't let him finish. They couldn't act in time to stop him killing her, but they could stop him carrying her down the darkened lawn and tipping her quietly into the river. This time she would not be carried away down her beloved river. This time she wouldn't suffer the disgrace of being defeated at last by the current and carried over the weir.

Janet did not finish up as Laura had finished up – her beautiful hair tangled, her beautiful body battered and wrenched and beautifully, bloodily pulped against the stakes of the breakwater.

Browdean Farm

A. M. Burrage

Most people with limited vocabularies such as mine would describe the house loosely and comprehensively as picturesque. But it was more than beautiful in its venerable age. It had certain subtle qualities which are called Atmosphere. It invited you, as you approached it along the rough and narrow road which is ignored by those maps which are sold for the use of motorists. In the language of very old houses it said plainly: 'Come in. Come in.'

It said 'Come in' to Rudge Jefferson and me. In one of the front windows there was a notice, inscribed in an illiterate hand, to the effect that the house was to be let, and that the keys were to be obtained at the first cottage down the road. We went and got them. The woman who handed them over to us remarked that plenty of people looked over the house, but nobody ever took it. It had been empty for years.

'Damp and falling to pieces, I suppose,' said Rudge as we returned. 'There's always a snag about these old places.'

The house – 'Browdean Farm' it was called – stood some thirty yards back from the road, at the end of a strip of garden not much wider than its façade. Most of the building was plainly Tudor, but part of it was even earlier. Time was when it had been the property of prosperous yeomen, but now its acres had been added to those of another farm, and it stood shorn of all its land save the small untended gardens in front and behind, and half an acre of apple orchard.

As in most houses of that description the kitchen was the largest room. It was long and lofty and its arched roof was supported by mighty beams which stretched across its breadth. There was a huge range with a noble oven. One could fancy, in the old days of plenty, a score of harvesters supping there after their work, and beer and cider flowing as freely as spring brooks.

To our surprise the place showed few signs of damp, considering the length of time it had been untenanted, and it needed little in the way of repairs. There was not a stick of furniture in the house, but we could tell that its last occupants had been people of refinement and taste. The wallpapers upstairs, the colours of the faded paints and distempers, the presence of a bathroom – that great rarity in old farmhouses – all pointed to the probability of its having been last in the hands of an amateur of country cottages.

Jefferson told me that he knew in his bones – and for once I agreed with his bones – that Nina would love the farm. He was engaged to my sister, and they were waiting until he had saved sufficient money to give them a reasonable material start in matrimony. Like most painstaking writers of no particular reputation Jefferson had to take care of the pence and the shillings, but, like Nina's, his tastes were inexpensive, and it was an understood thing that they were to live quietly together in the country.

We enquired about the rent. It was astonishingly low. Jefferson had to live somewhere while he finished a book, and he was already paying storage for the furniture which he had bought. I could look forward to some months of idleness before returning to India. There was a trout stream in the neighbourhood which would keep me occupied and out of mischief. We laid our heads together.

Jefferson did not want a house immediately, but bargains of that sort are not everyday affairs in these hard times. Besides, with me to share expenses for the next six months, the cost of living at Browdean Farm would be very low, and it seemed a profitable speculation to take the house then and there on a seven years' lease. This is just what Jefferson did – or rather, the agreement was signed by both parties within a week.

Rudge Jefferson and I were old enough friends to understand each other thoroughly, and make allowances for each other's temperaments. We were neither of us morose but often one or both of us would be anxious to talk. There were indefinite hours when Rudge felt either impelled or compelled to write. We found no difficulty in coming to a working agreement. We did not feel obliged to converse at meals. We could bring books to the table if we so wished. Rudge could go to his work when he chose, and I could go off fishing or otherwise amuse myself. Only when we were both inclined for companionship need we pay any attention to each other's existence.

And, from the April evening when we arrived half an hour after the men with the furniture, it worked admirably.

We lived practically in one room, the larger of the two front sitting-rooms. There we took our meals, talked and smoked and read. The smaller sitting-room Rudge commandeered for a study. He retired thither when the spirit moved him to invoke the muses and tap at his typewriter. Our only servant was the woman who had lately had charge of the keys. She came in every day to cook our meals and do the housework, and, as for convenience we dined in the middle of the day, we had the place to ourselves immediately after tea. The garden we decided to tend ourselves, but although we began digging and planting with the early enthusiasm of most amateurs we soon tired of the job and let wild nature take its course.

Our first month was ideal and idyllic. The weather was kind, and everything seemed to go in our favour. The trout gave me all the fun I could have hoped for, and Rudge was satisfied with the quality and quantity of his output. I had no difficulty in adapting myself to his little ways, and soon discovered that his best hours for working were in the mornings and the late evenings, so I left him to himself at those times. We took our last meal, a light cold supper, at about half past nine, and very often I stayed out until that hour.

You must not think that we lived like two recluses under the same roof. Sometimes Rudge was not in the mood for work and hinted at a desire for companionship. Then we went out for long walks, or he came to watch me fish. He was himself a ham-handed angler and seldom attempted to throw a fly. Often we went to drink the light ale at the village inn, a mile distant. And always after supper we smoked and talked for an hour or so before turning in.

It was then, while we were sitting quietly, that we discovered that the house, which was mute by day, owned strange voices which gave tongue after dark. They were the noises which, I suppose, one ought to expect to hear in an old house half full of timber when the world around it is hushed and sleeping. They might have been nerve-racking if one of us had been there alone, but as it was we took little notice at first. Mostly they proceeded from the kitchen, whence we heard the creaking of beams, sobbing noises, gasping noises and queer indescribable scufflings.

While neither of us believed in ghosts we laughingly agreed that the house ought to be haunted, and by something a little more sensational than the sounds of timber contracting and the wind in the kitchen chimney. We knew ourselves to be the unwilling hosts of a colony of rats, which was in itself sufficient to account for most nocturnal noises. Rudge said that he wanted to meet the ghost of an eighteenth century miser, who couldn't rest until he had shown where the money was hidden. There was some practical use in that sort of bogy. And although, as time went on, these night noises became louder and more persistent, we put them down to 'natural causes' and made no effort to investigate them. It occurred to us both that some more rats had discovered a good home, and although we talked of trapping them our talk came to nothing.

We had been at the farm about a month before Rudge Jefferson began to show symptoms of 'nerves'. All writers are the same. Neurotic brutes! But I said nothing to him and waited for him to diagnose his own trouble and ease up a little with his work.

It was at about that time that I, walking homewards one morning just about lunch-time, with my rod over my shoulder, encountered the local policeman just outside the village inn. He wished me a good day which was at once hearty and respectful, and at the same time passed the back of his hand over a thirsty-looking moustache. The hint was obvious, and only a heart of stone could have refrained from inviting him inside. Besides, I believe in keeping in with the police.

He was one of those country constables who become fixtures in quiet, out of the way districts, where they live and let live, and often go into pensioned retirement without bringing more than half a dozen cases before the petty sessions. This worthy was named Hicks, and I had already discovered that everybody liked him. He did not look for trouble. He had rabbits from the local poachers, beer from local cyclists who rode after dark without lights, and more beer from the landlord who chose to exercise his own discretion with regard to closing-time.

P.C. Hicks drank a pint of bitter with me and gave me his best respects. He asked me how we were getting on up at the farm. Admirably, I told him; and then he looked at me closely, as if to see if I were sincere, or, rather, to search my eyes for the passing of some afterthought.

Having found me guileless, as it seemed, he went on to tell of his length of service – he had been eighteen years on the one beat – and of how little trouble he had been to anybody. There was something pathetic in the protestations of the middle-aged Bobby that, to all the world, he had been a man and a brother. He seemed tacitly to be asking for reciprocity, and his own vagueness drew me out of my depth.

You know those beautifully vague men, who pride themselves for being diplomatists on the principle that a nod is as good as a wink to a blind horse? The people who will hint and hint and hint, the asses who will wander round and round and round the haystack with hardly a nibble at it? He was one of them. He wanted to tell me something without actually telling me, to exact from me a promise about something he chose not to mention.

I had found myself in dialectical tangles with him, and at last I laughingly gave up the task of trying to follow his labyrinthine thoughts. I ordered two more bitters and then he said:

'Well, sir, if anything 'appens up at the farm, you needn' get talkin' about it. We done our best. What's past is past, and can't be altered. There isn't no sense in settin' people against *us*.'

I knew from his inflection on the word that 'us' was the police. He did not look at me while he spoke. He was staring at something straight

across the counter, and I happened by sheer chance to follow the
direction of his gaze.

Opposite us, and hanging from a shelf so as to face the customers,
was a little tear-off calendar. The date recorded there was the nineteenth
of May.

*   *   *

Two evenings later – which is to say the evening of May 21st – I
returned home at half past nine full of suppressed excitement. I had a
story to tell Rudge, and I was yet not sure if I should be wise in telling it.
His nerves had grown worse during the past two days, but after all there
are nerves and nerves, and my tale might interest without harming him.

It was only just dusk and not a tithe of the stars were burning as I
walked up the garden path, inhaling the rank scents of those hardy
flowers which had sprung up untended in that miniature wilderness.
The sitting-room window was dark, but the subdued light of an oil lamp
burned behind the curtains of Rudge's study. I found the door
unbarred, walked in, and entered the study. You see, it was supper-
time, and Rudge might safely be intruded upon.

Rather to my surprise the room was empty, but I surmised that
Rudge had gone up to wash. That he had lately been at work was
evident from the fact that a sheet of paper, half used, lay in the roller of
the typewriter. I sat down in the revolving chair to see what he had
written – I was allowed that privilege – and was astonished to see that
he had ended in the middle of a sentence. In some respects he was
a methodical person, and this was unlike him. The last word he had
written was 'the', and the last letter of that word was black and
prominent as if he had slammed down the key with unnecessary force.

Two minutes later, while I was still reading, a probable explanation
was revealed to me. I heard the gate click and footfalls on the path.
Naturally I guessed that Rudge, temperamental as he was, had
suddenly tired of his work and gone out for a walk. I heard the footsteps
come to within a few yards of the house, when they left the path, fell
softer on grass and weeds, and approached the window. The curtain
obscured my view, but on the glass I heard the tap of finger-tips and the
clink of nails.

I did not pause to reflect that Rudge, if he had gone out, must know
that he had left the door on the latch, or that he could have no reason to
suppose that I was already in the house. One does not consider these
things in so brief a time. I just called out, 'Right ho,' and went round to
the front door to let him in.

Having opened the front door I leaned out and saw him – Rudge, I
imagined – peering in at the study window. He was no more than a
dark, bent shadow in the dusk, crowned by a soft felt hat, such as he

generally wore. 'Right ho,' I said again, and, leaving the door wide open for him, I hurried into the kitchen. There was some salad left in soak which had to be shaken and wiped before bringing it to the table. I remember that, as I walked through to the sink, one of the beams over my head creaked noisily.

I washed the salad and returned towards the dining-room. As I turned into the hall a gust of air from the still open door passed like a cool caress across my face. Then, before I had time to enter the dining-room, I heard the gate click at the end of the garden path, and footfalls on the gravel. I waited to see who it was. It was Rudge – and he was bareheaded.

He produced a book at supper, and sat scowling at it over his left arm while he ate. This was permitted by our rules, but I had something to tell him, and after a while I forced my voice upon his attention.

'Rudge,' I said, 'I've made a discovery this evening. I know how you got this place so cheap.'

He sat up with a start, stared at me, and winced.

'How?' he demanded.

'This is Stanley Stryde's old house. Don't you remember Stanley Stryde?'

He was pale already, but I saw him turn paler still.

'I remember the name vaguely,' he said. 'Wasn't he a murderer?'

'He was,' I answered. 'I didn't remember the case very well. But my memory's been refreshed today. Everybody here thought we knew, and the curious delicacy of the bucolic mind forbade mentioning it to us. It was rather a grisly business, and the odd thing is that local opinion is all in favour of Stryde's innocence, although he was hanged.'

Rudge's eyes had grown larger.

'I remember the name,' he said, 'but I forget the case. Tell me.'

'Well, Stanley Stryde was an artist who took this place. He was what we would call in common parlance a dirty dog. He'd got himself entangled with the daughter of a neighbouring farmer – the family has left here since – and then he found himself morally and socially compelled to marry her. At the same time he fell in love with another girl, so he lured the old one here and did her in. Don't you remember now?'

Rudge wrinkled his nose.

'Yes, vaguely,' he said. 'Didn't he bury the body and afterwards try to make out she'd committed suicide? So this is the house, is it? Funny nobody told us before?'

'They thought we knew,' I repeated, 'and nobody liked to mention it. As if it were some disgrace to *us*, you know! Oh, and, of course, the house is haunted.'

Rudge stared at me and frowned.

'I don't know about "haunted",' he said, 'but it's been a damned uncomfortable house to sit in for the past few evenings. I mean at twilight, when I've been waiting for you. My nerves have been pretty raw lately. Tonight I couldn't stand it, so I went out for a stroll.'

'Left in the middle of a sentence,' I remarked.

'Oh, so you noticed that, did you?'

'By the way,' I asked, 'what made you go out a second time?'

'I didn't.'

'But my dear chap, you did! Because the first time you came in you wore a hat, and two minutes later I saw you walking up the garden path without one.'

'That's when I did come back. I haven't wore a hat at all this evening.'

'Then who——' I began.

'And that reminds me,' he continued quickly, 'when *you* come in of an evening you needn't sneak up to the window and tap on it with your fingers. It doesn't frighten me, but it's disconcerting. You can always walk into the room to let me know you've come back.'

I sat and looked at him and laughed.

'But, my dear chap, I haven't done such a thing yet.'

'You old liar!' he exclaimed with an uneasy laugh, 'you've been doing it every evening for the past week – until tonight, when I didn't give you the chance.'

'I swear I haven't, Rudge. But if you thought that, it explains why you did the same thing to me tonight.'

I saw from his face that I had made some queer mistake, and interrupted his denial to ask:

'Then who was the man I saw peering in at the window? I saw him from the door. I thought you'd tapped at the window to be let in, not knowing that the door was open. So I went round and saw – I thought it was you – and called out, "Right ho".'

We looked at each other again and laughed uneasily.

'It seems we've got our ghost after all,' Rudge said half jestingly.

'Or somebody's trying to pull our leg,' I amended.

'I don't know that I should fancy meeting the ghost of a murderer. But, joking apart, the house *has* been getting on my nerves of late. And those noises we've always heard have been getting louder and more mysterious lately.'

As if to corroborate a statement which needed no evidence so far as I was concerned we heard a scuffling sound from the kitchen followed by the loud creaking of timber. We laughed again, puzzled uneasy laughter, for the thing was still half a joke.

'There you are!' said Rudge, and got upon his legs. 'I'm going to investigate this.'

He crossed the room and suddenly halted. I knew why. Then he turned about with an odd, shamed chuckle.

'No,' he said, 'there's no sense in it. I shall find nothing there. Why should I pander to my nerves?'

I had nothing to say. But I knew that in turning back he was pandering to cowardice, because just then I would have done almost anything rather than enter that kitchen. Had anybody asked me then where the murder was done, I could have told them with as much certainty as if I had just been reading about it in the papers.

Rudge sat down again.

'Don't laugh at me,' he said. 'I know this is all rot, but I've got a hideous feeling that things hidden and unseen around us are moving steadily to a crisis.'

'Cheerful brute,' I said, smiling.

'I know. It's only my nerves, of course. I don't want to infect you with them. But the noises we hear, and the fellow who comes and taps at the window – they want some explaining away, don't they?'

'Especially now that we know that somebody was murdered here,' I agreed. 'I'm beginning to wish we didn't know about that.'

Rudge went to bed early that night, but I sat up reading. As often happens to me I fell asleep over my book, and when I woke I was almost in darkness, for the lamp needed filling. The last jagged blue flame swelled and dwindled, fluttering like a moth and tapping against the glass. And as I watched it I became suddenly aware of the cause of my waking. I had heard the latch snap on the garden gate. And in that moment I began to hear them – the footfalls.

I heard the rhythmic crunch of gravel and then the swish of long grass and plantains, and then a shadow nodded on the blind. It loomed up large and suddenly became stationary. A loose pane rattled under the impact of fingers.

Perhaps there was a moon, perhaps not, but there was at least bright starlight in the world outside. The drawn blind looked like dim bluish glass, and the shadow of something outside was cut as cleanly as a silhouette clipped away with scissors. I saw only the head and shoulders of a man, who wore a dented felt hat. His head lolled over on to his left shoulder, just as I had always imagined a man's head would loll if – well, if he had been hanged. And I knew in my blood that he was a Horror and that he wanted me for something.

I felt my hair bristle and suddenly I was streaming with sweat. I don't remember turning and running, but I have a vague recollection of cannoning off the door-post and stumbling in the hall. And when I reached my bed I don't know if I fainted or fell asleep.

No, I didn't tell Rudge next day. His nerves were in a bad enough state already. Besides, in the fresh glory of a May morning it was easy to persuade myself that the episode had been an evil dream. But I did question Mrs Jaines, our charwoman, when she arrived, and I saw a look half stubborn and half guilty cross her face.

Yes, of course, she remembered the murder happening, but she didn't remember much about it. Mr Stryde was quite a nice gentleman, although rather a one of the ladies, and she had worked for him sometimes. Stryde's defence was that the poor girl had committed suicide and that he'd lost his head and buried the body when he found it. Lots of people thought that was true, but they'd hanged Mr Stryde for it all the same. And that was all I could get out of Mrs Jaines.

I smiled grimly to myself. As if the woman didn't remember every detail! As if the neighbourhood had talked of anything else for the two following years! And then I remembered the policeman's strange words and how he had been staring at the calendar while he spoke.

So that morning when I called at the inn for my usual glass of beer, I too looked at the calendar, and asked the landlord if he could tell me the date of the murder.

'Yes, sir,' he said, 'it was May the——' And then he stopped himself. 'Why, it was eight years ago, tonight!' he said.

* * *

I went out again that evening and came in at the usual hour. But that evening Rudge came down the path to meet me. He was white and sick-looking.

'He's been here again,' he said, 'half an hour ago.'

'You saw him this time?' I asked jerkily.

'Yes, I did as you did and went round to the door.' He paused and added quite soberly: 'He *is* a ghost, you know.'

'What happened?' I asked, looking uneasily around me.

'Oh! I went round to the door when I heard him tapping at the window, and there he was, as you saw him yesterday evening, trying to look through into the room. He must have heard me, for he turned and stared. His head was dropping all on one side, like a poppy on a broken stem. He came towards me, and I couldn't stand that, so I turned and ran into the house and locked the door.'

He spoke in a tone half weary, half matter of fact, and suddenly I knew that it was all true. I don't mean that I knew that just his story was true. I knew that the house was haunted and that the thing which we had both seen was part of the man who had once been Stanley Stryde.

When once one has accepted the hitherto incredible it is strange how soon one can adapt oneself to the altered point of view.

'This is the anniversary of the – the murder,' I said quietly. 'I should think something – something worse will happen tonight. Shall we see it through or shall we beat it?'

And almost in a whisper Rudge said:

'Poor devil! Oughtn't one to pity? He wants to tell us something, you know.'

'Yes,' I agreed, 'or show us something.'

Together we walked into the house. We were braver in each other's company, and we did not again discuss the problem of going or staying. We stayed.

I can pass over the details of how we spent that evening. They are of no importance to the story. We were left in peace until just after eleven o'clock, when once more we heard the garden gate being opened, and footfalls, which by this time we were able to recognize, came up the path and through the long grass to the window. We could see nothing, for our lamp was alight, but I knew what it looked like – the thing that stood outside and now tapped softly upon the glass. And in spite of having Rudge for company I lost my head and screamed at it.

'Get back to hell! Get back to hell, I tell you!' I heard myself shout.

And it was Rudge, Rudge the sensitive neurotic, who kept his head, for human psychology is past human understanding.

'No,' he called out in a thin quaver, 'come in. Come in, if we can help you.'

And then, as if regretting his courage on the instant, he caught my hand and held it, drawing me towards him.

The front door was locked, but it was no barrier to that which responded to the invitation. We heard slow footfalls shuffling through the hall, the footfalls, it seemed to me, of a man whose head was a burden to him. I died a thousand deaths as they approached the door of our room, but they passed and died away up the passage. And then I heard a whisper from Rudge.

'He's gone through into the kitchen. I think he wants us to follow.'

I shouldn't have gone if Rudge hadn't half dragged me by the hand. And as I went the sweat from the roots of my stiffened hair ran down my cheeks.

The kitchen door was closed, and we halted outside it, both of us breathing as if we had been running hard. Then Rudge held his breath for a moment, lifted the latch, and took a quick step across the threshold. And in that same instant he froze my chilled blood with a scream such as I had heard in war-time from a wounded horse.

He had almost fainted when he fell into my arms, but he had the presence of mind to pull the door after him, so that I saw nothing. I half dragged, half carried him into the dining-room and gave him brandy. And suddenly I became aware that a great peace had settled upon the house. I can only liken it to the freshness and the sweetness of the earth after a storm has passed. Rudge felt it too, for presently he began to talk.

'What was he – doing?' I asked in a whisper.

'He? He wasn't there – not in the kitchen.'

'Not in the kitchen? Then what – who——'

'It was She. Only She. She was kicking and struggling. From the middle beam, you know. And there was an overturned chair at her feet.'

He shuddered convulsively.

'She was worse than he,' he said presently – 'far worse.'

And then later:

'Poor devil! So he didn't do it, you see!'

*   *   *

Next morning we had it out with Mrs Jaines, and we did not permit her memory to be hazy or defective. She must have known that we had seen something and presently she burst into tears.

'He said he'd found her hanging in the kitchen, poor gentleman, and that he'd buried her because he was afraid people would say he'd done it. But the jury wouldn't believe him, and the doctors all said that it wasn't true, and that the marks on her neck were where he'd strangled her with a rope. I don't believe to this day he did it, I don't! But nothing can't ever bring him back.' She paused at that and added. 'Not back to life, I mean – real life, like you and me, I mean.'

And that was all we heard and all we wished to hear.

Afterwards Rudge said to me:

'For his sake, the truth as we know it ought to be told to everybody. I suppose the police know?'

'Yes,' I said, 'the police know – now. But as Mrs Jaines said, it can't bring him back.'

'Who wants to bring him back?' exclaimed Rudge with a shudder. 'But perhaps if people knew – as we know – it might let him rest. I am sure that was what he wanted – just that people should know.'

He paused and drew a long breath through his lips.

'You write it,' he said jerkily. 'I can't.'

And so I have.

The Ghoul
Hugh Clifford

We had been sitting up late upon the veranda of my bungalow at Kuâla Lîpis, which, from the top of a low hill covered with coarse grass, over-looked the long, narrow reach formed by the combined waters of the Lîpis and the Jĕlai. The moon had risen some hours earlier, and the river ran white between the black masses of forest, which seemed to shut it in on all sides, giving to it the appearance of an isolated tarn. The roughly cleared compound, with the tennis-ground which had never got beyond the stage of being dug over and weeded, and the rank growths beyond the bamboo fence, were flooded by the soft light, every tattered detail of their ugliness standing revealed as relentlessly as though it were noon. The night was very still, but the heavy, scented air was cool after the fierce heat of the day.

I had been holding forth to the handful of men who had been dining with me on the subject of Malay superstitions, while they manfully stifled their yawns. When a man has a working knowledge of anything which is not commonly known to his neighbours, he is apt to presuppose their interest in it when a chance to descant upon it occurs, and in those days it was only at long intervals that I had an opportunity of foregathering with other white men. Therefore, I had made the most of it, and looking back, I fear that I had occupied the rostrum during the greater part of that evening. I had told my audience of the *pĕnanggal* – the 'Undone One' – that horrible wraith of a woman who has died in childbirth, who comes to torment and prey upon small children in the guise of a ghastly face and bust, with a comet's tail of blood-stained entrails flying in her wake; of the *mâti-ânak*, the weird little white animal which makes beast noises round the graves of children, and is supposed to have absorbed their souls; and of the *pôlong*, familiar spirits, which men bind to their service by raising up from the corpses of babies that have been still-born, the tips of whose tongues they bite off and swallow after the infant has been brought to life by magic agencies. It was at this point that young Middleton began to pluck up his ears; and I, finding that one of my hearers was at last showing signs of being interested, launched out with renewed vigour, until my sorely tried companions, one by one, went off to bed, each to his own quarters.

Middleton was staying with me at the time, and he and I sat for a while in silence, after the others had gone, looking at the moonlight on the river. Middleton was the first to speak.

'That was a curious myth you were telling us about the *pôlong*,' he said. 'There is an incident connected with it which I have never spoken of before, and have always sworn that I would keep to myself; but I have a good mind to tell you about it, because you are the only man I know who will not write me down a liar if I do.'

'That's all right. Fire away,' I said.

'Well,' said Middleton. 'It was like this. You remember Juggins, of course? He was a naturalist, you know, dead nuts upon becoming an F.R.S. and all that sort of thing, and he came to stay with me during the close season* last year. He was hunting for bugs and orchids and things, and spoke of himself as an anthropologist and a botanist and a zoologist, and heaven knows what besides; and he used to fill his bedroom with all sorts of creeping, crawling things, kept in very indifferent custody, and my veranda with all kinds of trash and rotting green trade that he brought in from the jungle. He stopped with me for about ten days, and when he heard that duty was taking me upriver into the Sâkai country, he asked me to let him come, too. I was rather bored, for the tribesmen are mighty shy of strangers and were only just getting used to me; but he was awfully keen, and a decent beggar enough, in spite of his dirty ways, so I couldn't very well say "No." When we had poled upstream for about a week, and had got well up into the Sâkai country, we had to leave our boats behind at the foot of the big rapids, and leg it for the rest of the time. It was very rough going, wading up and down streams when one wasn't clambering up a hill-side or sliding down the opposite slope – you know the sort of thing – and the leeches were worse that I have ever seen them – thousands of them, swarming up your back, and fastening in clusters onto your neck, even when you had defeated those which made a frontal attack. I had not enough men with me to do more than hump the camp-kit and a few clothes, so we had to live on the country, which doesn't yield much up among the Sâkai except yams and tapioca roots and a little Indian corn, and soft stuff of that sort. It was all new to Juggins, and gave him fits; but he stuck to it like a man.

'Well, one evening when the night was shutting down pretty fast and rain was beginning to fall, Juggins and I struck a fairly large Sâkai camp in the middle of a clearing. As soon as we came out of the jungle, and began tight-roping along the felled timber, the Sâkai sighted us and

* 'Close season', *i.e.* from the beginning of November to the end of February, during which time the rivers on the eastern seaboard of the Malay Peninsula used to be closed to traffic on account of the North-East Monsoon.

bolted for covert *en masse*. By the time we reached the huts it was pelting in earnest, and as my men were pretty well fagged out, I decided to spend the night in the camp, and not to make them put up temporary shelters for us. Sâkai huts are uncleanly places at best, and any port has to do in a storm.

'We went into the largest of the hovels, and there we found a woman lying by the side of her dead child. She had apparently felt too sick to bolt with the rest of her tribe. The kid was as stiff as Herod, and had not been born many hours, I should say. The mother seemed pretty bad, and I went to her, thinking I might be able to do something for her; but she did not seem to see it, and bit and snarled at me like a wounded animal, clutching at the dead child the while, as though she feared I should take it from her. I therefore left her alone; and Juggins and I took up our quarters in a smaller hut near by, which was fairly new and not so filthy dirty as most Sâkai lairs.

'Presently, when the beggars who had run away found out that I was the intruder, they began to come back again. You know their way. First a couple of men came and peeped at us, and vanished as soon as they saw they were observed. Then they came a trifle nearer, bobbed up suddenly, and peeped at us again. I called to them in Sĕ-noi,* which always reassures them, and when they at last summoned up courage to approach, gave them each a handful of tobacco. Then they went back into the jungle and fetched the others, and very soon the place was crawling with Sâkai of both sexes and all ages.

'We got a meal of sorts, and settled down for the night as best we could; but it wasn't a restful business. Juggins swore with eloquence at the uneven flooring, made of very roughly trimmed boughs, which is an infernally uncomfortable thing to lied down upon, and makes one's bones ache as though they were coming out at the joints, and the Sâkai are abominably restless bedfellows as you know. I suppose one ought to realize that they have as yet only partially emerged from the animal, and that, like the beasts, they are still naturally nocturnal. Anyway, they never sleep for long at a stretch, though from time to time they snuggle down and snore among the piles of warm wood ashes round the central fireplace, and whenever you wake, you will always see half a dozen of them squatting near the blazing logs, half hidden by the smoke, and jabbering like monkeys. It is a marvel to me what they find to yarn about: food, or rather the patent impossibility of ever getting enough to eat, and the stony-heartedness of providence and of the neighbouring Malays must furnish the principal topics, I should fancy, with an

---

* *Sĕ-noi* – one of the two main branches into which the Sâkai are divided. The other is called *Tĕ-mi-au* by the *Sĕ-noi*. All the Sâkai dialects are variants of the languages spoken by these two principal tribes, which, though they have many words in common, differ from one another almost as much as, say, Italian from Spanish.

occasional respectful mention of beasts of prey and forest demons. That night they were more than ordinarily restless. The dead baby was enough to make them uneasy, and besides, they had got wet while hiding in the jungle after our arrival, and that always sets the skin disease, with which all Sâkai are smothered, itching like mad. Whenever I woke I could hear their nails going on their dirty hides; but I had had a hard day and was used to my hosts' little ways, so I contrived to sleep fairly sound. Juggins told me next morning that he had had *une nuit blanche*, and he nearly caused another stampede among the Sâkai by trying to get a specimen of the fungus or bacillus, or whatever it is, that occasions the skin disease. I do not know whether he succeeded. For my own part, I think it is probably due to chronic anaemia – the poor devils have never had more than a very occasional full meal for hundreds of generations. I have seen little brats, hardly able to stand, white with it, the skin peeling off in flakes, and I used to frighten Juggins out of his senses by telling him he had contracted it when his nose was flayed by the sun.

'Next morning I woke just in time to see the still-born baby put into a hole in the ground. They fitted its body into a piece of bark, and stuck it in the grave they had dug for it at the edge of the clearing. They buried a flint and steel and a wood-knife and some food, and a few other things with it, though no living baby could have had any use for most of them, let alone a dead one. Then the old medicine man of the tribe recited the ritual over the grave. I took the trouble to translate it once. It goes something like this:

'"O Thou, who hast gone forth from among those who dwell upon the surface of the earth, and hast taken for thy dwelling-place the land which is beneath the earth, flint and steel have we given thee to kindle thy fire, raiment to clothe thy nakedness, food to fill thy belly, and a wood-knife to clear thy path. Go, then, and make unto thyself friends among those who dwell beneath the earth, and come back no more to trouble or molest those who dwell upon the surface of the earth."

'It was short and to the point; and then they trampled down the soil, while the mother, who had got upon her feet by now, whimpered about the place like a cat that had lost its kittens. A mangy, half-starved dog came and smelt hungrily about the grave, until it was sent howling away by kicks from every human animal that could reach it; and a poor little brat, who chanced to set up a piping song a few minutes later, was kicked and cuffed and knocked about by all who could conveniently get at him with foot, hand or missile. Abstinence from song and dance for a period of nine days is the Sâkai way of mourning the dead, and any breach of this is held to give great offence to the spirit of the departed and to bring bad luck upon the tribe. It was considered necessary, therefore, to give the urchin who had done the wrong a fairly bad time of it in order to propitiate the implacable dead baby.

'Next the Sâkai set to work to pack all their household goods – not a very laborious business; and in about half an hour the last of the laden women, who was carrying so many cooking-pots and babies and rattan bags and carved bamboo-boxes and things, that she looked like the outside of a gipsy's cart at home, had filed out of the clearing and disappeared in the forest. The Sâkai always shift camp, like that, when a death occurs, because they think the ghost of the dead haunts the place where the body died. When an epidemic breaks out among them they are so busy changing quarters, building new huts, and planting fresh catch crops that they have not time to procure proper food, and half those who are not used up by the disease die of semi-starvation. They are a queer lot.

'Well, Juggins and I were left alone, but my men needed a rest, so I decided to trek no farther that day, and Juggins and I spent our time trying to get a shot at a *sêlâdang*,* but though we came upon great ploughed-up runs, which the herds had made going down to water, we saw neither hoof nor horn, and returned at night to the deserted Sâkai camp, two of my Malays fairly staggering under the piles of rubbish which Juggins called his botanical specimens. The men we had left behind had contrived to catch some fish, and with that and yams we got a pretty decent meal, and I was lying on my mat reading by the aid of a *dâmar* torch, and thinking how lucky it was that the Sâkai had cleared out, when suddenly old Juggins sat up, with his eyes fairly snapping at me through his gig-lamps in his excitement.

'"I say," he said. "I must have that baby. It would make a unique and invaluable ethnological specimen."

'"Rot," I said. "Go to sleep, old man. I want to read."

'"No, but I'm serious," said Juggins. "You do not realize the unprecedented character of the opportunity. The Sâkai have gone away, so their susceptibilities would not be outraged. The potential gain to science is immense – simply immense. It would be criminal to neglect such a chance. I regard the thing in the light of a duty which I owe to human knowledge. I tell you straight, I mean to have that baby whether you like it or not, and that is flat."

'Juggins was forever talking about human knowledge, as though he and it were partners in a business firm.

'"It is not only the Sâkai one has to consider," I said. "My Malays are sensitive about body-snatching, too. One has to think about the effect upon them."

* *Sêlâdang*. The gaur or wild buffalo. It is the same as the Indian variety but in the Malay Peninsula attains to a greater size than in any other part of Asia.

'"I can't help that," said Juggins resolutely. "I am going out to dig it up now."

'He had already put his boots on, and was sorting out his botanical tools in search of a trowel. I saw that there was no holding him.

'"Juggins," I said sharply. "Sit down. You are a lunatic, of course, but I was another when I allowed you to come up here with me, knowing as I did that you are the particular species of crank you are. However, I've done you as well as circumstances permitted, and as a mere matter of gratitude and decency, I think you might do what I wish."

'"I am sorry," said Juggins stiffly. "I am extremely sorry not to be able to oblige you. My duty as a man of science, however, compels me to avail myself of this God-sent opportunity of enlarging our ethnological knowledge of a little-known people."

'"I thought you did not believe in God," I said sourly: for Juggins added a militant agnosticism to his other attractive qualities.

'"I believe in my duty to human knowledge," he replied sententiously. "And if you will not help me to perform it, I must discharge it unaided."

'He had found his trowel, and again rose to his feet.

'"Don't be an ass, Juggins," I said. "Listen to me. I have forgotten more about the people and the country here than you will ever learn. If you go and dig up that dead baby, and my Malays see you, there will be the devil to pay. They do not hold with exhumed corpses, and have no liking for or sympathy with people who go fooling about with such things. They have not yet been educated up to the pitch of interest in the secrets of science which has made of you a potential criminal, and if they could understand our talk, they would be convinced that you needed the kid's body for some devilry or witchcraft business, and ten to one they would clear out and leave us in the lurch. Then who would carry your precious botanical specimens back to boats for you, and just think how the loss of them would knock the bottom out of human knowledge for good and all."

'"The skeleton of the child is more valuable still," repled Juggins. "It is well that you should understand that in this matter – which for me is a question of my duty – I am not to be moved from my purpose either by arguments or threats."

'He was as obstinate as a mule, and I was pretty sick with him; but I saw that if I left him to himself he would do the thing so clumsily that my fellows would get wind of it, and if that happened I was afraid that they might desert us. The tracks in that Sâkai country are abominably confusing, and quite apart from the fear of losing all our camp-kit, which we could not hump for ourselves, I was by no means certain that

I could find my own way back to civilization unaided. Making a virtue of necessity, there, I decided that I would let Juggins have his beastly specimen, provided that he would consent to be guided entirely by me in all details connected with the exhumation.

'"You are a rotter of the first water," I said frankly. "And if I ever get you back to my station, I'll have nothing more to do with you as long as I live. All the same, I am to blame for having brought you up here, and I suppose I must see you through."

'"You're a brick," said Juggins, quite unmoved by my insults. "Come on."

'"Wait," I replied repressively. "This thing cannot be done until my people are all asleep. Lie down on your mat and keep quiet. When it is safe, I'll give you the word."

'Juggins groaned, and tried to persuade me to let him go at once; but I swore that nothing would induce me to move before midnight, and with that I rolled over on my side and lay reading and smoking, while Juggins fumed and fretted as he watched the slow hands of his watch creeping round the dial.

'I always take books with me into the jungle, and the more completely incongruous they are to my immediate surroundings the more refreshing I find them. That evening, I remember, I happened to be re-reading Miss Florence Montgomery's *Misunderstood* with the tears running down my nose; and by the time my Malays were all asleep, this incidental wallowing in sentimentality had made me more sick with Juggins and his disgusting project than ever.

'I never felt so like a criminal as I did that night, as Juggins and I gingerly picked our way out of the hut across the prostrate forms of my sleeping Malays; nor had I realized before what a difficult job it is to walk without noise on an openwork flooring of uneven boughs. We got out of the place and down the crazy stair-ladder at last, without waking any of my fellows, and we then began to creep along the edge of the jungle that hedged the clearing about. Why did we think it necessary to creep? I don't know. Partly we did not want to be seen by the Malays, if any of them happened to wake; and besides that, the long wait and the uncanny sort of work we were after had set our nerves going a bit, I expect.

'The night was as still as most nights are in real, *pukka* jungle. That is to say, that it was as full of noises – little, quiet, half-heard beast and tree noises – as an egg is full of meat; and every occasional louder sound made me jump almost out of my skin. There was not a breath astir in the clearing, but miles up above our heads the clouds were racing across the moon, which looked as though it were scudding through them in the opposite direction at a tremendous rate, like a great white fire balloon. It was pitch dark along the edge of the clearing, for the jungle threw a heavy shadow; and Juggins kept knocking those great clumsy feet of his against the stumps, and swearing softly under his breath.

'Just as we were getting near the child's grave the clouds obscuring the moon became a trifle thinner, and the slightly increased light showed me something that caused me to clutch Juggins by the arm.

'"Hold hard!" I whispered, squatting down instinctively in the shadow, and dragging him after me. "What's that on the grave?"

'Juggins hauled out his six-shooter with a tug, and looking at his face, I saw that he was as pale as death and more than a little shaky. He was pressing up against me, too, as he squatted, a bit closer, I fancied, than he would have thought necessary at any other time, and it seemed to me that he was trembling. I whispered to him, telling him not to shoot; and we sat there for nearly a minute, I should think, peering through the uncertain light, and trying to make out what the creature might be which was crouching above the grave and making a strange scratching noise.

'Then the moon came out suddenly into a patch of open sky, and we could see clearly at last, and what it revealed did not make me, for one, feel any better. The thing we had been looking at was kneeling on the grave, facing us. It, or rather she, was an old, old Sâkai hag. She was stark naked, and in the brilliant light of the moon I could see her long, pendulous breasts swaying about like an ox's dewlap, and the creases and wrinkles with which her withered hide was criss-crossed, and the discoloured patches of foul skin disease. Her hair hung about her face in great matted locks, falling forward as she bent above the grave, and her eyes glinted through the tangle like those of some unclean and shaggy animal. Her long fingers, which had nails like claws, were tearing at the dirt of the grave, and her body was drenched with sweat, so that it glistened in the moonlight.

'"It looks as though someone else wanted your precious baby for a specimen, Juggins," I whispered; and a spirit of emulation set him floundering onto his feet, till I pulled him back. "Keep still, man," I added. "Let us see what the old hag is up to. It isn't the brat's mother, is it?"

'"No," panted Juggins. "This is a much older woman. Great God! What a ghoul it is!"

'Then we were silent again. Where we squatted we were hidden from the hag by a few tufts of rank *lâlang* grass, and the shadow of the jungle also covered us. Even if we had been in the open, however, I question whether the old woman would have seen us, she was so eagerly intent upon her work. For full five minutes, as near as I can guess, we squatted there watching her scrape and tear and scratch at the earth of the grave, with a sort of frenzy of energy; and all the while her lips kept

going like a shivering man's teeth, though no sound that I could hear
came from them.

'At length she got down to the corpse, and I saw her lift the bark
wrapper out of the grave, and draw the baby's body from it. Then she
sat back upon her heels, threw up her head, just like a dog, and bayed at
the moon. She did this three times, and I do not know what there was
about those long-drawn howls that jangled up one's nerves, but each
time the sound became more insistent and intolerable, and as I listened,
my hair fairly lifted. Then, very carefully, she laid the child's body
down in a position that seemed to have some connection with the points
of the compass, for she took a long time, and consulted the moon and the
shadows repeatedly before she was satisfied with the orientation of the
thing's head and feet.

'Then she got up, and began very slowly to dance round and round
the grave. It was not a reassuring sight, out there in the awful loneliness
of the night, miles away from everyone and everything, to watch that
abominable old beldam capering uncleanly in the moonlight, while
those restless lips of hers called noiselessly upon all the devils in hell,
with words that we could not hear. Juggins pressed up against me
harder than ever, and his hand on my arm gripped tighter and tighter.
He was shaking like a leaf, and I do not fancy that I was much steadier.
It does not sound very terrible, as I tell it to you here in comparatively
civilized surroundings; but at the time, the sight of that obscure figure
dancing silently in the moonlight with its ungainly shadow scared me
badly.

'She capered like that for some minutes, setting to the dead baby as
though she were inviting it to join her, and the intent purposefulness of
her made me feel sick. If anybody had told me that morning that I was
capable of being frightened out of my wits by an old woman, I should
have laughed; but I saw nothing outlandish in the idea while that
grotesque dancing lasted.

'Her movements, which had been very slow at first, became
gradually faster and faster, till every atom of her was in violent motion,
and her body and limbs were swaying this way and that, like the boughs
of a tree in a tornado. Then, all of a sudden, she collapsed to the ground,
with her back towards us, and seized the baby's body. She seemed to
nurse it, as a mother might nurse her child, and as she swayed from side
to side, I could see first the curve of the creature's head, resting on her
thin left arm, and then its feet near the crook of her right elbow. And
now she was crooning to it in a cracked falsetto chant that might have
been a lullaby or perhaps some incantation.

'She rocked the child at first, but very rapidly the pace quickened,
until her body was swaying to and fro from the hips, and from side to
side, at such a rate that, to me, she looked as though she was falling all

ways at once. And simultaneously her shrill chanting became faster and faster, and every instant more nerve-sawing.

'Next she suddenly changed the motion. She gripped the thing she was nursing by its arms, and began to dance it up and down, still moving with incredible agility, and crooning more damnably than ever. I could see the small, puckered face of the thing above her head every time she danced it up, and then, as she brought it down again, I lost sight of it for a second, until she danced it up once more. I kept my eyes fixed upon the thing's face every time it came into view, and I swear it was not an optical illusion – *it began to be alive*. Its eyes were open and moving, and its mouth was working, like that of a child which tries to laugh, but is too young to do it properly. Its face ceased to be like that of a new-born baby at all. It was distorted by a horrible animation. It was the most unearthly sight.

'Juggins saw it, too, for I could hear him drawing his breath harder and shorter than a healthy man should.

'Then, all in a moment, the hag did something. I did not see clearly precisely what it was, but it looked to me as though she bent forward and kissed it, and at that very instant a cry went up like the wail of a lost soul. It may have been something in the jungle, but I know my Malayan forests pretty thoroughly, and I have never heard any cry like it before nor since. The next thing we knew was that the old hag had thrown the body back into the grave, and was dumping down the earth and jumping on it, while that strange cry grew fainter and fainter. It all happened so quickly that I had not had time to think or move before I was startled back into full consciousness by the sharp crack of Juggins's revolver fired close to my ear.

'"She's burying it alive!" he cried.

'It was a queer thing for a man to say, who had seen the child lying stark and dead more than thirty hours earlier, but the same thought was in my mind too, as we both started forward on a run. The hag had vanished into the jungle as silently as a shadow. Juggins had missed her, of course. He was always a rotten bad shot. However, we had no thought for her. We just flung ourselves upon the grave, and dug at the earth with our hands, until the baby lay in our arms. It was cold and stiff, and putrefaction had already begun its work. I forced open its mouth, and saw something that I had expected. The tip of its tongue was missing. It looked as though it had been bitten off by a set of shocking bad teeth, for the edge left behind was like a saw.

'"The thing's quite dead," I said to Juggins.

'"But it cried – it cried!" whimpered Juggins. "I can hear it now. To think that we let that horrible creature murder it."

'He sat down with his head in his hands. He was utterly unmanned.

'Now that the fright was over, I was beginning to be quite brave again. It is a way I have.

'"Rot," I said. "The thing's been dead for hours, and anyway, here's your precious specimen if you want it."

'I had put it down, and now pointed at it from a distance. Its proximity was not pleasant. Juggins, however, only shuddered.

'"Bury it, in heaven's name,' he said, his voice broken by sobs. "I would not have it for the world. Besides, it *was* alive. I saw and heard it."

'Well, I put it back in its grave, and next day we left the Sâkai country. Juggins had a whacking dose of fever, and anyway we had had about enough of the Sâkai and all of their engaging habits to last us for a bit.

'We swore one another to secrecy as Juggins, when he got his nerve back, said that the accuracy of our observations was not susceptible of scientific proof, which, I understand, was the rock his religion had gone to pieces on, and I did not fancy being told that I was drunk or that I was lying. You, however, know something of the uncanny things of the East, so tonight I have broken our vow. Now I'm going to turn in. Don't give me away.'

Young Middleton died of fever and dysentery, somewhere up-country, a year or two later. His name was not Middleton, of course; so I am not really 'giving him away', as he called it, even now. As for his companion, though when I last heard of him he was still alive and a shining light in the scientific world, I have named him Juggins, and as the family is a large one, he will run no great risk of being identified.

The Horror Under Penmire
Adrian Cole

Penmire is strewn across the edge of one of the bleakest stretches of Cornish moorland in existence. Though the windswept houses are exposed constantly to the buffets of Atlantic gales, the withdrawn inhabitants live their lives in sheltered seclusion, rarely venturing beyond the proximities of their isolated haven. There are few trees in Penmire, or indeed for miles around on this spectral, misted countryside – the hard outcrops of granite permit only the barest growths of gorse and heather. Any who chance to pass this way would wonder how it is that the villagers live.

Yet it has been thus for years without number. In its long, un-chronicled history, Penmire has tenanted miners, farmers, even smug-glers from the secret coves of the not-too-distant coasts, where even today the caves and blow-holes shelter hidden secrets. There have always been people here in Penmire, perhaps from the dawn of man; sometimes it is whispered abroad on shadowed evenings that men worshipped at strange altars in the marshes behind the village, and some folks hold that Arthur took refuge here at one time, pursued across the moors by some hideous foe.

Only the tors of frowning granite know how long Penmire has stood, but the magic of distant ages still hangs wraith-like over the quaint dwellings, suggesting primal antiquity and forgotten knowledge. What scenes of ancient savagery did the inperturbable moon gaze down upon through ragged, storm-rent clouds? What dark arts were practised, what Neolithic sounds mingled with the roaring winds, to be torn and hurled across miles of barren wasteland?

Now the village seems to slumber, oblivious to the outside world, contemplating, perhaps, its fabled past.

Roy Baxter had long been fascinated by the lure of mystic Penmire. He was a hard-working engineer from Bristol, or 'up-country' as the locals termed it, but his hobby was this deep interest in folklore and mythology. It was a hobby which led him all over England, pottering around on ancient sites, and browsing through musty, faded records.

He was on holiday now, driving fairly aimlessly through the enchanting hamlets of Cornwall, the county that perhaps drew him most, and it was here in the tiny pubs that he first heard muted comments about Penmire. It was just the sort of guarded half-secret that he looked for, but no one was anxious to locate the place for him. His curiosity was fully aroused – he often found the local people non-committal concerning the old legends, despite their talkative natures – but an unnatural barrier of silence would always clamp down the moment he tried to bring Penmire into the conversation. In one little pub he saw a group of farmers down pints and fairly rush out into the night, though he may have imagined their rapid exit.

Baxter's fertile imagination worked further overtime when he tried to pinpoint Penmire on a map. All his efforts failed. There simply weren't any records of the place anywhere, on Ordnance Survey maps or local records.

Despite this disappointment, Baxter was thrilled. He was certain that the village existed and determined all the more to find it. Acting on the assumption from what little he had heard, that Penmire was somewhere on the central moorlands, he tried to cover as much of that foreboding landscape as he could, but it was a fruitless task. Thick fingers of fog obscured the hidden paths and narrow roadways that could have led him there. Infuriated, he came off the moors and drove into Bodmin, where he checked into a small hotel.

That evening he came down the creaking stairs, ducking under a thick beam, and came into the foyer.

'May I use the phone?' he asked his dumpy, rosy-cheeked hostess. She was a cheerful soul, ample-bosomed and bouncy, typical of the loquacious landlady.

''Course you can, Mr Baxter,' she chirped in a high voice, elongating her R's in the curious Cornish fashion.

'Fine. I want to call London, actually.'

'Oh, that's all right. Business, I s'pose?' Mrs Harcott was all smiles. She was already imagining Baxter to be a big-time executive or possibly a TV producer. Her gossip circles would shortly be afire with the news.

'Yes,' Baxter grinned, thinking it would all go on the bill anyway. 'Oh, by the way,' he added, trying to sound casual, 'uh, I noticed a turning on the moor for a place called – what was it? – ah, Penmire. Yes, that was it, Penmire. It seems I've heard of it in local customs and the like. Only I'm rather keen on that sort of thing. Do you know the place at all?' He had lied about that turn-off, but he wanted to see if Mrs Harcott would deny all knowledge of Penmire. Her mouth was slightly open, as though he had taken her by surprise. She began idly flicking through her guest-book, and Baxter knew he had found another peculiar link in the mysterious armour of that moorland village.

'Well, I 'ave 'eard of it, Mr Baxter, but I can't say as I know where 'tis. I 'spect you'd find out in the bar tonight, though. We do 'ave some of the local landowners in 'ere sometimes. But if 'tis on the moors, I'd keep away if I were you, Mr Baxter. 'Tis awful bleak up there, 'specially with the mist.'

'I see. Well, thanks anyway, Mrs Harcott. Perhaps you're right.' That was all he'd get out of her. So the place did exist.

'You're welcome,' she returned, but her air of pleasantness had dissipated. Baxter found the phone tucked away in a convenient niche, and after a series of brief interchanges eventually got through to a London number.

'Hallo, Phil? This is Roy.' There was a pause before he heard the voice of his life-long friend.

'Hallo, there. Long time no see. What have you been doing with yourself? Are you at home?' Philip Dayton's voice was warm, firm, painting a picture of a strong character.

'No, I'm in Cornwall, actually.'

'Ah, the legend-haunted south-west,' Dayton chuckled. He was more than familiar with his friend's obsession with mythology. Himself an expert in the field, he guessed the reason for this call at once. Roy was 'on to something'. Dayton grinned to himself as he thought of some of the ridiculous 'finds' his pal had unearthed in the last few years.

'Yes,' said Baxter. 'I've got a few weeks off to pursue my true calling as usual.'

'Very nice. And what have you dug up from the pixie-infested tin mines this time?'

'Well, nothing as yet. But I've come across an interesting case.'

'Oh?' Dayton was intrigued by his friend's tone, for, despite Baxter's ability to stumble across events of absolutely no importance whatsoever, he did occasionally find something interesting.

'Ever heard of Penmire?'

'Penmire? No, can't place it offhand.'

'It's a small village on Bodmin Moor, but I don't know where. If you can't direct me to it, no one can.' Baxter sounded urgent. He knew Philip Dayton's knowledge of legend and folklore was extensive; Dayton had written several authoritative books on the subject, and had read as much material as he could find.

'Ah, Penmire. It does ring the faintest of bells. Vaguely connected with Arthur, and with a history of Druidic dabbings to boot. Yes, I know of it, though I can't tell you the gory details until I've dredged them up.'

'Well, it's a start,' exclaimed Baxter. 'Where the blue blazes is the place?'

'That I don't know. In fact I think you're in a blind alley, old sport. As far as I remember the place is only legendary anyway. A bit like the evasive Camelot.'

'Oh no!' Baxter groaned. 'Don't tell me it doesn't exist!'

'I'm not sure. I'm not too well up in those channels. Tell you what, though.'

'Uh-huh?'

'Where are you exactly?'

Baxter gave his address and his friend took it down.

'Bodmin, eh? Right. You hang on down there, and perhaps have a scout round for our hidden Penmire. In the meantime I'll see what I can find out about it at this end, then I might just drive down and join you.'

'You needn't do that, Phil, thanks all the same. I don't want to drag you off on a wild-goose chase.'

There was a laugh from the other end of the line. 'Nonsense. I'm hooked. Matter of fact I'm at a loose end at the moment. I've just finished a series of University lectures, and I had thought about going up to the Yorkshire Moors for a spot of research. Witches and all that. But I must admit Bodmin Moor sounds just as enterprising.'

'Working on a new book?'

'Yup. Haven't done a damn thing yet, though. So your little find might furnish me with a few new tidbits. I could do with a break, and I haven't drunk a few jars with you for some time.'

'Great. In that case I'll stick around. When will you be here?'

'Oh, say three days. I should be able to ferret something out by then.'

'Right. Give my love to Annie and the kids.' Baxter rang off.

*   *   *

Philip Dayton scratched his head irritably and sipped his scotch, his thoughts running back once more to the events of the last few days. Where the hell was Roy? Five days ago he'd phoned him, enthusing about Penmire and its superstitious connotations. Two days ago, he, Dayton, had arrived here in Bodmin with enough information to help find the place, but Roy was nowhere to be found. That just wasn't like him.

Dayton now sat in the cramped bar of his friend's hotel, where he too had checked in. No one had been able to help. Mrs Harcott had seen Roy leave shortly after phoning him, and his few things were still in his room; she hadn't seen him since. Dayton had made several abortive attempts to eke information out of the people who used the bar, but he got the same shrugs from all of them. Hardly anyone had seen him, anyway, as he'd left the hotel shortly after checking in.

Dayton got little sleep that night; he began to get progressively more worried. His eyes turned again and again to the monolith on the hill above Bodmin, which stood out clearly against the purple skies. He turned this way and that in a restless half-slumber, while the brass pixies on the mantelpiece seemed to contort themselves into weird shapes. In the early hours of the morning, Dayton settled on a plan of action: he couldn't hang around lamely any longer. Roy must have found Penmire, otherwise he would have been back.

After a hurried breakfast, Dayton drove up on to Bodmin Moor and began searching the hedgeless side-roads and lesser tracks, from time to time consulting a rough map he had improvised in the records section of a London library. He pulled up at the base of a chain of huge, jutting tors, crowned with bare outcrops of wind-swept rock. According to his information, Penmire should be on the other side. There was an old road somewhere, but the chances were that it would be overgrown and hard to find.

Dayton got out, locking the car, and began the steep climb, his feet sinking slightly into the moss that dotted these lowest slopes. It was a gorgeous day; for once the sky was free of clouds and the sun beat down, giving the usually foreboding landscape a more welcoming quality. It was July, typically hot and windless. He could hear the skylarks twittering incessantly, though they were too high up to be seen against the glare. As he climbed he felt fresh and alive, at one with the land. His doubts about Roy dispersed in the joy of the climb.

As he reached the rock sentinels atop the tor, Dayton let out a deep sigh, mopped his brow and looked back at the clear vista below him. Far off he saw the sun glinting on the metal of speeding cars as they raced down the main road. You're missing it all, he thought. After a moment he turned and clambered through the dark rocks which were splotched here and there with thin patches of lichen. Once he'd crossed the top of the tor, he looked down with a satisfied grunt at the straggling houses below.

Unless I miss my guess, that'll be Penmire – picturesque little spot, he mused. A sparkling stream ran out of the distant village, twisting its way into the limits of his vision, where a dark mass of trees formed a wood at the edge of the moors. Before Penmire lay the marshes, a flattish area, peppered with bogs and mires, which the old records had mentioned, and behind them rose a series of rugged tors, leading off hazily into the heart of the moorland.

Dayton was about to start the descent, when he heard muffled voices

somewhere behind him. At least, he thought they had come from behind
him. He turned, half expecting to see a basking courting couple, but his
gaze encountered only the blank rocks. Damn fool, he said to himself.
On a day like this voices carry a long way.

He took off his jacket, slung it unceremoniously over his shoulder
and began to climb down into the broad valley. He hadn't noticed it,
but the skylarks were no longer audible. Looking down on Penmire,
he could see that it was oddly lifeless, as though it had been long
abandoned. That was strange, because according to Dayton's information it should be populated. Still, he was some way off yet, though he
couldn't see any vehicles or telephone wires. To all intents and purposes
the place was dead.

As he pressed on, expecting to see at least a sheep or two, Dayton
was suddenly aware of the silence, broken only by his passage through
the tufts of reed. He stood still and realized just how absurdly quiet it
was. He was reminded of Alice stepping though the looking glass. *So
where is the white rabbit?* He felt eyes on him too, though he had to
suppress a chuckle at his own nerves. Perhaps the villagers had seen him
approach – in a place as remote as this they wouldn't appreciate
strangers. But he should have been able to hear the birds or at least
the teeming insect life: the grasshoppers and crickets usually made a
terrific din.

Behind him, towering up into the sunlight, the rocks seemed to leer
down mockingly. Dayton shrugged and moved on. Roy's car should be
around somewhere, he told himself. He'd feel a lot easier when he saw
it. He heard the faintest suggestions of voices again and cursed himself;
he put it down to exertion – after all, he was not a young man. Penmire
was still some way off when he noticed a sudden chill in the air. The
psychical research boys would love this place. Then he laughed in-
wardly as he saw the reason for the drop in temperature.

Coming across the brow of a nearby tor was a thick mist, lapping
over the rocks and overspilling into the valley. These moor mists can be
frightening to those who don't know them – they appear from almost
nowhere and literally descend like blankets in a matter of minutes.
Dayton had tramped Dartmoor to the east, and knew how quickly he
would be enveloped by those swirling, silent tendrils.

He speeded up his descent, certain now that he could hear those
indefinable voices. It was uncanny, made even more so by this thickening mist. The stuff seemed to tremble with animation as it reached out
and engulfed him. Dayton calculated that he had about a mile to go.
He stumbled on, muttering obscenities, through the gathering coils.

There then burst on his ears a chorus of sounds that stopped him
dead in his tracks. He was in the heart of the mist when, as if at a
given signal, thousands of frogs burst into voice, the sound of their deep

croaking coming from all around the valley. Dayton reflected that it was the most chilling sound he had ever heard. He tried to see into the mist, but out of all those countless frogs he could see none. He was scared, no use in pretending otherwise, but he smiled grimly. The mist had probably alarmed them. Sitting at home in an armchair was one thing, but when you were alone in this lot it was a different matter.

Far off he heard a splashing vaguely over the cacophony of frogs. That would be the stream, etching its way through the boulders. But this was too rhythmic for a stream, more as though someone were sloshing their way through water or mud. An inhabitant at last? Dayton thought of shouting, but the sound appeared to recede, and, for some unaccountable reason, he thought it had gone *underground*. But so many odd things had occurred already that he cursed himself and carried on.

Abruptly the frogs were silent, and the abysmal silence supplanted their terrible racket. Dayton barked his shins more than once, now only vaguely certain of the direction in which Penmire lay. His progress had become far more difficult, for he had to skirt sinking clods of peat and slime-covered pools of mire. He was sweating profusely, his face damp with mist. Where was that blasted village? He leant on a huge granite slab and wheezed. *Roy, my son, heads shall roll for this.*

The events of the next few seconds were a total shock to him, and concrete proof that something was very much amiss with this weird valley. The rock on which he was leaning seemed to twitch, as the flank of a horse twitches when irritated by a fly. Dayton drew back in horrified alarm, half expecting something dark and malign to rear up out of the mire. Then the earth heaved, and he pitched forward into the soaking reeds. 'This is ridiculous!' he kept saying, over and over again, but the ground *rippled* as though it were water, and Dayton bit off a scream.

It must be an island of turf, he told himself desperately, for anything else would be far too alien to accept. He struggled to his feet and ran, though it was like standing in a small boat. He stumbled again before the movements stopped, then rushed on as far as the reeds and hidden rocks would allow. This time he could definitely hear voices, though they seemed as much inside of him as out in those sentient mists. The voices laughed, chuckling insanely at his plight: voices which he knew instinctively were not human.

The mist was now as thick as the fogs that he knew in London. God, how far away all that was. On and on he wandered, his shins bruised and bleeding from innumerable bumps on the hard granite that lay obscured everywhere he turned. A rumbling like distant thunder caught his attention, coming from the marsh, and again it seemed to come from *under* the earth. But that was unthinkable.

Dayton's progress had slowed right down, his breath coming in laboured gasps. The mist was playing tricks, though the sound had receded. Now all he could hear was the drip, drip of moisture on the reeds, faint though that sound was. Something dark and suggestive loomed up ahead, and he fell to his knees, heart pounding like a locomotive. *God, this is it.*

But it was only a house. He had reached the sanctuary of Penmire at last.

Painfully he limped between two houses, their eaves overhanging the path, their windows dark and shadowed. As he came into the street, he still had no idea where to start looking for Roy, assuming he was here. It was a relief to get off the marsh. Something stirred in the mist, and he recoiled in surprise. The skulking shape of a cat slunk past, eyes blazing with green hate, eyes that never left his own.

Where is everyone? Still the dense mist showed no signs of lifting. Dayton stumbled on up the badly-kept street, hands thrust deep in his pockets, numb with the cold, jacket pulled tight around him. He was conscious now of other cat-like shapes padding around the edge of his vision, but they were always obscured by the mist. At last he saw a dim light, and, coming upon what appeared to be an old inn, he pushed the thick wooden door and went inside.

Hostile eyes regarded him from at least five places as he closed the door. A bar ran the length of the far wall, while several tables were placed here and there around the little room. The walls were fitted with panelled cubicles, and nailed to the roof beams were brass horse-accoutrements, though Dayton couldn't see any horseshoes. He wasn't surprised.

An old woman sat at one of the tables, arms resting on a gnarled stick, a battered bag on the floor beside her slippered feet. Two weather-beaten men sat in one of the chipped cubicles in the corner, smoking and playing cards. The barman, a huge, shirt-sleeved character with a pink, freckled face and thinning, sandy hair, was talking to what appeared to be a local labourer. There was thick mud on his boots. The barman scowled at Dayton as he came forward.

'We aren't open yet,' he said gruffly in a very strong accent. Dayton noticed a grubby collie lying at the labourer's feet, regarding him disdainfully.

'That's all right. Only I, uh, lost my way in this ruddy mist. It's a bit marshy out there and I don't fancy trying to find my way back to the car until the mist lifts.' The old lady regarded him through her spectacles, but never blinked. She might have been carved from granite for all she moved. No one spoke. Dayton edged nearer the bar, wary of the dog. Its owner had turned to inspect him, his gaze as scathing as his animal's. The card players had stopped.

'I don't suppose you've a phone ...'

'No. There b'ain't none in Penmire,' returned the barman, taking a rag and wiping down the bar slowly and methodically.

'Oh. Well, I'm in a bit of a mess. Is there anywhere I can clean up?' The eyes stared questioningly. Christ, thought Dayton, what are they – zombies?

'From outside, be 'ee?' muttered the old girl beside him.

'Yes, that's right. London. I'm, er, looking for a friend of mine. I believe he's staying in Penmire.'

The woman nodded vaguely.

'I thought 'ee was from outside.'

'Hush, Mrs Dinnock,' muttered the barman. 'I think you're mistaken, sir. No one don't come to stay in Penmire.'

'Oh, but my friend expressly stated that he would be here.' Dayton watched the thick pipe-smoke curling up into the beams from the corner.

'No, I don't think so. No one has come. Only you.' Dayton shifted his gaze to the card players. They sat as though paralysed. What if Roy hadn't come here?

'Perhaps he'll turn up later. In the meantime, have you a gents handy? I must try and clean up a bit.'

'Through there,' grunted the barman reluctantly, pointing to a side door. Dayton nodded his thanks and went through. He found a tiny toilet and closed the flaking door behind him. There was an overpowering smell of fish exuding from the drain. Now what? he asked himself as he cleaned himself up in the battered sink. I was better off in the ruddy marsh.

He returned to the bar to find it empty, save for the inhospitable barman, who tried his damndest to ignore him.

'You get this mist often?'

'Ah.'

Dayton decided it was an affirmative. 'Like pea soup, eh?' he grinned, but it had no effect. Now I know how the lepers used to feel, he mused. 'Any chance of me buying a bite to eat?'

'Don't serve meals, sir. There's a shop down the street.'

'Hm. I'll hang on here till the mist lifts, I think. You, er, don't mind?' You hadn't better, he added to himself.

'May be down for a week. Often stops longer in the warm weather. My advice is to take the road off the moor, sir. You'll be all right. Folks in Penmire is wary of strangers.' The barman was fiddling about with glasses and glimpsing at a paper, anything to avoid being drawn into conversation.

'So I noticed. You, uh, sure about that friend of mine?'

'Positive.'

'O.K.' Dayton went over to one of the booths and sat down,

pretending to study a map that he carried. The barman eyed him coldly and began cleaning glasses again. Outside everything remained silent.

Dayton had been seated for only a short time, when he noticed a book of some description poking up from the back of the seat opposite. Gently he reached over, careful not to be seen by the barman who had for a moment turned to his shelves, and picked it up. It was a paperback entitled *Myths and Folklore of the South West*.

That clinched it! It must be Roy's. Hastily Dayton flicked through the book and found several underlined passages and notations, all in pencil and instantly recognizable as Roy's handwriting. He found a section on Druidic practices and certain other primitive rites said to have been handed down from earlier periods. The name Arthur cropped up here and there, along with the usual references to Tintagel, then Dayton found a very brief passage on Penmire.

'... a very old settlement, believed to be the one-time centre of a very primitive culture, centred around the worship of the Sea ... fantastic theory that the earliest inhabitants were settlers from the sinking of Atlantis ... seems a rather fanciful notion ... possibly the survivors from Lyonesse or counterpart ...' Pencilled beside the passage was the word: DAGON?

'I'm closing now,' boomed a voice above him, and Dayton slammed the book shut with a start.

'Oh. Oh, really? I'll be off then. Always carry some light reading matter, you know.' He knows, Dayton thought. *What are these people hiding?* He forced a grin, reflecting that it was still relatively early.

'Keep on the road, sir. One step off and you're likely to sink for good into the marshes.'

Dayton rose, pocketing the book. 'Uh-huh. I expect it'll brighten up soon. Sorry to be a nuisance.' He left as casually as he could, stepping once more into the dank, oppressive mist. The stench of fish came even more strongly to his nostrils now. Still, he'd resigned himself to expect anything in this eerie place, even pixies. But he *was* being observed, he knew at once, and far more intensely than before. Then he saw the glowing, baleful eyes of the cats, never for a moment averting their gaze.

Dayton watched them as he started down the street, having decided to stop at the shop. To his horror he saw that there were now a number of dogs in the mist, all plodding along quietly, as though waiting the command to attack. This was fast becoming a nightmare. What had Roy meant by the pencilled 'Dagon'? Dayton recognized the name as that of a mythical sea-dwelling creature, though as far as he knew it had only appeared in fiction.

Faintly-defined houses slipped past as he hastily moved on,

conscious now of several cats and dogs lurking at his heels, like a hungry pack. A flapping from above made him duck, to see a crow disappear into the gloom. Another house appeared ahead, but before he had taken another step he saw three pairs of eyes glowing in front of him.

What are they – wolves? He felt panic gripping him. They're trying to surround me! Dayton abruptly turned to his left and sprinted between the houses, anywhere to escape the lurking shadows. A bark behind him told him they were giving chase.

He came to the edge of the marsh, and for a moment he almost forgot the pursuit. He had found concrete proof that Roy had come to Penmire; one wheel and part of the front bumper of his Rover 2000 were sticking up out of the mire. Dayton had no time to speculate. Something heavy crashed into the back of his head and he plummeted into a bottomless well of oblivion.

*   *   *

Dayton came round with a splitting headache. His arms felt as though they were being torn from their sockets, and his mouth was horribly dry. Total darkness enveloped him; his surroundings swam in a blur as he tried to focus on something tangible. Vague thoughts on what had happened trickled back to him, but he was in no condition to struggle.

The first sound he heard was the plop-plop-plop of water somewhere near his head. He tried to move, only to find that he was chained up, back to a damp wall, somewhere in a cellar or cave. *Chained?* His mind raced as he tugged hopelessly in the chill, earthy air. There were scurrying sounds around his feet in response to his movements; he kicked out wildly, his toe digging into a number of squealing, furry bodies. The place was alive with rats, and as they ran hither and thither the air became permeated with the now familiar stink of rotting fish.

'Phil!' hissed a voice nearby, where more chains rattled in the acrid blackness.

'Roy? Is that you?' Dayton could not believe his ears.

''Fraid so, old pal. I was hoping you wouldn't get to find me.'

'What the devil's going on in this village? I've never encountered anything like it in all my travels.'

'I dread to think.' Baxter sounded very tired.

'The rudeness of the local goons I can stomach, but this is going too damn far.'

'Guess so. But save your strength, Phil. You'll probably need it.'

'I found a book of yours in the inn. I notice you've pencilled in a few notes. Have you any ideas on what's happening? Why the chains, for God's sake?' Rivulets of sweat trickled down Dayton's face despite the cold. His arms ached intolerably.

'Something very old and very evil has got Penmire in its grip, Phil. Whether they practise satanic rites or what, I don't know, but I've been shackled up here for bloody ages. I don't know for how long. I can't feel my arms. Some of the things I've heard ... God, it's incredible!' Baxter gasped with the effort.

'Where exactly are we?'

'Under the chapel. You may have noticed it. Sort of crypt. Judging by some of the chanting that goes on up there——' He broke off.

'What have you done for food? You must have been here for several days.'

'Oh, they keep me alive. Christ knows why, but they feed me. A robed figure in black appears now and again. It would be laughably melodramatic if it wasn't for the fact that I'm scared. Really scared, Phil. We're in a helluva situation.' Dayton admired his friend's strength of character; a lesser man would have cracked up in here. Even *he* might ...

'It's insane,' he growled. 'I know about witchcraft and most of its various cults, but I can't believe these people would do us any serious harm. It must be some sort of hoax – a festival, do you think?' Dayton's nerves were rapidly fraying. He had to keep talking.

'The pain's real enough.'

'They'd never get away with it.'

'Oh no? What's to stop the police finding us in the mire? Or not finding us in the mire? No one is safe on these moors. It's one of the bleakest parts of England. We may as well be on Mars.'

'Cheerful bugger!' They were silent for a moment; the humour soon vanished.

'Well,' grunted Dayton at length, 'what do we do?'

'God knows. We can't break these chains. We just wait.'

So they waited, their minds uselessly trying to fathom a way to escape, but there was absolutely none. The seconds slipped into minutes, marked by the ever-dripping, wet walls, and the minutes turned slowly into hours. There was only the pain and discomfort as the scampering rats kept vigil over the two incarcerated men. At last they heard sounds above them – feet shuffling to and fro in the chapel. Dayton, who had slipped to his knees, cocked an ear. Faintly came the strains of weird, ethereal music, like fluted pipes, drifting out from the old walls into the night.

'Roy. Are you awake?' There was a grunt. 'What's that noise?'

'It's them again. It happens every now and then – nights, I suppose ... Another ... ritual.'

'You OK?'

'I'll do. You know that passage I marked in the book? Did you see my reference to Dagon?'

'Yes, it's in my pocket.'

'Well, there could be something in it. It's a crazy notion, but now and again I've heard the name Dagon mentioned in the chanting. You listen for it once they start. One time I thought I heard something ... out in the marsh. Like a huge wave breaking. Yes, I know it sounds bloody daft, but there was something.'

'Maybe not so daft, Roy. I came here across that marsh and some of the things I heard were pretty odd.'

'Such as?'

'People splashing about. And frogs. God, I never heard so many. All at once they started up in unison.'

They fell silent again. Baxter broke the lull with a forced snort.

'Humph! We're probably behaving like kids. I know we're in a right mess, but the moor *is* spooky. There are probably the usual scientific explanations for it all.'

'Perhaps. But I'd like a good explanation for this.' Dayton rattled his chains. 'I'll create bloody hell when I get back to civilization.'

'Quiet a sec!' They both listened anew to the strange noises from above. A deep, somehow obscene chanting had begun, the words totally indecipherable, utterly alien.

'There they go again. They'll go on for hours, working themselves up into a frenzy. Just when you think it'll die down, they start up again.'

'Again, this is all new to me. I wish I had a tape-recorder.'

'I'd settle for a wrench,' Baxter replied, but neither of them laughed.

All that night the blasphemous sound swelled until, in the early hours of the morning, it reached a peak. There were sounds from around the prisoners, sounds of slopping footsteps, though nothing could be seen in the dark; the fish odour was overpowering. The climax of the terrible dirge above came in a resounding thunderclap which shook the very foundations of the chapel. Its echoes rolled away into the distance.

'Roy, that sound! It's going away beneath us! I'm sure of it.'

'Eh?' Roy Baxter was exhausted, very drowsy, having only partly registered the boom. He couldn't take much more of this.

'Have you heard anything underground?' persisted Dayton.

'Underground? No. Only from up there,' Baxter said sleepily. Dayton was thinking of the marsh and the rippling motion that he had seen.

'Probably an echo,' Baxter suggested. 'There are lots of caves under the, er, village.'

'Caves?'

'Umm. Well, tunnels. I saw a few when they dragged me here. All man-made, though.'

'But what about the mire?' Caves running under that would be
geologically impossible.

'I dunno. They seem to avoid that.' Baxter yawned. 'I expect they
all go straight down.'

'Curious.' Somehow the two men lapsed into fitful sleep; time had
ceased to exist for them in this rancid pit.

*   *   *

They languished for three days, three days of gruelling anguish which
were broken only by the brief appearance of a robed, half-glimpsed
figure who fed them. After that the villagers came for their prisoners.
Above the cellar, the voices had begun chanting again in mournful
unison. From out of the ether came whispered sounds of demonic
laughter. Baxter and Dayton were too spent to complain as their chains
were unlocked, and they were forced, staggering, through numerous
cold puddles of muddy water, pushed along by the sinister robed figures
of a score of unseen inhabitants.

They were led almost unconsciously along these subterranean,
winding tunnels until they came out eventually into the open. Their
bodies were weak and their spirits broken.

It was evening as they emerged; the sun was sinking into an orange
sea of clouds, tinting the surrounding tors with gold. Wisps of glistening
mist hung in shreds above the marsh, like steam rising from a sulphurous
pool. The two men registered little of this. They were some distance
from the village, at the edge of the marsh, and here they were thrust
forward on to a huge, flat slab of granite. Thin beards of stubble
darkened both their jaws, while their eyes were rimmed and bloodshot.
Neither had the strength to look up at the diminishing glory of the
sunset.

Roy Baxter began to mutter to himself, reciting the Lord's Prayer
under his breath. Dayton's head lay against cold rock. He regarded his
friend through pain-misted eyes; beside him the reeds trembled in the
cool breeze.

'Roy. Roy!' he whispered hoarsely. The other turned to him, still
praying. Above them the captors were still.

'We're done. Do you understand?'

'Listen!'

Far out over the marsh there came a gibbering of something
nebulous, as though the mire itself were alive. The frogs had begun
again that heart-stopping croaking – a hundred thousand throats swelling the chorus. Dayton turned his head, forcing a look back at the
village, framed between the arms of two of the gaunt figures in black.
There were scores of similarly-garbed people filing out of what he took

to be the chapel, all with arms raised in supplication, all walking like jerky dolls towards the two outsiders and the marsh.

To whom or what are they praying? Dayton asked himself, unable to credit his eyes. With a start of revulsion he saw that there were a number of dogs, cats and even a few sheep staring placidly out at the marsh. The spell on Penmire gripped even the animals. The chant swelled and the words became clear, though still incomprehensible.

'Ngah ohahgn, mnahn, ohahgn mnepn phatagn Dagon.
Ngah opahgan, rhantgna Dagon.
Ssna, ssna, phatagn Dagon.'

Over and over they repeated it. These were words not written for human mouths to speak. I must get out now. God knows what they'll do, thought Dayton.

'Roy!' he whispered. 'Roy!' But his friend had passed out over the altar-like stone. Dayton feigned the same, one eye on the chanting crowd. Those around had taken up the chant as well. Bloody mumbo-jumbo.

All around the valley the sound of the frogs was growing in volume; louder and louder it came, blending malefically with the ululations of the oncoming worshippers. From the marshes came a rising cloud of dense vapour, and with it the unbearable fish stench that Dayton had smelled so frequently. This time it seemed to pulse out from the marsh in disgusting waves, and he almost vomited.

Now he could see the frogs. They hopped around the stone as if mocking him – the marshes were teeming with them. Dayton shook himself. Beside him his captors were kneeling, arms outstretched in obeisance to the very heart of the marsh. What did they expect to see? Dayton craned his neck and gasped. Bubbles were bursting all over the surface as if it were boiling. He fought to control his sanity as he realized that the chanting was *attracting* something out in that festering pool of horror.

A movement beside him drew his attention back to his immediate dilemma. He turned to see some of these devilish acolytes stretching Roy, still unconscious, over the altar stone, preparing him for the very sacrifice he had feared. Dayton was stunned. *No, they can't mean it. Not today, 1974.* But they paid no attention to his torrent of invective. Dayton flung himself upon them with last reserves of energy, kicking, biting, hammering with his fists. But it was useless. He was flung contemptuously aside to roll pathetically into the reeds.

Stark terror gripped him now. He got up, his movement ignored by the still-chanting villagers, and fled into the treacherous mire, desperately trying to find a way through the numerous bogs. He looked back as he panted on, only to see a curved knife, glittering in the twilight with scarlet jewels, raised high. This is madness, *madness*. Dayton averted his gaze and felt his stomach heave, refusing to believe the knife would fall. But he heard it sink into Roy Baxter's flesh, and a shuddering satisfied sigh went up from the villagers.

> '*Abaghna pnam pnam Dagon.*
> *Accept our sacrifice, O Dagon.*
> *Ssna ssna, phatagn Dagon.*'

Tears of disbelief coursed in grimy runnels down Dayton's face. He shook his head in utter disgust at what they had done. Blood ran freely over the altar into the mud – Roy had died without a sound. Dayton fled farther into the marsh, hoping against hope to reach the tors before they came for him. But further diabolic events were unfolding. From even the farthest reaches of the marsh the fish smell was at its most foul; a new element of horror was emerging.

Unspeakable shapes were thrusting up out of the oozing mud and green scum, shapes so dreadful, so appalling, that only in the wildest fantasies of a madman could they have been conceived. Dayton bit into his hand to stifle a shriek. The constant chanting was taking its effect, as had the spilling of blood, drawing these vile monstrosities up from the depths like enchanted snakes. They were half human, half fish, or so it looked, for their features were a repulsive blend of both, with fins protruding from each jowl and long, plumed spines stretching right down their backs. There were gills in their man-like trunks, their eyes were the wide, filmy eyes of fish, and their arms were long and thin, tapering to webbed claws.

From these came the hellish smell. Dayton reached a boulder and leapt on to it, heart almost bursting with the effort. The mist was thickening, thankfully obscuring many of the beings, while the sun had set, leaving the world in rapidly gathering darkness. Dayton was surrounded by the fish-men, who still continued to rise from the muck like a legion from hell itself. As he stared in fascination, they began emitting croaking sounds of their own, frog-like and deep, until with a shudder Dayton realized that they were chanting in response to the people of Penmire.

From thick, fleshy lips came the same dread words that the villagers were chanting, spoken, he saw, by the very ones *to whom the language belonged*. Although he was some way out in the marsh, none of the terrible people came near. They just waved and writhed gently from side to side as though drugged, arms raised in ecstasy as were those of the villagers. Frogs jumped everywhere, their croaks adding to the swelling din.

Dayton ached with weariness; there was not a muscle in his body that didn't crave rest, but he knew that he must keep on whilst the horde were preoccupied with their incantations. He sprang from the rock and zigzagged his faltering way through islands of turf, constantly sinking to his knees into clinging mud. He wanted to lie down and sleep, but dare not. The thought of that dripping knife gave him more will to go on. Still the creatures were ignoring him, though he passed within feet of several, shutting everything out of his mind except the tors and escape.

Suddenly the ground heaved, pitching him forward into the gurgling slime, so that for terrifying seconds he crawled with cold, reptilian frogs. Within moments he was knee-deep, jerking himself upright and yanking at his arms to get them free. They came out with great sucking sounds, but his feet were held. He beat frantically at the swarming frogs, feeling them squirming beneath him in multitudes. Dayton struggled in despair. He was trapped. And still the chanting went on, rising in volume, driving him ever-closer to madness. Now the ground began rippling and pulsing like a great heart beating. A note of joy had entered the chanting.

Dayton heard, *felt*, the sound from below. He could not put a name to it, not dared to do so. Excitement spurred the invocations around him, and he tried to twist and see what exactly the villagers were doing: were they pursuing, or had they forgotten him in the midst of their insane revels? But he could not see. He was stuck firmly, sinking inexorably to a gruesome death.

> *'Ngah ohahgn, phatagn Dagon.*
> *Abaghna pnam pnan hnam Dagon.*
> *Accept our second sacrifice, O Dagon.*
> *Ssna ssna, phatagn Dagon.'*

Dayton heard the words of the people behind, and the terrible implication. He had escaped the knife, but the mire would take him. Unless ... With a last, vain effort, he stripped off his jacket, ready to throw it in front of him in one final attempt to heave himself out. Then he stopped, eyes wide in utter disbelief. Before him the marsh was heaving and thrashing like the cauldron of a volcano, sending great plumes of mud high into the mist. Dayton felt more tremors in the rumbling ground.

The chanting had abruptly ceased, together with the croaking of the frogs, as all eyes, all arms, had turned to the source of the disturbance. From out of the unknown depths of the mire, ringed by the evil-smelling fish-creatures, something huge, something unutterably ancient was rising. Dayton screamed now, his whole body shaking uncontrollably, unable to free itself from the fatal clutches of the marsh.

Higher and higher rose the mire-coated colossus, and worse grew the unholy stench of that awesome thing. For this was Dagon, Dagon the

ageless, summoned at last from an eternal sleep, summoned from the
refuge he had sought untold aeons before, when he and all his kind were
cursed upon earth.

Up, up rose the towering horror, a throbbing, glistening mass of
scaley, amorphous life. Waves of mud, spilling over with frogs, rippled
out from the growing monster. A score of thick, oily, tentacle-like pro-
tuberances, coated in contracting suckers, whipped up from beneath
the ooze in a welter of steaming filth, as the titanic creature rose higher,
exuding an aura of clinging vapours. Dayton coughed as he caught the
first whiffs of the poisonous diffusion; he had sunk waist deep before it,
his eyes riveted on this thing from before the dawn of men.

All around in the night the servants bowed down, eager to serve,
smiting themselves and yelling out in exultation. Dagon of the deeps had
come. Come to begin a new reign. The earth shook constantly, hissing
with escaping steam, and the mire overspilled its contaminated ooze
out into the village. Dayton closed his eyes and prayed fervently,
sinking lower, lower. Dagon stretched out his many arms to receive
the sacrifice that his people had prepared.

The Upper Berth
F. Marion Crawford

I am an old sailor, said Brisbane, and as I have to cross the Atlantic
pretty often, I have my favourites. Most men have their favourites. I
have seen a man wait in a Broadway bar for three-quarters of an hour
for a particular car which he liked. I believe the bar keeper made at
least one-third of his living by that man's preference. I have a habit of
waiting for certain ships when I am obliged to cross that duck pond. It
may be a prejudice, but I was never cheated out of a good passage but
once in my life. I remember it very well; it was a warm morning in June,
and the Customs House officials, who were hanging about waiting for a
steamer already on her way up from the Quarantine, presented a
peculiarly haze and thoughtful appearance. I had not much luggage – I
never have. I mingled with the crowd of passengers, porters, and
officious individuals in blue coats and brass buttons, who seemed to
spring up like mushrooms from the deck of a moored steamer to obtrude
their unnecessary services upon the independent passenger. I have often
noticed with a certain interest the spontaneous evolution of these
fellows. They are not there when you arrive; five minutes after the pilot
has called 'Go ahead!' they, or at least their blue coats and brass
buttons, have disappeared from deck and gangway as completely as
though they had been consigned to that locker which tradition
unanimously ascribes to Davy Jones. But, at the moment of starting,
they are there, clean shaved, blue coated, and ravenous for fees. I
hastened on board. The *Kamtschatka* was one of my favourite ships. I say
was, because she emphatically no longer is. I cannot conceive of any
inducement which could entice me to take another voyage in her. Yes, I
know what you are going to say. She is uncommonly clean in the run
aft, she has enough bluffing off in the bows to keep her dry, and the
lower berths are most of them double. She has a lot of advantages, but I
won't cross in her again. Excuse the digression. I got on board. I hailed
a steward, whose red nose and redder whiskers were equally familiar to
me.

'One hundred and five, lower berth,' said I, in the business-like tone peculiar to men who think no more of crossing the Atlantic than taking a whisky cocktail at down-town Delmonico's.

The steward took my portmanteau, greatcoat, and rug. I shall never forget the expression of his face. Not that he turned pale. It is maintained by the most eminent divines that even miracles cannot change the course of nature. I have no hesitation in saying that he did not turn pale; but, from his expression, I judged that he was either about to shed tears, to sneeze, or to drop my portmanteau. As the latter contained two bottles of particularly fine old sherry presented to me for my voyage by my old friend Snigginson van Pickyns, I felt extremely nervous. But the steward did none of these things.

'Well, I'm d———d!' he said in a low voice, and led the way.

I suppose my Hermes, as he led me to the lower regions, had had a little grog, but I said nothing, and followed him. 105 was on the port side, well aft. There was nothing remarkable about the state-room. The lower berth, like most of those upon the *Kamtschatka*, was double. There was plenty of room; there was the usual washing apparatus, calculated to convey an idea of luxury to the mind of a North American Indian; there was the usual inefficient racks of brown wood, in which it is more easy to hang a large-sized umbrella than the common tooth-brush of commerce. Upon the uninviting mattresses were carefully folded together those blankets which a great modern humorist has aptly compared to cold buckwheat cakes. The question of towels was left entirely to the imagination. The glass decanters were filled with a transparent liquid faintly tinged with brown, but from which an odour less faint, but not more pleasing, ascended to the nostrils, like a far off sea-sick reminiscence of oily machinery. Sand-coloured curtains half closed the upper berth. The hazy June daylight shed a faint illumination upon the desolate little scene. Ugh! How I hated that state-room!

The steward deposited my traps and looked at me, as though he wanted to get away – probably in search of more passengers and more fees. It is always a good plan to start in favour with those functionaries, and I accordingly gave him certain coins there and then.

'I'll try and make yer comfortable all I can,' he remarked, as he put the coins in his pocket. Nevertheless, there was a doubtful intonation in his voice which surprised me. Possibly his scale of fees had gone up, and he was not satisfied; but on the whole I was inclined to think that, as he himself would have expressed it, he was 'the better for a glass'. I was wrong, however, and did the man injustice.

* * *

Nothing especially worthy of mention occurred during that day. We left the pier punctually, and it was very pleasant to be fairly under way, for the weather was warm and sultry, and the motion of the steamer produced a refreshing breeze. Everybody knows what the first day at sea is like. People pace the decks and stare at each other, and occasionally meet acquaintances whom they did not know to be on board. There is the usual uncertainty as to whether the food will be good, bad, or indifferent, until the first two meals have put the matter beyond a doubt; there is the usual uncertainty about the weather, until the ship is fairly off Fire Island. The tables are crowded at first, and then suddenly thinned. Pale-faced people spring from their seats and precipitate themselves towards the door, and each old sailor breathes more freely as his sea-sick neighbour rushes from his side, leaving him plenty of elbow-room and an unlimited command over the mustard.

One passage across the Atlantic is very much like another, and we who cross very often do not make the voyage for the sake of novelty. Whales and icebergs are indeed always objects of interest, but, after all, one whale is very much like another whale, and one rarely sees an iceberg at close quarters. To the majority of us the most delightful moment of the day on board an ocean steamer is when we have taken our last turn on deck, have smoked our last cigar, and having succeeded in tiring ourselves, feel at liberty to turn in with a clear conscience. On that first night of the voyage I felt particularly lazy, and went to bed in 105 rather earlier than I usually do. As I turned in, I was amazed to see that I was to have a companion. A portmanteau, very like my own, lay in the opposite corner, and in the upper berth had been deposited a neatly folded rug, with a stick and umbrella. I had hoped to be alone, and I was disappointed; but I wondered who my room-mate was to be, and I determined to have a look at him.

Before I had been long in bed he entered. He was, as far as I could see, a very tall man, very thin, very pale, with sandy hair and whiskers and colourless grey eyes. He had about him, I thought, an air of rather dubious fashion; the sort of man you might see in Wall Street, without being able precisely to say what he was doing there – the sort of man who frequents the Café Anglais, who always seems to be alone and who drinks champagne; you might meet him on a racecourse, but he would never appear to be doing anything there either. A little over-dressed – a little odd. There are three or four of his kind on every ocean steamer. I made up my mind that I did not care to make his acquaintance, and I went to sleep saying to myself that I would study his habits in order to avoid him. If he rose early, I would rise late; if he went to bed late, I would go to bed early. I did not care to know him. If you once know people of that kind they are always turning up. Poor fellow! I need not have taken the trouble to come to so many decisions about him, for I never saw him again after that first night in 105.

I was sleeping soundly when I was suddenly waked by a loud noise.

To judge from the sound, my room-mate must have sprung with a single leap from the upper berth to the floor. I heard him fumbling with the latch and bolt of the door, which opened almost immediately, and then I heard his footsteps as he ran at full speed down the passage, leaving the door open behind him. The ship was rolling a little, and I expected to hear him stumble or fall, but he ran as though he were running for his life. The door swung on its hinges with the motion of the vessel, and the sound annoyed me. I got up and shut it, and groped my way back to my berth in the darkness. I went to sleep again; but I had no idea how long I slept.

When I awoke it was still quite dark, but I felt a disagreeable sensation of cold, and it seemed to me that the air was damp. You know the peculiar smell of a cabin which has been wet with sea-water. I covered myself up as well as I could and dozed off again, framing complaints to be made the next day, and selecting the most powerful epithets in the language. I could hear my room-mate turn over in the upper berth. He had probably returned while I was asleep. Once I thought I heard him groan, and I argued that he was sea-sick. That is particularly unpleasant when one is below. Nevertheless, I dozed off and slept till early daylight.

The ship was rolling heavily, much more than on the previous evening, and the grey light which came in through the porthole changed in tint with every movement according as the angle of the vessel's side turned the glass seawards or skywards. It was very cold – unaccountably so for the month of June. I turned my head and looked at the porthole, and I saw to my surprise that it was wide open and hooked back. I believe I swore audibly. Then I got up and shut it. As I turned back I glanced at the upper berth. The curtains were drawn close together; my companion had probably felt cold as well as I. It struck me that I had slept enough. The state-room was uncomfortable, though, strange to say, I could not smell the dampness which had annoyed me in the night. My room-mate was still asleep – excellent opportunity for avoiding him, so I dressed at once and went on deck. The day was warm and cloudy, with an oily smell on the water. It was seven o'clock as I came out – much later than I had imagined. I came across the doctor, who was taking his first sniff of the morning air. He was a young man from the west of Ireland – a tremendous fellow, with black hair and blue eyes, already inclined to be stout; he had a happy-go-lucky, healthy look about him which was rather attractive.

'Fine morning,' I remarked, by way of introduction.

'Well,' said he, eyeing me with an air of ready interest, 'it's a fine morning and it's not a fine morning. I don't think it's much of a morning.'

'Well, no – it is not so very fine,' said I.

'It's just what I call fuggly weather,' replied the doctor.

'It was very cold last night, I thought,' I remarked. 'However, when I looked about I found that the porthole was wide open. I had not noticed it when I went to bed. And the state-room was damp, too.'

'Damp!' said he. 'Whereabouts are you?'

'One hundred and five——'

To my surprise the doctor started visibly, and stared at me.

'What is the matter?' I asked.

'Oh – nothing,' he answered; 'only everybody has complained of that state-room for the last three trips.'

'I shall complain, too,' I said. 'It has certainly not been properly aired. It is a shame!'

'I don't believe it can be helped,' answered the doctor. 'I believe there is something – well, it is not my business to frighten passengers.'

'You need not be afraid of frightening me,' I replied. 'I can stand any amount of damp. If I should get a bad cold I will come to you.'

I offered the doctor a cigar, which he took and examined very critically.

'It is not so much the damp,' he remarked. 'However, I dare say you will get on very well. Have you a room-mate?'

'Yes; a deuce of a fellow, who bolts out in the middle of the night, and leaves the door open.'

Again the doctor glanced curiously at me. Then he lit the cigar and looked grave.

'Did he come back?' he asked presently.

'Yes. I was asleep, but I waked up and heard him moving. Then I felt cold and went to sleep again. This morning I found the porthole open.'

'Look here,' said the doctor quietly, 'I don't care much for this ship. I don't care a rap for her reputation. I tell you what I will do. I have a good-sized place up here. I will share it with you, though I don't know you from Adam.'

I was very much surprised at the proposition. I could not imagine why he should take such a sudden interest in my welfare. However, his manner as he spoke of the ship was peculiar.

'You are very good, Doctor,' I said. 'But, really, I believe even now the cabin could be aired, or cleaned out, or something. Why do you not care for the ship?'

'We are not superstitious in our profession, sir,' replied the doctor, 'but the sea makes people so. I don't want to prejudice you, and I don't want to frighten you, but if you will take my advice you will move in here. I would as soon see you overboard,' he added earnestly, 'as know that you or any other man was to sleep in 105.'

'Good gracious! Why?' I asked.

'Just because on the three last trips the people who have slept there actually have gone overboard,' he answered gravely.

The intelligence was startling and exceedingly unpleasant, I confess. I looked hard at the doctor to see whether he was making game of me, but he looked perfectly serious. I thanked him warmly for his offer, but told him I intended to be the exception to the rule by which everybody who slept in that particular state-room went overboard. He did not say much, but looked grave as ever, and hinted that, before we got across, I should probably reconsider his proposal. In the course of time we went to breakfast, at which only an inconsiderable number of passengers assembled. I noticed that one or two of the officers who breakfasted with us looked grave. After breakfast I went into by state-room in order to get a book. The curtains of the upper berth were still closely drawn. Not a word was to be heard. My room-mate was probably still asleep.

As I came out I heard the steward whose business it was to look after me. He whispered that the captain wanted to see me, and then scuttled away down the passage as if very anxious to avoid any questions. I went towards the captain's cabin, and found him waiting for me.

'Sir,' said he, 'I want to ask a favour of you.'

I answered that I would do anything to oblige him.

'Your room-mate has disappeared,' he said. 'He is known to have turned in early last night. Did you notice anything extraordinary in his manner?'

The question, coming as it did, in exact confirmation of the fears the doctor had expressed half an hour earlier, staggered me.

'You don't mean to say he has gone overboard?' I asked.

'I fear he has,' answered the captain.

'This is the most extraordinary thing——' I began.

'Why?' he asked.

'He is the fourth, then,' I explained. In answer to another question from the captain, I explained, without mentioning the doctor, that I had heard the story concerning 105. He seemed very much annoyed at hearing that I knew of it. I told him what had occurred in the night.

'What you say,' he replied, 'coincides almost exactly with what was told to me by the room-mates of two of the other three. They bolt out of bed and run down the passage. Two of them were seen to go overboard by the watch; we stopped and lowered boats, but they were not found. Nobody, however, saw or heard the man who was lost last night – if he is really lost. The steward, who is a superstitious fellow, perhaps, and expected something to go wrong, went to look for him this morning, and found his berth empty, but his clothes lying about, just as he had left them. The steward was the only man on board who knew him by sight, and he has been searching everywhere for him. He has disappeared! Now sir, I want to beg you not to mention the circumstance to any of the passengers; I don't want the ship to get a bad name, and nothing hangs about an ocean-goer like stories of suicides. You shall have your choice of any one of the officers' cabins you like, including my own, for the rest of the passage. Is that a fair bargain?'

'Very,' said I; 'and I am much obliged to you. But since I am alone, and have the state-room to myself, I would rather not move. If the steward will take out that unfortunate man's things, I would as lief stay where I am. I will not say anything about the matter, and I think I can promise you that I will not follow my room-mate.'

The captain tried to dissuade me from my intention, but I preferred having a state-room alone to being the chum of any officer on board. I do not know whether I acted foolishly, but if I had taken his advice I should have had nothing more to tell. There would have remained the disagreeable coincidence of several suicides occurring among men who had slept in the same cabin, but that would have been all.

That was not the end of the matter, however, by any means. I obstinately made up my mind that I would not be disturbed by such tales, and I even went so far as to argue the question with the captain. There was nothing wrong about the state-room, I said. It was rather damp. The porthole had been left open last night. My room-mate might have been ill when he came on board, and he might have become delirious after he went to bed. He might even now be hiding somewhere on board, and might be found later. The place ought to be aired and the fastening of the port looked to. If the captain would give me leave, I would see that what I thought necessary was done immediately.

'Of course you have a right to stay where you are if you please,' he replied, rather petulantly, 'but I wish you would turn out and let me lock the place up, and be done with it.'

I did not see it in the same light, and left the captain, after promising to be silent concerning the disappearance of my companion. The latter had had no acquaintances on board, and was not missed in the course of the day. Towards evening I met the doctor again, and he asked me whether I had changed my mind. I told him I had not.

'Then you will before long,' he said, very gravely.

*　　*　　*

We played whist in the evening, and I went to bed late. I will confess now that I felt a disagreeable sensation when I entered my state-room. I could not help thinking of the tall man I had seen on the previous night, who was now dead, drowned, tossing about in the long swell, two or three hundred miles astern. His face rose very distinctly before me as I undressed, and I even went so far as to draw back the curtains of the upper berth, as though to persuade myself that he was actually gone. I also bolted the door of the state-room. Suddenly I became aware that the porthole was open, and fastened back. This was more than I could stand. I hastily drew on my dressing-gown and went in search of Robert, the steward of my passage. I was very angry, I remember, and when I found him I dragged him roughly to the door of 105, and pushed him towards the open porthole.

'What the deuce do you mean, you scoundrel, by leaving that port open every night? Don't you know it is against the regulations? Don't you know that if the ship heeled and the water began to come in, ten men could not shut it? I will report you to the captain, you blackguard, for endangering the ship!'

I was exceedingly wroth. The man trembled and turned pale, and then began to shut the round glass plate with the heavy brass fittings.

'Why don't you answer me?' I said roughly.

'If you please, sir,' faltered Robert, 'there's nobody on board as can keep this 'ere port shut at night. You can try it yourself, sir, I ain't a-going to stop hany longer on board o' this vessel, sir; I ain't, indeed. But if I was you, sir, I'd just clear out and go and sleep with the surgeon, or something, I would. Look 'ere, sir, is that fastened what you may call securely, or not, sir? Try it, sir; see if it will move a hinch.'

I tried the port, and found it perfectly tight.

'Well, sir,' continued Robert triumphantly, 'I wager my reputation as an A1 steward that in 'arf an hour it will be open again; fastened back, too, sir, that's the horful thing – fastened back!'

I examined the great screw and the looped nut that ran on it.

'If I find it open in the night, Robert, I will give you a sovereign. It is not possible. You may go.'

'Soverin' did you say, sir? Very good, sir. Thank ye, sir. Goodnight, sir. Pleasant reepose, sir, and all manner of hinchantin' dreams, sir.'

Robert scuttled away, delighted at being released. Of course, I thought he was trying to account for his negligence by a silly story, intended to frighten me, and I disbelieved him. The consequence was that he got his sovereign, and I spent a very peculiarly unpleasant night.

I went to bed, and five minutes after I had rolled myself up in my blankets the inexorable Robert extinguished the light that burned steadily behind the ground-glass pane near the door. I lay quite still in the dark trying to go to sleep, but I soon found that impossible. It had been some satisfaction to be angry with the steward, and the diversion had banished that unpleasant sensation I had at first experienced when I thought of the drowned man who had been my chum; but I was no longer sleepy, and I lay awake for some time, occasionally glancing at the porthole, which I could just see from where I lay, and which, in the darkness, looked like a faintly luminous soup-plate suspended in blackness. I believe I must have lain there for an hour, and, as I remember, I was just dozing into sleep when I was roused by a draught of cold air, and by distinctly feeling the spray of the sea blown upon my face. I started to my feet, and not having allowed in the dark for the motion of the ship, I was instantly thrown violently across the state-room upon the couch which was placed beneath the porthole. I recovered myself immediately, however, and climbed upon my knees. The porthole was again wide open and fastened back!

Now these things are facts. I was wide awake when I got up, and I should certainly have been waked by the fall had I still been dozing. Moreover, I bruised my elbows and knees badly, and the bruises were there on the following morning to testify to the fact, if I myself had doubted it. The porthole was wide open and fastened back – a thing so unaccountable that I remember very well feeling astonishment rather than fear when I discovered it. I at once closed the plate again, and screwed down the loop-nut with all my strength. It was very dark in the state-room. I reflected that the port had certainly been opened within an hour after Robert had at first shut it in my presence, and I determined to watch it, and see whether it would open again. Those brass fittings are very heavy and by no means easy to move. I could not believe that the clump had been turned by the shaking of the screw. I stood peering out through the thick glass at the alternate white and grey streaks of the sea that foamed beneath the ship's side. I must have remained there a quarter of an hour.

Suddenly, as I stood, I distinctly heard something moving behind me in one of the berths, and a moment afterwards, just as I turned instinctively to look – though I could, of course, see nothing in the darkness – I heard a very faint groan. I sprang across the state-room, and tore the curtains of the upper berth aside, thrusting in my hands to discover if there were anyone there. There was someone.

I remember that the sensation as I put my hands forward was as though I were plunging them into the air of a damp cellar, and from behind the curtains came a gust of wind that smelled horribly of stagnant sea-water. I laid hold of something that had the shape of a man's arm, but was smooth, and wet, and icy cold. But suddenly, as I pulled, the creature sprang violently forward against me, a clammy, oozy mass, as it seemed to me, heavy and wet, yet endowed with a sort of supernatural strength. I reeled across the state-room, and in an instant the door opened and the thing rushed out. I had not had time to be frightened, and quickly recovered myself, I sprang through the door and gave chase at the top of my speed, but I was too late. Ten yards before me I could see – I am sure I saw it – a dark shadow moving in the dimly lighted passage, quickly as the shadow of a fast horse thrown before a dogcart by the lamp on a dark night. But in a moment it had disappeared, and I found myself holding on to the polished rail that ran along the bulkhead where the passage turned towards the companion. My hair stood on end, and the cold perspiration rolled down my face. I am not ashamed of it in the least: I was very badly frightened.

Still I doubted my senses, and pulled myself together. It was absurd, I thought. The Welsh rarebit I had eaten had disagreed with me. I had been in a nightmare. I made my way back to my state-room, and entered it with an effort. The whole place smelled of stagnant sea-water, as it had when I had waked on the previous evening. It required my utmost strength to go in, and grope among my things for a box of wax lights. As I lighted a railway reading lantern which I always carry in case I want to read after the lamps are out, I perceived that the porthole was again open, and a sort of creeping horror began to take possession of me which I never felt before, nor wish to feel again. But I got a light and proceeded to examine the upper berth, expecting to find it drenched with sea-water.

But I was disappointed. The bed had been slept in, and the smell of the sea was strong; but the bedding was as dry as a bone. I fancied that Robert had not had the courage to make the bed after the accident of the previous night – it had all been a hideous dream. I drew the curtains back as far as I could and examined the place very carefully. It was perfectly dry. But the porthole was open again. With a sort of dull bewilderment of horror I closed it and screwed it down, and thrusting my heavy stick through the brass loop, wrenched it with all my might, till the thick metal began to bend under the pressure. Then I hooked my reading lantern into the red velvet at the head of the couch, and sat down to recover my senses if I could. I sat there all night, unable to think of rest – hardly able to think at all. But the porthole remained closed, and I did not believe it would now open again without the application of a considerable force.

The morning dawned at last, and I dressed myself slowly, thinking over all that had happened in the night. It was a beautiful day and I went on deck, glad to get out into the early, pure sunshine, and to smell the breeze from the blue water, so different from the noisome, stagnant odour of my state-room. Instinctively I turned aft, towards the surgeon's cabin. There he stood, with a pipe in his mouth, taking his morning airing precisely as on the preceding day.

'Good morning,' said he quietly, but looking at me with evident curiosity.

'Doctor, you were quite right,' said I. 'There is something wrong about that place.'

'I thought you would change your mind,' he answered, rather triumphantly. 'You have had a bad night, eh? Shall I make you a pick-me-up? I have a capital recipe.'

'No, thanks,' I cried. 'But I would like to tell you what happened.'

I then tried to explain, as clearly as possible, precisely what had occurred, not omitting to state that I had been scared as I had never been scared in my whole life before. I dwelt particularly on the phenomenon of the porthole, which was a fact to which I could testify, even if the rest had been an illusion. I had closed it twice in the night, and the second time I had actually bent the brass in wrenching it with my stick. I believe I insisted a good deal on this point.

'You seem to think I am likely to doubt your story,' said the doctor, smiling at the detailed account of the state of the porthole. 'I do not doubt it in the least. I renew my invitation to you. Bring your traps here and take half my cabin.'

'Come and take half of mine for one night,' I said. 'Help me to get to the bottom of this thing.'

'You will get to the bottom of something else if you try,' answered the doctor.

'What?' I asked.

'The bottom of the sea. I am going to leave this ship. It is not canny.'

'Then you will not help to find out——'

'Not I,' said the doctor quickly. 'It is my business to keep my wits about me – not to go fiddling about with ghosts and things.'

'Do you really believe it is a ghost?' I enquired, rather contemptuously. But as I spoke I remembered very well the horrible sensation of the supernatural which had got possession of me during the night. The doctor turned sharply on me.

'Have you any reasonable explanation of these things to offer?' he asked. 'No; you have not. Well, you say you will find a explanation. I say that you won't, sir, simply because there is not any.'

'But, my dear sir,' I retorted, 'do you, a man of science, mean to tell me that such things cannot be explained?'

'I do,' he answered stoutly. 'And, if they could, I would not be concerned in the explanation.'

I did not care to spend another night alone in the state-room, and yet I was obstinately determined to get at the root of the disturbances. I do not believe there are many men who would have slept there alone, after passing two such nights. But I made up my mind to try it, if I could not get anyone to share a watch with me. The doctor was evidently not inclined for such an experiment. He said he was a surgeon, and that in case any accident occurred on board he must always be in readiness. He could not afford to have his nerves unsettled. Perhaps he was quite right, but I am inclined to think that his precaution was prompted by his inclination. On enquiry, he informed me that there was no one on board who would be likely to join me in my investigations, and after a little more conversation I left him. A little later I met the captain, and told my story. I said that, if no one would spend the night with me, I would ask leave to have the light burning all night, and would try it alone.

'Look here,' said he, 'I will tell you what I will do. I will share your watch myself, and we will see what happens. It is my belief that we can find out between us. There may be some fellow skulking on board who steals a passage by frightening the passengers. It is just possible that there may be something queer in the carpentering of that berth.'

I suggested taking the ship's carpenter below and examining the place; but I was overjoyed at the captain's offer to spend the night with me. He accordingly sent for the workman and ordered him to do anything I required. We went below at once. I had all the bedding cleared out of the upper berth, and we examined the place thoroughly to see if there was a board loose anywhere, or a panel which could be opened or pushed aside. We tried the planks everywhere, tapped the flooring, unscrewed the fittings of the lower berth and took it to pieces – in short, there was not a square inch of the state-room which was not searched and tested. Everything was in perfect order, and we put everything back in its place. As we were finishing out work, Robert came to the door and looked in.

'Well, sir – find anything, sir?' he asked, with a ghastly grin.

'You were right about the porthole, Robert,' I said, and gave him the promised sovereign. The carpenter did his work silently and skilfully, following my directions. When he had done he spoke.

'I'm a plain man, sir,' he said. 'But it's my belief you had better just turn out your things, and let me run a dozen four-inch screws through the door of this cabin. There's no good ever came o' this cabin yet, sir, and that's all about it. There's been four lives lost out o' here to my own remembrance, and that in four trips. Better give it up, sir – better give it up!'

'I will try it for one night more,' I said.

'Better give it up, sir – better give it up! It's a precious bad job,' repeated the workman, putting his tools in his bag and leaving the cabin.

But my spirits had risen considerably at the prospects of having the captain's company, and I made up my mind not to be prevented from going to the end of the strange business. I abstained from Welsh rarebits and grog that evening, and did not even join in the customary game of whist. I wanted to be quite sure of my nerves, and my vanity made me anxious to make a good figure in the captain's eyes.

* * *

The captain was one of those spendidly tough and cheerful specimens of seafaring humanity whose combined courage, hardihood, and calmness in difficulty leads them naturally into high positions of trust. He was not the man to be led away by an idle tale, and the mere fact that he was willing to join me in the investigation was proof that he thought there was something seriously wrong, which could not be accounted for on ordinary theories, nor laughed down as a common superstition. To some extent, too, his reputation was at stake, as well as the reputation of the ship. It is no light thing to lose passengers overboard, and he knew it.

About ten o'clock that evening, as I was smoking a last cigar, he came up to me, and drew me aside from the beat of the other passengers who were patrolling the deck in the warm darkness.

'This is a serious matter, Mr Brisbane,' he said. 'We must make up our minds either way – to be disappointed or to have a pretty rough time of it. You see I cannot afford to laugh at the affair, and I will ask you to sign your name to a statement of whatever occurs. If nothing happens tonight we will try it again tomorrow and next day. Are you ready?'

So we went below, and entered the state-room. As we went in I could see Robert the steward, who stood a little farther down the passage, watching us, with his usual grin, as though certain that something dreadful was about to happen. The captain closed the door behind us and bolted it.

'Supposing we put your portmanteau before the door,' he suggested. 'One of us can sit on it. Nothing can get out then. Is the port screwed down?'

I found it as I had left it in the morning. Indeed, without using a lever, as I had done, no one could have opened it. I drew back the curtains of the upper berth so that I could see well into it. By the captain's advice I lighted my reading lantern, and placed it so that it shone upon the white sheets above. He insisted upon sitting on the portmanteau, declaring that he wished to be able to swear that he had sat before the door.

Then he requested me to search the state-room thoroughly, an operation very soon accomplished, as it consisted merely in looking beneath the lower berth and under the couch below the porthole. The spaces were quite empty.

'It is impossible for any human being to get in,' I said, 'or for any human being to open the port.'

'Very good,' said the captain calmly. 'If we see anything now, it must be either imagination of something supernatural.'

I sat down on the edge of the lower berth.

'The first time it happened,' said the captain, crossing his legs and leaning back against the door, 'was in March. The passenger who slept here, in the upper berth, turned out to have been a lunatic – at all events, he was known to have been a little touched, and he had taken his passage without the knowledge of his friends. He rushed out in the middle of the night, and threw himself overboard, before the officer who had the watch could stop him. We stopped and lowered a boat; it was a quiet night, just before that heavy weather came on; but we could not find him. Of course his suicide was afterwards accounted for on the grounds of his insanity.'

'I suppose that often happens?' I remarked rather absently.

'Not often – no,' said the captain; 'never before in my experience, though I have heard of it happening on board other ships. Well, as I was saying, that occurred in March. On the very next trip—— What are you looking at?' he asked, stopping suddenly in his narration.

I believe I gave no answer. My eyes were riveted upon the porthole. It seemed to me that the brass loop-nut was beginning to turn very slowly upon the screw – so slowly, however, that I was not sure it moved at all. I watched it intently, fixing its position in my mind and trying to ascertain whether it changed. Seeing where I was looking, the captain looked, too.

'It moves!' he exclaimed, in a tone of conviction. 'No, it does not,' he added, after a minute.

'If it were the jarring of the screw,' said I, 'it would have opened during the day; but I found it this evening jammed tight as I left it this morning.'

I rose and tried the nut. It was certainly loosened, for by an effort I could move it with my hands.

'The queer thing,' said the captain, 'is that the second man who was lost is supposed to have got through that very port. We had a terrible time over it. It was in the middle of the night, and the weather was very heavy; there was an alarm that one of the ports was open and the sea running in. I came below and found everything flooded, the water pouring in every time she rolled, and the whole port swinging from the top bolts – not the porthole in the middle. Well, we managed to shut it, but the water did some damage. Ever since that the place smells of sea-water from time to time. We supposed the passenger had thrown himself out, though the Lord only knows how he did it. The steward kept telling me that he cannot keep anything shut here. Upon my word – I can smell it now, cannot you?' he enquired, sniffing the air suspiciously.

'Yes – distinctly,' I said, and I shuddered as that same odour of stagnant sea-water grew stronger in the cabin. 'Now, to smell like this, the place must be damp,' I continued, 'and yet when I examined it with the carpenter this morning everything was perfectly dry. It is most extraordinary – hallo!'

My reading lantern, which had been placed in the upper berth, was suddenly extinguished. There was still a good deal of light from the pane of ground glass near the door, behind which loomed the regulation lamp. The ship rolled heavily, and the curtain of the upper berth swung far out into the state-room and back again. I rose quickly from my seat on the edge of the bed, and the captain at the same moment started to his feet with a loud cry of surprise. I had turned with the intention of taking down the lantern to examine it, when I heard his exclamation, and immediately afterwards his call for help. I sprang towards him. He was wrestling with all his might with the brass loop of the port. It seemed to turn against his hands in spite of all his efforts. I caught up my cane, a heavy oak stick I always used to carry, and thrust it through the ring and bore on it with all my strength. But the strong wood snapped suddenly and I fell upon the couch. When I rose again the port was wide open, and the captain was standing with his back against the door, pale to the lips.

'There is something in that berth!' he cried, in a strange voice, his eyes almost starting from his head. 'Hold the door, while I look – it shall not escape us, whatever it is!'

But instead of taking his place, I sprang upon the lower bed, and seized something which lay in the upper berth.

It was something ghastly, horrible beyond words, and it moved in my grip. It was like the body of a man long drowned, and yet it moved, and had the strength of ten men living; but I gripped it with all my might – the slippery, oozy, horrible thing – the dead white eyes seemed to stare at me out of the dusk; the putrid odour of rank sea-water was about it, and its shiny hair hung in foul wet curls over its dead face. I wrestled with the dead thing; it thrust upon me and forced me back and nearly broke my arms; it wound its corpse's arms about my neck, the living death, and overpowered me, so that I, at last, cried aloud and fell, and left my hold.

As I fell the thing sprang across me, and seemed to throw itself upon the captain. When I last saw him on his feet his face was white and his lips set. It seemed to me that he struck a violent blow at the dead being, and then he, too, fell forward upon his face, with an inarticulate cry of horror.

The thing paused an instant, seeming to hover over his prostrate body, and I could have screamed again for very fright, but I had no voice left. The thing vanished suddenly, and it seemed to my disturbed senses that it made its exit through the open port, though how that was possible, considering the smallness of the aperture, is more than anyone can tell. I lay a long time upon the floor, and the captain lay beside me. At last I partially recovered my senses and moved, and instantly knew that my arm was broken – the small bone of the left forearm near the wrist.

I got upon my feet somehow, and with my remaining hand I tried to raise the captain. He groaned and moved, and at last came to himself. He was not hurt, but he seemed badly stunned.

Well, do you want to hear any more? There is nothing more. That is the end of my story. The carpenter carried out his scheme of running half a dozen four-inch screws through the door of 105; and if ever you take a passage in the *Kamtschatka*, you may ask for a berth in that stateroom. You will be told that it is engaged – yes – it is engaged by that dead thing.

I finished the trip in the surgeon's cabin. He doctored my broken arm, and advised me not to 'fiddle about with ghosts and things' any more. The captain was very silent, and never sailed again in that ship, though it is still running. And I will not sail in her either. It was a very disagreeable experience, and I was very badly frightened, which is a thing I do not like. That is all. That is how I saw a ghost – if it was a ghost. It was dead, anyhow.

The Signal-Man
Charles Dickens

'Halloa! Below there!'

When he heard a voice thus calling to him, he was standing at the door of his box, with a flag in his hand, furled round its short pole. One would have thought, considering the nature of the ground, that he could not have doubted from what quarter the voice came; but, instead of looking up to where I stood on the top of the steep cutting nearly over his head, he turned himself about and looked down the Line. There was something remarkable in his manner of doing so, though I could not have said, for my life, what. But, I know it was remarkable enough to attract my notice, even though his figure was foreshortened and shadowed, down in the deep trench, and mine was high above him, so steeped in the glow of an angry sunset that I had shaded my eyes with my hand before I saw him at all.

'Halloa! Below!'

From looking down the Line, he turned himself about again, and, raising his eyes, saw my figure high above him.

'Is there any path by which I can come down and speak to you?'

He looked up at me without replying, and I looked down at him without pressing him too soon with a repetition of my idle question. Just then, there came a vague vibration in the earth and air, quickly changing into a violent pulsation, and an oncoming rush that caused me to start back, as though it had force to draw me down. When such vapour as rose to my height from this rapid train had passed me and was skimming away over the landscape, I looked down again, and saw him re-furling the flag he had shown while the train went by.

I repeated my enquiry. After a pause, during which he seemed to regard me with fixed attention, he motioned with his rolled-up flag towards a point on my level, some two or three hundred yards distant. I called down to him, 'All right!' and made for that point. There, by dint of looking closely about me, I found a rough zigzag descending path notched out: which I followed.

The cutting was extremely deep, and unusually precipitate. It was

made through a clammy stone that became oozier and wetter as I went
down. For these reasons, I found the way long enough to give me time to
recall a singular air of reluctance or compulsion with which he had
pointed out the path.

When I came down low enough upon the zigzag descent, to see him
again, I saw that he was standing between the rails on the way by which
the train had lately passed, in an attitude as if he were waiting for me to
appear. He had his left hand at his chin, and that left elbow rested on his
right hand crossed over his breast. His attitude was one of such
expectation and watchfulness, that I stopped a moment, wondering at
it.

I resumed my downward way, and, stepping out upon the level of
the railroad and drawing nearer to him, saw that he was a dark sallow
man, with a dark beard and rather heavy eyebrows. His post was in as
solitary and dismal a place as ever I saw. On either side, a dripping wet
wall of jagged stone, excluding all view but a strip of sky; the perspective
one way, only a crooked prolongation of this great dungeon; the shorter
perspective in the other direction, terminating in a gloomy red light, and
the gloomier entrance to a black tunnel, in whose massive architecture
there was a barbarous, depressing and forbidding air. So little sunlight
ever found its way to this spot, that it had an earthy, deadly smell; and so
much cold wind rushed through it, that it struck chill to me, as if I had
left the natural world.

Before he stirred, I was near enough to him to have touched him. Not
even then removing his eyes from mine, he stepped back one step, and
lifted his hand.

This was a lonesome post to occupy (I said), and it had riveted my
attention when I looked down from up yonder. A visitor was a rarity, I
should suppose; not an unwelcome rarity, I hoped? In me, he merely saw
a man who had been shut up within narrow limits all his life, and who,
being at last set free, had a newly awakened interest in these great works.
To such purpose I spoke to him; but I am far from sure of the terms I
used, for, besides that I am not happy in opening any conversation,
there was something in the man that daunted me.

He directed a most curious look towards the red light near the
tunnel's mouth, and looked all about it, as if something were missing
from it, and then looked at me.

That light was part of his charge? Was it not?

He answered in a low voice: 'Don't you know it is?'

The monstrous thought came into my mind as I perused the fixed
eyes and the saturnine face, that this was a spirit, not a man. I have
speculated since, whether there may have been infection in his mind.

In my turn, I stepped back. But in making the action, I detected in
his eyes some latent fear of me. This put the monstrous thought to flight.

'You look at me,' I said, forcing a smile, 'as if you had a dread of me.'
'I was doubtful,' he returned, 'whether I had seen you before.'
'Where?'
He pointed to the red light he had looked at.
'There?' I said.
Intently watchful of me, he replied (but without sound), 'Yes.'
'My good fellow, what should I do there? However, be that as it may, I never was there, you may swear.'
'I think I may,' he rejoined. 'Yes. I am sure I may.'

His manner cleared, like my own. He replied to my remarks with readiness, and in well chosen words. Had he much to do there? Yes; that was to say, he had enough responsibility to bear; but exactness and watchfulness were what was required of him, and of actual work – manual labour he had next to none. To change that signal, to trim those lights, and to turn this iron handle now and then, was all he had to do under that head. Regarding those many long and lonely hours of which I seemed to make so much, he could only say that the routine of his life had shaped itself into that form, and he had grown used to it. He had taught himself a language down here – if only to know it by sight, and to have formed his own crude ideas of its pronunciation, could be called learning it. He had also worked at fractions and decimals, and tried a little algebra; but he was, and had been as a boy, a poor hand at figures. Was it necessary for him when on duty, always to remain in that channel of damp air, and could he never rise into the sunshine from between those high stone walls? Why, that depended upon times and circumstances. Under some conditions there would be less upon the Line than under others, and the same held good as to certain hours of the day and night. In bright weather, he did choose occasions for getting a little above these lower shadows; but, being at all times liable to be called by his electric bell, and at such times listening for it with redoubled anxiety, the relief was less than I would suppose.

He took me into his box, where there was a fire, a desk for an official book in which he had to make certain entries, a telegraphic instrument with its dial face and needles, and the little bell of which he had spoken. On my trusting that he would excuse the remark that he had been well educated, and (I hoped I might say without offence), perhaps educated above that station, he observed that instances of slight incongruity in such-wise would rarely be found wanting among large bodies of men; that he had heard it was so in workhouses, in the police force, even in that last desperate resource, the army; and that he knew it was so, more or less, in any great railway staff. He had been, when young (if I could believe it, sitting in that hut; he scarcely could), a student of natural philosophy, and had attended lectures; but he had run wild, misused his opportunities, gone down, and never risen again. He had no complaint to offer about that. He had made his bed, and he lay upon it. It was far too late to make another.

All that I have here condensed, he said in a quiet manner, with his grave dark regards divided between me and the fire. He threw in the word 'Sir' from time to time, and especially when he referred to his youth: as though to request me to understand that he claimed to be nothing but what I found him. He was several times interrupted by the little bell, and had to read off messages, and send replies. Once, he had to stand without the door, and display a flag as a train passed, and make some verbal communication to the driver. In the discharge of his duties I observed him to be remarkably exact and vigilant, breaking off his discourse at a syllable, and remaining silent until what he had to do was done.

In a word, I should have set this man down as one of the safest of men to be employed in that capacity, but for the circumstance that while he was speaking to me he twice broke off with a fallen colour, turned his face towards the little bell when it did *not* ring, opened the door of the hut (which was kept shut to exclude the unhealthy damp), and looked out towards the red light near the mouth of the tunnel. On both those occasions, he came back to the fire with the inexplicable air upon him which I had remarked, without being able to define, when we were so far asunder.

Said I when I rose to leave him: 'You almost make me think that I have met with a contented man.'

(I am afraid I must acknowledge that I said it to lead him on.)

'I believe I used to be so,' he rejoined, in the low voice in which he had first spoken; 'but I am troubled, sir, I am troubled.'

He would have recalled the words if he could. He had said them, however, and I took them up quickly.

'With what? What is your trouble?'

'It is very difficult to impart, sir. It is very, very difficult to speak of. If ever you make me another visit, I will try to tell you.'

'But I expressly intend to make you another visit. Say, when shall it be?'

'I go off early in the morning, and I shall be on again at ten tomorrow night, sir.'

'I will come at eleven.'

He thanked me, and went out at the door with me. 'I'll show my white light, sir,' he said, in his peculiar low voice, 'till you have found the way up. When you have found it, don't call out! And when you are at the top, don't call out!'

His manner seemed to make the place strike colder to me, but I said no more than 'Very well.'

'And when you come down tomorrow night, don't call out! Let me ask you a parting question. What made you cry "Halloa! Below there!" tonight?'

'Heaven knows,' said I. 'I cried something to that effect——'

'Not to that effect, sir. Those were the very words. I know them well.'

'Admit those were the very words. I said them, no doubt, because I saw you below.'

'For no other reason?'

'What other reason could I possibly have?'

'You had no feeling that they were conveyed to you in any supernatural way?'

'No.'

He wished me goodnight, and held up his light. I walked by the side of the down Line of rails (with a very disagreeable sensation of a train coming behind me), until I found the path. It was easier to mount than to descend, and I got back to my inn without any adventure.

Punctual to my appointment, I placed my foot on the first notch of the zigzag next night, as the distant clocks were striking eleven. He was waiting for me at the bottom, with his white light on. 'I have not called out,' I said, when we came close together; 'may I speak now?' 'By all means, sir.' 'Goodnight then, and here's my hand.' 'Goodnight, sir, and here's mine.' With that, we walked side by side to his box, entered it, closed the door, and sat down by the fire.

'I have made up my mind, sir,' he began, bending forward as soon as we were seated, and speaking in a tone but a little above a whisper, 'that you shall not have to ask me twice what troubles me. I took you for someone else yesterday evening. That troubles me.'

'That mistake?'

'No. That someone else.'

'Who is it?'

'I don't know.'

'Like me?'

'I don't know. I never saw the face. The left arm is across the face, and the right arm is waved. Violently waved. This way.'

I followed his action with my eyes, and it was the action of an arm gesticulating with the utmost passion and vehemence: 'For God's sake clear the way!'

'One moonlit night,' said the man, 'I was sitting here, when I heard a voice cry "Halloa! Below there!" I stared up, looked from that door, and saw this someone else standing by the red light near the tunnel, waving as I just now showed you. The voice seemed hoarse with shouting, and it cried, "Look out! Look out!" And then again "Halloa! Below there! Look out!" I caught up my lamp, turned it on red, and ran towards the figure, calling, "What's wrong? What has happened? Where?" It stood just outside the blackness of the tunnel. I advanced so close upon it that I wondered at its keeping the sleeve across its eyes. I ran right up at it, and had my hand stretched out to pull the sleeve away, when it was gone.'

'Into the tunnel,' said I.

'No. I ran on into the tunnel, five hundred yards. I stopped and held my lamp above my head, and saw the figures of the measured distance, and saw the wet stains stealing down the walls and trickling through the arch. I ran out again, faster than I had run in (for I had a mortal abhorrence of the place upon me), and I looked all round the red light with my own red light, and I went up the iron ladder to the gallery atop of it, and I came down again, and ran back here. I telegraphed both ways, "An alarm has been given. Is anything wrong?" The answer came back, both ways: "All well."'

Resisting the slow touch of a frozen finger tracing out my spine, I showed him how that this figure must be a deception of his sense of sight, and how that figures, originating in disease of the delicate nerves that minister to the functions of the eye, were known to have often troubled patients, some of whom had become conscious of the nature of their affliction, and had even proved it by experiments upon themselves. 'As to an imaginary cry,' said I, 'do but listen for a moment to the wind in this unnatural valley while we speak so low, and to the wild harp it makes of the telegraph wires!'

That was all very well, he returned, after we had sat listening for a while, and he ought to know something of the wind and the wires, he who so often passed long winter nights there, alone and watching. But he would beg to remark that he had not finished.

I asked his pardon, and he slowly added these words, touching my arm:

'Within six hours after the appearance, the memorable accident on this Line happened, and within ten hours the dead and wounded were brought along through the tunnel over the spot where the figure had stood.'

A disagreeable shudder crept over me, but I did my best against it. It was not to be denied, I rejoined, that this was a remarkable coincidence, calculated deeply to impress his mind. But it was unquestionable that remarkable coincidences did continually occur, and they must be taken into account in dealing with such a subject. Though to be sure I must admit, I added (for I thought I saw that he was going to bring the objection to bear upon me), men of common sense did not allow much for coincidences in making the ordinary calculations of life.

He again begged to remark that he had not finished.

I again begged his pardon for being betrayed into interruptions.

'This,' he said, again laying his hand upon my arm, and glancing over his shoulder with hollow eyes, 'was just a year ago. Six or seven months passed, and I had recovered from the surprise and shock, when one morning, as the day was breaking, I, standing at that door, looked towards the red light, and saw the spectre again.' He stopped, with a fixed look at me.

'Did it cry out?'

'No. It was silent.'

'Did it wave its arm?'

'No. It leaned against the shaft of the light, with both hands before the face. Like this.'

Once more, I followed his action with my eyes. It was an action of mourning. I have seen such an attitude in stone figures on tombs.

'Did you go up to it?'

'I came in and sat down, partly to collect my thoughts, partly because it had turned me faint. When I went to the door again, daylight was above me, and the ghost was gone.'

'But nothing followed? Nothing came of this?'

He touched me on the arm with his forefinger twice or thrice, giving a ghastly nod each time:

'That very day, as a train came out of the tunnel, I noticed, at a carriage window on my side, what looked like a confusion of hands and heads, and something waved. I saw it, just in time to signal the driver, Stop! He shut off, and put his brake on, but the train drifted past here a hundred and fifty yards or more. I ran after it, and, as I went along, heard terrible screams and cries. A beautiful young lady had died instantaneously in one of the compartments, and was brought in here, and laid down on this floor between us.'

Involuntarily, I pushed my chair back, as I looked from the boards at which he pointed, to himself.

'True, sir. True. Precisely as it happened, so I tell it you.'

I could think of nothing to say, to any purpose, and my mouth was very dry. The wind and the wires took up the story with a long lamenting wail.

He resumed. 'Now, sir, mark this, and judge how my mind is troubled. The spectre came back, a week ago. Ever since, it has been there, now and again, by fits and starts.'

'At the light?'

'At the Danger-light.'

'What does it seem to do?'

He repeated, if possible with increased passion and vehemence, that former gesticulation of 'For God's sake clear the way!'

Then, he went on. 'I have no peace or rest for it. It calls to me for many minutes together, in an agonized manner, "Below there! Look out! Look out!" It stands waving to me. It rings my little bell——'

I caught at that. 'Did it ring your bell yesterday evening when I was here, and you went to the door?'

'Twice.'

'Why, see,' said I, 'how your imagination misleads you. My eyes were on the bell, and my ears were open to the bell, and if I am a living man, it did *not* ring at those times. No, nor at any other time, except when it was rung in the natural course of physical things by the station communicating with you.'

He shook his head. 'I have never made a mistake as to that, yet, sir. I have never confused the spectre's ring with the man's. The ghost's ring is a strange vibration in the bell that it derives from nothing else, and I have not asserted that the bell stirs to the eye. I don't wonder that you failed to hear it. But *I* heard it.'

'And did the spectre seem to be there, when you looked out?'

'It was there.'

'Both times?'

He repeated firmly: 'Both times.'

'Will you come to the door with me, and look for it now?'

He bit his underlip as though he were somewhat unwilling, but arose. I opened the door, and stood on the step, while he stood in the doorway. There, was the Danger-light. There, was the dismal mouth of the tunnel. There, were the high wet stone walls of the cutting. There, were the stars above them.

'Do you see it?' I asked him, taking particular note of his face. His eyes were prominent and strained; but not very much more so, perhaps, than my own had been when I had directed them earnestly towards the same spot.

'No,' he answered. 'It is not there.'

'Agreed,' said I.

We went in again, shut the door, and resumed our seats. I was thinking how best to improve this advantage, if it might be called one, when he took up the conversation in such a matter of course way, so assuming that there could be no serious question of fact between us, that I felt myself placed in the weakest of positions.

'By this time you will fully understand, sir,' he said, 'that what troubles me so dreadfully, is the question, What does the spectre mean?'

I was not sure, I told him, that I did fully understand.

'What is its warning against?' he said, ruminating, with his eyes on the fire, and only by times turning them on me. 'What is the danger? Where is the danger? There is danger overhanging, somewhere on the Line. Some dreadful calamity will happen. It is not to be doubted this third time, after what has gone before. But surely this is a cruel haunting of *me*. What can *I* do?'

He pulled out his handkerchief, and wiped the drops from his heated forehead.

'If I telegraph Danger, on either side of me, or on both, I can give no reason for it,' he went on, wiping the palms of his hands. 'I should get into trouble, and do no good. They would think I was mad. This is the way it would work: Message: "Danger! Take care!" Answer: "What danger? Where?" Message: "Don't know. But for God's sake take care!" They would displace me. What else could they do?'

His pain of mind was most pitiable to see. It was the mental torture of a conscientious man, oppressed beyond endurance by an unintelligible responsibility involving life.

'When it first stood under the Danger-light,' he went on, putting his dark hair back from his head, and drawing his hands outwards across and across his temples in an extremity of feverish distress, 'why not tell me where that accident was to happen – if it must happen? Why not tell me how it could be averted – if it could have been averted? When on its second coming it hid its face, why not tell me instead: "She is going to die. Let them keep her at home"? If it came, on those two occasions, only to show me that its warnings were true, and so to prepare me for the third, why not warn me plainly now? And I, Lord help me! A mere poor signal-man on this solitary station! Why not go to somebody with credit to be believed, and power to act!'

When I saw him in this state, I saw that for the poor man's sake, as well as for the public safety, what I had to do for the time was, to compose his mind. Therefore, setting aside all question of reality or unreality between us, I represented to him that whoever thoroughly discharged his duty, must do well, and that at least it was his comfort that he understood his duty, though he did not understand these confounding appearances. In this effort I succeeded far better than in the attempt to reason him out of his conviction. He became calm; the occupations incidental to his post as the night advanced, began to make larger demands on his attention; and I left him at two in the morning. I had offered to stay through the night, but he would not hear of it.

That I more than once looked back at the red light as I ascended the pathway, that I did not like the red light, and that I should have slept but poorly if my bed had been under it, I see no reason to conceal. Nor did I like the two sequences of the accident and the dead girl. I see no reason to conceal that, either.

But, what ran most in my thoughts was the consideration how ought I to act, having become the recipient of this disclosure? I had proved the man to be intelligent, vigilant, painstaking and exact; but how long might he remain so, in his state of mind? Though in a subordinate position, still he held a most important trust, and would I (for instance) like to stake my own life on the chances of his continuing to execute it with precision?

Unable to overcome a feeling that there would be something treacherous in my communicating what he had told me to his superiors in the company, without first being plain with himself and proposing a middle course to him, I ultimately resolved to offer to accompany him (otherwise keeping his secret for the present) to the wisest medical practitioner we could hear of in those parts, and to take his opinion. A change in his time of duty would come round next night, he had apprised me, and he would be off an hour or two after sunrise, and on again soon after sunset. I had appointed to return accordingly.

Next evening was a lovely evening, and I walked out early to enjoy it. The sun was not yet quite down when I traversed the field-path near the top of the deep cutting. I would extend my walk for an hour, I said to myself, half an hour on and half an hour back, and it would then be time to go to my signal-man's box.

Before pursuing my stroll, I stepped to the brink, and mechanically looked down, from the point from which I had first seen him. I cannot describe the thrill that seized upon me, when, close at the mouth of the tunnel, I saw the appearance of a man, with his left sleeve across his eyes, passionately waving his right arm.

The nameless horror that oppressed me, passed in a moment, for in a moment I saw that this appearance of a man was a man indeed, and that there was a little group of other men standing at a short distance, to whom he seemed to be rehearsing the gesture he made. The Danger-light was not yet lighted. Against its shaft, a little low hut, entirely new to me, had been made of some wooden supports and tarpaulin. It looked no bigger than a bed.

With an irresistible sense that something was wrong – with a flashing self-reproachful fear that fatal mischief had come of my leaving the man there, and causing no one to be sent to overlook or correct what he did – I descended the notched path with all the speed I could make.

'What is the matter?' I asked the men.

'Signal-man killed this morning, sir.'

'Not the man belonging to that box?'

'Yes, sir.'

'Not the man I know?'

'You will recognize him, sir, if you knew him,' said the man who spoke for the others, solemnly uncovering his own head and raising an end of the tarpaulin, 'for his face is quite composed.'

'O! how did this happen, how did this happen?' I asked, turning from one to another as the hut closed in again.

'He was cut down by an engine, sir. No man in England knew his work better. But somehow he was not clear of the outer rail. It was just at broad day. He had struck the light, and had the lamp in his hand. As the engine came out of the tunnel, his back was towards her, and she cut him down. That man drove her, and was showing how it happened. Show the gentleman, Tom.'

The man who wore a rough dark dress, stepped back to his former place at the mouth of the tunnel!

'Coming round the curve in the tunnel, sir,' he said, 'I saw him at the end, like as if I saw him down a perspective-glass. There was no time to check speed, and I knew him to be very careful. As he didn't seem to take heed of the whistle, I shut it off when we were running down upon him, and called to him as loud as I could call.'

'What did you say?'

'I said, Below there! Look out! Look out! For God's sake clear the way!'

I started.

'Ah! it was a dreadful time, sir. I never left off calling to him. I put this arm before my eyes, not to see, and I waved this arm to the last; but it was no use.'

* * *

Without prolonging the narrative to dwell on any one of its curious circumstances more than on any other, I may, in closing it, point out the coincidence that the warning of the engine-driver included, not only the words which the unfortunate signal-man had repeated to me as haunting him, but also the words which I myself – not he – had attached, and that only in my own mind, to the gesticulation he had imitated.

The House of Balfother

William Croft Dickinson

'I sometimes wonder about those traditional immortals who live in secret chambers, like Earl Beardie at Glamis. Do they grow older and older? Do the years weary them? Or do they live on and on at exactly the same age? That's the worst of legends,' continued Drummond, addressing the company at large, 'they leave too much to the imagination.'

'Well, if Earl Beardie is growing older and older, his beard must be mighty long by now, after some four hundred years,' put in Sharples, with mock gravity. 'Unless at some point in time, or at some given length, a man's beard ceases to grow.'

'I know nothing about legends. Scottish history is too full of them,' said Petrie, critical as always. 'But, if someone will give me a long drink, I will tell you of one "immortal" who was certainly burdened by the years – so much so that he had declined into something worse than a second childhood. Yet from what I saw and experienced, I shudder to think what "life" would have meant to him had he not suffered an unnatural and terrible end.'

Someone got up to provide the drink.

'It will have to be a long one,' Petrie added quickly, 'for I shall have to tell you how I came to the House of Balfother, before I try to describe what happened there. And, after that, you will still have to hear the end of the tale.'

A very long drink was provided.

*　　*　　*

It all happened when I was a student at St Andrews – a 'magistrand', in my final year. And when I was also a great walker: which meant something more than the traditional ten-mile walk of St Andrews men, 'out by Cameron, and in by Grange'. To me, walking in those days meant striding across the hills by map and compass – the road to be taken only in times of sheer necessity – and never doing less than twenty miles a day. I can still do my twenty miles, but, in my student days, my long walks also meant trusting to hospitality, and hoping that the lonely farm or shepherd's cottage, marked with a small dot on the map, would somehow or other provide me with shelter for the night. Youth hostels were still unknown. Yet I was seldom turned away – even though, upon occasion, I must have been taken in at great inconvenience. And when I knew that that had been the case, I always strove to show my gratitude by giving any services I could on the following morning before setting out again – for I knew that any offer of payment would certainly be refused.

After the night of my strange experience, however, I left long before the day broke. And I was glad to be gone.

It was the Easter vacation of my final year and, faced with my examinations at the end of the coming summer term, I had decided upon a noble walk. I would take with me a copy of *Kidnapped*, and I would retrace David Balfour's route – partly that of 'the lad with the silver button', and partly that of David Balfour and Alan Breck when they 'took to the heather' after the murder of the 'Red Fox', Glenure. But I would do it in reverse, from North Queensferry to the Ross of Mull. Then back to Oban, and thence to St Andrews by train – to be at my books once more.

I had set out with high heart and, blessed with fine clear days, I was well ahead of my schedule when I reached the few small houses of Kilchonan, on Loch Rannoch-side. From there I walked the mile or so to the Bridge of Ericht and then struck northwards towards Loch Ericht. It was hardly midday, so I planned to go up the valley of the stream, skirt the loch on its western side (for I would find no Cluny's 'gillie' to row me across), and, with luck, find shelter for the night at Ben Alder Cottage. I knew I was giving myself something of a task for, according to the map, it was ten miles and a bit, with no habitation of any kind between Kilchonan and the Cottage. But I was in fine fettle, the day was glorious, and I had every confidence.

And then, for the first time, I found myself in difficulties. The way by the fast-running stream soon proved to be more troublesome than I had expected, so I struck up to the higher ground on the west. There I was beginning to make better progress, with a track to help me when, gradually, the sun paled and the afternoon grew colder. I knew well enough what that meant. I knew that before long I should be running the dangers of a mountain mist.

Wisely, I decided to turn back to Kilchonan. And then came the mist: thin at first, but soon, all too soon, thick and enveloping. I knew that all I had to do was to keep on due south. If I did that, I was bound to strike Loch Rannoch – and Kilchonan – again; or, if I had strayed too far west, I would strike the road that ran from the western end of the loch to Rannoch Station. After all, I had my compass – a fine prismatic one, with a luminous dial, a legacy of my father's service in the First World

War. More than once I had had to rely upon it amid the hills, and more
than once it had served me well. But, although I could keep on walking
in the right direction, I could not see where I was going; and almost
immediately I was reminded of a new danger. Stumbling badly on some
rough ground, I twisted my foot. Fortunately I was wearing heavy
boots, but there and then I pictured myself, with a sprained ankle, trying
painfully to make my way back and perhaps not succeeding, perhaps
not being found. I took greater care but, trying to pick my way slowly in
thick white mist, over ground that I could barely see ahead of me, meant
that before long I was chilled to the bone.

I cannot say that I was alarmed or dispirited. To the best of my
recollection, my first feeling was simply one of frustration – partly that I
had had to abandon my plan of reaching Ben Alder Cottage that night,
and partly at the enforced slowness of my return to Kilchonan. But as
the afternoon wore on, and still I had reached neither Loch Rannoch
nor the road, I began to feel worried. Also, I was tired out. My slow
groping through the mist would have tired anyone. But why had I made
such poor progress? I had kept steadily south. Where was I? By now, too,
although the mist was beginning to lift, darkness was taking its place.

And then, in the strange light that was half mist and half darkness, a
tall square-standing tower suddenly loomed up a few yards ahead of me.
Here was luck, indeed. Here I could find shelter for the night. Then
came a strange sense of puzzlement, perhaps even of disquiet. What was
this tower-house? It was certainly not marked on the map. There was no
house of this kind anywhere between Kilchonan and Loch Ericht. But
there it stood: a solid pile, much like a Border tower. It was no figment of
my imagination.

There was no surrounding wall of any kind, and I walked straight up
to the door. Again I was puzzled. The door was of solid oak, studded
with iron nails. Surely no house still boasted such a medieval defence? I
knocked as loudly as I could, but my knuckles seemed to make no sound
that would carry through the thick oak. Wondering what to do, I kicked
the door with my heavy boots, and knew that the noise I made was
bound to be heard. Standing there, cold and shivering, I kicked again
and again. And at last my demand was answered. I heard the drawing of
bars, the door opened slowly, and a man stood in the narrow opening as
though to contest any entry.

'For why are ye makand sic dunts on the door?' he asked.

'Could I have shelter for the night?' I replied.

'Na stranger enters Balfother. It's weel kent. The king's writ aye has
it so,' he answered, and would have closed the door.

But I was in no mood to be put off so easily and, being young and
impetuous, I thrust my foot into the gap.

'I'm sorry,' I said firmly, 'but you can't leave me out all night. I will be no trouble to you. I have food in my pack, and I can sleep on the kitchen floor, or in an outhouse if you have one. I want only that, and a fire to dry out my clothes.'

He seemed to hesitate, and then said again, almost as though it were a set phrase, 'Na stranger enters Balfother. The king's writ has it. It canna be.'

'But it must be,' I returned and, pushing against the door, I edged myself in.

'Bide ye there, then,' said the man, seeing that I had indeed entered Balfother, and apparently not wishing to dispute my entry. He shuffled away in the darkness of what I assumed to be some kind of entrance passage, and left me standing there. A minute or two later, however, he reappeared, carrying a lighted tallow candle on a dish. Beckoning me to follow him, he led the way up a winding stone stairway, opened a door, and ushered me into a small room. There he set the candle upon a rough table and, without a word, left me again.

I looked at my quarters for the night, and again I felt that strange sense of disquiet. The room was perhaps twelve feet square and completely empty save for the rough table on which the man had set my candle, and a bed that was even more roughly made and was completely devoid of bed-clothes of any kind. The stone walls were cold and bare; as also was the stone floor. Only a small window, high up in one of the walls, and a crude fire-place in the wall opposite the bed, broke the forbidding monotony of stone. More that that, the whole room smelled dank and musty, as though the one window had never been opened, and the room had never been used, for countless years.

'A chilly reception, if ever there was one,' I muttered resentfully. 'Surely there's a fire in the house, somewhere.'

But I did my reluctant host an injustice. I had barely muttered my resentment than he came into the room, bearing an armful of logs. Again without speaking he laid them in a neat pile in the fire-place and went out, returning a second time with a log that was still glowing from a fire elsewhere. He placed the glowing log in the centre of the pile, lay full length upon the floor and blew until the log broke into flames and began to set the other logs alight.

At any rate I shall have a fire, I thought, thankfully, as I watched him at his task. And then once more I was puzzled. What was this house with an ancient look about everything? Who was this man? And why did his coarse clothes seem so odd? Had he inherited them from a grandfather, or a great-grandfather?

As the man rose from his task, I thanked him sincerely for his attention to my wants. But he merely looked at me blankly and moved to the door. There, however, he turned before leaving.

'God keep ye through the night,' he said and, with that, he was gone.

'And what might that mean?' I wondered. Was it just a benison, or was it a warning? I had virtually commanded shelter for the night, but what sort of shelter had I taken? What sort of a night was I to have?

Dismissing various vague apprehensions which flitted through my mind, I opened my pack and took out the spare socks, shirt and underclothing which I always carried on my long walks. These I laid, like a hearth-rug, on the stone floor in front of the fire, and then stripped to the skin. Standing on my hearth-rug, I rubbed myself hard and long with my towel. Then I began to dry out my soaking clothes, first arranging them in small pyramids before the fire and then holding them up, one at a time, close to the flames. I knew I ran the risk of singeing them, but dry clothes I had to have if I was to sleep without blankets. For perhaps an hour I continued this task until all my clothes were dry. Then I dressed, ate some chocolate and plain biscuits, and felt completely refreshed.

I stress all this to show that I was fully alert and far from likely to 'imagine' things. Sitting on the edge of the bed I was ready to accept the shelter I had demanded and to face whatever the night might bring. Again taking out my map, I looked for a house somewhere in the hills to the south of Loch Ericht. No house was marked. But surely a tower-house like this was bound to be marked. What was this House of Balfother? And what had my queer host meant about 'na stranger', and 'the king's writ'? Well, I was ready for anything.

The fire was now burning low, but there was still life in the tallow candle. And then, just as I was debating whether or not to trust myself to the bed, and its possible vermin, I saw the door slowly opening. I flatter myself I was not in the least afraid. If robbery was intended, I felt in just the right mood to put up a good fight for my few pounds and pence. But it was not my host who entered. I was being visited by a large dog.

The animal, yellowish-white, and strangely devoid of fur, crawled slowly into the room and made straight for the fireplace and the warmth of the glowing embers there. But, instead of lying down, it *sat* down, much as a human would sit on the floor in front of a fire. Startled, I looked more closely at that strange posture. With a sudden feeling of revulsion, I realized that I was looking, not at a dog, but at a man.

He was completely naked. His skin was yellow, loose and wrinkled – much like a piece of faded paper that had been crumpled up and then roughly smoothed out again. Soon, as he sat there, warming himself before the fire, he began to make little noises, similar to those made by a baby before it first begins to talk. After a while, he stopped and, teetering to and fro, began to croon to himself: 'Robbie Norrie, Robbie Norrie canna die. Robbie Norrie wilna die.'

It is impossible to describe my feelings as I witnessed this complete degradation of humanity. And, as I wondered what to do, the man turned, and saw me sitting on the bed. With a gurgle of delight, he got up and crawled towards me. Never had I seen, never shall I see again such an old, old face. It looked as though it had aged through centuries. Now too, as he came close to me, I could smell his body – a horrible, indefinable smell of rank flesh.

'Robbie Norrie,' he gibbered. 'Robbie Norrie.'

I strove to push him away, and his body yielded to my hands like a soft sponge.

'Robbie Norrie. Robbie Norrie,' I heard in a kind of childish sing-song as I feverishly struggled to avoid an approach that sent shivers of horror through every nerve in my frame.

I have no idea how long I struggled with that degenerate lump of human flesh. I was contending with a creature (for that is the only appropriate name) that seemed to have risen in bodily form from an age-old grave; a creature that sought to nestle close to me and that I pushed away again and again.

'Robbie Norrie, Robbie Norrie.' The childish repetition, as the foul creature constantly returned and strove to nestle against me, suddenly snapped my control. I seized him by the throat, and might well have strangled him, had not the door opened, just in time.

I let go my hold as I saw my host enter the room. The creature dropped on all fours at my feet; my host gave a sharp word of command; and the horrible thing, that once had been a man, sidled slowly out. My host, without a word, followed it.

I am not ashamed to say that I was in a state of complete collapse. I was a strong, well-built youngster of twenty-two, and all I had had to do was to repulse a weak and decrepit creature, feeble alike in body and mind. Yet somehow, I felt that I had been struggling with something so unwholesome that I myself had been in danger of corruption. Perhaps people in the middle ages felt like that about contact with a leper. I do not know.

As I gradually became myself again, I decided there was only one course to take. I had had enough of Balfother. I put my things into my pack and, creeping out of the room, felt my way about until I had discovered the stairway. I stole quietly down, found the door, drew back the wooden bars, and literally ran out into the night. It was still dark, but the mist had cleared. Again I struck south by compass, this time not caring whether I sprained my ankle or not. And, to my surprise, I had been walking for barely a quarter of an hour when I reached Loch Rannoch. There I stayed until dawn, resting my back against a tree, pondering over my strange adventure and regaining peace of mind.

My walk was over, save for the few miles to Rannoch Station. I caught a train there, changed at Crianlarich, and journeyed slowly, across country, back to St Andrews.

* * *

A week or so after my return, I received a note from John Barnet, my professor of Greek, inviting me to his house for tea. Term had not yet started, and the only other guest at tea was Duncan Mackinnon, the senior lecturer in History. I had told Barnet of my intention to walk from North Queensferry to the Ross of Mull, and naturally his first question was to ask me how I had fared. You can easily understand that my immediate response was to tell the whole story of my night at Balfother. But I was not prepared for what followed.

'Balfother?' interrupted Mackinnon, when I told of my arrival at the house.

'Robert Norrie?' he asked, excitedly, a little later.

But he let me finish.

'You know something about all this?' queried Barnet, turning to Mackinnon, when my tale had ended.

'Wait!' he answered. 'I'll slip over to my house and bring back a document which goes some way towards an explanation – though even then the whole thing is incredible.'

Mackinnon went out, leaving us to await his return impatiently – wondering what his document could be, and what explanation it could possibly give.

About ten minutes later he was back.

'As you know,' he began, taking a folded paper from his pocket, 'I have been working on the Fortingall Papers in the Scottish Record Office. And as soon as Petrie mentioned Balfother I remembered a queer letter under the Privy Seal which I found in the Fortingall Papers and which intrigued me so much that I transcribed it in full.'

He unfolded his sheet of paper, and although I cannot give you the exact words – though I still have a copy of the document at home – what he read out to us ran roughly like this:

A letter made to William Fowler of Balfother, his heirs and assigns, making mention that for the good, true and thankful service done and to be done by the said William, his heirs and assigns, in the keeping and maintaining of Robert Norrie, the man to whom the French leech Damian gave the quintessence in the time of our sovereign Lord's predecessor King James IV, whom God assoil, and the said Robert Norrie being still on life, therefore our sovereign Lord grants to the said William, his heirs and assigns, an annual rent of five hundred shillings to be uptaken yearly of the lands of Dall and Finnart. Providing always that the said William Fowler, his heirs and assigns, shall keep the said Robert Norrie close from all other persons whatsomever that he may be scatheless and harmless in his bòdy, and that our sovereign Lord and, if God wills, our sovereign Lord's successors, may know to what age the said Robert shall live.

'Now you can understand my excitement,' continued Mackinnon. 'The date of that letter is April 3rd 1622. James IV died at Flodden in 1513. So already Robert Norrie had lived to at least the age of 109, and probably several years more – for the quintessence would hardly be given to him in his infancy. That had aroused my interest when I first read the extract; but, if Petrie saw the same Robert Norrie at Balfother, as he seems to have done, the man must now be more than 400 years old.'

For a minute or so we digested this in silence.

'He *was* centuries old,' I said. 'I felt it at the time.'

'And what's all this about the French leech Damian, and the quintessence?' asked Barnet.

'Oh, that part is straightforward enough,' answered Mackinnon. 'We know that James IV encouraged the experiments of a certain Damian who believed he could distil the "quintessence" – not only to turn base metals into gold but also to yield an elixir that would prolong man's life indefinitely. James IV even made him abbot of Tongland; and, if you are interested, you can find the materials which he used in his experiments, and for which the King paid, in the *Accounts of the Lord High Treasurer* from about 1501 to 1513. My extract proves conclusively that Robert Norrie, who had been given the "quintessence", lived to be at least 109. Is he still alive? At 400? What's more, when Petrie knocked at the door of Balfother he was told that no stranger could be admitted, and that the King's writ said so. Doesn't that mean that the same Robert Norrie is still being kept "close"?'

'We'll go to Balfother ourselves,' cried Barnet. 'And we'll ask James Waters to come with us. He takes so much interest in his anatomical reconstructions from the skulls and bones of men who have been dead for centuries that he's sure to be interested in the anatomy of a man who is still alive at the age of at least 400. All that puzzles me is how the affair has been kept secret for so long. Food – and even tallow candles – must be bought; and people are always curious about any queer goings-on in their neighbourhood. Surely the good folk of Kilchonan must know of the strange "creature" kept in Balfother. However, we'll see. I propose we ring up Waters and, if he's free, we'll drive to Kilchonan tomorrow.'

*   *   *

Waters was free. And Barnet was a good driver. We arrived at
Kilchonan about noon and, after a picnic lunch by the loch-side, the
four of us retraced my steps up the high ground to the west of the stream
that runs from Loch Ericht into Loch Rannoch. But we found no tower-
house. Reaching the point where I thought I had turned back, we
spread out, far wider than beaters on a grouse moor, and walked
southwards again. We met on the road by the Loch, and again we had
failed to find Balfother.

'Are you sure you didn't fall asleep and dream it all?' asked Barnet,
turning to me with a twinkle in his eye.

'I'm certain I didn't,' I replied, firmly.

'It can't have been a dream,' confirmed Mackinnon. 'Petrie had
never heard of Balfother and Robert Norrie. He knew nothing of a letter
under the Privy Seal – a "king's writ" – which banned the entry of
strangers.'

'Well,' said the practical Waters, 'I suggest we enquire at
Kilchonan. Perhaps we should have done so first of all.'

We enquired. But no one in Kilchonan had heard of a house called
Balfother. One encouragement, however, did emerge from our enquiries. It was suggested that we should call on a Mr Alastair
MacGregor, in Aberfeldy, who, we were told, was writing a local
history, and who, of all people, was the most likely to be of help to us.

We drove to Aberfeldy, and we found Mr MacGregor.

'Balfother?' he repeated. 'Yes, there was certainly a tower-house of
that name. It belonged to the Fowlers; but it was destroyed long ago. A
grim and tragic affair. Come in, and I'll tell you about it.'

*   *   *

Alastair MacGregor did not live long enough to see his book in print. I
can give you no reference to volume and page. But I am not likely to
forget his account.

It appears that in 1649 there was a veritable epidemic of witch-
huntings, witch-trials and witch-burnings throughout all Scotland from
one end of the country to the other. And, in the August of that year,
someone denounced William Fowler of Balfother, and Bessie Wilson, his
wife, of keeping a 'familiar'. The 'familiar' had been seen. It was in the
form of an old and naked man, who could not be clothed, and who ran
about on all fours like a dog.

A body of men, headed by a minister, went out to Balfother.
Apparently they had difficulty in gaining an entrance, but when, at last,
they had broken down the door, had entered the house, and had secured
Fowler and his wife, they began a search for the 'familiar'. And,
according to the story, they found it – an old and decrepit man, stark
naked, who babbled the words of some devilish incantation which put

them all in terror until the minister cried out: 'Get thee behind me, Satan,' when they rushed at it and bound it with strong cords.

William Fowler and Bessie Wilson were burned as agents of the devil and, with them, was burned their 'familiar'. It is said that William Fowler produced something which he called 'the king's writ', and which he offered in his defence. But the court refused to look at it, let alone accept it.

As for the house itself, after the burnings, the minister had preached a powerful sermon on the text, 'We will destroy this place ... and the Lord hath sent us to destroy it.' Whereupon all the people had marched out to Balfother and, with crowbars and irons, had pulled down the house, stone by stone, scattering the stones over the land. And yet, apparently, the sight of good cut freestone was too much for the people of a later time. According to MacGregor, many of the stones of Balfother were still to be seen in some of the walls in Kilchonan.

*   *   *

We left the knowledgeable MacGregor and we drove from Aberfeldy in silence.

'What a horrible story,' said Barnet, at last.

'Yes,' agreed Mackinnon. 'One of far too many. Horrible. And yet,' he continued with his historian's eye for dates, 'Robert Norrie must have lived to at least the age of 136. Is that possible, Waters?'

'Certainly it's possible,' replied Waters, crisply. 'All the same, I'm glad that modern medicine has not yet discovered the prescription for Damian's quintessence. Old age is already a social problem, without further complications from an elixir of life.'

'But,' I cried impatiently, 'can any of you explain how I came to the House of Balfother when the house was no longer there, and how Robert Norrie came to visit me when Robert Norrie had long been dead.'

No one answered me. And I know that no one ever will.

The Brown Hand
Arthur Conan Doyle

Everyone knows that Sir Dominick Holden, the famous Indian surgeon, made me his heir, and that his death changed me in an hour from a hard-working and impecunious medical man to a well-to-do landed proprietor. Many know also that there were at least five people between the inheritance and me, and that Sir Dominick's selection appeared to be altogether arbitrary and whimsical. I can assure them, however, that they are quite mistaken, and that, although I only knew Sir Dominick in the closing years of his life, there were none the less very real reasons why he should show his goodwill towards me. As a matter of fact, though I say it myself, no man ever did more for another than I did for my Indian uncle. I cannot expect the story to be believed, but it is so singular that I should feel that it was a breach of duty if I did not put it upon record – so here it is, and your belief or incredulity is your own affair.

Sir Dominick Holden, C.B., K.C.S.I., and I don't know what besides, was the most distinguished Indian surgeon of his day. In the Army originally, he afterwards settled down into civil practice in Bombay, and visited as a consultant every part of India. His name is best remembered in connection with the Oriental Hospital, which he founded and supported. The time came, however, when his iron constitution began to show signs of the long strain to which he had subjected it, and his brother practitioners (who were not, perhaps, entirely disinterested upon the point) were unanimous in recommending him to return to England. He held on so long as he could, but at last he developed nervous symptoms of a very pronounced character, and so came back, a broken man, to his native county of Wiltshire. He bought a considerable estate with an ancient manor-house upon the edge of Salisbury Plain, and devoted his old age to the study of Comparative Pathology, which had been his learned hobby all his life, and in which he was a foremost authority.

We of the family were, as may be imagined, much excited by the news of the return of this rich and childless uncle to England. On his part, although by no means exuberant in his hospitality, he showed some sense of his duty to his relations, and each of us in turn had an invitation to visit him. From the accounts of my cousins it appeared to be a melancholy business, and it was with mixed feelings that I at last received my own summons to appear at Rodenhurst. My wife was so carefully excluded in the invitation that my first impulse was to refuse it, but the interests of the children had to be considered, and so, with her consent, I set out one October afternoon upon my visit to Wiltshire, with little thought of what that visit was to entail.

My uncle's estate was situated where the arable land of the plains begins to swell upwards into the rounded chalk hills which are characteristic of the country. As I drove from Dinton Station in the waning light of that autumn day, I was impressed by the weird nature of the scenery. The few scattered cottages of the peasants were so dwarfed by the huge evidences of prehistoric life, that the present appeared to be a dream and the past to be the obtrusive and masterful reality. The road wound through the valleys, formed by a succession of grassy hills, and the summit of each was cut and carved into the most elaborate fortifications, some circular and some square, but all on a scale which has defied the winds and the rains of many centuries. Some call them Roman and some British, but their true origin and the reasons for this particular tract of country being so interlaced with entrenchments have never been finally made clear. Here and there on the long, smooth, olive-coloured slopes there rose small rounded barrows or tumuli. Beneath them lie the cremated ashes of the race which cut so deeply into the hills, but their graves tell us nothing save that a jar full of dust represents the man who once laboured under the sun.

It was through this weird country that I approached my uncle's residence of Rodenhurst, and the house was, as I found, in due keeping with its surroundings. Two broken and weather-stained pillars, each surmounted by a mutilated heraldic emblem, flanked the entrance to a neglected drive. A cold wind whistled through the elms which lined it, and the air was full of the drifting leaves. At the far end, under the gloomy arch of trees, a single yellow lamp burned steadily. In the dim half-light of the coming night I saw a long, low building stretching out two irregular wings, with deep eaves, a sloping gambrel roof, and walls which were criss-crossed with timber balks in the fashion of the Tudors. The cheery light of a fire flickered in the broad, latticed window to the left of the low-porched door, and this, as it proved, marked the study of my uncle, for it was thither that I was led by his butler in order to make my host's acquaintance.

He was cowering over his fire, for the moist chill of an English autumn had set him shivering. His lamp was unlit, and I only saw the red glow of the embers beating upon a huge, craggy face, with a Red

Indian nose and cheek, and deep furrows and seams from eye to chin, the sinister marks of hidden volcanic fires. He sprang up at my entrance with something of an old-world courtesy and welcomed me warmly to Rodenhurst. At the same time I was conscious, as the lamp was carried in, that it was a very critical pair of light-blue eyes which looked out at me from under shaggy eyebrows, like scouts beneath a bush, and that this outlandish uncle of mine was carefully reading off my character with all the ease of a practised observer and an experienced man of the world.

For my part I looked at him, and looked again, for I had never seen a man whose appearance was more fitted to hold one's attention. His figure was the framework of a giant, but he had fallen away until his coat dangled straight down in a shocking fashion from a pair of broad and bony shoulders. All his limbs were huge and yet emaciated, and I could not take my gaze from his knobby wrists, and long, gnarled hands, But his eyes – those peering light blue eyes – they were the most arrestive of any of his peculiarities. It was not their colour alone, nor was it the ambush of hair in which they lurked; but it was the expression which I read in them. For the appearance and bearing of the man were masterful, and one expected a certain corresponding arrogance in his eyes, but instead of that I read the look which tells of a spirit cowed and crushed, the furtive, expectant look of the dog whose master has taken the whip from the rack. I formed my own medical diagnosis upon one glance at those critical and yet appealing eyes. I believed that he was stricken with some mortal ailment, that he knew himself to be exposed to sudden death, and that he lived in terror of it. Such was my judgement – a false one, as the event showed; but I mention it that it may help you to realize the look which I read in his eyes.

My uncle's welcome was, as I have said, a courteous one, and in an hour or so I found myself seated between him and his wife at a comfortable dinner, with curious pungent delicacies upon the table, and a stealthy, quick-eyed Oriental waiter behind his chair. The old couple had come round to that tragic imitation of the dawn of life when husband and wife, having lost or scattered all those who were their intimates, find themselves face to face and alone once more, their work done, and the end nearing fast. Those who have reached that stage in sweetness and love, who can change their winter into a gentle Indian summer, have come as victors through the ordeal of life. Lady Holden was a small, alert woman, with a kindly eye, and her expression as she glanced at him was a certificate of character to her husband. And yet, though I read a mutual love in their glances, I read also a mutual horror, and recognized in her face some reflection of that stealthy fear which I detected in his. Their talk was sometimes merry and sometimes sad, but there was a forced note in their merriment and a naturalness in their sadness which told me that a heavy heart beat upon either side of me.

We were sitting over our first glass of wine, and the servants had left the room, when the conversation took a turn which produced a remarkable effect upon my host and hostess. I cannot recall what it was which started the topic of the supernatural, but it ended in my showing them that the abnormal in psychical experiences was a subject to which I had, like many neurologists, devoted a great deal of attention. I concluded by narrating my experiences when, as a member of the Psychical Research Society, I had formed one of a committee of three who spent the night in a haunted house. Our adventures were neither exciting nor convincing, but, such as it was, the story appeared to interest my auditors in a remarkable degree. They listened with an eager silence, and I caught a look of intelligence between them which I could not understand. Lady Holden immediately afterwards rose and left the room.

Sir Dominick pushed the cigar box over to me, and we smoked for some little time in silence. That huge bony hand of his was twitching as he raised it with his cheroot to his lips, and I felt that the man's nerves were vibrating like fiddle-strings. My instincts told me that he was on the verge of some intimate confidence, and I feared to speak lest I should interrupt it. At last he turned towards me with a spasmodic gesture like a man who throws his last scruple to the winds:

'From the little that I have seen of you it appears to me, Dr Hardacre,' said he, 'that you are the very man I have wanted to meet.'

'I am delighted to hear it, sir.'

'Your head seems to be cool and steady. You will acquit me of any desire to flatter you, for the circumstances are too serious to permit of insincerities. You have some special knowledge upon these subjects, and you evidently view them from that philosophical standpoint which robs them of all vulgar terror. I presume that the sight of an apparition would not seriously discompose you?'

'I think not, sir.'

'Would even interest you, perhaps?'

'Most intensely.'

'As a psychical observer, you would probably investigate it in as impersonal a fashion as an astronomer investigates a wandering comet?'

'Precisely.'

He gave a heavy sigh.

'Believe me, Dr Hardacre, there was a time when I could have spoken as you do now. My nerve was a by-word in India. Even the Mutiny never shook it for an instant. And yet you see what I am reduced to – the most timorous man, perhaps, in all this country of Wiltshire. Do not speak too bravely upon this subject, or you may find yourself subjected to as long-drawn a test as I am – a test which can only end in the madhouse or the grave.'

I waited patiently until he should see fit to go farther in his confidence. His preamble had, I need not say, filled me with interest and expectation.

'For some years, Dr Hardacre,' he continued, 'my life and that of my wife have been made miserable by a cause which is so grotesque that it borders upon the ludicrous. And yet familiarity has never made it more easy to bear – on the contrary, as time passes my nerves become more worn and shattered by the constant attrition. If you have no physical fears, Dr Hardacre, I should very much value your opinion upon this phenomenon which troubles us so.'

'For what it is worth my opinion is entirely at your service. May I ask the nature of the phenomenon?'

'I think that your experiences will have a higher evidential value if you are not told in advance what you may expect to encounter. You are yourself aware of the quibbles of unconscious cerebration and subjective impressions with which a scientific sceptic may throw a doubt upon your statement. It would be as well to guard against them in advance.'

'What shall I do, then?'

'I will tell you. Would you mind following me this way?' He led me out of the dining-room and down a long passage until we came to a terminal door. Inside there was a large bare room fitted as a laboratory, with numerous scientific instruments and bottles. A shelf ran along one side, upon which there stood a long line of glass jars containing pathological and anatomical specimens.

'You see that I still dabble in some of my old studies,' said Sir Dominick. 'These jars are the remains of what was once a most excellent collection, but unfortunately I lost the greater part of them when my house was burned down in Bombay in '92. It was a most unfortunate affair for me – in more ways than one. I had examples of many rare conditions, and my splenic collection was probably unique. These are the survivors.'

I glanced over them, and saw that they really were of a very great value and rarity from a pathological point of view: bloated organs, gaping cysts, distorted bones, odious parasites – a singular exhibition of the products of India.

'There is, as you see, a small settee here,' said my host. 'It was far from our intention to offer a guest so meagre an accommodation, but since affairs have taken this turn, it would be a great kindness upon your part if you would consent to spend the night in this apartment. I beg that you will not hesitate to let me know if the idea should be at all repugnant to you.'

'On the contrary,' I said, 'it is most acceptable.'

'My own room is the second on the left, so that if you should feel that you are in need of company a call would always bring me to your side.'

'I trust that I shall not be compelled to disturb you.'

'It is unlikely that I shall be asleep. I do not sleep much. Do not hesitate to summon me.'

And so with this agreement we joined Lady Holden in the drawing-room and talked of lighter things.

It was no affectation upon my part to say that the prospect of my night's adventure was an agreeable one. I have no pretence to greater physical courage than my neighbours, but familiarity with a subject robs it of those vague and undefined terrors which are the most appalling to the imaginative mind. The human brain is capable of only one strong emotion at a time, and if it be filled with curiosity or scientific enthusiasm, there is no room for fear. It is true that I had my uncle's assurance that he had himself originally taken this point of view, but I reflected that the breakdown of his nervous system might be due to his forty years in India as much as to any psychical experiences which had befallen him. I at least was sound in nerve and brain, and it was with something of the pleasurable thrill of anticipation with which the sportsman takes his position beside the haunt of his game that I shut the laboratory door behind me, and partially undressing, lay down upon the rug-covered settee.

It was not an ideal atmosphere for a bedroom. The air was heavy with many chemical odours, that of methylated spirit predominating. Nor were the decorations of my chamber very sedative. The odious line of glass jars with their relics of disease and suffering stretched in front of my very eyes. There was no blind to the window, and a three-quarter moon streamed its white light into the room, tracing a silver square with filigree lattices upon the opposite wall. When I had extinguished my candle this one bright patch in the midst of the general gloom had certainly an eerie and discomposing aspect. A rigid and absolute silence reigned throughout the old house, so that the low swish of the branches in the garden came softly and soothingly to my ears. It may have been the hypnotic lullaby of this gentle susurrus, or it may have been the result of my tiring day, but after many dozings and many efforts to regain my clearness of perception, I fell at last into a deep and dreamless sleep.

I was awakened by some sound in the room, and I instantly raised myself upon my elbow on the couch. Some hours had passed, for the square patch upon the wall had slid downwards and sideways until it lay obliquely at the end of my bed. The rest of the room was in deep shadow. At first I could see nothing. Presently, as my eyes became accustomed to the faint light, I was aware, with a thrill which all my scientific absorption could not entirely prevent, that something was moving slowly along the line of the wall. A gentle, shuffling sound, as of soft slippers, came to my ears, and I dimly discerned a human figure walking stealthily from the direction of the door. As it emerged into the patch of moonlight I was very clearly what it was and how it was employed. It was a man, short and squat, dressed in some sort of dark grey gown, which hung straight from his shoulders to his feet. The moon shone upon the side of his face, and I saw that it was chocolate-brown in colour, with a ball of black hair like a woman's at the back of his head. He walked slowly, and his eyes were cast upwards towards the line of bottles which contained those gruesome remnants of humanity. He seemed to examine each jar with attention, and then to pass on to the next. When he had come to the end of the line, immediately opposite my bed, he stopped, faced me, threw up his hands with a gesture of despair, and vanished from my sight.

I have said that he threw up his hands, but I should have said his arms, for at he assumed that attitude of despair I observed a singular peculiarity about his appearance. He had only one hand! As the sleeves drooped down from the up-flung arms I saw the left plainly, but the right ended in a knobby and unsightly stump. In every other way his appearance was so natural, and I had both seen and heard him so clearly, that I could easily have believed that he was an Indian servant of Sir Dominick's who had come into my room in search of something. It was only his sudden disappearance which suggested anything more sinister to me. As it was I sprang from my couch, lit a candle, and examined the whole room carefully. There were no signs of my visitor, and I was forced to conclude that there had really been something outside the normal laws of nature in his appearance. I lay awake for the remainder of the night, but nothing else occurred to disturb me.

I am an early riser, but my uncle was an even earlier one, for I found him pacing up and down the lawn at the side of the house. He ran towards me in his eagerness when he saw me come out from the door.

'Well, well!' he cried. 'Did you see him?'

'An Indian with one hand?'

'Precisely.'

'Yes, I saw him' – and I told him all that occurred. When I had finished, he led the way into his study.

'We have a little time before breakfast,' said he. 'It will suffice to give you an explanation of this extraordinary affair – so far as I can explain that which is essentially inexplicable. In the first place, when I tell you that for four years I have never passed one single night, either in Bombay, aboard ship, or here in England without my sleep being broken by this fellow, you will understand why it is that I am a wreck of my former self. His programme is always the same. He appears by my bedside, shakes me roughly by the shoulder, passes from my room into the laboratory, walks slowly along the line of my bottles, and then vanishes. For more than a thousand times he has gone through the same routine.'

'What does he want?'

'He wants his hand.'

'His hand?'

'Yes, it came about in this way. I was summoned to Peshawur for a consultation some years ago, and while there I was asked to look at the hand of a native who was passing through with an Afghan caravan. The fellow came from some mountain tribe living away at the back of beyond somewhere on the other side of Kaffiristan. He talked a bastard Pushtoo, and it was all I could do to understand him. He was suffering from a soft sarcomatous swelling of one of the metacarpal joints, and I made him realize that it was only by losing his hand that he could hope to save his life. After much persuasion he consented to the operation, and he asked me, when it was over, what fee I demanded. The poor fellow was almost a beggar, so that the idea of a fee was absurd, but I answered in jest that my fee should be his hand, and that I proposed to add it to my pathological collection.

'To my surprise he demurred very much to the suggestion, and he explained that according to his religion it was an all important matter that the body should be reunited after death, and so make a perfect dwelling for the spirit. This belief is, of course, an old one, and the mummies of the Egyptians arose from an analogous superstition. I answered him that his hand was already off, and asked him how he intended to preserve it. He replied that he would pickle it in salt and carry it about with him. I suggested that it might be safer in my keeping than in his, and that I had better means than salt for preserving it. On realizing that I really intended to keep it carefully, his opposition vanished instantly. 'But remember, sahib,' said he, 'I shall want it back when I am dead.' I laughed at the remark, and so the matter ended. I returned to my practice, and he no doubt in the course of time was able to continue his journey to Afghanistan.

'Well, as I told you last night, I had a bad fire in my house at Bombay. Half of it was burned down, and, among other things, my pathological collection was largely destroyed. What you see are the poor remains of it. The hand of the hillman went with the rest, but I gave the matter no particular thought at the time. That was six years ago.

'Four years ago – two years after the fire – I was awakened one night by a furious tugging at my sleeve. I sat up under the impression that my favourite mastiff was trying to arouse me. Instead of this, I saw my Indian patient of long ago, dressed in the long grey gown which was the

badge of his people. He was holding up his stump and looking
reproachfully at me. He then went over to my bottles, which at that
time I kept in my room, and he examined them carefully, after which he
gave a gesture of anger and vanished. I realized that he had just died,
and that he had come to claim my promise that I should keep his limb in
safety for him.

'Well, there you have it all, Dr Hardacre. Every night at the same
hour for four years this performance has been repeated. It is a simple
thing in itself, but it has worn me out like water dropping on a stone. It
has brought a vile insomnia with it, for I cannot sleep now for the
expectation of his coming. It has poisoned my old age and that of my
wife, who has been the sharer in this great trouble. But there is the
breakfast gong, and she will be waiting impatiently to know how it fared
with you last night. We are both much indebted to you for your
gallantry, for it takes something from the weight of our misfortune when
we share it, even for a single night, with a friend, and it reassures us as to
our sanity, which we are sometimes driven to question.'

This was the curious narrative which Sir Dominick confided to me –
a story which to many would have appeared to be a grotesque
impossibility, but which, after my experience of the night before, and
my previous knowledge of such things, I was prepared to accept as an
absolute fact. I thought deeply over the matter, and brought the whole
range of my reading and experience to bear upon it. After breakfast, I
surprised my host and hostess by announcing that I was returning to
London by the next train.

'My dear doctor,' cried Sir Dominick in great distress, 'you make me
feel that I have been guilty of a gross breach of hospitality in intruding
this unfortunate matter upon you. I should have borne my own
burden.'

'It is, indeed, that matter which is taking me to London,' I
answered; 'but you are mistaken, I assure you, if you think that my
experience of last night was an unpleasant one to me. On the contrary, I
am about to ask your permission to return in the evening and spend one
more night in your laboratory. I am very eager to see this visitor once
again.'

My uncle was exceedingly anxious to know what I was about to do,
but my fears of raising false hopes prevented me from telling him. I was
back in my own consulting room a little after luncheon, and was
confirming my memory of a passage in a recent book upon occultism
which had arrested my attention when I read it.

'In the case of earth-bound spirits,' said my authority, 'some one
dominant idea obsessing them at the hour of death is sufficient to hold
them to this material world. They are the amphibia of this life and of the
next, capable of passing from one to the other as the turtle passes from

land to water. The causes which may bind a soul so strongly to a life which its body has abandoned are any violent emotion. Avarice, revenge, anxiety, love, and pity have all been known to have this effect. As a rule it springs from some unfulfilled wish, and when the wish has been fulfilled the material bond relaxes. There are many cases upon record which show the singular persistence of these visitors, and also their disappearance when their wishes have been fulfilled, or in some cases when a reasonable compromise has been effected.'

'*A reasonable compromise effected*' – those were the words which I had brooded over all the morning, and which I now verified in the original. No actual atonement could be made here – but a reasonable compromise! I made my way as fast as a train could take me to the Shadwell Seamen's Hospital, where my old friend Jack Hewett was house-surgeon. Without explaining the situation I made him understand exactly what it was that I wanted.

'A brown man's hand!' said he, in amazement. 'What in the world do you want that for?'

'Never mind. I'll tell you some day. I know that your wards are full of Indians.'

'I should think so. But a hand——' He thought a little and then struck a bell.

'Travers,' said he to a student-dresser, 'what became of the hands of the Lascar which we took off yesterday? I mean the fellow from the East India Dock who got caught in the steam winch.'

'They are in the post-mortem room, sir.'

'Just pack one of them in antiseptics and give it to Dr Hardacre.'

And so I found myself back at Rodenhurst before dinner with this curious outcome of my day in town. I still said nothing to Sir Dominick, but I slept that night in the laboratory, and I placed the Lascar's hand in one of the glass jars at the end of my couch.

So interested was I in the result of my experiment that sleep was out of the question. I sat with a shaded lamp beside me and waited patiently for my visitor. This time I saw him clearly from the first. He appeared beside the door, nebulous for an instant, and then hardening into as distinct an outline as any living man. The slippers beneath his grey gown were red and heelless, which accounted for the low, shuffling sound which he made as he walked. As on the previous night he passed slowly along the line of bottles until he paused before that which contained the hand. He reached up to it, his whole figure quivering with expectation, took it down, examined it eagerly, and then, with a face which was convulsed with fury and disappointment, he hurled it down on the floor. There was a crash which resounded through the house, and when I looked up the mutilated Indian had disappeared. A moment later my door flew open and Sir Dominick rushed in.

'You are not hurt?' he cried.

'No – but deeply disappointed.'

He looked in astonishment at the splinters of glass, and the brown hand lying upon the floor.

'Good God!' he cried. 'What is this?'

I told him my idea and its wretched sequel. He listened intently, but shook his head.

'It was well thought of,' said he, 'but I fear that there is no such easy end to my sufferings. But one thing I now insist upon. It is that you shall never again upon any pretext occupy this room. My fears that something might have happened to you – when I heard that crash – have been the most acute of all the agonies which I have undergone. I will not expose myself to a repetition of it.'

He allowed me, however, to spend the remainder of that night where I was, and I lay there worrying over the problem and lamenting my own failure. With the first light of morning there was the Lascar's hand still lying upon the floor to remind me of my fiasco. I lay looking at it – and as I lay suddenly an idea flew like a bullet through my head and brought me quivering with excitement out of my couch. I raised the grim relic from where it had fallen. Yes, it was indeed so. The hand was the *left* hand of the Lascar.

By the first train I was on my way to town, and hurried at once to the Seamen's Hospital. I remembered that both hands of the Lascar had been amputated, but I was terrified lest the precious organ which I was in search of might have been already consumed in the crematory. My suspense was soon ended. It had still been preserved in the post-mortem room. And so I returned to Rodenhurst in the evening with my mission accomplished and the material for a fresh experiment.

But Sir Dominick Holden would not hear of my occupying the laboratory again. To all my entreaties he turned a deaf ear. It offended his sense of hospitality, and he could no longer permit it. I left the hand, therefore, as I had done its fellow the night before, and I occupied a comfortable bedroom in another portion of the house, some distance from the scene of my adventures.

But in spite of that my sleep was not destined to be uninterrupted. In the dead of night my host burst into my room, a lamp in his hand. His huge gaunt figure was enveloped in a loose dressing-gown, and his whole appearance might certainly have seemed more formidable to a weaknerved man than that of the Indian of the night before. But it was not his entrance so much as his expression which amazed me. He had turned suddenly younger by twenty years at least. His eyes were shining, his features radiant, and he waved one hand in triumph over his head. I sat up astounded, staring sleepily at this extraordinary visitor. But his words soon drove the sleep from my eyes.

'We have done it! We have succeeded!' he shouted. 'My dear
Hardacre, how can I ever in this world repay you?'

'You don't mean to say that it is all right?'

'Indeed I do. I was sure that you would not mind being awakened to
hear such blessed news.'

'Mind! I should think not indeed. But is it really certain?'

'I have no doubt whatever upon the point. I owe you such a debt,
my dear nephew, as I have never owed a man before, and never
expected to. What can I possibly do for you that is commensurate?
Providence must have sent you to my rescue. You have saved both my
reason and my life, for another six months of this must have seen me
either in a cell or a coffin. And my wife – it was wearing her out before
my eyes. Never could I have believed that any human being could have
lifted this burden off me.' He seized my hand and wrung it in his bony
grip.

'It was only an experiment – a forlorn hope – but I am delighted
from my heart that it has succeeded. But how do you know that it is all
right? Have you seen something?'

He seated himself at the foot of my bed.

'I have seen enough,' said he. 'It satisfies me that I shall be troubled
no more. What has passed is easily told. You know that at a certain hour
this creature always comes to me. Tonight he arrived at the usual time,
and aroused me with even more violence than is his custom. I can only
surmise that his disappointment of last night increased the bitterness of
his anger against me. He looked angrily at me, and then went on his
usual round. But in a few minutes I saw him, for the first time since this
persecution began, return to my chamber. He was smiling. I saw the
gleam of his white teeth through the dim light. He stood facing me at
the end of my bed, and three times he made the low Eastern salaam
which is their solemn leave-taking. And the third time that he bowed he
raised his arms over his head, and I saw his *two* hands outstretched in
the air. So he vanished, and, as I believe, for ever.'

*   *   *

So that is the curious experience which won me the affection and the
gratitude of my celebrated uncle, the famous Indian surgeon. His
anticipations were realized, and never again was he disturbed by the
visits of the restless hillman in search of his lost member. Sir Dominick
and Lady Holden spent a very happy old age, unclouded, so far as I
know, by any trouble, and they finally died during the great influenza
epidemic within a few weeks of each other. In his lifetime he always
turned to me for advice in everything which concerned that English life
of which he knew so little; and I aided him also in the purchase and
development of his estates. It was no great surprise to me, therefore, that

I found myself eventually promoted over the heads of five exasperated cousins, and changed in a single day from a hard-working country doctor into the head of an important Wiltshire family. I at least have reason to bless the memory of the man with the brown hand, and the day when I was fortunate enough to relieve Rodenhurst of his unwelcome presence.

The Phantom Coach
Amelia B. Edwards

The circumstances I am about to relate to you have truth to recommend them. They happened to myself, and my recollection of them is as vivid as if they had taken place only yesterday. Twenty years, however, have gone by since that night. During those twenty years I have told the story to but one other person. I tell it now with a reluctance which I find it difficult to overcome. All I entreat, meanwhile, is that you will abstain from forcing your own conclusions upon me. I want nothing explained away. I desire no arguments. My mind on this subject is quite made up, and, having the testimony of my own senses to rely upon, I prefer to abide by it.

Well! It was just twenty years ago, and within a day or two of the end of the grouse season. I had been out all day with my gun, and had had no sport to speak of. The wind was due east; the month, December; the place, a bleak wide moor in the far north of England. And I had lost my way. It was not a pleasant place in which to lose one's way, with the first feathery flakes of a coming snow-storm just fluttering down upon the heather, and the leaden evening closing in all around. I shaded my eyes with my hand, and stared anxiously into the gathering darkness, where the purple moorland melted into a range of low hills, some ten or twelve miles distant. Not the faintest smoke-wreath, not the tiniest cultivated patch, or fence, or sheep-track, met my eyes in any direction. There was nothing for it but to walk on, and take my chance of finding what shelter I could, by the way. So I shouldered my gun again, and pushed wearily forward; for I had been on foot since an hour after daybreak, and had eaten nothing since breakfast.

Meanwhile, the snow began to come down with ominous steadiness, and the wind fell. After this, the cold became more intense, and the night came rapidly up. As for me, my prospects darkened with the darkening sky, and my heart grew heavy as I thought how my young wife was already watching for me through the window of our little inn parlour, and thought of all the suffering in store for her throughout this weary night. We had been married four months, and, having spent our autumn in the Highlands, were now lodging in a remote little village situated just on the verge of the great English moorlands. We were very much in love, and, of course, very happy. This morning, when we parted, she had implored me to return before dusk, and I had promised her that I would. What would I not have given to have kept my word!

Even now, weary as I was, I felt that with a supper, an hour's rest, and a guide, I might still get back to her before midnight, if only guide and shelter could be found.

And all this time, the snow fell and the night thickened. I stopped and shouted every now and then, but my shouts seemed only to make the silence deeper. Then a vague sense of uneasiness came upon me, and I began to remember stories of travellers who had walked on and on in the falling snow until, wearied out, they were fain to lie down and sleep their lives away. Would it be possible, I asked myself, to keep on thus through all the long dark night? Would there not come a time when my limbs must fail, and my resolution give way? When I, too, must sleep the sleep of death. Death! I shuddered. How hard to die just now, when life lay all so bright before me! How hard for my darling, whose whole loving heart – but that thought was not to be borne! To banish it, I shouted again, louder and longer, and then listened eagerly. Was my shout answered, or did I only fancy that I heard a far-off cry? I hallooed again, and again the echo followed. Then a wavering speck of light came suddenly out of the dark, shifting, disappearing, growing momentarily nearer and brighter. Running towards it at full speed, I found myself, to my great joy, face to face with an old man and a lantern.

'Thank God!' was the exclamation that burst involuntarily from my lips.

Blinking and frowning, he lifted his lantern and peered into my face. 'What for?' growled he, sulkily.

'Well – for you. I began to fear I should be lost in the snow.'

'Eh, then, folks do get cast away hereabouts fra' time to time, an' what's to hinder you from bein' cast away likewise, if the Lord's so minded?'

'If the Lord is so minded that you and I shall be lost together, friend, we must submit,' I replied; 'but I don't mean to be lost without you. How far am I now from Dwolding?'

'A gude twenty mile, more or less.'

'And the nearest village?'

'The nearest village is Wuke, an' that's twelve mile t'other side.'

'Where do you live, then?'

'Out yonder,' said he, with a vague jerk of the lantern.

'You're going home, I presume?'

'Maybe I am.'

'Then I'm going with you.'

The old man shook his head, and rubbed his nose reflectively with the handle of the lantern.

'It ain't o' no use,' growled he. 'He 'ont let you in – not he.'

'We'll see about that,' I replied, briskly. 'Who is He?'

'The master.'

'Who is the master?'

'That's nowt to you,' was the unceremonious reply.

'Well, well; you lead the way, and I'll engage that the master shall give me shelter and a supper tonight.'

'Eh, you can try him!' muttered my reluctant guide; and, still shaking his head, he hobbled, gnome-like, away through the falling snow. A large mass loomed up presently out of the darkness, and a huge dog rushed out, barking furiously.

'Is this the house?' I asked.

'Ay, it's the house. Down, Bey!' And he fumbled in his pocket for the key.

I drew up close behind him, prepared to lose no chance of entrance, and saw in the little circle of light shed by the lantern that the door was heavily studded with iron nails, like the door of a prison. In another minute he had turned the key and I had pushed past him into the house.

Once inside, I looked round with curiosity, and found myself in a great raftered hall, which served, apparently, a variety of uses. One end was piled to the roof with corn, like a barn. The other was stored with flour-sacks, agricultural implements, casks, and all kinds of miscellaneous lumber; while from the beams overhead hung rows of hams, flitches, and bunches of dried herbs for winter use. In the centre of the floor stood some huge object gauntly dressed in a dingy wrapping-cloth, and reaching halfway to the rafters. Lifting a corner of this cloth, I saw, to my surprise, a telescope of very considerable size, mounted on a rude movable platform, with four small wheels. The tube was made of painted wood, bound round with bands of metal rudely fashioned; the speculum, so far as I could estimate its size in the dim light, measured at least fifteen inches in diameter. While I was yet examining the instrument, and asking myself whether it was not the work of some self-taught optician, a bell rang sharply.

'That's for you,' said my guide, with a malicious grin. 'Yonder's his room.'

He pointed to a low black door at the opposite side of the hall. I crossed over, rapped somewhat loudly, and went in, without waiting for an invitation. A huge, white-haired old man rose from a table covered with books and papers, and confronted me sternly.

'Who are you?' said he. 'How came you here? What do you want?'

'James Murray, barrister-at-law. On foot across the moor. Meat, drink and sleep.'

He bent his bushy brows into a portentous frown.

'Mine is not a house of entertainment,' he said, haughtily. 'Jacob, how dared you admit this stranger?'

'I didn't admit him,' grumbled the old man. 'He followed me over the muir, and shouldered his way in before me. I'm no match for six foot two.'

'And pray, sir, by what right have you forced an entrance into my house?'

'The same by which I should have clung to your boat, if I were drowning. The right of self-preservation.'

'Self-preservation?'

'There's an inch of snow on the ground already,' I replied, briefly; 'and it would be deep enough to cover my body before daybreak.'

He strode to the window, pulled aside a heavy black curtain, and looked out.

'It is true,' he said. 'You can stay, if you choose, till morning. Jacob, serve the supper.'

With this he waved me to a seat, resumed his own, and became at once absorbed in the studies from which I had disturbed him.

I placed my gun in a corner, drew a chair to the hearth, and examined my quarters at leisure. Smaller and less incongruous in its arrangements than the hall, this room contained, nevertheless, much to awaken my curiosity. The floor was carpetless. The whitewashed walls were in parts scrawled over with strange diagrams, and in others covered with shelves crowded with philosophical instruments, the uses of many of which were unknown to me. On one side of the fireplace, stood a bookcase filled with dingy folios; on the other, a small organ, fantastically decorated with painted carvings of medieval saints and devils. Through the half-opened door of a cupboard at the further end of the room, I saw a long array of geological specimens, surgical preparations, crucibles, retorts and jars of chemicals; while on the mantelshelf beside me, amid a number of small objects, stood a model of the solar system, a small galvanic battery and a microscope. Every chair had its burden. Every corner was heaped high with books. The very floor was littered over with maps, casts, papers, tracings and learned lumber of all conceivable kinds.

I stared about me with an amazement increased by every fresh object upon which my eyes chanced to rest. So strange a room I had never seen; yet seemed it stranger still, to find such a room in a lone farmhouse amid those wild and solitary moors! Over and over again, I looked from my host to his surroundings, and from his surroundings back to my host, asking myself who and what he could be? His head was singularly fine; but it was more the head of a poet than of a philosopher. Broad in the temples, prominent over the eyes, and clothed with a rough profusion of perfectly white hair, it had all the ideality and much of the ruggedness that characterizes the head of Ludwig van Beethoven. There were the same deep lines about the mouth, and the same stern furrows in the brow. There was the same concentration of expression. While I was yet observing him, the door opened, and Jacob brought in the supper. His master then closed his book, rose and, with more courtesy of manner than he had yet shown, invited me to the table.

A dish of ham and eggs, a loaf of brown bread and a bottle of admirable sherry were placed before me.

'I have but the homeliest farmhouse fare to offer you, sir,' said my entertainer. 'Your appetite, I trust, will make up for the deficiencies of our larder.'

I had already fallen upon the viands, and now protested, with the enthusiasm of a starving sportsman, that I had never eaten anything so delicious.

He bowed stiffly, and sat down to his own supper, which consisted, primitively, of a jug of milk and a basin of porridge. We ate in silence, and, when we had done, Jacob removed the tray. I then drew my chair back to the fireside. My host, somewhat to my surprise, did the same, and turning abruptly towards me, said:

'Sir, I have lived here in strict retirement for three-and-twenty years. During that time, I have not seen as many strange faces, and I have not read a single newspaper. You are the first stranger who has crossed my threshold for more than four years. Will you favour me with a few words of information respecting that outer world from which I have parted company so long?'

'Pray interrogate me,' I replied. 'I am heartily at your service.'

He bent his head in acknowledgement; leaned forward, with his elbows resting on his knees and his chin supported in the palms of his hands; stared fixedly into the fire; and proceeded to question me.

His enquiries related chiefly to scientific matters, with the later progress of which, as applied to the practical purposes of life, he was almost wholly unacquainted. No student of science myself, I replied as well as my slight information permitted; but the task was far from easy, and I was much relieved when, passing from interrogation to discussion, he began pouring forth his own conclusions upon the facts which I had been attempting to place before him. He talked, and I listened spellbound. He talked till I believe he almost forgot my presence, and only thought aloud. I had never heard anything like it then; I have never heard anything like it since. Familiar with all systems of all philosophies, subtle in analysis, bold in generalization, he poured forth his thoughts in an uninterrupted stream, and, still leaning forward in the same moody attitude with his eyes fixed upon the fire, wandered from topic to topic, from speculation to speculation, like an inspired dreamer. From practical science to mental philosophy; from electricity in the wire to electricity in the nerve; from Watts to Mesmer, from Mesmer to Reichenbach, from Reichenbach to Swedenborg, Spinoza, Condillac, Descartes, Berkeley, Aristotle, Plato and the Magi and mystics of the East, were transitions which, however bewildering in their variety and scope, seemed easy and harmonious upon his lips as sequences in music. By and by – I forgot now by what link of conjecture or illustration – he passed on to that field which lies beyond the boundary line of even conjectural philosophy, and reaches no man knows whither. He spoke of the soul and its aspirations; of the spirit and its powers; of second sight; of prophecy; of those phenomena which, under the names of ghosts, spectres and supernatural appearances, have been denied by the sceptics and attested by the credulous, of all ages.

'The world,' he said, 'grows hourly more and more sceptical of all that lies beyond its own narrow radius; and our men of science foster the fatal tendency. They condemn as fable all that resists experiment. They reject as false all that cannot be brought to the test of the laboratory or the dissecting-room. Against what superstition have they waged so long and obstinate a war, as against the belief in apparitions? And yet what superstition has maintained its hold upon the minds of men so long and so firmly? Show me any fact in physics, in history, in archaeology, which is supported by testimony so wide and so various. Attested by all races of men, in all ages and in all climates, by the soberest sages of antiquity, by the rudest savage of today, by the Christian, the Pagan, the Pantheist, the Materialist, this phenomenon is treated as a nursery tale by the philosophers of our century. Circumstantial evidence weighs with them as a feather in the balance. The comparison of causes with effects, however valuable in physical science, is put aside as worthless and unreliable. The evidence of competent witnesses, however conclusive in a court of justice, counts for nothing. He who pauses before he pronounces, is condemned as a trifler. He who believes, is a dreamer or a fool.'

He spoke with bitterness, and, having said thus, relapsed for some minutes into silence. Presently he raised his head from his hands, and added, with an altered voice and manner,

'I, sir, paused, investigated, believed and was not ashamed to state my convictions to the world. I, too, was branded as a visionary, held up to ridicule by my contemporaries, and hooted from that field of science in which I had laboured with honour during all the best years of my life. These things happened just three-and-twenty years ago. Since then, I have lived as you see me living now, and the world has forgotten me, as I have forgotten the world. You have my history.'

'It is a very sad one,' I murmured, scarcely knowing what to answer.

'It is a very common one,' he replied. 'I have only suffered for the truth, as many a better and wiser man has suffered before me.'

He rose, as if desirous of ending the conversation, and went over to the window.

'It has ceased snowing,' he observed, as he dropped the curtain, and came back to the fireside.

'Ceased!' I exclaimed, starting eagerly to my feet. 'Oh, if it were only possible – but no! it is hopeless. Even if I could find my way across the moor, I could not walk twenty miles tonight.'

'Walk twenty miles tonight!' repeated my host. 'What are you thinking of?'

'Of my wife,' I replied, impatiently. 'Of my young wife, who does not know that I have lost my way, and who is at this moment breaking her heart with suspense and terror.'

'Where is she?'

'At Dwolding, twenty miles away.'

'At Dwolding,' he echoed, thoughtfully. 'Yes, the distance, it is true, is twenty miles; but – are you so very anxious to save the next six or eight hours?'

'So very, very anxious, that I would give ten guineas at this moment for a guide and a horse.'

'Your wish can be gratified at a less costly rate,' said he, smiling. 'The night mail from the north, which changes horses at Dwolding, passes within five miles of this spot, and will be due at a certain cross-road in about an hour and a quarter. If Jacob were to go with you across the moor, and put you into the old coach-road, you could find your way, I suppose, to where it joins the new one?'

'Easily – gladly.'

He smiled again, rang the bell, gave the old servant his directions, and, taking a bottle of whisky and a wineglass from the cupboard in which he kept his chemicals, said:

'The snow lies deep, and it will be difficult walking tonight on the moor. A glass of usquebaugh before you start?'

I would have declined the spirit, but he pressed it on me, and I drank it. It went down my throat like liquid flame, and almost took my breath away.

'It is strong,' he said; 'but it will help to keep out the cold. And now you have no moments to spare. Goodnight!'

I thanked him for his hospitality, and would have shaken hands, but that he had turned away before I could finish my sentence. In another minute I had travelled the hall, Jacob had locked the outer door behind me, and we were out on the wide white moor.

Although the wind had fallen, it was still bitterly cold. Not a star glimmered in the black vault overhead. Not a sound, save the rapid crunching of the snow beneath our feet, disturbed the heavy stillness of the night. Jacob, not too well pleased with his mission, shambled on before in sullen silence, his lantern in his hand, and his shadow at his feet. I followed, with my gun over my shoulder, as little inclined for conversation as himself. My thoughts were full of my late host. His voice yet rang in my ears. His eloquence yet held my imagination captive. I remember to this day, with surprise, how my over-excited brain retained whole sentences and parts of sentences, troops of brilliant images, and fragments of splendid reasoning, in the very words in which he had uttered them. Musing thus over what I had heard, and striving to recall a lost link here and there, I strode on at the heels of my guide, absorbed and unobservant. Presently – at the end, as it seemed to me, of only a few minutes – he came to a sudden halt, and said:

'Yon's your road. Keep the stone fence to your right hand, and you can't fail of the way.'

'This, then, is the old coach-road?'

'Ay, 'tis the old coach-road.'

'And how far do I go, before I reach the cross-roads?'

'Nigh upon three mile.'

I pulled out my purse, and he became more communicative.

'The road's a fair road enough,' said he, 'for foot passengers; but 'twas over steep and narrow for the northern traffic. You'll mind where the parapet's broken away, close again the sign-post. It's never been mended since the accident.'

'What accident?'

'Eh, the night mail pitched right over into the valley below – a gude fifty feet an' more – just at the worst bit o' road in the whole county.'

'Hôrrible! Were many lives lost?'

'All. Four were found dead, and t'other two died next morning.'

'How long is it since this happened?'

'Just nine year.'

'Near the sign-post, you say? I will bear it in mind. Goodnight.'

'Gude night, sir, and thankee.' Jacob pocketed his half-crown, made a faint pretence of touching his hat, and trudged back by the way he had come.

I watched the light of his lantern till it quite disappeared, and then turned to pursue my way alone. This was no longer matter of the slightest difficulty, for, despite the dead darkness overhead, the line of stone fence showed distinctly enough against the pale gleam of the snow. How silent it seemed now, with only my footsteps to listen to; how silent and how solitary! A strange disagreeable sense of loneliness stole over me. I walked faster. I hummed a fragment of a tune. I cast up enormous sums in my head, and accumulated them at compound interest. I did my best, in short, to forget the startling speculations to which I had but just been listening, and, to some extent, I succeeded.

Meanwhile the night air seemed to become colder and colder, and though I walked fast I found it impossible to keep myself warm. My feet were like ice. I lost sensation in my hands, and grasped my gun mechanically. I even breathed with difficulty, as though, instead of traversing a quiet north country highway, I were scaling the uppermost heights of some gigantic Alp. This last symptom became presently so distressing, that I was forced to stop for a few minutes, and lean against the stone fence. As I did so, I chanced to look back up the road, and there, to my infinite relief, I saw a distant point of light, like the gleam of an approaching lantern. I at first concluded that Jacob had retraced his steps and followed me; but even as the conjecture presented itself, a second light flashed into sight – a light evidently parallel with the first, and approaching at the same rate of motion. It needed no second thought to show me that these must be the carriage-lamps of some private vehicle, though it seemed strange that any private vehicle should take a road professedly disused and dangerous.

There could be no doubt, however, of the fact, for the lamps grew larger and brighter every moment, and I even fancied I could already see the dark outline of the carriage between them. It was coming up very fast, and quite noiselessly, the snow being nearly a foot deep under the wheels.

And now the body of the vehicle became distinctly visible behind the lamps. It looked strangely lofty. A sudden suspicion flashed upon me. Was it possible that I had passed the cross-roads in the dark without observing the sign-post, and could this be the very coach which I had come to meet?

No need to ask myself that question a second time, for here it came round the bend of the road, guard and driver, one outside passenger, and four steaming greys, all wrapped in a soft haze of light, through which the lamps blazed out, like a pair of fiery meteors.

I jumped forward, waved my hat, and shouted. The mail came down at full speed, and passed me. For a moment I feared that I had not been seen or heard, but it was only for a moment. The coachman pulled up; the guard, muffled to the eyes in capes and comforters, and apparently sound asleep in the rumble, neither answered my hail nor made the slightest effort to dismount; the outside passenger did not even turn his head. I opened the door for myself, and looked in. There were but three travellers inside, so I stepped in, shut the door, slipped into the vacant corner, and congratualted myself on my good fortune.

The atmosphere of the coach seemed, if possible, colder than that of the outer air, and was pervaded by a singularly damp and disagreeable smell. I looked round at my fellow-passengers. They were all three, men, and all silent. They did not seem to be asleep, but each leaned back in his corner of the vehicle, as if absorbed in his own reflections. I attempted to open a conversation.

'How intensely cold it is tonight,' I said, addressing my opposite neighbour.

He lifted his head, looked at me, but made no reply.

'The winter,' I added, 'seems to have begun in earnest.'

Although the corner in which he sat was so dim that I could distinguish none of his features very clearly, I saw that his eyes were still turned full upon me. And yet he answered never a word.

At any other time I should have felt, and perhaps expressed, some annoyance, but at the moment I felt too ill to do either. The icy coldness of the night air had struck a chill to my very marrow, and the strange smell inside the coach was affecting me with an intolerable nausea. I shivered from head to foot, and, turning to my left-hand neighbour, asked if he had any objection to an open window?

He neither spoke nor stirred.

I repeated the question somewhat more loudly, but with the same result. Then I lost my patience, and let the sash down. As I did so, the leather strap broke in my hand, and I observed that the glass was covered with a thick coat of mildew, the accumulation, apparently, of years. My attention being thus drawn to the condition of the coach, I examined it more narrowly, and saw by the uncertain light of the outer lamps that it was in the last stage of dilapidation. Every part of it was not only out of repair, but in a condition of decay. The sashes splintered at a touch. The leather fittings were crusted over with mould, and literally rotting from the woodwork. The floor was almost breaking away beneath my feet. The whole machine, in short, was foul with damp, and had evidently been dragged from some outhouse in which it had been mouldering away for years, to do another day or two of duty on the road.

I turned to the third passenger, whom I had not yet addressed, and hazarded one more remark.

'This coach,' I said, 'is in a deplorable condition. The regular mail, I suppose, is under repair?'

He moved his head slowly, and looked me in the face, without speaking a word. I shall never forget that look while I live. I turned cold at heart under it. I turn cold at heart even now when I recall it. His eyes glowed with a fiery unnatural lustre. His face was livid as the face of a corpse. His bloodless lips were drawn back as if in the agony of death, and showed the gleaming teeth between.

The words that I was about to utter died upon my lips, and a strange horror – a dreadful horror – came upon me. My sight had by this time become used to the gloom of the coach, and I could see with tolerable distinctness. I turned to my opposite neighbour. He, too, was looking at me, with the same startling pallor in his face, and the same stony glitter in his eyes. I passed my hand across my brow. I turned to the passenger on the seat beside my own, and saw – oh Heaven! how shall I describe what I saw? I saw that he was no living man – that none of them were living men, like myself! A pale phosphorescent light – the light of putrefaction – played upon their awful faces; upon their hair, dank with the dews of the grave; upon their clothes, earth-stained and dropping to pieces; upon their hands, which were as the hands of corpses long buried. Only their eyes, their terrible eyes, were living; and those eyes were all turned menacingly upon me!

A shriek of terror, a wild unintelligible cry for help and mercy, burst from my lips as I flung myself against the door, and strove in vain to open it.

In that single instant, brief and vivid as a landscape beheld in the flash of summer lightning, I saw the moon shining down through a rift of stormy cloud – the ghastly sign-post rearing its warning finger by the wayside – the broken parapet – the plunging horses – the black gulf below. Then, the coach reeled like a ship at sea. Then, came a mighty crash – a sense of crushing pain – and then, darkness.

*　　*　　*

It seemed as if years had gone by when I awoke one morning from a deep sleep, and found my wife watching by my bedside. I will pass over the scene that ensued, and give you, in half a dozen words, the tale she told me with tears of thanksgiving. I had fallen over a precipice, close against the junction of the old coach-road and the new, and had only been saved from certain death by lighting upon a deep snowdrift that had accumulated at the foot of the rock beneath. In this snowdrift I was discovered at daybreak, by a couple of shepherds, who carried me to the nearest shelter, and brought a surgeon to my aid. The surgeon found me in a state of raving delirium, with a broken arm and a compound fracture of the skull. The letters in my pocket-book showed my name and address; my wife was summoned to nurse me; and, thanks to youth and a fine constitution, I came out of danger at last. The place of my fall, I need scarcely say, was precisely that at which a frightful accident had happened to the north mail nine years before.

I never told my wife the fearful events which I have just related to you. I told the surgeon who attended me; but he treated the whole adventure as a mere dream born of the fever in my brain. We discussed the question over and over again, until we found that we could discuss it with temper no longer, and then we dropped it. Others may form what conclusions they please – I *know* that twenty years ago I was the fourth inside passenger in that Phantom Coach.

Don't Tell Cissie
Celia Fremlin

'Friday, then. The six-ten from Liverpool Street,' said Rosemary, gathering up her gloves and bag. 'And don't tell Cissie!' she added, 'You *will* be careful about that, won't you, Lois?'

I nodded. People are always talking like this about Cissie, she's that kind of person. She was like that at school, and now, when we're all coming up towards retirement, she's like it still.

You know the kind of person I mean? Friendly, good-hearted, and desperately anxious to be in on everything, and yet with this mysterious knack of ruining things – of bringing every project grinding to a halt, simply by being there.

Because it wasn't ever her fault. Not really. 'Let me come! Oh, *please* let me come too!' she'd beg, when three or four of us from the Lower Fourth had schemed up an illicit trip to the shops on Saturday afternoon. And, because she was our friend (well, sort of – anyway, it was *our* set that she hovered on the fringe of all the time, not anyone else's) – because of this, we usually, let her come; and always it ended in disaster. *She'd* be the one to slip on the edge of the kerb outside Woolworth's, and cut her knee so that the blood ran, and a little crowd collected, and a kind lady rang up the school to have us fetched home. *She'd* be the one to get lost . . . to miss the bus . . . to arrive back at school bedraggled and tear-stained and late for evening preparation, hopelessly giving the game away for all of us.

You'd think, wouldn't you, that after a few such episodes she'd have given up, or at least have learned caution. But no. Her persistence (perhaps one would have called it courage if only it hadn't been so annoying) – well, her persistence, then, was indomitable. Neither school punishments nor the reproaches of her companions ever kept her under for long. 'Oh, *please* let me come!' she'd be pleading again, barely a week after the last débâcle, 'Oh, plee-ee-ease! Oh, don't be so *mean!*'

And so there, once again, she'd inexorably be, back in action once more. Throwing up in the middle of the dormitory feast. Crying with blisters as we trudged back from a ramble out of bounds. Soaked, and shivering, and starting pneumonia from having fallen through the ice of the pond we'd been forbidden to skate on.

So you can understand, can't you, why Rosemary and I didn't want Cissie with us when we went to investigate the ghost at Rosemary's new weekend cottage. Small as our chances might be of pinning down the ghost in any case, Cissie could have been counted on to reduce them to zero. Dropping a tray of tea things just as the rapping began . . . Calling out, 'What? *I* can't hear anything!' as we held our breaths trying to locate the ghostly sobbing . . . Falling over a tombstone as we tiptoed through the moonlit churchyard . . . No, Cissie must at all costs be kept out of our little adventure; and by now, after nearly half a century, we knew that the only way of keeping Cissie out of anything was to make sure that she knew nothing about it, right from the beginning.

*   *   *

But let me get back to Rosemary's new cottage. I say 'new', because Rosemary has only recently bought it – not because the cottage itself is new. Far from it. It is early eighteenth century, and damp, and dark, and built of the local stone, and Rosemary loves it (*did* love it, rather – but let me not get ahead of myself). Anyway, as I was saying, Rosemary loved the place, loved it on sight, and bought it almost on impulse with the best part of her life's savings. *Their* life's savings, I suppose I should say, because she and Norman are still married to each other, and it must have been his money just as much as hers. But Norman never seems to have much to do with these sort of decisions – indeed, he doesn't seem to have much to do with Rosemary's life at all, these days – certainly, he never comes down to the cottage. I think that was part of the idea, really – that they should be able to get away from each other at weekends. During the week, of course, it's all right, as they are both working full-time, and they both bring plenty of work home in the evenings. Rosemary sits in one room correcting history essays, while Norman sits in another working out export quotas, or something; and the mutual non-communication must be almost companionable, in an arid sort of a way. But the crunch will come, of course, when they both retire in a year or so's time. I think Rosemary was thinking of this when she bought the cottage; it would become a real port in a storm then – a bolthole from what she refers to as 'the last and worst lap of married life'.

At one time, we used to be sorry for Cissie, the only one of our set who never married. But now, when the slow revolving of the decades have left me a widow and Rosemary stranded among the flotsam of a dead marriage – now, lately I have begun wondering whether Cissie hasn't done just as well for herself as any of us, in the long run. Certainly, she has had plenty of fun on the fringes of other people's lives, over the years. She wangles invitations to silver-wedding parties; worms her way into other people's family holidays – and even if it ends up with the whole lot of them in quarantine at the airport because of Cissie coming out in spots – well, at least she's usually had a good run for her money first.

And, to be fair to her, it's not just the pleasures and luxuries of our lives that she tries to share; it's the problems and crises, too. I remember she managed to be present at the birth of my younger son, and if only she hadn't dropped the boiling kettle on her foot just as I went into the second stage of labour, her presence would have been a real help. As it was, the doctor and midwife were both busy treating her for shock in the kitchen, and binding up her scalded leg, while upstairs my son arrived unattended, and mercifully without fuss. Perhaps even the unborn are sensitive to atmosphere? Perhaps he sensed, even then, that, with Cissie around, it's just *no use* anyone else making a fuss about anything?

But let me get back to Rosemary's haunted cottage (or not haunted, as the case may be – let me not pre-judge the issue before I have given you all the facts). Of course, to begin with, we were half-playing a game, Rosemary and I. The tension tends to go out of life as you come up towards your sixties. Whatever problems once tore at you, and kept you fighting, and alive, and gasping for breath – they are solved now, or else have died, quietly, while you weren't noticing. Anyway, what with one thing and another, life can become a bit dull and flavourless when you get to our age; and, to be honest, a ghost was just what Rosemary and I were needing. A spice of danger; a spark of the unknown to re-activate these water-logged minds of ours, weighed down as they are by such a lifetime's accumulation of the known.

I am telling you this because I want to be absolutely honest. In evaluating the events I am to describe, you must remember, and allow for, the fact that Rosemary and I *wanted* there to be a ghost. Well, no, perhaps that's putting it too strongly; we wanted there to *might* be a ghost – if you see what I so ungrammatically mean. We wanted our weekend to bring us at least a small tingling of the blood; a tiny prickling of the scalp. We wanted our journey to reach a little way into the delicious outskirts of fear, even if it *did* have to start from Liverpool Street.

We felt marvellously superior, Rosemary and I, as we stood jam-packed in the corridor, rocking through the rainy December night. We glanced with secret pity at all those blank, commuter faces, trundling towards the security of their homes. *We* were different. *We* were travelling into the unknown.

*   *   *

Our first problems, of course, were nothing to do with ghosts. They were to do with milk, and bread, and damp firewood, and why Mrs Thorpe from the village hadn't come in to air the beds as she'd promised. She hadn't filled the lamps, either, or brought in the paraffin ... how did she think Rosemary was going to get it from the shed in all this rain and dark? And where were all those tins she'd stocked up with in the summer? They couldn't *all* have been eaten...?

I'm afraid I left it all to Rosemary. I know visitors are supposed to trot around at the heels of their hostesses, yapping helpfully, like terriers; but I just won't. After all, I know how little help it is to *me*, when I am a hostess, so why should I suppose that everyone else is different? Besides, by this time I was half frozen, what with the black, sodden fields and marsh-lands without, and the damp stone within; and so I decided to concentrate my meagre store of obligingness on getting a fire going.

What a job it was, though! It was as if some demon was working against me, spitting and sighing down the cavernous chimney, whistling wickedly along the icy, stone-flagged floor, blowing out each feeble flicker of flame as fast as I coaxed it from the damp balls of newspaper piled under the damper wood.

Fortunately there were plenty of matches, and gradually, as each of my abortive efforts left the materials a tiny bit drier than before, hope of success came nearer. Or maybe it was that the mischievous demon grew tired of his dance of obstruction – the awful sameness of frustrating me time and time again – anyway, for whatever reason, I at last got a few splinters of wood feebly smouldering. Bending close, and cupping my hands around the precious whorls to protect them from the sudden damp gusts and sputters of rain down the chimney, I watched, enchanted, while first one tiny speck of gold and then another glimmered on the charred wood. Another ... and yet another ... until suddenly, like the very dawn of creation, a flame licked upwards.

It was the first time in years and years that I had had anything to do with an open fire. I have lived in centrally-heated flats for almost all of my adult life, and I had forgotten this apocalyptic moment when fire comes into being under your hands. Like God on the morning of creation, I sat there, all-powerful, tending the spark I had created. A sliver more of wood here ... a knob of coal there ... soon my little fire was bright, and growing, and needing me no more.

But still I tended it – or pretended to – leaning over it, spreading my icy hands to the beginnings of warmth. Vaguely, in the background, I was aware of Rosemary blundering around the place, clutching in her left hand the only oil lamp that worked, peering disconsolately into drawers and cupboards, and muttering under her breath at each new evidence of disorder and depletion.

Honestly, it was no use trying to help. We'd have to manage somehow for tonight, and then tomorrow, with the coming of the blessed daylight, we'd be able to get everything to rights. Fill the lamps. Fetch food from the village. Get the place properly warm...

Warm! I shivered, and huddled closer into the wide chimney alcove. Although the fire was burning up nicely now, it had as yet made little impact on the icy chill of the room. It was cold as only these ancient, little-used cottages *can* be cold. The cold of centuries seems to be stored up in their old stones, and the idea that you can warm it away with a single brisk weekend of paraffin heaters and hastily-lit fires has always seemed to me laughable.

Not to Rosemary, though. She is an impatient sort of person, and it always seems to her that heaters *must* produce heat. That's what the word *means*! So she was first angered, then puzzled, and finally half-scared by the fact that she just *couldn't* get the cottage warm. Even in late August, when the air outside was still soft, and the warmth of summer lingered over the fields and marshes – even then, the cottage was like an ice-box inside. I remember remarking on it during my first visit – 'Marvellously cool!' was how I put it at the time, for we had just returned, hot and exhausted, from a long tramp through the hazy, windless countryside; and that was the first time (I think) that Rosemary mentioned to me that the place was supposed to be haunted.

'One of those tragic, wailing ladies that the past specializes in,' she explained, rather facetiously. 'She's supposed to have drowned herself away on the marsh somewhere – for love, I suppose; it always was, wasn't it? My God, though, what a thing to drown oneself for! – if only she'd *known*...!'

This set us off giggling, of course; and by the time we'd finished our wry reminiscences, and our speculations about the less than ecstatic love-lives of our various friends – by this time, of course, the end of the ghost story had rather got lost. Something about the woman's ghost moaning around the cottage on stormy nights (or was it moonlight ones?), and about the permanent, icy chill that had settled upon the cottage, and particularly upon the upstairs back bedroom, into which they'd carried her body, all dripping wet from the marsh.

'As good a tale as any, for when your tenants start demanding proper heating,' I remember remarking cheerfully (for Rosemary, at that time, had vague and grandiose plans for making a fortune by letting the place for part of the year) and we had both laughed, and that, it had seemed, was the end of it.

But when late summer became autumn, and autumn deepened into winter, and the North-East wind, straight from Siberia, howled in over the marshes, then Rosemary began to get both annoyed and perturbed.

'I just *can't* get the place warm,' she grumbled. 'I can't understand it! And as for that back room – the one that looks out over the marsh – it's uncanny how cold it is! Two oil heaters, burning day and night, and it's *still*...!'

I couldn't pretend to be surprised: as I say, I *expect* my friends' weekend cottages to be like this. But I tried to be sympathetic; and when, late in November, Rosemary confessed, half laughing, that she really *did* think the place was haunted, it was I who suggested that we should go down together and see if we could lay the ghost.

She welcomed the suggestion with both pleasure and relief.

'If it was just the cold, I wouldn't be bothering,' she explained. 'But there seems to be something eerie about the place – there really does, Lois! It's like being in the presence of the dead.' (Rosemary never has been in the presence of the dead, or she'd know it's not like that at all, but I let it pass.) 'I'm getting to hate being there on my own. Sometimes – I know it sounds crazy, but sometimes I really *do* seem to hear voices!' She laughed, uncomfortably. 'I must be in a bad way, mustn't I? *Hearing voices . . .! Me . . .!*'

To this day, I don't know how much she was really scared, and how much she was just trying to work a bit of drama into her lonely – and probably unexpectedly boring – trips down to her dream cottage. I don't suppose she even knows herself. All I can say for certain is that her mood of slightly factitious trepidation touched exactly on some deep need of my own, and at once we knew that we would go. And that it would be fun. And that Cissie must at all costs be kept out of it. Once *her* deep needs get involved, you've had it.

*   *   *

A little cry from somewhere in the shadows, beyond the circle of firelight, jerked me from my reveries, and for a moment I felt my heart pounding. Then, a moment later, I was laughing, for the cry came again:

'Spaghetti! Spaghetti Bolognese! Four whole tins of it, all stacked up under the sink! Now, *who* could have . . .?'

And who could care, anyway? Food, real food, was now within our grasp! Unless . . . Oh dear . . .!

'I bet you've lost the tin-opener!' I hazarded, with a sinking heart – for at the words 'Spaghetti Bolognese' I had realized just how hungry I was – and it was with corresponding relief that, in the flickering firelight, I saw a smug smile overspreading her face.

'See?' She held up the vital implement; it flickered through the shadows like a shining minnow as she gesticulated her triumph. '*See*? Though of course, if *Cissie* had been here . . .!'

We both began to giggle; and later, as we sat over the fire scooping spaghetti bolognese from pottery bowls, and drinking the red wine which Rosemary had managed to unearth – as we sat there, revelling in creature comforts, we amused ourselves by speculating on the disasters which would have befallen us by now had Cissie been one of the party. How she would have dropped the last of the matches into a puddle, looking for a lost glove ... would have left the front door swinging open in the wind, blowing out our only oil lamp. And the tin-opener, of course, would have been a write-off from the word go; if she hadn't lost it in some dark corner, it would certainly have collapsed into two useless pieces under her big, willing hands... By now, we would have been without light, heat or food...

This depressing picture seemed, somehow, to be the funniest thing imaginable as we sat there, with our stomachs comfortably full and with our third helping of red wine gleaming jewel-like in the firelight.

'To absent friends!' we giggled, raising our glasses. 'And let's hope they *remain* absent.' I added, wickedly, thinking of Cissie; and while we were both still laughing over this cynical toast, I saw Rosemary suddenly go rigid, her glass an inch from her lips, and I watched the laughter freeze on her face.

'Listen!' she hissed. 'Listen, Lois! Do you *hear*?'

For long seconds, we sat absolutely still, and the noises of the night impinged, for the first time, on my consciousness. The wind, rising now, was groaning and sighing around the cottage, moaning in the chimney and among the old beams. The rain spattered in little gusts against the windows, which creaked and rattled on their old hinges. Beyond them, in the dark, overgrown garden, you could hear the stir and rustle of bare twigs and sodden leaves ... and beyond that again there was the faint, endless sighing of the marsh, mile upon mile of it, half-hidden under the dry, winter reeds.

'No...' I began, in a whisper; but Rosemary made a sharp little movement, commanding silence. '*Listen!*' she whispered once more; and this time – or was it my imagination? – I did begin to hear something.

'Ee ... ee ... ee ...!' came the sound, faint and weird upon the wind. 'Ee ... ee ... ee ...!' – and for a moment it sounded so human, and so imploring, that I, too, caught my breath. It must be a trick of the wind, of course; it *must* – and as we sat there, tensed almost beyond bearing by the intentness of our listening, another sound impinged upon our preternaturally sharpened senses – a sound just as faint, and just as far away, but this time very far from ghostly.

'Pr-rr-rr! Ch-ch-ch......!' – the sound grew nearer ... unmistakable... The prosaic sound of a car, bouncing and crunching up the rough track to the cottage.

Rosemary and I looked at each other.

'Norman?' she hazarded, scrambling worriedly to her feet. 'But it *can't* be Norman, he *never* comes! And at this time of night, too! Oh dear, I wonder what can have happened ...?' By this time she had reached the window, and she parted the curtains just as the mysterious vehicle screeched to a halt outside the gate. All I could see, from where I sat, was the triangle of darkness between the parted curtains, and Rosemary's broad back, rigid with disbelief and dismay.

Then, she turned on me.

'Lois!' she hissed. 'How *could* you...!'

I didn't ask her what she meant. Not after all these years.

'I didn't! Of course I didn't! What do you take me for?' I retorted, and I don't doubt that by now my face was almost as white as hers.

For, of course, she did not need to tell me who it was who had arrived. Not after nearly half a century of this sort of thing. Besides, who else was there who slammed a car door as if slapping down an invasion from Mars? Who else would announce her arrival by yelling 'Yoo-hoo!' into the midnight air, and bashing open the garden gate with a hat-box, so that latch and socket hurtled together into the night?

'Oops – sorry!' said Cissie, for perhaps the fifty-thousandth time in our joint lives; and she blundered forward towards the light, like an untidy grey moth. For by now we had got the front door open, and lamplight was pouring down the garden path, lighting up her round, radiant face and her halo of wild grey curls, all a-glitter with drops of rain.

'You naughty things! Fancy not *telling* me!' she reproached us, as she surged through the lighted doorway, dumping her luggage to left and right. It was, as always, like a one-man army of occupation. Always, she manages to fill any situation so totally with herself, and her belongings, and her eagerness, that there simply isn't *room* for anyone else's point of view. It's not selfishness, exactly; it's more like being a walking take-over bid, with no control over one's operations.

'A real, live ghost! Isn't it thrilling!' she babbled, as we edged her into the firelit room. 'Oh, but you *should* have told me! You *know* how I love this sort of thing ...!'

On and on she chattered, in her loud, eager, unstoppable voice ... and this, too, we recognized as part of her technique of infiltration. By the time her victims have managed to get a word in edgeways, their first fine fury has already began to wilt ... the cutting edge of their protests has been blunted ... their sense of outrage has become blurred. And anyway, by that time she is *there*. Inescapably, irreversibly, *there*!

Well, what can you do? By the time Rosemary and I got a chance to put a word in, Cissie already had her coat off, her luggage spilling on to the floor, and a glass of red wine in her hand. There she was, reclining in the big easychair (mine), the firelight playing on her face, exactly as if she had lived in the place for years.

'But, Cissie, how did you find *out*?' was the nearest, somehow, that we could get to a reproof; and she laughed her big, merry laugh, and the bright wine sloshed perilously in her raised glass.

'Simple, you poor Watsons!' she declared. 'You see, I happened to be

phoning Josie, and Josie happened to mention that Mary had said that
Phyllis had told her that she'd heard from Ruth, and...'

See what I mean? You can't win. You might as well try to dodge the
Recording Angel himself.

'And when I heard about the ghost, then of course I just *had* to come!'
she went on. 'It sounded just *too* fascinating! You see, it just happens that
at the moment I know a good deal about ghosts, because...'

Well, of course she did. It was her knowing a good deal about
Classical Greek architecture last spring that had kept her arguing with
the guide on the Parthenon for so long that the coach went off without
us. And it was precisely because she'd boned up so assiduously on rare
Alpine plants that she'd broken her leg trying to reach one of them a
couple of years ago, and we had to call out the Mountain Rescue for her.
The rest of us had thought it was just a daisy.

'Yes, well, we don't even know yet that there *is* a ghost,' said
Rosemary, dampingly; but not dampingly enough, evidently, for we
spent the rest of the evening – and indeed far into the small hours –
trying to dissuade Cissie from putting into practice, then and there,
various uncomfortable and hazardous methods of ghost-hunting of
which she had recently informed herself – methods which ranged from
fixing a tape-recorder on the thatched roof, to ourselves lying all night in
the churchyard, keeping our minds a blank.

By two o'clock, our minds were blank anyway – well, Rosemary's
and mine were – and we could think about nothing but bed. Here,
though, there were new obstacles to be overcome, for not only was
Cissie's arrival unexpected and unprepared-for, but she insisted on
being put in the haunted room. If it *was* haunted – anyway, the room
that was coldest, dampest, and most uncomfortable, and therefore
entitled her (well, what can you do?) to the only functioning oil-heater,
and more than her share of the blankets.

'Of course, I shan't *sleep!*' she promised (as if this was some sort of
special treat for me and Rosemary). 'I shall be keeping vigil all night
long! And tomorrow night, darlings, as soon as the moon rises, we must
each take a white willow twig, and pace in silent procession through the
garden...'

We nodded, simply because we were too sleepy to argue; but beyond
the circle of lamplight, Rosemary and I exchanged glances of undiluted
negativism. I mean, apart from anything else, you'd have to be crazy to
embark on any project which depended for its success on Cissie's not
falling over something.

But we did agree, without too much reluctance, to her further
suggestion that tomorrow morning we should call on the vicar and ask
him if we might look through the parish archives. Even Cissie, we
guardedly surmised, could hardly wreck a call on a vicar.

But the next morning, guess what? Cissie was laid up with lumbago, stiff as a board, and unable even to get out of bed, let alone go visiting.

'Oh dear – Oh, please don't bother!' she kept saying, as we ran around with hot water bottles and extra pillows. 'Oh dear, I do so hate to be a nuisance!'

We hated her to be a nuisance, too, but we just managed not to say so; and after a bit our efforts, combined with her own determination not to miss the fun (yes, she was still counting it fun) – after a bit, all this succeeded in loosening her up sufficiently to let her get out of bed and on to her feet; and at once her spirits rocketed sky-high. She decided, gleefully, that her affliction was a supernatural one, consequent on sleeping in the haunted room.

'Damp sheets, more likely!' said Rosemary, witheringly. 'If people *will* turn up unexpectedly like this...'

But Cissie is unsquashable. *Damp sheets?* When the alternative was the ghost of a lady who'd died two hundred years ago? Cissie has never been one to rest content with a likely explanation if there is an *un*likely one to hand.

'I know what I'm talking about!' she retorted. 'I know more about this sort of thing than either of you. I'm a sensitive, you see. I only discovered it just recently, but it seems I'm one of those people with a sort of sixth sense when it comes to the supernatural. It makes me more *vulnerable*, of course, to this sort of thing – look at my bad back – but it also makes me more *aware*. I can *sense* things. Do you know, the moment I walked into this room last night, I could tell that it was haunted! I could feel the ... Ouch!'

Her back had caught her again; all that gesticulating while she talked had been a mistake. However, between us we got her straightened up once more, and even managed to help her down the stairs – though I must say it wasn't long before we were both wishing we'd left well alone – if I may put it so uncharitably. For Cissie, up, was far, far more nuisance than Cissie in bed. In bed, her good intentions could harm no one; but once up and about, there seemed no limit to the trouble she could cause in the name of 'helping'. Trying to lift pans from shelves above her head; trying to rake out cinders without bending, and setting the hearth brush on fire in the process; trying to fetch paraffin in cans too heavy for her to lift, and slopping it all over the floor. Rosemary and I seemed to be forever clearing up after her, or trying to un-crick her from some position she'd got stuck in for some maddening, altruistic reason.

* * *

Disturbingly, she seemed to get worse as the day went on, not better. The stiffness increased, and by afternoon she looked blue with cold, and was scarcely able to move. But nothing would induce her to let us call a doctor, or put her to bed.

'What, and miss all the fun?' she protested, through numbed lips. 'Don't you realize that this freezing cold is *significant*? It's the chilling of the air that you always get before the coming of an apparition . . . !'

By now, it was quite hard to make out what she was saying, so hoarse had her voice become, and so stiff her lips; but you could still hear the excitement and triumph in her croaked exhortations:

'Isn't it thrilling! This is the chill of death, you know, darlings! It's the warning that the dead person is now about to appear! Oh, I'm so thrilled! Any moment now, and we're going to know the truth . . . !

*   *   *

We did, too. A loud knocking sounded on the cottage door, and Rosemary ran to answer it. From where I stood, in the living-room doorway, I could see her framed against the winter twilight – already the short December afternoon was nearly at an end. Beyond her, I glimpsed the uniforms of policemen, heard their solemn voices.

' "Miss Cecily Curtis"? – Cissie? Yes, of course we know her!' I heard Rosemary saying, in a frightened voice; and then came the two deeper voices, grave and sympathetic.

I could hardly hear their words from where I was standing, yet somehow the story wasn't difficult to follow. It was almost as if, in some queer way, I'd known it all along. How last night, at about 10.30 p.m., a Miss Cecily Curtis had skidded while driving – too fast – along the dyke road, and had plunged, car and all, into deep water. The body had only been recovered and identified this morning.

As I say, I did not really need to hear the men's actual words. Already the picture was in my mind, the picture which has never left it: the picture of Cissie, all lit up with curiosity and excitement, belting through the rain and dark to be in on the fun. Nothing would keep her away, not even death itself . . .

A little sound in the room behind me roused me from my state of shock, and I turned to see Cissie smiling that annoying smile of hers, for the very last time. It's maddened us for years, the plucky way she smiles in the face of whatever adversity she's got us all into.

'You see?' she said, a trifle smugly, 'I've been dead ever since last night – it's no wonder I've been feeling so awful!' – and with a triumphant little toss of her head she turned, fell over her dressing-gown cord, and was gone.

Yes, gone. We never saw her again. The object they carried in, wet and dripping from the marsh, seemed to be nothing to do with her at all.

*   *   *

We never discovered whether the cottage had been haunted all along; but it's haunted now, all right. I don't suppose Rosemary will go down there much any more – certainly, we will never go ghost-hunting there again. Apart from anything else, we are too scared. There is so much that might go wrong. It was different in the old days, when we could plan just any wild escapade we liked, confident that whatever went wrong would merely be the fault of our idiotic, infuriating, impossible, irreplaceable friend.

The Horsehair Trunk
Davis Grubb

To Marius the fever was like a cloud of warm river fog around him.
Or like the blissful vacuum that he had always imagined death would
be. He had lain for nearly a week like this in the big corner room while
the typhoid raged and boiled inside him. Mary Ann was a dutiful wife.
She came and fed him his medicine and stood at the foot of the brass
bed when the doctor was there, clasping and unclasping her thin hands;
and sometimes from between hot, heavy lids Marius could glimpse her
face, dimly pale and working slowly in prayer. Such a fool she was, a
praying, stupid fool that he had married five years ago. He could
remember thinking that even in the deep, troubled delirium of the
fever.

'You want me to die,' he said to her one morning when she came
with his medicine. 'You want me to die, don't you?'

'Marius! Don't say such a thing! Don't ever——'

'It's true, though,' he went on, hearing his voice miles above him at
the edge of the quilt. 'You want me to die. But I'm not going to. I'm
going to get well, Mary Ann. I'm not going to die. Aren't you
disappointed?'

'No! No! It's not true! It's not!'

Now, though he could not see her face through the hot blur of fever,
he could hear her crying; sobbing and shaking with her fist pressed tight
against her teeth. Such a fool.

*   *   *

On the eighth morning Marius woke full of a strange, fiery brilliance as
if all his flesh were glass not yet cool from the furnace. He knew the fever
was worse, close to its crisis, and yet it no longer had the quality of
darkness and mists. Everything was sharp and clear. The red of his
necktie hanging in the corner of the bureau mirror was a flame. And
he could hear the minutest stirrings down in the kitchen, the breaking

of a match stick in Mary Ann's fingers as clear as pistol shots outside
his bedroom window. It was a joy.

Marius wondered for a moment if he might have died. But if it was
death it was certainly more pleasant than he had ever imagined death
would be. He could rise from the bed without any sense of weakness
and he could stretch his arms and he could even walk out through the
solid door into the upstairs hall. He thought it might be fun to tiptoe
downstairs and give Mary Ann a fright, but when he was in the
parlour he remembered suddenly that she would be unable to see him.
Then when he heard her coming from the kitchen with his medicine he
thought of an even better joke. With the speed of thought Marius was
back in his body under the quilt again, and Mary Ann was coming into
the bedroom with her large eyes wide and worried.

'Marius,' she whispered, leaning over him and stroking his hot forehead with her cold, thin fingers. 'Marius, are you better?'

He opened his eyes as if he had been asleep.

'I see,' he said, 'that you've moved the pianola over to the north
end of the parlour.'

Mary Ann's eyes widened and the glass of amber liquid rattled
against the dish.

'Marius!' she whispered. 'You haven't been out of bed! You'll kill
yourself! With a fever like——'

'No,' said Marius faintly, listening to his own voice as if it were in
another room. 'I haven't been out of bed, Mary Ann.'

His eyelids flickered weakly up at her face, round and ghostlike,
incredulous. She quickly set the tinkling glass of medicine on the little
table.

'Then how——?' she said. 'Marius, how could you know?'

Marius smiled weakly up at her and closed his eyes, saying nothing,
leaving the terrible question unanswered, leaving her to tremble and
ponder over it for ever if need be. She was such a fool.

It had begun that way, and it had been so easy he wondered why
he had never discovered it before. Within a few hours the fever broke
in great rivers of sweat, and by Wednesday, Marius was able to sit up
in the chair by the window and watch the starlings hopping on the front
lawn. By the end of the month he was back at work as editor of the
Daily Argus. But even those who knew him least were able to detect in
the manner of Marius Lindsay that he was a changed man – and a
worse one. And those who knew him best wondered how so malignant a
citizen, such a confirmed and studied misanthrope as Marius, could
possibly change into anything worse than he was. Some said that
typhoid always burned the temper from the toughest steel and that
Marius's mind had been left a dark and twisted thing. At prayer
meeting on Wednesday nights the wives used to watch Marius's young

wife and wonder how she endured her cross. She was such a pretty thing.

*　　*　　*

One afternoon in September, as he dozed on the bulging leather couch of his office, Marius decided to try it again. The secret, he knew, lay somewhere on the brink of sleep. If a man knew that – any man – he would know what Marius did. It wasn't more than a minute later that Marius knew that all he would have to do to leave his body was to get up from the couch. Presently he was standing there, staring down at his heavy, middle-aged figure sunk deep into the cracked leather of the couch, the jowls of the face under the close-cropped moustache sagging deep in sleep, the heart above his heavy gold watch chain beating solidly in its breast.

I'm not dead, he thought, delighted. But here is my soul – my damned, immortal soul standing looking at its body!

It was as simple as shedding a shoe. Marius smiled to himself, remembering his old partner Charlie Cunningham and how they had used to spend long hours in the office, in this very room, arguing about death and atheism and the whither of the soul. If Charlie were still alive, Marius thought, I would win from him a quart of the best Kentucky bourbon in the county. As it was, no one would ever know. He would keep his secret even from Mary Ann, especially from Mary Ann, who would go to her grave with the superstitious belief that Marius had died for a moment, that for an instant fate had favoured her; that she had been so close to happiness, to freedom from him for ever. She would never know. Still, it would be fun to use as a trick, a practical joke to set fools like his wife at their wits' edge. If only he could *move* things. If only the filmy substance of his soul could grasp a tumbler and send it shattering at Mary Ann's feet on the kitchen floor some morning. Or tweak a copy boy's nose. Or snatch a cigar from the teeth of Judge John Robert Gants as he strolled home some quiet evening from the fall session of the district court.

Well, it was, after all, a matter of will, Marius decided. It was his own powerful and indomitable will that had made the trick possible in the first place. He walked to the edge of his desk and grasped at the letter opener on the dirty, ancient blotter. His fingers were like wisps of fog that blew through a screen door. He tried again, willing it with all his power, grasping again and again at the small brass dagger until at last it moved a fraction of an inch. A little more. On the next try it lifted four inches in the air and hung for a second on its point before it dropped. Marius spent the rest of the afternoon practising until at last he could lift the letter opener in his fist, fingers tight around the haft, the thumb pressing the cold blade tightly, and drive it through the blotter so deeply that it bit into the wood of the desk beneath.

Marius giggled in spite of himself and hurried around the office picking things up like a pleased child. He lifted a tumbler off the dusty water cooler and stared laughing at it, hanging there in the middle of nothing. At that moment he heard the copy boy coming for the proofs of the morning editorials and Marius flitted quickly back into the cloak of his flesh. Nor was he a moment too soon. Just as he opened his eyes, the door opened and he heard the glass shatter on the floor.

'I'm going to take a nap before supper, Mary Ann,' Marius said that evening, hanging his black hat carefully on the elk-horn hatrack.

'Very well,' said Mary Ann. He watched her young, unhappy figure disappearing into the gloom of the kitchen and he smiled to himself again, thinking what a fool she was, his wife. He could scarcely wait to get to the davenport and stretch out in the cool, dark parlour with his head on the beaded pillow.

Now, thought Marius. Now.

And in a moment he had risen from his body and hurried out into the hallway, struggling to suppress the laughter that would tell her he was coming. He could already anticipate her white, stricken face when the pepper pot pulled firmly from between her fingers cut a clean figure eight in the air before it crashed against the ceiling.

He heard her voice and was puzzled.

'You must go,' she was murmuring. 'You musn't ever come here when he's home. I've told you that before, Jim. What would you do if he woke up and found you here!'

Then Marius, as he rushed into the kitchen, saw her bending through the doorway into the dusk with the saucepan of greens clutched in her white knuckles.

'What would you do? You must go!'

Marius rushed to her side; careful not to touch her, careful not to let either of them know he was there, listening, looking, flaming hatred growing slowly inside him.

* * *

The man was young and dark and well built and clean-looking. He leaned against the half-open screen door, holding Mary Ann's free hand between his own. His round, dark face bent to hers, and she smiled with a tenderness and passion that Marius had never seen before.

'I know,' the man said. 'I know all that. But I just can't stand it no more, Mary Ann. I just can't stand it thinking about him beating you up that time. He might do it again, Mary Ann. He might! He's worse, they say, since he had the fever. Crazy, I think. I've heard them say he's crazy.'

'Yes. Yes. You must go away now, though,' she was whispering frantically, looking back over her shoulder through Marius's dark face. 'We'll have time to talk it all over again, Jim. I – I know I'm going to leave him but—— Don't rush me into things, Jim dear. Don't make me do it till I'm clear with myself.'

'Why not now?' came the whisper. 'Why not tonight? We can take a steamboat to Lou'ville and you'll never have to put up with him again. You'll be shed of him for ever, honey. Look! I've got two tickets for Lou'ville right here in my pocket on the *Nancy B. Turner*. My God, Mary Ann, don't make me suffer like this – lyin' abed nights dreaming about him comin' at you with his cane and beatin' you – maybe killin' you!'

The woman grew silent and her face softened as she watched the fireflies dart their zigzags of cold light under the low trees along the street. She opened her mouth, closed it, and stood biting her lip hard. Then she reached up and pulled his face down to hers, seeking his mouth.

'All right,' she whispered then. 'All right. I'll do it! Now go! Quick!'

'Meet me at the wharf at nine,' he said. 'Tell him that you're going to prayer meeting. He'll never suspicion anything. Then we can be together without all this sneakin' around. Oh, honey, if you ever knew how much I——'

The words were smeared in her kiss as he pulled her down through the half-open door and held her.

'All right. All right,' she gasped. 'Now go! Please!'

And he walked away, his heels ringing boldly on the bricks, lighting a cigarette, the match arching like a shooting star into the darkness of the shrubs. Mary Ann stood stiff for a moment in the shadow of the porch vines, her large eyes full of tears, and the saucepan of greens grown cold in her hands. Marius drew back to let her pass. He stood then and watched her for a moment before he hurried back into the parlour and lay down again within his flesh and bone in time to be called for supper.

* * *

Captain Joe Alexander of the *Nancy B. Turner* was not curious that Marius should want a ticket for Louisville. He remembered years later that he had thought nothing strange about it at the time. It was less than two months till the elections and there was a big Democratic convention there.

Everyone had heard of Marius Lindsay and the power he and his *Daily Argus* held over the choices of the people. But Captain Alexander did remember thinking it strange that Marius should insist on seeing the passenger list of the *Nancy B.* that night and that he should ask particularly after a man named Jim. Smith, Marius had said, but there was no Smith. There was a Jim though, a furniture salesman from Wheeling: Jim O'Toole, who had reserved two staterooms, No. 3 and No. 4.

'What do you think of the Presidential chances this term, Mr Lindsay?' Captain Alexander had said. And Marius had looked absent for a moment (the captain had never failed to recount that detail) and then said that it would be Cleveland, that the Republicans were done for ever.

Captain Alexander had remembered that conversation and the manner of its delivery years later and it had become part of the tale that rivermen told in wharf boats and water-street saloons from Pittsburgh to Cairo long after that night had woven itself into legend.

Then Marius had asked for Stateroom No. 5, and that had been part of the legend, too, for it was next to the room that was to be occupied by Jim O'Toole, the furniture salesman from Wheeling.

'Say nothing,' said Marius, before he disappeared down the stairway from the captain's cabin, 'to anyone about my being aboard this boat tonight. My trip to Louisville is connected with the approaching election and is, of necessity, confidential.'

'Certainly, sir,' said the captain, and he listened as Marius made his way awkwardly down the gilded staircase, lugging his small horsehair trunk under his arm. Presently the door to Marius's stateroom snapped shut and the bolt fell to.

At nine o'clock sharp, two rockaway buggies rattled down the brick pavement of Water Street and met at the wharf. A man jumped from one, and a woman from the other.

'You say he wasn't home when you left,' the man was whispering as he helped the woman down the rocky cobbles, the two carpetbags tucked under his arms.

'No. But it's all right,' Mary Ann said. 'He always goes down to the office this time of night to help set up the morning edition.'

'You reckon he suspicions anything?'

The woman laughed, a low, sad laugh.

'He always suspicions everybody,' she said. 'Marius has the kind of a mind that always suspicions; and the kind of life he leads, I guess he has to. But I don't think he knows about us – tonight. I don't think he ever *knew* about us – ever.'

They hurried up the gangplank together. The water lapped and gurgled against the wharf, and off over the river, lightning scratched the dark rim of mountains like the sudden flare of a kitchen match.

'I'm Jim O'Toole,' Jim said to Captain Alexander, handing him the tickets. 'This is my wife——'

Mary Ann bit her lip and clutched the strap of her carpet-bag till her knuckles showed through the flesh.

'——she has the stateroom next to mine. Is everything in order?'

'Right, sir,' said Captain Alexander, wondering in what strange ways the destinies of this furniture salesman and his wife were meshed with the life of Marius Lindsay.

They tiptoed down the worn carpet of the narrow, white hallway, counting the numbers on the long, monotonous row of doors to either side.

'Goodnight, dear,' said Jim, glancing unhappily at the Negro porter dozing on the split-bottom chair under the swinging oil lantern by the door. 'Goodnight, Mary Ann. Tomorrow we'll be on our way. Tomorrow you'll be shed of Marius for ever.'

*   *   *

Marius lay in his bunk, listening as the deep-throated whistle shook the quiet valley three times. Then he lay smiling and relaxed as the great drive shafts tensed and plunged once forward and backward, gathering into their dark, heavy rhythm as the paddles bit the black water. The *Nancy B. Turner* moved heavily away into the thick current and headed downstream for the Devil's elbow and the open river. Marius was stiff. He had lain for nearly four hours waiting to hear the voices. Every sound had been as clear to him as the tick of his heavy watch in his vest pocket. He had heard the dry, rasping racket of the green frogs along the shore and the low, occasional words of boys fishing in their skiffs down the shore under the willows.

Then he had stiffened as he heard Mary Ann's excited murmur suddenly just outside his stateroom door and the voice of the man answering her, comforting her. Lightning flashed and flickered out again over the Ohio hills and lit the river for one clear moment. Marius saw all of his stateroom etched suddenly in silver from the open porthole. The mirror, washstand, bowl and pitcher. The horsehair trunk beside him on the floor. Thunder rumbled in the dark and Marius smiled to himself, secure again in the secret darkness, thinking how easy it would be, wondering why no one had thought of such a thing before. Except for the heavy pounding rhythm of the drive shafts and the chatter of the drinking glass against the washbowl as the boat shuddered through the water, everything was still. The Negro porter dozed in his chair under the lantern by the stateroom door. Once Marius thought he heard the lovers' voices in the next room, but he knew then that it was the laughter of the cooks down in the galley.

Softly he rose and slipped past the sleeping porter, making his way for the white-painted handrail at the head of the stairway. Once Marius laughed aloud to himself as he realized that there was no need

to tiptoe with no earthly substance there to make a sound. He crept
down the narrow stairway to the galley. The Negro cooks bent around
the long wooden table eating their supper. Marius slid his long shadow
along the wall towards the row of kitchen knives lying, freshly washed
and honed, on the zinc table by the pump. For a moment, he hovered
over them, dallying, with his finger in his mouth, like a child before an
assortment of equally tempting sweets, before he chose the longest of
them all, and the sharpest, a knife that would sheer the ham clean from
a hog with one quick upward sweep. There was, he realized suddenly,
the problem of getting the knife past human eyes even if he himself
was invisible. The cooks laughed then at some joke one of them had
made and all of them bent forward, their heads in a dark circle of
merriment over their plates.

In that instant Marius swept the knife soundlessly from the zinc
table and darted into the gloomy companionway. The Negro porter
was asleep still, and Marius laughed to himself to imagine the man's
horror at seeing the butcher's knife, its razor edge flashing bright in the
dull light, inching itself along the wall. But it was a joke he could not
afford. He bent at last and slipped the knife cautiously along the threadbare rug under the little ventilation space beneath the stateroom door;
and then, rising, so full of hate that he was half afraid he might shine
forth in the darkness, Marius passed through the door and picked the
knife up quickly again in his hand.

Off down the Ohio the thunder throbbed again. Marius stepped
carefully across the worn rug towards the sleeping body on the bunk.
He felt so gay and light he almost laughed aloud. In a moment it would
be over and there would be one full-throated cry, and Mary Ann would
come beating on the locked door. And when she saw her lover ...

*   *   *

With an impatient gesture, Marius lifted the knife and felt quickly for
the sleeping, pulsing throat. The flesh was warm and living under his
fingers as he held it taut for the one quick stroke. His arm flashed. It
was done. Marius, fainting with excitement, leaned in the darkness to
brace himself. His hand came to rest on the harsh, rough surface of the
horsehair trunk.

'My God!' screamed Marius. 'My God!'

And at his cry the laughing murmur in the galley grew still and
there was a sharp scrape of a chair outside the stateroom door.

'The wrong room!' screamed Marius. 'The wrong room!' And he
clawed with fingers of smoke at the jetting fountain of his own blood.

A Vindictive Woman

R. Chetwynd-Hayes

Robert C. Hogg was a sparse, shy little man who ambled through life with lowered head and cautious steps, as though harbouring grave suspicions about the suburban paving stones. He lived at the very top of the house, in a miserable two-roomed flat with sagging ceilings, shrunken window-frames and walls that had long ago shed their cheap wallpaper.

It was difficult to define his age, but he must have been at least sixty-five, as I once saw him in the post office drawing his state pension. Nevertheless, his receding, mouse-coloured hair was only just flecked with silver, his pale, narrow face, save for two deep furrows on either side of the thin-lipped mouth, was unlined, and his small, grey eyes were bright with undiminished intelligence. Nothing other than the bowed shoulders and slow walk suggested that a growing burden of years was gradually taking its toll.

The only mail addressed to him that I ever saw on the hall table was the familiar buff envelope from the football pools, which at least testified that he was not lacking a certain element of optimism. He went for a walk every morning: mainly a slow stroll round the town, which generally terminated in one of the many pubs, where he sat nursing a half-pint glass of brown ale. The rest of his time appeared to be spent in that top-floor flat, doing I knew not what.

It might be as well if I were to stress that, although the house was sub-divided into seven – for want of a better term – living units, in fact Robert C. Hogg and I appeared to be the only people living there. Five other unknown and rarely seen tenants either rented a room as an accommodation address, or used it to spend the odd night whenever business brought them into the area. I, needing space that could be used as a place of work and residence, rented the entire basement, and – a completely unwarranted piece of extravagance – the massive back garden as well.

I worked in the back and front rooms alternately, being of the opinion that a change of scene helps to keep the creative stream flowing, and thus did not always see Robert C. Hogg mount the front steps. But sometimes, when the night was overcast and I had yet to close my curtains, I knew he was in his flat, for a rectangular slab of yellowish light lay across the lawn – an almost perfect facsimile of a lighted window, complete with four black-edged squares that bordered each pane – plus a bowed shadow-figure that kept passing back and forth across this illuminated frame.

I often thought how disconcerting it would be for a permanent occupant in the room below to hear this continuous pacing, and I wondered what troubled line of thought prompted the little man to do it. Perhaps he was beset by some problem which required such deep concentration that it could only be maintained by constant movement. Whatever the reason, I soon became a little disturbed by the spectacle and took to closing my curtains whenever the block of light flashed into being.

One night in early January, when the moon illuminated the thirty or so feet of lawn, transforming the slightly frosted grass into a gleaming silver carpet and obliterating every shadow, save for the dense cluster that lurked under two old elm trees at the far end, I walked two-thirds of the way up the garden, then turned and cast a cursory glance at the uppermost windows. Why I took the trouble to come out on such a cold night, I can't think; idle curiosity, I suspect, prompted by an urge to see if my neighbour still paced in front of his window, even when conditions did not allow his silhouette to be projected onto the lawn.

On this night his lights were out, but, even so, I detected the faint outline of a figure that might have been standing some little way back from the curtainless window, staring down, either at me, or at the two trees that were some way to my rear. Embarrassed by being caught out in an act of blatant nosiness, I swung round and pretended to examine the trees myself. I soon came to the conclusion that they were scarcely worthy of attention. Bleak and naked against the cold, steel-grey sky, their skeletal branches creaked forlornly when disturbed by the gentle easterly wind. Then I lowered my eyes and became uncomfortably aware of the dense block of shadow that seemed to be an extension of the sturdy trunks, a thick splodge of darkness that, if viewed in a certain way, took on the form of a black-clad figure.

I quickly switched my gaze back to Hogg's windows, but now they were gleaming mirrors that reflected the bright moonlight, and there was no way of deciding if an unseen spectator still lurked behind the shining façade. My tiny stock of courage was seeping away when I again faced the two trees and dared to ask a simple question.

'Is there anyone there?'

An answer would have been a precious gift from whatever saint watches over frightened men, while the ensuing silence was surely more terrifying even than the shriek of a doomed soul riding in on the wind.

With my head turned to the far right, my left eye had an oblique view of the furthermost tree, and it seemed as though I could see a dark shape that might have been that of a woman dressed in black and wearing a long head-shawl. An inch either side, and the vision was lost, becoming merely a slab of shadow that merged into the tree trunk.

Without further words or thought, I ran to warmth and transient security, without looking up or back. I locked doors and closed curtains in an endeavour to prove that anything which could not be seen did not exist.

*   *   *

Robert C. Hogg made his first tenuous approach the following evening.

There came a timid tap on my hall door which, when opened, revealed the bent-shouldered little figure standing on the bottom stair. Without raising his head, he said quietly:

'My lights have gone out.'

His voice was unexpectedly cultured, in some inexplicable way adding to the air of oddness that was manifest in every line of his body.

I said: 'I expect your fuse has blown. Have you examined it?'

'I know very little about such things. Where exactly will I find the fuse?'

'Would you like me to look at it for you?' I asked.

'If you would be so kind.'

I collected fuse wire, a pair of pliers, a screwdriver, and, as an afterthought, an electric torch, and followed him up three flights of stairs. A strip-light on the top landing enabled me to see the open door of his flat and part of the tiny kitchen beyond, but I was completely unprepared for the unpleasant smell that seemed to waiting to pounce the moment I set foot over the threshold. It had a sweetish, cloying quality that can only be associated with a rotting corpse, and it was so intense that I only just managed to suppress a snort of disgust.

I turned on the torch and was relieved to see that the main switch and its attendant fuse box were just by the door. I lost no time in removing the cover, pulling out the china fuse and replacing the burnt strip of wire. The entire operation took no more than two minutes, but to me, knowing that a still, silent figure was watching from the shadows, it seemed as if my fumbling fingers would never complete the job. Then I pushed the fuse home and instantly a twenty-five-watt bulb that dangled from the bulging ceiling sprang into dingy life. I got up, brushed my trouser legs and gradually became aware of a bone-numbing coldness that had, so to speak, been demanding recognition for some time.

It seemed to grow more intense by the second, and I heard my voice, loud, shrill with something akin to fear, demand:

'Good God, man, haven't you lit a fire?'

He remained unmoving, silent, and I, motivated by irritation and alarm – and perhaps some slight curiosity – walked into the small bed-sitting-room and looked around with incredulous eyes.

An extremely ancient gas fire spluttered angrily from behind a cracked tiled hearth, but for all the heat it sent out, a solitary candle might have been more effective. However, it was the almost terrifying cleanness of the place which attracted my full attention. He had scrubbed the bare floorboards snow-white, a result that can only be achieved by using boiling water well dosed with soda, a potent mixture that can be very tough on the fingernails, as my early days in the army had taught me. The narrow bed, which lurked against one wall, had been stripped, and the blankets (sheets were conspicuous by their absence) folded into neat squares and placed one on top of the other. He had even taken the trouble to clean the gas tap so that it gleamed like a fragment of burnished gold. Walls and ceiling were covered with a thick coating of whitewash that, when supplemented by a naked electric light bulb, dazzled the eye and created the illusion that the room had been carved out of snow.

I detected no concession to comfort. One plain wooden chair crouched in front of the ineffective fire and gave the impression that it would freeze the backside of anyone who was so foolhardy as to sit on it. The only other item of furniture was a plain deal table with a surface that might have been even more well scrubbed than the floor. I managed to laugh and say:

'You certainly keep the place neat.'

He gave me a strange, part anxious, part sly look.

'There are no stains?'

'None that I can see. But how can you stand this cold? It's enough to freeze the what's-its off the proverbial.'

He looked round at his chilly domain and sighed deeply.

'Cold preserves. But there is still the corruption of the soul.'

I shivered and edged towards the door. 'That's too profound for me. How about a cup of tea? I could most certainly do with one.'

He hesitated and for a moment appeared to be on the point of refusing, then slowly nodded.

'That is very kind of you. Yes, I'd like to very much.'

When we reached my flat I motioned him to an armchair and went into the kitchen where I brewed a large pot of tea, deciding the poor wretch needed well thawing out before again ascending to that ice-box. Determined to demonstrate how civilized people live, I placed teapot, cups and saucers, spoons, sugar-basin and slop bowl on to a rather grand trolley I had just acquired and wheeled it into my sitting-room. I found him seated well forward on the chair, hands outstretched, while he gazed almost reproachfully at my elaborate gas fire. He looked up as I entered and produced a rare smile.

'You really shouldn't have gone to all this trouble. Extraordinarily kind of you.'

'Not at all,' I replied, moving a low table beside his chair. 'I have a cup myself at this time. You take sugar?'

He shook his head violently.

'Oh, dear no! That would never do. She would not ...'

He stopped short and my – perhaps – unfortunate lust for knowledge received a little fillip of encouragement. So there was a woman in the background? It was only to be expected, although I had rather imagined him to be a confirmed bachelor.

'Biscuits?' I enquired. 'I've some passable digestives.'

One might have assumed I had just invited him to accept the united crowns of Great Britain.

'Really, that would be too much.'

'Nonsense,' I replied and went to fetch the tin.

We sat and drank tea and nibbled a vast amount of biscuits (at least, he did) while I tried to light a fire of informative conversation. I have often thought that those urbane interviewers on television would soon be out of a job if all of their questions were answered by a plain yes or no. Mr Hogg almost proved my point.

'I assume,' I murmured, with what I could only hope was an air of polite interest, 'you are not married.'

Mr Hogg waited until he had masticated a biscuit before replying.

'Not now.'

'But you have been?'

'Yes.'

The affirmative could be considered a tiny step forward along the path of enquiry. The fellow was either a widower or divorced. I decided to assume the former.

'I'm sorry. You must be very lonely.'

'Yes.'

It was then that he, with a rather ironic smile, posed his own question.

'And you, Mr ... ?'

'Glynn,' I replied, feeling as if I was parting with a state secret. 'Henry Glynn.'

'And you, Mr Glynn – you, too, are alone?'

I shrugged. 'I've had several trial runs, but have yet to discover a woman who does not bore me after three weeks. I'm willing to concede that this may be the result of a flaw in my character.'

He shook his head and emitted a quaint chuckle of amusement.

'How indeed extraordinary! To think that a woman can bore you. Imagine, Mr Glynn, if the shoe was on the other foot. Suppose you bored them.'

'Not an impossibility,' I replied drily. 'I must have often been the subject of a feminine yawn.'

He began to display more animation than I would have thought possible. So much so that he upset his teacup. He was at once profusely apologetic.

'How careless of me! Really unforgivable. If you will fetch a cloth ...'

'Forget it,' I ordered brusquely, alarmed less this mishap deprive me of much-desired information. 'Tea is good for the carpet. You were about to say?'

He replaced the cup carefully on the side table, then wiped his hands on a spotless handkerchief. He spoke slowly, as though savouring each word.

'Suppose, Mr Glynn, you fell hopelessly in love with a woman much younger than yourself and experienced a kind of unsurpassable delight when she agreed to marry you. Then, having given her your all – house, not insignificant savings, devotion, self-respect – suppose one day she yawns in your face and orders you out of the house. What would you do, Mr Glynn?'

'Reach for the nearest hairbrush,' I replied without hesitation.

It was then that he said something which at the time I assumed to be a joke.

'Not a poker, Mr Glynn?'

I shook my head. 'No. The use of a poker could turn out to be more than corrective – it might even be fatal. Another cup of tea, Mr Hogg.'

'You are indeed very kind.' He waited until I had refilled his cup before continuing. 'I sometimes have a fanciful notion that life is a narrow plank that stretches from the cradle to the grave, and if God is kind to us we cross without serious mishap. But one false step, one moment of inattention – and we spend eternity in a black pit of despair.' He looked up. 'Would you say women are vindictive, Mr Glynn?'

'Some,' I replied warily. 'I've met one or two.'

He took a dainty sip from his cup and gazed thoughtfully into the fire. A full two minutes passed before he spoke again.

'Believe me, a really vindictive woman has much in common with a hungry tiger. She will stalk you to perdition, and no amount of penance will placate her.' His voice sank to a thrilling whisper and, despite the warm room, I shivered. 'At first she keeps her distance, and the victim is only permitted to see her a long way off. At the end of a railway platform, on a bridge, looking down – at the bottom of a garden. Then she moves in for the kill.'

He lapsed into silence, and for the first time I became really alarmed and wished the hell I had never let him into the flat. The memory of that shape under the trees was still fresh. At last I was able to marshal words into a number one question.

'And are you ... you, Mr Hogg, pursued by such a woman?'

This time he dropped the cup and was much too agitated to apologize. I thought for a moment he was going to be sick over my best carpet. Then speech came tumbling over lax lips.

'Why do you ask? Have you seen her?'

I spoke slowly while watching him through narrowed eyes.

'Last night I thought I saw someone under the trees.'

And that was it. He got up, his face a mask of pure terror, and all but ran for the door. I called after him: 'It might have been my imagination,' but he took no notice and left me as near dumbfounded as at any time in my life. But he must have slowed down on reaching the hall, for I heard him creeping up the second flight of stairs as though reluctant to reach the top landing.

No power in this world or the next could stop me going into the bedroom and drawing back the curtains. The lighted shadow-window was back, laid out like an illuminated picture across the grass, with the silhouette of my recent guest passing to and fro, much as the imaginary tiger he had used to define a vindictive woman. But it was the almost imperceptible shape that stood just beyond the lighted square that clothed doubt in the cold raiment of reality.

Now there was no need to adjust the angle of vision, for I could dimly see a slim figure that wore some kind of long evening dress and probably a black lace head-shawl. I might even have caught a brief glimpse of a pale blur of a face, although this was uncertain. The thought slipped unbidden into my brain: 'Oh, my God! She's moved nearer!' just before Hogg turned out his light and complete darkness erased both shadow-window and whatever did – or did not – stand beyond.

Some minutes later I made what was probably the most shrewd observation of my life.

'The coldness is fear ... the stench is death.'

Next morning I tried to dismiss the entire business as the result of auto-suggestion.

*   *   *

An entire week passed before I saw Robert C. Hogg again.

I was seated at my desk in the sitting-room, having developed a distaste for looking out over the back garden, when I saw the little man climbing the front steps, his hat pulled well down over his ears, and gripping the handrail with grim determination. At the same time I was aware that someone else was just behind him and well over to the left, allowing me to catch a glimpse of a bobbing head that wore a black lace shawl. I had the ridiculous feeling that if that unseen person were to move one or two inches to the right, I would probably lose my sanity. Then I heard Hogg insert his key into the Yale lock. The door crashed back against the wall, and this was closely followed by him running along the hall. And I do mean running. A terrifying, foot-stamping, ceiling-shaking gallop that continued up two flights of stairs and was finally terminated by the distant slam of a door.

Presently I went upstairs and found the front door open. Having closed it, I ascended to the first-floor landing – now an expanse of shadow-haunted gloom. I peered up at the one above, toying with the unworthy intention of mounting the third flight and possibly pressing my ear against a closed door. But this piece of nefarious behaviour never came to fruition, for scarcely had I put foot to the first step when the merest suggestion of a black shape looking down over the banisters sent me racing back to my own domain.

It would seem that whoever pursued Robert C. Hogg was now in the house. But not yet in his flat. She was up there on the top landing – waiting.

*   *   *

Mr Hogg paid his second and last visit the following night.

The tapping on my hall door was timid but insistent, and finally I had to draw the bolts and open up. As he entered and walked silently to the fireside chair, I shrank back.

Face as white as snow in moonlight, head well forward, he stared into the fire, his limbs twitching in a most frightful manner. At that moment I hated him, alive to a fearsome possibility that something I did not want to see might come through the closed door after him. I shouted, shook clenched fists and even considered the idea of grabbing his scrawny neck and marching him out of the front door.

'For God's sake go! I can't help you. No one can. We all walk in our own hells.'

His face was a mask of frozen terror, and although his mouth opened and closed, it seemed as if speech was beyond him. I knew he was trying to tell me something that he considered to be of extreme importance, but – God help me – I didn't want to know. I could only decide that he must be very ill and that the right place for him was a hospital, so I turned my back on those bulging eyes and constantly writhing mouth and grabbed the telephone receiver. I was irrationally irritated by the number of questions that I had to answer before being informed that an ambulance would be there in the quickest possible time.

When I again looked at him, his eyes were still watching me, his mouth gaping, one hand outstretched, but now there was no movement of any kind. I thought: 'He's dead!' only he didn't really look dead. Just paralysed by fright. To remain in the same room as that ... that thing, was an impossibility, so I wandered around the flat, even occasionally opening the front door, vainly hoping to hear the approaching sound of a siren that would inform me that the dreadful wait was over. Then, possibly to delay having to return to the sitting-room, I strayed into the bedroom and, without thinking of what I was doing, walked over to the window.

There was no moon, and the rectangular slab of light lay across the lawn: the shadow-edged squares – one might almost say the ghost – of that fearful window. And, oh, most merciful God, a shadow figure was passing back and forth, a shape that wore a shawl on its graceful head. Then it suddenly stopped, and another shadow joined it – and I'd recognize that head anywhere – damn you, I could even make out the receding hair, the bloody thin face – but I must have been mad, for wasn't he seated in the next room? And that woman – the bloody, vindictive woman – was hitting him with something – and it might have been a poker – and I could actually see his mouth opening and closing, screaming ... screaming ... *only the screams were coming from my sitting-room.*

Then the light went out and so did I and mercifully knew no more until the ambulance men kicked my door in.

*   *   *

They had to break Robert C. Hogg's arms and legs, for apparently he was frozen stiff and that was the only way his corpse could be put into the zip-fastened stretcher-bag. Later, the police asked a lot of questions: how long had he lived in the house, did he have any visitors, and so on. I did not tell them about the woman who finally caught up with him.

He was traced back to a nice little house situated on the outskirts of Swindon. In it was discovered the body of his young wife, attired in a black evening dress, with a lace-shawl draped about her lovely, if a trifle dented, head. She was in an excellent state of preservation, as he had folded her, more or less neatly, before stowing her in the freezer.

All of which is, I suppose, as good a reason as any for a woman to become vindictive.

The Furnished Room
O. Henry

Restless, shifting, fugacious as time itself is a certain vast bulk of the population of the red brick district of the lower West Side. Homeless, they have a hundred homes. They flit from furnished room to furnished room, transients forever – transients in abode, transients in heart and mind. They sing 'Home, Sweet Home' in ragtime; they carry their *lares et penates* in a bandbox; their vine is entwined about a picture hat; a rubber plant is their fig tree.

Hence the houses of this district, having had a thousand dwellers, should have a thousand tales to tell, mostly dull ones, no doubt; but it would be strange if there could not be found a ghost or two in the wake of all these vagrant guests.

One evening after dark a young man prowled among these crumbling red mansions, ringing their bells. At the twelfth he rested his lean hand-baggage upon the step and wiped the dust from his hat-band and forehead. The bell sounded faint and far away in some remote, hollow depths.

To the door of this, the twelfth house whose bell he had rung, came a housekeeper who made him think of an unwholesome, surfeited worm that had eaten its nut to a hollow shell and now sought to fill the vacancy with edible lodgers.

He asked if there was a room to let.

'Come in,' said the housekeeper. Her voice came from her throat; her throat seemed lined with fur. 'I have the third-floor back, vacant since a week back. Should you wish to look at it?'

The young man followed her up the stairs. A faint light from no particular source mitigated the shadows of the halls. They trod noiselessly upon a stair carpet that its own loom would have forsworn. It seemed to have become vegetable; to have degenerated in that rank, sunless air to lush lichen or spreading moss that grew in patches to the staircase and was viscid under the foot like organic matter. At each turn of the stairs were vacant niches in the wall. Perhaps plants had once been set within them. If so they had died in that foul and tainted air. It may be that statues of the saints had stood there, but it was not difficult to conceive that imps and devils had dragged them forth in the darkness and down to the unholy depths of some furnished pit below.

'This is the room,' said the housekeeper, from her furry throat. 'It's a nice room. It ain't often vacant. I had some most elegant people in it last summer – no trouble at all, and paid in advance to the minute. The water's at the end of the hall. Sprowls and Mooney kept it three months. They done a vaudeville sketch. Miss B'retta Sprowls – you may have heard of her – Oh, that was just the stage names – right there over the dresser is where the marriage certificate hung, framed. The gas is here, and you see there is plenty of closet room. It's a room everybody likes. It never stays idle long.'

'Do you have many theatrical people rooming here?' asked the young man.

'They comes and goes. A good proportion of my lodgers is connected with the theatres. Yes, sir, this is the theatrical district. Actor people never stays long anywhere. I get my share. Yes, they comes and they goes.'

He engaged the room, paying for a week in advance. He was tired, he said, and would take possession at once. He counted out the money. The room had been made ready, she said, even to towels and water. As the housekeeper moved away he put, for the thousandth time, the question that he carried at the end of his tongue.

'A young girl – Miss Vashner – Miss Eloise Vashner – do you remember such a one among your lodgers? She would be singing on the stage, most likely. A fair girl, of medium height, and slender, with reddish, gold hair and a dark mole near her left eyebrow.'

'No, I don't remember the name. Them stage people has names they change as often as their rooms. They comes and they goes. No, I don't call that one to mind.'

No. Always no. Five months of ceaseless interrogation and the inevitable negative. So much time spent by day in questioning managers, agents, schools and choruses; by night among the audiences of theatres from all-star casts down to music halls so low that he dreaded to find what he most hoped for. He who had loved her best had tried to find her. He was sure that since her disappearance from home this great, water-girt city held her somewhere, but it was like a monstrous quicksand, shifting its particles constantly, with no foundation, its upper granules of today buried tomorrow in ooze and slime.

The furnished room received its latest guest with a first glow of pseudo-hospitality, a hectic, haggard, perfunctory welcome like the specious smile of a demi-rep. The sophistical comfort came in reflected gleams from the decayed furniture, the ragged brocade upholstery of a couch and two chairs, a foot-wide cheap pier glass between the two windows, from one or two gilt picture frames and a brass bedstead in a corner.

The guest reclined, inert, upon a chair, while the room, confused in speech as though it were an apartment in Babel, tried to discourse to him of its divers tenantry.

A polychromatic rug like some brilliant-flowered, rectangular tropical islet lay surrounded by a billowy sea of soiled matting. Upon the gay-papered wall were those pictures that pursue the homeless one from house to house – *The Huguenot Lovers, The First Quarrel, The Wedding Breakfast, Psyche at the Fountain*. The mantel's chastely severe outline was ingloriously veiled behind some pert drapery drawn rakishly askew like the sashes of the Amazonian ballet. Upon it was some desolate flotsam cast aside by the room's marooned when a lucky sail had borne them to a fresh port – a trifling vase or two, pictures of actresses, a medicine bottle, some stray cards out of a deck.

One by one, as the characters of a cryptograph become explicit, the little signs left by the furnished room's procession of guests developed a significance. The threadbare space in the rug in front of the dresser told that lovely women had marched in the throng. Tiny finger prints on the wall spoke of little prisoners trying to feel their way to sun and air. A splattered stain, raying like a shadow of a bursting bomb, witnessed where a hurled glass or bottle had splintered with its contents against the wall. Across the pier glass had been scrawled with a diamond in staggering letters the name 'Marie'. It seemed that the succession of dwellers in the furnished room had turned in fury – perhaps tempted beyond forbearance by its garish coldness – and wreaked upon it their passions. The furniture was chipped and bruised; the couch, distorted by bursting springs, seemed a horrible monster that had been slain during the stress of some grotesque convulsion. Some more potent upheaval had cloven a great slice from the marble mantel. Each plank in the floor owned its particular cant and shriek as from a separate and individual agony. It seemed incredible that all this malice and injury had been wrought upon the room by those who had called it for a time their home; and yet it may have been the cheated home instinct surviving blindly, the resentful rage at false household gods that had kindled their wrath. A hut that is our own we can sweep and adorn and cherish.

The young tenant in the chair allowed these thoughts to file, soft-shod, through his mind, while there drifted into the room furnished sounds and furnished scents. He heard in one room a tittering and incontinent, slack laughter; in others the monologue of a scold, the rattling of dice, a lullaby, and one crying dully; above him a banjo tinkled with spirit. Doors banged somewhere, the elevated trains roared intermittently; a cat yowled miserably upon a back fence. And he breathed the breath of the house – a dank savour rather than a smell – a cold, musty effluvium as from underground vaults mingled with the reeking exhalations of linoleum and mildewed and rotten woodwork.

Then, suddenly, as he rested there, the room was filled with the strong, sweet odour of mignonette. It came as upon a single buffet of wind with such sureness and fragrance and emphasis that it almost seemed a living visitant. And the man cried aloud: 'What, dear?' as if he had been called, and sprang up and faced about. The rich odour clung to him and wrapped him around. He reached out his arms for it, all his senses for the time confused and commingled. How could one be peremptorily called by an odour? Surely it must have been a sound. But, was it not the sound that had touched, that had caressed him?

'She has been in the room,' he cried, and he sprang to wrest from it a token, for he knew he would recognize the smallest thing that had belonged to her or that she had touched. This enveloping scent of mignonette, the odour that she had loved and made her own – whence came it?

The room had been but carelessly set in order. Scattered upon the flimsy dresser scarf were half a dozen hairpins – those discreet, indistinguishable friends of womankind, feminine of gender, infinite of mood and uncommunicative of tense. These he ignored, conscious of their triumphant lack of identity. Ransacking the drawers of the dresser he came upon a discarded, tiny, ragged handkerchief. He pressed it to his face. It was racy and insolent with heliotrope; he hurled it to the floor. In another drawer he found odd buttons, a theatre programme, a pawnbroker's card, two lost marshmallows, a book on the divination of dreams. In the last was a woman's black satin hair-bow, which halted him, poised between ice and fire. But the black satin hair-bow also is femininity's demure, impersonal, common ornament, and tells no tales.

And then he traversed the room like a hound on the scent, skimming the walls, considering the corners of the bulging matting on his hands and knees, rummaging mantel and tables, the curtains and hangings, the drunken cabinet in the corner, for a visible sign, unable to perceive that she was there beside, around, against, within, above him, clinging to him, wooing him, calling him so poignantly through the finer senses that even his grosser ones became cognisant of the call. Once again he answered loudly: 'Yes dear!' and turned, wild-eyed, to gaze on vacancy, for he could not yet discern form and colour and love and outstretched arms in the odour of mignonette. Oh, God! whence that odour, and since when have odours had a voice to call? Thus he groped.

He burrowed in crevices and corners, and found corks and cigarettes. These he passed in passive contempt. But once he found in a fold of the matting a half-smoked cigar, and this he ground beneath his heel with a green and trenchant oath. He sifted the room from end to end. He found dreary and ignoble small records of many a peripatetic tenant;

but of her whom he sought, and who may have lodged there, and whose spirit seemed to hover there, he found no trace.

And then he thought of the housekeeper.

He ran from the haunted room downstairs and to a door that showed a crack of light. She came out to his knock. He smothered his excitement as best he could.

'Will you tell me, madam,' he besought her, 'who occupied the room I have before I came?'

'Yes, sir. I can tell you again. 'Twas Sprowls and Mooney, as I said. Miss B'retta Sprowls it was in the theatres, but Missis Mooney she was. My house is well known for respectability. The marriage certificate hung, framed, on a nail over——'

'What kind of lady was Miss Sprowls – in looks, I mean?'

'Why, black-haired, sir, short, and stout, with a comical face. They left a week ago Tuesday.'

'And before they occupied it?'

'Why, there was a single gentleman connected with the draying business. He left owing me a week. Before him was Missis Crowder and her two children, they stayed four months; and back of them was old Mr Doyle, whose sons paid for him. He kept the room six months. That goes back a year, sir, and further I do not remember.'

He thanked her and crept back to his room. The room was dead. The essence that had vivified it was gone. The perfume of mignonette had departed. In its place was the old, stale odour of mouldy house furniture, of atmosphere in storage.

The ebbing of his hope drained his faith. He sat staring at the yellow, singing gaslight. Soon he walked to the bed and began to tear the sheets into strips. With the blade of his knife he drove them tightly into every crevice around windows and door. When all was snug and taut he turned out the light, turned the gas full on again and laid himself gratefully upon the bed.

* * *

It was Mrs McCool's night to go with the can for beer. So she fetched it and sat with Mrs Purdy in one of those subterranean retreats where housekeepers forgather and the worm dieth seldom.

'I rented out my third floor, back, this evening,' said Mrs Purdy, across a fine circle of foam. 'A young man took it. He went up to bed two hours ago.'

'Now, did ye, Missis Purdy, ma'am?' said Mrs McCool, with intense admiration. 'You do be a wonder for rentin' rooms of that kind. And did ye tell him, then?' she concluded in a husky whisper, laden with mystery.

'Rooms,' said Mrs Purdy, in her furriest tones, 'are furnished for to rent. I did not tell him, Mrs McCool.'

''Tis right ye are, ma'am; 'tis by renting rooms we kape alive. Ye have the rale sense for business, ma'am. There be many people will rayjict the rentin' of a room if they be tould a suicide has been after dyin' in the bed of it.'

'As you say, we has our living to be making,' remarked Mrs Purdy.

'Yis, ma'am, 'tis true. 'Tis just one wake ago this day I helped ye lay out the third floor, back. A pretty slip of a collen she was to be killin' herself wid the gas – a swate little face she had, Mrs Purdy, ma'am.'

'She'd a-been called handsome, as you say,' said Mrs Purdy, assenting but critical, 'but for that mole she had a-growin' by her left eyebrow. Do fill up your glass again, Missis McCool.'

The Whistling Room
William Hope Hodgson

Carnacki shook a friendly fist at me as I entered late. Then he opened the door into the dining-room, and ushered the four of us – Jessop, Arkright, Taylor and myself – in to dinner.

We dined well, as usual, and, equally as usual, Carnacki was pretty silent during the meal. At the end, we took our wine and cigars to our accustomed positions, and Carnacki – having got himself comfortable in his big chair – began without any preliminary:

'I have just got back from Ireland again,' he said. 'And I thought you chaps would be interested to hear my news. Besides, I fancy I shall see the thing clearer, after I have told it all out straight. I must tell you this, though, at the beginning – up to the present moment, I have been utterly and completely "stumped". I have tumbled upon one of the most peculiar cases of "haunting" – or devilment of some sort – that I have come against. Now listen.

'I have been spending the last few weeks at Iastrae Castle, about twenty miles north-east of Galway. I got a letter about a month ago from a Mr Sid K. Tassoc, who it seemed had bought the place lately, and moved in, only to find that he had got a very peculiar piece of property.

'When I reached there, he met me at the station, driving a jaunting-car, and drove me up to the castle, which, by the way, he called a "house-shanty". I found that he was "pigging it" there with his boy brother and another American, who seemed to be half servant and half companion. It appears that all the servants had left the place, in a body, as you might say; and now they were managing among themselves, assisted by some day-help.

'The three of them got together a scratch feed, and Tassoc told me all about the trouble, whilst we were at table. It is most extraordinary, and different from anything that I have had to do with; though that Buzzing Case was very queer, too.

'Tassoc began right in the middle of his story. "We've got a room in this shanty," he said, "which has got a most infernal whistling in it; sort of haunting it. The thing starts any time: you never know when, and it goes on until it frightens you. All the servants have gone, as I've told you. It's not ordinary whistling, and it isn't the wind. Wait till you hear it."

'"We're all carrying guns," said the boy; and slapped his coat pocket.

'"As bad as that?" I said; and the older brother nodded. "I may be soft," he replied; "but wait till you've heard it. Sometimes I think it's some infernal thing, and the next moment, I'm just as sure that someone's playing a trick on us."

'"Why?" I asked. "What is to be gained?"

'"You mean," he said, "that people usually have some good reason for playing tricks as elaborate as this. Well, I'll tell you. There's a lady in this province, by the name of Miss Donnehue, who's going to be my wife, this day two months. She's more beautiful than they make them, and so far as I can see, I've just stuck my head into an Irish hornet's nest. There's about a score of hot young Irishmen been courting her these two years gone, and now that I've come along and cut them out, they feel raw against me. Do you begin to understand the possibilities?"

'"Yes," I said. "Perhaps I do in a vague sort of way; but I don't see how all this affects the room?"

'"Like this," he said. "When I'd fixed it up with Miss Donnehue, I looked out for a place, and bought this little house-shanty. Afterwards, I told her – one evening during dinner, that I'd decided to tie up here. And then she asked me whether I wasn't afraid of the whistling room. I told her it must have been thrown in gratis, as I'd heard nothing about it. There were some of her men friends present, and I saw a smile go round. I found out, after a bit of questioning, that several people have bought this place during the last twenty odd years. And it was always on the market again, after a trial.

'"Well, the chaps started to bait me a bit, and offered to take bets after dinner that I'd not stay six months in this shanty. I looked once or twice to Miss Donnehue, so as to be sure I was 'getting the note' of the talkee-talkee; but I could see that she didn't take it as a joke, at all. Partly, I think, because there was a bit of a sneer in the way the men were tackling me, and partly because she really believes there is something in this yarn of the whistling room.

'"However, after dinner, I did what I could to even things up with the others. I nailed all their bets, and screwed them down good and safe. I guess some of them are going to be hard hit, unless I lose; which I don't mean to. Well, there you have practically the whole yarn."

'"Not quite," I told him. "All that I know, is that you have bought a castle, with a room in it that is in some way 'queer', and that you've been doing some betting. Also, I know that your servants have got frightened, and run away. Tell me something about the whistling?"

'"Oh, that!" said Tassoc; "that started the second night we were in. I'd had a good look round the room in the daytime, as you can understand; for the talk up at Arlestrae – Miss Donnehue's place – had made me wonder a bit. But it seems just as usual as some of the other rooms in the old wing, only perhaps a bit more lonesome feeling. But that may be only because of the talk about it, you know.

'"The whistling started about ten o'clock, on the second night, as I said. Tom and I were in the library, when we heard an awfully queer whistling, coming along the East Corridor—— The room is in the East Wing, you know.

'"That blessed ghost!" I said to Tom, and we collared the lamps off the table, and went up to have a look. I tell you, even as we dug along the corridor, it took me a bit in the throat, it was so beastly queer. It was a sort of tune, in a way; but more as if a devil or some rotten thing were laughing at you, and going to get round at your back. That's how it makes you feel.

'"When we got to the door, we didn't wait; but rushed it open; and then I tell you the sound of the thing fairly hit me in the face. Tom said he got it the same way – sort of felt stunned and bewildered. We looked all round, and soon got so nervous, we just cleared out, and I locked the door.

'"We came down here, and had a stiff peg each. Then we landed fit again, and began to feel we'd been nicely had. So we took sticks, and went out into the grounds, thinking after all it must be some of these confounded Irishmen working the ghost-trick on us. But there was not a leg stirring.

'"We went back into the house, and walked over it, and then paid another visit to the room. But we simply couldn't stand it. We fairly ran out, and locked the door again. I don't know how to put it into words; but I had a feeling of being up against something that was rottenly dangerous. You know! We've carried our guns ever since.

'"Of course, we had a real turn-out of the room next day, and the whole house-place; and we even hunted the grounds; but there was nothing queer. And now I don't know what to think; except that the sensible part of me tells me that it's some plan of these wild Irishmen to try to take a rise out of me."

'"Done anything since?" I asked him.

'"Yes," he said. "Watched outside of the door of the room at nights, and chased round the grounds, and sounded the walls and floor of the room. We've done everything we could think of; and it's beginning to get on our nerves; so we sent for you."

'By this, we had finished eating. As we rose from the table, Tassoc suddenly called out: "Ssh! Hark!"

'We were instantly silent, listening. Then I heard it, an extraordinary hooning whistle, monstrous and inhuman, coming from far away through corridors to my right.

'"By God!" said Tassoc; "and it's scarcely dark yet! Collar those candles, both of you, and come along."

'In a few moments, we were all out of the door and racing up the stairs. Tassoc turned into a long corridor, and we followed, shielding our candles as we ran. The sound seemed to fill all the passages as we drew near, until I had the feeling that the whole air throbbed under the power of some wanton Immense Force – a sense of an actual taint, as you might say, of monstrosity all about us.

'Tassoc unlocked the door; then, giving it a push with his foot, jumped back, and drew his revolver. As the door flew open, the sound beat out at us, with an effect impossible to explain to one who has not heard it – with a certain, horrible personal note in it; as if in there in the darkness you could picture the room rocking and creaking in a mad, vile glee to its own filthy piping and whistling and hooning; and yet all the time aware of you in particular. To stand there and listen, was to be stunned by Realization. It was as if someone showed you the mouth of a vast pit suddenly, and said: That's Hell. And you *knew* that they had spoken the truth. Do you get it, even a little bit?

'I stepped a pace into the room, and held the candle over my head, and looked quickly around. Tassoc and his brother joined me, and the man came up at the back, and we all held our candles high. I was deafened with the shrill, piping hoon of the whistling; and then, clear in my ear, something seemed to be saying to me: "Get out of here – quick! Quick! Quick!"

'As you chaps know, I never neglect that sort of thing. Sometimes it may be nothing but nerves; but as you will remember, it was just such a warning that saved me in the "Grey Dog" Case, and in the "Yellow Finger" Experiments; as well as other times. Well, I turned sharp round to the others: "Out!" I said. "For God's sake, *out* quick!" And in an instant I had them into the passage.

'There came an extraordinary yelling scream into the hideous whistling, and then, like a clap of thunder, an utter silence. I slammed the door, and locked it. Then, taking the key, I looked round at the others. They were pretty white, and I imagine I must have looked that way too. And there we stood a moment, silent.

'"Come down out of this, and have some whisky," said Tassoc, at last, in a voice he tried to make ordinary; and he led the way. I was the back man, and I knew we all kept looking over our shoulders. When we got downstairs, Tassoc passed the bottle round. He took a drink himself, and slapped his glass onto the table. Then sat down with a thud.

'"That's a lovely thing to have in the house with you, isn't it!" he said. And directly afterwards: "What on earth made you hustle us all out like that, Carnacki?"

'"Something seemed to be telling me to get out, *quick,*" I said. "Sounds a bit silly superstitious, I know; but when you are meddling with this sort of thing, you've got to take notice of queer fancies, and risk being laughed at."

'I told him then about the "Grey Dog" business, and he nodded a lot to that. "Of course," I said, "this may be nothing more than those would-be rivals of yours playing some funny game; but, personally, though I'm going to keep an open mind, I feel that there is something beastly and dangerous about this thing."

'We talked for a while longer, and then Tassoc suggested billiards, which we played in a pretty half-hearted fashion, and all the time cocking an ear to the door, as you might say, for sounds; but none came, and later, after coffee, he suggested early bed, and a thorough overhaul of the room on the morrow.

'My bedroom was in the newer part of the castle, and the door opened into the picture gallery. At the east end of the gallery was the entrance to the corridor of the east wing; this was shut off from the gallery by two old and heavy oak doors, which looked rather odd and quaint beside the more modern doors of the various rooms.

'When I reached my room, I did not go to bed; but began to unpack my instrument trunk, of which I had retained the key. I intended to take one or two preliminary steps at once, in my investigation of the extraordinary whistling.

'Presently, when the castle had settled into quietness, I slipped out of my room, and across to the entrance of the great corridor. I opened one of the low, squat doors, and threw the beam of my pocket searchlight down the passage. It was empty, and I went through the doorway, and pushed-to the oak behind me. Then along the great passageway, throwing my light before and behind, and keeping my revolver handy.

'I had hung a "protection belt" of garlic round my neck, and the smell of it seemed to fill the corridor and give me assurance; for, as you all know, it is a wonderful "protection" against the more usual Aeiirii forms of semi-materialization, by which I supposed the whistling might be produced; though, at that period of my investigation, I was still quite prepared to find it due to some perfectly natural cause; for it is astonishing the enormous number of cases that prove to have nothing abnormal in them.

'In addition to wearing the necklet, I had plugged my ears loosely with garlic, and as I did not intend to stay more than a few minutes in the room, I hoped to be safe.

'When I reached the door, and put my hand into my pocket for the key, I had a sudden feeling of sickening funk. But I was not going to back out, if I could help it. I unlocked the door and turned the handle. Then I gave the door a sharp push with my foot, as Tassoc had done, and drew my revolver, though I did not expect to have any use for it, really.

'I shone the searchlight all round the room, and then stepped inside, with a disgustingly horrible feeling of walking slap into a waiting danger. I stood a few seconds, expectant, and nothing happened, and the empty room showed bare from corner to corner. And then, you know, I realized that the room was full of an abominable silence; can you understand that? A sort of purposeful silence, just as sickening as any of the filthy noises the Things have power to make. Do you remember what I told you about that "Silent Garden" business? Well, this room had just that same *malevolent* silence – the beastly quietness of a thing that is looking at you and not seeable itself, and thinks that it has got you. Oh, I recognized it instantly, and I whipped the top off my lantern, so as to have light over the *whole* room.

'Then I set to, working like fury, and keeping my glance all about me. I sealed the two windows with lengths of human hair, right across, and sealed them at every frame. As I worked, a queer, scarcely perceptible tenseness stole into the air of the place, and the silence seemed, if you can understand me, to grow more solid. I knew then that I had no business there without "full protection"; for I was practically certain that this was no mere Aeiirii development; but one of the worst forms, as the Saiitii; like that "Grunting Man" case – you know.

'I finished the window, and hurried over to the great fireplace. This is a huge affair, and has a queer gallows-iron, I think they are called, projecting from back of the arch. I sealed the opening with seven human airs – the seventh crossing the six others.

'Then, just as I was making an end, a low, mocking whistle grew in the room. A cold, nervous prickling went up my spine, and round my forehead from the back. The hideous sound filled all the room with an extraordinary, grotesque parody of human whistling, too gigantic to be human – as if something gargantuan and monstrous made the sounds softly. As I stood there a last moment, pressing down the final seal, I had little doubt but that I had come across one of those rare and horrible cases of the *Inanimate* reproducing the functions of the *Animate*. I made a grab for my lamp and went quickly to the door, looking over my shoulder, and listening for the thing that I expected. It came, just as I got my hand upon the handle – a low squeal of incredible, malevolent anger, piercing through the low hooning of the whistling. I dashed out, slamming the door and locking it.

'I leant a little against the opposite wall of the corridor, feeling rather funny; for it had been a hideously narrow squeak... "Theyr be noe sayfetie to be gained bye gayrds of holieness when the monyster hath pow'r to speak throe woode and stoene." So runs the passage in the

Sigsand MS., and I proved it in that "Nodding Door" business. There is no protection against this particular form of monster, except, possibly, for a fractional period of time; for it can reproduce itself in, or take to its purpose, the very protective material which you may use, and has power to "*forme* wythine the pentycle"; though not immediately. There is, of course, the possibility of the Unknown Last Line of the Saaamaaa Ritual being uttered; but it is too uncertain to count upon, and the danger is too hideous; and even then it has no power to protect for more than "maybee fyve beats of the harte", as the Sigsand has it.

'Inside of the room, there was now a constant, meditative, hooning whistling; but presently this ceased, and the silence seemed worse; for there is such a sense of hidden mischief in a silence.

'After a little, I sealed the door with crossed hairs, and then cleared off down the great passage, and so to bed.

'For a long time I lay awake; but managed eventually to get some sleep. Yet, about two o'clock I was waked by the hooning whistling of the room coming to me, even through the closed doors. The sound was tremendous, and seemed to beat through the whole house with a presiding sense of terror. As if (I remember thinking) some monstrous giant had been holding mad carnival with itself at the end of that great passage.

'I got up and sat on the edge of the bed, wondering whether to go along and have a look at the seal; and suddenly there came a thump on my door, and Tassoc walked in, with his dressing-gown over his pyjamas.

'"I thought it would have waked you, so I came along to have a talk," he said. "*I* can't sleep. Beautiful! Isn't it?"

'"Extraordinary!" I said, and tossed him my case.

'He lit a cigarette, and we sat and talked for about an hour; and all the time that noise went on, down at the end of the big corridor.

'Suddenly Tassoc stood up:

'"Let's take our guns, and go and examine the brute," he said, and turned towards the door.

'"No!" I said. "By Jove – NO! I can't say anything definite yet; but I believe that room is about as dangerous as it well can be."

'"Haunted – *really* haunted?" he asked, keenly and without any of his frequent banter.

'I told him, of course, that I could not say a definite *yes* or *no* to such a question; but that I hoped to be able to make a statement, soon. Then I gave him a little lecture on the False Re-materialization of the Animate Force through the Inanimate Inert. He began then to understand the particular way in which the room might be dangerous, if it were really the subject of a manifestation.

'About an hour later, the whistling ceased quite suddenly and

Tassoc went off again to bed. I went back to mine, also, and eventually got another spell of sleep.

'In the morning, I walked along to the room. I found the seals on the door intact. Then I went in. The window seals and the hair were all right; but the seventh hair across the great fireplace was broken. This set me thinking. I knew that it might, very possibly, have snapped, through my having tensioned it too highly; but then, again, it might have been broken by something else. Yet it was scarcely possible that a man, for instance, could have passed between the six unbroken hairs; for no one would ever have noticed them, entering the room that way, you see; but just walked through them, ignorant of their very existence.

'I removed the other hairs, and the seals. Then I looked up the chimney. It went up straight, and I could see blue sky at the top. It was a big open flue, and free from any suggestion of hiding-places or corners. Yet, of course, I did not trust to any such casual examination, and after breakfast, I put on my overalls, and climbed to the very top, sounding all the way; but I found nothing.

'Then I came down, and went over the whole of the room – floor, ceiling, and walls, mapping them out in six-inch squares, and sounding with both hammer and probe. But there was nothing unusual.

'Afterwards, I made a three-weeks' search of the whole castle, in the same thorough way; but I found nothing. I went even further then; for at night, when the whistling commenced, I made a microphone test. You see, if the whistling were mechanically produced, this test would have made evident to me the working of the machinery, if there were any such concealed within the walls. It certainly was an up to date method of examination, as you must allow.

'Of course, I did not think that any of Tassoc's rivals had fixed up any mechanical contrivance; but I thought it just possible that there had been some such thing for producing the whistling, made away back in the years, perhaps with the intention of giving the room a reputation that would ensure its being free of inquisitive folk. You see what I mean? Well, of course, it was just possible, if this were the case, that someone knew the secret of the machinery, and was utilizing the knowledge to play this devil of a prank on Tassoc. The microphone test of the walls would certainly have made this known to me, as I have said; but there was nothing of the sort in the castle; so that I had practically no doubt at all now, but that it was a genuine case of what is popularly termed "haunting".

'All this time, every night, and sometimes most of each night, the hooning whistling of the room was intolerable. It was as if an Intelligence there knew that steps were being taken against it, and piped and hooned in a sort of mad mocking contempt. I tell you, it was as extraordinary as it was horrible. Time after time I went along –

tiptoeing noiselessly on stockinged feet – to the sealed door (for I always kept the room sealed). I went at all hours of the night, and often the whistling, inside, would seem to change to a brutally jeering note, as though the half-animate monster saw me plainly through the shut door. And all the time, as I would stand watching, the hooning of the whistling would seem to fill the whole corridor, so that I used to feel a precious lonely chap, messing about there with one of Hell's mysteries.

'And every morning I would enter the room, and examine the different hairs and seals. You see, after the first week I had stretched parallel hairs all along the walls of the room, and along the ceiling; but over the floor, which was of polished stone, I had set out little colourless wafers, tacky-side uppermost. Each wafer was numbered, and they were arranged after a definite plan, so that I should be able to trace the exact movements of any living thing that went across.

'You will see that no material being or creature could possibly have entered that room, without leaving many signs to tell me about it. But nothing was ever disturbed, and I began to think that I should have to risk an attempt to stay a night in the room, in the Electric Pentacle. Mind you, I *knew* that it would be a crazy thing to do; but I was getting stumped, and ready to try anything.

'Once, about midnight, I did break the seal on the door and have a quick look in; but, I tell you, the whole room gave one mad yell, and seemed to come towards me in a great belly of shadows, as if the walls had bellied in towards me. Of course, that must have been fancy. Anyway, the yell was sufficient, and I slammed the door, and locked it, feeling a bit weak down my spine. I wonder whether you know the feeling.

'And then, when I had got to that state of readiness for anything, I made what, at first, I thought was something of a discovery.

'It was about one in the morning, and I was walking slowly round the castle, keeping in the soft grass. I had come under the shadow of the east front, and far above me, I could hear the vile hooning whistling of the room, up in the darkness of the unlit wing. Then, suddenly, a little in front of me, I heard a man's voice, speaking low, but evidently in glee:

'"By George! You chaps; but I wouldn't care to bring a wife home to that!" it said, in the tone of the cultured Irish.

'Someone started to reply; but there came a sharp exclamation, and then a rush, and I heard footsteps running in all directions. Evidently, the men had spotted me.

'For a few seconds I stood there, feeling an awful ass. After all, *they* were at the bottom of the haunting! Do you see what a big fool it made me seem? I had no doubt but that they were some of Tassoc's rivals; and here I had been feeling in every bone that I had hit a genuine Case! And then, you know, there came the memory of hundreds of details, that made me just as much in doubt, again. Anyway, whether it was natural, or ab-natural, there was a great deal yet to be cleared up.

'I told Tassoc, next morning, what I had discovered, and through the whole of every night, for five nights, we kept a close watch round the east wing; but there was never a sign of anyone prowling about; and all the time, almost from evening to dawn, that grotesque whistling would hoon incredibly, far above us in the darkness.

'On the morning after the fifth night, I received a wire from here, which brought me home by the next boat. I explained to Tassoc that I was simply bound to come away for a few days; but I told him to keep up the watch round the castle. One thing I was very careful to do, and that was to make him absolutely promise never to go into the Room between sunset and sunrise. I made it clear to him that we knew nothing definite yet, one way or the other; and if the room were what I had first thought it to be, it might be a lot better for him to die first, than enter it after dark.

'When I got here, and had finished my business, I thought you chaps would be interested; and also I wanted to get it all spread out clear in my mind; so I rang you up. I am going over again tomorrow, and when I get back I ought to have something pretty extraordinary to tell you. By the way, there is a curious thing I forgot to tell you. I tried to get a phonographic record of the whistling; but it simply produced no impression on the wax at all. That is one of the things that has made me feel queer.

'Another extraordinary thing is that the microphone will not magnify the sound – will not even transmit it; seems to take no account of it; and acts as if it were non-existent. I am absolutely and utterly stumped, up to the present. I am a wee bit curious to see whether any of your dear clever heads can make daylight of it. *I* cannot – not yet.'

He rose to his feet.

'Goodnight, all,' he said, and began to usher us out abruptly, but without offence, into the night.

*   *   *

A fortnight later, he dropped us each a card, and you can imagine that I was not late this time. When we arrived, Carnacki took us straight into dinner, and when we had finished, and all made ourselves comfortable, he began again, where he had left off:

'Now just listen quietly; for I have got something very queer to tell you. I got back late at night, and I had to walk up to the castle, as I had not warned them I was coming. It was bright moonlight; so that the walk was rather a pleasure than otherwise. When I got there, the whole place was in darkness, and I thought I would go round outside, to see whether Tassoc or his brother was keeping watch. But I could not find them anywhere, and concluded that they had got tired of it, and gone off to bed.

'As I returned across the lawn that lies below the front of the east wing, I caught the hooning whistling of the room, coming down strangely clear through the stillness of the night. It had a peculiar note in it, I remember – low and constant, queerly meditative. I looked up at the window, bright in the moonlight, and got a sudden thought to bring a ladder from the stable-yard, and try to get a look into the room, from the outside.

'With this notion, I hunted round at the back of the castle, among the straggle of offices, and presently found a long, fairly light ladder; though it was heavy enough for one, goodness knows! I thought at first that I should never get it reared. I managed at last, and let the ends rest very quietly against the wall, a little below the sill of the larger window. Then, going silently, I went up the ladder. Presently, I had my face above the sill, and was looking in, alone with the moonlight.

'Of course, the queer whistling sounded louder up there; but it still conveyed that peculiar sense of something whistling quietly to itself – can you understand? Though, for all the meditative lowness of the note, the horrible, gargantuan quality was distinct – a mighty parody of the human; as if I stood there and listened to the whistling from the lips of a monster with a man's soul.

'And then, you know, I saw something. The floor in the middle of the huge, empty room, was puckered upwards in the centre into a strange, soft-looking mound, parted at the top into an ever-changing hole, that pulsated to that great, gentle hooning. At times, as I watched, I saw the heaving of the indented mound gap across with a queer inward suction, as with the drawing of an enormous breath; then the thing would dilate and pout once more to the incredible melody. And suddenly, as I stared, dumb, it came to me that the thing was living. I was looking at two enormous, blackened lips, blistered and brutal, there in the pale moonlight . . .

'Abruptly, they bulged out to a vast, pouting mound of force and sound, stiffened and swollen, and hugely massive and clean-cut in the moonbeams. And a great sweat lay heavy on the vast upper lip. In the same moment of time, the whistling had burst into a mad screaming note, that seemed to stun me, even where I stood, outside of the window. And then, the following moment, I was staring blankly at the solid, undisturbed floor of the room – smooth, polished stone flooring, from wall to wall. And there was an absolute silence.

'You can imagine me staring into the quiet room, and knowing what I knew. I felt like a sick, frightened child, and I wanted to slide *quietly* down the ladder, and run away. But in that very instant, I heard Tassoc's voice calling to me from within the room, for help, *help*. My

God! but I got such an awful dazed feeling; and I had a vague bewildered notion that, after all, it was the Irishmen who had got him in there, and were taking it out of him. And then the call came again, and I burst the window, and jumped in to help him. I had a confused idea that the call had come from within the shadow of the great fireplace, and I raced across to it; but there was no one there.

'"Tassoc!" I shouted, and my voice went empty-sounding round the great apartment; and then, in a flash, *I knew that Tassoc had never called.* I whirled round, sick with fear, towards the window, and as I did so a frightful, exultant whistling scream burst through the room. On my left, the end wall had bellied in towards me, in a pair of gargantuan lips, black and utterly monstrous, to within a yard of my face. I fumbled for a mad instant at my revolver; not for *it*, but myself; for the danger was a thousand times worse than death. And then, suddenly, the Unknown Last Line of the Saaamaaa Ritual was whispered quite audibly in the room. Instantly, the thing happened that I have known once before. There came a sense as of dust falling continually and monotonously, and I knew that my life hung uncertain and suspended for a flash, in a brief reeling vertigo of unseeable things. Then *that* ended, and I knew that I might live. My soul and body blended again, and life and power came to me. I dashed furiously at the window, and hurled myself out head foremost; for I can tell you that I had stopped being afraid of death. I crashed down on to the ladder, and slithered, grabbing and grabbing; and so came some way or other alive to the bottom. And there I sat in the soft, wet grass, with the moonlight all about me; and far above, through the broken window of the room, there was a low whistling.

'That is the chief of it. I was not hurt, and I went round to the front, and knocked Tassoc up. When they let me in, we had a long yarn, over some good whisky – for I was shaken to pieces – and I explained things as much as I could. I told Tassoc that the room would have to come down, and every fragment of it be burned in a blast-furnace, erected within a pentacle. He nodded. There was nothing to say. Then I went to bed.

'We turned a small army on to the work, and within ten days, that lovely thing had gone up in smoke, and what was left was calcined and clean.

'It was when the workmen were stripping the panelling, that I got hold of a sound notion of the beginnings of that beastly development. Over the great fireplace, after the great oak panels had been torn down, I found that there was let into the masonry a scrollwork of stone, with on it an old inscription, in ancient Celtic, that here in this room was burned Dian Tiansay, Jester of King Alzof, who made the Song of Foolishness upon King Ernore of the Seventh Castle.

'When I got the translation clear, I gave it to Tassoc. He was

tremendously excited; for he knew the old tale, and took me down to the
library to look at an old parchment that gave the story in detail.
Afterwards, I found that the incident was well known about the
countryside; but always regarded more as a legend than as history. And
no one seemed ever to have dreamt that the old east wing of Iastrae
Castle was the remains of the ancient Seventh Castle.

'From the old parchment, I gathered that there had been a pretty
dirty job done, away back in the years. It seems that King Alzof and
King Ernore had been enemies by birthright, as you might say truly; but
that nothing more than a little raiding had occurred on either side for
years, until Dian Tiansay made the Song of Foolishness upon King
Ernore, and sang it before King Alzof; and so greatly was it appreciated
that King Alzof gave the jester one of his ladies to wife.

'Presently, all the people of the land had come to know the song, and
so it came at last to King Ernore, who was so angered that he made war
upon his old enemy, and took and burned him and his castle; but Dian
Tiansay, the jester, he brought with him to his own place, and having
torn his tongue out because of the song which he had made and sung he
imprisoned him in the room in the east wing (which was evidently used
for unpleasant purposes), and the jester's wife he kept for himself, having
a fancy for her prettiness.

'But one night Dian Tiansay's wife was not to be found, and in the
morning they discovered her lying dead in her husband's arms, and he
sitting, whistling the Song of Foolishness, for he had no longer the power
to sing it.

'Then they roasted Dian Tiansay in the great fireplace – probably
from that selfsame "gallows-iron" which I have already mentioned.
And until he died, Dian Tiansay "ceased not to whistle" the Song of
Foolishness, which he could no longer sing. But afterwards, "in that
room" there was often heard at night the sound of something whistling;
and there "grew a power in that room", so that none dared to sleep in it.
And presently, it would seem, the King went to another castle; for the
whistling troubled him.

'There you have it all. Of course, that is only a rough rendering of the
translation from the parchment. It's a bit quaint! Don't you think so?'

*   *   *

'Yes,' I said, answering for the lot. 'But how did the thing grow to such a
tremendous manifestation?'

'One of those cases of continuity of thought producing a positive
action upon the immediate surrounding material,' replied Carnacki.
'The development must have been going forward through centuries, to
have produced such a monstrosity. It was a true instance of Saiitii
manifestation, which I can best explain by likening it to a living spiritual

fungus, which involves the very structure of the aether-fibre itself, and, of course, in so doing, acquires an essential control over the "material-substance" involved in it. It is impossible to make it plainer in a few words.'

'What broke the seventh hair?' asked Taylor.

But Carnacki did not know. He thought it was probably nothing but being too severely tensioned. He also explained that they found out that the men who had run away had not been up to mischief; but had come over secretly merely to hear the whistling, which, indeed, had suddenly become the talk of the whole countryside.

'One other thing,' said Arkright, 'have you any idea what governs the use of the Unknown Last Line of the Saaamaaa Ritual? I know, of course, that it was used by the Ab-human Priests in the Incantation of Raaaee; but what used it on your behalf, and what made it?'

'You had better read Harzam's Monograph, and my Addenda to it, on "Astral and Astarral Co-ordination and Interference", said Carnacki. 'It is an extraordinary subject, and I can only say here that the human vibration may not be insulated from the "astarral" (as is always believed to be the case, in interferences by the Ab-human) without immediate action being taken by those Forces which govern the spinning of the outer circle. In other words, it is being proved, time after time, that there is some inscrutable Protective Force constantly intervening between the human soul (not the body, mind you) and the Outer Monstrosities. Am I clear?'

'Yes, I think so,' I replied. 'And you believe that the room had become the material expression of the ancient jester – that his soul, rotted with hatred, had bred into a monster – eh?' I asked.

'Yes,' said Carnacki, nodding. 'I think you've put my thought rather neatly. It is a queer coincidence that Miss Donnehue is supposed to be descended (so I have heard since) from the same King Ernore. It makes one think some rather curious thoughts, doesn't it? The marriage coming on, and the room waking to fresh life. If she had gone into that room, ever . . . eh? IT had waited a long time. Sins of the fathers. Yes, I've thought of that. They're to be married next week, and I am to be best man, which is a thing I hate. And he won his bets, rather! Just think *if* ever she had gone into that room. Pretty horrible, eh?'

He nodded his head grimly, and we four nodded back. Then he rose and took us collectively to the door, and presently thrust us forth in friendly fashion on to the Embankment, and into the fresh night air.

'Goodnight,' we all called back, and went to our various homes.

If she had, eh? If she had? That is what I kept thinking.

Magic Man
Robert Holdstock

Crouched in the mouth of the shrine-cave, One Eye, the painter, shivered as black storm clouds skated overhead and the wind whipped down from the northern ice-wastes to plague the grasslands with its bitter touch.

The tribe should be gathered together before the darkening skies could loose their volleys of rain and lightening; then they would huddle into the cliff wall and wail and moan their misery. When the rains passed the women would come, invading the shrine-cave and screeching at One Eye because he had not stopped their soaking.

He squatted, looking out across the grasslands to the man-high rushes that waved and danced in the biting winds. Stupid women, he thought. Stupid, stupid women. They should understand that his drawings were for the spirit of the hunt, not for their own comfort. They should be pleased when their men brought home bison, deer and, increasingly, the reindeer that strayed from the snows of the north valleys.

'One Eye!' hailed a child's voice. One Eye looked down to where a small boy scrambled up the slopes of the cliff towards the cave.

'Go away, child. Go away!' shouted the old man angrily. But he knew it would be no use. The boy, brown and dusty, crawled into the mouth of the cave and squatted there, breathing heavily. The sight of One Eye's empty eye socket staring at him no longer perturbed the would-be painter as once it had.

'I want to draw.'

One Eye let his grey hair fall over his one good eye, clenched his mouth tight in an obstinate gesture of annoyance and shook his head, 'Go away, child. Wait for the hunters.' Outside the wind howled against the cliff and the dark sky grew perceptibly darker.

'I want to *draw*.' Big eyes stared at the old man, childish features, open, honest. The boy was filthy; his hair was lank and filled with grass from his earlier romping. 'I'm tired of making *these*!' He threw the

inaccurately made axe from his hand and it clattered down the slopes to
land heavily among the women below. One of them looked up and
shouted angrily. She was cleaning a skin and had blood up to her
elbows. The fire around which the group squatted burned low, and
charred bones and wood poked blackly from the pile of ashes. An
adolescent girl, underdeveloped and sulky, prodded the dying embers
with a spear. The boy, in the shrine-cave above, was angry. 'I want to
draw a bear. One Eye, please! Let me draw a bear, please?'

'Look,' snapped One Eye, pointing. Black shapes against the grey
sky, the hunters returned. They walked slowly, spears clutched tightly,
animals slung over their shoulders. Leading them came He Who
Carries a Red Spear, his scarred face angry, bleeding from gashes on his
cheeks. He waved his red-ochred spear at the group and the women
stood, shouting their greeting. Red Spear, thought One Eye. How I
wish a bison would get *you*. The tall hunter strode into the camp. He
had a deer slung over his shoulders. His fur and leather tunic had been
torn away and he walked naked, black hair coating his body from neck
to toe, acting as a fur in itself. He was unaware of the death-thoughts of
the old man above his head. Today he had not killed a bison. Today the
hunt, for him, had failed. He was angry.

The men dropped their kills close in to the cliff wall and then
dragged the skins and axe baskets from where they had been distributed
about the fire. The women crouched against the sloping wall of the
overhang and giggled as the hunters covered them with taut skins,
making rough and ready tents against the cliff face. They hammered
special narrow points through the skins to hold them down, propping
them up in the middle with spears. The skies darkened, distant thunder
rolled and the grass whispered and sang as it bowed to the groaning
winds.

'Go down,' snapped One Eye. 'Into the tents with you. Leave me in
peace, brat. Leave me.'

The boy darted back into the cave and laughed as One Eye
screeched with surprise. He waited for the painter to come after him,
but One Eye had fallen suddenly quiet, watching the slope below him.
There was the sound of someone climbing up to the cave. The boy
crawled to the entrance and began to shake as he saw his father coming
up towards them.

He Who Carries a Red Spear crouched beside One Eye and snarled.
'What happened to your magic today, old man? Why didn't I kill a
bison, uh?' Mouth stretched back into a hideous grin, eyes narrowed,
Red Spear struck fear into the heart of One Eye. One Eye cowered
back, but a hairy and powerful hand reached out and grabbed him by
the neck. The hunter snarled, increased the grip until the bone nearly
snapped, then released the painter, looking back into the cave.

'Drawings! Paintings!' Hard eyes turned on One Eye. 'Only *spears* kill animals, you old fool. Spears, stones ... and *these.*' He held up his bare hands, the fingers curved with the power they possessed. 'I have killed bison with my bare hands, old man. I have twisted their heads, their necks twice the thickness of my body. I have twisted them until the bones snapped and splintered, the muscle tore and the blood spurted over my body. Drawings! Pah!' He smashed One Eye across the face. 'If it weren't that *they,* stupid fools, believed this nonsense, I should kill you. I should break your neck between my thumb and forefinger. I should snap you in two and throw your useless body to the scavengers. I should give you to the Grunts to devour.'

'My paintings,' mumbled One Eye, 'show the hunt. They protect you. They give you power over beasts.'

Red Spear laughed. Behind him a hunter climbed into the cave and touched the bitter man on his arm. 'Your wife waits, Red Spear. She is eager.'

He Who Carries a Red Spear grunted. 'Hear that, old man? My wife waits for me. All the women in this tribe I could have if I so desired. Because I am the best hunter!' He pounded his naked chest and inched towards the painter, the stench of his body strong and sickening. 'I hunt with weapons, not with paintings ...' And as he said it he clutched dirt in his hand and threw it over the ochred walls. He took his son by the arm and threw him down the slope before him, sliding down and disappearing into the tent.

The other hunter looked sympathetically at the old man. 'He killed no bison today. You must forgive his anger.'

One Eye shook his head. 'He is the sire of a Grunt – that explains much to me.' Thunder crashed nearby and the black skies flared with the streaking lightning to the north. 'He sneers at the magic of my paintings,' One Eye murmured. 'The paintings bring luck, they bring kills.' He looked at the blood-smeared hunter. 'They don't say *who* shall make the kills. They bring kills to the tribe. He *must* understand that ...' He looked away. 'But I fear he never shall – he cannot understand, just as none of his father's spore can understand, that beasts and men have spirit.'

The hunter nodded. 'He only understands *kill*. And soon, One Eye, he will kill *you*. Be careful.' The hunter turned to go. One Eye reached out a hand and stopped him, 'How many kills today? How many?'

'Ten,' said the hunter. 'More than enough. But we shall go into the herds again tomorrow.' His eyes flickered beyond One Eye to the cave walls. 'Paint us luck, old man.'

Then he was gone and the storm broke, rain sheeting down and drumming off the taut animal hide tents below. The women moaned and cried and the men laughed and loved. One Eye sat in the darkness at the back of the cave and thought over and over of the ten dead animals he had drawn the day before.

Always it was the same. The number he drew was the number killed. And yet, he felt he had no real power. But one day *true* power over the paintings would come to one of the tribe, and then, from here to the seas in the south, beasts would be at the mercy of men – and men, perhaps, would no longer be at the mercy of the moving ice-wastes to the north. The tribe must never die, One Eye realized, not with the inherent power it contained, hidden somewhere in the bodies of its hunters.

*　　*　　*

With the breaking of the sun above the eastern horizon the boy came scrambling up to the shrine-cave. He found One Eye hard at work, drawing the shapes of hunters with a charred wood stick.

'Why don't you draw them full?' asked the boy as he sat, absorbed by the growing picture of a hunt. 'Why so thin? And black?'

'Men are black,' said One Eye mysteriously. Then, pausing to glance at the boy, he lifted his eye to the cave entrance. 'Inside ... we are thin and shallow.' His glance dropped to the boy. 'Beasts kill other beasts in a *natural* way. Man kills beasts with more than his hands. He uses spears and slings, and traps and nets. Man is more than a beast, but he has lost his goodness.' The old man looked at the coloured portraits of his animals. 'They have goodness and they are full and whole. But man is shallow.' He turned to the boy. 'That is why I draw the hunters thin.'

The boy did not understand the old man's talk. But he knew he was right. And when he, too, was a great painter, magicking animals into the traps, on to the spears, of his brothers, he would follow the tradition of One Eye.

'Let me draw. Please. Let me draw.'

One Eye muttered with annoyance but he passed the yellow and red pastes he had made that dawn. The boy dipped his fingers in and smudged the wall with yellow. With his left hand he used a charred stick to draw an outline around the smear. He remembered how the ribs of the bison stood out and he drew them in. He drew the legs and the way the muscles rippled with the power of the beast. One Eye concentrated on his own drawing, but again and again he glanced at the bison taking form at the hands of the boy. Finally he stopped and watched as his small apprentice drew a spear, thrust deep into the neck of the animal.

'It is good,' said One Eye. 'You have skill.' He smiled.

The boy beamed, 'May I draw a bear? Please?'

One Eye shook his head with finality. 'The bear is a hunter of man and he must never be drawn in the shrine-cave – he is beyond our magic.'

'A bear is just a beast,' argued the boy.

'The bear is *more* than a beast. We must only draw animals that *run* from man. Never those that attack him. Do you understand?'

The boy nodded, bitterly disappointed.

'Old man!' He Who Carries a Red Spear crawled into the cave. 'How many kills today, old man?' He sneered. 'You, down!' He looked angrily at his son and the boy left the cave. Red Spear raised a fist at One Eye. 'If I find him here too many more times I shall begin to think you are stopping him from being a great hunter, like me. I shall be forced to kill you ... hear me?'

He was gone before One Eye could answer. The hunters gathered together their spears and furs and walked from the cliff towards the plains where they would find bison and deer, and smaller animals to eat on the way home.

The boy, grinning, scampered back into the cave. One Eye ignored him, staying in the mouth of the cave, watching the distant figures and wishing he was going with them. Behind him he heard charred wood scrape on the wall. He ignored it. The scraping ended and there was silence. Eventually One Eye looked round. 'What do you draw, child?'

The boy said nothing but continued working. One Eye crawled over to him.

What he saw made him gasp with horror. He slapped the boy away from the wall and reached out to try and erase the fully-drawn man from the painting of the hunt.

'No!' cried the boy, but he fell silent. The ochre was too dry; only the arm was erased. One Eye sat and looked at the man with one arm. Then he looked at the bison with the spear in its neck. Then he looked at the boy and his face was white beneath its dusty covering.

When the hunt returned, one of the hunters was dead. They carried him in, stretched on a fur and laid across two poles. His left arm had been severed above the elbow and he had bled to death. One Eye heard the word 'bear' and he knew what had happened. Then his eye wandered to the kills of the day, to the bison still with a spear-head buried deep in its neck.

The women mourned that night. The hunter lay in a shallow pit at the edge of the camp and his wife rubbed ochre into his ice-cold body, groaning and keening with every pass of her hand across her dead husband's strong chest. The fire burned high in the still night and the faces of the children and women who squatted around its warmth were solemn and drawn. Red Spear sat apart from the tribe and time and again his eyes flicked up to the dark cave mouth, where he could see One Eye squatting, watching the gathering.

Suddenly he jumped towards the fire and kicked the burning wood. 'What happened to your magic today, old man?' he screamed up at the figure in the cave. 'Why didn't you save him?' He turned to look at the dead hunter, and there were tears in his eyes, but tears of frustrated anger rather than sorrow. 'He was a *good* hunter. He killed many beasts for the tribe. Nearly as many as me!' Swinging round he raised one clenched fist. 'If you can work magic Old Man, why couldn't you have saved him?'

A hunter jumped up from the ring and caught Red Spear by the shoulders. 'One Eye cannot know the unknowable! He merely spirits the animals into our traps!'

He Who Carries a Red Spear flung the man aside. 'He does *nothing!*' he cried angrily. 'We no longer need One Eye and his stupid paintings.'

As he ran through the circle of seated hunters and their women, a feminine hand reached out and tripped him. Furious, he twisted on the ground and reached for the woman who had insulted him. He stared into the calm face of his wife, brown eyes insolently watching him. 'Leave the old man,' she said softly. 'He does no harm and many here believe him possessed of magical power. Why waste energy and respect on killing the useless?' Her smile was the last straw in the cooling of angry fires in the hunter. He leered up at One Eye and shook his fist. But he spared him.

A wood torch burned in the shrine-cave. A wolf pack howled somewhere on the tundra, and as the night progressed so the sound of their baying moved farther away to the south. One Eye was oblivious to their cries, he was oblivious to the howling wind and the sound of rocks falling outside the cave mouth. He worked on his picture. The boy knelt beside him, watching. He had begged to be allowed to draw, but One Eye had said no, not yet. The anticipation kept the boy silent and now he watched as animals took shape upon the cave wall, overlapped animals that had been drawn in the past, but that did not matter because those animals had been killed and now they were just ochre smears, without meaning, without consequence.

As he worked, One Eye repeatedly glanced at the attentive boy. There was a strange look in the old man's eye, an expression of awe.

Well into the night, when the boy was beginning to yawn, One Eye sat back and handed the charred wood to his apprentice. Wrapped tightly in animals' skins, still One Eye shivered as he began to guide the boy's hand in the drawing of men on the wall scheme. The boy, with small furs round his shoulders, hardly noticed his chill. He was enthralled.

'Draw ... your father, here. That's right,' breathed One Eye as the boy's hand traced the pin shape. 'Arch the back, that's right. Throw the arms up ... no, don't stop ...'

'I don't understand . . .' murmured the boy.

'See,' explained the painter, 'see how he scares the bison into the traps – see, they run before him and he has no weapon. Red Spear *needs* no weapon.'

The boy nodded, satisfied, and continued the picture.

'Tomorrow,' said One Eye, 'I shall accompany the hunters. That surprises you?' His whiskered face broke into a smile at the expression on the boy's face. 'I used to be a hunter, long years ago. This hunt . . . see how it spreads across the wall. Tomorrow will be a *great* day for the tribe. There will be *many* kills . . .' His voice trailed off. 'Many kills. And I wish to join in on such an occasion. Now.' He guided the tiny hand to the wall. 'Draw me, here. See, standing *behind* your father. Draw me a spear. See how I throw it at the bison your father scares . . .'

Pin shapes took form upon the grey wall. The boy, excited, creating, drew as the old man instructed him. When it was finished he was beaming. One Eye was satisfied. The boy settled against the cave wall and One Eye looked at the picture of the hunt and dreamt of the kill that would be least expected toworrow. And by the boy's magic hand it had been depicted so! He closed his eyes and slept.

When he was sure One Eye was asleep, the boy crawled to the wall and picked up the charred wood. Carefully he drew more hunters. But he was tired and they didn't form as they should – they were too small, too stooped . . . like Grunts. Uncomfortable at what he had done, the boy smudged them away. They remained, shadows on the wall.

*   *   *

A fine mist hung over the grasslands as the hunters, followed by One Eye, moved off towards the grazing herds. There was the feel of snow in the air and the women had wrapped up tightly and insisted that their men put thicker skins around their shoulders, binding them into place with extra thongs. Silently, feet trudging across the cold, dewy grass, the band moved off, away from the cliff, and was swallowed by the mist.

The boy watched them go, and when they were out of sight he scrambled up to the shrine-cave and disappeared inside.

The hunters had moved silently across the mist-covered land for several hours when the first feelings of unease came to them. The fog was dense and they could see only a few paces around them. They grouped together and Red Spear motioned them to silence. One Eye watched him, breath steamy with the cold, as he pricked his ears to the low winds and listened.

There was movement all around them, shuffling, the sound of invisible feet padding across the frozen grass.

A stir went through the hunters. Was it Grunts, was it the squat and ugly men who lived in the shadow of the moving snow walls? Clutching

his red-ochred spear, Red Spear motioned for the band to move on.
One Eye, his own spear held, ready to stab, followed, but now his eye
was wide and watchful, his heart thundering. Grunts were unpredict-
able. They might pass by or they might attack. There was no way of
telling.

The hunters spread out as they neared where they could hear the
bison grazing. Still the wall of white separated them from anything that
lay ahead or behind. Each hunter was a vague grey shape as he moved
through the mist, spear held ready, head turning from side to side.
Behind them the sound of creatures grew louder.

'Look!' breathed a hunter close to One Eye. His voice caused them
all to stop and turn. What they saw made them howl with fear . . .

White shapes, running through the mist. Ghosts, shimmering and
flickering in and out of vision. Ghostly spears held high, mouths open in
a silent war cry. Grunts, spirits, the spirits of the ugly creatures that had
died at the hands of the hunters over the years gone by.

One Eye ran. He ran hard and he ran fast and he was aware of the
other hunters running beside him, breathing fast and hard, eyes wide
and constantly turned to regard the apparitions that pursued them.

All at once they were among the bison. Their approach, not the
most silent, had been muffled by the heavy air, and the animals were
taken by surprise. The huge black head of a male bison looked upon
One Eye, and the creature stood, for a moment, stunned. Then it
snorted and turned, scampering heavily away and out of sight.

From his left there came a scream and the sound of flesh torn. One
Eye moved over and saw the shape of a hunter spreadeagled on the
ground, being gored by the huge leader of the herd. And beyond the
sight of the man threshing against the veil of death, the white ghosts of
dead men came running through the fog.

One Eye staggered backwards, his head turning frantically from
right to left as he searched for a way out. The silent shapes were all
around and now he could see their tiny eyes, black orbs in the white of
their spectral faces. Their bodies were naked, squat and heavy, their
brows huge and jutting, giving them a peculiarly blind look.

They ran through the fog, and ghostly spears flew from ghostly
hands, sailing silently past the hunters and vanishing as they flew from
sight. The bison snorted and raged and ran amok among the terrified
hunters. One Eye came up to the steaming flank of a small animal, and
when it saw him it turned on him. He stabbed at it with his spear and
felt the point sink into flesh. The bison roared and thundered away.
One Eye stood alone, surrounded by the shifting wall of white. He could
see the ghosts moving closer, their bodies swaying as they neared him,
mouths open, screaming their silent screams of anger.

Behind him he heard the thunderous approach of a large bison and ran to avoid its maddened gallop. Distantly, a hunter screamed, and the scream was cut off as his life ended at the razor tip of a bison's horn. One Eye ran towards the scream, and as he ran he passed bewildered and terrified hunters who stood still, now, almost ready for the death that was overtaking so many of the tribe.

A bison snorted close by and lumbered out of the mist, its flank catching One Eye and sending him sprawling. As he staggered to his feet a new sound reached his ears. He paused, on his knees, breath coming short and painfully. There was blood on his tightly-wrapped fur breeches, but he felt no pain.

A throaty growl, like no sound he had ever heard in his life. And it was near, very near. A hunter screamed, and it was a scream of terror, not of death. One Eye jumped to his feet and crouched with his spear-point centred unwaveringly on where he could hear something big and cumbersome moving in his direction. The hunter who had screamed so loudly came running out of the mist, face smeared with blood and sweat, eyes open, mouth open. He carried no spear and ran past One Eye as if he hadn't seen him. He disappeared into the mist and a moment later One Eye heard a grunt and a gasp. The hunter reappeared, staggering, a red-ochred spear thrust deep into his belly.

The roar of the animal that approached came again, nearer. One Eye backed away carefully and his eye searched the fog for any sign of what it could be. The ghosts appeared again, dancing towards the lost hunters, and now they seemed almost ... taunting.

Behind One Eye there was the snort of a bison. He swung round but could see nothing. As he walked forward, ears keened for the sound of the beast behind him, he came to He Who Carries a Red Spear, standing with his back to One Eye, crouched and waiting for the bison to charge. One Eye could hear its snorting in the mist and realized that any moment it would tear into sight and Red Spear would either kill or be killed. But that could not be! Remembering how he had drawn the hunt, how he had spirited Red Spear's life into his own hands, One Eye edged forward.

He raised his spear high and threw it with all his strength at the centre of the leader's naked back. Red Spear screamed and arched over backwards, and One Eye saw two feet of spear protruding beyond the other man's chest. Naked, blood pumping down his glistening limbs, Red Spear lay dead at One Eye's feet.

A shadow fell across One Eye and, as he was about to defile the body with his hand axe, he froze. Straightening up, he became aware of the heavy breathing close behind, of the rumbling roar of a wild beast ...

'NO!' he screamed, flinging his body round and staring up at the black creature which towered over him. 'NO!' His hands flew to his face and he staggered backwards, tripping over the body of Red Spear. The monster lumbered forward, rising onto its hindlegs and reaching down with its front paws. Claws as long as a man's forearm glinted and slashed down at the painter, caught him just below his throat and ripped downwards, disembowelling him and throwing him twenty feet across the grass with a last jerk of a bloodstained paw. One Eye had a brief second to assess his killer. It was like a bear, yet so unlike a bear – the muzzle was long and twisted, the teeth too long, too white. The eyes, huge, staring, were the eyes of a dead man, not a living beast. And the fur... the fur was unlike the fur of any bear that One Eye had ever seen. It was black and red! Black and red!

Then there was only pain for One Eye, intense pain and the sight of his own blood and entrails seeping on to the grass. Followed by the blackness of death.

*   *   *

Crouched in the mouth of the shrine-cave, the boy shivered as black storm clouds skated overhead and icy winds whipped down from the northern ice-wastes, driving the mist before them, clearing the grass-lands to the eyes of the desperate women.

The hunters were late, very late. The women were frightened and they wailed. The fire burned high as a beacon for their men, and soon, tired and bloody, spearless and without a single kill between them, the few hunters that survived returned to the camp.

The boy crawled into the deep of the cave where a small fire burned and illuminated the drawings and paintings on the wall. He reached out a hand and traced the figure of his father, moving his finger to the outline of One Eye poised, ready to throw the spear. Then the boy's fingers traced the great bear that reared up on its hind legs, body finished with red ochre and black charred wood, teeth pearly white with root gum ... It had taken him a long time to draw and he was proud of it. That it was not a realistic likeness of one of the bears which roamed the tundra he was not to know, for he had never seen a bear.

He settled back and regarded the towering shape as it seemed to swoop on the little figure of One Eye, dancing among the smudges of the hunters the boy had drawn earlier.

The boy laughed as he reached out and smudged away the black drawing of his teacher. One Eye would not be coming back. The tribe had a new painter, now.

The Spectre Bridegroom
Washington Irving

'*He that supper for is dight,*
He lyes full cold, I trow, this night!
Yestreen to chamber I him led,
This night Gray-steel has made his bed!'
—*Sir Eger, Sir Grahame* and *Sir Gray-steel*

On the summit of one of the heights of the Odenwald, a wild and romantic tract of Upper Germany that lies not far from the confluence of the Main and the Rhine, there stood, many, many years since, the Castle of the Baron Von Landshort. It is now quite fallen to decay, and almost buried among beech trees and dark firs; above which, however, its old watch-tower may still be seen struggling, like the former possessor I have mentioned, to carry a high head, and look down upon a neighbouring country.

The Baron was a dry branch of the great family of Katzenellenbogen, and inherited the relics of the property and all the pride of his ancestors. Though the warlike disposition of his predecessors had much impaired the family possessions, yet the Baron still endeavoured to keep up some show of former state. The times were peaceable, and the German nobles, in general, had abandoned their inconvenient old castles, perched like eagles' nests among the mountains, and had built more convenient residences in the valleys; still the Baron remained proudly drawn up in his little fortress, cherishing with hereditary inveteracy all the old family feuds; so that he was on ill terms with some of his nearest neighbours, on account of disputes that had happened between their great-great-grandfathers.

The Baron had but one child, a daughter; but nature, when she grants but one child, always compensates by making it a prodigy; and so it was with the daughter of the Baron. All the nurses, gossips and country cousins, assured her father that she had not her equal for beauty in all Germany; and who should know better than they? She had, moreover, been brought up with great care, under the superintendence of two maiden aunts, who had spent some years of their early life at one of the little German courts, and were skilled in all the branches of knowledge necessary to the education of a fine lady. Under their instructions, she became a miracle of accomplishments. By the time she was eighteen she could embroider to admiration, and had worked whole histories of the saints in tapestry with such strength of expression in their countenances that they looked like so many souls in purgatory. She could read without great difficulty, and had spelled her way through several church legends, and almost all the chivalric wonders of the *Heldenbuch*. She had even made considerable proficiency in writing, could sign her own name without missing a letter, and so legibly that her aunts could read it without spectacles. She excelled in making little good-for-nothing ladylike knick-knacks of all kinds; was versed in the most abstruse dancing of the day; played a number of airs on the harp and guitar; and knew all the tender ballads of the *Minne-lieders* by heart.

Her aunts, too, having been great flirts and coquettes in their younger days, were admirably calculated to be vigilant guardians and strict censors of the conduct of their niece; for there is no duenna so rigidly prudent, and inexorably decorous, as a superannuated coquette. She was rarely suffered out of their sight; never went beyond the domains of the castle, unless well attended, or, rather, well watched; had continual lectures read to her about strict decorum and implicit obedience; and, as to the men – pah! she was taught to hold them at such distance and distrust that, unless properly authorized, she would not have cast a glance upon the handsomest cavalier in the world – no, not if he were even dying at her feet.

The good effects of this system were wonderfully apparent. The young lady was a pattern of docility and correctness. While others were wasting their sweetness in the glare of the world, and liable to be plucked and thrown aside by every hand, she was coyly blooming into fresh and lovely womanhood under the protection of those immaculate spinsters, like a rosebud blushing forth among guardian thorns. Her aunts looked upon her with pride and exultation, and vaunted that though all the other young ladies in the world might go astray, yet, thank Heaven, nothing of the kind could happen to the heiress of Katzenellenbogen.

But however scantily the Baron Von Landshort might be provided with children, his household was by no means a small one, for Providence had enriched him with abundance of poor relations. They, one and all, possessed the affectionate disposition common to humble relatives; were wonderfully attached to the Baron, and took every possible occasion to come in swarms and enliven the castle. All family festivals were commemorated by these good people at the Baron's expense; and when they were filled with good cheer, they would declare that there was nothing on earth so delightful as these family meetings, these jubilees of the heart.

The Baron, though a small man, had a large soul, and it swelled with satisfaction at the consciousness of being the greatest man in the little world about him. He loved to tell long stories about the stark old warriors whose portraits looked grimly down from the walls around, and he found no listeners equal to those who fed at his expense. He was much given to the marvellous, and a firm believer in all those supernatural tales with which every mountain and valley in Germany abounds. The faith of his guests even exceeded his own. They listened to every tale of wonder with open eyes and mouth, and never failed to be astonished, even though repeated for the hundredth time. Thus lived the Baron Von Landshort, the oracle of his table, the absolute monarch of his little territory, and happy, above all things, in the persuasion that he was the wisest man of the age.

At the time of which my story treats there was a great family gathering at the castle, on an affair of the utmost importance: it was to receive the destined bridegroom of the Baron's daughter. A negotiation had been carried on between the father and an old nobleman of Bavaria, to unite the dignity of their houses by the marriage of their children. The preliminaries had been conducted with proper punctilio. The young people were betrothed without seeing each other, and the time was appointed for the marriage ceremony. The young Count Von Altenburg had been recalled from the army for the purpose, and was actually on his way to the Baron's to receive his bride. Missives had even been received from him, from Wurtzburg, where he was accidentally detained, mentioning the day and hour when he might be expected to arrive.

The castle was in a tumult of preparation to give him a suitable welcome. The fair bride had been decked out with uncommon care. The two aunts had superintended her toilet, and quarrelled the whole morning about every article of her dress. The young lady had taken advantage of their contest to follow the bent of her own taste; and fortunately it was a good one. She looked as lovely as a youthful bridegroom could desire; and the flutter of expectation heightened the lustre of her charms.

The suffusions that mantled her face and neck, the gentle heaving of the bosom, the eye now and then lost in reverie, all betrayed the soft tumult that was going on in her little heart. The aunts were continually hovering around her; for maiden aunts are apt to take great interest in affairs of this nature: they were giving her a world of staid counsel, how to deport herself, what to say, and in what manner to receive the expected lover.

The Baron was no less busied in preparations. He had, in truth, nothing exactly to do; but he was naturally a fuming, bustling little man, and could not remain passive when all the world was in a hurry. He worried from top to bottom of the castle, with an air of infinite anxiety; he continually called the servants from their work to exhort them to be diligent, and buzzed about every hall and chamber, as idle, restless and importunate as a bluebottle fly on a warm summer's day.

In the meantime, the fatted calf had been killed; the forests had rung with the clamour of the huntsmen; the kitchen was crowded with good cheer; the cellars had yielded up whole oceans of *Rhein-wein* and *Ferne-wein*, and even the great Heidelberg Tun had been laid under contribution. Everything was ready to receive the distinguished guest with *Saus und Braus* in the true spirit of German hospitality – but the guest delayed to make his appearance. Hour rolled after hour. The sun that had poured his downward rays upon the rich forests of the Odenwald, now just gleamed along the summits of the mountains. The Baron mounted the highest tower, and strained his eyes in hopes of catching a distant sight of the Count and his attendants. Once he thought he beheld them; the sound of horns came floating from the valley, prolonged by the mountain echoes: a number of horsemen were seen far below, slowly advancing along the road; but when they had nearly reached the foot of the mountain they suddenly struck off in a different direction. The last ray of sunshine departed – the bats began to flit by in the twilight – the road grew dimmer and dimmer to the view; and nothing appeared stirring in it but now and then a peasant lagging homeward from his labour.

While the old castle of Landshort was in this state of perplexity, a very interesting scene was transacting in a different part of the Odenwald.

The young Count Von Altenburg was tranquilly pursuing his route in that sober jog-trot way in which a man travels towards matrimony when his friends have taken all the trouble and uncertainty of courtship off his hands, and a bride is waiting for him, as certainly as a dinner, at the end of his journey. He had encountered at Wurtzburg a youthful companion in arms, with whom he had seen some service on the frontiers: Herman Von Starkenfaust, one of the stoutest hands and worthiest hearts of German chivalry, who was now returning from the army. His father's castle was not far distant from the old fortress of Landshort, although a hereditary feud rendered the families hostile and strangers to each other.

In the warm-hearted moment of recognition, the young friends related all their past adventures and fortunes, and the Count gave the whole history of his intended nuptials with a young lady whom he had never seen, but of whose charms he had received the most enrapturing descriptions.

As the route of the friends lay in the same direction, they agreed to perform the rest of their journey together; and, that they might do it more leisurely, set off from Wurtzburg at an early hour, the Count having given directions for his retinue to follow and overtake him.

They beguiled their wayfaring with recollections of their military scenes and adventures; but the Count was apt to be a little tedious, now and then, about the reputed charms of his bride, and the felicity that awaited him.

In this way they had entered among the mountains of the Odenwald, and were traversing one of its most lonely and thickly wooded passes. It is well known that the forests of Germany have always been as much infested with robbers as its castles, by spectres; and, at this time, the former were particularly numerous, from the hordes of disbanded soldiers wandering about the country. It will not appear extraordinary, therefore, that the cavaliers were attacked by a gang of these stragglers in the midst of the forest. They defended themselves with bravery, but were nearly overpowered when the Count's retinue arrived to their assistance. At sight of them the robbers fled, but not until the Count had received a mortal wound. He was slowly and carefully conveyed back to the city of Wurtzburg, and a friar summoned from a neighbouring convent, who was famous for his skill in administering to both soul and body. But half of his skill was superfluous; the moments of the unfortunate Count were numbered.

With his dying breath he entreated his friend to repair instantly to the castle of Landshort, and explain the fatal cause of his not keeping his appointment with his bride. Though not the most ardent of lovers, he was one of the most punctilious of men, and appeared earnestly solicitous that his mission should be speedily and courteously executed. 'Unless this is done,' said he, 'I shall not sleep quietly in my grave!' He repeated these last words with peculiar solemnity. A request, at a moment so impressive, admitted no hesitation. Starkenfaust endeavoured to soothe him to calmness; promised faithfully to execute his wish, and gave him his hand in solemn pledge. The dying man pressed it in acknowledgment, but soon lapsed into delirium – raved about his bride – his engagement – his plighted word; ordered his horse, that he might ride to the castle of Landshort, and expired in the fancied act of vaulting into the saddle.

Starkenfaust bestowed a sigh and a soldier's tear on the untimely fate of his comrade; and then pondered on the awkward mission he had undertaken. His heart was heavy, and his head perplexed; for he was to present himself an unbidden guest among hostile people, and to damp their festivity with tidings fatal to their hopes. Still there was certain whisperings of curiosity in his bosom to see this far-famed beauty of Katzenellenbogen so cautiously shut up from the world; for he was a passionate admirer of the sex, and there was a dash of eccentricity and enterprise in his character that made him fond of all singular adventure.

Previous to his departure, he made all due arrangements with the holy fraternity of the convent for the funeral solemnities of his friend, who was to be buried in the cathedral of Wurtzburg, near some of his illustrious relatives; and the mourning retinue of the Count took charge of his remains.

It is now high time that we should return to the ancient family of Katzenellenbogen, who were impatient for their guest, and still more for their dinner; and to the worthy little Baron, whom we left airing himself on the watch-tower.

Night closed in, but still no guest arrived. The Baron descended from the tower in despair. The banquet, which had been delayed from hour to hour, could no longer be postponed. The meats were already overdone, the cook in an agony, and the whole household had the look of a garrison that had been reduced by famine. The Baron was obliged reluctantly to give orders for the feast without the presence of the guest. All were seated at table, and just on the point of commencing, when the sound of a horn from without the gate gave notice of the approach of a stranger. Another long blast filled the old courts of the castle with its echoes, and was answered by the warder from the walls. The Baron hastened to receive his future son-in-law.

The drawbridge had been let down, and the stranger was before the gate. He was a tall gallant cavalier, mounted on a black steed. His countenance was pale, but he had a beaming, romantic eye, and an air of stately melancholy. The Baron was a little mortified that he should have come in this simple, solitary style. His dignity for a moment was ruffled, and he felt disposed to consider it a want of proper respect for the important occasion, and the important family with which he was to be connected. He pacified himself, however, with the conclusion that it must have been youthful impatience which had induced him thus to spur on sooner than his attendants.

'I am sorry,' said the stranger, 'to break in upon you thus unseasonably——'

Here the Baron interrupted him with a world of compliments and greetings; for, to tell the truth, he prided himself upon his courtesy and his eloquence. The stranger attempted, once or twice, to stem the torrent of words, but in vain; so he bowed his head and suffered it to flow on. By the time the Baron had come to a pause they had reached the inner court of the castle; and the stranger was again about to speak, when he was once more interrupted by the appearance of the female part of the family, leading forth the shrinking and blushing bride. He gazed on her for a moment as one entranced; it seemed as if his whole soul beamed forth in the gaze, and rested upon that lovely form. One of the maiden aunts whispered something in her ear; she made an effort to speak; her moist blue eye was timidly raised, gave a shy glance of enquiry on the stranger, and was cast again to the ground. The words died away; but there was a sweet smile playing about her lips, and a soft dimpling of the cheek, that showed her glance had not been unsatisfactory. It was impossible for a girl of the fond age of eighteen, highly predisposed for love and matrimony, not to be pleased with so gallant a cavalier.

The late hour at which the guest had arrived left no time for parley. The Baron was peremptory, and deferred all particular conversation until the morning, and led the way to the untasted banquet.

It was served up in the great hall of the castle. Around the walls hung the hard-favoured portraits of the heroes of the house of Katzenellenbogen, and the trophies which they had gained in the field and in the chase. Hacked corselets, splintered jousting spears, and tattered banners were mingled with the spoils of sylvan warfare: the jaws of the wolf and the tusks of the boar grinned horribly among crossbows and battleaxes, and a huge pair of antlers branched immediately over the head of the youthful bridegroom.

The cavalier took but little notice of the company or the entertainment. He scarcely tasted the banquet, but seemed absorbed in admiration of his bride. He conversed in a low tone, that could not be overheard – for the language of love is never loud; but where is the female ear so dull that it cannot catch the softest whisper of the lover? There was a mingled tenderness and gravity in his manner that appeared to have a powerful effect upon the young lady. Her colour came and went, as she listened with deep attention. Now and then she made some blushing reply, and when his eye was turned away she would steal a sidelong glance at his romantic countenance, and heave a gentle sigh of tender happiness. It was evident that the young couple were completely enamoured. The aunts, who were deeply versed in the mysteries of the heart, declared that they had fallen in love with each other at first sight.

The feast went on merrily, or at least noisily, for the guests were all blessed with those keen appetites that attend upon light purses and mountain air. The Baron told his best and longest stories, and never had he told them so well, or with such great effect. If there was anything marvellous, his auditors were lost in astonishment; and if anything facetious, they were sure to laugh exactly in the right place. The Baron, it is true, like most great men, was too dignified to utter any joke but a dull one: it was always enforced, however, by a bumper of excellent *Hoch-heimer*; and even a dull joke, at one's own table, served up with jolly old wine, is irresistible. Many good things were said by poorer and keener wits that would not bear repeating, except on similar occasions; many sly speeches whispered in ladies' ears that almost convulsed them with suppressed laughter; and a song or two roared out by a poor, but merry and broad-faced cousin of the Baron, that absolutely made the maiden aunts hold up their fans.

Amid all this revelry, the stranger-guest maintained a most singular and unseasonable gravity. His countenance assumed a deeper cast of dejection as the evening advanced, and, strange as it may appear, even the Baron's jokes seemed only to render him the more melancholy. At times he was lost in thought, and at times there was a perturbed and restless wandering of the eye that bespoke a mind but ill at ease. His conversation with the bride became more and more earnest and mysterious. Lowering clouds began to steal over the fair serenity of her brow, and tremors to run through her tender frame.

All this could not escape the notice of the company. Their gaiety was chilled by the unaccountable gloom of the bridegroom; their spirits were infected; whispers and glances were interchanged, accompanied by shrugs and dubious shakes of the head. The song and the laugh grew less and less frequent, there were dreary pauses in the conversation, which were at length succeeded by wild tales and supernatural legends. One dismal story produced another still more dismal, and the Baron nearly frightened some of the ladies into hysterics with the history of the goblin horseman that carried away the fair Leonora – a dreadful, but true story, which has since been put into excellent verse, and is read and believed by all the world.

The bridegroom listened to this tale with profound attention. He kept his eyes steadily fixed on the Baron and, as the story drew to a close, began gradually to rise from his seat, growing taller and taller, until, in the Baron's entranced eye, he seemed almost to tower into a giant. The moment the tale was finished, he heaved a deep sigh, and took a solemn farewell of the company. They were all amazement. The Baron was perfectly thunderstruck.

'What! going to leave the castle at midnight? Why, everything is prepared for your reception; a chamber is ready for you if you wish to retire.'

The stranger shook his head mournfully and mysteriously: 'I must lay my head in a different chamber tonight!'

There was something in this reply, and the tone in which it was uttered, that made the Baron's heart misgive him; but he rallied his forces, and repeated his hospitable entreaties. The stranger shook his head silently, but positively, at every offer; and, waving his farewell to the company, stalked slowly out of the hall. The maiden aunts were absolutely petrified – the bride hung her head, and a tear stole to her eye.

The Baron followed the stranger to the great court of the castle, where the black charger stood pawing the earth and snorting with impatience. When they had reached the portal, whose deep archway was dimly lighted by a cresset, the stranger paused, and addressed the Baron in a hollow tone of voice, which the vaulted roof rendered still more sepulchral. 'Now that we are alone,' said he, 'I will impart to you the reason of my going. I have a solemn, an indispensable engagement——'

'Why,' said the Baron, 'cannot you send someone in your place?'

'It admits of no substitute – I must attend it in person – I must away to Wurtzburg cathedral——'

'Ay,' said the Baron, plucking up spirit, 'but not until tomorrow – tomorrow you shall take your bride there.'

'No! no!' replied the stranger, with tenfold solemnity, 'my engagement is with no bride – the worms! the worms expect me! I am a dead man – I have been slain by robbers – my body lies at Wurtzburg – at midnight I am to be buried – the grave is waiting for me – I must keep my appointment!'

He sprang on his black charger, dashed over the drawbridge, and the clattering of his horse's hoofs was lost in the whistling of the night-blast.

The Baron returned to the hall in the utmost consternation, and related what had passed. Two ladies fainted outright; others sickened at the idea of having banqueted with a spectre. It was the opinion of some that this might be the wild huntsman famous in German legend. Some talked of mountain sprites, of wood-demons, and of other supernatural beings, with which the good people of Germany have been so grievously harassed since time immemorial. One of the poor relations ventured to suggest that it might be some sportive evasion of the young cavalier, and that the very gloominess of the caprice seemed to accord with so melancholy a personage. This, however, drew on him the indignation of the whole company, and especially of the Baron, who looked upon him as little better than an infidel; so that he was fain to abjure his heresy as speedily as possible, and come into the faith of the true believers.

But, whatever may have been the doubts entertained, they were completely put to an end by the arrival, next day, of regular missives confirming the intelligence of the young Count's murder, and his interment in Wurtzburg cathedral.

The dismay at the castle may well be imagined. The Baron shut himself up in his chamber. The guests who had come to rejoice with him could not think of abandoning him in his distress. They wandered about the courts, or collected in groups in the hall, shaking their heads and shrugging their shoulders at the troubles of so good a man; and sat longer than ever at table, and ate and drank more stoutly than ever, by way of keeping up their spirits. But the situation of the widowed bride was the most pitiable. To have lost a husband before she had even embraced him

– and such a husband! If the very spectre could be so gracious and noble, what must have been the living man? She filled the house with lamentations.

On the night of the second day of her widowhood, she had retired to her chamber, accompanied by one of her aunts, who insisted on sleeping with her. The aunt, who was one of the best tellers of ghost stories in all Germany, had just been recounting one of her longest, and had fallen asleep in the very midst of it. The chamber was remote, and overlooked a small garden. The niece lay pensively gazing at the beams of the rising moon, as they trembled on the leaves of an aspen tree before the lattice. The castle clock had just told midnight, when a soft strain of music stole up from the garden. She rose hastily from her bed and stepped lightly to the window. A tall figure stood among the shadows of the trees. As it raised its head, a beam of moonlight fell upon the countenance. Heaven and earth! She beheld the Spectre Bridegroom! A loud shriek at that moment burst upon her ear, and her aunt, who had been awakened by the music, and had followed her silently to the window, fell into her arms. When she looked again, the spectre had disappeared.

Of the two females, the aunt now required the most soothing, for she was perfectly beside herself with terror. As to the young lady, there was something, even in the spectre of her lover, that seemed endearing. There was still the semblance of manly beauty; and though the shadow of a man is but little calculated to satisfy the affections of a lovesick girl, yet, where the substance is not to be had, even that is consoling. The aunt declared that she would never sleep in that chamber again; the niece, for once, was refractory, and declared as strongly that she would sleep in no other in the castle: the consequence was that she had to sleep in it alone; but she drew a promise from her aunt not to relate the story of the spectre, lest she should be denied the only melancholy pleasure left her on earth – that of inhabiting the chamber over which the guardian shade of her lover kept its nightly vigils.

How long the good old lady would have observed this promise is uncertain, for she dearly loved to talk of the marvellous, and there is a triumph in being the first to tell a frightful story; it is, however, still quoted in the neighbourhood, as a memorable instance of female secrecy, that she kept it to herself for a whole week; when she was suddenly absolved from all further restraint by intelligence brought to the breakfast-table one morning that the young lady was not to be found. Her room was empty – the bed had not been slept in – the window was open – and the bird had flown!

The astonishment and concern with which the intelligence was received can only be imagined by those who have witnessed the agitation which the mishaps of a great man cause among his friends. Even the poor relations paused for a moment from the indefatigable labours of the trencher; when the aunt, who had at first been struck speechless, wrung her hands and shrieked out, 'The goblin! the goblin! She's carried away by the goblin!'

In a few words she related the fearful scene of the garden, and concluded that the spectre must have carried off his bride. Two of the domestics corroborated the opinion, for they had heard the clattering of a horse's hoofs down the mountain about midnight, and had no doubt that it was the spectre on his black charger, bearing her away to the tomb. All present were struck with the direful probability; for events of the kind are extremely common in Germany, as many well-authenticated histories bear witness.

What a lamentable situation was that of the poor Baron! What a heartrending dilemma for a fond father, and a member of the great family of Katzenellenbogen! His only daughter had either been rapt away to the grave, or he was to have some wood-demon for a son-in-law and, perchance, a troop of goblin grandchildren. As usual, he was completely bewildered, and all the castle in an uproar. The men were ordered to take horse and scour every road and path and glen of the Odenwald. The Baron himself had just drawn on his jack-boots, girded on his sword, and was about to mount his steed to sally forth on the doubtful quest, when he was brought to a pause by a new apparition. A lady was seen approaching the castle, mounted on a palfrey attended by a cavalier on horseback. She galloped up to the gate, sprang from her horse, and falling at the Baron's feet, embraced his knees. It was his lost daughter, and her companion – the Spectre Bridegroom! The Baron was astounded. He looked at his daughter, then at the spectre, and almost doubted the evidence of his senses. The latter, too, was wonderfully improved in his appearance, since his visit to the world of spirits. His dress was splendid, and set off a noble figure of manly symmetry. He was no longer pale and melancholy. His fine countenance was flushed with the glow of youth, and joy rioted in his large dark eye.

The mystery was soon cleared up. The cavalier (for, in truth, as you must have known all the while, he was no goblin) announced himself as Sir Herman Von Starkenfaust. He related his adventure with the young Count. He told how he had hastened to the castle to deliver the unwelcome tidings, but that the eloquence of the Baron had interrupted him in every attempt to tell his tale. How the sight of the bride had completely captivated him, and that to pass a few hours near her he had tacitly suffered the mistake to continue. How he had been sorely perplexed in what way to make a decent retreat, until the Baron's goblin stories had suggested his eccentric exit. How, fearing the feudal hostility of the family, he had repeated his visits by stealth – had haunted the garden beneath the young lady's window – had wooed – had won – had borne away in triumph – and, in a word, had wedded, the fair.

Under any other circumstances the Baron would have been inflexible, for he was tenacious of paternal authority and devoutly obstinate in all family feuds; but he loved his daughter; he had lamented her as lost; he rejoiced to find her still alive; and, though her husband was of a hostile house, yet, thank heaven, he was not a goblin. There was something, it must be acknowledged, that did not exactly accord with his notions of strict veracity, in the joke the knight had passed upon him of his being a dead man; but several old friends present, who had served in the wars, assured him that every stratagem was excusable in love, and that the cavalier was entitled to especial privilege, having lately served as a trooper.

Matters, therefore, were happily arranged. The Baron pardoned the young couple on the spot. The revels at the castle were resumed. The poor relations overwhelmed this new member of the family with loving-kindness; he was so gallant, so generous – and so rich. The aunts, it is true, were somewhat scandalized that their system of strict seclusion and passive obedience should be so badly exemplified, but attributed all to their negligence in not having the windows grated. One of them was particularly mortified at having her marvellous story marred, and that the only spectre she had ever seen should turn out a counterfeit; but the niece seemed perfectly happy at having found him substantial flesh and blood – and so the story ends.

Lost Hearts

M. R. James

It was, as far as I can ascertain, in September of the year 1811 that a post-chaise drew up before the door of Aswarby Hall, in the heart of Lincolnshire. The little boy who was the only passenger in the chaise, and who jumped out as soon as it had stopped, looked about him with the keenest curiosity during the short interval that elapsed between the ringing of the bell and the opening of the hall door. He saw a tall, square, red-brick house, built in the reign of Anne; a stone-pillared porch had been added in the purer classical style of 1790; the windows of the house were many, tall and narrow, with small panes and thick white woodwork. A pediment, pierced with a round window, crowned the front. There were wings to right and left, connected by curious glazed galleries, supported by colonnades, with the central block. These wings plainly contained the stables and offices of the house. Each was surmounted by an ornamental cupola with a gilded vane.

An evening light shone on the building, making the window-panes glow like so many fires. Away from the Hall in front stretched a flat park studded with oaks and fringed with firs, which stood out against the sky. The clock in the church tower, buried in trees on the edge of the park, only its golden weather-cock catching the light, was striking six, and the sound came gently beating down the wind. It was altogether a pleasant impression, though tinged with the sort of melancholy appropriate to an evening in early autumn, that was conveyed to the mind of the boy who was standing in the porch waiting for the door to open to him.

The post-chaise had brought him from Warwickshire, where, some six months before, he had been left an orphan. Now, owing to the generous offer of his elderly cousin, Mr Abney, he had come to live at Aswarby. The offer was unexpected, because all who knew anything of Mr Abney looked upon him as a somewhat austere recluse, into whose steady-going household the advent of a small boy would import a new and, it seemed, incongruous element. The truth is that very little was known of Mr Abney's pursuits or temper. The Professor of Greek at

Cambridge had been heard to say that no one knew more of the religious beliefs of the later pagans than did the owner of Aswarby. Certainly his library contained all the then available books bearing on the Mysteries, the Orphic poems, the worship of Mithras, and the Neo-Platonists. In the marble-paved hall stood a fine group of Mithras slaying a bull, which had been inherited from the Levant at great expense by the owner. He had contributed a description of it to the *Gentleman's Magazine*, and he had written a remarkable series of articles in the *Critical Museum* on the superstitions of the Romans of the Lower Empire. He was looked upon, in fine, as a man wrapped up in his books, and it was a matter of great surprise among his neighbours that he should ever have heard of his orphan cousin, Stephen Elliott, much more that he should have volunteered to make him an inmate of Aswarby Hall.

Whatever may have been expected by his neighbours, it is certain that Mr Abney – the tall, the thin, the austere – seemed inclined to give his young cousin a kindly reception. The moment the front door was opened he darted out of his study, rubbing his hands with delight.

'How are you, my boy? – how are you? How old are you?' said he – 'that is, you are not too much tired, I hope, by your journey to eat your supper?'

'No, thank you sir,' said Master Elliott; 'I am pretty well.'

'That's a good lad,' said Mr Abney. 'And how old are you, my boy?'

It seemed a little odd that he should have asked the question twice in the first two minutes of their acquaintance.

'I'm twelve years old next birthday, sir,' said Stephen.

'And when is your birthday, my dear boy? Eleventh of September, eh? That's well – that's very well. Nearly a year hence, isn't it? I like – ha, ha! – I like to get these things down in my book. Sure it's twelve? Certain?'

'Yes, quite sure, sir.'

'Well, well! Take him to Mrs Bunch's room, Parkes, and let him have his tea – supper – whatever it is.'

'Yes, sir,' answered the staid Mr Parkes; and conducted Stephen to the lower regions.

Mrs Bunch was the most comfortable and human person whom Stephen had as yet met in Aswarby. She made him completely at home; they were great friends in a quarter of an hour; and great friends they remained. Mrs Bunch had been born in the neighbourhood some fifty-five years before the date of Stephen's arrival, and her residence at the Hall was of twenty years' standing. Consequently, if anyone knew the ins and outs of the house and the district, Mrs Bunch knew them; and she was by no means disinclined to communicate her information.

Certainly there were plenty of things about the Hall and the Hall gardens which Stephen, who was of an adventurous and enquiring turn, was anxious to have explained to him. 'Who built the temple at the end of the laurel walk? Who was the old man whose picture hung on the staircase, sitting at a table, with a skull under his hand?' These and many similar points were cleared up by the resources of Mrs Bunch's powerful intellect. There were others, however, of which the explanations furnished were less satisfactory.

One November evening Stephen was sitting by the fire in the housekeeper's room reflecting on his surroundings.

'Is Mr Abney a good man, and will he go to heaven?' he suddenly asked, with the peculiar confidence which children possess in the ability of their elders to settle these questions, the decision of which is believed to be reserved for other tribunals.

'Good? – bless the child?' said Mrs Bunch. 'Master's as kind a soul as ever I see! Didn't I never tell you of the little boy as he took in out of the street, as you may say, this seven years back? and the little girl, two years after I first come here?'

'No. Do tell me all about them, Mrs Bunch – now this minute!'

'Well,' said Mrs Bunch, 'the little girl I don't seem to recollect so much about. I know master brought her back with him from his walk one day, and give orders to Mrs Ellis, as was housekeeper then, as she should be took every care with. And the pore child hadn't no one belonging to her – she told me so her own self – and here she lived with us a matter of three weeks it might be; and then, whether she were something of a gypsy in her blood or what not, but one morning she out of her bed afore any of us had opened a eye, and neither track nor yet trace of her have I set eyes on since. Master was wonderful put about, and had all the ponds dragged; but it's my belief she was had away by them gipsies, for there was singing round the house for as much as an hour the night she went, and Parkes, he declare as he heard them a-calling in the woods all that afternoon. Dear, dear! a hodd child she was, so silent in her ways and all, but I was wonderful taken up with her, so domesticated she was – surprising.'

'And what about the little boy?' said Stephen.

'Ah, that pore boy!' sighed Mrs Bunch. 'He were a foreigner – Jevanny he called hisself – and he come a-tweaking his 'urdy-gurdy round and about the drive one winter day, and master 'ad him in that minute, and ast all about where he came from, and how old he was, and how he made his way, and where was his relatives, and all as kind as heart could wish. But it went the same way with him. They're a hunruly lot, them foreign nations, I do suppose, and he was off one fine morning just the same as the girl. Why he went and what he done was our question for as much as a year after; for he never took his 'urdy-gurdy, and there it lays on the shelf.'

The remainder of the evening was spent by Stephen in miscellaneous cross-examination of Mrs Bunch and in efforts to extract a tune from the hurdy-gurdy.

That night he had a curious dream. At the end of the passage at the top of the house, in which his bedroom was situated, there was an old disused bathroom. It was kept locked, but the upper half of the door was glazed, and, since the muslin curtains which used to hang there had long been gone, you could look in and see the lead-lined bath affixed to the wall on the right hand, with its head towards the window.

On the night of which I am speaking, Stephen Elliott found himself, as he thought, looking through the glazed door. The moon was shining through the window, and he was gazing at a figure which lay in the bath.

His description of what he saw reminds me of what I once beheld myself in the famous vaults of St Michan's Church in Dublin, which possesses the horrid property of preserving corpses from decay for centuries. A figure inexpressibly thin and pathetic, of a dusty leaden colour, enveloped in a shroud-like garment, the thin lips crooked into a faint and dreadful smile, the hands pressed tightly over the region of the heart.

As he looked upon it, a distant, almost inaudible moan seemed to issue from its lips, and the arms began to stir. The terror of the sight forced Stephen backwards and he awoke to the fact that he was indeed standing on the cold boarded floor of the passage in the full light of the moon. With a courage which I do not think can be common among boys of his age, he went to the door of the bathroom to ascertain if the figure of his dream were really there. It was not, and he went back to bed.

Mrs Bunch was much impressed next morning by his story, and went so far as to replace the muslin curtain over the glazed door of the bathroom. Mr Abney, moreover, to whom he confided his experiences at breakfast, was greatly interested, and made notes of the matter in what he called 'his book'.

The spring equinox was approaching, as Mr Abney frequently reminded his cousin, adding that this had been always considered by the ancients to be a critical time for the young: that Stephen would do well to take care of himself, and to shut his bedroom window at night; and that Censorinus had some valuable remarks on the subject. Two incidents that occurred about this time made an impression upon Stephen's mind.

The first was after an unusually uneasy and oppressed night that he had passed – though he could not recall any particular dream that he had had.

The following evening Mrs Bunch was occupying herself in mending his nightgown.

'Gracious me, Master Stephen!' she broke forth rather irritably, 'how do you manage to tear your nightdress all to flinders this way? Look here, sir, what trouble you do give to poor servants that have to darn and mend after you!'

There was indeed a most destructive and apparently wanton series of slits or scorings in the garment, which would undoubtedly require a skilful needle to make good. They were confined to the left side of the chest – long, parallel slits, about six inches in length, some of them not quite piercing the texture of the linen. Stephen could only express his entire ignorance of their origin: he was sure they were not there the night before.

'But,' he said, 'Mrs Bunch, they are just the same as the scratches on the outside of my bedroom door: and I'm sure I never had anything to do with making *them*.'

Mrs Bunch gazed at him open-mouthed, then snatched up a candle, departed hastily from the room, and was heard making her way upstairs. In a few minutes she came down.

'Well,' she said, 'Master Stephen, it's a funny thing to me how them marks and scratches can 'a' come there – too high up for any cat or dog to 'ave made 'em, much less a rat: for all the world like a Chinaman's finger-nails, as my uncle in the tea trade used to tell us of when we was girls together. I wouldn't say nothing to master, not if I was you, Master Stephen, my dear; and just turn the key of the door when you go to your bed.'

'I always do, Mrs Bunch, as soon as I've said my prayers.'

'Ah, that's a good child: always say your prayers, and then no one can't hurt you.'

Herewith Mrs Bunch addressed herself to mending the injured nightgown, with intervals of meditation, until bedtime. This was on a Friday night in March 1812.

On the following evening the usual duet of Stephen and Mrs Bunch was augmented by the sudden arrival of Mr Parkes, the butler, who as a rule kept himself rather to himself in his own pantry. He did not see that Stephen was there: he was, moreover, flustered and less slow of speech than was his wont.

'Master may get up his own wine, if he likes, of an evening,' was his first remark. 'Either I do it in the daytime or not at all, Mrs Bunch. I don't know what it may be: very like it's the rats, or the wind got into the cellars; but I'm not so young as I was, and I can't go through with it as I have done.'

'Well, Mr Parkes, you know it is a surprising place for the rats, is the Hall.'

'I'm not denying that, Mrs Bunch; and, to be sure, many a time I've heard the tale from the men in the shipyards about the rat that could speak. I never laid no confidence in that before; but tonight, if I'd demeaned myself to lay my ear to the door of the further bin, I could pretty much have heard what they was saying.'

'Oh, there, Mr Parkes, I've no patience with your fancies! Rats talking in the wine-cellar indeed!'

'Well, Mrs Bunch, I've no wish to argue with you: all I say is, if you choose to go to the far bin, and lay your ear to the door, you may prove my words this minute.'

'What nonsense you do talk, Mr Parkes – not fit for children to listen to! Why, you'll be frightening Master Stephen there out of his wits.'

'What! Master Stephen?' said Parkes, awaking to the consciousness of the boy's presence. 'Master Stephen knows well enough when I'm a-playing a joke with you, Mrs Bunch.'

In fact, Master Stephen knew much too well to suppose that Mr Parkes had in the first instance intended a joke. He was interested, not altogether pleasantly, in the situation; but all his questions were unsuccessful in inducing the butler to give any more detailed account of his experiences in the wine-cellar.

*   *   *

We have now arrived at March 24th 1812. It was a day of curious experiences for Stephen: a windy, noisy day, which filled the house and the gardens with a restless impression. As Stephen stood by the fence of the grounds, and looked out into the park, he felt as if an endless procession of unseen people were sweeping past him on the wind, borne on resistlessly and aimlessly, vainly striving to stop themselves, to catch at something that might arrest their flight and bring them once again into contact with the living world of which they had formed a part. After luncheon that day Mr Abney said:

'Stephen, my boy, do you think you could manage to come to me tonight as late as eleven o'clock in my study? I shall be busy until that time, and I wish to show you something connected with your future life which it is most important that you should know. You are not to mention this matter to Mrs Bunch nor to anyone else in the house; and you had better go to your room at the usual time.'

Here was a new excitement added to life: Stephen eagerly grasped at the opportunity of sitting up till eleven o'clock. He looked in at the library door on his way upstairs that evening, and saw a brazier, which He had often noticed in the corner of the room, moved out before the fire: an old silver-gilt cup stood on the table, filled with red wine, and some written sheets of paper lay near it. Mr Abney was sprinkling some incense on the brazier from a round silver box as Stephen passed, but did not seem to notice his step.

The wind had fallen, and there was a still night and a full moon. At about ten o'clock Stephen was standing at the open window of his bedroom, looking out over the country. Still as the night was, the mysterious population of the distant moon-lit woods was not yet lulled to rest. From time to time strange cries as of lost and despairing wanderers sounded from across the mere. They might be the notes of owls or water-birds, yet they did not quite resemble either sound. Were not they coming nearer? Now they sounded from the nearer side of the water, and in a few moments they seemed to be floating about among the shrubberies. Then they ceased; but just as Stephen was thinking of shutting the window and resuming his reading of *Robinson Crusoe,* he caught sight of two figures standing on the gravelled terrace that ran along the garden side of the Hall – the figures of a boy and a girl, as it seemed; they stood side by side, looking up at the windows. Something in the form of the girl recalled irresistibly his dream of the figure in the bath. The boy inspired him with more acute fear.

Whilst the girl stood still, half smiling, with her hands clasped over her heart, the boy, a thin shape, with black hair and ragged clothing, raised his arms in the air with an appearance of menace and of unappeasable hunger and longing. The moon shone upon his almost transparent hands, and Stephen saw that the nails were fearfully long and that the light shone through them. As he stood with his arms thus raised, he disclosed a terrifying spectacle. On the left side of his chest there opened a black and gaping rent; and there fell upon Stephen's brain, rather than upon his ear, the impression of one of those hungry and desolate cries that he had heard resounding over the woods of Aswarby all that evening. In another moment this dreadful pair had moved swiftly and noiselessly over the dry gravel, and he saw them no more.

Inexpressibly frightened as he was, he determined to take his candle and go down to Mr Abney's study, for the hour appointed for their meeting was near at hand. The study or library opened out of the front hall on one side, and Stephen, urged on by his terrors, did not take long in getting there. To effect an entrance was not so easy. It was not locked, he felt sure, for the key was on the outside of the door as usual. His repeated knocks produced no answer. Mr Abney was engaged: he was speaking. What! why did he try to cry out? and why was the cry choked in his throat? Had he, too, seen the mysterious children? But now everything was quiet, and the door yielded to Stephen's terrified and frantic pushing.

*   *   *

On the table in Mr Abney's study certain papers were found which explained the situation to Stephen Elliott when he was of an age to understand them. The most important sentences were as follows:

'It was a belief very strongly and generally held by the ancients – of whose wisdom in these matters I have had such experience as induces me to place confidence in their assertions – that by enacting certain processes, which to us moderns have something of a barbaric complexion, a very remarkable enlightenment of the spiritual faculties in man may be attained: that, for example, by absorbing the personalities of a certain number of his fellow creatures, an individual may gain a complete ascendancy over those orders of spiritual beings which control the elemental forces of our universe.

'It is recorded of Simon Magnus that he was able to fly in the air, to become invisible, or to assume any form he pleased, by the agency of the soul of a boy whom, to use the libellous phrase employed by the author of the *Clementine Recognitions*, he had "murdered". I find it set down, moreover, with considerable detail in the writings of Hermes Trismegistus, that similar happy results may be produced by the absorption of the hearts of not less than three human beings below the age of twenty-one years. To the testing of the truth of this receipt I have devoted the greater part of the last twenty years, selecting as the *corpora vilia* of my experiment such persons as could conveniently be removed without occasioning a sensible gap in society. The first step I effected by the removal of one Phoebe Stanley, a girl of gipsy extraction, on March 24th 1792. The second, by the removal of a wandering Italian lad, named Giovanni Paoli, on the night of March 23rd 1805. The final "victim" – to employ a word repugnant in the highest degree to my feelings – must be my cousin, Stephen Elliott. His day must be this March 24th 1812.

'The best means of effecting the required absorption is to remove the heart from the *living* subject, to reduce it to ashes, and to mingle them with about a pint of some red wine, preferably port. The remains of the first two subjects, at least, it will be well to conceal: a disused bathroom or wine-cellar will be found convenient for such a purpose. Some annoyance may be experienced from the psychic portion of the subjects, which the popular language dignifies with the name of ghosts. But the man of philosophic temperament – to whom alone the experiment is appropriate – will be little prone to attach importance to the feeble efforts of these beings to wreak their vengeance on him. I contemplate with the liveliest satisfaction the enlarged and emancipated existence which the experiment, if successful, will confer on me; not only placing me beyond the reach of human justice (so-called), but eliminating to a great extent the prospect of death itself.'

*   *   *

Mr Abney was found in his chair, his head thrown back, his face stamped with an expression of rage, fright, and mortal pain. In his left side was a terrible lacerated wound, exposing the heart. There was no blood on his hands, and a long knife that lay on the table was perfectly clean. A savage wildcat might have inflicted the injuries. The window of the study was open, and it was the opinion of the coroner that Mr Abney had met his death by the agency of some wild creature. But Stephen Elliott's study of the papers I have quoted led him to a very different conclusion.

Carnival on the Downs
Gerald Kersh

We are a queer people: I do not know what to make of us. Whatever anyone says for us is right; whatever anyone says against us is right. A conservative people, we would turn out our pockets for a rebel; and prim as we are, we love an eccentric.

We are an eccentric people. For example: we make a cult of cold baths – and of our lack of plumbing – and a boast of such characters as Dirty Dick of Bishopsgate, and Mr Lagg who is landlord of The White Swan at Wettendene.

Dirty Dick of Bishopsgate had a public house, and was a dandy, once upon a time. But it seems that on the eve of his marriage to a girl with whom he was in love he was jilted, with the wedding breakfast on the table. Thereafter, everything had, by his order, to be left exactly as it was on that fatal morning. The great cake crumbled, the linen mouldered, the silver turned black. The bar became filthy. Spiders spun their webs, which grew heavy and grey with insects and dirt. Dick never changed his wedding suit, nor his linen, either. His house became a byword for dirt and neglect ... whereupon, he did good business there, and died rich.

Mr Lagg, who had a public house in Wettendene, which is in Sussex, seeing The Green Man redecorated and furnished with chromium chairs, capturing carriage trade, was at first discouraged. His house, The White Swan, attracted the local men who drank nothing but beer – on the profit of which, at that time, a publican could scarcely live.

Lagg grew depressed; neglected the house. Spiders spun their webs in the cellar, above and around the empty, mouldering barrels, hogsheads, kilderkins, nipperkins, casks and pins. He set up a bar in this odorous place – and so made his fortune. As the dirtiest place in Sussex, it became a meeting place for people who bathed every day. An American from New Orleans started the practice of pinning visiting cards to the beams. Soon, everybody who had a card pinned it up, so that Lagg's cellar was covered with them.

When he went to town, Lagg always came back with artificial spiders and beetles on springy wires, to hang from the low ceiling; also, old leather jacks, stuffed crocodiles and spiky rays from the Caribbean gulfs, and even a dried human head from the Amazon. Meanwhile, the cards accumulated, and so did the bills advertising local attractions – cattle shows, flower shows, theatricals, and what not.

And the despisers of what they called the 'great Unwashed' congregated there – the flickers-away of specks of dust – the ladies and gentlemen who could see a thumb print on a plate. Why? Homesickness for the gutter, perhaps – it is an occupational disease of people who like strong perfumes.

I visited the White Swan, in passing, on holiday. The people in Wettendene called it – not without affection – The Mucky Duck. There was the usual vociferous gathering of long-toothed women in tight-cut tweeds, and ruddy men with two slits to their jackets howling confidences, while old Lagg, looking like a half-peeled beetroot, brooded under the cobwebs.

He took notice of me when I offered him something to drink, and said: 'Stopping in Wettendene, sir?'

'Overnight,' I said. 'Anything doing?'

He did not care. 'There's the flower show,' he said, flapping about with a loose hand. 'There's the Christian Boys' Sports. All pinned up. Have a dekko. See for yourself.'

So I looked about me.

That gentleman from New Orleans, who had pinned up the first card on the lowest beam, had started a kind of chain reaction. On the beams, the ceiling, and the very barrels, card jostled card, and advertisement advertisement. I saw the card of the Duke of Chelsea overlapped by the large, red-printed trade card of one George Grape, Rat-Catcher; a potato-crisp salesman's card half overlaid by that of the Hon. Iris Greene. The belly of a stuffed trout was covered with cards as an autumn valley with leaves.

But the great hogshead, it seemed, was set aside for the bills advertising local attractions. Many of these were out of date – for example, an advertisement of a Baby Show in 1932, another of a Cricket Match in 1934, and yet another for 'Sports' in 1923. As Mr Lagg had informed me, there were the printed announcements of the Christian Boys' affair and the Flower Show.

Under the Flower Show, which was scheduled for 14 August, was pinned a wretched little bill advertising, for the same date, a 'Grand Carnival' in Wagnall's Barn on Long Meadow, Wettendene. Everything was covered with dust.

It is a wonderful place for dust. It is necessary, in The Mucky Duck cellar, to take your drink fast or clasp your hand over the top of the glass before it accumulates a grey scum or even a dead spider: the nobility and

gentry like it that way. The gnarled old four-ale drinkers go to The
Green Man: they have no taste for quaintness.

I knew nobody in Wettendene, and am shy of making new
acquaintances. The 'Grand Carnival' was to begin at seven o'clock;
entrance fee sixpence, children half price. It could not be much of a
show, I reflected, at that price and in that place: a showman must be
hard up, indeed, to hire a barn for his show in such a place. But I like
carnivals and am interested in the people that follow them; so I set off at
five o'clock.

Long Meadow is not hard to find: you go to the end of Wettendene
High Street, turn sharp right at Scott's Corner where the village ends,
and take the winding lane, Wettendene Way. This will lead you,
through a green tunnel, to Long Meadow, where the big Wagnall's Barn
is.

Long Meadow was rich grazing land in better times, but now it is
good for nothing but a pitiful handful of sheep that nibble the coarse
grass. There has been no use for the barn these last two generations. It
was built to last hundreds of years; but the land died first. This had
something to do with water – either a lack or an excess of it. Long
Meadow is good for nothing much, at present, but the Barn stands firm
and four-square to the capricious rains and insidious fogs of Wettendene
Marsh. (If it were not for the engineers who dammed the river, the
whole area would, by now, be under water.) However, the place is dry,
in dry weather.

Still, Long Meadow has the peculiarly dreary atmosphere of a
swamp and Wagnall's Barn is incongruously sturdy in that wasteland. It
is a long time since any produce was stocked in Wagnall's Barn. Mr
Etheridge, who owns it, rents it for dances, amateur theatrical shows
and what not.

That playbill aroused my curiosity. It was boldly printed in red, as
follows:

!!! JOLLY JUMBO'S CARNIVAL !!!
!! THE ONE AND ONLY !!
COME AND SEE
!! GORGON, The Man Who Eats Bricks & Swallows Glass !!
!! THE HUMAN SKELETON !!
!! THE INDIA RUBBER BEAUTY –
She Can Put Her Legs Around Her Neck & Walk On
Her Hands !!
!! A LIVE MERMAID !!
!! ALPHA, BETA, AND DOT.
The World-Famous Tumblers
With The Educated Dog!!
! JOLLY JUMBO !
!! JOLLY JUMBO !!

I left early, because I like to look behind the scenes, and have a chat with a wandering freak or two. I remembered a good friend of mine who had been a Human Skeleton – six foot six and weighed a hundred pounds – ate five meals a day, and was as strong as a bull. He told good stories in that coffee-bar that is set up where the Ringling Brothers and Barnum and Bailey Combined Circuses rest in Florida for the winter. I 'tasted sawdust', as the saying goes, and had a yearning to sit on the ground and hear strange stories. Not that I expected much of Wettendene. All the same the strangest people turn up at the unlikeliest places...

Then the rain came down, as it does in an English summer. The sky sagged, rumbled a borborygmic threat of thunderstorms, which seemed to tear open clouds like bags of water.

Knowing our English summer, I had come prepared with a mackintosh, which I put on as I ran for the shelter of the barn.

I was surprised to find it empty. The thunder was loud, now, and there were zigzags of lightning in the east; the pelting rain sounded on the meadow like a maracca. I took off my raincoat and lit a cigarette – and then, in the light of the match flame, I caught a glimpse of two red-and-green eyes watching me, in a far corner, about a foot away from the floor.

It was not yet night, but I felt in that moment such a pang of horror as comes only in the dark; but I am so constituted that, when frightened, I run forward. There was something unholy about Wagnall's Barn, but I should have been ashamed not to face it, whatever it might be. So I advanced, with my walking-stick; but then there came a most melancholy whimper, and I knew that the eyes belonged to a dog.

I made a caressing noise and said: 'Good dog, good doggie! Come on, doggo!' – feeling grateful for his company. By the light of another match, I saw a grey poodle, neatly clipped in the French style. When he saw me, he stood up on his hindlegs and danced.

In the light of that same match I saw, also, a man squatting on his haunches with his head in his hands. He was dressed only in trousers and a tattered shirt. Beside him lay a girl. He had made a bed for her of his clothes and, the rain falling softer, I could hear her breathing, harsh and laborious. The clouds lifted. A little light came into the barn. The dog danced, barking, and the crouching man awoke, raising a haggard face.

'Thank God you've come,' he said. 'She can't breathe. She's got an awful pain in her chest, and a cough. She can't catch her breath, and she's burning. Help her, Doctor – Jolly Jumbo has left us high and dry.'

'What?' I said. 'Went on and left you here, all alone?'

'Quite right, Doctor.'

I said: 'I'm not a doctor.'

'Jumbo promised to send a doctor from the village,' the man said, with a laugh more unhappy than tears. 'Jolly Jumbo promised! I might have known. I did know. Jolly Jumbo never kept his word. Jumbo lives for hisself. But he didn't ought to leave us here in the rain, and Dolores in a bad fever. No, nobody's got the right. No!'

I said: 'You might have run down to Wettendene yourself, and got the doctor.'

'"Might" is a long word, mister. I've broke my ankle and my left wrist. Look at the mud on me, and see if I haven't tried... Third time, working my way on my elbows – and I am an agile man – I fainted with the pain, and half drowned in the mud... But Jumbo swore his Bible oath to send a physician for Dolores. Oh, dear me!'

At this the woman between short, agonized coughs, gasped: '*Alma de mi corazan* – heart of my soul – not leave? So cold, so hot, so cold. Please, not go?'

'I'll see myself damned first,' the man said, 'and so will Dot. Eh, Dot?'

At this the poodle barked and stood on its hindlegs, dancing.

The man said, drearily: 'She's a woman, do you see, sir. But one of the faithful kind. She come out of Mexico. That *alma de mi corazan* – she means it. Actually, it means "soul of my heart". There's nothing much more you can say to somebody you love, if you mean it... So you're not a doctor? More's the pity! I'd hoped you was. But oh, sir, for the sake of Christian charity, perhaps you'll give us a hand.

'She and me, we're not one of that rabble of layabouts, and gyppos, and what not. Believe me, sir, we're artists of our kind. I know that a gentleman like you doesn't regard us, because we live rough. But it would be an act of kindness for you to get a doctor up from Wettendene, because my wife is burning and coughing, and I'm helpless.

'I'll tell you something, guv'nor – poor little Dot, who understands more than the so-called Christians in these parts, she knew, *she* knew! She ran away. I called her: "Dot – Dot – Dot!" – but she run on. I'll swear she went for a doctor, or something.

'And in the meantime Jolly Jumbo has gone and left us high and dry. Low and wet is the better word, sir, and we haven't eaten this last two days.'

The girl, gripping his wrist, sighed: 'Please, not to go, not to leave?'

'Set your heart at ease, sweetheart,' the man said. 'Me and Dot, we are with you. And here's a gentleman who'll get us a physician. Because, to deal plainly with you, my one and only, I've got a bad leg now and a bad arm, and I can't make it through the mud to Wettendene. The dog tried and she come back with a bloody mouth where somebody kicked her...'

I said: 'Come on, my friends, don't lose heart. I'll run down to Wettendene and get an ambulance, or at least a doctor. Meanwhile,' I said, taking off my jacket, 'peel off some of those damp clothes. Put this on her. At least it's dry. Then I'll run down and get you some help.'

He said: 'All alone? It's a dretful thing, to be all alone. Dot'll go with you, if you will, God love you! But it's no use, I'm afraid.'

He said this in a whisper, but the girl heard him, and said, quite clearly: 'No use. Let him not go. Kind voice. Talk' – this between rattling gasps.

He said: 'All right, my sweet, he'll go in a minute.'

The girl said: 'Only a minute. Cold. Lonely——'

'What, Dolores, lonely with me and Dot?'

'Lonely, lonely, lonely.'

So the man forced himself to talk. God grant that no circumstances may compel any of you who read this to talk in such a voice. He was trying to speak evenly; but from time to time, when some word touched his heart, his voice broke like a boy's, and he tried to cover the break with a laugh that went inward, a sobbing laugh.

Holding the girl's hand and talking for her comfort, interrupted from time to time by the whimpering of the poodle Dot, he went on:

They call me Alpha, you see, because my girl's name is Beta. That is her real name – short for Beatrice Dolores. But my real name is Alfred, and I come from Hampshire.

They call us 'tumblers', sir, but Dolores is an artist. I can do the forward rolls and the triple back-somersaults; but Dolores is the genius. Dolores, and that dog, Dot, do you see?

It's a hard life, sir, and it's a rough life. I used to be a Joey – a kind of a clown – until I met Dolores in Southampton, where she'd been abandoned by a dago that run a puppet show, with side-shows, as went broke and left Dolores high and dry. All our lives, from Durham to Land's End, Carlisle to Brighton, north, south, east, west, I've been left high and dry when the rain came down and the money run out. Not an easy life, sir. A hard life, as a matter of fact. You earn your bit of bread, in this game.

Ever since Dolores and me joined Jolly Jumbo's Carnival, there was a run of bad luck. At Immersham, there was a cloudburst; Jumbo had took Grote's Meadow – we was two foot under water. The weather cleared at Athelboro' and they all came to see Pollux, the Strong Man, because, do you see, the blacksmith at Athelboro' could lift an anvil over his head, and there was a fi'-pun prize

for anybody who could out-lift Pollux (his name was really
Michaels).

Well, as luck would have it, at Athelboro' Pollux sprained his
wrist. The blacksmith out-lifted him, and Jolly Jumbo told him to
come back next morning for his fiver. We pulled out about midnight:
Jumbo will never go to Athelboro' again. Then, in Pettydene,
something happened to Gorgon, the man that eats bricks and
swallows glass. His act was to bite lumps out of a brick, chew them
up, wash them down with a glass of water, and crunch up and
swallow the glass. We took the Drill Hall at Pettydene, and
had a good house. And what happens, but Gorgon breaks a
tooth!

I tell you, sir, we had no luck: After that, at Firestone, something
went wrong with the Mermaid. She was my property, you know – an
animal they call a manatee – I bought her for a round sum from a
man who caught her in South America. A kind of seal, but with
breasts like a woman, and almost a human voice. She got a cough,
and passed away.

There was never such a round. Worst of all, just here, Dolores
caught a cold.

I dare say you've heard of my act, Alpha, Beta and Dot? . . . Oh, a
stranger here; are you sir? I wish you could have seen it. Dolores is
the genius – her and Dot. I'm only the under-stander. I would come
rolling and somersaulting in, and stand. Then Dolores'd come
dancing in and take what looked like a standing jump – I gave her a
hand-up – on to my shoulders, so we stood balanced. Then, in comes
poor little Dot, and jumps; first on to my shoulder, then on to
Dolores' shoulder from mine, and so on to Dolores' head where Dot
stands on her hind legs and dances . . .

The rain comes down, sir. Dolores has got a cold in the chest. I
beg her: 'Don't go on, Dolores – don't do it!' But nothing will satisfy
her, bless her heart: the show must go on. And when we come on, she
was burning like a fire. Couldn't do the jump. I twist sidewise to take
the weight, but her weight is kind of a deadweight, poor girl! My
ankle snaps, and we tumbles.

Tried to make it part of my act – making funny business, carrying
the girl in my arms, hopping on one foot, with good old Dot
dancing after us.

That was the end of us in Wettendene. Jolly Jumbo says to us:
'Never was such luck. The brick-eater's bust a tooth. The mermaid's
good and dead. The strong-man has strained hisself . . . and I'm not
sure but that blacksmith won't be on my trail, with a few pals, for
that fi'pun note. I've got to leave you to it, Alph, old feller. I'm off to
Portsmouth.'

I said: 'And what about my girl? I've only got one hand and one foot, and she's got a fever.'

He said: 'Wait a bit, Alph, just wait a bit. My word of honour, and my Bible oath, I'll send a sawbones up from Wettendene.'

'And what about our pay?' I ask.

Jolly Jumbo says: 'I swear on my mother's grave, Alph, I haven't got it. But I'll have it in Portsmouth, on my Bible oath. You know me. Sacred word of honour! I'll be at The Hope and Anchor for a matter of weeks, and you'll be paid in full. And I'll send you a doctor, by my father's life I will. Honour bright! In the meantime, Alph, I'll look after Dot for you.'

And so he picked up the dog – I hadn't the strength to prevent him – and went out, and I heard the whips cracking and the vans squelching in the mud.

But little Dot got away and came back...

I've been talking too much, sir. I thought you was the doctor. Get one for the girl, if you've a heart in you – and a bit of meat for the dog. I've got a few shillings on me.

I said: 'Keep still. I'll be right back.' And I ran in the rain, closely followed by the dog Dot, down through that dripping green tunnel into Wettendene, and rang long and loud at a black door to which was affixed the brass plate, well worn, of one Dr MacVitie, M.R.C.S., L.R.C.P.

The old doctor came out, brushing crumbs from his waistcoat. There was an air of decrepitude about him. He led me into his surgery. I saw a dusty old volume of *Gray's Anatomy*, two fishing rods, four volumes of the Badminton Library – all unused these past twenty years. There were also some glass-stoppered bottles that seemed to contain nothing but sediment; a spirit lamp without spirit; some cracked test-tubes; and an ancient case-book into the cover of which was stuck a rusty scalpel.

He was one of the cantankerous old Scotch school of doctors that seem incapable of graciousness, and grudging even of a civil word. He growled: 'I'm in luck this evening. It's six months since I sat down to my bit of dinner without the bell going before I had the first spoonful of soup half-way to my mouth. Well, you've let me finish my evening meal. Thank ye.'

He was ponderously ironic, this side of offensiveness. 'Well, out with it. What ails ye? Nothing, I'll wager. Nothing ever ails 'em hereabouts that a dose of castor oil or an aspirin tablet will not cure – excepting always rheumatism. Speak up, man!'

I said: 'There's nothing wrong with me at all. I've come to fetch you to treat two other people up at Wagnall's Barn. There's a man with a broken ankle and a girl with a congestion of the lungs. So get your bag and come along.'

He snapped at me like a turtle, and said: 'And since when, may I ask, were you a diagnostician? And who are you to be giving a name to symptoms? In any case, young fellow, I'm not practising. I'm retired. My son runs the practice, and he's out on a child-bed case . . . Damn that dog – he's barking again!'

The poodle, Dot, was indeed barking hysterically and scratching at the front door.

I said: 'Doctor, these poor people are in desperate straits.'

'Aye, poor people always are. And who's to pay the bill?'

'I'll pay,' I said, taking out my wallet.

'Put it up, man, put it up! Put your hand in your pocket for all the riff-raff that lie about in barns and ye'll end in the workhouse.'

He got up laboriously, sighing: 'Alex is over Iddlesworth way with the car. God give us strength to bear it. I swore my oath and so I'm bound to come, Lord preserve us!'

'If——' I said, 'if you happen to have a bit of meat in the house for the dog, I'd be glad to pay for it——'

'– And what do you take this surgery for? A butcher's shop?' Then he paused. 'What sort of a dog, as a matter of curiosity would ye say it was?'

'A little grey French poodle.'

'Oh, aye? Very odd. Ah well, there's a bit of meat on the chop bones, so I'll put 'em in my pocket for the dog, if you like . . . Wagnall's Barn, did ye say? A man and a girl, is that it? They'll be some kind of vagrant romanies, or gyppos, no doubt?'

I said: 'I believe they are some kind of travelling performers. They are desperately in need of help. Please hurry, Doctor.'

His face was sour and his voice harsh, but his eyes were bewildered, as he said: 'Aye, no doubt. I dare say, very likely. A congestion of the lungs, ye said? And a fractured ankle, is that it? Very well.' He was throwing drugs and bandages into his disreputable-looking black bag. I helped him into his immense black mackintosh.

He said: 'As for hurrying, young man, I'm seventy-seven years old, my arteries are hard, and I could not hurry myself for the crack of doom. Here, carry the bag. Hand me my hat and my stick, and we'll walk up to Wagnall's Barn on this fool's errand of yours. Because a fool's errand it is, I fancy. Come on.'

The little dog, Dot, looking like a bit of the mud made animate, only half distinguishable in the half dark, barked with joy, running a little way backwards and a long way forwards, leading us back to the Barn through that darkened green tunnel.

The doctor had a flash-lamp. We made our way to the barn, he grumbling and panting and cursing the weather. We went in. He swung the beam of his lamp from corner to corner, until it came to rest on my jacket. It lay as I had wrapped it over poor Dolores, but it was empty.

I shouted: 'Alpha, Beta! Here's the doctor!'

The echo answered: '*Octor!*'

I could only pick up my jacket and say: 'They must have gone away.'

Dr MacVitie said, drily: 'Very likely, if they were here at all.'

'Here's my jacket, damp on the inside and dry on the outside,' I said. 'And I have the evidence of my own eyes——'

'No doubt. Very likely. In a lifetime of practice I have learned, sir, to discredit the evidence of my eyes, and my other four senses, besides. Let's away. Come!'

'But where have they gone?'

'Ah, I wonder!'

'And the dog, where's the dog?' I cried.

He said, in his dour way: 'For that, I recommend you consult Mr Lindsay, the vet.'

So we walked down again, without exchanging a word until we reached Dr MacVitie's door. Then he said: 'Where did you spend your evening?'

I said: 'I came straight to the Barn from The White Swan.'

'Well, then,' he said, 'I recommend ye go back, and take a whisky and water, warm; and get ye to bed in a dry night-shirt. And this time take a little more water with it. Goodnight to ye——' and slammed the door in my face.

I walked the half mile to The White Swan, which was still open. The landlord, Mr Lagg, looked me up and down, taking notice of my soaking wet clothes and muddy boots. 'Been out?' he asked.

In Sussex they have a way of asking unnecessary, seemingly innocent questions of this nature which lead to an exchange of witticisms – for which, that night, I was not in the mood.

I said: 'I went up to Wagnall's Barn for Jolly Jumbo's Carnival. but he pulled out, it seems, and left a man, a woman, and a dog——'

'You hear that, George?' said Mr Lagg to a very old farmer whose knobbed ash walking-stick seemed to have grown out of the knobbed root of his earthy, arthritic hand, and who was smoking a pipe mended in three places with insulating tape.

'I heerd,' said old George, with a chuckle. 'Dat gen'lemen'll been a liddle bit late for dat carnival, like.'

At this they both laughed. But then Mr Lagg said, soothingly, as to a cash customer: 'Didn't you look at the notice on the bill, sir? Jolly Jumbo was here all right, and flitted in a hurry too. And he did leave a man and

a girl (not lawfully married, I heerd) and one o' them liddle shaved
French dogs.

'I say, you'm a liddle late for Jolly Jumbo's Carnival, sir. 'Cause if
you look again at Jolly Jumbo's bill, you'll see – I think the programme
for the Cricket Match covers up the corner – you'll see the date
on it is August the fourteenth, 1904. I was a boy at the time; wasn't
I, George?'

'Thirteen-year-old,' old George said, 'making you sixty-three to
my seventy-two. Dat were a sad business, but as ye sow, so shall ye
reap, they says. Live a vagabond, die a vagabond. Live in sin, die
in sin——'

'All right, George,' said Mr Lagg, 'you're not in chapel now ... I
don't know how you got at it, sir, but Jolly Jumbo (as he called hisself)
lef' two people and a dog behind. Hauled out his vans, eleven o'clock at
night, and left word with Dr MacVitie (the old one, that was) to go up to
Wagnall's Barn.

'But he was in the middle o' dinner, and wouldn't go. Then he was
called out to the Squire's place, and didn't get home till twelve o'clock
next night. And there was a liddle dog that kep' barking and barking,
and trying to pull him up the path by the trousis-leg. But Dr Mac-
Vitie——'

'Dat were a mean man, dat one, sure enough!'

'You be quiet, George. Dr MacVitie kicked the liddle dog into the
ditch, and unhooked the bell, and tied up the knocker, and went to bed.
Couple o' days later, Wagnall, going over his land, has a look at that
barn, and he sees a young girl stone dead, a young fellow dying, and a
poor liddle dog crying fit to break your heart. Oh, he got old Dr
MacVitie up to the barn then all right, but t'was too late. The fellow, he
died in the Cottage Hospital.

'They tried to catch the dog, but nobody could. It stood off and on,
like, until that pair was buried by the parish. Then it run off into the
woods, and nobody saw it again——'

'Oh, but didn't they, though?' said old George.

Mr Lagg said: 'It's an old wives' tale, sir. They *do* say that this here
liddle grey French dog comes back every year on August the fourteenth
to scrat and bark at the doctor's door, and lead him to Wagnall's Barn.
And be he in the middle of his supper or be he full, be he weary or rested,
wet or dry, sick or well, go he must ... *He* died in 1924, so you see it's
nothing but an old wives' tale——'

'Dey did used to git light-headed, like, here on the marshes,' said old
George, 'but dey do say old Dr MacVitie mustn't rest. He mus' pay dat
call to dat empty barn, every year, because of his hard heart. Tomorrow,
by daylight, look and see if doctor's door be'nt all scratted up,
like.'

'George, you're an old woman in your old age,' said Mr Lagg. 'We take no stock of such things in these parts, sir. Would you like to come up to the lounge and look at the television until closing time?'

The Mark of the Beast

Rudyard Kipling

Your Gods and my Gods – do you or I know which are the stronger?
Native Proverb

East of Suez, some hold, the direct control of providence ceases; man being there handed over to the power of the gods and devils of Asia, and the Church of England providence only exercising an occasional and modified supervision in the case of Englishmen.

This theory accounts for some of the more unnecessary horrors of life in India: it may be stretched to explain my story.

My friend Strickland of the police who knows as much of natives of India as is good for any man, can bear witness to the facts of the case. Dumiose, our doctor, also saw what Strickland and I saw. The inference which he drew from the evidence was entirely incorrect. He is dead now; he died in a rather dubious manner, which has been elsewhere described.

When Fleete came to India he owned a little money and some land in the Himalayas, near a place called Dharmsala. Both properties had been left him by an uncle, and he came out to finance them. He was a big, heavy, genial and inoffensive man. His knowledge of natives was, of course, limited, and he complained of the difficulties of the language.

He rode in from his place in the hills to spend New Year in the station, and he stayed with Strickland. On New Year's Eve there was a big dinner at the club, and the night was excusably wet. When men foregather from the uttermost ends of the Empire, they have a right to be riotous. The Frontier had sent down a contingent of 'Catch-'em-Alive-O's' who had not seen twenty white faces for a year, and were used to riding fifteen miles to dinner at the next fort at the risk of a Khyberee bullet where their drink should lie. They profited by their new security, for they tried to play pool with a curled up hedgehog found in the garden, and one of them carried the marker round the room in his teeth. Half a dozen planters had come in from the south and

were talking 'horse' to the biggest liar in Asia, who was trying to cap all
their stories at once. Everybody was there, and there was a general
closing up of ranks and taking stock of our losses in dead or disabled that
had fallen during the past year. It was a very wet night, and I remember
that we sang 'Auld Lang Syne' with our feet in the Polo Championship
Cup, and our heads among the stars, and swore that we were all dear
friends. Then some of us went away and annexed Burma, and some
tried to open up the Soudan and were opened up by Fuzzies in that
cruel scrub outside Suakim, and some found stars and medals, and some
were married, which was bad, and some did other things which were
worse, and the others of us stayed in our chains and strove to make
money on insufficient experiences.

Fleete began the night with sherry and bitters, drank champagne
steadily up to dessert, then raw, rasping Capri with all the strength of
whisky, took Benedictine with his coffee, four or five whiskys and sodas
to improve his pool strokes, beer and bones at half past two, winding up
with old brandy. Consequently, when he came out, at half past three in
the morning, into fourteen degrees of frost, he was very angry with his
horse for coughing, and tried to leapfrog into the saddle. The horse
broke away and went to his stables; so Strickland and I formed a guard
of dishonour to take Fleete home.

Our road lay through the bazaar, close to a little temple of
Hanuman, the monkey-god, who is a leading divinity worthy of respect.
All gods have good points, just as have all priests. Personally I attach
much importance to Hanuman, and am kind to his people – the
great grey apes of the hills. One never knows when one may want a
friend.

There was a light in the temple, and as we passed we could hear
voices of men chanting hymns. In a native temple the priests rise at all
hours of the night to do honour to their god. Before we could stop him,
Fleete dashed up the steps, patted two priests on the back, and was
gravely grinding the ashes of his cigar butt into the forehead of the red
stone image of Hanuman. Strickland tried to drag him out, but he sat
down and said solemnly:

'Shee that? Mark of the B-beasht! *I* made it. Ishn't it fine?'

In half a minute the temple was alive and noisy, and Strickland,
who knew what came of polluting gods, said that things might occur.
He, by virtue of his official position, long residence in the country, and
weakness for going among the natives, was known to the priests, and he
felt unhappy. Fleete sat on the ground and refused to move. He said
that 'good old Hanuman' made a very soft pillow.

Then, without any warning, a silver man came out of a recess
behind the image of the god. He was perfectly naked in that bitter,
bitter cold, and his body shone like frosted silver, for he was what the

Bible calls 'a leper as white as snow'. Also he had no face, because he was a leper of some years' standing, and his disease was heavy upon him. We two stooped to haul Fleete up, and the temple was filling and filling with folk who seemed to spring from the earth, when the silver man ran in under our arms, making a noise exactly like the mewing of an otter, caught Fleete round the body and dropped his head on Fleete's breast before we could wrench him away. Then he retired to a corner and sat mewing while the crowd blocked all the doors.

The priests were very angry until the silver man touched Fleete. That nuzzling seemed to sober them.

At the end of a few minutes' silence one of the priests came to Strickland and said, in perfect English, 'Take your friend away. He has done with Hanuman, but Hanuman has not done with him.' The crowd gave room and we carried Fleete into the road.

Strickland was very angry. He said that we might all three have been knifed, and that Fleete should thank his stars that he had escaped without injury.

Fleete thanked no one. He said that he wanted to go to bed. He was gorgeously drunk.

We moved on, Strickland silent and wrathful, until Fleete was taken with violent shivering fits and sweating. He said that the smells of the bazaar were overpowering, and he wondered why slaughter-houses were permitted so near English residences. 'Can't you smell the blood?' said Fleete.

We put him to bed at last, just as the dawn was breaking, and Strickland invited me to have another whisky and soda. While we were drinking he talked of the trouble at the temple, and admitted that it baffled him completely. Strickland hates being mystified by natives, because his business in life is to overmatch them with their own weapons. He has not yet succeeded in doing this, but in fifteen or twenty years he will have made some small progress.

'They should have mauled us,' he said, 'instead of mewing at us. I wonder what they meant. I don't like it one little bit.'

I said that the managing committee of the temple would in all probability bring a criminal action against us for insulting their religion. There was a section of the Indian Penal Code which exactly met Fleete's offence. Strickland said he only hoped and prayed that they would do this. Before I left I looked into Fleete's room, and saw him lying on his right side, scratching his left breast. Then I went to bed, cold, depressed, and unhappy, at seven o'clock in the morning.

At one o'clock I rode over to Strickland's house to enquire after Fleete's head. I imagined it would be a sore one. Fleete was breakfasting and seemed unwell. His temper was gone, for he was abusing the cook for not supplying him with an underdone chop. A man who can eat raw meat after a wet night is a curiosity. I told Fleete this, and he laughed.

'You breed queer mosquitoes in these parts,' he said. 'I've been bitten to pieces, but only in one place.'

'Let's have a look at the bite,' said Strickland. 'It may have gone down since this morning.'

While the chops were being cooked, Fleete opened his shirt and showed us, just over his left breast, a mark, the perfect double of the black rosettes – the five or six irregular blotches arranged in a circle – on a leopard's hide. Strickland looked and said, 'It was only pink this morning. It's gone black now.'

Fleete ran to a glass.

'By Jove!' he said, 'this is nasty. What is it?'

We could not answer. Here the chops came in, all red and juicy, and Fleete bolted three in a most offensive manner. He ate on his right grinders only, and threw his head over his right shoulder as he snapped the meat. When he had finished, it struck him that he had been behaving strangely, for he said apologetically, 'I don't think I ever felt so hungry in my life. I've bolted like an ostrich.'

After breakfast Strickland said to me, 'Don't go. Stay here, and stay for the night.'

Seeing that my house was not three miles from Strickland's, this request was absurd. But Strickland insisted, and was going to say something when Fleete interrupted by declaring in a shamefaced way that he felt hungry again. Strickland sent a man to my house to fetch over my bedding and a horse, and we three went down to Strickland's stables to pass the hours until it was time to go out for a ride. The man who has a weakness for horses never wearies of inspecting them; and when two men are killing time in this way they gather knowledge and lies, the one from the other.

There were five horses in the stables, and I shall never forget the scene as we tried to look them over. They seemed to have gone mad. They reared and screamed and nearly tore up their pickets; they sweated and shivered and lathered and were distraught with fear. Strickland's horses used to know him as well as his dogs; which made the matter more curious. We left the stables for fear of the brutes throwing themselves in their panic. Then Strickland turned back and called me. The horses were still frightened, but they let us 'gentle' and make much of them, and put their heads in our bosoms.

'They aren't afraid of *us*,' said Strickland. 'D'you know, I'd give three months' pay if Outrage here could talk.'

But Outrage was dumb, and could only cuddle up to his master and blow out his nostrils, as is the custom of horses when they wish to explain things but can't. Fleete came up when we were in the stalls, and as soon as the horses saw him their fright broke out afresh. It was all we could do to escape from the place unkicked. Strickland said, 'They don't seem to love you, Fleete.'

'Nonsense,' said Fleete; 'my mare will follow me like a dog.' He went to her; she was in a loose box; but as he slipped the bars she plunged, knocked him down, and broke away into the garden. I laughed, but Strickland was not amused. He took his moustache in both fists, and pulled at it till it nearly came out. Fleete, instead of going off to chase his property, yawned, saying that he felt sleepy. He went to the house to lie down, which was a foolish way of spending New Year's Day.

Strickland sat with me in the stables and asked if I had noticed anything peculiar in Fleete's manner. I said that he ate his food like a beast; but that this might have been the result of living alone in the hills out of the reach of society as refined and elevating as ours, for instance. Strickland was not amused. I do not think that he listened to me, for his next sentence referred to the mark on Fleete's breast, and I said that it might have been caused by blister flies, or that it was possibly a birth-mark newly born and now visible for the first time. We both agreed that it was unpleasant to look at, and Strickland found occasion to say that I was a fool.

'I can't tell you what I think now,' said he, 'because you would call me a madman; but you must stay with me for the next few days, if you can. I want you to watch Fleete, but don't tell me what you think till I have made up my mind.'

'But I am dining out tonight,' I said.

'So am I,' said Strickland, 'and so is Fleete. At least if he doesn't change his mind.'

We walked about the garden smoking, but saying nothing – because we were friends, and talking spoils good tobacco – till our pipes were out. Then we went to wake up Fleete. He was wide awake and fidgeting about his room.

'I say, I want some more chops,' he said. 'Can I get them?'

We laughed and said, 'Go and change. The ponies will be round in a minute.'

'All right,' said Fleete. 'I'll go when I get the chops – underdone ones, mind.'

He seemed to be quite in earnest. It was four o'clock, and we had breakfast at one; still, for a long time, he demanded those underdone chops. Then he changed into riding clothes and went out onto the verandah. His pony – the mare had not been caught – would not let him come near. All three horses were unmanageable – mad with fear – and finally Fleete said that he would stay at home and get something to eat. Strickland and I rode out wondering. As we passed the temple of Hanuman, the silver man came out and mewed at us.

'He is not one of the regular priests of the temple,' said Strickland. 'I think I should peculiarly like to lay my hands on him.'

There was no spring in our gallop on the race course that evening. The horses were stale, and moved as though they had been ridden out.

'The fright after breakfast has been too much for them,' said Strickland.

That was the only remark he made through the remainder of the ride. Once or twice I think he swore to himself; but that did not count.

We came back in the dark at seven o'clock, and saw that there were no lights in the bungalow. 'Careless ruffians my servants are!' said Strickland.

My horse reared at something on the carriage-drive and Fleete stood up under its nose.

'What are you doing, grovelling about the garden?' said Strickland.

But both horses bolted and nearly threw us. We dismounted by the stables and returned to Fleete, who was on his hands and knees under the orange-bushes.

'What the devil's wrong with you?' said Strickland.

'Nothing, nothing in the world,' said Fleete, speaking very quickly and thickly. 'I've been gardening – botanizing, you know. The smell of the earth is delightful. I think I'm going for a walk – long walk – all night.'

Then I saw that there was something excessively out of order somewhere, and I said to Strickland, 'I am not dining out.'

'Bless you!' said Strickland. 'Here, Fleete, get up. You'll catch fever there. Come in to dinner and let's have the lamps lit. We'll all dine at home.'

Fleete stood up unwillingly, and said, 'No lamps – no lamps. It's much nicer here. Let's dine outside and have some more chops – lots of 'em and underdone – bloody ones with gristle.'

Now a December evening in Northern India is bitterly cold, and Fleete's suggestion was that of a maniac.

'Come in,' said Strickland sternly. 'Come in at once.'

Fleete came, and when the lamps were brought, we saw that he was literally plastered with dirt from head to foot. He must have been rolling in the garden. He shrank from the light and went to his room. His eyes were horrible to look at. There was a green light behind them, not in them, if you understand, and the man's lower lip hung down.

Strickland said, 'There is going to be trouble – big trouble – tonight. Don't you change your riding things.'

We waited and waited for Fleete's reappearance, and ordered dinner in the meantime. We could hear him moving about his own room, but there was no light there. Presently from the room came the long-drawn howl of a wolf.

People write and talk lightly of blood running cold and hair standing up and things of that kind. Both sensations are too horrible to be trifled with. My heart stopped as though a knife had been driven through it, and Strickland turned as white as the table-cloth.

The howl was repeated and was answered by another howl far across the fields.

That set the gilded roof on the horror. Strickland dashed into Fleete's room. I followed, and we saw Fleete getting out of the window. He made beast noises in the back of his throat. He could not answer us when we shouted at him. He spat.

I don't quite remember what followed, but I think that Strickland must have stunned him with the long boot-jack or else I should never have been able to sit on his chest. Fleete could not speak, he could only snarl, and his snarls were those of a wolf, not of a man. The human spirit must have been giving way all day and have died out with the twilight. We were dealing with a beast that had once been Fleete.

The affair was beyond any human and rational experience. I tried to say 'Hydrophobia', but the word wouldn't come, because I knew I was lying.

We bound this beast with leather thongs of the punkah-rope, and tied its thumbs and big toes together, and gagged it with a shoe horn, which makes a very efficient gag if you know how to arrange it. Then we carried it into the dining-room and sent a man to Dumoise, the doctor, telling him to come over at once. After we had despatched the messenger and were drawing breath, Strickland said, 'It's no good. This isn't any doctor's work.' I, also, knew that he spoke the truth.

The beast's head was free, and it threw it about from side to side. Anyone entering the room would have believed that we were curing a wolf's pelt. That was the most loathsome accessory of all.

Strickland sat with his chin in the heel of his fist, watching the beast as it wriggled on the ground, but saying nothing. The shirt had been torn open in the scuffle and showed the black rosette mark on the left breast. It stood out like a blister.

In the silence of the watching we heard something without, mewing like a she-otter. We both rose to our feet, and, I answer for myself, not Strickland, felt sick – actually and physically sick. We told each other, as did the men in 'Pingafore', that it was the cat.

Dumoise arrived, and I never saw a little man so unprofessionally shocked. He said that it was a heartrending case of hydrophobia and that nothing could be done. At least any palliative measures would only prolong the agony. The beast was foaming at the mouth. Fleete, as we told Dumoise, had been bitten by dogs once or twice. Any man who keeps half a dozen terriers must expect a nip now and again. Dumoise could offer no help. He could only certify that Fleete was dying of hydrophobia. The beast was then howling, for it had managed to spit out the shoe horn. Dumoise said that he would be ready to certify to the cause of death, and that the end was certain. He was a good little man, and he offered to remain with us; but Strickland refused the kindness. He did not wish to poison Dumoise's New Year. He would only ask him not to give the real cause of Fleete's death to the public.

So Dumoise left, deeply agitated; and as soon as the noise of the cart-wheels had died away, Strickland told me, in a whisper, his suspicions. They were so wildly improbable that he dared not say them aloud; and I, who entertained all Strickland's beliefs, was so ashamed of owning to them that I pretended to disbelieve.

'Even if the silver man had bewitched Fleete for polluting the image of Hanuman, the punishment could not have fallen so quickly.'

As I was whispering this the cry outside the house rose again, and the beast fell into a fresh paroxysm of struggling till we were afraid that the thongs that held it would give way.

'Watch!' said Strickland. 'If this happens six times I shall take the law into my own hands. I order you to help me.'

He went into his room and came out in a few minutes with the barrels of an old shotgun, a piece of fishing-line, some thick cord, and his heavy wooden bedstead. I reported that the convulsions had followed the cry by two seconds in each case, and the beast seemed perceptibly weaker.

Strickland muttered, 'But he can't take away the life! He can't take away the life!'

I said, though I knew that I was arguing against myself, 'It may be a cat. It must be a cat. If the silver man is responsible, why does he dare to come here?'

Strickland arranged the wood on the hearth, put the gun-barrels into the glow of the fire, spread the twine on the table, and broke a walking-stick in two. There was one yard of fishing-line, gut, lapped with wire, such as is used for *mahseer*-fishing, and he tied the two ends together in a loop.

Then he said, 'How can we catch him? He must be taken alive and unhurt.'

I said that we must trust in Providence, and go out softly with polo-sticks into the shrubbery at the front of the house. The man or animal that made the cry was evidently moving round the house as regularly as a night-watchman. We could wait in the bushes till he came by, and knock him over.

Strickland accepted this suggestion, and we slipped out from a bathroom window onto the front verandah and then across the carriage-drive into the bushes.

In the moonlight we could see the leper coming round the corner of the house. He was perfectly naked, and from time to time he mewed and stopped to dance with his shadow. It was an unattractive sight, and thinking of poor Fleete, brought to such degradation by so foul a creature, I put away all my doubts and resolved to help Strickland from the heated gun-barrels to the loop of twine – from the loins to the head and back again – with all tortures that might be needful.

The leper halted in the front porch for a moment and we jumped out on him with the sticks. He was wonderfully strong, and we were afraid that he might escape or be fatally injured before we caught him. We had an idea that lepers were frail creatures, but this proved to be incorrect. Strickland knocked his legs from under him, and I put my foot on his neck. He mewed hideously, and even through my riding-boots I could feel that his flesh was not the flesh of a clean man.

He struck at us with his hand and feet stumps. We looped the lash of a dog-whip round him, under the armpits, and dragged him backwards into the hall and so into the dining-room where the beast lay. There we tied him with trunk-straps. He made no attempt to escape, but mewed.

When we confronted him with the beast the scene was beyond description. The beast doubled backwards into a bow, as though he had been poisoned with strychnine, and moaned in the most pitiable fashion. Several other things happened also, but they cannot be put down here.

'I think I was right,' said Strickland. 'Now we will ask him to cure this case.'

But the leper only mewed. Strickland wrapped a towel round his hand and took the gun-barrels out of the fire. I put the half of the broken walking-stick through the loop of fishing-line and buckled the leper comfortably to Strickland's bedstead. I understood then how men and women and little children can endure to see a witch burnt alive; for the beast was moaning on the floor, and though the silver man had no face, you could see horrible feelings passing through the slab that took its place, exactly as waves of heat play across red-hot iron gun-barrels for instance.

Strickland shaded his eyes with his hands for a moment, and we got to work. This part is not to be printed.

The dawn was beginning to break when the leper spoke. His mewings had not been satisfactory up to that point. The beast had fainted from exhaustion, and the house was very still. We unstrapped the leper and told him to take away the evil spirit. He crawled to the beast and laid his hand upon the left breast. That was all. Then he fell face down and whined, drawing in his breath as he did so.

We watched the face of the beast, and saw the soul of Fleete coming back into the eyes. Then a sweat broke out on the forehead, and the eyes

– they were human eyes – closed. We waited for an hour, but Fleete still slept. We carried him to his room and bade the leper go, giving him the bedstead, and the sheet on the bedstead to cover his nakedness, the gloves and the towels with which we had touched him, and the whip that had been hooked round his body. He put the sheet about him and went out into the early morning without speaking or mewing.

Strickland wiped his face and sat down. A night-gong, far away in the city, made seven o'clock.

'Exactly four-and-twenty hours!' said Strickland. 'And I've done enough to ensure my dismissal from the service, besides permanent quarters in a lunatic asylum. Do you believe that we are awake?'

The red-hot gun-barrel had fallen on the floor and was singeing the carpet. The smell was entirely real.

That morning at eleven we two together went to wake up Fleete. We looked and saw that the black leopard-rosette on his chest had disappeared. He was very drowsy and tired, but as soon as he saw us, he said, 'Oh! Confound you fellows. Happy New Year to you. Never mix your liquors. I'm nearly dead.'

'Thanks for your kindness, but you're over time,' said Strickland. 'Today is the morning of the second. You've slept the clock round with a vengeance.'

The door opened, and little Dumoise put his head in. He had come on foot, and fancied that we were laying out Fleete.

'I've brought a nurse,' said Dumoise. 'I suppose that she can come in for ... what is necessary.'

'By all means,' said Fleete cheerily, sitting up in bed. 'Bring on your nurses.'

Dumoise was dumb. Strickland led him out and explained that there must have been a mistake in the diagnosis. Dumoise remained dumb and left the house hastily. He considered that his professional reputation had been injured, and was inclined to make a personal matter of the recovery. Strickland went out too. When he came back, he said that he had been to call on the temple of Hanuman to offer redress for the pollution of the god, and had been solemnly assured that no white man had ever touched the idol, and that he was an incarnation of all the virtues labouring under a delusion. 'What do you think?' said Strickland.

I said, 'There are more things ...'

But Strickland hates that quotation. He says that I have worn it threadbare.

One other curious thing happened which frightened me as much as anything in all the night's work. When Fleete was dressed he came into the dining-room and sniffed. He had a quaint trick of moving his nose when he sniffed. 'Horrid doggy smell, here,' said he. 'You should really keep those terriers of yours in better order. Try sulphur, Strick.'

But Strickland did not answer. He caught hold of the back of a chair, and, without warning, went into an amazing fit of hysterics. It is terrible to see a strong man overtaken with hysteria. Then it struck me that we had fought for Fleete's soul with the silver man in that room, and that we had disgraced ourselves as Englishmen for ever, and I laughed and gasped and gurgled just as shamefully as Strickland, while Fleete thought that we had both gone mad. We never told him what we had done.

Some years later, when Strickland had married and was a church-going member of society for his wife's sake, we reviewed the incident dispassionately, and Strickland suggested that I should put it before the public.

I cannot myself see that this step is likely to clear up the mystery; because, in the first place, no one will believe a rather unpleasant story, and, in the second, it is well known to every right-minded man that the gods of the heathen are stone and brass, and any attempt to deal with them otherwise is justly condemned.

An Account of Some Strange Disturbances in Aungier Street

J. Sheridan Le Fanu

It is not worth telling, this story of mine – at least, not worth writing. Told, indeed, as I have sometimes been called upon to tell it, to a circle of intelligent and eager faces, lighted up by a good after-dinner fire on a winter's evening, with a cold wind rising and wailing outside, and all snug and cosy within, it has gone off – though I say it, who should not – indifferent well. But it is a venture to do as you would have me. Pen, ink and paper are cold vehicles for the marvellous, and a 'reader' decidedly a more critical animal than a 'listener'. If, however, you can induce your friends to read it after nightfall, and when the fireside talk has run for a while on thrilling tales of shapeless terror; in short, if you will secure me the *mollia tempora fandi*, I will go to my work, and say my say, with better heart. Well, then, these conditions presupposed, I shall waste no more words, but tell you simply how it all happened.

My cousin (Tom Ludlow) and I studied medicine together. I think he would have succeeded, had he stuck to the profession; but he preferred the Church, poor fellow, and died early, a sacrifice to contagion, contracted in the noble discharge of his duties. For my present purpose, I say enough of his character when I mention that he was of a sedate but frank and cheerful nature; very exact in his observance of truth, and not by any means like myself – of an excitable or nervous temperament.

My Uncle Ludlow – Tom's father – while we were attending lectures, purchased three or four old houses in Aungier Street, one of which was unoccupied. *He* resided in the country, and Tom proposed that we should take up our abode in the untenanted house, so long as it should continue unlet; a move which would accomplish the double end of settling us nearer alike to our lecture-rooms and to our amusements, and of relieving us from the weekly charge of rent for our lodgings.

Our furniture was very scant – our whole equipage remarkably modest and primitive; and, in short, our arrangements pretty nearly as simple as those of a bivouac. Our new plan was, therefore, executed almost as soon as conceived. The front drawing-room was our sitting-room. I had the bedroom over it, and Tom the back bedroom on the same floor, which nothing could have induced me to occupy.

The house, to begin with, was a very old one. It had been, I believe, newly fronted about fifty years before; but with this exception, it had nothing modern about it. The agent who bought it and looked into the titles for my uncle, told me that it was sold, along with much other forfeited property, at Chichester House, I think, in 1702; and had belonged to Sir Thomas Hacket, who was Lord Mayor of Dublin in James II's time. How old it was *then*, I can't say; but, at all events, it had seen years and changes enough to have contracted all that mysterious and saddened air, at once exciting and depressing, which belongs to most old mansions.

There had been very little done in the way of modernizing details; and, perhaps, it was better so; for there was something queer and bygone in the very walls and ceilings – in the shape of doors and windows – in the odd diagonal site of the chimney-pieces – in the beams and ponderous cornices – not to mention the singular solidity of all the woodwork, from the banisters to the window-frames, which hopelessly defied disguise, and would have emphatically proclaimed their antiquity through any conceivable amount of modern finery and varnish.

An effort had, indeed, been made, to the extent of papering the drawing-rooms; but, somehow, the paper looked raw and out of keeping; and the old woman, who kept a little dirt-pie of a shop in the lane, and whose daughter – a girl of two-and-fifty – was our solitary handmaid, coming in at sunrise, and chastely receding again as soon as she had made all ready for tea in our state apartment – this woman, I say, remembered it, when old Judge Horrocks (who, having earned the reputation of a particularly 'hanging judge', ended by hanging himself, as the coroner's jury found, under an impulse of 'temporary insanity', with a child's skipping-rope, over the massive old banisters) resided there, entertaining good company, with fine venison and rare old port. In those halcyon days, the drawing-rooms were hung with gilded leather, and, I dare say, cut a good figure, for they were really spacious rooms.

The bedrooms were wainscoted, but the front one was not gloomy; and in it the cosiness of antiquity quite overcame its sombre associations. But the back bedroom, with its two queerly placed melancholy windows, staring vacantly at the foot of the bed, and with the shadowy recess to be found in most old houses in Dublin, like a large ghostly closet, which, from congeniality of temperament, had amalgamated with the bedchamber, and dissolved the partition. At night-time, this 'alcove' – as our 'maid' was wont to call it – had, in my eyes, a specially sinister and suggestive character. Tom's distant and solitary candle glimmered vainly into its darkness. *There* it was always overlooking him

– always itself impenetrable. But this was only part of the effect. The whole room was, I can't tell how, repulsive to me. There was, I suppose, in its proportions and features, a latent discord – a certain mysterious and indescribable relation, which jarred indistinctly upon some secret sense of the fitting and the safe, and raised indefinable suspicions and apprehensions of the imagination. On the whole, as I began by saying, nothing could have induced me to pass a night alone in it.

I had never pretended to conceal from poor Tom my superstitious weakness; and he, on the other hand, most unaffectedly ridiculed my tremors. The sceptic was, however, destined to receive a lesson as you shall hear.

We had not been very long in occupation of our respective dormitories when I began to complain of uneasy nights and disturbed sleep. I was, I suppose, the more impatient under this annoyance, as I was usually a sound sleeper, and by no means prone to nightmares. It was now, however, my destiny, instead of enjoying my customary repose, every night to 'sup full of horrors'. After a preliminary course of disagreeable and frightful dreams, my troubles took a definite form, and the same vision, without an appreciable variation in a single detail, visited me at least (on an average) every second night in the week.

Now, this dream, nightmare or infernal illusion – which you please – of which I was the miserable sport, was on this wise:

I saw or thought I saw, with the most abominable distinctness, although at the time in profound darkness, every article of furniture and accidental arrangement of the chamber in which I lay. This, as you know, is incidental to ordinary nightmare. Well, while in this clair-voyant condition, which seemed but the lighting up of the theatre in which was to be exhibited the monotonous tableau of horror, which made my nights insupportable, my attention invariably became, I know not why, fixed upon the windows opposite the foot of my bed; and, uniformly with the same effect, a sense of dreadful anticipation always took slow but sure possession of me. I became somehow conscious of a sort of horrid but undefined preparation going forward in some unknown quarter, and by some unknown agency, for my torment; and, after an interval, which always seemed to me of the same length, a picture suddenly flew up to the window, where it remained fixed, as if by an electrical attraction, and my discipline of horror then commenced, to last perhaps for hours. The picture thus mysteriously glued to the window-panes, was the portrait of an old man, in a crimson flowered silk dressing-gown, the folds of which I could now describe, with a countenance embodying a strange mixture of intellect, sen-suality, and power, but withal sinister and full of malignant omen. His nose was hooked, like the beak of a vulture; his eyes large, grey, and prominent, and lighted up with a more than mortal cruelty and coldness. These features were surmounted by a crimson velvet cap, the hair that peeped from under which was white with age, while the eyebrows retained their original blackness. Well I remember every line, hue and shadow of the stony countenance, and well I may! The gaze of this hellish visage was fixed upon me, and mine returned it with the inexplicable fascination of nightmare, for what appeared to me to be hours of agony. At last

'*The cock he crew, away then flew*'

the fiend who had enslaved me through the awful watches of the night; and, harassed and nervous, I rose to the duties of the day.

I had – I can't say exactly why, but it may have been from the exquisite anguish and profound impressions of unearthly horror, with which this strange phatasmagoria was associated – an insurmountable antipathy to describing the exact nature of my nightly troubles to my friend and comrade. Generally, however, I told him that I was haunted by abominable dreams; and, true to the imputed materialism of medicine, we put our heads together to dispel my horrors, not by exorcism, but by a tonic.

I will do this tonic justice, and frankly admit that the accursed portrait began to intermit its visits under its influence. What of that? Was this singular apparition – as full of character as of terror – therefore the creature of my fancy, or the invention of my poor stomach? Was it, in short, *subjective* (to borrow the technical slang of the day) and not the palpable aggression and intrusion of an external agent? That, good friend, as we will both admit, by no means follows. The evil spirit, who enthralled my senses in the shape of that portrait, may have been just as near me, just as energetic, just as malignant, though I saw him not. What means the whole moral code of revealed religion regarding the due keeping of our own bodies, soberness, temperance, etc.? Here is an obvious connection between the material and the invisible; the healthy tone of the system, and its unimpaired energy, may, for aught we can tell, guard us against influences which would otherwise render life itself terrific. The mesmerist and the electro-biologist will fail upon an average with nine patients out of ten – so may the evil spirit. Special conditions of the corporeal system are indispensable to the production of certain spiritual phenomena. The operation succeeds sometimes – sometimes fails – that is all.

I found afterwards that my would-be sceptical companion had his troubles too. But of these I knew nothing yet. One night, for a wonder, I was sleeping soundly, when I was roused by a step on the lobby outside my room, followed by the loud clang of what turned out to be a large brass candlestick, flung with all his force by poor Tom Ludlow over the banisters, and rattling with a rebound down the second flight of stairs; and almost concurrently with this, Tom burst open my door and bounced into my room backwards, in a state of extraordinary agitation.

I had jumped out of bed and clutched him by the arm before I had any distinct idea of my own whereabouts. There we were – in our shirts – standing before the open door – staring through the great old banister opposite, at the lobby window, through which the sickly light of a clouded moon was gleaming.

'What's the matter, Tom? What's the matter with you? What the devil's the matter with you, Tom?' I demanded, shaking him with nervous impatience.

He took a long breath before he answered me, and then it was not very coherently.

'It's nothing, nothing at all – did I speak? – what did I say? – where's the candle, Richard? It's dark; I – I had a candle!'

'Yes, dark enough,' I said; 'but what's the matter? – what *is* it? – why don't you speak, Tom? – have you lost your wits? – what is the matter?'

'The matter? – oh, it is all over. It must have been a dream – nothing at all but a dream – don't you think so? It could not be anything more than a dream.'

'Of *course*,' said I, feeling uncommonly nervous, 'it *was* a dream.'

'I thought,' he said, 'there was a man in my room, and – and I jumped out of bed; and – and – where's the candle?'

'In your room, most likely,' I said. 'Shall I go and bring it?'

'No; stay here – don't go; it's no matter – don't, I tell you; it was all a dream. Bolt the door, Dick; I'll stay here with you – I feel nervous. So, Dick, like a good fellow, light your candle and open the window – I am in a *shocking state*.'

I did as he asked me, and robing himself like Granuaile in one of my blankets, he seated himself close beside my bed.

Everybody knows how contagious is fear of all sorts, but more especially that particular kind of fear under which poor Tom was at that moment labouring. I would not have heard, nor I believe would he have recapitulated, just at that moment, for half the world, the details of the hideous vision which had so unmanned him.

'Don't mind telling me anything about your nonsensical dream, Tom,' said I, affecting contempt, really in a panic; 'let us talk about something else; but it is quite plain that this dirty old house disagrees with us both, and hang me if I stay here any longer, to be pestered with indigestion and – and – bad nights, so we may as well look out for lodgings – don't you think so? – at once.'

Tom agreed, and, after an interval, said:

'I have been thinking, Richard, that it is a long time since I saw my father, and I have made up my mind to go down tomorrow and return in a day or two, and you can take rooms for us in the meantime.'

I fancied that this resolution, obviously the result of the vision which had so profoundly scared him, would probably vanish next morning with the damps and shadows of night. But I was mistaken. Off went Tom at peep of day to the country, having agreed that so soon as I had secured suitable lodgings, I was to recall him by letter from his visit to my Uncle Ludlow.

Now, anxious as I was to change my quarters, it so happened, owing to a series of petty procrastinations and accidents, that nearly a week elapsed before my bargain was made and my letter of recall on the wing to Tom; and, in the meantime, a trifling adventure or two had occurred to your humble servant, which, absurd as they now appear, diminished by distance, did certainly at the time serve to whet my appetite for change considerably.

A night or two after the departure of my comrade, I was sitting by my bedroom fire, the door locked, and the ingredients of a tumbler of hot whiskey-punch upon the spider-table; for, as the best mode of keeping the

> *'Black spirits and white,*
> *Blue spirits and grey,'*

with which I was environed, at bay, I had adopted the practice recommended by the wisdom of my ancestors, and 'kept my spirits up by pouring spirits down'. I had thrown aside my volume of Anatomy, and was treating myself by way of a tonic, preparatory to my punch and bed, to half a dozen pages of the *Spectator*, when I heard a step on the flight of stairs descending from the attics. It was two o'clock, and the streets were as silent as a churchyard – the sounds were, therefore, perfectly distinct. There was a slow, heavy tread, characterized by the emphasis and deliberation of age, descending by the narrow staircase from above; and, what made the sound more singular, it was plain that the feet which produced it were perfectly bare, measuring the descent with something between a pound and flop, very ugly to hear.

I knew quite well that my attendant had gone away many hours before, and that nobody but myself had any business in the house. It was quite plain also that the person who was coming downstairs had no intention whatever of concealing his movements; but, on the contrary, appeared disposed to make even more noise, and proceed more deliberately, than was at all necessary. When the step reached the foot of the stairs outside my room, it seemed to stop; and I expected every moment to see my door open spontaneously and give admission to the original of my detested portrait. I was, however, relieved in a few seconds by hearing the descent renewed, just in the same manner, upon the staircase leading down to the drawing-rooms, and thence, after another pause, down the next flight, and so on to the hall, whence I heard no more.

Now, by the time the sound had ceased, I was wound up, as they say, to a very unpleasant pitch of excitement. I listened, but there was not a stir. I screwed up my courage to a decisive experiment – opened my door, and in a stentorian voice bawled over the banisters, 'Who's there?' There was no answer, but the ringing of my own voice through the empty old house – no renewal of the movement; nothing, in short, to give my unpleasant sensations a definite direction. There is, I think, something most disagreeably disenchanting in the sound of one's own voice under such circumstances, exerted in solitude and in vain. I redoubled my sense of isolation, and my misgivings increased on perceiving that the door, which I certainly thought I had left open, was closed behind me; in a vague alarm, lest my retreat should be cut off, I got again into my room as quickly as I could, where I remained in a state of imaginary blockade, and very uncomfortable indeed, till morning.

Next night brought no return of my barefooted fellow-lodger; but the night following, being in my bed, and in the dark – somewhere, I suppose, about the same hour as before, I distinctly heard the old fellow again descending from the garrets.

This time I had my punch, and the *morale* of the garrison was consequently excellent. I jumped out of bed, clutched the poker as I passed the expiring fire, and in a moment was upon the lobby. The sound had ceased by this time – the dark and chill were discouraging; and, guess my horror when I saw, or thought I saw, a black monster, whether in the shape of a man or a bear I could not say, standing with its back to the wall, on the lobby, facing me, with a pair of great greenish eyes shining dimly out. Now, I must be frank, and confess that the cupboard which displayed our plates and cups stood just there, though at the moment I did not recollect it. At the same time I must honestly say, that making every allowance for an excited imagination, I never could satisfy myself that I was made the dupe of my own fancy in this matter; for this apparition, after one or two shiftings of shape, as if in the act of incipient transformation, began, as it seemed on second thoughts, to advance upon me in its original form. From an instinct of terror rather than of courage, I hurled the poker, with all my force, at its head; and to the music of a horrid crash made my way into my room, and double-locked the door. Then, in a minute more, I heard the horrid bare feet walk down the stairs, till the sound ceased in the hall, as on the former occasion.

If the apparition of the night before was an ocular delusion of my fancy sporting with the dark outlines of our cupboard, and if its horrid eyes were nothing but a pair of inverted teacups, I had, at all events, the satisfaction of having launched the poker with admirable effect, and in true 'fancy' phrase, 'knocked its two daylights into one', as the commingled fragments of my tea-service testified. I did my best to gather comfort and courage from these evidences; but it would not do. And then what could I say of those horrid bare feet, and the regular tramp, tramp, tramp, which measured the distance of the entire staircase through the solitude of my haunted dwelling, and at an hour when no good influence was stirring? Confound it! – the whole affair was abominable. I was out of spirits, and dreaded the approach of night.

It came, ushered ominously in with a thunderstorm and dull torrents of depressing rain. Earlier than usual the streets grew silent; and by twelve o'clock nothing but the comfortless pattering of the rain was to be heard.

I made myself as snug as I could. I lighted *two* candles instead of one. I forswore bed, and held myself in readiness for a sally, candle in hand; for, *coûte que coûte*, I was resolved to *see* the being, if visible at all, who troubled the nightly stillness of my mansion. I was fidgety and nervous, and tried in vain to interest myself with my books. I walked up and down my room, whistling in turn martial and hilarious music, and listening ever and anon for the dreaded noise. I sat down and stared at the square label on the solemn and reserved-looking black bottle, until 'FLANAGAN & CO.'s BEST OLD MALT WHISKEY' grew into a sort of subdued accompaniment to all the fantastic and horrible speculations which chased one another through my brain.

Silence, meanwhile, grew more silent, and darkness darker. I listened in vain for the rumble of a vehicle, or the dull clamour of a distant row. There was nothing but the sound of a rising wind, which had succeeded the thunderstorm that had travelled over the Dublin mountains quite out of hearing. In the middle of this great city I began to feel myself alone with nature, and Heaven knows what beside. My courage was ebbing. Punch, however, which makes beasts of so many, made a man of me again – just in time to hear with tolerable nerve and firmness the lumpy, flabby, naked feet deliberately descending the stairs again.

I took a candle, not without a tremor. As I crossed the floor I tried to extemporize a prayer, but stopped short to listen, and never finished it. The steps continued. I confess I hesitated for some seconds at the door before I took heart of grace and opened it. When I peeped out the lobby was perfectly empty – there was no monster standing on the staircase; and as the detested sound ceased, I was reassured enough to venture forward nearly to the banisters. Horror of horrors! within a stair or two beneath the spot where I stood the unearthly tread smote the floor. My eye caught something in motion; it was about the size of Goliath's foot – it was grey, heavy and flapped with a dead weight from one step to another. As I am alive, it was the most monstrous grey rat I ever beheld or imagined.

Shakespeare says: 'Some men there are cannot abide a gaping pig, and some that are mad if they behold a cat.' I went well-nigh out of my wits when I beheld this *rat*; for, laugh at me as you may, it fixed upon me, I thought, a perfectly human expression of malice; and, as it shuffled about and looked up into my face almost from between my feet, I saw, I could swear it – I felt it then, and know it now, the infernal gaze and the accursed countenance of my old friend in the portrait, transfused into the visage of the bloated vermin before me.

I bounced into my room again with a feeling of loathing and horror I cannot describe, and locked and bolted my door as if a lion had been at the other side. D——n him or *it*; curse the portrait and its original! I felt in my soul that the rat – yes, the *rat*, the RAT I had just seen, was that evil being in masquerade, and rambling through the house upon some infernal night lark.

Next morning I was early trudging through the miry streets; and, among other transactions, posted a peremptory note recalling Tom. On my return, however, I found a note from my absent 'chum', announcing his intended return next day. I was doubly rejoiced at this, because I had succeeded in getting rooms; and because the change of scene and return of my comrade were rendered specially pleasant by the last night's half ridiculous half horrible adventure.

I slept extemporaneously in my new quarters in Digges' Street that night, and next morning returned for breakfast to the haunted mansion, where I was certain Tom would call immediately on his arrival.

I was quite right – he came; and almost his first question referred to the primary object of our change of residence.

'Thank God,' he said with genuine fervour, on hearing that all was arranged. 'On *your* account I am delighted. As to myself, I assure you that no earthly consideration could have induced me ever again to pass a night in this disastrous old house.'

'Confound the house!' I ejaculated, with a genuine mixture of fear and detestation, 'we have not had a pleasant hour since we came to live here'; and so I went on, and related incidentally my adventure with the plethoric old rat.

'Well, if that were *all*,' said my cousin, affecting to make light of the matter, 'I don't think I should have minded it very much.'

'Ay, but its eye – its countenance, my dear Tom,' urged I; 'if you had seen *that*, you would have felt it might be *anything* but what it seemed.'

'I am inclined to think the best conjurer in such a case would be an able-bodied cat,' he said, with a provoking chuckle.

'But let us hear your own adventure,' I said tartly.

At this challenge he looked uneasily round him. I had poked up a very unpleasant recollection.

'You shall hear it, Dick; I'll tell it to you,' he said. 'Begad, sir, I should feel quite queer, though, telling it *here*, though we are too strong a body for ghosts to meddle with just now.'

Though he spoke this like a joke, I think it was serious calculation. Our Hebe was in a corner of the room, packing our cracked Delf tea- and dinner-services in a basket. She soon suspended operations, and with mouth and eyes wide open became an absorbed listener. Tom's experiences were told nearly in these words:

'I saw it three times. Dick – three distinct times; and I am perfectly certain it meant me some infernal harm. I was, I say, in danger – in *extreme* danger; for, if nothing else had happened, my reason would most certainly have failed me, unless I had escaped so soon. Thank God. I *did* escape.

'The first night of this hateful disturbance, I was lying in the attitude of sleep, in that lumbering old bed. I hate to think of it. I was really wide awake, though I had put out my candle, and was lying as quietly as if I had been asleep; and although accidentally restless, my thoughts were running in a cheerful and agreeable channel.

'I think it must have been two o'clock at least when I thought I heard a sound in that – that odious dark recess at the far end of the bedroom. It was as if someone was drawing a piece of cord slowly along the floor, lifting it up, and dropping it softly down again in coils. I sat up once or twice in my bed, but could see nothing so I concluded it must be mice in the wainscot. I felt no emotion graver than curiosity, and after a few minutes ceased to observe it.

'While lying in this state, strange to say, without at first a suspicion of anything supernatural, on a sudden I saw an old man, rather stout and square, in a sort of roan-red dressing-gown, and with a black cap on his head, moving stiffly and slowly in a diagonal direction, from the recess, across the floor of the bedroom, passing my bed at the foot, and entering the lumber-closet at the left. He had something under his arm; his head hung a little at one side; and merciful God! when I saw his face.'

Tom stopped for a while, and then said:

'That awful countenance, which living or dying I never can forget, disclosed what he was. Without turning to the right or left, he passed beside me, and entered the closet by the bed's head.

'While this fearful and indescribable type of death and guilt was passing, I felt that I had no more power to speak or stir than if I had been myself a corpse. For hours after it had disappeared I was too terrified and weak to move. As soon as daylight came, I took courage and examined the room, and especially the course which the frightful intruder had seemed to take, but there was not a vestige to indicate anybody's having passed there; no sign of any disturbing agency visible among the lumber that strewed the floor of the closet.

'I now began to recover a little. I was fagged and exhausted, and at last, overpowered by a feverish sleep, I came down late; and finding you out of spirits on account of your dreams about the portrait, whose *original* I am now certain disclosed himself to me, I did not care to talk about the infernal vision. In fact, I was trying to persuade myself that the whole thing was an illusion, and I did not like to revive in their intensity the hated impressions of the past night – or to risk the constancy of my scepticism by recounting the tale of my sufferings.

'It required some nerve, I can tell you, to go to my haunted chamber next night, and lie down quietly in the same bed,' continued Tom. 'I did so with a degree of trepidation, which, I am not ashamed to say, a very little matter would have sufficed to stimulate to downright panic. This night, however, passed off quietly enough, as also the next; and so too did two or three more. I grew more confident and began to fancy that I believed in the theories of spectral illusions, with which I had at first vainly tried to impose upon my convictions.

'The apparition had been, indeed, altogether anomalous. It had crossed the room without any recognition of my presence: I had not disturbed *it*, and *it* had no mission to *me*. What, then, was the imaginable use of its crossing the room in a visible shape at all? Of course it might have *been* in the closet instead of *going* there, as easily as it introduced itself into the recess without entering the chamber in a shape discernible by the senses. Besides, how the deuce *had* I seen it? It was a dark night; I had no candle; there was no fire; and yet I saw it as distinctly, in colouring and outline, as ever I beheld human form! A cataleptic dream would explain it all; and I was determined that a dream it should be.

'One of the most remarkable phenomena connected with the practice of mendacity is the vast number of deliberate lies we tell ourselves, whom, of all persons, we can least expect to deceive. In all this, I need hardly tell you, Dick, I was simply lying to myself, and did not believe one word of the wretched humbug. Yet I went on, as men will do, like persevering charlatans and impostors, who tire people into credulity by the mere force of reiteration; so I hoped to win myself over at last to a comfortable scepticism about the ghost.

'He had not appeared a second time – that certainly was a comfort; and what, after all, did I care for him and his queer old toggery and strange looks? Not a fig! I was nothing the worse for having seen him, and a good story the better. So I tumbled into bed, put out my candle, and, cheered by a loud drunken quarrel in the back lane, went fast asleep.

'From this deep slumber I awoke with a start. I knew I had had a horrible dream; but what it was I could not remember. My heart was thumping furiously; I felt bewildered and feverish; I sat up in the bed and looked about the room. A broad flood of moonlight came in through the curtainless window; everything was as I had last seen it; and though the domestic squabble in the back lane was, unhappily for me, allayed, I yet could hear a pleasant fellow singing, on his way home, the then popular comic ditty called "Murphy Delany". Taking advantage of this diversion, I lay down again, with my face towards the fireplace and, closing my eyes, did my best to think of nothing else but the song, which was every moment growing fainter in the distance:

> "'Twas Murphy Delany, so funny and frisky,
>   Stept into a shebeen shop to get his skin full;
> He reeled out again pretty well lined with whiskey,
>   As fresh as a shamrock, as blind as a bull."

'The singer, whose condition I dare say resembled that of his hero, was soon too far off to regale my ears any more; and as his music died away, I myself sank into a doze, neither sound nor refreshing. Somehow the song had got into my head, and I went meandering on through the adventures of my respectable fellow-countryman, who, on emerging from the "shebeen shop", fell into a river, from which he was fished up to be "sat upon" by a coroner's jury, who having learned from a "horse-doctor" that he was "dead as a door-nail, so there was an end", returned their verdict accordingly, just as he returned to his senses, when an angry altercation and a pitched battle between the body and the coroner winds up the lay with due spirit and pleasantry.

'Through this ballad I continued with a weary monotony to plod, down to the very last line, and then *da capo*, and so on, in my uncomfortable half-sleep, for how long, I can't conjecture. I found myself at last, however, muttering, "*dead* as a door-nail, so there was an end"; and something like another voice within me, seemed to say, very faintly, but sharply, "dead! dead! *dead!* and may the Lord have mercy on your soul!" and instantaneously I was wide awake, and staring right before me from the pillow.

'Now – will you believe it, Dick? – I saw the same accursed figure standing full front, and gazing at me with its stony and fiendish countenance, not two yards from the bedside.'

Tom stopped here and wiped the perspiration from his face. I felt very queer. The girl was as pale as Tom; and, assembled as we were in the very scene of these adventures, we were all, I dare say, equally grateful for the clear daylight and the resuming bustle out of doors.

'For about three seconds only I saw it plainly; then it grew indistinct; but for a long time there was something like a column of dark vapour where it had been standing between me and the wall; and I felt sure that he was still there. After a good while, this appearance went too. I took my clothes downstairs to the hall, and dressed there, with the door half open; then went out into the street, and walked about town till morning, when I came back, in a miserable state of nervousness and exhaustion. I was such a fool, Dick, as to be ashamed to tell you how I came to be so upset. I thought you would laugh at me; especially as I had always talked philosophy, and treated *your* ghosts with contempt. I concluded you would give me no quarter; and so kept my tale of horror to myself.

'Now, Dick, you will hardly believe me when I assure you that for many nights after this last experience I did not go to my room at all. I used to sit up for a while in the drawing-room after you had gone up to your bed; and then steal down softly to the hall-door, let myself out, and sit in the "Robin Hood" tavern until the last guest went off; and then I got through the night like a sentry, pacing the streets till morning.

'For more than a week I never slept in bed. I sometimes had a snooze on a form in the "Robin Hood", and sometimes a nap in a chair during the day; but regular sleep I had absolutely none.

'I was quite resolved that we should get into another house; but I could not bring myself to tell you the reason, and I somehow put it off from day to day, although my life was, during every hour of this procrastination, rendered as miserable as that of a felon with the constables on his track. I was growing absolutely ill from this wretched mode of life.

'One afternoon I determined to enjoy an hour's sleep upon your bed. I hated mine; so that I had never, except in a stealthy visit every day to unmake it, lest Martha should discover the secret of my nightly absence, entered the ill-omened chamber.

'As ill luck would have it, you had locked your bedroom and taken away the key. I went into my own to unsettle the bed-clothes, as usual, and give the bed the appearance of having been slept in. Now, a variety of circumstances concurred to bring about the dreadful scene through which I was that night to pass. In the first place, I was literally overpowered with fatigue and longing for sleep; in the next place, the effect of this extreme exhaustion upon my nerves resembled that of a narcotic and rendered me less susceptible than, perhaps, I should in any other condition have been of the exciting fears which had become habitual to me. Then again, a little bit of the window was open, a pleasant freshness pervaded the room and, to crown all, the cheerful sun of day was making the room quite pleasant. What was to prevent my enjoying an hour's nap *here?* The whole air was resonant with the cheerful hum of life, and the broad matter-of-fact light of day filled every corner of the room.

'I yielded – stifling my qualms – to the almost overpowering temptation; and merely throwing off my coat and loosening my cravat, I lay down, limiting myself to *half* an hour's doze in the unwonted enjoyment of a feather bed, a coverlet, and a bolster.

'It was horribly insidious; and the demon, no doubt, marked my infatuated preparations. Dolt that I was, I fancied, with mind and body worn out for want of sleep, and an arrear of a full week's rest to my credit, that such measure as *half* an hour's sleep, in such a situation, was possible. My sleep was death-like, long and dreamless.

'Without a start or fearful sensation of any kind, I waked gently, but completely. It was, as you have good reason to remember, long past midnight – I believe, about two o'clock. When sleep has been deep and long enough to satisfy nature thoroughly, one often wakens in this way, suddenly, tranquilly and completely.

'There was a figure seated in that lumbering, old sofa-chair, near the fireplace. Its back was rather towards me, but I could not be mistaken; it turned slowly round, and, merciful heavens! there was the stony face, with its infernal lineaments of malignity and despair, gloating on me. There was now no doubt as to its consciousness of my presence, and the hellish malice with which it was animated, for it arose and drew close to the bedside. There was a rope about its neck, and the other end, coiled up, it held stiffly in its hand.

'My good angel nerved me for this horrible crisis. I remained for some seconds transfixed by the gaze of this tremendous phantom. He came close to the bed and appeared on the point of mounting upon it. The next instant I was upon the floor at the far side, and in a moment more was, I don't know how, upon the lobby.

'But the spell was not yet broken; the valley of the shadow of death was not yet traversed. The abhorred phantom was before me there; it was standing near the banisters, stooping a little, and with one end of the rope round its own neck, was poising a noose at the other, as if to throw over mine; and while engaged in this baleful pantomime, it wore a smile so sensual, so unspeakably dreadful, that my senses were nearly overpowered. I saw and remember nothing more until I found myself in your room.

'I had a wonderful escape, Dick – there is no disputing *that* – an escape for which, while I live, I shall bless the mercy of heaven. No one can conceive or imagine what it is for flesh and blood to stand in the presence of such a thing, but one who has had the terrific experience. Dick, Dick, a shadow has passed over me – a chill has crossed my blood and marrow, and I will never be the same again – never, Dick – never!'

Our handmaid, a mature girl of two-and-fifty, as I have said, stayed her hand, as Tom's story proceeded, and by little and little drew near to us, with open mouth, and her brows contracted over her little, beady black eyes, till, stealing a glance over her shoulder now and then, she established herself close behind us. During the relation, she had made various earnest comments, in an undertone; but these and her ejaculations, for the sake of brevity and simplicity, I have omitted in my narration.

'It's often I heard tell of it,' she now said, 'but I never believed it right till now – though, indeed, why should not I? Does not my mother, down there in the lane, know quare stories, God bless us, beyant telling about it? But you ought not to have slept in the back bedroom. She was loath to let me be going in and out of that room even in the daytime, let alone for any Christian to spend the night in it; for sure she says it was his own bedroom.'

'Whose own bedroom?' we asked, in a breath.

'Why, *his* – the ould Judge's – Judge Horrocks', to be sure, God rest his sowl'; and she looked fearfully round.

'Amen!' I muttered. 'But did he die there?'

'Die there! No, not quite *there*,' she said. 'Shure, was not it over the banisters he hung himself, the ould sinner, God be merciful to us all? and was not it in the alcove they found the handles of the skipping-rope cut off, and the knife where he was settling the cord, God bless us, to hang himself with? It was his housekeeper's daughter owned the rope, my mother often told me, and the child never throve after, and used to be starting up out of her sleep, and screeching in the night-time, wid dhrames and frights than cum an her; and they said how it was the speerit of the ould Judge that was tormentin' her; and she used to be roaring and yelling out to hould back the big ould fellow with the crooked neck; and then she'd screech "Oh, the master! the master! he's stampin' at me and beckoning to me! Mother, darling, don't let me go!" And so the poor crathure died at last, and the docthers said it was wather on the brain, for it was all they could say.'

'How long ago was all this?' I asked.

'Oh, then, how would I know?' she answered. 'But it must be a wondherful long time ago, for the housekeeper was an ould woman, with a pipe in her mouth, and not a tooth left, and better nor eighty years ould when my mother was first married; and they said she was a rale buxom, fine-dressed woman when the ould Judge come to his end; an', indeed, my mother's not far from eighty years ould herself this day; and what made it worse for the unnatural ould villain, God rest his soul, to frighten the little girl out of the world the way he did, was what was mostly thought and believed by everyone. My mother says how the poor little crathure was his own child; for he was by all accounts an ould villain every way, an' the hangin'est judge that ever was known in Ireland's ground.'

'From what you said about the danger of sleeping in that bedroom,' said I, 'I suppose there were stories about the ghost having appeared there to others.'

'Well, there *was* things said – quare things, surely,' she answered, as it seemed, with some reluctance. 'And why would not there? Sure was it not up in that same room he slept for more than twenty years? and was it not in the *alcove* he got the rope ready that done his own business at last, the way he done many a betther man's in his lifetime? – and was not the body lying in the same bed after death, and put in the coffin there, too, and carried out to his grave from it in Pether's churchyard, after the coroner was done? But there was quare stories – my mother has them all – about how one Nicholas Spaight got into trouble on the head of it.'

'And what did they say of this Nicholas Spaight?' I asked.

'Oh, for that matther, it's soon told,' she answered.

And she certainly did relate a very strange story, which so piqued my curiosity that I took occasion to visit the ancient lady, her mother, from whom I learned many very curious particulars. Indeed, I am tempted to tell the tale, but my fingers are weary, and I must defer it. But if you wish to hear it another time, I shall do my best.

When we heard the strange tale I have *not* told you, we put one or two further questions to her about the alleged spectral visitations, to which the house had, ever since the death of the wicked old Judge, been subjected.

'No one ever had luck in it,' she told us. 'There was always cross accidents, sudden deaths, and short times in it. The first that tuck it was family – I forget their name – but at any rate there was two young ladies and their papa. He was about sixty, and a stout, healthy gentleman as you'd wish to see at that age. Well, he slept in that unlucky back bedroom; and, God between us an' harm! sure enough he was found dead one morning, half out of the bed, with his head as black as a sloe, and swelled like a puddin', hanging down near the floor. It was a fit, they said. He was as dead as a mackerel, and so *he* could not say what it was; but the ould people was all sure that it was nothing at all but the ould Judge, God bless us! that frightened him out of his senses and his life together.

'Some time after there was a rich old maiden lady took the house. I don't know which room *she* slept in, but she lived alone; and at any rate, one morning, the servants going down early to their work, found her sitting on the passage-stairs, shivering and talkin' to herself, quite mad;

and never a word more could any of *them* or her friends get from her ever afterwards but "Don't ask me to go, for I promised to wait for him". They never made out from her who it was she meant by *him*, but of course those that knew all about the ould house were at no loss for the meaning of all that happened to her.

'Then afterwards, when the house was let out in lodgings, there was Micky Byrne that took the same room, with his wife and three little children; and sure I heard Mrs Byrne telling how the children used to be lifted up in the bed at night, she could not see by what mains; and how they were starting and screeching every hour, just all as one as the housekeeper's little girl that died, till at last one night poor Micky had a dhrop in him, the way he used now and again; and what do you think in the middle of the night he thought he heard a noise on the stairs, and being in liquor, nothing less id do him but out he must go himself to see what was wrong. Well, after that, all she ever heard of him was himself sayin', "Oh, God!" and a tumble that shook the very house; and there, sure enough, he was lying on the lower stairs, under the lobby, with his neck smashed double undher him, where he was flung over the banisters.'

Then the handmaiden added:

'I'll go down to the lane and send up Joe Gavvey to pack up the rest of the taythings, and bring all the things across to your new lodgings.'

And so we all sallied out together, each of us breathing more freely, I have no doubt, as we crossed that ill-omened threshold for the last time.

Now, I may add thus much, in compliance with the immemorial usage of the realm of fiction, which sees the hero not only through his adventures, but fairly out of the world. You must have perceived that what the flesh, blood and bone hero of romance proper is to the regular compounder of fiction, this old house of brick, wood and mortar is to the humble recorder of this true tale. I therefore relate, as in duty bound, the catastrophe which ultimately befell it, which was simply this – that about two years ago subsequently to my story it was taken by a quack doctor, who called himself Baron Duhlestoerf, and filled the parlour windows with bottles of indescribable horrors preserved in brandy, and the newspapers with the usual grandiloquent and mendacious advertisements. This gentleman among his virtues did not reckon sobriety, and one night, being overcome with much wine, he set fire to his bed curtains, partially burned himself, and totally consumed the house. It was afterwards rebuilt, and for a time an undertaker established himself in the premises.

I have now told you my own and Tom's adventures, together with some valuable collateral particulars; and having acquitted myself of my engagement, I wish you a very goodnight, and pleasant dreams.

The Moon-Bog
H. P. Lovecraft

Somewhere, to what remote and fearsome region I know not, Denys Barry has gone. I was with him the last night he lived among men, and heard his screams when the thing came to him; but all the peasants and police in County Meath could never find him, or the others, though they searched long and far. And now I shudder when I hear the frogs piping in swamps, or see the moon in lonely places.

I had known Denys Barry well in America, where he had grown rich, and had congratulated him when he bought back the old castle by the bog at sleepy Kilderry. It was from Kilderry that his father had come, and it was there that he wished to enjoy his wealth among ancestral scenes. Men of his blood had once ruled over Kilderry and built and dwelt in the castle, but those days were very remote, so that for generations the castle had been empty and decaying. After he went to Ireland Barry wrote to me often, and told me how under his care the grey castle was rising tower by tower to its ancient splendour, how the ivy was climbing slowly over the restored walls as it had climbed so many centuries ago, and how the peasants blessed him for bringing back the old days with his gold from over the sea. But in time there came troubles, and the peasants ceased to bless him, and fled away instead as from a doom. And then he sent a letter and asked me to visit him, for he was lonely in the castle with no one to speak to save the new servants and labourers he had brought from the North.

The bog was the cause of all these troubles, as Barry told me the night I came to the castle. I had reached Kilderry in the summer sunset, as the gold of the sky lighted the green of the hills and groves and the blue of the bog, where on a far islet a strange olden ruin glistened spectrally. The sunset was very beautiful, but the peasants at Ballylough had warned me against it and said that Kilderry had become accursed, so that I almost shuddered to see the high turrets of the castle gilded with fire. Barry's motor had met me at the Ballylough station, for Kilderry is off the railway. The villagers had shunned the car and the driver from the

North, but had whispered to me with pale faces when they saw I was going to Kilderry. And that night, after our reunion, Barry told me why.

The peasants had gone from Kilderry because Denys Barry was to drain the great bog. For all his love of Ireland, America had not left him untouched, and he hated the beautiful wasted space where peat might be cut and land opened up. The legends and superstitions of Kilderry did not move him, and he laughed when the peasants first refused to help, and then cursed him and went away to Ballylough with their few belongings as they saw his determination. In their place he sent for labourers from the North, and when the servants left he replaced them likewise. But it was lonely among strangers, so Barry had asked me to come.

When I heard the fears which had driven the people from Kilderry I laughed as loudly as my friend had laughed, for these fears were of the vaguest, wildest and most absurd character. They had to do with some preposterous legend of the bog, and of a grim guardian spirit that dwelt in the strange olden ruin on the far islet I had seen in the sunset. There were tales of dancing lights in the dark of the moon, and of chill winds when the night was warm; of wraiths in white hovering over the waters, and of an imagined city of stone deep down below the swampy surface. But hovering over the waters, and of an imagined absolute unanimity, was that of the curse awaiting him who should dare to touch or drain the vast reddish morass. There were secrets, said the peasants, which must not be uncovered; secrets that had lain hidden since the plague came to the children of Partholan in the fabulous years beyond history. In the *Book of Invaders* it is told that these sons of the Greeks were all buried at Tallaght, but old men in Kilderry said that one city was overlooked save by its patron moon-goddess; so that only the wooded hills buried it when the men of Nemed swept down from Scythia in their thirty ships.

Such were the idle tales which had made the villagers leave Kilderry, and when I heard them I did not wonder that Denys Barry had refused to listen. He had, however, a great interest in antiquities, and proposed to explore the bog thoroughly when it was drained. The white ruins on the islet he had often visited, but though their age was plainly great, and their contour very little like that of most ruins in Ireland, they were too dilapidated to tell the days of their glory. Now the work of drainage was ready to begin, and the labourers from the North were soon ready to strip the forbidden bog of its green moss and red heather, and kill the tiny shell-paved streamlets and quiet blue pools fringed with rushes.

After Barry had told me these things I was very drowsy, for the travels of the day had been wearying and my host had talked late into the night. A manservant showed me to my room, which was in a remote tower overlooking the village, and the plain at the edge of the bog, and the bog itself; so that I could see from my windows in the moonlight the silent roofs from which the peasants had fled and which now sheltered the labourers from the North, and too, the parish church with its antique spire and far out across the brooding bog the remote olden ruin on the islet gleaming white and spectral. Just as I dropped to sleep I fancied I heard faint sounds from the distance; sounds that were wild and half musical, and stirred me with a weird excitement which coloured my dreams. But when I awakened next morning I felt it had all been a dream, for the visions I had seen were more wonderful than any sounds of wild pipes in the night. Influenced by the legends that Barry had related, my mind had in slumber hovered around a stately city in a green valley, where marble streets and statues, villas and temples, carvings and inscriptions, all spoke in certain tones the glory that was Greece. When I told this dream to Barry we both laughed; but I laughed the louder, because he was perplexed about his labourers from the North. For the sixth time they had all overslept, waking very slowly and dazedly, and acting as if they had not rested, although they were known to have gone early to bed the night before.

That morning and afternoon I wandered alone through the sun-gilded village and talked now and then with idle labourers, for Barry was busy with the final plans for beginning his work of drainage. The labourers were not as happy as they might have been, for most of them seemed uneasy over some dream which they had had, yet which they tried in vain to remember. I told them of my dream, but they were not interested till I spoke of the weird sounds I thought I had heard. Then they looked oddly at me, and said that they seemed to remember weird sounds, too.

In the evening Barry dined with me and announced that he would begin the drainage in two days. I was glad, for although I disliked to see the moss and the heather and the little streams and lakes depart, I had a growing wish to discern the ancient secrets the deep-matted peat might hide. And that night my dreams of piping flutes and marble peristyle came to a sudden and disquieting end; for upon the city in the valley I saw a pestilence descend, and then a frightful avalanche of wooded slopes that covered the dead bodies in the streets and left unburied only the temples of Artemis on the high peak, where the aged moon-priestess Cleis lay cold and silent with a crown of ivory on her silver head.

I had said that I awakened suddenly and in alarm. For some time I could not tell whether I was waking or sleeping, for the sound of flutes still rang shrilly in my ears; but when I saw on the floor the icy moonbeams and the outlines of a latticed Gothic window I decided I must be awake and in the castle of Kilderry. Then I heard a clock from some remote landing below strike the hour of two, and knew I was awake. Yet still there came that monotonous piping from afar; wild, weird airs that made me think of some dance of fauns on distant

Maenalus. It would not let me sleep, and in impatience I sprang up and paced the floor. Only by chance did I go to the north window and look out upon the silent village and the plain at the edge of the bog. I had no wish to gaze abroad, for I wanted to sleep; but the flutes tormented me, and I had to do or see something. How could I have suspected the thing I was to behold?

There in the moonlight that flooded the spacious plain was a spectacle which no mortal, having seen it, could ever forget. To the sound of reedy pipes that echoed over the bog there glided silently and eerily a mixed throng of swaying figures, reeling through such a revel as the Sicilians may have danced to Demeter in the old days under the harvest moon beside the Cyane. The wide plain, the golden moonlight, the shadowy moving forms, and above all the shrill monotonous piping, produced an effect which almost paralysed me; yet I noted amidst my fear that half of these tireless, mechanical dancers were the labourers whom I had thought asleep, whilst the other half were strange airy beings in white, half-indeterminate in nature, but suggesting pale wistful naiads from the haunted fountains of the bog. I do not know how long I gazed at this sight from the lonely turret window before I dropped suddenly in a dreamless swoon, out of which the high sun of morning aroused me.

My first impulse on awaking was to communicate all my fears and observations to Denys Barry, but as I saw the sunlight glowing through the latticed east window I became sure that there was no reality in what I thought I had seen. I am given to strange phantasms, yet am never weak enough to believe in them; so on this occasion contented myself with questioning the labourers, who slept very late and recalled nothing of the previous night save misty dreams of shrill sounds. This matter of the spectral piping harassed me greatly, and I wondered if the crickets of autumn had come before their time to vex the night and haunt the visions of men. Later in the day I watched Barry in the library pouring over his plans for the great work which was to begin on the morrow, and for the first time felt a touch of the same kind of fear that had driven the peasants away. For some unknown reason I dreaded the thought of disturbing the ancient bog and its sunless secrets, and pictured terrible sights lying black under the unmeasured depth of age-old peat. That these secrets should be brought to light seemed injudicious, and I began to wish for an excuse to leave the castle and the village. I went so far as to talk casually to Barry on the subject, but did not dare continue after he gave his resounding laugh. So I was silent when the sun set fulgently over the far hills, and Kilderry blazed all red and gold in a flame that seemed a portent.

Whether the events of that night were reality or illusion I shall never ascertain. Certainly they transcend anything we dream of in nature and the universe; yet in no normal fashion can I explain those disappearances which were known to all men after it was over. I retired early and full of dread, and for a long time could not sleep in the uncanny silence of the tower. It was very dark, for although the sky was clear the moon was now well on the wane, and would not rise till the small hours. I thought as I lay there of Denys Barry, and of what would befall that bog when the day came, and found myself almost frantic with an impulse to rush out into the night, take Barry's car, and drive madly to Ballylough out of the menaced lands. But before my fears could crystallize into action, I had fallen asleep, and gazed in dreams upon the city in the valley, cold and dead under a shroud of hideous shadow.

Probably it was the shrill piping that awaked me, yet that piping was not what I noticed first when I opened my eyes. I was lying with my back to the east window overlooking the bog, where the waning moon would rise, and therefore expected to see light cast on the opposite wall before me; but I had not looked for such a sight as now appeared. Light indeed glowed on the panels ahead, but it was not any light that the moon gives. Terrible and piercing was the shaft of ruddy refulgence that streamed through the Gothic window, and the whole chamber was brilliant with a splendour intense and unearthly. My immediate actions were peculiar for such a situation, but it is only in tales that a man does the dramatic and foreseen thing. Instead of looking out across the bog, towards the source of the new light. I kept my eyes from the window in panic and fear, and clumsily drew on my clothing with some dazed idea of escape. I remember seizing my revolver and hat, but before it was over I had lost them both without firing the one or donning the other. After a time the fascination of the red radiance overcame my fright, and I crept to the east window and looked out whilst the maddening, incessant piping whined and reverberated through the castle and over all the village.

Over the bog was a deluge of flaring light, scarlet and sinister, and pouring from the strange olden ruin on the far islet. The aspect of that ruin I cannot describe – I must have been mad, for it seemed to rise majestic and undecayed, splendid and column-cinctured, the flame-reflecting marble of its entablature piercing the sky like the apex of a temple on a mountain-top. Flutes shrieked and drums began to beat, and as I watched in awe and terror I thought I saw dark saltant forms silhouetted grotesquely against the vision of marble and effulgence. The effect was titanic – altogether unthinkable – and I might have stared indefinitely had not the sound of the piping seemed to grow stronger at my left. Trembling with a terror oddly mixed with ecstasy I crossed the circular room to the north window from which I could see the village and the plain at the edge of the bog. There my eyes dilated again with a wild wonder as great as if I had not just turned from a scene beyond the pale of nature, for on the ghastly red-lit plain was moving a procession of beings in such a manner as none ever saw before save in night-mares.

Half-gliding, half-floating in the air, the white-clad bog-wraiths were slowly retreating towards the still waters and the island ruin in fantastic formations suggesting some ancient and solemn ceremonial dance. Their waving translucent arms, guided by the detestable piping of those unseen flutes, beckoned in uncanny rhythm of a throng of lurching labourers who followed doglike with blind, brainless, flounder-ing steps as if dragged by a clumsy but resistless demon-will. As the naiads neared the bog, without altering their course, a new line of stumbling stragglers zigzagged drunkenly out of the castle from some door far below my window, groped sightlessly across the courtyard and through the intervening bit of village, and joined the floundering column of labourers on the plain. Despite their distance below me I at once knew they were the servants brought from the North, for I recognized the ugly and unwieldy form of the cook, whose very absurdness had now become unutterably tragic. The flutes piped horribly, and again I heard the beating of the drums from the direction of the island ruin. Then silently and gracefully the naiads reached the water and melted one by one into the ancient bog; while the line of followers, never checking their speed, splashed awkwardly after them and vanished amidst a tiny vortex of unwholesome bubbles which I could barely see in the scarlet light. And as the last pathetic straggler, the fat cook, sank heavily out of sight in that sullen pool, the flutes and the drums grew silent, and the blinding red rays from the ruins snapped instantaneously out, leaving the village of doom lone and desolate in the wan beams of a new-risen moon.

My condition was now one of indescribable chaos. Not knowing whether I was mad or sane, sleeping or waking, I was saved only by a merciful numbness. I believe I did ridiculous things such as offering prayers to Artemis, Latona, Demeter, Persephone and Plouton. All that I recalled of a classical youth came to my lips as the horrors of the situation roused my deepest superstitions. I felt that I had witnessed the death of a whole village, and knew I was alone in the castle with Denys Barry, whose boldness had brought down a doom. As I thought of him new terrors convulsed me, and I fell to the floor, not fainting, but physically helpless. Then I felt the icy blast from the east window where the moon had risen, and began to hear the shrieks in the castle far below me. Soon these shrieks had attained a magnitude and quality which cannot be written of, and which make me faint as I think of them. All I can say is that they came from something I had known as a friend.

At some time during this shocking period the cold wind and the screaming must have roused me, for my next impression is of racing madly through inky rooms and corridors and out across the courtyard into the hideous night. They found me at dawn wandering mindless near Ballylough, but what unhinged me utterly was not any of the horrors I had seen or heard before. What I muttered about as I came slowly out of the shadows was a pair of fantastic incidents which occurred in my flight: incidents of no significance, yet which haunt me unceasingly when I am alone in certain marshy places or in the moonlight.

As I fled from that accursed castle along the bog's edge I heard a new sound: common, yet unlike any I had heard before at Kilderry. The stagnant waters, lately quite devoid of animal life, now teemed with a horde of enormous, slimy frogs which piped shrilly and incessantly in tones strangely out of keeping with their size. They glistened bloated and green in the moonbeams, and seemed to gaze up at the fount of light. I followed the gaze of one very fat and ugly frog, and saw the second of the things which drove my senses away.

Stretching directly from the strange olden ruin on the far islet to the waning moon, my eyes seemed to trace a beam of faint quivering radiance having no reflection in the waters of the bog. And upward along that pallid path my fevered fancy pictured a thin shadow slowly writhing, a vague contorted shadow struggling as if drawn by unseen demons. Crazed as I was, I saw in that awful shadow a monstrous resemblance – a nauseous, unbelievable caricature – a blasphemous effigy of him who had been Denys Barry.

A Fair Lady
Roger Malisson

The sight of her made his day.

She had long blonde hair and long brown legs, the tall slim girl dressed in brief denim shorts and what looked like a liberty bodice. She also had a bulging rucksack, a cheap camera slung round her neck, and a cross expression.

''Morning, miss,' said Jack, getting an eyeful as he wheeled his bike towards her over the grass verge.

'How far is it to Seachester, Officer?' she demanded, pushing her hair away from her face impatiently.

'Ten miles or so, straight down the road,' he answered.

'Is there much traffic later in the day?'

'Not a lot, but you may be lucky.'

'Bloody hell.' She shaded her eyes and scowled at the sea, sparkling peacefully in the July sun, then turned abruptly and jerked her head at the rolling countryside opposite.

'Not much point in going that way, then? Only bloody tractors and things, I suppose.' Her voice was faintly Cockney.

''Fraid so,' he said, smiling slightly. Her sulking, vapid stare reminded him of a model's in a glossy magazine; she had to be all of sixteen.

'If you don't mind my mentioning it, miss,' he said, recalling his duty, 'it's a bit dangerous for attractive girls to go hitch-hiking on their own. There's a bus goes from Hobston to Seachester every hour, and——'

'Hobston? Where's that?'

'The village just down the road. You can get a cup of tea, and the buses ...'

She was already striding away.

'I can take care of myself,' she snapped over her shoulder.

Suppressing a sarcastic retort, Jack watched her neat figure until she disappeared round a bend in the road. She couldn't help being rude. To kids like her he was just 'the fuzz', a hated symbol of a world they despised, criticized and coveted. She also made him feel quite piqued and old.

It was too bright a day for depressing thoughts. Jack remounted his bicycle and set off along the road on his rounds. The sun beat down on his shoulders; the heat would be fierce later on. They'd said on the radio it was the warmest summer since nineteen-something.

His route took him past a couple of farms and a trendy pub. A farm worker waved at him from a field. He exchanged a pleasantry with the trendy pub's landlord and set off back down the same road towards Hobston. Sometimes he felt as if he'd wandered into a soap opera, cast as Mr Plod; it was that blasted girl who'd disturbed him, he decided. She reminded him of city life – and 'life' was the word – London especially, before his return home to Hobston as the village bobby. Cycling along the smooth road with the shimmering sea lapping the beach below on his right and the rich green pastures spreading to the horizon on his left, Jack Merril, thirty-four and healthy, being the envy of his mates on the force as one who had unquestionably got it made, surrendered to wistful reminiscences.

He remembered the dingy, smoky offices and the city slums, the degradation, corruption, ingenuity and, above all, the vast quantity of crime there. He'd seen everything in the last ten years from high-life vice to sordid murder: the blackmailers and the cat-burglars, the tarts and the freaks, that spy case where the Specials had turned nasty, the nutcase with the hamner . . . How glad and relieved he'd been when he had landed this job at Hobston, where the last felony had been a breaking and entering at the off-licence two years ago, and that had been down to some drunken tourist. He'd been nine when his parents had moved away from the village; it was only because he'd been born here that he was accepted back, along with Sheila and the kids.

Cycling round a bend in the road, his musings were scattered by a terrible shock. It wasn't the sort of horrific fright that makes the hair prickle and the mouth open in an involuntary scream, but that spasm of tension experienced by every animal when suddenly confronted by a long-dreaded, potentially threatening, stronger animal. And so Jack's stomach contracted, his head jerked upright, his shoulders squared themselves – not easy on a bike – his pulse and heart rate accelerated as the adrenalin flowed, and he glanced down surreptitiously to see whether his shoes were polished. The creature which had caused these atavistic reactions advanced with an air of regal authority; it was his old headmistress. She stopped as he approached, her keen eyes undimmed with sixty years of clean living, and her memory circuits snapped into action.

'Jack Merril.'

Jack dismounted and straightened his tie. 'Miss Brophy.'

'Well, Jack, you've returned to Hobston, I see.'

Jack smiled foolishly and nodded, recalling her undeniable gift for making unanswerable statements.

'I hear you've done well in the Force. Inspector, aren't you?'

'No, sergeant.' Due for promotion soon, he nearly added, but checked himself in time. She wouldn't be interested in possibilities.

''H'm. You're married, aren't you?'

'Yes, they've given us one of the workers' cottages at the north end. A bit small, but it's rent-free.'

'Good. I hope you settle in.' Nodding curtly, she continued on her way, leaving him with the clear impression that she'd never thought he would ever amount to much, and by God she'd been right. Pedalling humbly down the road, Jack marvelled at the fact that the teacher, with her short grey hair and neat tweeds, hadn't altered a day in twenty years. By some alchemy, Miss Brophy seemed to have discovered the secret of eternal middle-age.

Funny old life, as Sid Fletcher would say. He was heading towards Sid's farm now, a mile or so past the spot where he'd met the hitch-hiker earlier. 'Fletcher's Farm' was a euphemism really. Sid owned a decrepit cottage and an acre or so on which he raised a few vegetables, a cow and some chickens – a smallholding by means of which Sid scraped a living. He also sold watery lemonade and rather dry biscuits to the tourists who wandered down from Seachester in the summer. Jack grinned to himself as he caught sight of the stone wall which surrounded Sid's place. Old Sid never could build a wall properly, and he was too stubborn to get professional help. Every winter, without fail, the searing North Yorkshire storms smashed his barrier, and the wind-lashed seas flooded his land. Every spring, Sid was to be seen painstakingly cementing his wall again and cursing his ill-luck. Sid wasn't very bright, in fact he was something of a local joke.

'Hey up, lad. Fancy a cuppa?'

'Nay, Sid, I s'll have to get back to t' station.'

The exchange was becoming a morning ritual. Jack waved and rode on towards Hobston, grinning to himself. It was easy to slip back into the dialect, and he did it half-ironically.

One of the Hobston job's perks was getting home for a decent lunch while John Duncan, the village's junior guardian of the law, minded the shop. Farewell to the curling cellophane-wrapped sandwich, hello to homemade steak and kidney pie. Hello to a spreading waistline, come to that.

'I took the kids to school this morning,' chattered Sheila as she shovelled an omelette onto a plate. 'Jamie was fretful, – just first-day nerves, I think – but Sally will look after him. She's good that way.'

'How about you? Do you think you're going to like it here?' Jack asked. His wife was cheerful, strong and capable, but Hobston didn't readily take to strangers.

'Oh, I think so.' Sheila turned from the cooking and shook her hair from her eyes, a mannerism that reminded him for a moment of the girl he'd met that morning.

'They're a bit old-fashioned, though, aren't they? Eccentric, almost. I saw a dark-haired man on a horse when I was doing the shopping, and one of the farm workers all but touched his cap as he passed.'

'That would be Dick Hobston,' answered Jack. 'I went to primary school with him. His family owned the whole area a hundred years ago. Then his father sold off most of the land and went into plastics. The people round here still look up to the Hobstons.'

'Sounds feudal,' commented Sheila, busy at the stove.

Jack stretched in his chair and yawned. 'Look 'ee, there be young Squire Hobston, a-gallopin' off on his foam-flecked mare. A devil for the ladies be young Squire. Ar.'

Sheila laughed dutifully and served his lunch before broaching her favourite topic of the moment.

'This house is rather small, isn't it, Jack? And there's no proper garden. I could save a fortune if we grew our own vegetables. Do you think we could buy a place of our own, maybe next year?'

Jack blanched at the thought of cutting into their savings.

'I like small houses,' he said petulantly, then, seeing Sheila's crest-fallen face, he added: 'Oh, we'll see.'

But Jack's domestic plans were abruptly forgotten when news came of the hitch-hiker's disappearance. The girl never reached her destination; Jack was the last person known to have seen her alive. During the weary days and weeks of questioning and search – the Seachester C.I.D. combing the area like rabbits – he was profoundly grateful for the villagers' silent support. Never once was a whisper of gossip or glance of suspicion directed against him, though the grilling he had from his superiors left him feeling like a criminal. Eventually the police de-camped, the case unsolved. The locals were glad to see the back of them; nobody born and bred outside of Hobston could possibly be up to any good, ran their philosophy.

Jack wasn't sorry to see them go, either. He took the family for a pre-lunch drink to the Hobston Arms the following Sunday, slipping easily into the village custom.

'This is the life, Sheila,' he said, stretching luxuriously in his wicker chair.

She smiled, adjusting her sunglasses. 'It's the first time I've seen you relaxed in weeks.'

Jamie, who was only six, began to fidget.

'I want to play at Droos, Sally! Let's play at Droos!'

'Druids, he means,' explained his sister. 'We learned about them in History.'

Jack ruffled his son's hair. 'I'll bet you don't want to be a fireman any more. I bet you're going to be a Druid when you leave school, right?'

Sally shrieked with laughter. 'Don't be silly, Daddy, it takes *years*!'

'Well, whatever do they teach you kids these days?' Jack teased her. 'Turning you into a right couple of little pagans, by the sound of – oh, ah – hello, Miss Brophy.'

He smiled weakly as the teacher settled herself and her dry sherry primly at a nearby table.

'Good morning to you. Lovely day. I see James and Sarah are looking much healthier than when they arrived, Mrs Merril.'

'Yes, they love it here,' Sheila agreed as the children ran off to their game. 'Talking of health, how's old Sid Fletcher now?'

'He'll be better soon.' Miss Brophy sniffed. 'The man's a weakling. Always was.'

Bet she's never been ill in her life, thought Jack, and marvelled again at the ease with which his wife had settled into this tight little community. She was a clever girl, and Sally was 'promising fair' to grow up just like her.

'See this, Jack?' Arthur Bell, the landlord, handed him a tabloid as he served their drinks.

MY DESPAIR, shouted the headline. *Heartbroken Mother in Police Row Drama. Mrs Cynthia Brown, 40, wept yesterday as she told of her agony over 'police delays and cover-ups' in the case of her missing daughter. 'I have now given up hope of seeing her again. Lynda and I were very close. I know in my heart she will never be found alive.'*

Attractive 16-year-old Lynda Brown, who vanished while hitch-hiking from London to Darlington, was last seen in the Hobston area of Seachester. Harrassed Chief Inspector Lewis, who led the search for Lynda, said last night, 'This is a very worrying case. We are doing everything possible to trace the missing girl.'

Jack threw down the paper. He knew what the woman was getting at, of course; she'd decided the moment she saw him that Jack was implicated, and that his colleagues were concealing the facts. Two and two make sixty-four, don't they, Mrs Brown?

'She might have got amnesia,' he muttered aloud. 'She might just have taken off – some bloke she met on the road ...'

'She's dead,' said Sheila calmly, and with such conviction that he started, suddenly aware of the rapt and sympathetic attention of every person there.

'Oh yes? Sure of that, are you?'

Sheila bent her blonde head over her glass. 'It's obvious,' she said slowly. 'A good-looking girl like that, *dressed* like that, hitch-hiking alone. Surely——'

'You're quite right, Mrs Merril.' Miss Brophy's brittle voice broke in. 'These modern young people! No discipline, no religion. They think the old ways are foolish, but they learn, they learn.'

During the totally predictable murmur of agreement from the rest of them, Jack rose to his feet and called the kids.

'Well – time to go, Sheila. 'Bye, all.' See you next week, he thought bitterly. See all of you next week, same time, same bloody place.

'Don't worry, old chap,' said Dick Hobston as they walked together out of the gate. 'Bound to be upsetting, but it'll blow over soon. These things always do, you know.'

He was right, of course. The summer weeks stretched on with sunny monotony and Hobston thrived. For a hobby, Sheila began to study ancient history at Miss Brophy's evening class and nagged gently for a place of their own. The children, apple-cheeked and tanned, did well at school. Dick Hobston wrote off his racing car and walked unscathed from the wreck. The dairyfarming Dobsons turned down an enormous offer for some of their land from a man who wanted to build a hotel. Mrs Dobson reported the theft of her purse, which was later found intact by the postman in the field where she had dropped it, and Sid Fletcher grew a little more potty every day. Jack worried about his chances of promotion, and occasionally wondered whether Lynda Brown was raving it up on the Continent or rotting quietly in some makeshift grave.

Autumn arrived with wind and rain. The children chattered constantly of the Harvest Festival, an important date in Hobston's calendar. It was always held in the village hall, or on the green in fine weather, as the nearest church was a couple of miles away. Jack missed it. He was called to Seachester that day for a meeting with his superiors. The meeting turned out to be a waste of time for him, and he came home tired, cold and dispirited. Sheila hadn't had time to cook anything hot, and he started a row over the meal before slamming out to the pub. It was all very well for her and the kids – they loved the village – but he was sick of the same faces and routine, and the clannishness of the place was beginning to get on his nerves.

There was a mood of celebration in the Hobston Arms that evening, and Jack was quick to catch it.

'Here's to prosperity,' he said, raising his glass.

'Oh, we'll prosper all right,' said the landlord jubilantly. 'All the proper rites have been observed today, so there's no reason why we shouldn't.'

Jack laughed. 'Rites? You can't be serious, Arthur. What have you all been doing, sacrificing white cockerels? I never took you for a superstitious bloke.'

Arthur reddened. 'Look, Jack, you can't argue with bloody——'

'"There are more things in heaven and earth, Horatio,"' drawled Dick Hobston. 'Isn't that right, Arthur?'

Miss Brophy put her oar in. 'I'm surprised at your scoffing, Jack Merril. You know we've always valued our traditions in Hobston, and with the world in the state it is today we are all in favour of a return to the old ways. It's just ignorance that——'

Her harangue was left unfinished as the door crashed open and a shabby, dishevelled man stumbled into the room, his face so distorted with fear that it took Jack some moments to recognize Sid Fletcher. He stood swaying, with pleading desperation in his bloodshot eyes, then collapsed into a chair and covered his face, keening quietly to himself.

'What's up, Sid? What's happened?' Jack broke the silence.

'He's drunk again,' said someone contemptuously.

'Come on, Sid. Tell us what's the matter.'

The old man clutched his arm, staring inwards.

'It's coming closer,' he whispered. 'Every day, a bit closer. And I can't stop it. It's horrible, Jack.'

'Take a grip on yourself, man!' snapped Miss Brophy. 'Nothing's going to harm you as long as you keep some control!'

'It's too late,' mourned Sid. 'I should never have listened. You don't know what it's like ...'

'Look, will someone start talking sense?' said Jack in exasperation. 'What's going on?'

'Quite simple, old lad,' Dick Hobston replied smoothly. 'Poor old Sid's taken to the bottle and he's seeing things. Ghosts, isn't it, Sid? Sad, really.'

'You're a feeble-minded old fool, Sid Fletcher!' said Miss Brophy brutally. 'Get home to your bed – it's all you're fit for.'

'Just a minute.' Jack looked at the woman with real loathing. 'Arthur, give me a double brandy. Right ... Get that down you, Sid, and I'll take you home.'

Ignoring the disapproving glances and mutterings all around him, he sat while Sid gulped his drink, then steered him out of the door and down the coast road that led to the farm. Sid was drunk, and kept up a low, desultory monologue all the way to his gate, but he'd stopped shaking and could walk reasonably steadily.

'You should see a doctor, Sid.'

'What for? All right, I am. Just keep going. It'll work, lad. Very angry, see – and that's good ... only I can't take it, Jack ... shouldn't have been me, no, it shouldn't. I'm sick, and too old ...'

'What's angry, Sid?' Jack interrupted gently. 'You, or this ghost you think you're seeing?'

Sid stared at him, and his eyes in the moonlight were crafty and mad.

'No more!' he shouted suddenly. 'Not much longer now. The old ways! The old ways!'

With a curious, tattered dignity, he walked the last few yards to his door.

Jack watched him with mingled pity and irritation. The village idiot, he thought, but what had happened to turn his brain like this? Idly, he turned his steps towards the beach. He didn't feel like going home yet. The glint of the moon on the dark waves reminded him for a moment of the sunlight's gleam on the girl's bright hair, that summer day ... Poor Sid ...

He turned sharply, staring at the cottage. Suppose the old fool had murdered that girl? What if guilt feelings were responsible for the illusion of her ghost? No, that was nonsense; no motive. There wasn't any money involved, and if she'd been rude her insults would have been met with bewilderment, not fury. And he couldn't figure old Sid for a sex murderer. Still, he decided on the way home to mention Sid's strange behaviour to Inspector Lewis next time they met. Opening the door of his own silent house, he walked inside and made a bed of the sofa.

Three days later Sid was found dead in his fireside chair. His heart had given out, and he must have died in some anguish, for the look on his face was far from peaceful. He was scarcely cold when Sheila began to talk of buying the farm, improving the cottage and cultivating a vegetable garden. Jack's opposition was confounded with relentless logic. The house was going cheap because it was so decrepit, a unique chance to make a worthwhile investment, good for the kids ...

'What about the flooding?' argued Jack. 'Your precious vegetables will be ruined every time that wall gives way.'

'It won't,' said Sheila.

'Oh?'

Sheila just smiled.

'Of course, dear, you know best, as always,' Jack said sarcastically. 'I suppose you'll be selling lemonade to the tourists, as well.'

'Why not?' said Sheila happily, and before he knew it Jack was stripping walls and putting up shelves in his spare time, while she scrubbed the place clean and made trips to Seachester for carpets and extra furniture.

They moved in on a Friday morning, only two months after Sid Fletcher's death. The conveyancing had gone smoothly, and the cottage, newly-decorated and shining, was waiting for them. Some essential renovating had been done; the rest could wait till they had more cash. The children were thrilled and ran about the house and garden with noisy delight. Sheila was all sunshine and surveyed her home with the expression of a woman whose nest-building instincts had found fulfilment.

Jack, on the other hand, couldn't care less. The atmosphere of the cottage, laden with old associations, was as cold to him as the bitter winter outside. He remembered sneaking into the place as a kid, tears streaking his dirty face and his hands tingling from Miss Brophy's strap. Sid had always been kind, and wasn't in the least concerned with things like talking in class or getting homework sums wrong. Jack remembered Sid's harmless swearing when his wall was knocked down during the storms, in the years before his stubborn habits had hardened into eccentricity. But he was gone now. Jack shivered suddenly at the thought of the old man's lonely, frightened death, here in this very room. He stared out through the window at Sid's wall, thick and solid, which was braving a savage wind from the east. Blow down, you fool, he thought angrily. Prove to Sheila that she was wrong about you at least.

Sally ran in from the garden.

'Daddy!' she cried, 'we're going to the shops with Mummy to buy things for the housewarming party tomorrow. Are you coming with us?'

'You realize all this could be a waste of time.' Jack ignored Sally and spoke directly to his wife. 'I might get promoted soon and we'd have to move out of the area.'

'Commute, then,' Sheila snapped. 'I'm staying.' Taking the children by the hand she walked out of the house, leaving Jack to his gloomy contemplation of the weather and his marriage.

Despite an uneasy truce with Sheila – no quarrelling when the kids were present – Jack had trouble sleeping that first night. After his third semi-nightmare he gave up and went downstairs for a drink. He stood at the window with his coffee and cigarette, staring moodily at the moonlit front garden, the stone wall and the sheet of grey sea beyond.

He shivered, and rubbed his eyes. Must be still half-asleep, because that white, nebulous thing moving slowly across the wall was surely pure imagination ... old Sid and his ghosts ... It's moving to and fro before the wall now – helpless, agitated, such a waste, such a pity ... catching at his thoughts ... And now it had stopped, and turned, as if it saw him, and he was the sole focus of its inimicable will. A silent roaring filled his brain, and his numbed limbs began to shake with shock and terror. The thin, luminous shape was moving towards him, a demonic embodiment of hatred, rage and destruction, and he thought he saw the eyes alight with all the fury and torment of hell, eager to rend his soul. It was getting closer, advancing across the garden towards the window. Brick walls would not stop it. Not this confused thought, but a mortal dread of encountering the face that might belong to that sinister being overcame the paralysis of fear. He ran from the room like a hunted hare and up the stairs to his bedroom. It was empty; Sheila had gone.

As in moments of physical danger, Jack thrust the panic from his mind and waited for the hammering of his heart to subside. Then, gathering all his courage, he forced himself to walk along the landing to the children's room, which faced on to the front of the house. Opening the door quietly, he stepped inside. A low, unintelligible sing-song met his ears, like plain chant. By the window stood a woman, ghostly in the moonlight. Keeping a firm hold of his consciousness Jack walked towards her, melting in wordless relief as he saw it was Sheila. But his wife had become a stranger in this weird, midnight world. She was staring into the garden and murmuring in a foreign tongue. From where he stood he thought he could see the malignant spirit recoil, and go back, leave them alone – at least, he thought he could ... Out of here, kids still sleeping, thank God, back along the landing and here was his bed ... mustn't pass out ...

'Are you all right, Jack? I just went to see if the kids were OK. Couldn't you sleep?' Sheila's voice was soothing as she climbed into bed.

'Sheila, you saw it, didn't you? The thing in the garden?'

'What? You've been having nightmares. Poor old Jack, never mind. Sure you're all right? You sound drunk. Try to get some sleep.'

Jack laughed mirthlessly. 'I only drank coffee,' he said. Turning his back upon the stranger in the bed, he fell asleep.

It was a relief the next day to be out of the house and alone at the station. His constable, John Duncan, had been requested yet again to help out in Seachester, much to John's disgust. But Inspector Lewis's word was, of course, law. Jack concentrated fiercely on overdue reports and tried to convince himself that he had dreamed all last night's events. He didn't succeed, but managed to keep his mind off any of the implications, real or imaginary. He had no evidence that anything untoward had occurred; he wasn't trained to deal with irrational hocus-pocus and old-fashioned superstition. He must wait for developments. That was right, wasn't it? He lunched off a chocolate bar and a packet of crisps and continued working.

But the evening brought a different mood. At six o'clock, he locked the filing cabinet, dragged on his overcoat and made straight for the Hobston Arms.

'Bit empty tonight, aren't you, Arthur?' he asked, nursing his pint.

The landlord gave him a strange look.

'Not surprising. They're all over at your place for the house-warming. Hope to be looking in myself later on.'

'Good God. I'd forgotten the bloody party.'

Arthur winced – perhaps he disapproved of swearing – as Jack knocked back his drink and hurried home, bent against the cutting wind that howled inland from the sea.

Jamie came running up the pathway to meet him.

'The party, Daddy! The party!'

'Cheers,' he said gloomily, allowing himself to be dragged into the house. And everyone was there, of course: Sheila, looking dishy, amazingly grown-up Sally, Miss Brophy, John Duncan, Dick Hobston, Harry Dobson, old Uncle Tom Cobley and all ...

'You're late, Jack,' Sheila remarked.

'Acutely observed, my dear.'

Sheila smiled winningly and dragged him to one side.

'Look, if you're in *that* mood – well, just don't show me up in front of the guests, do you hear? What's the matter with you, anyway? Have you been drinking?'

'Not really, but we'll soon remedy that, as they say.'

It was a fair-to-horrible party, but Jack was determined to struggle through it with the aid of several large scotches. One good thing, he thought, if that ghost comes again tonight I won't see it, I'll be dead to the world after all this booze. What ghost? Just imagination. More to the point, what booze? His glass was empty again. Only eight o'clock; two or three hours to go yet, at the least. Hold on, lad. Smile and chat to them all, from Dick Hobston to his stable lad, play the host. Good harvest, wasn't it? Rotten weather, isn't it? Quite.

What were they really thinking?

Nothing, from the look of it. A normal crowd of provincial people enjoying themselves at a well-organized party. You had to hand it to Sheila.

Sally and the older children were singing in a corner of the room, watched with approval by a group of adults.

'*Build it up with wood and clay ...*'

What's this? Can't have people bunched up like that at a party.

'*Wood and clay will wash away, wash away, wash away.*'

Other kids of her age are singing pop songs.

'*Set a watchman at the gate ...*'

'You're a bit old for nursery rhymes, Sally,' he said loudly.

There was a painful silence, and Sally blushed scarlet.

'Oh, Daddy! It's not really a nursery rhyme, it's part of a very old ballad, and——'

'Rubbish,' he said loftily. 'If you must sing, pick something cheerful and modern, for Heaven's sake. Ballad, my foot! It's a baby song.'

But adolescent dignity was affronted, and Sally was determined to carry her point.

'It *is* an old ballad, Daddy, truly – no one knows how old.' She was almost sobbing now, battling against the easy tears of childhood. 'You *must* know about it. I wish you wouldn't tease!'

'Tell me,' said Jack softly.

'Well, the people always knew that the water spirits would be offended if they built bridges and things on their stretch of water. So They had to offer human sacrifices to propitiate them, and the people who were sacrificed had to be young and, you know, untouched, so they'd be really angry at all they'd missed, their whole life, really, and they would guard their territory against the water gods, so the bridge or whatever it was would keep standing. Like Stonehenge. They found skulls and things there, and that's still standing, and – don't look like that, Daddy, please!'

'But this is all – this is nonsense.'

'No, dear,' said Sheila. 'There's a castle in Brittany where they found the skeleton of a four-year-old bricked into the wall with a candle in one hand and a piece of bread in the other, to keep him awake and nourished ... It happened all over Europe. Don't you think this sort of thing is worth investigating?'

Jack was cold, suddenly freezing cold. He gazed around the room, seeing his neighbours as if from another plane, as though he were looking at them down the centuries. Sickened, his mind recoiled from the primeval, reptilian cruelty in their ageless eyes as they stared back at him, their set smiles seeming to mock him while he turned from one familiar face to another. The atmosphere was stagnant, rancid, suffocating. He broke the spell by moving, first like a sleepwalker, then breaking into a run as he left the house.

Sheila made to follow him; Miss Brophy laid a restraining hand on her arm.

'Let him go, dear. He has to know sooner or later.'

Jack found his spade in the shed. He hurried to the wall that kept out the sea and began to dig like someone demented, jabbing hard at the stiff, frosty soil.

His family and friends watched with concern, then, smiling, shrugging, resumed their party. Dick, as usual, got a little drunk; Arthur, when he arrived, told them some funny stories. Sally, recovering, handed round cold snacks, and everyone complimented Sheila on her cooking.

Outside, Jack dug and dug into the hard, sandy soil, and the cold spade rubbed his palms raw. He had to pause often, to fight off waves of nausea and to chafe his freezing arms. He finally stopped, just as the moon was beginning to rise, at the moment when his spade struck something hard and rebounded, a matted hank of blonde hair clinging to its edge.

As he stood spent and motionless in the moonlight, there came the

high, clear, timeless sound of children's voices, drifting across the
garden:

> *'London Bridge is falling down,*
> *Falling down, falling down ...*

A gurgling laugh broke from his lips, and hoarsely, discordantly, he
raised his voice.

> *'Who will build it up again?*
> *My fair lady.'*

Who Knows?

Guy de Maupassant
Translated by H. N. P. Sloman

Merciful heaven! At last I've made up my mind to put on record what I've been through! But shall I ever be able to do it, shall I have the courage? It's all so mysterious, so inexplicable, so unintelligible, so crazy!

If I were not sure of what I've seen, certain that there has been no flaw in my reasoning, no mistake in my facts, no gap in the strict sequence of my observations, I should consider myself merely the victim of a hallucination, the sport of some strange optical delusion.

After all, who knows?

Today I am in a mental home, but I went there of my own free will, as a precaution, because I was afraid. Only one man knows my story, the House Doctor. Now I'm going to put it on paper, I really don't quite know why. Perhaps in order to shake off the obsession, which haunts me like some ghastly nightmare.

Anyhow, here it is:

I have always been a lonely man, a dreamer, a kind of solitary: good-natured, easily satisfied, harbouring no bitterness against mankind and no grudge against heaven. I have always lived alone, because of a sort of uneasiness, which the presence of others sets up in me. How can I explain it? I can't. It's not that I shun society; I enjoy conversation, and dining with my friends, but when I am conscious of them near me, even the most intimate, for any length of time, I feel tired, exhausted, on edge, and I am aware of a growing and distressing desire to see them go away or to go away myself and be alone.

This desire is more than a mere craving, it is an imperative necessity. And if I had to remain in their company, if I had to go on, I do not say listening to, but merely hearing their conversation, I am sure something dreadful would happen. What? Who knows? Possibly, yes, probably, I should simply collapse.

I am so fond of being alone that I cannot even endure the proximity of other human beings sleeping under the same roof; I cannot live in Paris; it is a long, drawn-out fight for life to me. It is spiritual death: this huge, swarming crowd living all round me, even in its sleep, causes me physical and nervous torture. Indeed, other people's sleep is even more painful to me than their conversation. And I can never rest, when I know or feel that there are living beings, on the other side of the wall, suffering this nightly suspension of consciousness.

Why do I feel like this? Who knows? Perhaps the reason is quite simple: I get tired very quickly of anything outside myself. And there are many people like me.

There are two kinds of human beings. Those who need others, who are distracted, amused, soothed by company, while loneliness, such as the ascent of some forbidding glacier or the crossing of a desert, worries them, exhausts them, wears them out: and those whom, on the contrary, the society of their fellows wearies, bores, irritates, cramps, while solitude gives them peace and rest in the unshackled world of their phantasy.

It is, in fact, a recognized psychological phenomenon. The former are equipped to lead the life of the extrovert, the latter that of the introvert. In my own case my ability to concentrate on things outside myself is limited and quickly exhausted, and as soon as this limit is reached I am conscious of unbearable physical and mental discomfort. The result of this has been that I am, or rather I was, very much attached to inanimate objects, which take on for me the importance of human beings, and that my house has, or rather had, become a world in which I led a lonely but purposeful life, surrounded by things, pieces of furniture and ornaments that I knew and loved like friends. I had gradually filled my home and decorated it with them, and in it I felt at peace, contented, completely happy as in the arms of a loving wife, the familiar touch of whose caressing hand has become a comforting, restful necessity.

I had had this house built in a beautiful garden, standing back from the road, not far from a town, where I could enjoy the social amenities, of which I felt the need from time to time. All my servants slept in a building at the far end of a walled kitchen-garden. In the silence of my home, deep hidden from sight beneath the foliage of tall trees, the enveloping darkness of the nights was so restful and so welcome that every evening I put off going to bed for several hours in order to prolong my enjoyment of it.

That evening there had been a performance of *Sigurd* at the local theatre. It was the first time I had heard this beautiful fairy play with music and I had thoroughly enjoyed it.

I was walking home briskly, with scraps of melody running in my head and the entrancing scenes still vivid in my memory. It was dark, pitch dark, and when I say that, I mean I could hardly see the road, and several times I nearly fell headlong into the ditch. From the toll-gate to my house is a little more than half a mile, or about twenty minutes' slow walking. It was one o'clock in the morning, one o'clock or half past one; suddenly the sky showed slightly luminous in front of me, and the crescent moon rose, the melancholy crescent of the waning moon. The moon in its first quarter, when it rises at four or five o'clock in the evening, is bright, cheerful, silvery; but in the last quarter, when it rises after midnight, it is copper-coloured, gloomy and foreboding, a real Witches' Sabbath moon. Anyone given to going out much at night must have noticed this. The first quarter's crescent, even when slender as a thread, sheds a faint but cheering gleam, at which the heart lifts, and throws clearly defined shadows on the ground: the last quarter's crescent gives a feeble, fitful light, so dim that it casts almost no shadow.

The dark outline of my garden loomed ahead, and for some reason I felt an odd disinclination to go in. I slackened my pace. The night was very mild. The great mass of trees looked like a tomb, in which my house lay buried.

I opened the garden gate and entered the long sycamore drive leading to the house with the trees meeting overhead; it stretched before me like a lofty tunnel through the black mass of the trees and past lawns, on which the flower-beds showed up in the less intense darkness as oval patches of no particular colour.

As I approached the house an unaccountable uneasiness gripped me. I paused. There was not a sound, not a breath of air stirring in the leaves. 'What has come over me?' I thought. For ten years I had been coming home like this without the least feeling of nervousness. I was not afraid. I have never been afraid in the dark. The sight of a man, a thief or a burglar, would merely have thrown me into a rage, and I should have closed with him, unhesitatingly. Moreover, I was armed; I had my revolver. But I did not put my hand on it, for I wanted to resist this feeling of fear stirring within me.

What was it? A presentiment? That unaccountable presentiment which grips a man's mind at the approach of the supernatural? Perhaps. Who knows?

As I went on, I felt shivers running down my spine, and when I was close to the wall of my great shuttered house, I felt I must pause for a few moments before opening the door and going in. Then I sat down on a garden seat under my drawing-room windows. I stayed there, my heart thumping, leaning my head against the wall, staring into the blackness of the foliage. For the first few minutes I noticed nothing unusual. I *was* aware of a kind of rumbling in my ears, but that often happens to me. I sometimes think I can hear trains passing, bells ringing, or the tramp of a crowd.

But soon the rumbling became more distinct, more definite, more unmistakable. I had been wrong. It was not the normal throbbing of my arteries which was causing this buzzing in my ears, but a quite definite though confused noise, coming, without any question, from inside my house. I could hear it through the wall, a continuous noise, a rustling rather than a noise, a faint stirring, as of many objects being moved about, as if someone were shifting all my furniture from its usual place and dragging it about gently.

Naturally, for some time I did not trust my hearing. But after putting my ear close to the shutters in order to hear the strange noises in the house more clearly, I remained quite firmly convinced that something abnormal and inexplicable was going on inside. I was not afraid, but – how can I express it? – startled by the sheer surprise of the thing. I did not slip the safety-catch of my revolver, somehow feeling certain it would be of no use. I waited.

I waited a long while, unable to come to any decision, with my mind perfectly clear but deeply disturbed. I waited motionless, listening all the time to the growing noise, which swelled at times to a violent crescendo, and then seemed to turn to an impatient, angry rumble, which made one feel that some outburst might follow at any minute.

Then, suddenly, ashamed of my cowardice, I seized my bunch of keys, picked out the one I wanted, thrust it into the lock, turned it twice, and pushing the door with all my force, hurled it back against the inside wall.

The bang echoed like a gunshot, and immediately the crash was answered by a terrific uproar from cellar to attic. It was so sudden, so terrifying, so deafening, that I stepped back a few paces and, though I realized it was useless, I drew my revolver from its holster.

I waited again, but not for long. I could now distinguish an extraordinary sound of trampling on the stairs, parquet floors and carpets, a trampling, not of human feet or boot soles, but of crutches, wooden crutches and iron crutches, that rang with the metallic insistence of cymbals. And then, suddenly, on the threshold of the front door, I saw an armchair, my big reading chair, come waddling out; it moved off down the drive. It was followed by others from the drawing-room, then came the sofas, low on the ground and crawling along like crocodiles on their stumpy legs, then all the rest of my chairs, leaping like goats, and the little stools loping along like rabbits.

Imagine my feelings! I slipped into a clump of shrubs, where I crouched, my legs glued all the time to the procession of my furniture, for it was all on the way out, one piece after the other, quickly or slowly, according to its shape and weight. My piano, my concert grand, galloped past like a runaway horse, with a faint jangle of wires inside; the smaller objects, brushes, cut glass and goblets, slid over the gravel like ants, gleaming like glow-worms in the moonlight. The carpets and hangings crawled away, sprawling pools of living matter, for all the world like devil-fish. I saw my writing-desk appear, a rare eighteenth century collector's piece, containing all my letters, the whole record of anguished passion long since spent. And in it were also my photographs.

Suddenly all fear left me; I threw myself upon it, and grappled with it, as one grapples with a burglar; but it went on its way irresistibly and, in spite of my furious efforts, I could not even slow it up. As I wrestled like a madman against this terrible strength, I fell to the ground in the struggle. Then it rolled me over and over, and dragged me along the gravel, and already the pieces of furniture behind were beginning to tread on me, trampling and bruising my legs; then, when I let go, the others swept over me, like a cavalry charge over an unhorsed soldier.

At last, mad with terror, I managed to drag myself off the main drive and hide again among the trees, watching the disappearance of the smallest, tiniest, humblest pieces that I had ever owned, whose very existence I had forgotten.

Then I heard, in the distance, inside the house, which was full of echoes like an empty building, a terrific din of doors being shut. They banged from attic to basement, and last of all the hall door slammed, which I had foolishly opened myself to allow the exodus.

Then I fled and ran towards the town, and I didn't recover myself till I got to the streets, and met people going home late. I went and rang at the door of a hotel where I was known. I had beaten my clothes with my hands to shake the dust out of them, and I made up a story that I had lost my bunch of keys with the key of the kitchen-garden, where my servants slept in a house by itself, behind the garden wall which protected my fruit and vegetables from thieves.

I pulled the bed-clothes up to my eyes in the bed they gave me; but I couldn't sleep, and I waited for dawn, listening to the violent beating of my heart. I had given orders for my servants to be informed as soon as it was light, and my valet knocked at my door at seven o'clock in the morning. His face showed how upset he was.

'An awful thing has happened during the night, sir,' he said.

'What is it?'

'All your furniture has been stolen, sir, absolutely everything, down to the smallest objects.'

Somehow I was relieved to hear this. Why? I don't know. I had complete control of myself; I knew I could conceal my feelings, tell no one what I had seen, hide it, bury it in my breast like some ghastly secret. I replied:

'Then they are the same people who stole my keys. The police must be informed at once. I'm getting up, and I'll be with you in a few minutes at the police station.'

The enquiry lasted five months. Nothing was brought to light.

Neither the smallest of my ornaments nor the slightest trace of the thieves was ever found. Good heavens! If I had told them what I knew ... If I had told ... they would have shut up, not the thieves, but me, the man who could have seen such a thing.

Of course, I knew how to keep my mouth shut. But I never furnished my house again. It was no good. The same thing would have happened. I never wanted to go back to it again. I never did go back. I never saw it again. I went to a hotel in Paris, and consulted doctors about the state of my nerves, which·had been causing me considerable anxiety since that dreadful night.

They prescribed travel and I took their advice.

*   *   *

I began with a trip to Italy. The sun did me good. For six months I wandered from Genoa to Venice, from Venice to Florence, from Florence to Rome, from Rome to Naples. Then I toured Sicily, an attractive country, from the point of view of both scenery and monuments, the remains left by the Greeks and the Normans. I crossed to Africa, and travelled at my leisure through the great sandy, peaceful desert, where camels, gazelles and nomad Arabs roam, and where, in the clear, dry air, no obsession can persist either by day or by night.

I returned to France via Marseilles, and, in spite of the Provençal gaiety, the diminished intensity of the sunlight depressed me. On my return to Europe I had the old feeling of a patient who thinks he is cured, but is suddenly warned, by a dull pain, that the seat of the trouble is still active.

Then I went back to Paris. After a month I got bored. It was autumn, and I decided to take a trip, before the winter, through Normandy, which was new ground to me.

I began with Rouen, of course, and for a week I wandered about, intrigued, charmed, thrilled, in this medieval town, this amazing museum of rare specimens of Gothic art.

Then one evening, about four o'clock, as I was entering a street that seemed too good to be true, along which flows an inky-black stream called the Eau de Robec, my attention, previously centred on the unusual, old-fashioned aspect of the houses, was suddenly arrested by a number of second-hand furniture shops next door to one another.

They had, indeed, chosen their haunt well, these seedy junk dealers, in this fantastic alley along this sinister stream, under pointed roofs of tile or slate, on which the weather-vanes of a vanished age still creaked.

Stacked in the depths of the cavernous shops could be seen carved chests, china from Rouen, Nevers and Moustiers, statues, some painted, some in plain oak, crucifixes, Madonnas, Saints, church ornaments, chasubles, copes, even chalices, and an old tabernacle of gilded wood, now vacated by its Almighty tenant. What astonishing caverns there were in these great, lofty houses, packed from cellar to attic with pieces of every kind, whose usefulness seemed finished, and which had outlived their natural owners, their century, their period, their fashion, to be bought as curios by later generations!

My passion for old things was reviving in this collector's paradise. I went from shop to shop, crossing in two strides the bridges made of four rotten planks thrown over the stinking water of the Eau de Robec. And then – Mother of God! My heart leapt to my mouth. I caught sight of one of my finest cabinets at the edge of a vault crammed with junk, that looked like the entrance to the catacombs of some cemetery of old furniture. I went towards it trembling all over, trembling to such an extent that I did not dare touch it. I stretched out my hand, then I hesitated. It *was* mine, there was no question about it, a unique Louis XIII cabinet, unmistakable to anyone who had ever seen it. Suddenly, peering farther into the sombre depths of this gallery, I noticed three of my arm-chairs covered with *petit point* embroidery, then farther off my two Henry II tables, which were so rare that people came specially from Paris to see them.

Imagine, just imagine my feelings!

Then I went forward, dazed and faint with excitement, but I went in, for I am no coward, I went in like a knight in the dark ages entering a witches' kitchen. As I advanced, I found all my belongings, my chandeliers, my books, my pictures, my hangings and carpets, my weapons, everything except the writing-desk containing my letters, which I could not discover anywhere.

I went on, downstairs, along dark passages, and then up again to the floors above. I was alone. I called, but there was no answer. I was quite alone; there was no one in this huge, winding labyrinth of a house.

Night came on, and I had to sit down in the dark on one of my own chairs, for I wouldn't go away. At intervals I shouted: 'Hullo! Hullo! Anybody there?'

I had been there, I am sure, more than an hour, when I heard footsteps, light, slow steps: I could not tell where they came from. I nearly ran away, but, bracing myself, I called again, and I saw a light in the next room.

'Who's there?' said a voice.

I answered:

'A customer.'

The answer came:

'It's very late, we're really closed.'

I retorted:

'I've been waiting for you an hour.'

'You could have come back tomorrow.'

'Tomorrow I shall have left Rouen.'

I did not dare to move, and he did not come to me. All this time I saw the reflection of his light shining on a tapestry, in which two angels were flying above the dead on a battlefield. That, too, belonged to me.

I said:

'Well, are you coming?'

He replied:

'I'm waiting for you.'

I got up and went towards him.

In the centre of a large room stood a very short man, very short and very fat, like the fat man at a show, and hideous into the bargain. He had a sparse, straggling, ill-kept, dirty-yellow beard, and not a hair on his head, not a single one. As he held his candle raised at arm's length in order to see me, the dome of his bald head looked like a miniature moon in this huge room stacked with old furniture. His face was wrinkled and bloated, his eyes mere slits.

After some bargaining I bought three chairs that were really mine, and paid a large sum in cash, merely giving the number of my room at the hotel. They were to be delivered next morning before nine o'clock. Then I left the shop. He showed me to the door most politely. I went straight to the Head Police Station, where I told the story of the theft of my furniture and the discovery I had just made.

The Inspector telegraphed, on the spot, for instructions, the Public Prosecutor's Office, where the investigation into the theft had been held, asking me to wait for the answer. An hour later it was received, completely confirming my story.

'I'll have this man arrested and questioned at once,' he said, 'for he may have become suspicious, and he might move your belongings. I suggest you go and dine, and come back in two hours' time: I'll have him here, and I'll put him through a second examination in your presence.'

'Excellent, Inspector! I'm more than grateful to you.'

I went and dined at my hotel, and my appetite was better than I should have thought possible. But I was pretty well satisfied. They had got him.

Two hours later I was back at the police station, where the officer was waiting for me.

'Well, sir,' he said, when he saw me, 'we haven't got your friend. My men haven't been able to lay hands on him.'

'Do you mean...?'

A feeling of faintness came over me.

'But ... you *have* found the house?' I asked.

'Oh yes! And it will, of course, be watched and guarded till he comes back. But he has disappeared.'

'Disappeared?'

'Yes, disappeared. He usually spends the evening with his next-door neighbour, a queer old hag, a widow called Mrs Bidoin, a second-hand dealer like himself. She hasn't seen him this evening and can't give any information about him. We shall have to wait till tomorrow.'

I went away. The streets of Rouen now seemed sinister, disturbing, haunted.

I slept badly, with nightmares every time I dropped off.

As I didn't want to seem unduly anxious, or in too much of a hurry, I waited next morning till ten o'clock before going round to the police station.

The dealer had not reappeared: his shop was still closed.

The Inspector said to me:

'I've taken all the necessary steps. The Public Prosecutor's Department has been informed; we'll go together to the shop and have it opened: you can show me what belongs to you.'

We drove to the place. Policemen were on duty, with a locksmith, in front of the door, which had been opened.

When I went in, I saw neither my cabinet nor my armchairs, nor my tables, not a single one of all the contents of my house, though the evening before I could not take a step without running into something of mine.

The Chief Inspector, in surprise, at first looked at me suspiciously.

'Well, I must say, Inspector, the disappearance of this furniture coincides oddly with that of the dealer,' I said.

He smiled:

'You're right! You made a mistake buying and paying for your pieces yesterday. It was that gave him the tip.'

I replied:

'What I can't understand is that all the space occupied by my furniture is now filled with other pieces.'

'Oh well,' answered the Inspector, 'he had the whole night before him, and accomplices too, no doubt. There are sure to be means of communication with the houses on either side. Don't be alarmed, sir, I shall leave no stone unturned. The thief won't evade us for long, now we've got his hide-out.'

My heart was beating so violently that I thought it would burst.

*   *   *

I stayed on in Rouen for a fortnight. The man did not come back. God knows, nobody could outwit or trap a man like that.

Then on the following morning I got this strange letter from my gardener, who was acting as caretaker of my house, which had been left unoccupied since the robbery:

Dear Sir,
I beg to inform you that something happened last night, which we can't
explain, nor the police neither. All the furniture has come back, absolutely
everything, down to the smallest bits. The house is now just as it was the
evening before the burglary. It's fit to send you off your head. It all happened
on the night between Friday and Saturday. The paths are cut up, as if every-
thing had been dragged from the garden gate to the front door. It was just the
same the day it all disappeared.

I await your return and remain,
Yours respectfully,
PHILIP RAUDIN.

No! No! No! I will *not* return there!

I took the letter to the Chief Inspector of Rouen.

'It's a very neat restitution,' he said. 'We'll lie doggo, and we'll nab
the fellow one of these days.'

*   *   *

But he has not been nabbed. No! They've never got him, and now I'm
afraid of him, as if a wild animal were loose on my track.

He can't be found! He'll never be found, this monster with the bald
head like a full moon. They'll never catch him. He'll never go back to his
shop. Why should he? Nobody but me *can* meet him, and I won't. I
won't! I won't! I won't!

And if he does go back, if he returns to his shop, who will be able to
prove that my furniture was ever there? There's only my evidence, and
I've a feeling that that is becoming suspect.

No! My life was getting impossible. And I couldn't keep the secret of
what I had seen. I couldn't go on living like everyone else, with the fear
that this sort of thing might begin again at any moment.

I went and consulted the doctor who keeps this mental home, and
told him the whole story.

After putting me through a lengthy examination, he said:

'My dear sir, would you be willing to stay here for a time?'

'I should be very glad to.'

'You're not short of money?'

'No, Doctor.'

'Would you like a bungalow to yourself?'

'Yes, I should.'

'Would you like your friends to come and see you?'

'No, Doctor, no one. The man from Rouen might venture to follow
me here to get even with me.'

*   *   *

And I have been here alone for three months, absolutely alone. I have practically no anxieties. I am only afraid of one thing ... Supposing the second-hand dealer went mad ... and suppose he was brought to this home ...? Even prisons are not absolutely safe...

John Charrington's Wedding
E. Nesbit

No one ever thought that May Forster would marry John Charrington; but he thought differently, and things which John Charrington intended had a queer way of coming to pass. He asked her to marry him before he went up to Oxford. She laughed and refused him. He asked her again next time he came home. Again she laughed, tossed her dainty blonde head and again refused. A third time he asked her; she said it was becoming a confirmed bad habit, and laughed at him more than ever.

John was not the only man who wanted to marry her: she was the belle of our village coterie, and we were all in love with her more or less; it was a sort of fashion, like heliotrope ties or Inverness capes. Therefore we were as much annoyed as surprised when John Charrington walked into our little local Club – we held it in a loft over the saddler's, I remember – and invited us all to his wedding.

'Your wedding?'

'You don't mean it?'

'Who's the happy pair? When's it to be?'

John Charrington filled his pipe and lighted it before he replied. Then he said:

'I'm sorry to deprive you fellows of your only joke – but Miss Forster and I are to be married in September.'

'You don't mean it?'

'He's got the mitten again, and it's turned his head.'

'No,' I said, rising, 'I see it's true. Lend me a pistol someone – or a first-class fare to the other end of Nowhere. Charrington has bewitched the only pretty girl in our twenty-mile radius. Was it mesmerism, or a love-potion, Jack?'

'Neither, sir, but a gift you'll never have – perseverance – and the best luck a man ever had in this world.'

There was something in his voice that silenced me, and all chaff of the other fellows failed to draw him further.

The queer thing about it was that when we congratulated Miss

Forster, she blushed and smiled and dimpled, for all the world as though she were in love with him, and had been in love with him all the time. Upon my word, I think she had. Women are strange creatures.

We were all asked to the wedding. In Brixham everyone who was anybody knew everybody else who was anyone. My sisters were, I truly believe, more interested in the *trousseau* than the bride herself, and I was to be best man. The coming marriage was much canvassed at afternoon tea-tables, and at our little Club over the saddler's, and the question was always asked, 'Does she care for him?'

I used to ask that question myself in the early days of their engagement, but after a certain evening in August I never asked it again. I was coming home from the Club through the churchyard. Our church is on a thyme-grown hill, and the turf about it is so thick and soft that one's footsteps are noiseless.

I made no sound as I vaulted the low lichened wall, and threaded my way between the tombstones. It was at the same instant that I heard John Charrington's voice, and saw her. May was sitting on a low flat gravestone, her face turned towards the full splendour of the western sun. Its expression ended, at once and for ever, any question of love for him; it was transfigured to a beauty I should not have believed possible, even to that beautiful little face.

John lay at her feet, and it was his voice that broke the stillness of the golden August evening.

'My dear, my dear, I believe I should come back from the dead if you wanted me!'

I coughed at once to indicate my presence, and passed on into the shadow fully enlightened.

The wedding was to be early in September. Two days before I had to run up to town on business. The train was late, of course, for we are on the South-Eastern, and as I stood grumbling with my watch in my hand, whom should I see but John Charrington and May Forster. They were walking up and down the unfrequented end of the platform, arm in arm, looking into each other's eyes, careless of the sympathetic interest of the porters.

Of course I knew better than to hesitate a moment before burying myself in the booking-office, and it was not till the train drew up at the platform, that I obtrusively passed the pair with my Gladstone, and took the corner in a first-class smoking-carriage. I did this with as good an air of not seeing them as I could assume. I pride myself on my discretion, but if John were travelling alone I wanted his company. I had it.

'Hullo, old man,' came his cheery voice as he swung his bag into my carriage; 'here's luck; I was expecting a dull journey!'

'Where are you off to?' I asked, discretion still bidding me turn my eyes away, though I saw, without looking, that hers were red-rimmed.

'To old Branbridge's,' he answered, shutting the door and leaning out for a last word with his sweetheart.

'Oh, I wish you wouldn't go, John,' she was saying in a low, earnest voice. 'I feel certain something will happen.'

'Do you think I should let anything happen to keep me, and the day after tomorrow our wedding day?'

'Don't go,' she answered, with a pleading intensity which would have sent my Gladstone on to the platform and me after it. But she wasn't speaking to me. John Charrington was made differently: he rarely changed his opinions, never his resolutions.

He only stroked the little ungloved hands that lay on the carriage door.

'I must, May. The old boy's been awfully good to me, and now he's dying I must go and see him, but I shall come home in time for——' the rest of the parting was lost in a whisper and in the rattling lurch of the starting train.

'You're sure to come?' she spoke as the train moved.

'Nothing shall keep me,' he answered; and we steamed out. After he had seen the last of the little figure on the platform he leaned back in his corner and kept silence for a minute.

When he spoke it was to explain to me that his godfather, whose heir he was, lay dying at Peasmarsh Place, some fifty miles away, and had sent for John, and John had felt bound to go.

'I shall be surely back tomorrow,' he said, 'or, if not, the day after, in heaps of time. Thank heaven, one hasn't to get up in the middle of the night to get married nowadays!'

'And suppose Mr Branbridge dies?'

'Alive or dead I mean to be married on Thursday!' John answered, lighting a cigar and unfolding *The Times*.

At Peasmarsh station we said 'goodbye', and he got out, and I saw him ride off; I went on to London, where I stayed the night.

When I got home the next afternoon, a very wet one, by the way, my sister greeted me with:

'Where's Mr Charrington?'

'Goodness knows,' I answered testily. Every man, since Cain, has resented that kind of question.

'I thought you might have heard from him,' she went on, 'as you're to give him away tomorrow.'

'Isn't he back?' I asked, for I had confidently expected to find him at home.

'No, Geoffrey,' my sister Fanny always had a way of jumping to conclusions, especially such conclusions as were least favourable to her fellow-creatures – 'he has not returned, and, what is more, you may depend upon it he won't. You mark my words, there'll be no wedding tomorrow.'

My sister Fanny has a power of annoying me which no other human being possesses.

'You mark my words,' I retorted with asperity, 'you had better give up making such a thundering idiot of yourself. There'll be more wedding tomorrow than ever you'll take the first part in.' A prophecy which, by the way, came true.

But though I could snarl confidently to my sister, I did not feel so comfortable when late that night, I, standing on the doorstep of John's house, heard that he had not returned. I went home gloomily through the rain. Next morning brought a brilliant blue sky, gold sun, and all such softness of air and beauty of cloud as go to make up a perfect day. I woke with a vague feeling of having gone to bed anxious, and of being rather averse to facing that anxiety in the light of full wakefulness.

But with my shaving-water came a note from John which relieved my mind and sent me up to the Forsters with a light heart.

May was in the garden. I saw her blue gown through the hollyhocks as the lodge gates swung to behind me. So I did not go up to the house, but turned aside down the turfed path.

'He's written to you too,' she said, without preliminary greeting, when I reached her side.

'Yes, I'm to meet him at the station at three, and come straight on to the church.'

Her face looked pale, but there was a brightness in her eyes, and a tender quiver about the mouth that spoke of renewed happiness.

'Mr Branbridge begged him so to stay another night that he had not the heart to refuse,' she went on. 'He is so kind, but I wish he hadn't stayed.'

I was at the station at half past two. I felt rather annoyed with John. It seemed a sort of slight to the beautiful girl who loved him, that he should come as it were out of breath, and with the dust of travel upon him, to take her hand, which some of us would have given the best years of our lives to take.

But when the three o'clock train glided in, and glided out again having brought no passengers to our little station, I was more than annoyed. There was no other train for thirty-five minutes; I calculated that, with much hurry, we might just get to the church in time for the ceremony; but, oh, what a fool to miss that first train! What other man could have done it?

That thirty-five minutes seemed a year, as I wandered round the station reading the advertisements and the timetables, and the company's bye-laws, and getting more and more angry with John Charrington. This confidence in his own power of getting everything he wanted the minute he wanted it was leading him too far. I hate waiting. Everyone does, but I believe I hate it more than anyone else. The three thirty-five was late, of course.

I ground my pipe between my teeth and stamped with impatience as I watched the signals. Click. The signal went down. Five minutes later I flung myself into the carriage that I had brought for John.

'Drive to the church!' I said, as someone shut the door. 'Mr Charrington hasn't come by this train.'

Anxiety now replaced anger. What had become of the man? Could he have been taken suddenly ill? I had never known him have a day's illness in his life. And even so he might have telegraphed. Some awful accident must have happened to him. The thought that he had played her false never – no, not for a moment – entered my head. Yes, something terrible had happened to him, and on me lay the task of telling his bride. I almost wished the carriage would upset and break my head so that someone else might tell her, not I, who – but that's nothing to do with this story.

It was five minutes to four as we drew up at the churchyard gate. A double row of eager onlookers lined the path from lychgate to porch. I sprang from the carriage and passed up between them. Our gardener had a good front place near the door. I stopped.

'Are they waiting still, Byles?' I asked, simply to gain time, for of course I knew they were by the waiting crowd's attentive attitude.

'Waiting, sir? No, no, sir; why, it must be over by now.'

'Over! Then Mr Charrington's come?'

'To the minute, sir; must have missed you somehow, and I say, sir,' lowering his voice, 'I never see Mr John the least bit so afore, but my opinion is he's been drinking pretty free. His clothes was all dusty and his face like a sheet. I tell you I didn't like the looks of him at all, and the folks inside are saying all sorts of things. You'll see, something's gone very wrong with Mr John, and he's tried liquor. He looked like a ghost, and in he went with his eyes straight before him, with never a look or a word for none of us: him that was always such a gentleman!'

I had never heard Byles make so long a speech. The crowd in the churchyard were talking in whispers and getting ready rice and slippers to throw at the bride and bridegroom. The ringers were ready with their hands on the ropes to ring out the merry peal as the bride and bridegroom should come out.

A murmur from the church announced them; out they came. Byles was right. John Charrington did not look himself. There was dust on his coat, his hair was disarranged. He seemed to have been in some row, for there was a black mark above his eyebrow. He was deathly pale. But his pallor was not greater than that of the bride, who might have been carved in ivory – dress, veil, orange blossoms, face and all.

As they passed out the ringers stooped – there were six of them – and then, on the ears expecting the gay wedding peal, came the slow tolling of the passing bell.

A thrill of horror at so foolish a jest from the ringers passed through us all. But the ringers themselves dropped the ropes and fled like rabbits out into the sunlight. The bride shuddered, and grey shadows came about her mouth, but the bridegroom led her on down the path where the people stood with the handfuls of rice; but the handfuls were never thrown, and the wedding bells never rang. In vain the ringers were urged to remedy their mistake: they protested with many whispered expletives that they would see themselves further first.

In a hush like the hush in the chamber of death the bridal pair passed into their carriage and its door slammed behind them.

Then the tongues were loosed. A babel of anger, wonder, conjecture from the guests and the spectators.

'If I'd seen his condition, sir,' said old Forster to me as we drove off, 'I would have stretched him on the floor of the church, sir, by heaven I would, before I'd have let him marry my daughter!'

Then he put his head out of the window.

'Drive like hell,' he cried to the coachman; 'don't spare the horses.'

He was obeyed. We passed the bride's carriage. I forbore to look at it, and old Forster turned his head away and swore. We reached home before it.

We stood in the doorway, in the blazing afternoon sun, and in about half a minute we heard wheels crunching the gravel. When the carriage stopped in front of the steps old Forster and I ran down.

'Great heaven, the carriage is empty! And yet——'

I had the door open in a minute, and this is what I saw ...

No sign of John Charrington; and of May, his wife, only a huddled heap of white satin lying half on the floor of the carriage and half on the seat.

'I drove straight here, sir,' said the coachman, as the bride's father lifted her out; 'and I'll swear no one got out of the carriage.'

We carried her into the house in her bridal dress and drew back her veil. I saw her face. Shall I ever forget it? White, white and drawn with agony and horror, bearing such a look of terror as I have never seen since except in dreams. And her hair, her radiant blonde hair, I tell you it was white like snow.

As we stood, her father and I, half mad with the horror and mystery of it, a boy came up the avenue – a telegraph boy. They brought the orange envelope to me. I tore it open.

Mr Charrington was thrown from the dogcart on his way to the station at half past one. Killed on the spot!

And he was married to May Forster in our parish church at *half past three*, in presence of half the parish.

'*I shall be married, dead or alive!*'

What had passed in that carriage on the homeward drive? No one knows – no one will ever know. Oh, May! oh, my dear!

Before a week was over they laid her beside her husband in our little churchyard on the thyme-covered hill – the churchyard where they had kept their love-trysts.

Thus was accomplished John Charrington's wedding.

The Facts in the Case of M. Valdemar
Edgar Allan Poe

Of course I shall not pretend to consider it any matter for wonder, that the extraordinary case of M. Valdemar has excited discussion. It would have been a miracle had it not – especially under the circumstances. Through the desire of all parties concerned, to keep the affair from the public, at least for the present, or until we had further opportunities for investigation – through our endeavours to effect this – a garbled or exaggerated account made its way into society, and became the source of many unpleasant misrepresentations, and, very naturally, of a great deal of disbelief.

It is now rendered necessary that I give the *facts* – as far as I comprehend them myself. They are, succinctly, these:

My attention, for the last three years, had been repeatedly drawn to the subject of Mesmerism; and, about nine months ago, it occurred to me, quite suddenly, that in the series of experiments made hitherto, there had been a very remarkable and most unaccountable omission – no person had as yet been mesmerised *in articulo mortis*. It remained to be seen, first, whether, in such condition, there existed in the patient any susceptibility to the magnetic influence; secondly, whether, if any existed, it was impaired or increased by the condition; thirdly, to what extent, or for how long a period, the encroachments of death might be arrested by the process. There were other points to be ascertained, but these most excited my curiosity – the last in especial, from the immensely important character of its consequences.

In looking around me for some subject by whose means I might test these particulars, I was brought to think of my friend, M. Ernest Valdemar, the well-known compiler of the *Bibliotheca Forensica,* and author (under the *nom de plume* of Issachar Marx) of the Polish versions of *Wallenstein* and *Gargantua*. M. Valdemar, who has resided principally at Harlem, N.Y., since the year 1839, is (or was) particularly noticeable for the extreme spareness of his person – his lower limbs much resembling those of John Randolph; and, also, for the whiteness of his whiskers, in violent contrast to the blackness of his hair. His temperament was markedly nervous, and rendered him a good subject for mesmeric experiment. On two or three occasions I had put him to sleep with little difficulty, but was disappointed in other results which his peculiar constitution had naturally led me to anticipate. His will was at no period positively, or thoroughly, under my control, and in regard to *clairvoyance*, I could accomplish with him nothing to be relied upon. I always attributed my failure at these points to the disordered state of his health. For some months previous to my becoming acquainted with him, his physicians had declared him in a confirmed phthisis. It was his custom, indeed, to speak calmly of his approaching dissolution, as of a matter neither to be avoided nor regretted.

When the ideas to which I have alluded first occurred to me, it was of course very natural that I should think of M. Valdemar. I knew the steady philosophy of the man too well to apprehend any scruples from *him*; and he had no relatives in America who would be likely to interfere. I spoke to him frankly upon the subject; and, to my surprise, his interest seemed vividly excited. I say to my surprise; for, although he had always yielded his person freely to my experiments, he had never before given me any tokens of sympathy with what I did. His disease was of that character which would admit of exact calculation in respect to the epoch of its termination in death; and it was finally arranged between us that he would send for me about twenty-four hours before the period announced his physicians as that of his decease.

It is now rather more than seven months since I received, from M. Valdemar himself, the subjoined note:

> My Dear P——,
> You may as well come *now*. D—— and F—— are agreed that I cannot hold out beyond to-morrow midnight; and I think they have hit the time very nearly.
>
> Valdemar.

I received this note within half an hour after it was written, and in fifteen minutes more I was in the dying man's chambers. I had not seen him for ten days, and was appalled by the fearful alteration which the brief interval had wrought in him. His face wore a leaden hue; the eyes were utterly lustreless; and the emaciation was so extreme that the skin had been broken through by the cheek bones. His expectoration was excessive. The pulse was barely perceptible. He retained, nevertheless, in a very remarkable manner, both his mental power and a certain degree of physical strength. He spoke with distinctness – took some palliative medicines without aid – and, when I entered the room, was occupied in pencilling memoranda in a pocket-book. He was propped up in the bed by pillows. Doctors D—— and F—— were in attendance.

After pressing Valdemar's hand, I took these gentlemen aside, and obtained from them a minute account of the patient's condition. The left lung had been for eighteen months in a semi-osseous or cartilaginous state, and was, of course, entirely useless for all purposes of vitality. The right, in its upper portion, was also partially, if not thoroughly, ossified, while the lower region was merely a mass of purulent tubercles, running one into another. Several extensive perforations existed; and, at one point, permanent adhesion to the ribs had taken place. These appearances in the right lobe were of comparatively recent date. The ossification had proceeded with very unusual rapidity; no sign of it had been discovered a month before, and the adhesion had only been observed during the three previous days. Independently of the phthisis, the patient was suspected of aneurism of the aorta; but on this point the osseous symptoms rendered an exact diagnosis impossible. It was the opinion of both physicians that M. Valdemar would die about midnight on the morrow (Sunday). It was then seven o'clock on Saturday evening.

On quitting the invalid's bedside to hold conversation with myself, Doctors D—— and F—— had bidden him a final farewell. It had not been their intention to return; but, at my request, they agreed to look in upon the patient about ten the next night.

When they had gone, I spoke freely with M. Valdemar on the subject of his approaching dissolution, as well as, more particularly, of the experiment proposed. He still professed himself quite willing and even anxious to have it made, and urged me to commence it at once. A male and female nurse were in attendance; but I did not feel myself altogether at liberty to engage in a task of this character with no more reliable witnesses than these people, in case of sudden accident, might prove. I therefore postponed operations until about eight the next night, when the arrival of a medical student with whom I had some acquaintance (Mr Theodore L——l), relieved me from further embarrassment. It had been my design, originally, to wait for the physicians; but I was induced to proceed, first, by the urgent entreaties of M. Valdemar, and secondly, by my conviction that I had not a moment to lose, as he was evidently sinking fast.

Mr L——l was so kind as to accede to my desire that he would take notes of all that occurred; and it is from his memoranda that what I now have to relate is, for the most part, either condensed or copied *verbatim*.

It wanted about five minutes of eight when, taking the patient's hand, I begged him to state, as distinctly as he could, to Mr L——l, whether he (M. Valdemar) was entirely willing that I should make the experiment of mesmerizing him in his then condition.

He replied feebly, yet quite audibly, 'Yes, I wish to be mesmerized' – adding immediately afterwards, 'I fear you have deferred it too long.'

While he spoke thus, I commenced the passes which I had already found most effectual in subduing him. He was evidently influenced with the first lateral stroke of my hand across his forehead; but although I exerted all my powers, no further perceptible effect was induced until some minutes after ten o'clock, when Doctors D—— and F—— called, according to appointment. I explained to them, in a few words, what I designed, and as they opposed no objection, saying that the patient was already in the death agony, I proceeded without hesitation – exchanging, however, the lateral passes for downward ones, and directing my gaze entirely into the right eye of the sufferer.

By this time his pulse was imperceptible and his breathing was stertorous, and at intervals of half a minute.

This condition was nearly unaltered for a quarter of an hour. At the expiration of this period, however, a natural although a very deep sigh escaped the bosom of the dying man, and the stertorous breathing ceased – that is to say, its stertorousness was no longer apparent; the intervals were undiminished. The patient's extremities were of an icy coldness.

At five minutes before eleven I perceived unequivocal signs of the mesmeric influence. The glassy roll of the eye was changed for that expression of uneasy *inward* examination which is never seen except in cases of sleep-walking, and which it is quite impossible to mistake. With a few rapid lateral passes I made the lids quiver, as in incipient sleep, and with a few more I closed them altogether. I was not satisfied, however, with this, but continued the manipulations vigorously, and with the fullest exertion of the will, until I had completely stiffened the limbs of the slumberer, after placing them in a seemingly easy position. The legs were at full length; the arms were nearly so, and reposed on the bed at a moderate distance from the loins. The head was very slightly elevated.

When I had accomplished this, it was fully midnight, and I requested the gentlemen present to examine M. Valdemar's condition. After a few experiments, they admitted him to be in an unusually perfect state of mesmeric trance. The curiosity of both the physicians was greatly excited. Dr D—— resolved at once to remain with the patient all night, while Dr F—— took leave with a promise to return at daybreak. Mr L——l and the nurses remained.

We left M. Valdemar entirely undisturbed until about three o'clock in the morning, when I approached him and found him in precisely the same condition as when Dr F—— went away – that is to say, he lay in the same position; the pulse was imperceptible; the breathing was gentle (scarcely noticeable, unless through the application of a mirror to the lips); the eyes were closed naturally; and the limbs were as rigid and as cold as marble. Still, the general appearance was certainly not that of death.

As I approached M. Valdemar I made a kind of half effort to influence his right arm into pursuit of my own, as I passed the latter gently to and fro above his person. In such experiments with this patient I had never perfectly succeeded before, and assuredly I had little thought of succeeding now; but to my astonishment, his arm very readily, although feebly, followed every direction I assigned it with mine. I determined to hazard a few words of conversation.

'M. Valdemar,' I said, 'are you asleep?' He made no answer, but I perceived a tremor about the lips, and was thus induced to repeat the question, again and again. At its third repetition, his whole frame was agitated by a very slight shivering; the eyelids unclosed themselves so far as to display a white line of the ball; the lips moved sluggishly, and from between them, in a barely audible whisper, issued the words:

'Yes – asleep now. Do not wake me! – let me die so!'

I here felt the limbs and found them as rigid as ever. The right arm, as before, obeyed the direction of my hand. I questioned the sleep-walker again:

'Do you still feel pain in the breast, M. Valdemar?'

The answer now was immediate, but even less audible than before:

'No pain – I am dying.'

I did not think it advisable to disturb him further just then, and nothing more was said or done until the arrival of Dr F——, who came a little before sunrise, and expressed unbounded astonishment at finding the patient still alive. After feeling the pulse and applying a mirror to the lips, he requested me to speak to the sleep-walker again. I did so, saying:

'M. Valdemar, do you still sleep?'

As before, some minutes elapsed ere a reply was made; and during the interval the dying man seemed to be collecting his energies to speak. At my fourth repetition of the question, he said very faintly, almost inaudibly:

'Yes; still asleep – dying.'

It was now the opinion, or rather the wish, of the physicians, that M. Valdemar should be suffered to remain undisturbed in his present apparently tranquil condition, until death should supervene – and this, it was generally agreed, must now take place within a few minutes. I concluded, however, to speak to him once more, and merely repeated my previous question.

While I spoke, there came a marked change over the countenance of the sleep-waker. The eyes rolled themselves slowly open, the pupils disappearing upwardly; the skin generally assumed a cadaverous hue, resembling not so much parchment as white paper; and the circular hectic spots which, hitherto, had been strongly defined in the centre of each cheek, went out at once. I use this expression, because the suddenness of their departure put me in mind of nothing so much as the extinguishment of a candle by a puff of the breath. The upper lip, at the same time, writhed itself away from the teeth, which it had previously covered completely; while the lower jaw fell with an audible jerk, leaving the mouth widely extended, and disclosing in full view the swollen and blackened tongue. I presume that no member of the party then present had been unaccustomed to death-bed horrors; but so hideous beyond conception was the appearance of M. Valdemar at this moment, that there was a general shrinking back from the region of the bed.

I now feel that I have reached a point of this narrative at which every reader will be startled into positive disbelief. It is my business, however, simply to proceed.

There was no longer the faintest sign of vitality in M. Valdemar; and concluding him to be dead, we were consigning him to the charge of the nurses, when a strong vibratory motion was observable in the tongue. This continued for perhaps a minute. At the expiration of this period, there issued from the distended and motionless jaws a voice – such as it would be madness in me to attempt describing. There are, indeed, two or three epithets which might be considered as applicable to it in parts; I might say for example, that the sound was harsh, and broken, and hollow; but the hideous whole is indescribable, for the simple reason that no similar sounds have ever jarred upon the ear of humanity. There were two particulars, nevertheless, which I thought then, and still think, might fairly be stated as characteristic of the intonation – as well adapted to convey some idea of its unearthly peculiarity. In the first place, the voice seemed to reach our ears – at least mine – from a vast distance, or from some deep cavern within the earth. In the second place, it impressed me (I fear, indeed, that it will be impossible to make myself comprehended) as gelatinous or glutinous matters impress the sense of touch.

I have spoken both of 'sound' and of 'voice.' I mean to say that the sound was one of distinct – of even wonderfully, thrillingly distinct – syllabification. M. Valdemar *spoke* – obviously in reply to the question I had propounded to him a few minutes before. I had asked him, it will be remembered, if he still slept. He now said:

'Yes – no – I *have been* sleeping – and no – now – *I am dead.*'

No person present even affected to deny, or attempted to repress, the unutterable, shuddering horror which these few words, thus uttered, were so well calculated to convey. Mr L——l (the student) swooned. The nurses immediately left the chamber, and could not be induced to return. For nearly an hour, we busied ourselves, silently – without the utterance of a word – in endeavours to revive Mr L——l. When he came to himself, we addressed ourselves again to an investigation of M. Valdemar's condition.

It remained in all respects as I have last described it, with the exception that the mirror no longer afforded evidence of respiration. An attempt to draw blood from the arm failed. I should mention, too, that this limb was no further subject to my will. I endeavoured in vain to make it follow the direction of my hand. The only real indication, indeed, of the mesmeric influence, was now found in the vibratory movement of the tongue, whenever I addressed M. Valdemar a question. He seemed to be making an effort to reply, but had no longer sufficient volition. To queries put to him by any other person than myself he seemed utterly insensible – although I endeavoured to place each member of the company in mesmeric *rapport* with him. I believe that I have now related all that is necessary to an understanding of the sleep-waker's state at this epoch. Other nurses were procured; and at ten o'clock I left the house in company with the two physicians and Mr L——l.

In the afternoon we all called again to see the patient. His condition remained precisely the same. We had now some discussion as to the propriety and feasibility of awakening him; but we had little difficulty in agreeing that no good purpose would be served by so doing. It was evident that, so far, death (or what is usually termed death) had been arrested by the mesmeric process. It seemed clear to us all that to awaken M. Valdemar would be merely to insure his instant, or at least his speedy dissolution.

From this period until the close of last week – *an interval of nearly seven months* – we continued to make daily calls at M. Valdemar's house, accompanied, now and then, by medical and other friends. All this time the sleep-waker remained *exactly* as I have last described him. The nurses' attentions were continual.

It was on Friday last that we finally resolved to make the experiment of awakening, or attempting to awaken him; and it is the (perhaps) unfortunate result of this latter experiment which has given rise to so much discussion in private circles – to so much of what I cannot help thinking unwarranted popular feeling.

For the purpose of relieving M. Valdemar from the mesmeric trance, I made use of the customary passes. These, for a time, were unsuccessful. The first indication of revival was afforded by a partial descent of the iris. It was observed, as especially remarkable, that this lowering of the pupil was accompanied by the profuse out-flowing of a yellowish ichor (from beneath the lids with a pungent and highly offensive odour.

It was now suggested that I should attempt to influence the patient's arm, as heretofore. I made the attempt and failed. Dr F—— then intimated a desire to have me put a question. I did so, as follows:

'M. Valdemar, can you explain to us what are your feelings or wishes now?'

There was an instant return of the hectic circles on the cheeks; the tongue quivered, or rather rolled violently in the mouth (although the jaws and lips remained rigid as before); and at length the same hideous voice which I have already described, broke forth:

'For God's sake – quick! – quick! – put me to sleep – or, quick! – waken me! – quick! – *I say to you that I am dead!*'

I was thoroughly unnerved, and for an instant remained undecided what to do. At first I made an endeavour to recompose the patient; but, failing in this through total abeyance of the will, I retraced my steps and as earnestly struggled to awaken him. In this attempt I soon saw that I should be successful – or at least I soon fancied that my success would be complete – and I am sure that all in the room were prepared to see the patient awaken.

For what really occurred, however, it is quite impossible that any human being could have been prepared.

As I rapidly made the mesmeric passes, amid ejaculations of 'dead! dead!' absolutely *bursting* from the tongue and not from the lips of the sufferer, his whole frame at once – within the space of a single minute, or even less, shrunk – crumbled – absolutely *rotted* away beneath my hands. Upon the bed, before that whole company, there lay a nearly liquid mass of loathsome – of detestable putridity.

A Story of Don Juan
V. S. Pritchett

It is said that on one night of his life Don Juan slept alone, though I think
the point has been disputed. Returning to Seville in the spring he was
held up, some hours' ride from the city, by the floods of the
Quadalquiver, a river as dirty as an old lion after the rains, and was
obliged to stay at the *finca* of the Quintero family. The doorway, the
walls, the windows of the house were hung with the black and violet
draperies of mourning when he arrived there. God rest her soul (the
peasants said), the lady of the house was dead. She had been dead a year.
The young Quintero was a widower. Nevertheless Quintero took him in
and even smiled to see a gallant spattered and drooping in the rain like a
sodden cockerel. There was malice in that smile, for Quintero was mad
with loneliness and grief; the man who had possessed and discarded all
women, was received by a man demented because he had lost only one.

'My house is yours,' said Quintero, speaking the formula. There was
bewilderment in his eyes; those who grieve do not find the world and its
people either real or believable. Irony inflects the voices of mourners,
and there was malice, too, in Quintero's further greetings; for grief
appears to put one at an advantage, the advantage (in Quintero's case)
being the macabre one that he could receive Juan now without that fear,
that terror which Juan brought to the husbands of Seville. It was perfect,
Quintero thought, that for once in his life Juan should have arrived at an
empty house.

There was not even (as Juan quickly ascertained) a maid, for
Quintero was served only by a manservant, being unable any longer to
bear the sight of women. This servant dried Don Juan's clothes and in an
hour or two brought in a bad dinner, food which stamped up and down
in the stomach like people waiting for a coach in the cold. Quintero was
torturing his body as well as his mind, and as the familiar pains arrived
they agonized him and set him off about his wife. Grief had also made
Quintero an actor. His eyes had that hollow, taper-haunted dusk of the
theatre as he spoke of the beautiful girl. He dwelled upon their
courtship, on details of her beauty and temperament, and how he had

rushed her from the church to the marriage bed like a man racing a tray of diamonds through the streets into the safety of a bank vault. The presence of Don Juan turned every man into an artist when he was telling his own love story – one had to tantalize and surpass the great seducer – and Quintero, rolling it all off in the grand manner, could not resist telling that his bride had died on her marriage night.

'Man!' cried Don Juan. He started straight off on stories of his own. But Quintero hardly listened; he had returned to the state of exhaustion and emptiness which is natural to grief. As Juan talked, the madman followed his own thoughts like an actor preparing and mumbling the next entrance; and the thought he had had when Juan had first appeared at his door returned to him: that Juan must be a monster to make a man feel triumphant that his own wife was dead. Half-listening, and indigestion aiding, Quintero felt within himself the total hatred of all the husbands of Seville for this diabolical man. And as Quintero brooded upon this it occurred to him that it was probably not a chance that he had it in his power to effect the most curious revenge on behalf of the husbands of Seville.

The decision was made. The wine being finished Quintero called for his manservant and gave orders to change Don Juan's room.

'For,' said Quintero drily, 'his Excellency's visit is an honour and I cannot allow one who has slept in the most delicately scented room in Spain to pass the night in a chamber which stinks to heaven of goat.'

'The closed room?' said the manservant, astonished that the room which still held the great dynastic marriage bed and which had not been used more than half a dozen times by his master since the lady's death – and then only at the full moon when his frenzy was worst – was to be given to a stranger.

Yet to this room Quintero led his guest and there parted from him with eyes so sparkling with ill-intention that Juan, who was sensitive to this kind of point, understood perfectly that the cat was being let into the cage only because the bird had long ago flown out. The humiliation was unpleasant. Juan saw the night stretching before him like a desert.

What a bed to lie in: so wide, so unutterably vacant, so malignantly inopportune! Juan took off his clothes, snuffed the lamp wick. He lay down conscious that on either side of him lay wastes of sheet, draughty and uninhabited except by the nomadic bug. A desert. To move an arm one inch to the side, to push out a leg, however cautiously, was to enter desolation. For miles and miles the foot might probe, the fingers or the knee explore a friendless Antarctica. Yet to lie rigid and still was to have a foretaste of the grave. And here, too, he was frustrated; for though the wine kept him yawning, that awful food romped in his stomach, jolting him back from the edge of sleep the moment he got there.

There is an art in sleeping alone in a double bed but, naturally, this art was unknown to Juan; he had to learn it. The difficulty is easily solved. If you cannot sleep on one side of the bed, you move over and try the other. Two hours or more must have passed before this occurred to Juan. Sullen-headed he advanced into the desert and the night air lying chill between the sheets flapped, and made him shiver. He stretched out his arm and crawled towards the opposite pillow. Mother of God, the coldness, the more than virgin frigidity of linen! Juan put down his head and, drawing up his knees, he shivered. Soon, he supposed, he would be warm again, but in the meantime, ice could not have been colder. It was unbelievable.

Ice was the word for that pillow and those sheets. Ice. Was he ill? Had the rain chilled him that his teeth must chatter like this and his legs tremble? Far from getting warmer he found the cold growing. Now it was on his forehead and his cheeks, like arms of ice on his body, like legs of ice upon his legs. Suddenly in superstition he got up on his hands and stared down at the pillow in the darkness, threw back the bed-clothes and looked down upon the sheet; his breath was hot, yet blowing against his cheeks was a breath colder than the grave, his shoulders and body were hot, yet limbs of snow were drawing him down; and just as he would have shouted his appalled suspicion, lips like wet ice unfolded upon his own and he sank down to a kiss, unmistakably a kiss, which froze him like a winter.

In his own room Quintero lay listening. His mad eyes were exalted and his ears were waiting. He was waiting for the scream of horror. He knew the apparition. There would be a scream, a tumble, hands fighting for the light, fists knocking at the door. And Quintero had locked the door. But when no scream came, Quintero lay talking to himself, remembering the night the apparition had first come to him and had made him speechless and left him choked and stiff. It would be even better if there were no scream! Quintero lay awake through the night building castle after castle of triumphant revenge and receiving, as he did so, the ovations of the husbands of Seville. 'The stallion is gelded!' At an early hour Quintero unlocked the door and waited downstairs impatiently. He was a wreck after a night like that.

Juan came down at last. He was (Quintero observed) pale. Or was he pale?

'Did you sleep well?' Quintero asked furtively.

'Very well,' Juan replied.

'I do not sleep well in strange beds myself,' Quintero insinuated. Juan smiled and replied that he was more used to strange beds than his own. Quintero scowled.

'I reproach myself: the bed was large,' he said. But the large, Juan said, were necessarily as familiar to him as the strange. Quintero bit his nails. Some noise had been heard in the night – something like a scream, a disturbance. The manservant had noticed it also. Juan answered him that disturbances in the night had indeed bothered him at the beginning of his career, but now he took them in his stride. Quintero dug his nails into the palms of his hands. He brought out the trump.

'I am afraid,' Quintero said, 'it was a cold bed. You must have *frozen*.'

'I am never cold for long,' Juan said, and, unconsciously anticipating the manner of a poem that was to be written in his memory two centuries later, declaimed: 'The blood of Don Juan is hot, for the sun is the blood of Don Juan'.

Quintero watched. His eyes jumped like flies to every movement of his guest. He watched him drink his coffee. He watched him tighten the stirrups of his horse. He watched Juan vault into the saddle. Don Juan was humming and when he went off was singing, was singing in that intolerable tenor of his which was like a cock crow in the olive groves.

Quintero went into the house and rubbed his unshaven chin. Then he went out again to the road where the figure of Don Juan was now only a small smoke of dust between the eucalyptus trees. Quintero went up to the room where Juan had slept and stared at it with accusations and suspicions. He called the manservant.

'I shall sleep here tonight,' Quintero said.

The manservant answered carefully. Quintero was mad again and the moon was still only in its first quarter. The man watched his master during the day looking towards Seville. It was too warm after the rains, the country steamed like a laundry.

And then, when the night came, Quintero laughed at his doubts. He went up to the room and as he undressed he thought of the assurance of those ice-cold lips, those icicle fingers and those icy arms. She had not come last night; oh what fidelity! To think, he would say in his remorse to the ghost, that malice had so disordered him that he had been base and credulous to use the dead for a trick.

Tears were in his eyes as he lay down and for some time he dared not turn on his side and stretch out his hand to touch what, in his disorder, he had been willing to betray. He loathed his heart. He craved – yet how could he hope for it now? – the miracle of recognition and forgiveness. It was this craving which moved him at last. His hands went out. And they were met.

The hands, the arms, the lips moved out of their invisibility and soundlessness towards him. They touched him, they clasped him, they drew him down, but – what was this? He gave a shout, he fought to get away, kicked out and swore; and so the manservant found him wrestling with the sheets, striking out with fists and knees, roaring that he was in hell. Those hands, those lips, those limbs, he screamed, were *burning* him. They were of ice no more. They were of fire.

The Open Window
Saki

'My aunt will be down presently, Mr Nuttel,' said a very self-possessed young lady of fifteen; 'in the meantime you must try and put up with me.'

Framton Nuttel endeavoured to say the correct something which should duly flatter the niece of the moment without unduly discounting the aunt that was to come. Privately he doubted more than ever whether these formal visits on a succession of total strangers would do much towards helping the nerve cure which he was supposed to be undergoing.

'I know how it will be,' his sister had said when he was preparing to migrate to this rural retreat; 'you will bury yourself down there and not speak to a living soul, and your nerves will be worse than ever from moping. I shall just give you letters of introduction to all the people I know there. Some of them, as far as I can remember, were quite nice.'

Framton wondered whether Mrs Sappleton, the lady to whom he was presenting one of the letters of introduction, came into the nice division.

'Do you know many of the people round here?' asked the niece, when she judged that they had had sufficient silent communion.

'Hardly a soul,' said Framton. 'My sister was staying here, at the rectory, you know, some four years ago, and she gave me letters of introduction to some of the people here.'

He made the last statement in a tone of distinct regret.

'Then you know practically nothing about my aunt?' pursued the self-possessed young lady.

'Only her name and address,' admitted the caller. He was wondering whether Mrs Sappleton was in the married or widowed state. An undefinable something about the room seemed to suggest masculine habitation.

'Her great tragedy happened just three years ago,' said the child; 'that would be since your sister's time.'

'Her tragedy?' asked Framton; somehow in this restful country spot tragedies seemed out of place.

'You may wonder why we keep that window wide open on an October afternoon,' said the niece, indicating a large French window that opened on to a lawn.

'It is quite warm for the time of the year,' said Framton; 'but has that window got anything to do with the tragedy?'

'Out through that window, three years ago to a day, her husband and her two young brothers went off for their day's shooting. They never came back. In crossing the moor to their favourite snipe-shooting ground they were all three engulfed by a treacherous piece of bog. It had been that dreadful wet summer, you know, and places that were safe in other years gave way suddenly without warning. Their bodies were never recovered. That was the dreadful part of it.' Here the child's voice lost its self-possessed note and became falteringly human. 'Poor aunt always thinks that they will come back some day, they and the little brown spaniel that was lost with them, and walk in at that window just as they used to do. That is why the window is kept open every evening till it is quite dusk. Poor dear aunt, she has often told me how they went out, her husband with his white waterproof coat over his arm, and Ronnie, her youngest brother, singing "Bertie, why do you bound?" as he always did to tease her, because she said it got on her nerves. Do you know, sometimes on still, quiet evenings like this, I almost get a creepy feeling that they will all walk in through that window——'

She broke off with a little shudder. It was a relief to Framton when the aunt bustled into the room with a whirl of apologies for being late in making her appearance.

'I hope Vera has been amusing you?' she said.

'She has been very interesting,' said Framton.

'I hope you don't mind the open window,' said Mrs Sappleton briskly; 'my husband and brothers will be home directly from shooting, and they always come in this way. They've been out for snipe in the marshes today, so they'll make a fine mess over my poor carpets. So like you men-folk, isn't it?'

She rattled on cheerfully about the shooting and the scarcity of birds, and the prospects for duck in the winter. To Framton it was all purely horrible. He made a desperate but only partially successful effort to turn the talk on to a less ghastly topic; he was conscious that his hostess was giving him only a fragment of her attention, and her eyes were constantly straying past him to the open window and the lawn beyond. It was certainly an unfortunate coincidence that he should have paid his visit on this tragic anniversary.

'The doctors agree in ordering me complete rest, an absence of mental excitement, and avoidance of anything in the nature of violent physical exercise,' announced Framton, who laboured under the tolerably widespread delusion that total strangers and chance acquaintances are hungry for the least detail of one's ailments and infirmities, their cause and cure. 'On the matter of diet they are not so much in agreement,' he continued.

'No?' said Mrs Sappleton, in a voice which only replaced a yawn at the last moment. Then she suddenly brightened into alert attention – but not to what Framton was saying.

'Here they are at last!' she cried. 'Just in time for tea, and don't they look as if they were muddy up to the eyes!'

Framton shivered slightly, and turned towards the niece with a look intended to convey sympathetic comprehension. The child was staring out through the open window with dazed horror in her eyes. In a chill shock of nameless fear Framton swung round in his seat and looked in the same direction.

In the deepening twilight three figures were walking across the lawn towards the window; they all carried guns under their arms, and one of them was additionally burdened with a white coat hung over his shoulders. A tired brown spaniel kept close at their heels. Noiselessly they neared the house, and then a hoarse young voice chanted out of the dusk:

'I said, Bertie, why do you bound?'

Framton grabbed wildly at his stick and hat; the hall door, the gravel drive, and the front gate were dimly-noted stages in his headlong retreat. A cyclist coming along the road had to run into the hedge to avoid imminent collision.

'Here we are, my dear,' said the bearer of the white mackintosh, coming in through the window; 'fairly muddy, but most of it's dry. Who was that who bolted out as we came up?'

'A most extraordinary man, a Mr Nuttel,' said Mrs Sappleton; 'could only talk about his illnesses, and dashed off without a word of goodbye or apology when you arrived. One would think he had seen a ghost.'

'I expect it was the spaniel,' said the niece calmly; 'he told me he had a horror of dogs. He was once hunted into a cemetery somewhere on the banks of the Ganges by a pack of pariah dogs, and had to spend the night in a newly-dug grave with the creatures snarling and grinning and foaming just above him. Enough to make anyone lose their nerve.'

Romance at short notice was her speciality.

A Woman Seldom Found

William Sansom

Once a young man was on a visit to Rome.

It was his first visit; he came from the country – but he was neither on the one hand so young nor on the other so simple as to imagine that a great and beautiful capital should hold out finer promises than anywhere else. He already knew that life was largely illusion, that though wonderful things could happen, nevertheless as many disappointments came in compensation: and he knew, too, that life could offer a quality even worse – the probability that nothing would happen at all. This was always more possible in a great city intent on its own business.

Thinking in this way, he stood on the Spanish steps and surveyed the momentous panorama stretched before him. He listened to the swelling hum of the evening traffic and watched, as the lights went up against Rome's golden dusk. Shining automobiles slunk past the fountains and turned urgently into the bright Via Condotti, neon-red signs stabbed the shadows with invitation; the yellow windows of buses were packed with faces intent on going somewhere – everyone in the city seemed intent on the evening's purpose. He alone had nothing to do.

He felt himself the only person alone of everyone in the city. But searching for adventure never brought it – rather kept it away. Such a mood promised nothing. So the young man turned back up the steps, passed the lovely church, and went on up the cobbled hill towards his hotel. Wine-bars and food-shops jostled with growing movement in those narrow streets. But out on the broad pavements of the Vittorio Veneto, under the trees mounting to the Borghese Gardens, the high world of Rome would be filling the most elegant cafés in Europe to enjoy with apéritifs the twilight. That would be the loneliest of all! So the young man kept to the quieter, older streets on his solitary errand home.

In one such street, a pavementless alley between old yellow houses, a street that in Rome might suddenly blossom into a secret piazza of fountain and baroque church, a grave secluded treasure-place – he noticed that he was alone but for the single figure of a woman walking down the hill towards him.

As she drew nearer, he saw that she was dressed with taste, that in her carriage was a soft Latin fire, that she walked for respect. Her face was veiled, but it was impossible to imagine that she would not be beautiful. Isolated thus with her, passing so near to her, and she symbolizing the adventure of which the evening was so empty – a greater melancholy gripped him. He felt wretched as the gutter, small, sunk, pitiful. So that he rounded his shoulders and lowered his eyes – but not before casting one furtive glance into hers.

He was so shocked at what he saw that he paused, he stared, shocked, into her face. He had made no mistake. She was smiling. Also – she too had hesitated. He thought instantly: 'Whore?' But no – it was not that kind of smile, though as well it was not without affection. And then amazingly she spoke:

'I – I know I shouldn't ask you ... but it is such a beautiful evening – and perhaps you are alone, as alone as I am ...'

She was very beautiful. He could not speak. But a growing elation gave him the power to smile. So that she continued, still hesitant, in no sense soliciting:

'I thought ... perhaps ... we could take a walk, an apéritif ...'

At last the young man achieved himself:

'Nothing, *nothing* would please me more. And the Veneto is only a minute up there.'

She smiled again:

'My home is just here ...'

They walked in silence a few paces down the street, to a turning that young man had already passed. This she indicated. They walked to where the first humble houses ended in a kind of recess. In the recess was set the wall of a garden, and behind it stood a large and elegant mansion. The woman, about whose face shone a curious glitter – something fused of the transparent pallor of fine skin, of grey but brilliant eyes, of dark eyebrows and hair of lucent black – inserted her key in the garden gate.

They were greeted by a servant in velvet livery. In a large and exquisite salon, under chandeliers of fine glass and before a moist green courtyard where water played, they were served with a frothy wine. They talked. The wine – iced in the warm Roman night – filled them with an inner warmth of exhilaration. But from time to time the young man looked at her curiously.

With her glances, with many subtle inflections of teeth and eyes she was inducing an intimacy that suggested much. He felt he must be careful. At length he thought the best thing might be to thank her – somehow thus to root out whatever obligation might be in store. But here she interrupted him, first with a smile, then with a look of some sadness. She begged him to spare himself any perturbation: she knew it was strange, that in such a situation he might suspect some second purpose: but the simple truth remained that she was lonely and – this with a certain deference – something perhaps in him, perhaps in that moment of dusk in the street, had proved to her inescapably attractive. She had not been able to help herself.

The possibility of a perfect encounter – a dream that years of disillusion will never quite kill – decided him. His elation rose beyond control. He believed her. And thereafter the perfections compounded. At her invitation they dined. Servants brought food of great delicacy; shell-fish, fat bird-flesh, soft fruits. And afterwards they sat on a sofa near the courtyard, where it was cool. Liqueurs were brought. The servants retired. A hush fell upon the house. They embraced.

A little later, with no word, she took his arm and led him from the room. How deep a silence had fallen between them! The young man's heart beat fearfully – it might be heard, he felt, echoing in the hall whose marble they now crossed, sensed through his arm to hers. But such excitement rose now from certainty. Certainty that at such a moment, on such a charmed evening – nothing could go wrong. There was no need to speak. Together they mounted the great staircase.

In her bedroom, to the picture of her framed by the bed curtains and dimly naked in a silken shift, he poured out his love; a love that was to be eternal, to be always perfect, as fabulous as this their exquisite meeting.

Softly she spoke the return of his love. Nothing would ever go amiss, nothing would ever come between them. And very gently she drew back the bedclothes for him.

But suddenly, at the moment when at last he lay beside her, when his lips were almost upon hers – he hesitated.

Something was wrong. A flaw could be sensed. He listened, felt – and then saw the fault was his. Shaded, soft-shaded lights by the bed – but he had been so careless as to leave on the bright electric chandelier in the centre of the ceiling. He remembered the switch was by the door. For a fraction, then, he hesitated. She raised her eyelids – saw his glance at the chandelier, understood.

Her eyes glittered. She murmured:

'My beloved, don't worry – don't move ...'

And she reached out her hand. Her hand grew larger, her arm grew longer and longer, it stretched out through the bed-curtains, across the long carpet, huge and overshadowing the whole of the long room, until at last its giant fingers were at the door. With a terminal click, she switched out the light.

The Body Snatcher
Robert Louis Stevenson

Every night in the year, four of us sat in the small parlour of the George
at Debenham – the undertaker, and the landlord, and Fettes, and
myself. Sometimes there would be more; but blow high, blow low, come
rain or snow or frost, we four would be each planted in his own
particular armchair. Fettes was an old drunken Scotsman, a man of
education obviously, and a man of some property, since he lived in
idleness. He had come to Debenham years ago, while still young, and by
a mere continuance of living and grown to be an adopted townsman. His
blue camlet cloak was a local antiquity, like the church-spire. His place
in the parlour at the George, his absence from church, his old, crapulous,
disreputable vices, were all things of course in Debenham. He had some
vague Radical opinions and some fleeting infidelities, which he would
now and again set forth and emphasize with tottering slaps upon the
table. He drank rum – five glasses regularly every evening; and for the
greater portion of his nightly visit to the George sat, with his glass in his
right hand, in a state of melancholy alcoholic saturation. We called him
the Doctor, for he was supposed to have some special knowledge of
medicine and had been known, upon a pinch, to set a fracture or reduce
a dislocation; but beyond these slight particulars, we had no knowledge
of his character and antecedents.

One dark winter night – it had struck nine some time before the
landlord joined us – there was a sick man in the George, a great
neighbouring proprietor suddenly struck down with apoplexy on his
way to Parliament; and the great man's still greater London doctor had
been telegraphed to his bedside. It was the first time that such a thing
had happened in Debenham, for the railway was but newly open, and
we were all proportionately moved by the occurrence.

'He's come,' said the landlord, after he had filled and lighted his
pipe.

'He?' said I. 'Who? – not the doctor?'

'Himself,' replied our host.

'What is his name?'

'Dr Macfarlane,' said the landlord.

Fettes was far through this third tumbler, stupidly fuddled, now nodding over, now staring mazily around him; but at the last word he seemed to awaken and repeated the name 'Macfarlane' twice, quietly enough the first time, but with sudden emotion at the second.

'Yes,' said the landlord, 'that's his name, Doctor Wolfe Macfarlane.'

Fettes became instantly sober; his eyes awoke, his voice became clear, loud and steady, his language forcible and earnest. We were all startled by the transformation, as if a man had risen from the dead.

'I beg your pardon,' he said, 'I am afraid I have not been paying much attention to your talk. Who is this Wolfe Macfarlane?' And then, when he had heard the landlord out, 'It cannot be, it cannot be,' he added; 'and yet I would like well to see him face to face.'

'Do you know him, Doctor?' asked the undertaker, with a gasp.

'God forbid!' was the reply. 'And yet the name is a strange one; it were too much to fancy two. Tell me, landlord, is he old?'

'Well,' said the host, 'he's not a young man, to be sure, and his hair is white; but he looks younger than you.'

'He is older, though; years older. But,' with a slap upon the table, 'it's the rum you see in my face – rum and sin. This man, perhaps, may have an easy conscience and a good digestion. Conscience! Hear me speak. You would think I was some good, old, decent Christian, would you not? But no, not I; I never canted. Voltaire might have canted if he'd stood in my shoes; but the brains' – with a rattling fillip on his bald head – 'the brains were clear and active and I saw and made no deductions.'

'If you know this doctor,' I ventured to remark, after a somewhat awful pause, 'I should gather that you do not share the landlord's good opinion.'

Fettes paid no regard to me.

'Yes,' he said, with sudden decision, 'I must see him face to face.'

There was another pause and then a door was closed rather sharply on the first floor and a step was heard upon the stair.

'That's the doctor,' cried the landlord. 'Look sharp and you can catch him.'

It was but two steps from the small parlour to the door of the old George inn; the wide oak staircase landed almost in the street; there was room for a Turkey rug and nothing more between the threshold and the last round of the descent; but this little space was every evening brilliantly lit up, not only by the light upon the stair and the great signal-lamp below the sign, but by the warm radiance of the bar-room window. The George thus brightly advertised itself to passers-by in the cold street. Fettes walked steadily to the spot and we, who were hanging behind, beheld the two men meet, as one of them had phrased it, face to face. Dr Macfarlane was alert and vigorous. His white hair set off his pale and placid, although energetic, countenance. He was richly dressed in the finest of broadcloth and the whitest of linen, with a great gold watch-chain, and studs and spectacles of the same precious material. He wore a broad-folded tie, white and speckled with lilac, and he carried on his arm a comfortable driving-coat of fur. There was no doubt but he became his years, breathing, as he did, of wealth and consideration; and it was a surprising contrast to see our parlour sot – bald, dirty, pimpled and robed in his old camlet cloak – confront him at the bottom of the stairs.

'Macfarlane!' he said somewhat loudly, more like a herald than a friend.

The great doctor pulled up short on the fourth step, as though the familiarity of the address surprised and somewhat shocked his dignity.

'Toddy Macfarlane!' repeated Fettes.

The London man almost staggered. He stared for the swiftest of seconds at the man before him, glanced behind him with a sort of scare, and then in a startled whisper, 'Fettes!' he said, 'you!'

'Ay,' said the other, 'me! Did you think I was dead too? We are not so easy shut of our acquaintance.'

'Hush, hush!' exclaimed the doctor. 'Hush, hush! this meeting is so unexpected – I can see you are unmanned. I hardly knew you, I confess, at first, but I am overjoyed – overjoyed to have this opportunity. For the present it must be how-d'ye-do and goodbye in one, for my fly is waiting and I must not fail the train; but you shall – let me see – yes – you shall give me your address and you can count on early news of me. We must do something for you, Fettes. I fear you are out at elbows; but we must see to that for auld lang syne, as once we sang at suppers.'

'Money!' cried Fettes; 'money from you! The money that I had from you is lying where I cast it in the rain.'

Dr Macfarlane had talked himself into some measure of superiority and confidence, but the uncommon energy of this refusal cast him back into his first confusion.

A horrible, ugly look came and went across his almost venerable countenance. 'My dear fellow,' he said, 'be it as you please; my last thought is to offend you. I would intrude on none. I will leave you my address, however——'

'I do not wish it – I do not wish to know the roof that shelters you,' interrupted the other. 'I heard your name; I feared it might be you; I wished to know if, after all, there were a God; I know now that there is none. Begone!'

He still stood in the middle of the rug, between the stair and the doorway; and the great London physician, in order to escape, would be forced to step to one side. It was plain that he hesitated before the thought of this humiliation. White as he was, there was a dangerous glitter in his spectacles; but while he still paused uncertain, he became aware that the driver of his fly was peering in from the street at this unusual scene and caught a glimpse at the same time of our little body from the parlour, huddled by the corner of the bar. The presence of so many witnesses decided him at once to flee. He crouched together, brushing on the wainscot, and made a dart like a serpent, striking for the door. But his tribulation was not yet entirely at an end, for even as he was passing Fettes clutched him by the arm and these words came in a whisper, and yet painfully distinct, 'Have you seen it again?'

The great rich London doctor cried out aloud with a sharp, throttling cry; he dashed his questioner across the open space, and, with his hands over his head, fled out of the door like a detected thief. Before it had occurred to one of us to make a movement, the fly was already rattling towards the station. The scene was over like a dream, but the dream had left proofs and traces of its passage. Next day the servant found the fine gold spectacles broken on the threshold, and that very night we were all standing breathless by the bar-room window, and Fettes at our side, sober, pale, and resolute in look.

'God protect us, Mr Fettes!' said the landlord, coming first into possession of his customary senses. 'What in the universe is all this? These are strange things you have been saying.'

Fettes turned towards us; he looked us each in succession in the face. 'See if you can hold your tongues,' said he. 'That man Macfarlane is not safe to cross; those that have done so already have repented it too late.'

And then, without so much as finishing his third glass, far less waiting for the other two, he bade us goodbye and went forth, under the lamp of the hotel, into the black night.

We three turned to our places in the parlour, with the big red fire and four clear candles; and as we recapitulated what had passed the first chill of our surprise soon changed into a glow of curiosity. We sat late; it was the latest session I have known in the old George. Each man, before we parted, had his theory that he was bound to prove; and none of us had any nearer business in this world than to track out the past of our condemned companion, and surprise the secret that he shared with the great London doctor. It was no great boast, but I believe I was a better hand at worming out a story than either of my fellows at the George; and perhaps there is now no other man alive who could narrate to you the following foul and unnatural events.

In his young days Fettes studied medicine in the schools of Edinburgh. He had talent of a kind, the talent that picks up swiftly what it hears and readily retails it for its own. He worked little at home; but he was civil, attentive, and intelligent in the presence of his masters. They soon picked him out as a lad who listened closely and remembered well;

nay, strange as it seemed to me when I first heard it, he was in those days well favoured, and pleased by his exterior. There was, at that period, a certain extramural teacher of anatomy, whom I shall here designate by the letter K. His name was subsequently too well known. The man who bore it skulked through the streets of Edinburgh in disguise, while the mob that applauded at the execution of Burke called loudly for the blood of his employer. But Mr K—— was then at the top of his vogue; he enjoyed a popularity due partly to his own talent and address, partly to the incapacity of his rival, the university professor. The students, at least, swore by his name, and Fettes believed himself, and was believed by others, to have laid the foundations of success when he had acquired the favour of this meteorically famous man. Mr K—— was a *bon vivant* as well as an accomplished teacher; he liked a sly allusion no less than a careful preparation. In both capacities Fettes enjoyed and deserved his notice, and by the second year of his attendance he held the half-regular position of second demonstrator or sub-assistant in his class.

In this capacity, the charge of the theatre and lecture room devolved in particular upon his shoulders. He had to answer for the cleanliness of the premises and the conduct of the other students, and it was a part of his duty to supply, receive, and divide the various subjects. It was with a view to this last – at that time very delicate – affair that he was lodged by Mr K—— in the same wynd, and at last in the same building, with the dissecting rooms. Here, after a night of turbulent pleasures, his hand still tottering, his sight still misty and confused, he would be called out of bed in the black hours before the winter dawn by the unclean and desperate interlopers who supplied the table. He would open the door to these men, since infamous throughout the land. He would help them with their tragic burthen, pay them their sordid price, and remain alone, when they were gone, with the unfriendly relics of humanity. From such a scene he would return to snatch another hour or two of slumber, to repair the abuses of the night, and refresh himself for the labours of the day.

Few lads could have been more insensible to the impressions of a life thus passed among the ensigns of mortality. His mind was closed against all general considerations. He was incapable of interest in the fate and fortunes of another, the slave of his own desires and low ambitions. Cold, light and selfish in the last resort, he had that modicum of prudence, miscalled morality, which keeps a man from inconvenient drunkenness or punishable theft. He coveted, besides, a measure of consideration from his masters and his fellow-pupils, and he had no desire to fail conspicuously in the external parts of life. Thus he made it his pleasure to gain some distinction in his studies, and day after day rendered unimpeachable eye-service to his employer, Mr K——. For his day of work he indemnified himself by nights of roaring, blackguardly enjoyment; and when that balance had been struck, the organ that he called his conscience declared itself content.

The supply of subjects was a continual trouble to him as well as to his master. In that large and busy class, the raw material of the anatomists kept perpetually running out; and the business thus rendered necessary was not only unpleasant in itself, but threatened dangerous consequences to all who were concerned. It was the policy of Mr K—— to ask no questions in his dealings with the trade. 'They bring the body, and we pay the price,' he used to say, dwelling on the alliteration – '*quid pro quo.*' And again, and somewhat profanely, 'Ask no questions,' he would tell his assistants, 'for conscience' sake.' There was no understanding that the subjects were provided by the crime of murder. Had that idea been broached to him in words, he would have recoiled in horror; but the lightness of his speech upon so grave a matter was, in itself, an offence against good manners, and a temptation to the men with whom he dealt. Fettes, for instance, had often remarked to himself upon the singular freshness of the bodies. He had been struck again and again by the hang-dog, abominable looks of the ruffians who came to him before the dawn; and, putting things together clearly in his private thoughts, he perhaps attributed a meaning too immoral and too categorical to the unguarded counsels of his master. He understood his duty, in short, to have three branches: to take what was brought, to pay the price, and to avert the eye from any evidence of crime.

One November morning this policy of silence was put sharply to the test. He had been awake all night with a racking toothache – pacing his room like a caged beast or throwing himself in fury on his bed – and had fallen at last into that profound, uneasy slumber that so often follows on a night of pain, when he was awakened by the third or fourth angry repetition of the concerted signal. There was a thin, bright moonshine: it was bitter cold, windy, and frosty; the town had not yet awakened, but an indefinable stir already preluded the noise and business of the day. The ghouls had come later than usual, and they seemed more than usually eager to be gone. Fettes, sick with sleep, lighted them upstairs. He heard their grumbling Irish voices through a dream; and as they stripped the sack from their sad merchandise he leaned dozing with his shoulder propped against the wall; he had to shake himself to find the men their money. As he did so his eyes lighted on the dead face. He started; he took two steps nearer, with the candle raised.

'God Almighty!' he cried. 'That is Jane Galbraith!'

The men answered nothing, but they shuffled nearer the door.

'I know her, I tell you,' he continued. 'She was alive and hearty yesterday. It's impossible she can be dead; it's impossible you should have got this body fairly.'

'Sure, sir, you're mistaken entirely,' asserted one of the men.

But the other looked Fettes darkly in the eyes, and demanded the money on the spot.

It was impossible to misconceive the threat or to exaggerate the danger. The lad's heart failed him. He stammered some excuses, counted out the sum, and saw his hateful visitors depart. No sooner were they gone than he hastened to confirm his doubts. By a dozen unquestionable marks he identified the girl he had jested with the day before. He saw, with horror, marks upon her body that might well betoken violence. A panic seized him, and he took refuge in his room. There he reflected at length over the discovery that he had made; considered soberly the bearing of Mr K——'s instructions and the danger to himself of interference in so serious a business, and at last, in sore perplexity, determined to wait for the advice of his immediate superior, the class assistant.

This was a young doctor, Wolfe Macfarlane, a high favourite among all the restless students, clever, dissipated, and unscrupulous to the last degree. He had travelled and studied abroad. His manners were agreeable and a little forward. He was an authority on the stage, skilful on the ice or the links with skate or golf-club; he dressed with nice audacity, and, to put the finishing touch upon his glory, he kept a gig and a strong trotting-horse. With Fettes he was on terms of intimacy; indeed their relative positions called for some community of life; and when subjects were scarce the pair would drive far into the country in Macfarlane's gig, visit and desecrate some lonely graveyard, and return before dawn with their booty to the door of the dissecting room.

On that particular morning Macfarlane arrived somewhat earlier than his wont. Fettes heard him, and met him on the stairs, told him his story, and showed him the cause of his alarm. Macfarlane examined the marks on her body.

'Yes,' he said with a nod, 'it looks fishy.'

'Well, what should I do?' asked Fettes.

'Do?' repeated the other. 'Do you want to do anything? Least said soonest mended, I should say.'

'Someone else might recognize her,' objected Fettes. 'She was as well known as the Castle Rock.'

'We'll hope not,' said Macfarlane, 'and if anybody does – well you didn't, don't you see, and there's an end. The fact is, this has been going on too long. Stir up the mud, and you'll get K—— into the most unholy trouble; you'll be in a shocking box yourself. So will I, if you come to that. I should like to know how any one of us would look, or what the devil we should have to say for ourselves, in any Christian witness-box. For me, you know there's one thing certain – that, practically speaking, all our subjects have been murdered.'

'Macfarlane!' cried Fettes.

'Come now!' sneered the other. 'As if you hadn't suspected it yourself!'

'Suspecting is one thing——'

'And proof another. Yes, I know; and I'm as sorry as you are this should have come here,' tapping the body with his cane. 'The next best thing for me is not to recognize it; and,' he added coolly, 'I don't. You may, if you please. I don't dictate, but I think a man of the world would do as I do; and I may add, I fancy that is what K—— would look for at our hands. The question is, why did he choose us two for his assistants? And I answer, because he didn't want old wives.'

This was the tone of all others to affect the mind of a lad like Fettes. He agreed to imitate Macfarlane. The body of the unfortunate girl was duly dissected, and no one remarked or appeared to recognize her.

One afternoon, when his day's work was over, Fettes dropped into a popular tavern and found Macfarlane sitting with a stranger. This was a small man, very pale and dark, with coal-black eyes. The cut of his features gave a promise of intellect and refinement which was but feebly realized in his manners, for he proved, upon a nearer acquaintance, coarse, vulgar, and stupid. He exercised, however, a very remarkable control over Macfarlane; issued orders like the Great Bashaw; became inflamed at the least discussion or delay, and commented rudely on the servility with which he was obeyed. This most offensive person took a fancy to Fettes on the spot, plied him with drinks, and honoured him with unusual confidences on his past career. If a tenth part of what he confessed were true, he was a very loathsome rogue; and the lad's vanity was tickled by the attention of so experienced a man.

'I'm a pretty bad fellow myself,' the stranger remarked, 'but Macfarlane is the boy – Toddy Macfarlane I call him. Toddy, order your friend another glass.' Or it might be, 'Toddy, you jump up and shut the door.' 'Toddy hates me,' he said again. 'Oh, yes, Toddy, you do!'

'Don't call me that confounded name,' growled Macfarlane.

'Hear him! Did you ever see the lads play knife? He would like to do that all over my body,' remarked the stranger.

'We medicals have a better way than that,' said Fettes. 'When we dislike a dead friend of ours, we dissect him.'

Macfarlane looked up sharply, as though this jest was scarcely to his mind.

The afternoon passed. Gray, for that was the stranger's name, invited Fettes to join them at dinner, ordered a feast so sumptuous that the tavern was thrown in commotion, and when all was done commanded Macfarlane to settle the bill. It was late before they separated; the man Gray was incapably drunk. Macfarlane, sobered by his fury, chewed the cud of the money he had been forced to squander and the slights he had been obliged to swallow. Fettes, with various liquors singing in his head, returned home with devious footsteps and a mind entirely in abeyance. Next day Macfarlane was absent from the class, and Fettes smiled to himself as he imagined him still squiring the intolerable Gray from tavern to tavern. As soon as the hour of liberty had struck he posted from place to place in quest of his last night's companions. He could find them, however, nowhere; so returned early to his rooms, went early to bed, and slept the sleep of the just.

At four in the morning he was awakened by the well known signal. Descending to the door, he was filled with astonishment to find Macfarlane with his gig, and in the gig one of those long and ghastly packages with which he was so well acquainted.

'What?' he cried. 'Have you been out alone? How did you manage?'

But Macfarlane silenced him roughly, bidding him turn to business. When they had got the body upstairs and laid it on the table, Macfarlane made at first as if he were going away. Then he paused and seemed to hesitate; and then, 'You had better look at the face,' said he, in tones of some constraint. 'You had better,' he repeated, as Fettes only stared at him in wonder.

'But where, and how, and when did you come by it?' cried the other.

'Look at the face,' was the only answer.

Fettes was staggered; strange doubts assailed him. He looked from the young doctor to the body, and then back again. At last, with a start, he did as he was bidden. He had almost expected the sight that met his eyes, and yet the shock was cruel. To see, fixed in the rigidity of death and naked on that coarse layer of sack-cloth, the man whom he had left well-clad and full of meat and sin upon the threshold of a tavern, awoke, even in the thoughtless Fettes, some of the terrors of the conscience. It was a *cras tibi* which re-echoed in his soul, that two whom he had known should have come to lie upon these icy tables. Yet these were only secondary thoughts. His first concern regarded Wolfe. Unprepared for a challenge so momentous, he knew not how to look his comrade in the face. He durst not meet his eye, and he had neither words nor voice at his command.

It was Macfarlane himself who made the first advance. He came up quietly behind and laid his hand gently but firmly on the other's shoulder.

'Richardson,' said he, 'may have the head.'

Now Richardson was a student who had long been anxious for that portion of the human subject to dissect. There was no answer, and the murderer resumed: 'Talking of business, you must pay me; your accounts, you see, must tally.'

Fettes found a voice, the ghost of his own: 'Pay you!' he cried. 'Pay you for that?'

'Why, yes, of course you must. By all means and on every possible account, you must,' returned the other. 'I dare not give it for nothing, you dare not take it for nothing; it would compromise us both. This is another case like Jane Galbraith's. The more things are wrong the more we must act as if all were right. Where does old K—— keep his money——'

'There,' answered Fettes hoarsely, pointing to a cupboard in the corner.

'Give me the key, then,' said the other, calmly, holding out his hand.

There was an instant's hesitation, and the die was cast. Macfarlane could not suppress a nervous twitch, the infinitesimal mark of an immense relief, as he felt the key turn between his fingers. He opened the cupboard, brought out pen and ink and a paper-book that stood in one compartment, and separated from the funds in a drawer a sum suitable to the occasion.

'Now, look here,' he said, 'there is the payment made – first proof of you good faith: first step to your security. You have now to clinch it by a second. Enter the payment in your book, and then you for your part may defy the devil.'

The next few seconds were for Fettes an agony of thought; but in balancing his terrors it was the most immediate that triumphed. Any future difficulty seemed almost welcome if he could avoid a present quarrel with Macfarlane. He set down the candle which he had been carrying all the time, and with a steady hand entered the date, the nature, and the amount of the transaction.

'And now,' said Macfarlane, 'it's only fair that you should pocket the lucre. I've had my share already. By-the-by, when a man of the world falls into a bit of luck, he has a few shillings extra in his pocket – I'm ashamed to speak of it, but there's a rule of conduct in the case. No treating, no purchase of expensive class-books, no squaring of old debts; borrow, don't lend.'

'Macfarlane,' began Fettes, still somewhat hoarsely. 'I have put my neck in a halter to oblige you.'

'To oblige me?' cried Wolfe. 'Oh, come! You did, as near as I can see the matter, what you downright had to do in self defence. Suppose I got into trouble, where would you be? This second little matter flows clearly from the first. Mr Gray is the continuation of Miss Galbraith. You can't begin and then stop. If you begin, you must keep on beginning; that's the truth. No rest for the wicked.'

A horrible sense of blackness and the treachery of fate seized hold upon the soul of the unhappy student.

'My God!' he cried, 'but what have I done? and when did I begin? To be made a class assistant – in the name of reason, where's the

harm in that? Service wanted the position; Service might have got it.
Would *he* have been where *I* am now?'

'My dear fellow,' said Macfarlane, 'what a boy you are! What harm
has come to you? What harm *can* come to you if you hold your tongue?
Why, man, do you know what this life is? There are two squads of us –
the lions and the lambs. If you're a lamb, you'll come to lie upon these
tables like Gray or Jane Galbraith; if you're a lion, you'll live and drive a
horse like me, like K——, like all the world with any wit or courage.
You're staggered at the first. But look at K——! My dear fellow, you're
clever, you have pluck. I like you, and K—— likes you. You were born
to lead the hunt: and I tell you, on my honour and my experience of life,
three days from now you'll laugh at all these scarecrows like a high school
boy at a farce.'

And with that Macfarlane took his departure and drove off up the
wynd in his gig to get under cover before daylight. Fettes was thus left
alone with his regrets. He saw the miserable peril in which he stood
involved. He saw, with inexpressible dismay, that there was no limit to
his weakness, and that, from concession to concession, he had fallen from
the arbiter of Macfarlane's destiny to his paid and helpless accomplice.
He would have given the world to have been a little braver at the time,
but it did not occur to him that he might still be brave. The secret
of Jane Galbraith and the cursed entry in the daybook closed his
mouth.

Hours passed; the class began to arrive; the members of the unhappy
Gray were dealt out to one and to another, and received without
remark. Richardson was made happy with the head; and before the
hour of freedom rang Fettes trembled with exultation to perceive how
far they had already gone towards safety.

For two days he continued to watch, with increasing joy, the
dreadful process of disguise.

On the third day Macfarlane made his appearance. He had been ill,
he said; but he made up for lost time by the energy with which he
directed the students. To Richardson in particular he extended the most
valuable assistance and advice, and that student, encouraged by the
praise of the demonstrator, burned high with ambitious hopes, and saw
the medal already in his grasp.

Before the week was out Macfarlane's prophecy had been fulfilled.
Fettes had outlived his terrors and had forgotten his baseness. He began
to plume himself upon his courage, and had so arranged the story in his
mind that he could look back on these events with an unhealthy pride.
Of his accomplice he saw but little. They met, of course, in the business
of the class; they received their orders together from Mr K——. At times
they had a word or two in private, and Macfarlane was from first to last
particularly kind and jovial. But it was plain that he avoided any

reference to their common secret; and even when Fettes whispered to him that he had cast in his lot with the lions and forsworn the lambs, he only signed to him smilingly to hold his peace.

At length an occasion arose which drew the pair once more into a closer union. Mr K—— was again short of subjects; pupils were eager, and it was a part of this teacher's pretensions to be always well supplied. At the same time there came the news of a burial in the rustic graveyard of Glencorse. Time has little changed the place in question. It stood then, as now, upon the crossroad, out of call of human habitations, and buried fathom deep in the foliage of six cedar trees. The cries of the sheep upon the neighbouring hills, the streamlets upon either hand, one loudly singing among pebbles, the other dripping furtively from pond to pond, the stir of the wind in mountainous old flowering chestnuts, and once in seven days the voice of the bell and the old tunes of the precentor, were the only sounds that disturbed the silence around the rural church. The Resurrection Man – to use a by-name of the period – was not to be deterred by any of the sanctities of customary piety. It was part of his trade to despise and desecrate the scrolls and trumpets of old tombs, the paths worn by the feet of worshippers and mourners, and the offerings and the inscriptions of bereaved affection. To rustic neighbourhoods, where love is more than commonly tenacious, and where some bonds of blood or fellowship unite the entire society of a parish, the body-snatcher, far from being repelled by natural respect, was attracted by the ease and safety of the task. To bodies that had been laid in earth, in joyful expectation of a far different awakening, there came that hasty, lamp-lit, terror-haunted resurrection of the spade and mattock. The coffin was forced, the cerements torn, and the melancholy relics, clad in sackcloth, after being rattled for hours on moonless by-ways, were at length exposed to uttermost indignities before a class of gaping boys.

Somewhat as two vultures may swoop upon a dying lamb, Fettes and Macfarlane were to be let loose upon a grave in that green and quiet resting place. The wife of a farmer, a woman who had lived for sixty years, and been known for nothing but good butter and a godly conversation, was to be rooted from her grave at midnight and carried, dead and naked, to that far away city that she had always honoured with her Sunday best; the place beside her family was to be empty till the crack of doom; her innocent and almost venerable members to be exposed to that last curiosity of the anatomist.

Late one afternoon the pair set forth, well wrapped in cloaks and furnished with a formidable bottle. It rained without remission – a cold, dense, lashing rain. Now and again there blew a puff of wind, but these sheets of falling water kept it down. Bottle and all, it was a sad and silent drive as far as Penicuik, where they were to spend the evening. They stopped once, to hide their implements in a thick bush not far from the churchyard, and once again at the Fisher's Tryst, to have a toast before the kitchen fire and vary their nips of whisky with a glass of ale. When they reached their journey's end the gig was housed, the horse was fed and comforted, and the two young doctors in a private room sat down to the best dinner and the best wine the house afforded. The lights, the fire, the beating rain upon the window, the cold, incongruous work that lay before them, added zest to their enjoyment of the meal. With every glass their cordiality increased. Soon Macfarlane handed a little pile of gold to his companion.

'A compliment,' he said. 'Between friends these little damned accommodations ought to fly like pipe-lights.'

Fettes pocketed the money, and applauded the sentiment to the echo. 'You are a philosopher,' he cried. 'I was an ass till I knew you. You and K—— between you, by the Lord Harry! but you'll make a man of me.'

'Of course we shall,' applauded Macfarlane. 'A man? I tell you, it required a man to back me up the other morning. There are some big, brawling, forty-year-old cowards who would have turned sick at the look of the damned thing; but not you – you kept your head. I watched you.'

'Well, and why not?' Fettes thus vaunted himself. 'It was no affair of mine. There was nothing to gain on the one side but disturbance, and on the other I could count on your gratitude, don't you see?' And he slapped his pocket till the gold pieces rang.

Macfarlane somehow felt a certain touch of alarm at these unpleasant words. He may have regretted that he had taught his young companion so successfully, but he had no time to interfere, for the other noisily continued in this boastful strain:

'The great thing is not to be afraid. Now, between you and me, I don't want to hang – that's practical; but for all cant, Macfarlane, I was born with a contempt. Hell, God, Devil, right, wrong, sin, crime, and all the old gallery of curiosities – they may frighten boys, but men of the world, like you and me, despise them. Here's to the memory of Gray!'

It was by this time growing somewhat late. The gig, according to order, was brought round to the door with both lamps brightly shining, and the young men had to pay their bill and take the road. They announced that they were bound for Peebles, and drove in that direction till they were clear of the last houses of the town; then, extinguishing the lamps, returned upon their course, and followed a by-road towards Glencorse. There was no sound but that of their own passage, and the incessant, strident pouring of the rain. It was pitch dark; here and there a white gate or a white stone in the wall guided them for a short space across the night; but for the most part it was at a foot pace, and almost groping, that they picked their way through that resonant blackness to their solemn and isolated destination. In the sunken woods that traverse the neighbourhood of the burying ground the last glimmer failed them, and it became necessary to kindle a match and re-illumine one of the lanterns of the gig. Thus, under the dripping trees, and environed by huge and moving shadows, they reached the scene of their unhallowed labours.

They were both experienced in such affairs, and powerful with the spade; and they had scarce been twenty minutes at their task before they were rewarded by a dull rattle on the coffin lid. At the same moment Macfarlane, having hurt his hand upon a stone, flung it carelessly above his head. The grave, in which they now stood almost to the shoulders, was close to the edge of the plateau of the graveyard; and the gig lamp had been propped, the better to illuminate their labours, against a tree, and on the immediate verge of the steep bank descending to the stream. Chance had taken a sure aim with the stone. Then came a clang of broken glass; night fell upon them; sounds alternately dull and ringing announced the bounding of the lantern down the bank, and its occasional collision with the trees. A stone or two, which it had dislodged in its descent rattled behind it into the profundities of the glen; and then silence, like night, resumed its sway; and they might bend their hearing to its utmost pitch, but naught was to be heard except the rain, now marching to the wind, now steadily falling over miles of open country.

They were so nearly at an end of their abhorred task that they judged it wisest to complete it in the dark. The coffin was exhumed and broken open; the body inserted in the dripping sack and carried between them to the gig; one mounted to keep it in its place, and the other, taking the horse by the mouth, groped along by the wall and bush until they reached the wider road by the Fisher's Tryst. Here was a faint disused radiancy, which they hailed like daylight; by that they pushed the horse to a good pace and began to rattle along merrily in the direction of the town.

They had both been wetted to the skin during their operations, and now, as the gig jumped among the deep ruts, the thing that stood propped between them fell now upon one and now upon the other. At every repetition of the horrid contact each instinctively repelled it with greater haste; and the process, natural although it was, began to tell upon the nerves of the companions. Macfarlane made some ill-favoured jest about the farmer's wife, but it came hollowly from his lips, and was allowed to drop in silence. Still their unnatural burthen bumped from side to side; and now the head would be laid, as if in confidence, upon their shoulders; and now the drenching sackcloth would flap icily about their faces. A creeping chill began to possess the soul of Fettes. He peered at the bundle, and it seemed somehow larger than at first. All over the countryside, and from every degree of distance, the farm dogs accompanied their passage with tragic ululations; and it grew and grew upon his mind that some unnatural miracle had been achieved, that some nameless change had befallen the dead body, and that it was in fear of their unholy burthen that the dogs were howling.

'For God's sake,' said he, making a great effort to arrive at speech, 'for God's sake, let's have a light!'

Seemingly Macfarlane was affected in the same direction; for though he made no reply, he stopped the horse, passed the reins to his companion, got down, and proceeded to kindle the remaining lamp. They had by that time got no farther than the crossroad down to Auchendinny. The rain still poured as though the deluge were returning, and it was no easy matter to make a light in such a world of wet and darkness. When at last the flickering blue flame had been transferred to the wick and began to expand and clarify, and shed a wide circle of misty brightness round the gig, it became possible for the two young men to see each other and the thing they had along with them. The rain had moulded the rough sacking to the outlines of the body underneath; the head was distinct from the trunk, the shoulders plainly modelled; something at once spectral and human riveted their eyes upon the ghastly comrade of their drive.

For some time Macfarlane stood motionless, holding up the lamp. A nameless dread was swathed, like a wet sheet, about the body, and tightened the white skin upon the face of Fettes; a fear that was meaningless, a horror of what could not be, kept mounting to his brain. Another beat of the watch, and he had spoken. But his comrade forestalled him.

'That is not a woman,' said Macfarlane, in a hushed voice.

'It was a woman when we put her in,' whispered Fettes.

'Hold that lamp,' said the other. 'I must see her face.'

And as Fettes took the lamp his companion untied the fastenings of the sack and drew down the cover from the head. The light fell very clear upon the dark, well-moulded features and smooth-shaven cheeks of a too familiar countenance, often beheld in dreams of both of these young men. A wild yell rang up into the night; each leaped from his own side into the roadway; the lamp fell, broke, and was extinguished; and the horse, terrified by this unusual commotion, bounded and went off towards Edinburgh at a gallop, bearing along with it, sole occupant of the gig, the body of the dead and long-dissected Gray.

A Ghost Story
Mark Twain

I took a large room, far up New York's Broadway, in a huge old building whose upper storeys had been wholly unoccupied for years until I came. The place had long been given up to dust and cobwebs, to solitude and silence. I seemed groping among the tombs and invading the privacy of the dead, that first night I climbed up to my quarters. For the first time in my life a superstitious dread came over me; and as I turned a dark angle of the stairway and an invisible cobweb swung its slazy woof in my face and clung there, I shuddered as one who had encountered a phantom.

I was glad enough when I reached my room and locked out the mould and the darkness. A cheery fire was burning in the grate, and I sat down before it with a comfortable sense of relief. For two hours I sat there, thinking of bygone times; recalling old scenes, and summoning half-forgotten faces out of the mists of the past; listening, in fancy, to voices that long ago grew silent for all time, and to once familiar songs that nobody sings now. And as my reverie softened down to a sadder and sadder pathos, the shrieking of the winds outside softened to a wail, the angry beating of the rain against the panes diminished to a tranquil patter, and one by one the noises in the street subsided, until the hurrying footsteps of the last belated straggler died away in the distance and left no sound behind.

The fire had burned low. A sense of loneliness crept over me. I arose and undressed, moving on tiptoe about the room, doing stealthily what I had to do, as if I were environed by sleeping enemies whose slumbers it would be fatal to break. I covered up in bed, and lay listening to the rain and wind and the faint creaking of distant shutters, till they lulled me to sleep.

I slept profoundly, but how long I do not know. All at once I found myself awake, and filled with a shuddering expectancy. All was still. All but my own heart – I could hear it beat. Presently the bedclothes began to slip slowly towards the foot of the bed, as if some one were pulling

them! I could not stir; I could not speak. Still the blankets slipped
deliberately away, till my chest was uncovered. Then with a great effort
I seized them and drew them over my head. I waited, listened, waited.
Once more that steady pull began, and once more I lay torpid a century
of dragging seconds till my chest was once more uncovered. At last I
roused my energies and snatched the covers back to their place and held
them with a strong grip. I waited. By and by I felt a faint tug, and took a
fresh grip. The tug strengthened to a steady strain – it grew stronger and
stronger. My hold parted, and for the third time the blankets slid away.
I groaned. An answering groan came from the foot of the bed! Beaded
drops of sweat stood upon my forehead. I was more dead than alive.
Presently I heard a heavy footstep in my room – the step of an elephant,
it seemed to me – it was not like anything human. But it was moving
from me – there was relief in that. I heard it approach the door – pass out
without moving bolt or lock – and wander away among the dismal
corridors, straining the floors and joists till they creaked again as it
passed – and then silence reigned once more.

When my excitement had calmed, I said to myself, 'This is a dream
– simply a hideous dream.' And so I lay thinking it over until I
convinced myself that it *was* a dream, and then a comforting laugh
relaxed my lips and I was happy again. I got up and struck a light; and
when I found that the locks and bolts were just as I had left them,
another soothing laugh welled in my heart and rippled from my lips. I
took my pipe and lit it, and was just sitting down before the fire, when –
down went the pipe out of my nerveless fingers, the blood forsook my
cheeks, and my placid breathing was cut short with a gasp! In the ashes
on the hearth, side by side with my own bare footprint, was another, so
vast that in comparison mine was but an infant's! Then I *had* had a
visitor, and the elephantine tread was explained.

I put out the light and returned to bed, palsied with fear. I lay a long
time, peering into the darkness, and listening. Then I heard a grating
noise overhead, like the dragging of a heavy body across the floor; then
the throwing down of the body, and the shaking of my windows in
response to the concussion. In distant parts of the building I heard the
muffled slamming of doors. I heard, at intervals, stealthy footsteps
creeping in and out among the corridors, and up and down the stairs.
Sometimes these noises approached my door, hesitated, and went away
again. I heard the clanking of chains faintly, in remote passages, and
listened while the clanking grew nearer – while it wearily climbed the
stairways, marking each move by the loose surplus of chain that fell with
an accented rattle upon each succeeding step as the goblin that bore it
advanced. I heard muttered sentences; half uttered screams that seemed
smothered violently; and the swish of invisible garments, the rush of
invisible wings. Then I became conscious that my chamber was invaded

– that I was not alone. I heard sighs and breathings about my bed, and mysterious whisperings. Three little spheres of soft phosphorescent light appeared on the ceiling directly over my head, clung and glowed there a moment, and then dropped – two of them upon my face and one upon the pillow. They spattered liquidly and felt warm. Intuition told me they had turned to gouts of blood as they fell – I needed no light to satisfy myself of that. Then I saw pallid faces, dimly luminous, and white uplifted hands, floating bodiless in the air – floating a moment and then disappearing. The whispering ceased, and the voices and the sounds, and a solemn stillness followed. I waited and listened. I felt that I must have light or die. I was weak with fear. I slowly raised myself towards a sitting posture, and my face came in contact with a clammy hand! All strength went from me apparently, and I fell back like a stricken invalid. Then I heard the rustle of a garment – it seemed to pass to the door and go out.

When everything was still once more, I crept out of bed, sick and feeble, and lit the gas with a hand that trembled as if it were aged with a hundred years. The light brought some little cheer to my spirits. I sat down and fell into a dreamy contemplation of that great footprint in the ashes. By and by its outlines began to waver and grow dim. I glanced up and the broad gas-flame was slowly wilting away. In the same moment I heard that elephantine tread again. I noted its approach, nearer and nearer, along the musty halls, and dimmer and dimmer the light waned. The tread reached my very door and paused – the light had dwindled to a sickly blue, and all things about me lay in a spectral twilight. The door did not open, and yet I felt a faint gust of air fan my cheek, and presently was conscious of a huge, cloudy presence before me. I watched it with fascinated eyes. A pale glow stole over the Thing; gradually its cloudy folds took shape – an arm appeared, then legs, then a body, and last a great sad face looked out of the vapour. Stripped of its filmy housings, naked, muscular and comely, that petrified, prehistoric man, the so-called Cardiff Giant loomed above me!

All my misery vanished – for a child might know that no harm could come with that benignant countenance. My cheerful spirits returned at once, and in sympathy with them the gas flamed up brightly again. Never was a lonely outcast so glad to welcome company as I was to greet the friendly giant. I said:

'Why, is it nobody but you? Do you know, I have been scared to death for the last two or three hours? I am most honestly glad to see you. I wish I had a chair—— Here, here, don't try to sit down in that thing!'

But it was too late. He was in it before I could stop him, and down he went – I never saw a chair so shivered in my life.

'Stop, stop, you'll ruin ev——'

Too late again. There was another crash, and another chair was resolved into its original elements.

'Confound it, haven't you got any judgement at all? Do you want to ruin all the furniture in the place? Here, here, you petrified fool——'

But it was no use. Before I could arrest him he had sat down on the bed, and it was a melancholy ruin.

'Now what sort of a way is that to do? First you come lumbering about the place bringing a legion of vagabond goblins along with you to worry me to death, and when I overlook an indelicacy of costume, which would not be tolerated anywhere by cultivated people except in a respectable theatre, and not even there if the nudity were of *your* sex, you repay me by wrecking all the furniture you can find to sit down on. And why will you? You damage yourself as much as you do me. You have broken off the end of your spinal column, and littered up the floor with chips of your hams till the place looks like a marble yard. You ought to be ashamed of yourself – you are big enough to know better.'

'Well, I will not break any more furniture. But what am I to do? I have not had a chance to sit down for a century.' And the tears came into his eyes.

'Poor devil,' I said, 'I should not have been so harsh with you. And you are an orphan too, no doubt. But sit down on the floor here – nothing else can stand your weight – and besides, we cannot be sociable with you away up there above me; I want you down where I can perch on this high counting-house stool and gossip with you face to face.'

So he sat down on the floor, and lit a pipe which I gave him, threw one of my red blankets over his shoulders, inverted my hip-bath on his head, helmet fashion, and made himself picturesque and comfortable. Then he crossed his ankles, while I renewed the fire, and exposed the flat, honeycombed bottoms of his prodigious feet to the grateful warmth.

'What is the matter with the bottom of your feet and the back of your legs, that they are gouged up so?'

'Infernal chilblains – I caught them clear up to the back of my head, roosting out there under Newell's farm where they dug me up. But I love the place; love it as one loves his old home. There is no peace like the peace I feel when I am there.'

We talked along for half an hour, and then I noticed that he looked tired, and spoke of it.

'Tired?' said he. 'Well, I should think so. And now I will tell you all about it, since you have treated me so well. I am the spirit of the petrified man that lies across the street there in the museum. I am the ghost of the Cardiff Giant. I can have no rest, no peace, till they have given that poor body burial again. Now what was the most natural thing for me to do, to make men satisfy this wish? Terrify them into it! –

haunt the place where the body lay! So I haunted the museum night after night. I even got other spirits to help me. But it did no good, for nobody ever came to the museum at midnight. Then it occurred to me to come over the way and haunt this place a little. I felt that if I ever got a hearing I must succeed, for I had the most efficient company that perdition could furnish. Night after night we have shivered around through these mildewed halls, dragging chains, groaning, whispering, tramping up and down stairs, till, to tell you the truth, I am almost worn out. But when I saw a light in your room tonight I roused my energies again and went at it with a deal of the old freshness. But I'm tired out – entirely fagged out. Give me, I beseech you, give me some hope!'

I lit off my perch in a burst of excitement, and exclaimed:

'This transcends everything! Everything that ever did occur. Why, you poor blundering old fossil, you have had all your trouble for nothing – you have been haunting a *plaster cast* of yourself – the real Cardiff Giant is in Albany! Confound it, don't you know your own remains?'

It was a fact. The original fraud was ingeniously and fraudulently duplicated, and exhibited in New York as the 'only genuine' Cardiff Giant (to the unspeakable disgust of the owners of the real colossus) at the very same time that the latter was drawing crowds at a museum in Albany.

Well, when I explained all this, I never saw such an eloquent look of shame, of pitiable humiliation, overspread a countenance before.

The petrified man rose slowly to his feet, and said:

'Honestly, *is* that true?'

'As true as I am sitting here.'

He took the pipe from his mouth and laid it on the mantel, then stood irresolute a moment, dropping his chin on his chest, and finally said:

'Well – I *never* felt so absurd before. The petrified man has sold everybody else, and now the mean fraud has ended by selling its own ghost! My son, if there is any charity left in your heart for a poor friendless phantom like me, don't let this get out. Think how *you* would feel if you had made such an ass of yourself.'

I heard his stately tramp die away, step by step down the stairs and out into the deserted street, and felt sorry that he was gone, poor fellow – and sorrier still that he had carried off my red blanket and my bath-tub.

Mrs Lunt
Hugh Walpole

'Do you believe in ghosts?' I asked Runciman. I had to ask him this very
platitudinous question more because he was so difficult a man to spend
an hour with rather than for any other reason. You know his books,
perhaps, or more probably you don't know them – *The Running Man,
The Elm Tree*, and *Crystal and Candlelight.* He is one of those little men
who are constant enough in this age of immense overproduction of
books, men who publish every autumn their novel, who arouse by that
publication in certain critics eager appreciation and praise, who have a
small and faithful public, whose circulation is very small indeed, who,
when you meet them, have little to say, are often shy and nervous,
pessimistic and remote from daily life. Such men do fine work, are made
but little of in their own day, and perhaps fifty years after their death
are rediscovered by some digging critic and become a sort of cult with a
new generation.

I asked Runciman that question because, for some unknown
reason, I had invited him to dinner at my flat, and was now faced with a
long evening filled with that most tiresome of all conversations, talk that
dies every two minutes and has to be revived with terrific exertions.
Being myself a critic, and having on many occasions praised
Runciman's work, he was the more nervous and shy with me; had I
abused it, he would perhaps have had plenty to say – he was that kind of
man. But my question was a lucky one: it roused him instantly, his long,
bony body became full of a new energy, his eyes stared into a rich and
exciting reminiscence, he spoke without pause, and I took care not to
interrupt him. He certainly told me one of the most astounding stories I
have ever heard. Whether it was true or not I cannot, of course, say:
these ghost stories are nearly always at second or third hand. I had, at
any rate, the good fortune to secure mine from the source. Moreover,
Runciman was not a liar: he was too serious for that. He himself
admitted that he was not sure, at this distance of time, as to whether the

thing had gained as the years passed. However, here it is as he told it.

'It was some fifteen years ago,' he said. 'I went down to Cornwall to stay with Robert Lunt. Do you remember his name? No, I suppose you do not. He wrote several novels; some of those half-and-half things that are not quite novels, not quite poems, rather mystical and picturesque, and are the very devil to do well. De la Mare's *Return* is a good example of the kind of thing. I had reviewed somewhere his last book, and reviewed it favourably, and received from him a really touching letter showing that the man was thirsting for praise, and also, I fancied, for company. He lived in Cornwall somewhere on the sea coast, and his wife had died some two years before; he said he was quite alone there, and would I come and spend Christmas with him; he hoped I would not think this impertinent; he expected that I would be engaged already, but he could not resist the chance. Well, I wasn't engaged; far from it. If Lunt was lonely, so was I; if Lunt was a failure, so was I; I was touched, as I have said, by his letter, and I accepted his invitation. As I went down in the train to Penzance I wondered what kind of a man he would be. I had never seen any photographs of him; he was not the sort of author whose picture the newspapers publish. He must be, I fancied, about my own age – perhaps rather older. I know when we're lonely how some of us are for ever imagining that a friend will somewhere turn up, that ideal friend who will understand all one's feelings, who will give one affection without being sentimental, who will take an interest in one's affairs without being impertinent – yes, the sort of friend one never finds.

'I fancy that I became quite romantic about Lunt before I reached Penzance. We would talk, he and I, about all those literary questions that seemed to me at that time so absorbing; we would, perhaps, often stay together and even travel abroad on those little journeys that are so swiftly melancholy when one is alone, so delightful when one has a perfect companion. I imagined him as sparse and delicate and refined, with a sort of wistfulness and rather childish play of fancy. We had both, so far, failed in our careers, but perhaps together we would do great things.

'When I arrived at Penzance it was almost dark, and the snow, threatened all day by an overhanging sky, had begun gently and timorously to fall. He had told me in his letter that a fly would be at the station to take me to his house; and there I found it – a funny old weather-beaten carriage with a funny old weather-beaten driver. At this distance of time my imagination may have created many things, but I fancy that from the moment I was shut into that carriage some dim suggestion of fear and apprehension attacked me. I fancy that I had some absurd impulse to get out of the thing and take the night train back to London again – an action that would have been very unlike me, as I had always a sort of obstinate determination to carry through anything that I had begun. In any case, I was uncomfortable in that carriage; it had, I remember, a nasty, musty smell of damp straw and stale eggs, and it seemed to confine me so closely as though it were determined that, once I was in, I should never get out again. Then, it was bitterly cold; I was colder during that drive than I have ever been before or since. It was that penetrating cold that seems to pierce your very brain, so that I could not think with any clearness, but only wish again and again that I hadn't come. Of course, I could see nothing – only feel the jolt over the uneven road – and once and again we seemed to fight our way through dark paths, because I could feel the overhanging branches of the trees knock against the cab with mysterious taps, as though they were trying to give me some urgent message.

'Well, I mustn't make more of it than the facts allow, and I mustn't see into it all the significance of the events that followed. I only know that as the drive proceeded I became more and more miserable: miserable with the cold of my body, the misgivings of my imagination, the general loneliness of my case.

'At last we stopped. The old scarecrow got slowly off his box, with many heavings and sighings, came to the cab door, and, with great difficulty and irritating slowness, opened it. I got out of it, and found that the snow was now falling very heavily indeed, and that the path was lightened with its soft, mysterious glow. Before me was a humped and ungainly shadow: the house that was to receive me. I could make nothing of it in that darkness, but only stood there shivering while the old man pulled at the doorbell with a sort of frantic energy as though he were anxious to be rid of the whole job as quickly as possible and return to his own place. At last, after what seemed an endless time, the door opened, and an old man, who might have been own brother to the driver, poked out his head. The two old men talked together, and at last my bag was shouldered and I was permitted to come in out of the piercing cold.

'Now this, I know, is not imagination. I have never at any period of my life hated at first sight so vigorously any dwelling-place into which I have entered as I did that house. There was nothing especially disagreeable about my first vision of the hall. It was a large, dark place, lit by two dim lamps, cold and cheerless; but I got no particular impression of it because at once I was conducted out of it, led along a passage, and then introduced into a room which was, I saw at once, as warm and comfortable as the hall had been dark and dismal. I was, in fact, so eagerly pleased at the large and leaping fire that I moved towards it at once, not noting, at the first moment, the presence of my host; and when I did see him I could not believe that it was he. I have told you the kind of man that I had expected; but, instead of the sparse, sensitive artist, I found facing me a large burly man, over six foot, I should fancy, as broad-shouldered as he was tall, giving evidence of great muscular strength, the lower part of his face hidden by a black, pointed beard.

'But if I was astonished at the sight of him, I was double amazed when he spoke. His voice was thin and piping, like that of some old woman, and the little nervous gestures that he made with his hands were even more feminine than his voice. But I had to allow, perhaps, for excitement, for excited he was; he came up to me, took my hand in both of his, and held it as though he would never let it go. In the evening, when we sat over our port, he apologized for this. 'I was so glad to see you,' he said; 'I couldn't believe that really you would come; you are the first visitor of my own kind that I have had here for ever so long. I was ashamed indeed of asking you, but I had to snatch at the chance – it means so much to me."

'His eagerness, in fact, had something disturbing about it; something pathetic, too. He simply couldn't do too much for me: he led me through funny crumbling old passages, the boards creaking under us at every step, up some dark stairs, the walls hung, so far as I could see in the dim light, with faded yellow photographs of places, and showed me into my room with a deprecating agitated gesture as though he expected me at the first sight of it to turn and run. I didn't like it any more than I liked the rest of the house; but that was not my host's fault. He had done everything he possibly could for me: there was a large fire flaming in the open fireplace, there was a hot bottle, as he explained to me, in the big four-poster bed, and the old man who had opened the door to me was already taking my clothes out of my bag and putting them away. Lunt's nervousness was almost sentimental. He put both his hands on my shoulders and said, looking at me pleadingly: "If only you knew what it is for me to have you here, the talks we'll have. Well, well, I must leave you. You'll come down and join me, won't you, as soon as you can?"

'It was then, when I was left alone in my room, that I had my second impulse to flee. Four candles in tall old silver candlesticks were burning brightly, and these, with the blazing fire, gave plenty of light; and yet the room was in some way dim, as though a faint smoke pervaded it, and I remember that I went to one of the old lattice windows and threw it open for a moment as though I felt stifled. Two things quickly made me close it. One was the intense cold which, with a fluttering scamper of snow, blew into the room; the other was the quite deafening roar of the sea, which seemed to fling itself at my very face as though it wanted to knock me down. I quickly shut the window, turned round, and saw an old woman standing just inside the door. Now every story of this kind depends for its interest on its verisimilitude. Of course, to make my tale convincing I should be able to prove to you that I saw that old woman; but I can't. I can only urge upon you my rather dreary reputation of probity. You know that I'm a teetotaller, and always have been, and, most important evidence of all, I was not expecting to see an old woman; and yet I hadn't the least doubt in the world but that it was an old woman I saw. You may talk about shadows, clothes hanging on the back of the door, and the rest of it. I don't know. I've no theories about this story, I'm not a spiritualist. I don't know that I believe in anything especially, except the beauty of beautiful things. We'll put it, if you like, that I fancied that I saw an old woman, and my fancy was so strong that I can give you to this day a pretty detailed account of her appearance. She wore a black silk dress and on her breast was a large, ugly, gold brooch; she had black hair, brushed back from her forehead and parted down the middle; she wore a collar of some white stuff round her throat; her face was one of the wickedest, most malignant, and furtive that I have ever seen – very white in colour. She was shrivelled enough now, but might once have been rather beautiful. She stood there quietly, her hands at her side. I thought that she was some kind of housekeeper. "I have everything I want, thank you," I said. "What a splendid fire!" I turned for a moment towards it, and when I looked back she was gone. I thought nothing of this, of course, but drew up an old chair covered with green faded tapestry, and thought that I would read a little from some book that I had brought down with me before I went to join my host. The fact was that I was not very intent upon joining him before I must. I didn't like him, I had already made up my mind that I would find some excuse to return to London as soon as possible. I can't tell you why I didn't like him, except that I was myself very reserved and had, like many Englishmen, a great distrust of demonstrations, especially from another man. I hadn't cared for the way in which he had put his hands on my shoulders, and I felt perhaps that I wouldn't be able to live up to all his eager excitement about me.

'I sat in my chair and took up my book, but I had not been reading for more than two minutes before I was conscious of a most unpleasant smell. Now, there are all sorts of smells – healthy and otherwise – but I think the nastiest is that chilly odour that comes from bad sanitation and stuffy rooms combined; you meet it sometimes at little country inns and decrepit town lodgings. This smell was so definite that I could almost locate it; it came from near the door. I got up, approached the door, and at once it was as though I were drawing near to somebody who, if you'll forgive the impoliteness, was not accustomed to taking too many baths. I drew back just as I might had an actual person been there. Then, quite suddenly, the smell was gone, the room was fresh, and I saw, to my surprise, that one of the windows had opened and that snow was again blowing in. I closed it and went downstairs.

'The evening that followed was odd enough. My host was not in himself an unlikeable man; he did his very utmost to please me. He had a fine culture and a wide knowledge of books and things. He became quite cheerful as the evening went on; gave me a good dinner in a funny little old dining-room hung with some admirable mezzotints. The old serving man looked after us – a funny old man, with a long white beard like a goat – and, oddly enough, it was from him that I first recaught my earlier apprehension. He had just put the dessert on the table, had arranged my plate in front of me, when I saw him give a start and look towards the door. My attention was attracted to this because his hand, as it touched the plate, suddenly trembled. My eyes followed, but I could see nothing. That he was frightened of something was perfectly clear, and then (it may, of course, very easily have been fancy) I thought that I detected once more that strange unwholesome smell.

'I forgot this again when we were both seated in front of a splendid fire in the library. Lunt had a very fine collection of books, and it was delightful to him, as it is to every book collector, to have somebody with him who could really appreciate them. We stood looking at one book after another and talking eagerly about some of the minor early English novelists who were my especial hobby – Bage, Godwin, Henry Mackenzie, Mrs Shelley, Mat Lewis, and others – when once again he affected me most unpleasantly by putting his arm round my shoulders. I have all my life disliked intensely to be touched by certain people. I suppose we all feel like this. It is one of those inexplicable things; and I disliked this so much that I abruptly drew away.

'Instantly he was changed into a man of furious and ungovernable rage; I thought that he was going to strike me. He stood there quivering all over, the words pouring out of his mouth incoherently, as though he were mad and did not know what he was saying. He accused me of insulting him, of abusing his hospitality, of throwing his kindness back into his face, and of a thousand other ridiculous things; and I can't tell you how strange it was to hear all this coming out in that shrill, piping voice as though it were from an agitated woman, and yet to see with one's eyes that big, muscular frame, those immense shoulders, and that dark bearded face.

'I said nothing. I am, physically, a coward. I dislike, above anything else in the world, any sort of quarrel. At last I brought out, "I am very sorry. I didn't mean anything. Please forgive me," and then hurriedly turned to leave the room. At once he changed again; now he was almost in tears. He implored me not to go; said it was his wretched temper, but that he was so miserable and unhappy, and had for so long now been alone and desolate that he hardly knew what he was doing. He begged me to give him another chance, and if I would only listen to his story, I would perhaps be more patient with him.

'At once, so oddly is man constituted, I changed in my feelings towards him. I was very sorry for him. I saw that he was a man on the edge of his nerves, and that he really did need some help and sympathy, and would be quite distracted if he could not get it. I put my hand on his shoulder to quieten him and to show him that I bore no malice, and I felt that his great body was quivering from head to foot. We sat down again, and in an odd, rambling manner he told me his story. It amounted to very little, and the gist of it was that, rather to have some sort of companionship than from any impulse of passion, he had married some fifteen years before the daughter of a neighbouring clergyman. They had had no very happy life together, and at the last, he told me quite frankly, he had hated her. She had been mean, overbearing, and narrow-minded; it had been, he confessed, nothing but a relief to him when, just a year ago, she had suddenly died from heart failure. He had thought, then, that things would go better with him, but they had not; nothing had gone right with him since. He hadn't been able to work, many of his friends had ceased to come to see him, he had found it even difficult to get servants to stay with him, he was desperately lonely, he slept badly – that was why his temper was so terribly on edge. He had no one in the house with him save the old man, who was, fortunately, an excellent cook, and a boy – the old man's grandson. "Oh, I thought," I said, "that that excellent meal tonight was cooked by your housekeeper." "My housekeeper?" he answered. "There's no woman in the house." "Oh, but one came to my room," I replied, "this evening – an old ladylike looking person in a black silk dress." "You were mistaken," he answered in the oddest voice, as though he were exerting all the strength that he possessed to keep himself quiet and controlled. "I am sure that I saw her," I answered. "There couldn't be any mistake." And I described her to him. "You were mistaken," he repeated again. "Don't you see that you must have been when I tell you there is no woman in the house?" I reassured him quickly lest there should be another outbreak of rage. Then there followed the oddest kind of appeal. Urgently, as though his very life depended upon it, he begged me to stay with him for a few days. He implied, although he said nothing definitely, that he was in great trouble, that if only I would stay for a few days all would be well, that if ever in all my life I had had a chance of doing a kind action I had one now, that he couldn't expect me to stop in so dreary a place, but that he would never forget it if I did. He spoke in a voice of such urgent distress that I reassured him as I might a child, promising that I would stay and shaking hands with him on it as though it were a kind of solemn oath between us.

*   *   *

'I am sure that you would wish me to give you this incident as it occurred, and if the final catastrophe seems to come, as it were, accidentally, I can only say to you that that was how it happened. It is since the event that I have tried to put two and two together, and that they don't altogether make four is the fault that mine shares, I suppose, with every true ghost story.

'But the truth is that after that very strange episode between us I had a very good night. I slept the sleep of all justice, cosy and warm, in my four-poster, with the murmur of the sea beyond the windows to rock my slumbers. Next morning, too, was bright and cheerful, the sun sparkling down on the snow, and the snow sparkling back to the sun as though they were glad to see one another. I had a very pleasant morning looking at Lunt's books, talking to him, and writing one or two letters. I must say that, after all, I liked the man. His appeal to me on the night before had touched me. So few people, you see, had ever appealed to me about anything. His nervousness was there and the constant sense of apprehension, yet he seemed to be putting the best face on it, doing his utmost to set me at my ease in order to induce me to stay, I suppose, and to give him a little of that company that he so terribly needed. I dare say if I had not been so busy about the books I would not have been so happy. There was a strange eerie silence about that house if one ever stopped to listen; and once, I remember, sitting at the old bureau writing a letter, I raised my head and looked up, and caught Lunt watching as though he wondered whether I had heard or noticed anything. And so I listened too, and it seemed to me as though someone were on the other side of the library door with their hand raised to knock; a quaint notion, with nothing to support it, but I could have sworn that if I had gone to the door and opened it suddenly someone would have been there.

'However, I was cheerful enough, and after lunch quite happy. Lunt asked me if I would like a walk, and I said I would; and we started out in the sunshine over the crunching snow towards the sea. I don't remember of what we talked; we seemed to be now quite at our ease with one another. We crossed the fields to a certain point, looked down at the sea – smooth now, like silk – and turned back. I remember that I was so cheerful that I seemed suddenly to take a happy view of all my prospects. I began to confide in Lunt, telling him of my little plans, of my hopes for the book that I was then writing, and even began rather timidly to suggest to him that perhaps we should do something together; that what we both needed was a friend of common taste with ourselves. I know that I was talking on, that we had crossed a little village street, and were turning up the path towards the dark avenue of trees that led to his house, when suddenly the change came.

'What I first noticed was that he was not listening to me; his gaze

was fixed beyond me, into the very heart of the black clump of trees that
fringed the silver landscape. I looked too, and my heart bounded. There
was, standing just in front of the trees, as though she were waiting for us,
the old woman whom I had seen in my room the night before. I
stopped. "Why, there she is!" I said. "That's the old woman of whom I
was speaking – the old woman who came to my room." He caught my
shoulder with his hand. "There's nothing there," he said. "Don't you
see that that's a shadow? What's the matter with you? Can't you see
that there's nothing?" I stepped forward, and there was nothing, and I
wouldn't, to this day, be able to tell you whether it was hallucination or
not. I can only say that, from that moment, the afternoon appeared to
become dark. As we entered into the avenue of trees, silently, and
hurrying as though someone were behind us, the dusk seemed to have
fallen so that I could scarcely see my way. We reached the house
breathless. He hastened into his study as though I were not with him,
but I followed and, closing the door behind me, said, with all the force
that I had at command: "Now, what is this? What is it that's troubling
you? You must tell me! How can I help you if you don't?" And he
replied, in so strange a voice that it was as though he had gone out of his
mind: "I tell you there's nothing! Can't you believe me when I tell you
there's nothing at all? I'm quite all right . . . Oh, my God! – my God! . . .
don't leave me! . . . This is the very day – the very night she said . . . But I
did nothing, I tell you – I did nothing – it's only her beastly malice . . ."
He broke off. He still held my arm with his hand. He made strange
movements, wiping his forehead as though it were damp with sweat,
almost pleading with me; then suddenly angry again, then beseeching
once more, as though I had refused him the one thing he wanted.

'I saw that he was truly not far from madness, and I began myself to
have a sudden terror of this damp, dark house, this great, trembling
man, and something more that was worse than they. But I pitied him.
How could you or any man have helped it? I made him sit down in the
armchair beside the fire, which had now dwindled to a few glimmering
red coals. I let him hold me close to him with his arm and clutch my
hand with his, and I repeated, as quietly as I might: "But tell me; don't
be afraid, whatever if is you have done. Tell me what danger it is you
fear, and then we can face it together." "Fear! Fear!" he repeated; and
then, with a mighty effort which I could not but admire, he summoned
all his control. "I'm off my head," he said, "with loneliness and
depression. My wife died a year ago on this very night. We hated one
another. I couldn't be sorry when she died, and she knew it. When that
last heart attack came on, between her gasps she told me that she would
return, and I've always dreaded this night. That's partly why I asked
you to come, to have anyone here, anybody, and you've been very
kind – more kind than I had any right to expect. You must think me

insane going on like this, but see me through tonight and we'll have splendid times together. Don't desert me now – now, of all times!" I promised that I would not. I soothed him as best I could. We sat there, for I know not how long, through the gathering dark; we neither of us moved, the fire died out, and the room was lit with a strange dim glow that came from the snowy landscape beyond the uncurtained windows. Ridiculous, perhaps, as I look back at it. We sat there, I in a chair close to his, hand in hand, like a couple of lovers; but, in real truth, two men terrified, fearful of what was coming, and unable to do anything to meet it.

'I think that that was perhaps the strangest part of it; a sort of paralysis that crept over me. What would you or anyone else have done – summoned the old man, gone down to the village inn, fetched the local doctor? I could do nothing, but see the snowshine move like trembling water about the furniture and hear, through the urgent silence, the faint hoot of an owl from the trees in the wood.

*　　*　　*

'Oddly enough, I can remember nothing, try as I may, between that strange vigil and the moment when I myself, wakened out of a brief sleep, sat up in bed to see Lunt standing inside my room holding a candle. He was wearing a night-shirt, and looked huge in the candle-light, his black beard falling intensely dark on the white stuff of his shirt. He came very quietly towards my bed, the candle throwing flickering shadows about the room. When he spoke it was in a voice low and subdued, almost a whisper. "Would you come," he asked, "only for half an hour – just for half an hour?" he repeated, staring at me as though he didn't know me. "I'm unhappy without somebody – very unhappy." Then he looked over his shoulder, held the candle high above his head, and stared piercingly at every part of the room. I could see that something had happened to him, that he had taken another step into the country of Fear – a step that had withdrawn him from me and from every other human being. He whispered: "When you come, tread softly; I don't want anyone to hear us." I did what I could. I got out of bed, put on my dressing-gown and slippers, and tried to persuade him to stay with me. The fire was almost dead, but I told him that we would build it up again, and that we would sit there and wait for the morning; but no, he repeated again and again: "It's better in my own room; we're safer there." "Safe from what?" I asked him, making him look at me. "Lunt, wake up! You're as though you were asleep. There's nothing to fear. We've nobody but ourselves. Stay here and let us talk, and have done with this nonsense." But he wouldn't answer; only drew me forward down the dark passage, and then turned into his room, beckoning me to follow. He got into bed and sat hunched up there, his hands holding his knees, staring at the door, and every once and again shivering with a little tremor. The only light in the room was that from the candle, now burning low, and the only sound was the purring whisper of the sea.

'It seemed to make little difference to him that I was there. He did not look at me, but only at the door, and when I spoke to him he did not answer me nor seem to hear what I had said. I sat down beside the bed and, in order to break the silence, talked on about anything, about nothing, and was dropping off, I think, into a confused doze, when I heard his voice breaking across mine. Very clearly and distinctly he said: "If I killed her, she deserved it; she was never a good wife to me, not from the first; she shouldn't have irritated me as she did – she knew what my temper was. She had a worse one than mine, though. She can't touch me; I'm as strong as she is." And it was then, as clearly as I can now remember, that his voice suddenly sank into a sort of gentle whisper, as though he were almost glad that his fears had been confirmed. He whispered: "She's there!" I cannot possibly describe to you how that whisper seemed to let fear loose like water through my body. I could see nothing – the candle was flaming high in the last moments of its life – I could see nothing; but Lunt suddenly screamed, with a shrill cry like a tortured animal in agony: "Keep her off me, keep her away from me, keep her off – keep her off!" He caught me, his hands digging into my shoulders; then, with an awful effect of constricted muscles, as though rigor had caught and held him, his arms slowly fell away, he slipped back on to the bed as though someone were pushing him, his hands fell against the sheet, his whole body jerked with a convulsive effort, and then he rolled over. I saw nothing; only, quite distinctly, in my nostrils was that same fetid odour that I had known on the preceding evening. I rushed to the door, opened it, shouted down the long passage again and again, and soon the old man came running. I sent him for the doctor, and then could not return to the room, but stood there listening, hearing nothing save the whisper of the sea, the loud ticking of the hall clock. I flung open the window at the end of the passage; the sea rushed in with its precipitant roar; some bells chimed the hour. Then at last, beating into myself more courage, I turned back towards the room . . .'

'Well?' I asked as Runciman paused. 'He was dead, of course?'

'Dead, the doctor afterwards said, of heart failure.'

'Well?' I asked again.

'That's all.' Runciman paused. 'I don't know whether you can even call it a ghost story. My idea of the old woman may have been all hallucination. I don't even know whether his wife was like that when she was alive. She may have been large and fat. Lunt died of an evil conscience.'

'Yes,' I said.

'The only thing,' Runciman added at last, after a long pause, 'is that on Lunt's body there were marks – on his neck especially, some on his chest – as of fingers pressing in, scratches and dull blue marks. He may, in his terror, have caught at his own throat ...'

'Yes,' I said again.

'Anyway' – Runciman shivered – 'I don't like Cornwall – beastly country. Queer things happen there – something in the air ...'

'So I've heard,' I answered. 'And now have a drink. We both will.'

All Souls'
Edith Wharton

Queer and inexplicable as the business was, on the surface it appeared fairly simple – at the time, at least; but with the passing of years, and owing to there not having been a single witness of what happened except Sara Clayburn herself, the stories about it have become so exaggerated, and often so ridiculously inaccurate, that it seems necessary that someone connected with the affair, though not actually present – I repeat that when it happened my cousin was (or thought she was) quite alone in her house – should record the few facts actually known.

In those days I was often at Whitegates (as the place had always been called) – I was there, in fact, not long before, and almost immediately after, the strange happenings of those thirty-six hours. Jim Clayburn and his widow were both my cousins, and because of that, and of my intimacy with them, both families think I am more likely than anybody else to be able to get at the facts, as far as they can be called facts, and as anybody can get at them. So I have written down, as clearly as I could, the gist of the various talks I had with cousin Sara, when she could be got to talk – it wasn't often – about what occurred during that mysterious weekend.

*   *   *

I read the other day in a book by a fashionable essayist that ghosts went out when electric light came in. What nonsense! The writer, though he is fond of dabbling, in a literary way, in the supernatural, hasn't even reached the threshold of his subject. As between turreted castles patrolled by headless victims with clanking chains, and the comfortable suburban house with a refrigerator and central heating where you feel, as soon as you're in it, *that there's something wrong*, give me the latter for sending a chill down the spine! And, by the way, haven't you noticed that it's generally not the high-strung and imaginative who see ghosts, but the calm matter-of-fact people who don't believe in them, and are sure they wouldn't mind if they did see one? Well, that was the case with

Sara Clayburn and her house. The house, in spite of its age – it was built, I believe, about 1780 – was open, airy, high-ceilinged, with electricity, central heating and all the modern appliances: and its mistress was – well, very much like her house. And, anyhow, this isn't exactly a ghost story and I've dragged in the analogy only as a way of showing you what kind of woman my cousin was, and how unlikely it would have seemed that what happened at Whitegates should have happened just there – or to her.

* * *

When Jim Clayburn died the family all thought that, as the couple had no children, his widow would give up Whitegates and move either to New York or Boston – for being of good Colonial stock, with many relatives and friends, she would have found a place ready for her in either. But Sally Clayburn seldom did what other people expected, and in this case she did exactly the contrary; she stayed at Whitegates.

'What, turn my back on the old house – tear up all the family roots, and go and hang myself up in a bird-cage flat in one of those new skyscrapers in Lexington Avenue, with a bunch of chickweed and a cuttlefish to replace my good Connecticut mutton? No, thank you. Here I belong, and here I stay till my executors hand the place over to Jim's next of kin – that stupid fat Presley boy ... Well, don't let's talk about him. But I tell you what – I'll keep him out of here as long as I can.' And she did – for being still in the early fifties when her husband died, and a muscular, resolute figure of a woman, she was more than a match for the fat Presley boy, and attended his funeral a few years ago, in correct mourning, with a faint smile under her veil.

Whitegates was a pleasant hospitable-looking house, on a height overlooking the stately windings of the Connecticut River; but it was five or six miles from Norrington, the nearest town, and its situation would certainly have seemed remote and lonely to modern servants. Luckily, however, Sara Clayburn had inherited from her mother-in-law two or three old stand-bys who seemed as much a part of the family tradition as the roof they lived under; and I never heard of her having any trouble in her domestic arrangements.

The house, in Colonial days, had been foursquare, with four spacious rooms on the ground floor, an oak-floored hall dividing them, the usual kitchen extension at the back, and a good attic under the roof. But Jim's grandparents, when interest in the 'Colonial' began to revive, in the early eighties, had added two wings, at right angles to the south front, so that the old 'circle' before the front door became a grassy court, enclosed on three sides, with a big elm in the middle. Thus the house was turned into a roomy dwelling, in which the last three generations of Clayburns had exercised a large hospitality; but the architect had respected the character of the old house, and the enlargement made it more comfortable without lessening its simplicity. There was a lot of land about it, and Jim Clayburn, like his fathers before him, farmed it, not without profit, and played a considerable and respected part in state politics. The Clayburns were always spoken of as a 'good influence' in the country, and the townspeople were glad when they learned that Sara did not mean to desert the place – 'though it must be lonesome, winters, living all alone up there atop of that hill' – they remarked as the days shortened, and the first snow began to pile up under the quadruple row of elms along the common.

Well, if I've given you a sufficiently clear idea of Whitegates and the Clayburns – who shared with their old house a sort of reassuring orderliness and dignity – I'll efface myself, and tell the tale, not in my cousin's words, for they were too confused and fragmentary, but as I built it up gradually out of her half-avowals and nervous reticences. If the thing happened at all – and I must leave you to judge of that – I think it must have happened in this way ...

*   *   *

The morning had been bitter, with a driving sleet – though it was only the last day of October – but after lunch a watery sun showed for a while through banked-up woolly clouds, and tempted Sara Clayburn out. She was an energetic walker, and given, at that season, to tramping three or four miles along the valley road, and coming back by way of Shaker's wood. She had made her usual round, and was following the main drive to the house when she overtook a plainly-dressed woman walking in the same direction. If the scene had not been so lonely – the way to Whitegates at the end of an autumn day was not a frequented one – Mrs Clayburn might not have paid any attention to the woman, for she was in no way noticeable, but when she caught up with the intruder my cousin was surprised to find that she was a stranger – for the mistress of Whitegates prided herself on knowing, at least by sight, most of her country neighbours. It was almost dark, and the woman's face was hardly visible, but Mrs Clayburn told me she recalled her as middle-aged, plain and rather pale.

Mrs Clayburn greeted her, and then added: 'You're going to the house?'

'Yes, ma'am,' the woman answered, in a voice that the Connecticut Valley in old days would have called 'foreign', but that would have been unnoticed by ears used to the modern multiplicity of tongues. 'No, I couldn't say where she came from,' Sara always said, 'What struck me as queer was that I didn't know her.'

She asked the woman, politely, what she wanted, and the woman answered: 'Only to see one of the girls.' The answer was natural enough, and Mrs Clayburn nodded and turned off from the drive to the lower part of the gardens, so that she saw no more of the visitor then or afterwards. And, in fact, a half hour later something happened which put the stranger entirely out of her mind. The brisk and light-footed Mrs Clayburn, as she approached the house, slipped on a frozen puddle, turned her ankle and lay suddenly helpless.

* * *

Price, the butler, and Agnes, the dour old Scottish maid whom Sara had inherited from her mother-in-law, of course knew exactly what to do. In no time they had their mistress stretched out on a lounge, and Dr Selgrove had been called up from Norrington. When he arrived, he ordered Mrs Clayburn to bed, did the necessary examining and bandaging, and shook his head over her ankle, which he feared was fractured. He thought, however, that if she would swear not to get up, or even shift the position of her leg, he could spare her the discomfort of putting it in plaster. Mrs Clayburn agreed, the more promptly as the doctor warned her that any rash movement would prolong her immobility. Her quick imperious nature made the prospect trying, and she was annoyed with herself for having been so clumsy. But the mischief was done, and she immediately thought what an opportunity she would have for going over her accounts and catching up with her correspondence. So she settled down resignedly in her bed.

'And you won't miss much, you know, if you have to stay there a few days. It's beginning to snow, and it looks as if we were in for a good spell of it,' the doctor remarked, glancing through the window as he gathered up his implements. 'Well, we don't often get snow here as early as this; but winter's got to begin some time,' he concluded philosophically. At the door he stopped to add: 'You don't want me to send up a nurse from Norrington? Not to nurse you, you know; there's nothing much to do till I see you again. But this is a pretty lonely place when the snow begins, and I thought maybe——'

Sara Clayburn laughed. 'Lonely? With my old servants? You forget how many winters I've spent here alone with them. Two of them were with me in my mother-in-law's time.'

'That's so,' Dr Selgrove agreed. 'You're a good deal luckier than most people, that way. Well, let me see; this is Saturday. We'll have to let the inflammation go down before we can X-ray you. Monday morning, first thing, I'll be here with the X-ray man. If you want me sooner, call me up.' And he was gone.

* * *

The foot, at first, had not been very painful; but towards the small hours Mrs Clayburn began to suffer. She was a bad patient, like most healthy

and active people. Not being used to pain she did not know how to bear
it, and the hours of wakefulness and immobility seemed endless. Agnes,
before leaving her, had made everything as comfortable as possible. She
had put a jug of lemonade within reach, and had even (Mrs Clayburn
thought it odd afterwards) insisted on bringing in a tray with sandwiches and a thermos of tea. 'In case you're hungry in the night,
madam.'

'Thank you; but I'm never hungry in the night. And I certainly
shan't be tonight – only thirsty. I think I'm feverish.'

'Well, there's the lemonade, madam.'

'That will do. Take the other things away, please.' (Sara had always
hated the sight of unwanted food 'messing about' in her room.)

'Very well, madam. Only you might——'

'Please take it away,' Mrs Clayburn repeated irritably.

'Very good, madam.' But as Agnes went out, her mistress heard
her set the tray down softly on a table behind the screen which shut off
the door.

'Obstinate old goose!' she thought, rather touched by the old
woman's insistence.

Sleep, once it had gone, would not return, and the long black hours
moved more and more slowly. How late the dawn came in November!
'If only I could move my leg,' she grumbled.

She lay still and strained her ears for the first steps of the servants.
Whitegates was an early house, its mistress setting the example; it would
surely not be long now before one of the women came. She was tempted
to ring for Agnes, but refrained. The woman had been up late, and this
was Sunday morning, when the household was always allowed a little
extra time. Mrs Clayburn reflected restlessly: 'I was a fool not to let her
leave the tea beside the bed, as she wanted to. I wonder if I could get up
and get it?' But she remembered the doctor's warning, and dared not
move. Anything rather than risk prolonging her imprisonment ...

Ah, there was the stable clock striking. How loud it sounded in the
snowy stillness! One – two – three – four – five ...

What? Only five? Three hours and a quarter more before she could
hope to hear the door handle turned ... After a while she dozed off
again, uncomfortably.

Another sound aroused her. Again the stable clock. She listened. But
the room was still in deep darkness, and only six strokes fell ... She
thought of reciting something to put her to sleep; but she seldom read
poetry, and being naturally a good sleeper, she could not remember any
of the usual devices against insomnia. The whole of her leg felt like lead
now. The bandages had grown terribly tight – her ankle must have
swollen ... She lay staring at the dark windows, watching for the first
glimmer of dawn. At last she saw a pale filter of daylight through the

shutters. One by one the objects between the bed and the window recovered first their outline, then their bulk, and seemed to be stealthily regrouping themselves, after goodness knows what secret displacements during the night. Who that has lived in an old house could possibly believe that the furniture in it stays still all night? Mrs Clayburn almost fancied she saw one little slender-legged table slipping hastily back into its place.

'It knows Agnes is coming, and it's afraid,' she thought whimsically. Her bad night must have made her imaginative for such nonsense as that about the furniture had never occurred to her before ...

At length, after hours more, as it seemed, the stable clock struck eight. Only another quarter of an hour. She watched the hand moving slowly across the face of the little clock beside her bed ... ten minutes ... five ... only five! Agnes was as punctual as destiny ... in two minutes now she would come. The two minutes passed, and she did not come. Poor Agnes – she had looked pale and tired the night before. She had overslept herself, no doubt – or perhaps she felt ill, and would send the housemaid to replace her. Mrs Clayburn waited.

She waited half an hour; then she reached up to the bell at the head of the bed. Poor old Agnes – her mistress felt guilty about waking her. But Agnes did not appear – and after a considerable interval Mrs Clayburn, now with a certain impatience, rang again. She rang once; twice; three times – but still no one came.

Once more she waited; then she said to herself: 'There must be something wrong with the electricity.' Well – she could find out by switching on the bed lamp at her elbow (how admirably the room was equipped with every practical appliance!). She switched it on – but no light came. Electric current off; and it was Sunday, and nothing could be done about it till the next morning. Unless it turned out to be just a burnt-out fuse, which Price could remedy. Well, in a moment now some one would surely come to her door.

It was nine o'clock before she admitted to herself that something uncommonly strange must have happened in the house. She began to feel a nervous apprehension; but she was not the woman to encourage it. If only she had had the telephone put in her room, instead of out on the landing! She measured mentally the distance to be travelled, remembered Dr Selgrove's admonition, and wondered if her broken ankle would carry her there. She dreaded the prospect of being put in plaster, but she had to get to the telephone, whatever happened.

She wrapped herself in her dressing-gown, found a walking-stick, and, resting heavily on it, dragged herself to the door. In her bedroom the careful Agnes had closed and fastened the shutters, so that it was not much lighter there than at dawn; but outside in the corridor the cold whiteness of the snowy morning seemed almost reassuring. Mysterious things – dreadful things – were associated with darkness; and here was the wholesome prosaic daylight come again to banish them. Mrs Clayburn looked about her and listened. A deep nocturnal silence in that day-lit house, in which five people were presumably coming and going about their work. It was certainly strange ... She looked out of the window, hoping to see someone crossing the court or coming along the drive. But no one was in sight, and the snow seemed to have the place to itself: a quiet steady snow. It was still falling, with a business-like regularity, muffling the outer world in layers on layers of thick white velvet, and intensifying the silence within. A noiseless world – were people so sure that absence of noise was what they wanted? Let them first try a lonely country house in a November snowstorm!

She dragged herself along the passage to the telephone. When she unhooked the receiver she noticed that her hand trembled.

She rang up the pantry – no answer. She rang again. Silence – more silence! It seemed to be piling itself up like the snow on the roof and in the gutters. Silence. How many people that she knew had any idea what silence was – and how loud it sounded when you really listened to it?

Again she waited: then she rang up 'Central'. No answer. She tried three times. After that she tried the pantry again ... The telephone was cut off, then; like the electric current. Who was at work downstairs, isolating her thus from the world? Her heart began to hammer. Luckily there was a chair near the telephone, and she sat down to recover her strength – or was it her courage?

Agnes and the housemaid slept in the nearest wing. She would certainly get as far as that when she had pulled herself together. Had she the courage——? Yes, of course she had. She had always been regarded as a plucky woman; and had so regarded herself. But this silence——

It occurred to her that by looking from the window of a neighbouring bathroom she could see the kitchen chimney. There ought to be smoke coming from it at that hour; and if there were she thought she would be less afraid to go on. She got as far as the bathroom and looking through the window saw that no smoke came from the chimney. Her sense of loneliness grew more acute. Whatever had happened below-stairs must have happened before the morning's work had begun. The cook had not had time to light the fire, the other servants had not yet begun their round. She sank down on the nearest chair, struggling against her fears. What next would she discover if she carried on her investigations?

The pain in her ankle made progress difficult; but she was aware of it now only as an obstacle to haste. No matter what it cost her in physical suffering, she must find out what was happening below-stairs – or had happened. But first she would go to the maid's room. And if that were empty – well, somehow she would have to get herself downstairs.

She limped along the passage, and on the way steadied herself by resting her hand on a radiator. It was stone-cold. Yet in that well-ordered house in winter the central heating, though damped down at night, was never allowed to go out, and by eight in the morning a mellow warmth pervaded the rooms. The icy chill of the pipes startled her. It was the chauffeur who looked after the heating – so he too was involved in the mystery, whatever it was, as well as the house-servants. But this only deepened the problem.

*   *   *

At Agnes's door Mrs Clayburn paused and knocked. She expected no answer, and there was none. She opened the door and went in. The room was dark and very cold. She went to the window and flung back the shutters; then she looked slowly around, vaguely apprehensive of what she might see. The room was empty but what frightened her was not so much its emptiness as its air of scrupulous and undisturbed order. There was no sign of anyone having lately dressed in it – or undressed the night before. And the bed had not been slept in.

Mrs Clayburn leaned against the wall for a moment; then she crossed the floor and opened the cupboard. That was where Agnes kept her dresses; and the dresses were there, neatly hanging in a row. On the shelf above were Agnes's few and unfashionable hats, rearrangements of her mistress's old ones. Mrs Clayburn, who knew them all, looked at the shelf, and saw that one was missing. And so also was the warm winter coat she had given to Agnes the previous winter.

The woman was out, then; had gone out, no doubt, the night before, since the bed was unslept in, the dressing and washing appliances untouched. Agnes, who never set foot out of the house after dark, who despised the movies as much as she did the wireless, and could never be persuaded that a little innocent amusement was a necessary element in life, had deserted the house on a snowy winter night, while her mistress lay upstairs, suffering and helpless! Why had she gone, and where had she gone? When she was undressing Mrs Clayburn the night before, taking her orders, trying to make her more comfortable, was she already planning this mysterious nocturnal escape? Or had something – the mysterious and dreadful Something for the clue of which Mrs Clayburn was still groping – occurred later in the evening, sending the maid downstairs and out of doors into the bitter night? Perhaps one of the men at the garage – where the chauffeur and gardener lived – had been suddenly taken ill, and someone had run up to the house for Agnes. Yes – that must be the explanation ... Yet how much it left unexplained.

Next to Agnes's room was the linen room; beyond that was the housemaid's door. Mrs Clayburn went to it and knocked. 'Mary!' No one answered, and she went in. The room was in the same immaculate order as her maid's, and here too the bed was unslept in, and there were no signs of dressing or undressing. The two women had no doubt gone out together – gone where?

More and more the cold unanswering silence of the house weighed down on Mrs Clayburn. She had never thought of it as a big house, but now, in this snowy winter light, it seemed immense, and full of ominous corners around which one dared not look.

Beyond the housemaid's room were the back stairs. It was the nearest way down, and every step that Mrs Clayburn took was increasingly painful; but she decided to walk slowly back, the whole length of the passage, and go down by the front stairs. She did not know why she did this; but she felt that at the moment she was past reasoning, and had better obey her instinct.

More than once she had explored the ground floor alone in the small hours, in search of unwonted midnight noises; but now it was not the idea of noises that frightened her, but that inexorable and hostile silence, the sense that the house had retained in full daylight its nocturnal mystery, and was watching her as she was watching it; that in entering those empty orderly rooms she might be disturbing some unseen confabulation on which beings of flesh and blood had better not intrude.

The broad oak stairs were beautifully polished, and so slippery that she had to cling to the rail and let herself down tread by tread. And as she descended, the silence descended with her – heavier, denser, more absolute. She seemed to feel its steps just behind her, softly keeping time with hers. It had a quality she had never been aware of in any other silence, as though it were not merely an absence of sound, a thin barrier between the ear and the surging murmur of life just beyond, but an impenetrable substance made out of the world-wide cessation of all life and all movement.

Yes, that was what laid a chill on her: the feeling that there was no limit to this silence, no outer margin, nothing beyond it. By this time she had reached the foot of the stairs and was limping across the hall to the drawing-room. Whatever she found there, she was sure, would be mute and lifeless; but what would it be? The bodies of her dead servants, mown down by some homicidal maniac? And what if it were her turn next – if he were waiting for her behind the heavy curtains of the room she was about to enter? Well, she must find out – she must face whatever lay in wait. Not impelled by bravery – the last drop of courage had oozed out of her – but because anything, anything was better than to remain shut up in that snow-bound house without knowing whether she was alone in it or not, 'I must find that out, I must find that out,' she repeated to herself in a sort of meaningless sing-song.

The cold outer light flooded the drawing-room. The shutters had not been closed, nor the curtains drawn. She looked about her. The room was empty, and every chair in its usual place. Her armchair was pushed up by the chimney, and the cold hearth was piled with the ashes of the fire at which she had warmed herself before starting on her ill-fated walk. Even her empty coffee cup stood on a table near the armchair. It was evident that the servants had not been in the room since she had left it the day before after luncheon. And suddenly the conviction entered into her that, as she found the drawing-room, so she would find the rest of the house; cold, orderly – and empty. She would find nothing, she would find no one. She no longer felt any dread or ordinary human dangers lurking in those dumb spaces ahead of her. She knew she was utterly alone under her own roof. She sat down to rest her aching ankle, and looked slowly about her.

There were the other rooms to be visited, and she was determined to go through them all – but she knew in advance that they would give no answer to her question. She knew it, seemingly, from the quality of the silence which enveloped her. There was no break, no thinnest crack in it anywhere. It had the cold continuity of the snow which was still falling steadily outside.

She had no idea how long she waited before nerving herself to continue her inspection. She no longer felt the pain in her ankle, but was only conscious that she must not bear her weight on it, and therefore moved very slowly, supporting herself on each piece of furniture in her path. On the ground floor no shutter had been closed, no curtain drawn, and she progressed without much difficulty from room to room: the library, her morning-room, the dining-room. In each of them, every piece of furniture was in its usual place. In the dining-room, that table had been laid for the dinner of the previous evening, and the candel-abra, with candles unlit, stood reflected in the dark mahogany. She was not the kind of woman to nibble a poached egg on a tray when she was alone, but always came down to the dining-room, and had what she called a civilized meal.

The back premises remained to be visited. From the dining-room she entered the pantry, and there too everything was in irreproachable order. She opened the door and looked down the back passage with its neat linoleum floor-covering. The deep silence accompanied her; she still felt it moving watchfully at her side, as though she were its prisoner and it might throw itself upon her if she attempted to escape. She limped on towards the kitchen. That of course would be empty too, and immaculate. But she must see it.

She leaned a minute in the embrasure of a window in the passage. 'It's like the *Marie Celeste* – a *Marie Celeste* on terra firma,' she thought, recalling the unsolved sea mystery of her childhood. 'No one ever knew what happened on board the *Marie Celeste*. And perhaps no one will ever know what happened here. Even I shan't know.'

At the thought her latent fear seemed to take on a new quality. It was like an icy liquid running through every vein, and lying in a pool about her heart. She understood now that she had never before known what fear was, and that most of the people she had met had probably never known either. For this sensation was something quite different . . .

It absorbed her so completely that she was not aware how long she remained leaning there. But suddenly a new impulse pushed her forward, and she walked on towards the scullery. She went there first because there was a service slide in the wall, through which she might peep into the kitchen without being seen; and some indefinable instinct told her that the kitchen held the clue to the mystery. She still felt strongly that whatever had happened in the house must have its source and centre in the kitchen.

In the scullery, as she had expected, everything was clean and tidy. Whatever had happened, no one in the house appeared to have been taken by surprise; there was nowhere any sign of confusion or disorder. 'It looks as if they'd know beforehand, and put everything straight,' she thought. She glanced at the wall facing the door, and saw that the slide was open. And then, as she was approaching it, the silence was broken. A voice was speaking in the kitchen – a man's voice, low but emphatic, and which she had never heard before.

She stood still, cold with fear. But this fear was again a different one. Her previous terrors had been speculative, conjectured, a ghostly emanation of the surrounding silence. This was a plain everyday dread of evil-doers. Oh, God, why had she not remembered her husband's revolver, which ever since his death had lain in a drawer in her room?

She turned to retreat across the smooth slippery floor but halfway her stick slipped from her, and crashed down on the tiles. The noise seemed to echo on and on through the emptiness, and she stood still, aghast. Now that she had betrayed her presence, flight was useless. Whoever was beyond the kitchen door would be upon her in a second . . .

But to her astonishment the voice went on speaking. It was as though neither the speaker nor his listeners had heard her. The invisible stranger spoke so low that she could not make out what he was saying, but the tone was passionately earnest, almost threatening. The next moment she realized that he was speaking in a foreign language, a language unknown to her. Once more her terror was surmounted by the urgent desire to know what was going on, so close to her yet unseen. She crept to the slide, peered cautiously through into the kitchen, and saw that it was as orderly and empty as the other rooms. But in the middle of the carefully scoured table stood a portable wireless, and the voice she heard came out of it ...

She must have fainted then, she supposed; at any rate she felt so weak and dizzy that her memory of what happened next remained indistinct. But in the course of time she groped her way back to the pantry, and there found a bottle of spirits – brandy or whisky, she could not remember which. She found a glass, poured herself a stiff drink, and while it was flushing through her veins, managed, she never knew with how many shuddering delays, to drag herself through the deserted ground floor, up the stairs and down the corridor to her own room. There, apparently, she fell across the threshold, again unconscious ...

When she came to, she remembered, her first care had been to lock herself in; then to recover her husband's revolver. It was not loaded, but she found some cartridges, and succeeded in loading it. Then she remembered that Agnes, on leaving her the evening before, had refused to carry away the tray with the tea and sandwiches, and she fell on them with a sudden hunger. She recalled also noticing that a flask of brandy had been put beside the thermos, and being vaguely surprised. Agnes's departure, then, had been deliberately planned, and she had known that her mistress, who never touched spirits, might have need of a stimulant before she returned. Mrs Clayburn poured some of the brandy into her tea, and swallowed it greedily.

After that (she told me later) she remembered that she had managed to start a fire in her grate, and after warming herself, had got back into her bed, piling on it all the coverings she could find. The afternoon passed in a haze of pain, out of which there emerged now and then a dim shape of fear – the fear that she might lie there alone and untended till she died of cold, and of the terror of her solitude. For she was sure by this time that the house was empty – completely empty, from garret to cellar. She knew it was so, she could not tell why; but again she felt that it must be because of the peculiar quality of the silence – the silence which had dogged her steps wherever she went, and was now folded down on her like a pall. She was sure that the nearness of any other human being, however dumb and secret, would have made a faint crack in the texture of that silence, flawed it as a sheet of glass is flawed by a pebble thrown against it ...

*　　　*　　　*

'Is that easier?' the doctor asked, lifting himself from bending over her ankle. He shook his head disapprovingly. 'Looks to me as if you'd disobeyed orders – eh? Been moving about, haven't you? And I guess Dr Selgrove told you to keep quiet till he saw you again, didn't he?'

The speaker was a stranger, whom Mrs Clayburn knew only by name. Her own doctor had been called away that morning to the bedside of an old patient in Baltimore, and had asked this young man, who was beginning to be known at Norrington, to replace him. The newcomer was shy, and somewhat familiar, as the shy often are, and Mrs Clayburn decided that she did not much like him. But before she could convey this by the tone of her reply (and she was past mistress of the shades of disapproval) she heard Agnes speaking – yes, Agnes, the same, the usual Agnes, standing behind the doctor, neat and stern-looking as ever. 'Mrs Clayburn must have got up and walked about in the night instead of ringing for me, as she'd ought to.' Agnes intervened severely.

This was too much! In spite of the pain, which was now exquisite, Mrs Clayburn laughed. 'Ringing for you? How could I, with the electricity cut off?'

'The electricity cut off?' Agnes's surprise was masterly. 'Why, when was it cut off?' She pressed her finger on the bell beside the bed, and the call tinkled through the quiet room. 'I tried that bell before I left you last night, madam, because if there'd been anything wrong with it I'd have come and slept in the dressing-room sooner than leave you here alone.'

Mrs Clayburn lay speechless, staring up at her. 'Last night? But last night I was all alone in the house.'

Agnes's firm features did not alter. She folder her hands resignedly across her trim apron. 'Perhaps the pain's made you a little confused, madam.' She looked at the doctor, who nodded.

'The pain in your foot must have been pretty bad,' he said.

'It was,' Mrs Clayburn replied. 'But it was nothing to the horror of being left alone in this empty house since the day before yesterday, with the heat and the electricity cut off, and the telephone not working.'

The doctor was looking at her in evident wonder. Agnes's sallow face flushed slightly, but only as if in indignation at an unjust charge. 'But, madam, I made up your fire with my own hands last night – and look, it's smouldering still. I was getting ready to start it again just now, when the doctor came.'

'That's so. She was down on her knees before it,' the doctor corroborated.

Again Mrs Clayburn laughed. Ingeniously as the tissue of lies was being woven about her, she felt she could still break through it. 'I made up the fire myself yesterday – there was no one else to do it,' she said, addressing the doctor, but keeping her eyes on her maid. 'I got up twice to put on more coal, because the house was like a sepulchre. The central heating must have been out since Saturday afternoon.'

At this incredible statement Agnes's face expressed only a polite distress; but the new doctor was evidently embarrassed at being drawn into an unintelligible controversy with which he had no time to deal. He said he had brought the X-ray photographer with him, but the ankle was too much swollen to be photographed at present. He asked Mrs Clayburn to excuse his haste, as he had all Dr Selgrove's patients to visit besides his own, and promised to come back that evening to decide whether she could be X-rayed then, and whether, as he evidently feared, the ankle would have to be put in plaster. Then, handing his prescriptions to Agnes, he departed.

Mrs Clayburn spent a feverish and suffering day. She did not feel well enough to carry on the discussion with Agnes; she did not ask to see the other servants. She grew drowsy, and understood that her mind was confused with fever. Agnes and the housemaid waited on her as attentively as usual, and by the time the doctor returned in the evening her temperature had fallen; but she decided not to speak of what was on her mind until Dr Selgrove reappeared. He was to be back the following evening, and the new doctor preferred to wait for him before deciding to put the ankle in plaster – though he feared this was now inevitable.

* * *

That afternoon Mrs Clayburn had me summoned by telephone, and I arrived at Whitegates the following day. My cousin, who looked pale and nervous, merely pointed to her foot, which had been put in plaster, and thanked me for coming to keep her company. She explained that Dr Selgrove had been taken suddenly ill in Baltimore, and would not be back for several days, but that the young man who replaced him seemed fairly competent. She made no allusion to the strange incidents I have set down, but I felt at once that she had received a shock which her accident, however painful, could not explain.

Finally, one evening, she told me the story of her strange weekend, as it had presented itself to her unusually clear and accurate mind, and as I have recorded it above. She did not tell me this till several weeks after my arrival; but she was still upstairs at the time, and obliged to divide her days between her bed and a lounge. During those endless intervening weeks, she told me, she had thought the whole matter over: and though the events of the mysterious thirty-six hours were still vivid to her, they had already lost something of their haunting terror, and she had finally decided not to reopen the question with Agnes, or to touch on it in speaking to the other servants. Dr Selgrove's illness had been not only serious but prolonged. He had not yet returned, and it was reported that as soon as he was well enough he would go on a West Indian cruise, and not resume his practice at Norrington till the spring. Dr Selgrove, as my cousin was perfectly aware, was the only person who could prove that thirty-six hours had elapsed between his visit and that of his successor; and the latter, a shy young man, burdened by the heavy additional practice suddenly thrown on his shoulders, told me (when I

risked a little private talk with him) that in the haste of Dr Selgrove's
departure the only inŝtructions he had given about Mrs Clayton
were summed up in the brief memorandum: 'Broken ankle. Have X-
rayed.'

Knowing my cousin's authoritative character, I was surprised at her
decision not to speak to the servants of what had happened; but on
thinking it over I concluded she was right. They were all exactly as they
had been before that unexplained episode: efficient, devoted, respectful
and respectable. She was dependent on them and felt at home with
them, and she evidently preferred to put the whole matter out of her
mind, as far as she could. She was absolutely certain that something
strange had happened in her house, and I was more than ever
convinced that she had received a shock which the accident of a broken
ankle was not sufficient to account for; but in the end I agreed that
nothing was to be gained by cross-questioning the servants or the new
doctor.

I was at Whitegates off and on that winter and during the following
summer, and when I went home to New York for good early in October
I left my cousin in her old health and spirits. Dr Selgrove had been
ordered to Switzerland for the summer, and this further postponement
of his return to his practice seemed to have put the happenings of the
strange weekend out of her mind. Her life was going on as peacefully
and normally as usual, and I left her without anxiety, and indeed
without a thought of the mystery, which was now nearly a year old.

I was living then in a small flat in New York by myself, and I had
hardly settled into it when, very late one evening – on the last day of
October – I heard my bell ring. As it was my maid's evening out, and I
was alone, I went to the door myself, and on the threshold, to my
amazement, I saw Sara Clayburn. She was wrapped in a fur cloak, with
a hat drawn down over her forehead, and a face so pale and haggard
that I saw something dreadful must have happened to her. 'Sara,' I
gasped, not knowing what I was saying, 'where in the world have you
come from at this hour?'

'From Whitegates. I missed the last train and came by car.' She
came in and sat down on the bench near the door. I saw that she could
hardly stand, and sat down beside her, putting my arm about her. 'For
heaven's sake, tell me what happened.'

She looked at me without seeming to see me. 'I telephoned to
Nixon's and hired a car. It took me five hours and a quarter to get here.'
She looked about her. 'Can you take me in for the night? I've left my
luggage downstairs.'

'For as many nights as you like. But you look so ill——'

She shook her head. 'No; I'm not ill. I'm only frightened – deathly
frightened,' she repeated in a whisper.

Her voice was so strange, and the hands I was pressing between mine were so cold, that I drew her to her feet and led her straight to my little guest-room. My flat was in an old-fashioned building, not many stories high, and I was on more human terms with the staff than is possible in one of the modern Babels. I telephoned down to have my cousin's bags brought up, and meanwhile I filled a hot water bottle, warmed the bed, and got her into it as quickly as I could. I had never seen her as unquestioning and submissive, and that alarmed me even more than her pallor. She was not the woman to let herself be undressed and put to bed like a baby; but she submitted without a word, as though aware that she had reached the end of her tether.

'It's good to be here,' she said in a quieter tone, as I tucked her up and smoothed the pillows. 'Don't leave me yet, will you – not just yet.'

'I'm not going to leave you for more than a minute – just to get you a cup of tea,' I reassured her; and she lay still. I left the door open, so that she could hear me stirring about in the little pantry across the passage, and when I brought her the tea she swallowed it gratefully, and a little colour came into her face. I sat with her in silence for some time; but at last she began: 'You see it's exactly a year——'

I should have preferred to have her put off till the next morning whatever she had to tell me; but I saw from her burning eyes that she was determined to rid her mind of what was burdening it, and that until she had done so it would be useless to proffer the sleeping draft I had ready.

'A year since what?' I asked stupidly, not yet associating her precipitate arrival with the mysterious occurrences of the previous year at Whitegates.

She looked at me in surprise. 'A year since I met that woman. Don't you remember – the strange woman who was coming up the drive the afternoon when I broke my ankle? I didn't think of it at the time, but it was on All Souls' eve that I met her.'

Yes, I said, I remembered that it was.

'Well – all this is All Souls' eve, isn't it? I'm not as good as you are on Church dates, but I thought it was.'

'Yes. This is All Souls' eve.'

'I thought so ... Well, this afternoon I went out for my usual walk, I'd been writing letters, and paying bills, and didn't start till late; not till it was nearly dusk. But it was a lovely clear evening. And as I got near the gate, there was the woman coming in – the same woman ... going towards the house ...'

I pressed my cousin's hand, which was hot and feverish now. 'If it was dusk, could you be perfectly sure it was the same woman?' I asked.

'Oh, perfectly sure, the evening was so clear. I knew her and she knew me; and I could see she was angry at meeting me. I stopped her and asked: "Where are you going?" just as I had asked her last year. And she said, in the same queer half-foreign voice. "Only to see one of the girls", as she had before. Then I felt angry all of a sudden, and I said: "You shan't set foot in my house again. Do you hear me? I order you to leave." And she laughed: yes, she laughed – very low, but distinctly. By that time it had got quite dark, as if a sudden storm was sweeping up over the sky, so that though she was so near me I could hardly see her. We were standing by the clump of hemlocks at the turn of the drive, and as I went up to her, furious at her impertinence, she passed behind the hemlocks, and when I followed her she wasn't there . . . No; I swear to you she wasn't there . . . And in the darkness I hurried back to the house, afraid that she would slip by me and get there first. And the queer thing was that as I reached the door the black cloud vanished, and there was the transparent twilight again. In the house everything seemed as usual, and the servants were busy about their work; but I couldn't get it out of my head that the woman, under the shadow of that cloud, had somehow got there before me.' She paused for breath, and began again. 'In the hall I stopped at the telephone and rang up Nixon, and told him to send me a car at once to go to New York, with a man he knew to drive me. And Nixon came with the car himself . . .'

Her head sank back on the pillow and she looked at me like a frightened child. 'It was good of Nixon,' she said.

'Yes; it was very good of him. But when they saw you leaving – the servants, I mean . . .'

'Yes. Well, when I got upstairs to my room I rang for Agnes. She came, looking just as cool and quiet as usual. And when I told her I was starting for New York in half an hour – I said it was on account of a sudden business call – well, then her presence of mind failed her for the first time. She forgot to look surprised, she even forgot to make an objection – and you know what an objector Agnes is. And as I watched her I could see a little secret spark of relief in her eyes, though she was so on her guard. And she just said: "Very well, madam," and asked me what I wanted to take with me. Just as if I were in the habit of dashing off to New York after dark on an autumn night to meet a business engagement! No, she made a mistake not to show any surprise – and not even to ask me why I didn't take my own car. And her losing her head in that way frightened me more than anything else. For I saw she was so thankful I was going that she hardly dared speak, for fear she should betray herself, or I should change my mind.'

After that Mrs Clayburn lay a long while silent, breathing less unrestfully; and at last she closed her eyes, as though she felt more at ease now that she had spoken, and wanted to sleep. As I got up quietly to leave her, she turned her head a little and murmured: 'I shall never go back to Whitegates again.' Then she shut her eyes and I saw that she was falling asleep.

*   *   *

I have set down above, I hope without omitting anything essential, the record of my cousin's strange experience as she told it to me. Of what happened at Whitegates that is all I can personally vouch for. The rest – and of course there is a rest – is pure conjecture; and I give it only as such.

My cousin's maid, Agnes, was from the Isle of Skye, and the Hebrides, as everyone knows, are full of the supernatural – whether in the shape of ghostly presences, or the almost ghostlier sense of unseen watchers peopling the long nights of those stormy solitudes. My cousin, at any rate, always regarded Agnes as the – perhaps unconscious, at any rate irresponsible – channel through which communications from the other side of the veil reached the submissive household at Whitegates. Though Agnes had been with Mrs Clayburn for a long time without any peculiar incident revealing this affinity with the unknown forces, the power to communicate with them may all the while have been latent in the woman, only awaiting a kindred touch; and that touch may have been given by the unknown visitor whom my cousin, two years in succession, had met coming up the drive at Whitegates on the eve of All Souls'. Certainly the date bears out my hypothesis; for I suppose that, even in this unimaginative age, a few people still remember that All Souls' eve is the night when the dead can walk – and when, by the same token, other spirits, piteous or malevolent, are also freed from the restrictions which secure the earth to the living on the other days of the year.

If the recurrence of this date is more than a coincidence – and for my part I think it is – then I take it that the strange woman who twice came up the drive at Whitegates on All Souls' eve was either a 'fetch', or else, more probably, and more alarmingly, a living woman inhabited by a witch. The history of witchcraft, as is well known, abounds in such cases, and such a messenger might well have been delegated by the powers who rule in these matters to summon Agnes and her fellow servants to a midnight 'Coven' in some neighbouring solitude. To learn what happens at Covens, and the reason of the irresistible fascination they exercise over the timorous and superstitious, one need only address oneself to the immense body of literature dealing with these mysterious rites. Anyone who has once felt the faintest curiosity to assist at a Coven apparently soon finds the curiosity increase to desire, the desire to an uncontrollable longing, which, when the opportunity presents itself, breaks down all inhibitions; for those who have once taken part in a Coven will move heaven and earth to take part again.

*   *   *

Such is my – conjectural – explanation of the strange happenings at Whitegates. My cousin always said she could not believe that incidents which might fit into the desolate landscape of the Hebrides could occur in the cheerful and populous Connecticut Valley; but if she did not believe, she at least feared – such moral paradoxes are not uncommon – and though she insisted that there must be some natural explanation of the mystery, she never returned to investigate it.

'No, no,' she said with a little shiver, whenever I touched on the subject of her going back to Whitegates, 'I don't want ever to risk seeing that woman again ...' And she never went back.

Acknowledgements

The publishers wish to thank the following for permission to reprint previously published material. Every effort has been made to locate all persons having any rights in the stories appearing in this book. Any omissions will be corrected in future reprints upon written notification to the publishers.

'The Drifting Snow' by August Derleth, first published by Arkham House, copyright © 1948 by August Derleth. Reprinted by permission of Arkham House, Inc.

'The Mindworm' by C. M. Kornbluth. From *The Best of C. M. Kornbluth* by C. M. Kornbluth. Copyright © 1976 by Mary Kornbluth, John Kornbluth and David Kornbluth. Reprinted by permission of Ballantine Books, a division of Random House, Inc.

'The Living Dead' by Robert Bloch, copyright © Robert Bloch, 1967. Reprinted by permission of the author and Scott Meredith Literary Agency, Inc., 845 Third Avenue, New York, New York 10022.

'Ringing the Changes' from *Dark Entries*, by Robert Aickman, first published 1964. Copyright © The Estate of Robert Aickman.

'Couching at the Door' from *Couching at the Door* by D. K. Broster, reprinted by permission of William Heinemann Ltd.

'Don't You Dare' by John Burke, from *Don't You Dare*, reprinted by permission of the author and the Hutchinson Publishing Group, Ltd.

'The Horror Under Penmire' by Adrian Cole, © 1974, reprinted by permission of the author.

'The House of Balfother' from *Dark Encounters*, by William Croft Dickinson, reprinted by permission of John Goodchild, Publishers.

'Don't Tell Cissie', from *By Horror Haunted*, by Celia Fremlin, copyright © Celia Fremlin 1974. Reprinted by permission of the author.

Acknowledgements

'The Horsehair Trunk' by Davis Grubb, reprinted by permission of the Peters Fraser & Dunlop Group.

'The Moon-Bog' by H. P. Lovecraft, reprinted by permission of the estate of the late H. P. Lovecraft, and the publishers.

'A Story of Don Juan' by V. S. Pritchett, reprinted by permission of the Peters Fraser & Dunlop Group.

'A Woman Seldom Found' by William Sansom. Reprinted by permission of Elaine Greene, Ltd.